Rohinton Mistry was born in Bombay in 1952 and has lived in Canada since 1975. His first novel, *Such a Long Journey*, was shortlisted for the Booker Prize and won the Commonwealth Writers Prize for Best Book, the Governor General's Award, and the W. H. Smith/Books in Canada First Novel Award. *A Fine Balance* was shortlisted for the Booker Prize and won the Commonwealth Writers Prize for Best Book.

More praise for *A Fine Balance*:

'A brave, wildly imaginative book . . . Full of bleak messages, it is also extraordinarily funny.' *Spectator*

'The novel works wonderfully well and is a distinguished addition to the mythologizing of Bombay.' *Times Literary Supplement*

'Mistry combines the old-fashioned storyteller's precise craftsmanship with the film director's art of scanning the vastness and complexity of India without the need to use tricky literary devices.' *Evening Standard*

'*A Fine Balance* is, in almost every respect, an admirable book . . . both hugely ambitious and touchingly simple. Mistry tells his story with the honesty of a writer who knows he has a story worth telling.' *Sunday Telegraph*

'Rohinton Mistry, who both won the Commonwealth Writers Prize and was shortlisted for the Booker with his first novel, *Such a Long Journey*, has more than confirmed his promise in this capacious yet utterly readable successor . . . this most sympathetic and loving of novels.' *Daily Telegraph*

'This is Mistry's great gift: gradual enlightenment through the patient accumulation of detail. Nothing is obvious, everything significant. The slightest disclosure may change the whole perspective . . . Mistry writes with exquisite clarity. He uses language to dignify life . . . Modesty is a rare virtue in contemporary fiction. Mistry has it in abundance. He makes himself invisible, never allowing his prose to draw attention to itself . . . *A Fine Balance* is a masterpiece of illumination and grace. Like all great fiction, it transforms our understanding of life.' *Guardian by the same author*

SUCH A LONG JOURNEY
TALES FROM FIROZSHA BAAG

ROHINTON MISTRY

A Fine Balance

faber and faber
LONDON · BOSTON

First published in Great Britain in 1996
by Faber and Faber Limited
3 Queen Square London WC1N 3AU
Open market paperback edition first published in 1996
This paperback edition first published in 1997

Printed and bound in Great Britain by Mackays of Chatham plc,
Chatham, Kent

© Rohinton Mistry, 1995

Rohinton Mistry is hereby identified as author of this
work in accordance with Section 77 of the Copyright,
Designs and Patents Act 1988

*This book is sold subject to the condition that it shall not, by way of
trade or otherwise, be lent, resold, hired out or otherwise circulated
without the publisher's prior consent in any form of binding or cover other
than that in which it is published and without a similar condition including
this condition being imposed on the subsequent purchaser*

A CIP record for this book
is available from the British Library

ISBN 0-571-17936-3

'Holding this book in your hand, sinking back in your soft arm-chair, you will say to yourself: perhaps it will amuse me. And after you have read this story of great misfortunes, you will no doubt dine well, blaming the author for your own insensitivity, accusing him of wild exaggeration and flights of fancy. But rest assured: this tragedy is not a fiction. All is true.'

Honoré de Balzac, *Le Père Goriot*

Contents

Prologue: 1975 1

I City by the Sea 13

II For Dreams to Grow 71

III In a Village by a River 93

IV Small Obstacles 165

V Mountains 197

VI Day at the Circus, Night in the Slum 255

VII On the Move 291

VIII Beautification 319

IX What Law There Is 349

X Sailing Under One Flag 377

XI The Bright Future Clouded 407

XII Trace of Destiny 435

XIII Wedding, Worms, and Sanyas 463

XIV Return of Solitude 487

XV Family Planning 513

XVI The Circle Is Completed 545

Epilogue: 1984 577

Prologue: 1975

THE MORNING EXPRESS bloated with passengers slowed to a crawl, then lurched forward suddenly, as though to resume full speed. The train's brief deception jolted its riders. The bulge of humans hanging out of the doorway distended perilously, like a soap bubble at its limit.

Inside the compartment, Maneck Kohlah held on to the overhead railing, propped up securely within the crush. He felt someone's elbow knock his textbooks from his hand. In the seats nearby, a thin young fellow was catapulted into the arms of the man opposite him. Maneck's textbooks fell upon them.

'Ow!' said the young fellow, as volume one slammed into his back.

Laughing, he and his uncle untangled themselves. Ishvar Darji, who had a disfigured left cheek, helped his nephew out of his lap and back onto the seat. 'Everything all right, Om?'

'Apart from the dent in my back, everything is all right,' said Omprakash Darji, picking up the two books covered in brown paper. He hefted them in his slender hands and looked around to find who had dropped them.

Maneck acknowledged ownership. The thought of his heavy textbooks thumping that frail spine made him shudder. He remembered the sparrow he had killed with a stone, years ago; afterwards, it had made him sick.

His apology was frantic. 'Very sorry, the books slipped and –'

'Not to worry,' said Ishvar. 'Wasn't your fault.' To his nephew he added, 'Good thing it didn't happen in reverse, hahn? If I fell in your lap, my weight would crack your bones.' They laughed again, Maneck too, to supplement his apology.

Ishvar Darji was not a stout man; it was the contrast with Omprakash's skinny limbs that gave rise to their little jokes about his size. The wisecracks originated sometimes with one and sometimes the other. When they had their evening meal, Ishvar would be sure to spoon out a larger portion onto his nephew's enamel plate; at a roadside dhaba, he would wait till Omprakash went for water, or to the latrine, then swiftly scoop some of his own food onto the other leaf.

If Omprakash protested, Ishvar would say, 'What will they think in our village when we return? That I starved my nephew in the city and ate all the food myself? Eat, eat! Only way to save my honour is by fattening you!'

'Don't worry,' Omprakash would tease back. 'If your honour weighs even half as much as you, that will be ample.'

Omprakash's physique, however, defied his uncle's efforts and stayed matchstick thin. Their fortunes, too, stubbornly retained a lean and hungry aspect, and a triumphal return to the village remained a distant dream.

The southbound express slowed again. With a pneumatic hiss, the bogies clanked to a halt. The train was between stations. Its air brakes continued to exhale wheezily for a few moments before dying out.

Omprakash looked through the window to determine where they had stopped. Rough shacks stood beyond the railroad fence, alongside a ditch running with raw sewage. Children were playing a game with sticks and stones. An excited puppy danced around them, trying to join in. Nearby, a shirtless man was milking a cow. They could have been anywhere.

The acrid smell of a dung-fire drifted towards the train. Just ahead, a crowd had gathered near the level-crossing. A few men jumped off the train and began walking down the tracks.

'Hope we reach in time,' said Omprakash. 'If someone gets there before us, we're finished for sure.' ·

Maneck Kohlah asked if they had far to go. Ishvar named the station. 'Oh, that's the same one I want,' said Maneck, fingering his sparse moustache.

Hoping to spot a watch dial, Ishvar looked up into a thicket of wrists growing ceilingward. 'Time, please?' he asked someone over his shoulder. The man shot his cuff stylishly and revealed his watch: a quarter to nine.

'Come on, yaar, move!' said Omprakash, slapping the seat between his thighs.

'Not as obedient as the bullocks in our village, is it?' said his uncle, and Maneck laughed. Ishvar added it was true – ever since he was a child, their village had never lost a bullock-cart race when there were competitions on festival days.

'Give the train a dose of opium and it will run like the bullocks,' said Omprakash.

A combseller, twanging the plastic teeth of a large comb, pushed his way through the crowded compartment. People grumbled and snarled at him, resenting the bothersome presence.

'Oi!' said Omprakash to get his attention.

'Plastic hairband, unbreakable, plastic hairclip, flower shape, butterfly

4

shape, colourful comb, unbreakable.' The combseller recited in a half-hearted monotone, uncertain whether this was a real customer or just a joker passing the time. 'Big comb and small comb, pink, orange, maroon, green, blue, yellow comb – unbreakable.'

Omprakash gave them a test run through his hair before selecting a red specimen, pocket-sized. He dug into his trousers and extracted a coin. The combseller suffered hostile elbows and shoulders while searching for change. He used his shirtsleeve to wipe hair oil off the rejected combs, then returned them to his satchel, keeping in his hand the big dual-toothed one to resume his soft twanging through the compartment.

'What happened to the yellow comb you had?' asked Ishvar.

'Broke in two.'

'How?'

'It was in my back pocket. I sat on it.'

'That's the wrong place for a comb. It's meant for your head, Om, not your bottom.' He always called his nephew Om, using Omprakash only when he was upset with him.

'If it was your bottom, the comb would have smashed into a hundred pieces,' returned his nephew, and Ishvar laughed. His disfigured left cheek was no hindrance, standing firm like a mooring around which his smiles could safely ripple.

He chucked Omprakash under the chin. Most of the time their ages – forty-six and seventeen – were a misleading indicator of their actual relationship. 'Smile, Om. Your angry mouth does not suit your hero hairstyle.' He winked at Maneck to include him in the fun. 'With a puff like that, lots of girls will be after you. But don't worry, Om, I'll select a nice wife for you. A woman big and strong, with flesh enough for two.'

Omprakash grinned and administered a flourish to his hair with the new comb. The train still showed no sign of moving. The men who had wandered outside came back with news that yet another body had been found by the tracks, near the level-crossing. Maneck edged towards the door to listen. A nice, quick way to go, he thought, as long as the train had struck the person squarely.

'Maybe it has to do with the Emergency,' said someone.

'What emergency?'

'Prime Minister made a speech on the radio early this morning. Something about country being threatened from inside.'

'Sounds like one more government tamasha.'

'Why does everybody have to choose the railway tracks only for dying?' grumbled another. 'No consideration for people like us.

Murder, suicide, Naxalite-terrorist killing, police-custody death – everything ends up delaying the trains. What is wrong with poison or tall buildings or knives?'

The long-anticipated rumble at last rippled through the compartments, and the train shivered down its long steel spine. Relief lit the passengers' faces. As the compartments trundled past the level-crossing, everyone craned to see the cause of their delay. Three uniformed policemen stood by the hastily covered corpse awaiting its journey to the morgue. Some passengers touched their foreheads or put their hands together and murmured, 'Ram, Ram.'

Maneck Kohlah descended behind the uncle and nephew, and they exited the platform together. 'Excuse me,' he said, taking a letter from his pocket. 'I am new in the city, can you tell me how to get to this address?'

'You are asking the wrong people,' said Ishvar without reading it. 'We are also new here.'

But Omprakash glanced at the letter and said, 'Look, it's the same name!'

Ishvar pulled a square of ragged paper out of his own pocket and compared it. His nephew was right, there it was: Dina Dalal, followed by the address.

Omprakash regarded Maneck with sudden hostility. 'Why are you going to Dina Dalal? Are you a tailor?'

'Me, tailor? No, she is my mother's friend.'

Ishvar tapped his nephew's shoulder. 'See, simply you were panicking. Come on, let's find the building.'

Maneck did not understand what they meant, till Ishvar explained outside the station. 'You see, Om and I are tailors. Dina Dalal has work for two tailors. We are going to apply.'

'And you thought I was running there to steal your job.' Maneck smiled. 'Don't worry, I am just a student. Dina Dalal and my mother used to be in school together. She's letting me stay with her for a few months, that's all.'

They asked a paanwalla for directions, and walked down the street that was pointed out. Omprakash was still a little suspicious. 'If you are staying with her for a few months, where is your trunk, your belongings? Only two books you have?'

'Today I'm just going to meet her. I will shift my things from the college hostel next month.'

They passed a beggar slumped upon a small wooden platform fitted with castors, which raised him four inches off the ground. His fingers and thumbs were missing, and his legs were amputated almost to the buttocks. 'O babu, ek paisa day-ray!' he sang, shaking a tin can between his bandaged palms. 'O babu! Hai babu! Aray babu, ek paisa day-ray!'

'That's one of the worst I've seen since coming to the city,' said Ishvar, and the others agreed. Omprakash paused to drop a coin in the tin.

They crossed the road, asking again for directions. 'I've been living in this city for two months,' said Maneck, 'but it's so huge and confusing. I can recognize only some big streets. The little lanes all look the same.'

'We have been here six months and still have the same problem. In the beginning we were completely lost. The first time, we couldn't even get on a train – two or three went by before we learned how to push.'

Maneck said he hated it here, and could not wait to return to his home in the mountains, next year, when he finished college.

'We have also come for a short time only,' said Ishvar. 'To earn some money, then go back to our village. What is the use of such a big city? Noise and crowds, no place to live, water scarce, garbage everywhere. Terrible.'

'Our village is far from here,' said Omprakash. 'Takes a whole day by train – morning till night – to reach it.'

'And reach it, we will,' said Ishvar. 'Nothing is as fine as one's native place.'

'My home is in the north,' said Maneck. 'Takes a day and night, plus another day, to get there. From the window of our house you can see snow-covered mountain peaks.'

'A river runs near our village,' said Ishvar. 'You can see it shining, and hear it sing. It's a beautiful place.'

They walked quietly for a while, occupied with home thoughts. Omprakash broke the silence by pointing out a watermelon-sherbet stand. 'Wouldn't that be nice, on such a hot day.'

The vendor stirred his ladle in the tub, tinkling chunks of ice afloat in a sea of dark red. 'Let's have some,' said Maneck. 'It looks delicious.'

'Not for us,' said Ishvar quickly. 'We had a big breakfast this morning,' and Omprakash erased the longing from his face.

'Okay,' said Maneck doubtfully, ordering one large glass. He studied the tailors who stood with eyes averted, not looking at the tempting tub or his frosted glass. He saw their tired faces, how poor their clothes were, the worn-out chappals.

He drank half and said, 'I'm full. You want it?'

They shook their heads.

'It will go to waste.'

'Okay, yaar, in that case,' said Omprakash, and took the sherbet. He gulped some, then passed it to his uncle.

Ishvar drained the glass and returned it to the vendor. 'That was so tasty,' he said, beaming with pleasure. 'It was very kind of you to share it with us, we really enjoyed it, thank you.' His nephew gave him a disapproving look to tone it down.

How much gratitude for a little sherbet, thought Maneck, how starved they seemed for ordinary kindness.

═══

The verandah door had a brass nameplate: *Mr. & Mrs. Rustom K. Dalal*, the letters enriched by years of verdigris. Dina Dalal answered their ring and accepted the scrap of crumpled paper, recognizing her own handwriting.

'You are tailors?'

'Hahnji,' said Ishvar, nodding vigorously. All three entered the verandah at her invitation and stood awkwardly.

The verandah, which used to be an open gallery, had been converted into an extra room when Dina Dalal's late husband was still a child – his parents had decided it would be a playroom to supplement the tiny flat. The portico was bricked and fitted with an iron-grilled window.

'But I need only two tailors,' said Dina Dalal.

'Excuse me, I'm not a tailor. My name is Maneck Kohlah.' He stepped forward from behind Ishvar and Omprakash.

'Oh, you are Maneck! Welcome! Sorry, I couldn't recognize you. It's been years since I last saw your mummy, and you I have never, ever, seen.'

She left the tailors on the verandah and took him inside, into the front room. 'Can you wait here for a few minutes while I deal with those two?'

'Sure.'

Maneck took in the shabby furnishings around him: the battered sofa, two chairs with fraying seats, a scratched teapoy, a dining table with a cracked and faded rexine tablecloth. She mustn't live here, he decided, this was probably a family business, a boarding house. The walls were badly in need of paint. He played with the discoloured plaster blotches, the way he did with clouds, imagining animals and landscapes. Dog shaking hands. Hawk diving sharply. Man with walking-stick climbing mountain.

On the verandah, Dina Dalal ran a hand over her black hair, as yet uninvaded by grey, and turned her attention to the tailors. At forty-two, her forehead was still smooth, and sixteen years spent fending for herself had not hardened the looks which, a long time ago, used to make her brother's friends vie to impress her.

She asked for names and tailoring experience. The tailors claimed to know everything about women's clothes. 'We can even take measurements straight from the customer's body and make any fashion you like,' said Ishvar confidently, doing all the talking while Omprakash nodded away.

'For this job, there will be no customers to measure,' she explained. 'The sewing will be straight from paper patterns. Each week you have to make two dozen, three dozen, whatever the company wants, in the same style.'

'Child's play,' said Ishvar. 'But we'll do it.'

'What about you?' she addressed Omprakash, whose look was disdainful. 'You have not said a word.'

'My nephew speaks only when he disagrees,' said Ishvar. 'His silence is a good sign.'

She liked Ishvar's face, the type that put people at ease and encouraged conversation. But there was the other tight-lipped fellow, who frightened away the words. His chin was too small for his features, though when he smiled everything seemed in proportion.

She stated the terms of employment: they would have to bring their own sewing-machines; all sewing would be piecework. 'The more dresses you make, the more you earn,' she said, and Ishvar agreed that that was fair. Rates would be fixed according to the complexity of each pattern. The hours were from eight a.m. to six p.m. – less than that would not do, though they were welcome to work longer. And there would be no smoking or paan-chewing on the job.

'Paan we don't chew only,' said Ishvar. 'But sometimes we like to smoke a beedi.'

'You will have to smoke it outside.'

The conditions were acceptable. 'What is the address of your shop?' asked Ishvar. 'Where do we bring the sewing-machines?'

'Right here. When you come next week, I will show you where to put them, in the back room.'

'Okayji, thank you, we will definitely come on Monday.' They waved to Maneck as they left. 'We will see you again soon, hanh.'

'Sure,' said Maneck, waving back. Noticing Dina Dalal's silent inquiry, he explained about their meeting on the train.

'You must be careful who you talk to,' she said. 'Never know what kind of crooks you might run into. This is not your little hamlet in the mountains.'

'They seemed very nice.'

'Hmm, yes,' she said, reserving judgement. Then she apologized again for assuming he was a tailor. 'I could not see you properly because you were standing behind them, my eyes are weak.' How silly of me, she thought, mistaking this lovely boy for a bowlegged tailor. And so sturdy too. Must be the famous mountain air they talk about, the healthy food and water.

She peered a little closer, tilting her head to one side. 'It has been over twenty years, but I can recognize your mummy in your face. You know Aban and I were in school together.'

'Yes,' he said, uncomfortable under her intense scrutiny. 'Mummy told me in her letter. She also wanted to let you know I'll move in from next month, and she'll mail you the rent cheque.'

'Yes, yes, that's all right,' she said, dismissing his concern about the details and drifting again into the past. 'Real little terrors we used to be in our school-days. And a third girl, Zenobia. When we three were together, it was trouble with a capital t, the teachers would say.' The memory brought a wistful smile to her face. 'Anyway, let me show you my house, and your room.'

'You live here as well?'

'Where else?' As she led him through the dingy little flat, she asked what he was taking at college.

'Refrigeration and air-conditioning.'

'I hope you will do something about this hot weather then, make my home more comfortable.'

He smiled feebly, saddened by the place in which she resided. Not much better than the college hostel, he thought. And yet, he was looking forward to it. Anything would do, after what had happened there. He shuddered and tried to think of something else.

'This one will be your room.'

'It's very nice. Thank you, Mrs. Dalal.'

There was a cupboard in one corner with a scratched, misshapen suitcase on top. A small desk stood beside the cupboard. Here, as in the front room, the ceiling was dark and flaking, the walls discoloured, missing chunks of plaster in several places. Other stark patches, recently cemented, stood out like freshly healed wounds. Two single beds lay at right angles along the walls. He wondered if she would sleep in the same room.

'I will move one bed into the other room for myself.'

He looked through the door beyond and glimpsed a room tinier and in worse condition, crowded by a cupboard (also with a suitcase on top), a rickety table, two chairs, and three rusting trunks stacked on a trestle.

'I am turning you out of your own room,' mumbled Maneck, the surroundings depressing him rapidly.

'Don't be silly.' Her tone was brisk. 'I wanted a paying guest, and it is my great good luck to get a nice Parsi boy – the son of my schoolfriend.'

'It's very kind of you, Mrs. Dalal.'

'And that's another thing. You must call me Dina Aunty.'

Maneck nodded.

'You can bring your things here any time. If you are not happy with the hostel, this room is ready – we don't have to wait for a special date next month.'

'No, it's all right, but thank you, Mrs. –'

'Ahn, careful.'

'I mean, Dina Aunty.' They smiled.

When Maneck left her flat, she began pacing the room, suddenly restless, as though about to embark on a long voyage. No need now to visit her brother and beg for next month's rent. She took a deep breath. Once again, her fragile independence was preserved.

Tomorrow she would bring home the first batch of sewing from Au Revoir Exports.

1 City by the Sea

DINA DALAL SELDOM indulged in looking back at her life with regret or bitterness, or questioning why things had turned out the way they had, cheating her of the bright future everyone had predicted for her when she was in school, when her name was still Dina Shroff. And if she did sink into one of these rare moods, she quickly swam out of it. What was the point of repeating the story over and over and over, she asked herself – it always ended the same way; whichever corridor she took, she wound up in the same room.

Dina's father had been a doctor, a GP with a modest practice who followed the Hippocratic oath somewhat more passionately than others of his profession. During the early years of Dr. Shroff's career, his devotion to his work was diagnosed, by peers, family members, and senior physicians, as typical of youthful zeal and vigour. 'How refreshing, this enthusiasm of the young,' they smiled, nodding sagely, confident that time would douse the fires of idealism with a healthy dose of cynicism and family responsibilities.

But marriage, and the arrival of a son, followed eleven years later by a daughter, changed nothing for Dr. Shroff. Time only sharpened the imbalance between his fervour to ease suffering and his desire to earn a comfortable income.

'How disappointing,' said friends and relatives, shaking their heads. 'Such high hopes we had for him. And he keeps slaving like a clerk, like a fanatic, refusing to enjoy life. Poor Mrs. Shroff. Never a vacation, never a party – no fun at all in her existence.'

At fifty-one, when most GPs would have begun considering options like working half-time, hiring an inexpensive junior, or even selling the practice in favour of early retirement, Dr. Shroff had neither the bank balance nor the temperament to permit such indulgences. Instead, he volunteered to lead a campaign of medical graduates bound for districts in the interior. There, where typhoid and cholera, unchallenged by science or technology, were still reaping their routine harvest of villagers, Dr. Shroff would try to seize the deadly sickles or, at the very least, to blunt them.

But Mrs. Shroff undertook a different sort of campaign: to dissuade her husband from going into what she felt were the jaws of certain death. She attempted to coach Dina with words to sway her father. After all, Dina, at twelve, was Daddy's darling. Mrs. Shroff knew that her son, Nusswan, could be of no help in this enterprise. Enlisting him would have ruined any chance of changing her husband's mind.

The turning point in the father-and-son relationship had come seven years ago, on Nusswan's sixteenth birthday. Uncles and aunts had been invited to dinner, and someone said, 'Well, Nusswan, you will soon be studying to become a doctor, just like your father.'

'I don't want to be a doctor,' Nusswan answered. 'I'll be going into business – import and export.'

Some of the uncles and aunts nodded approvingly. Others recoiled in mock horror, turning to Dr. Shroff. 'Is this true? No father-son partnership?'

'Of course it's true,' he said. 'My children are free to do whatever they please.'

But five-year-old Dina had seen the hurt on her father's face before he could hide it. She ran to him and clambered onto his lap. 'Daddy, I want to be a doctor, just like you, when I grow up.'

Everyone laughed and applauded, and said, Smart little girl, knows how to get what she wants. Later, they whispered that the son was obviously not made of the same solid stuff as the father – no ambition, wouldn't amount to much.

Dina had repeated her wish in the years to come, continuing to regard her father as some kind of god who gave people good health, who struggled against illness, and who, sometimes, succeeded in temporarily thwarting death. And Dr. Shroff was delighted with his bright child. On parents' night at the convent school, the principal and teachers always had the highest praise for her. She would succeed if she wanted to, Dr. Shroff knew it for certain.

Mrs. Shroff also knew, for certain, that her daughter was the one to recruit in the campaign against Dr. Shroff's foolish philanthropic plan of working in remote, Godforsaken villages. But Dina refused to cooperate; she did not approve of devious means to keep her beloved father home.

Then Mrs. Shroff resorted to other methods, using not money or his personal safety or his family to persuade him, for she knew these would fail hopelessly. Instead, she invoked his patients, claiming he was abandoning them, old and frail and helpless. 'What will they do if you go so far away? They trust you and rely on you. How can you be so cruel? You have no idea how much you mean to them.'

'No, that is not the point,' said Dr. Shroff. He was familiar with the anfractuous arguments that her love for him could prompt her to wield. Patiently he explained there were GPs galore in the city who could take care of the assorted aches and pains – where he was going, the people had no one. He comforted her that it was only a temporary assignment, hugging and kissing her much more than was usual for him. 'I promise to be back soon,' he said. 'Before you even grow used to my absence.'

But Dr. Shroff could not keep his promise. Three weeks into the medical campaign he was dead, not from typhoid or cholera, but from a cobra's bite, far from the lifesaving reach of antivenins.

Mrs. Shroff received the news calmly. People said it was because she was a doctor's wife, more familiar with death than other mortals. They reasoned that Dr. Shroff must have often carried such tidings to her regarding his own patients, thus preparing her for the inevitable.

When she took brisk charge of the funeral arrangements, managing everything with superb efficiency, people wondered if there was not something a little abnormal about her behaviour. Between disbursing funds from her handbag for the various expenses, she accepted condolences, comforted grieving relatives, tended the oil lamp at the head of Dr. Shroff's bed, washed and ironed her white sari, and made sure there was a supply of incense and sandalwood in the house. She personally instructed the cook about the special vegetarian meal for the next day.

After the full four days of death ceremonies, Dina was still crying. Mrs. Shroff, who was busy tallying the prayer-bungalow charges from the Towers of Silence, said briskly, 'Come, my daughter, be sensible now. Daddy would not like this.' So Dina did her best to control herself.

Then Mrs. Shroff continued absentmindedly, writing out the cheque. 'You could have stopped him if you wanted. He would have listened to you,' she said.

Dina's sobs burst out with renewed intensity. In addition to the grief for her father, her tears now included anger towards her mother, even hatred. It would take her a few months to understand that there was no malice or accusation contained in what had been said, just a sad and simple statement of fact as seen by her mother.

Six months after Dr. Shroff's death, after being the pillar that everyone could lean on, Mrs. Shroff gradually began to crumble. Retreating from daily life, she took very little interest in the running of her household or in her own person.

It made little difference to Nusswan, who was twenty-three and busy planning his own future. But Dina, at twelve, could have done with a parent for a few more years. She missed her father dreadfully. Her mother's withdrawal made it much worse.

===

Nusswan Shroff had earned his own living as a businessman for two years prior to his father's death. He was still single, living at home, saving his money while searching for a suitable flat and a suitable wife. With his father's passing and his mother's reclusion, he realized that the pursuit of a flat was unnecessary, and a wife, urgent.

He now assumed the role of head of the family, and legal guardian to Dina. All their relatives agreed this was as it should be. They praised his selfless decision, admitting they had been wrong about his capabilities. He also took over the family finances, promising that his mother and sister would want for nothing; he would look after them out of his own salary. But, even as he spoke, he knew there was no need for this. The money from the sale of Dr. Shroff's dispensary was sufficient.

Nusswan's first decision as head of the family was to cut back on the hired help. The cook, who came for half the day and prepared the two main meals, was kept on; Lily, the live-in servant, was let go. 'We cannot continue in the same luxury as before,' he declared. 'I just can't afford the wages.'

Mrs. Shroff expressed some doubt about the change. 'Who will do the cleaning? My hands and feet don't work like before.'

'Don't worry, Mamma, we will all share it. You can do easy things, like dusting the furniture. We can wash our own cups and saucers, surely. And Dina is a young girl, full of energy. It will be good for her, teach her how to look after a home.'

'Yes, maybe you are right,' said Mrs. Shroff, vaguely convinced of the need for money-saving measures.

But Dina knew there was more to it. The week before, while passing the kitchen on her way to the WC well past midnight, she had noticed her brother with the ayah: Lily sitting on one end of the kitchen table, her feet resting on the edge; Nusswan, his pyjamas around his ankles, stood between Lily's thighs, clasping her hips to him. Dina watched his bare buttocks with sleepy curiosity, then crept back to bed without using the toilet, her cheeks flushed. But she must have lingered a moment too long, for Nusswan had seen her.

Not a word was spoken about it. Lily departed (with a modest bonus, unbeknownst to Mrs. Shroff), tearfully declaring that she would never find as nice a family to work for ever again. Dina felt sorry for her, and also despised her.

Then the new household arrangement got under way. Everyone made an honest effort. The experiment in self-reliance seemed like fun. 'It's a little like going camping,' said Mrs. Shroff.

'That's the spirit,' said Nusswan.

With the passing of days, Dina's chores began to increase. As a token of his participation, Nusswan continued to wash his cup, saucer, and breakfast plate before going to work. Beyond that, he did nothing.

One morning, after swallowing his last gulp of tea, he said, 'I'm very late today, Dina. Please wash my things.'

'I'm not your servant! Wash your own dirty plates!' Weeks of pent-up resentment came gushing. 'You said we would each do our own work! All your stinking things you leave for me!'

'Listen to the little tigress,' said Nusswan, amused.

'You mustn't speak like that to your big brother,' chided Mrs. Shroff gently. 'Remember, we must share and share alike.'

'He's cheating! He doesn't do any work! I do everything!'

Nusswan hugged his mother: 'Bye-bye, Mamma,' and gave Dina a friendly pat on the shoulder to make up. She shrank from him. 'The tigress is still angry,' he said and left for the office.

Mrs. Shroff tried to soothe Dina, promising to discuss it later with Nusswan, maybe convince him to hire a part-time ayah, but her resolve melted within hours. Matters continued as before. As weeks went by, instead of restoring fairness in the household, she began turning into one of the chores on her daughter's ever-growing list.

Now Mrs. Shroff had to be told what to do. When food was placed before her, she ate it, though it did her little good, for she kept losing weight. She had to be reminded to bathe and change her clothes. If toothpaste was squeezed out and handed to her on the brush, she brushed her teeth. For Dina, the most unpleasant task was helping her mother wash her hair – it fell out in clumps on the bathroom floor, and more followed when she combed it for her.

Once every month, Mrs. Shroff attended her husband's prayers at the fire-temple. She said it gave her great comfort to hear the elderly Dustoor Framji's soothing tones supplicating for her husband's soul. Dina missed school to accompany her mother, worried about her wandering off somewhere.

Before commencing the ceremony, Dustoor Framji unctuously shook Mrs. Shroff's hand and gave Dina a prolonged hug of the sort he reserved for girls and young women. His reputation for squeezing and fondling had earned him the title of Dustoor Daab-Chaab, along with the hostility of his colleagues, who resented not so much his actions but his lack of subtlety, his refusal to disguise his embraces with fatherly or spiritual concern. They feared that one day he would go too far, drool over his victim or something, and disgrace the fire-temple.

Dina squirmed in his grasp as he patted her head, rubbed her neck, stroked her back and pressed himself against her. He had a very short beard, stubble that resembled flakes of grated coconut, and it scraped her cheeks and forehead. He released her just when she had summoned enough courage to tear her trapped body from his arms.

After the fire-temple, for the rest of the day at home Dina tried to make her mother talk, asking her advice about housework or recipes, and when that failed, about Daddy, and the days of their newlywed lives. Faced with her mother's dreamy silences, Dina felt helpless. Soon, her concern for her mother was tempered by the instinct of youth which held her back – she would surely receive her portion of grief and sorrow in due course, there was no need to take on the burden prematurely.

And Mrs. Shroff spoke in monosyllables or sighs, staring into Dina's face for answers. As for dusting the furniture, she could never proceed beyond wiping the picture frame containing her husband's graduation photograph. She spent most of her time gazing out the window.

Nusswan preferred to regard his mother's disintegration as a widow's appropriate renunciation, wherein she was sloughing off the dross of life to concentrate on spiritual matters. He focused his attention on the raising of Dina. The thought of the enormous responsibility resting on his shoulders worried him ceaselessly.

He had always perceived his father to be a strict disciplinarian; he had stood in awe of him, had even been a little frightened of him. If he was to fill his father's shoes, he would have to induce the same fear in others, he decided, and prayed regularly for courage and guidance in his task. He confided to the relatives – the uncles and aunts – that Dina's defiance, her stubbornness, was driving him crazy, and only the Almighty's help gave him the strength to go forward in his duty.

His sincerity touched them. They promised to pray for him too. 'Don't worry, Nusswan, everything will be all right. We will light a lamp at the fire-temple.'

Heartened by their support, Nusswan began taking Dina with him to the fire-temple once a week. There, he thrust a stick of sandalwood in her hand and whispered fiercely in her ear, 'Now pray properly – ask Dadaji to make you a good girl, ask Him to make you obedient.'

While she bowed before the sanctum, he travelled along the outer wall hung with pictures of various dustoors and high priests. He glided from display to display, stroking the garlands, hugging the frames, kissing the glass, and ending with the very tall picture of Zarathustra to which he glued his lips for a full minute. Then, from the vessel of ashes placed in the sanctum's doorway, he smeared a pinch on his forehead, another bit across the throat, and undid his top two shirt buttons to rub a fistful over his chest.

Like talcum powder, thought Dina, watching from the corner of her eye, from her bowed position, straining to keep from laughing. She did not raise her head till he had finished his antics.

'Did you pray properly?' he demanded when they were outside.

She nodded.

'Good. Now all the bad thoughts will leave your head, you will feel peace and quiet in your heart.'

Dina was no longer allowed to spend time at her friends' houses during the holidays. 'There is no need to,' said Nusswan. 'You see them every day in school.' They could visit her after being granted his permission, but this was not much fun since he always hovered around.

Once, he overheard her in the next room with her friend Zenobia, making fun of his teeth. It only served to confirm his belief that the little devils needed monitoring. Zenobia was saying he looked like a horse.

'Yes, a horse with cheap dentures,' added Dina.

'An elephant would be proud of that much ivory,' continued Zenobia, raising the stakes.

They were helpless with laughter when he entered the room. He fixed each one with a black stare before turning away with menacing slowness, leaving behind silence and misery. Yes, it worked, he realized with surprise and triumph – fear worked.

Nusswan had always been sensitive about his bad teeth and, in his late teens, had tried to get them straightened. Dina, only six or seven then, had teased him mercilessly. But the orthodontic treatment was too painful, and he abandoned it, complaining that with a doctor for a father, it was surprising his condition had not been taken care of in childhood. As evidence of partiality, he would point to Dina's perfect mouth.

Distressed by his hurt, their mother had tried to explain. 'It's all my fault, son, I didn't know that children's teeth should be massaged daily, gently pressed inward. The old nurse at Dina's birth taught me the trick, but it was too late for you.'

Nusswan had never been convinced. And now, after Dina's friend left, she paid the price. He asked her to repeat what was said. She did, boldly.

'You have always had the habit of blurting whatever comes into your loose mouth. But you are no longer a child. Someone has to teach you respect.' He sighed, 'It is my duty, I suppose,' and without warning he began slapping her. He stopped when a cut opened her lower lip.

'You pig!' she wept. 'You want to make me look ugly like you!' Whereupon, he got a ruler and whacked her wherever he could, as she ran around trying to escape the blows.

For once, Mrs. Shroff noticed that something was wrong. 'Why are you crying, my daughter?'

'That stupid Dracula! He hit me and made me bleed!'

'Tch-tch, my poor child.' She hugged Dina and returned to her seat by the window.

Two days after this row, Nusswan tried to make peace by bringing Dina a collection of ribbons. 'They will look lovely in your plaits,' he said.

She went to her school satchel, got out her arts-and-crafts scissors, and snipped the ribbons into small pieces.

'Look, Mamma!' he said, almost in tears. 'Look at your vindictive daughter! My hard-earned money I spend on her, and this is the thanks.'

The ruler became Nusswan's instrument of choice in his quest for discipline. His clothes were the most frequent cause of Dina's punishment. After washing, ironing, and folding them, she had to stack four separate piles in his cupboard: white shirts, coloured shirts, white trousers, coloured trousers. Sometimes she would strategically place a pinstriped shirt with the whites, or liberate a pair of pants with a hound's-tooth check among the white trousers. Despite the beatings, she never tired of provoking him.

'The way she behaves, I feel that Sataan himself has taken refuge in her heart,' he said wearily to the relatives who asked for updates. 'Maybe I should just pack her off to a boarding school.'

'No, no, don't take that drastic step,' they pleaded. 'Boarding school has been the ruination of many Parsi girls. Rest assured, God will repay you for your patience and devotion. And Dina will also thank you when she is old enough to understand it's for her own good.' They went away murmuring the man was a saint – every girl should be fortunate enough to have a brother like Nusswan.

His spirit restored by their encouragement, Nusswan persevered. He bought all of Dina's clothes, deciding what was appropriate for a young girl. The purchases were usually ill-fitting, for she was not allowed to be present while he shopped. 'I don't want tiresome arguments in the shopkeeper's presence,' he said. 'You always embarrass me.' When she needed new uniforms, he went to school with her on the day the tailors were coming, to supervise the measurements. He quizzed the tailors about rates and fabrics, trying to work out the principal's kickbacks.

Dina dreaded this annual event, wondering what new mortification would be visited upon her before her classmates.

All her friends were now wearing their hair short, and she begged to be allowed the same privilege. 'If you let me cut my hair, I'll swab the dining room every day instead of alternate days,' she tried to bargain. 'Or I can polish your shoes every night.'

'No,' said Nusswan. 'Fourteen is too young for fancy hairstyles, plaits are good for you. Besides, I cannot afford to pay for the hairdresser.' But he promptly added shoe-polishing to her list of chores.

A week after her final appeal, with the help of Zenobia in the school bathroom, Dina lopped off the plaits. Zenobia's ambition was to be a hairstylist, and she was overwhelmed by the good fortune that delivered her friend's head into her hands. 'Let's cut off the whole jing-bang lot,' she said. 'Let's bob it really short.'

'Are you crazy?' said Dina. 'Nusswan will jump over the moon.' So they settled for a pageboy, and Zenobia trimmed the hair to roughly an inch above the shoulders. It looked a bit ragged, but both girls were delighted with the results.

Dina hesitated about throwing the severed plaits in the dustbin. She put them in her satchel and raced home. Parading proudly about the house, she went repeatedly past the many mirrors to catch glimpses of her head from different angles. Then she visited her mother's room and waited – for her surprise, or delight, or something. But Mrs. Shroff noticed nothing.

'Do you like my new hairstyle, Mummy?' she asked at last.

Mrs. Shroff stared blankly for a moment. 'Very pretty, my daughter, very pretty.'

Nusswan got home late that evening. He greeted his mother, and said there had been so much work at the office. Then he saw Dina. He took a deep breath and put a hand to his forehead. Exhausted, he wished there was some way to deal with this without another fight. But her insolence, her defiance, could not go unpunished; or how would he look himself in the mirror?

'Please come here, Dina. Explain why you have disobeyed me.'

She scratched her neck where tiny hair clippings were making her skin itch. 'How did I disobey you?'

He slapped her. 'Don't question me when I ask you something.'

'You said you couldn't afford my haircut. This was free, I did it myself.'

He slapped her again. 'No back talk, I'm warning you.' He got the ruler and struck her with it flat across the palms, then, because he deemed the offence extremely serious, with the edge over her knuckles. 'This will teach you to look like a loose woman.'

'Have you seen your hair in the mirror? You look like a clown,' she said, refusing to be intimidated.

Nusswan's haircut, in his own opinion, was a statement of dignified elegance. He wore a centre parting, imposing order on either side of it with judicious applications of heavy pomade. Dina's taunt unleashed the fury of the disciplinarian. With lashes of the ruler across her calves and arms, he drove her to the bathroom, where he began tearing off her clothes.

'I don't want another word from you! Not a word! Today you have crossed the limit! Take a bath first, you polluted creature! Wash off those hair clippings before you spread them around the house and bring misfortune upon us!'

'Don't worry, your face will frighten away any misfortune.' She was standing naked on the tiles now, but he did not leave. 'I need hot water,' she said.

He stepped back and flung a mugful of cold water at her from the bucket. Shivering, she stared defiantly at him, her nipples stiffening. He pinched one, hard, and she flinched. 'Look at you with your little breasts starting to grow. You think you are a woman already. I should cut them right off, along with your wicked tongue.'

He was eyeing her strangely, and she grew afraid. She understood that her sharp answers were enraging him, that it was vaguely linked to the way he was staring at the newfledged bloom of hair where her legs met. It would be safer to seem submissive, to douse his anger. She turned away and started to cry, her hands over her face.

Satisfied, he left. Her school satchel, lying on her bed, drew his attention. He opened it for a random inspection and found the plaits sitting on top. Dangling one between thumb and forefinger, he gritted his teeth before a smile slowly eased his angry features.

When Dina had finished her bath, he fetched a roll of black electrical tape and fastened the plaits to her hair. 'You will wear them like this,' he said. 'Every day, even to school, till your hair has grown back.'

She wished she had thrown the wretched things away in the school toilet. It felt like dead rats were hanging from her head.

Next morning, she secretly took the roll of tape to school. The plaits were pulled off before going to class. It was painful, with the black tape clutching hard. When school was over, she fixed them back with Zenobia's help. In this way she evaded Nusswan's punishment on weekdays.

But a few days later riots started in the city, in the wake of Partition and the British departure, and Dina was stuck at home with Nusswan. There were day-and-night curfews in every neighbourhood. Offices, businesses, colleges, schools, all stayed closed, and there was no respite from the detested plaits. He allowed her to remove them only while bathing, and supervised their reattachment immediately after.

Cooped up inside the flat, Nusswan lamented the country's calamity, grumbling endlessly. 'Every day I sit at home, I lose money. These bloody uncultured savages don't deserve independence. If they must hack one another to death, I wish they would go somewhere else and do it quietly. In their villages, maybe. Without disturbing our lovely city by the sea.'

When the curfew was lifted, Dina flew off to school, happy as an uncaged bird, eager for her eight hours of Nusswan less existence. And he, too, was relieved to return to his office. On the first evening of normalcy in the city, he came home in a most cheerful mood. 'The curfew is over, and your punishment is over. We can throw away your plaits now,' he said, adding generously, 'You know, short hair does suit you.'

He opened his briefcase and took out a new hairband. 'You can wear this now instead of electrical tape,' he joked.

'Wear it yourself,' she said, refusing to take it.

Three years after his father's death, Nusswan married. A few weeks later, his mother's withdrawal from life was complete. Where before she had responded obediently to instructions – get up, drink your tea, wash your hands, swallow your medicine – now there was only a wall of incomprehension.

The task of caring for her had outgrown Dina's ability. When the smell from Mrs. Shroff's room was past ignoring, Nusswan timidly broached the subject with his wife. He did not dare ask her directly to help, but hoped that her good nature might persuade her to volunteer. 'Ruby, dear, Mamma is getting worse. She needs a lot of attention, all the time.'

'Put her in a nursing home,' said Ruby. 'She'll be better off there.'

He nodded placatingly, and did something less expensive and more human than shipping his mother to the old-age factory – as some unkind relatives would doubtless have put it – he hired a full-time nurse.

The nurse's assignment was short-lived; Mrs. Shroff died later that year, and people finally understood that a doctor's wife was no more immune to grief than other mortals. She died on the same day of the Shahenshahi calendar as her husband. Their prayers were performed consecutively at the same fire-temple by Dustoor Framji. By this time, Dina had learned how to evade the trap of his overfriendly hugs. When he approached, she held out a polite hand and took a step back, and another, and another. Short of pursuing her around the prayer-hall amid the large thuribles of flaming sandalwood, he could only smile foolishly and give up the chase.

After the first month's prayer ceremonies for Mrs. Shroff were completed, Nusswan decided there was no point in Dina matriculating. Her last report card was quite wretched. She would have been kept back were it not for the principal who, loyal to the memory of Dr. Shroff, preferred to see the marks as a temporary aberration.

'Very decent of Miss Lamb to promote you,' said Nusswan. 'But the fact remains that your results are hopeless. I'm not going to waste money on school fees for another year.'

'You make me clean and scrub all the time, I cannot study for even one hour a day! What do you expect?'

26

'Don't make excuses. A strong young girl, doing a little housework – what's that got to do with studying? Do you know how fortunate you are? There are thousands of poor children in the city, doing boot-polishing at railway stations, or collecting papers, bottles, plastic – plus going to school at night. And you are complaining? What's lacking in you is the desire for education. This is it, enough schooling for you.'

Dina was not willing to concede without a struggle. She also hoped that Nusswan's wife would intervene on her behalf. But Ruby preferred to stay out of the quarrel, so next morning when she was sent to market with a shopping list, Dina ran to her grandfather's flat.

Grandfather lived with one of her uncles, in a room that smelled of stale balm. She held her breath and hugged him, then poured out her troubles in a torrent of words. 'Please, Grandpa! Please tell him to stop treating me like this!'

Already started on the road to senility, he took a while to realize who Dina was exactly, and longer to understand what she wanted. His dentures were not in, making it difficult to decipher his speech. 'Shall I get your teeth, Grandpa?' she offered.

'No, no, no!' He raised his hands and shook them vehemently. 'No teeth. All crooked, and paining in the mouth. Bastard stupid dentist, useless fellow. My carpenter could make better teeth.'

She repeated everything slowly, and at last he grasped the issue. 'Matric? Who, you? Of course you must do your matric. Of course. Of course. You must matriculate. And then college. Yes, of course I will tell that shameless rascal to send you, I will order that Nauzer. No, Nevil – that Nusswan, yes, I will force him.'

He dispatched a servant with a message for Nusswan to visit him as soon as possible. Nusswan could not refuse. He cared deeply about the family's opinion of him. After delaying for several days, citing too much work at the office, he went, taking Ruby along to have an ally by his side. She was instructed to ingratiate herself with the old man in any way possible.

Grandfather had misplaced more of his memory since Dina's visit. He remembered nothing of their conversation. He was wearing his teeth this time but had very little to say. With much prompting and reminiscing he appeared to recognize them. Then, ignoring Ruby altogether, he abruptly decided that Nusswan and Dina were man and wife. He refused to relinquish this belief, however much Dina coaxed and cajoled.

Ruby sat on the sofa holding the old man's hand. She asked if he would like her to massage his feet. Without waiting for an answer she grabbed the left one and began kneading it. The toenails were yellow, long overdue for a clipping.

Enraged, he tore his foot from her grasp. 'Kya karta hai? Chalo, jao!'

Too startled at being addressed in Hindi, Ruby sat there gaping. Grandfather turned to Nusswan, 'Doesn't she understand? What language does your ayah speak? Tell her to get off my sofa, wait in the kitchen.'

Ruby rose in a huff and stood by the door. 'Rude old man!' she hissed. 'Just because my skin is a little dark!'

Nusswan said a gruff goodbye and followed his wife, stopping to turn and look triumphantly at Dina, who was trying to sort out the confusion. She stayed behind, hoping Grandpa would summon some hidden resource and come to her rescue. An hour later she too gave up, kissed his forehead, and left.

It was the last time she saw him alive. He died in his sleep the following month. At the funeral, Dina wondered how much longer Grandpa's toenails had grown under the white sheet that hid everything from view but his face.

———

For four years, Nusswan had been faithfully putting money aside for Dina's wedding expenses. A considerable sum had collected, and he planned to get her married in the near future. He was certain he would have no trouble finding a good husband – as he proudly said to himself, Dina had grown into a beautiful young woman, she deserved nothing less than the best. It would be a lavish celebration, befitting the sister of a successful businessman, and people would talk about it for a long time to come.

When she turned eighteen, he started inviting eligible bachelors to their home. She invariably found them repugnant; they were her brother's friends, and reminded her of Nusswan in all they said and did.

Nusswan was convinced that sooner or later there would be one she liked. He could no longer place restrictions on her comings and goings – she had outgrown those adolescent controls. So long as she did the housework and daily shopping according to Ruby's lists, relative calm prevailed in the house. Nowadays the quarrelling, if there was any, was between Ruby and Dina, as though Nusswan had delegated this function to his wife.

At the market Dina sometimes used her initiative and substituted cauliflower for cabbage; or she felt a sudden yearning for chickoos and bought them instead of oranges. Then Ruby promptly accused her of sabotaging the carefully planned meals, 'Wicked, malicious woman, ruining my husband's dinner.' She delivered the charge and the verdict in a matter-of-fact, mechanical manner, all part of her role as the dutiful wife.

But it was not always squabbles and bickering between them. More and more, the two women worked together amicably. Among the items that Ruby had brought to the house following her marriage was a small sewing-machine with a hand crank. She showed Dina how to use it, teaching her to make simple items like pillowcases, bedsheets, curtains.

When Ruby's first child was born, a son who was named Xerxes, Dina helped to look after him. She sewed baby clothes and knitted little caps and pullovers. For her nephew's first birthday she produced a pair of bootees. On that happy morning they garlanded Xerxes with roses and lilies, and made a large red teelo on his forehead.

'What a sweetie pie he is,' said Dina, laughing with delight.

'And those bootees you made – just too cute!' said Ruby, giving her a huge hug.

But it was the rare day that passed entirely without argument. Once the chores were done, Dina preferred to spend as much time out of the house as possible. Her resources for her outings were limited to what she could squeeze from the shopping money. Her conscience was clear; she regarded it as part-payment for her drudgery, barely a fraction of what was owed her.

Ruby demanded an account down to the last paisa. 'I want to see the bills and receipts. For every single item,' she pounded her fist on the kitchen table, rattling the saucepan's lid.

'Since when do fishmongers and vegetable-women on the footpath give receipts?' fired back Dina, throwing at her the bills for shop purchases, along with the change kept ready after juggling undocumented prices. She left the kitchen while her sister-in-law searched the floor to retrieve and count the coins.

The savings were sufficient to pay for bus fares. Dina went to parks, wandered in museums and markets, visited cinemas (just from the outside, to look at posters), and ventured timidly into public libraries. The heads bent over books made her feel out of place; everyone in there seemed so learned, and she hadn't even matriculated.

This impression was dispelled when she realized that the reading material in the hands of these grave individuals could range from something unpronounceable like *Areopagitica* by John Milton to *The Illustrated Weekly of India*. Eventually, the enormous old reading rooms, with their high ceilings, creaky floorboards and dark panelling, became her favourite sanctuary. The stately ceiling fans that hung from long poles swept the air with a comforting whoosh, and the deep leather chairs, musty smells, and rustle of turning pages were soothing. Best of all, people spoke in whispers. The only time Dina heard a shout was when the doorman scolded a beggar trying to sneak inside. Hours passed as she flipped through encyclopaedias, gazed into art books, and curiously opened dusty medical tomes, rounding off the visit by sitting for a few minutes with eyes closed in a dark corner of the old building, where time could stand still if one wanted it to.

The more modern libraries were equipped with music rooms. They also had fluorescent lights, Formica tables, air-conditioning, and brightly painted walls, and were always crowded. She found them cold and inhospitable, going there only if she wanted to listen to records. She knew very little about music – a few names like Brahms, Mozart, Schumann, and Bach, which her ears had picked up in childhood when her father would turn on the radio or put something on the gramophone, take her in his lap and say, 'It makes you forget the troubles of this world, doesn't it?' and Dina would nod her head seriously.

In the library she selected records at random, trying to memorize the names of the ones she enjoyed so she could play them again another day. It was tricky, because the symphonies and concertos and sonatas were distinguished only by numbers that were preceded by letters like Op. and K. and BWV, and she did not know what any of it meant. If she was lucky she found something with a name that resonated richly in her memory; and when the familiar music filled her head, the past was conquered for a brief while, and she felt herself ache with the ecstasy of completion, as though a missing limb had been recovered.

She both desired and dreaded these intense musical experiences. The perfect felicity of the music room was always replaced by an unfocused anger when she returned to life with Nusswan and Ruby. The bitterest fights took place on days when she had visited the record collection.

Magazines and newspapers were far less complicated. Through reading the dailies, she discovered there were several cultural groups that sponsored concerts and recitals in the city. Many of these performances – usually the ones by local amateurs or obscure foreigners – were free. She started using her bus fares to go to these concerts, and found them a welcome variation on the library. The performers, too, were no doubt grateful for her presence at these meagrely attended evenings.

She lingered at the periphery of the crowd in the foyer, feeling like an imposter. Everyone else seemed to know so much about music, about the evening's performers, judging from the sophisticated way they held their programmes and pointed to items inside. She longed for the doors to open, for the dim lights within to disguise her shortcomings.

In the recital hall the music did not have the power to touch her the way it did during her solitary hours in the library. Here, the human comedy shared equal time with the music. And after a few recitals she began to recognize the regulars in the audience.

There was an old man who, at every concert, fell asleep at precisely four minutes into the first piece; latecomers skirted his row out of consideration, to avoid bumping his knees. At seven minutes, his spectacles began sliding down his nose. And at eleven minutes (if the piece was that long and he hadn't yet been wakened by applause), his dentures were protruding. He reminded Dina of Grandpa.

Two sisters, in their fifties, tall and lean with pointed chins, always sat in the first row and often clapped at the wrong moment, unnecessarily disturbing the old man's nap. Dina herself did not understand about sonatas and movements, but realized that a performance was not over just because there was a pause in the music. She took the lead from a goateed individual in round wire-rimmed glasses who wore a beret, looked like an expert, and always knew when to clap.

Then there was an amusing middle-aged fellow who wore the same brown suit at every concert, and was everyone's friend. He dashed around madly in the foyer, greeting people, his head bobbing wildly, assuring them what a splendid evening it was going to be. His ties were the subject of constant speculation. On some evenings they hung long, dominating his front, flapping over his crotch. At other times they barely reached his diaphragm. The knots ranged in size from microscopic to a bulky samosa. And he did not walk from one person to the next so much as prance, keeping his comments brief because, as he liked to explain, there were just a few minutes before the curtain went up, and still so many he had to greet.

Dina noticed in the lobby a young man who, like her, was engaged in observing from the edges the merry mingling of their fellow concert-goers. Since she usually arrived early, anxious to get away from home, she was there to see him sail up to the entrance on his bicycle, dismount cleanly, and wheel it in through the gates. The gateman allowed him this liberty in exchange for a tip. At the side of the building, he padlocked the bicycle, making sure to remove the briefcase from the rear carrier. He snapped the clips off his trousers and slipped them into the briefcase. Then he retired to his favourite corner of the lobby to study the programme and the public.

Sometimes their eyes met, and there was a recognition of their tacit conspiracy. The funny man in the brown suit left Dina alone but included him in his round of greetings. 'Hello, Rustom! How are you?'

he bellowed, and thus Dina learned the young man's name.

'Very well, thank you,' said Rustom, looking over the shoulder of the brown suit at Dina watching amusedly.

'Tell me, what do you think of the pianist today? Is he capable of the depth required in the slow movement? Do you think that the largo – oh, excuse me, excuse me, I'll be back in a moment, soon as I say hello to Mr. Medhora over there,' and he was off. Rustom smiled at Dina and shook his head in mock despair.

The bell rang and the auditorium doors opened. The two tall sisters hastened to the first row with synchronized hopping steps, unfolded the maroon-upholstered seats, and flopped down triumphantly, beaming at each other for once again winning their secret game of musical chairs. Dina took her usual centre aisle seat, roughly midway down the hall.

As the place began to fill, Rustom came up beside her. 'Is this one free?' She nodded.

He sat down. 'That Mr. Toddywalla is a real character, isn't he?'

'Oh, is that his name? Yes, he is very funny.'

'Even if the recital is so-so, you can always rely on him for entertainment.'

The lights dimmed, and the two performers appeared on stage to scattered applause. 'By the way, I'm Rustom Dalal,' he said, leaning closer and holding out his hand while the flute received the piano's silver A and offered its own golden one in return.

She whispered 'Dina Shroff' without taking his hand, for in the dark she did not immediately notice it being held out. When she did, it was too late; he had begun to withdraw it.

During the interval Rustom asked if she would like coffee or a cold drink.

'No, thank you.'

They watched the audience in the aisles, bound for the bathrooms and refreshments. He crossed his legs and said, 'You know, I see you regularly at these concerts.'

'Yes, I enjoy them very much.'

'Do you play yourself? The piano, or –?'

'No, I don't.'

'Oh. You have such lovely fingers, I was sure you played the piano.'

'No, I don't,' she repeated. Her cheeks felt a little hot, and she looked down at her fingers. 'I don't know anything about music, I just enjoy listening to it.'

'That's the best way, I think.'

She wasn't sure what he meant, but nodded. 'And what about you? Do you?'

'Like all good Parsi parents, mine made me take violin lessons when I was little,' he laughed.

'You don't play it anymore?'

'Oh, once in a while. When I feel like torturing myself, I take it out of its case to make it screech and wail.'

She smiled. 'At least it must make your parents happy, to hear you play.'

'No, they are dead. I live alone.'

Her smile collapsed as she prepared to say she was sorry, but he quickly added, 'Only the neighbours suffer when I play,' and they laughed again.

They always sat together after that, and the following week she accepted a Mangola during the interval. While they were in the lobby, sipping from the chilled bottles, watching moisture beads embellish the glass, Mr. Toddywalla came up to them.

'So, Rustom, what did you think of the first half? In my opinion, a borderline performance. That flautist should do some breathing exercises before he ever thinks of a recital again.' He lingered long enough to be introduced to Dina, which was why he had come in the first place. Then he was off, gambolling towards his next victims.

After the concert Rustom walked her to the bus stop, wheeling his bicycle. The departing audience had their eyes on them. To break the silence she asked, 'Are you ever nervous about cycling in this traffic?'

He shook his head. 'I've been doing it for years. It's second nature to me.' He waited for her bus to arrive, then rode behind the red double-decker till their ways parted. He could not see her watching him from the upper deck. She followed his diminishing figure, her eyes sometimes losing him, then finding him under a streetlamp, travelling with him till he became a speck that only her imagination could claim was Rustom.

In a few weeks the concert regulars came to regard them as a couple. Their every move was viewed with concern and curiosity. Rustom and Dina were amused by the attention but preferred to dismiss it in the same category as Mr. Toddywalla's antics.

Once, on arriving, Rustom looked around to find Dina in the crowd. One of the first-row sisters immediately came up to his elbow and whispered coyly, 'She is here, do not fear. She has just gone to the ladies' room.'

It had been raining heavily, and Dina, soaked, was trying to tidy herself up in the ladies' but her tiny hanky was not equal to the task. The towel on the rod looked uninviting. She did the best she could, then went out, her hair still dripping.

'What happened?' asked Rustom.

'My umbrella was blown inside out. I couldn't get it straight quickly enough.'

He offered her his large handkerchief. The significance of this proposal was not lost on the observers around them: would she or wouldn't she?

'No, thanks,' she said, running her fingers through the wet hair. 'It will soon be dry.' The concertgoers held their breath.

'My hanky is clean, don't worry,' he smiled. 'Look, go in and dry yourself, I'll buy two hot coffees for us.' When she still hesitated, he threatened to take off his shirt and towel her head with it in the lobby. Laughing, she accepted the handkerchief and returned to the ladies' room. The regulars sighed happily.

Inside, Dina rubbed her hair with the handkerchief. It had a nice smell to it, she thought. Not perfume, but a clean human smell. His smell. The same one she perceived sometimes while sitting next to him. She put it against her nose and breathed deeply, then folded it away, embarrassed.

It was still raining lightly when the concert ended. They walked to the bus stop. The drizzle hissed in the trees, as though the leaves were sizzling. Dina shivered.

'Are you cold?'

'Just a little.'

'Hope you're not getting a fever. All that soaking. Listen, why don't you put on my raincoat, and I'll take your umbrella.'

'Don't be silly, it's broken. Anyway, how can you ride your cycle with an umbrella?'

'Of course I can. I can ride it standing on my head if necessary.' He insisted, and in the bus shelter they undertook the exchange. He helped her into the Duckback raincoat and his hand grazed her shoulder. His fingers felt warm to her cold skin. The sleeves were a bit long, otherwise it fitted quite well. And nicely heated up by his body, she realized, as it slowly got the chill out of her.

They stood close together, watching the fine needles of rain slanting in the light of the streetlamp. Then they held hands for the first time, and it seemed the most natural thing to do. It was hard to let go when the bus came.

From now on, Rustom used his bicycle only to get to and from work. In the evenings he came by bus, so they could travel together and he could see her home.

Dina was happier meeting him without the bicycle. She felt he should give it up altogether, it was too dangerous in the city traffic.

'I'm going to get married,' announced Dina at the dinner table.

'Ah,' beamed her brother. 'Good, good. Which one is it, Solly or Porus?' – these two being the gents he had most recently introduced.

Dina shook her head.

'Then it must be either Dara or Firdosh,' said Ruby, smiling meaningfully. 'They are both crazy about you.'

'His name is Rustom Dalal.'

Nusswan was surprised; the name did not belong among the numerous candidates he had brought before Dina over the past three years. Perhaps it was someone she had met at one of the family gatherings he so detested. 'And where did we come across him?'

'We didn't. I did.'

Nusswan did not like the answer. He was offended that all his efforts, all his choices, were being spurned by her for a total stranger. 'Just like that you want to marry this fellow? What do you know about him and his family? What does he know about you, your family?'

'Everything,' said Dina in a tone that made him anxious. 'I've been seeing Rustom for a year and a half now.'

'I see. A well-kept secret,' he said, affecting sarcasm. 'And what does he do, this Dalal fellow, your Rustom-in-hiding?'

'He's a pharmaceutical chemist.'

'Hah! Pharmaceutical chemist! A bloody compounder! Why don't you use the proper word? That's what he is, mixing prescription powders all day long behind a counter.'

He reminded himself there was no sense in losing his temper just yet. 'So, when are we going to meet this Father Forty-Lakhs of yours?'

'Why? So you can insult him in person?'

'I have no reason to insult him. But it is my duty to meet him, and then advise you properly. In the end it's up to you.'

On the appointed day, Rustom arrived with a box of sweetmeats for Nusswan and Ruby, which he placed in the hands of little Xerxes, who was almost three now. For Dina, he brought a new umbrella. The significance was not lost on her, and she smiled. He winked at her when the others were not looking.

35

'It's gorgeous,' she said, opening it up. 'What a lovely pagoda shape.' The fabric was sea green, and the shaft was stainless steel, with a formidable spike at the end.

'That's a dangerous weapon,' joked Nusswan. 'Be careful who you point it at.'

They had tea, with cheese sandwiches and butter biscuits prepared by Ruby and Dina, and the time passed without unpleasantness. But that night, after the visitor left, Nusswan said he could not understand for one moment what was in his sister's head – brains or sawdust.

'Selecting someone without looks, without money, without prospects. Some fiancés give diamond rings. Others a gold watch, or at least a little broach. What does your fellow bring? A bloody umbrella! To think I wasted so much time and energy introducing you to solicitors, chartered accountants, police superintendents, civil engineers. All from respectable families. How will I hold my head up when people hear that my sister married an unambitious medicine-mixing fool? Don't expect me to rejoice or come to the wedding. For me it will be a day of deep, dark mourning.'

It was sad, he lamented, that in order to hurt him she was ruining her own life. 'Mark my words, your spite will come back to haunt you. I am powerless to stop you, you are twenty-one, no longer a little girl I can look after. And if you are determined to throw your life away in the gutter, I can only watch helplessly while you do it.'

Dina had expected all this. The words washed over her and gurgled into oblivion, leaving her untouched. The way the rain had rolled off Rustom's lovely raincoat, she remembered, on that beautiful night. But she wondered again, as she had so many times, where her brother had learned to rave so proficiently. Neither their mother nor father had had much talent for it.

In a few days Nusswan grew calmer. If Dina was getting married and leaving for good, better that it should happen amicably, without too much fuss. Secretly he was also pleased that Rustom Dalal was no great catch. It would have been unbearable if his friends had been rejected in favour of someone superior.

He participated in the wedding plans with more enthusiasm and generosity than Dina expected. He wanted to book a hall for the reception and pay for everything out of the money he had been collecting for her. 'We'll have the wedding after sunset, and then dinner. We'll show them how it's done – everyone will envy you. A four-piece band, floral decorations, lights. I can afford about three hundred guests. But no liquor – too expensive and too risky. Prohibition police are everywhere, you bribe one and ten more show up for their share.'

That night in bed, Ruby, who was pregnant with their second child, expressed dismay at Nusswan's extravagance. 'It's up to Rustom Dalal to spend, if they want to get married. Not your responsibility – especially when she wouldn't even let you select the husband. She never appreciates anything you do for her.'

Rustom and Dina, however, had simpler preferences. The wedding took place in the morning. At Dina's request, it was a quiet ceremony in the same fire-temple where her parents' prayers were performed on each death anniversary. Dustoor Framji, old and stoop-shouldered, watched from the shadows, upset that he had not been asked to conduct the marriage rites. Time was slowing him down, and the flesh of young women was rarely caught now in his once-dexterous embraces. But the name of Dustoor Daab-Chaab clung to his autumnal years even as all else was withering. 'It's disgraceful,' he grumbled to a colleague. 'Especially after my long association with the Shroff family. For death, they come to me – for saros-nu-paatru, for afargan, baaj, faroksy. But for a happy occasion, for wedding ashirvaad, I am not wanted. It's a matter of shamefulness.'

In the evening there was a party at the Shroff residence. Nusswan insisted on at least this much celebration, and arranged for a caterer. There were forty-eight guests, of which six were Rustom's friends, plus his Shirin Aunty and Darab Uncle. The rest were from Nusswan's circle, including extended family members who could not be left out without risking criticism from relatives – the insinuating, whispered kind of criticism to which he was so sensitive.

The dining room, drawing room, Nusswan's study, and the four bedrooms were rearranged to allow mingling and movement, with tables set up for food and drink. Little Xerxes and his friends ran from room to room in a frenzy of adventure and discovery, screaming and laughing. They were thrilled by the sudden freedom they enjoyed in a house where their previous visits had felt like time spent in prison, grimly supervised by the very strict daddy of Xerxes. Nusswan himself groaned inwardly each time one of them collided with him, but smiled and patted the child on its way.

During the course of the evening he produced four bottles of Scotch whisky to general applause. 'Now we will put some life in the evening, and into this newly married pair!' said the men to one another, with much nodding and laughter, and the whispering of things not meant for women's ears.

'Okay, brother-in-law,' said Nusswan, clinking two empty glasses before Rustom. 'You're the expert, better start mixing a dose of Johnnie

Walker medicine for everyone.'

'Sure,' said Rustom good-naturedly, and took the glasses.

'Just joking, just joking,' said Nusswan, holding on to the bottle. 'How can the bridegroom be allowed to work at his own wedding?' It was his only pharmaceutical dig during the evening.

An hour after the Scotch was taken, Ruby went to the kitchen; it was time to serve dinner. The dining table had been moved against the wall and set up for a buffet. The caterer's men staggered in with hot, heavy dishes, calling 'Side please! Side please!' to get through. Everyone reverently made way for the food.

The aromas that had been filling the house with appetizing hints all evening, teasing nostrils and taunting palates, suddenly overwhelmed the gathering. A hush fell across the room. Someone chuckled loudly that where Parsis were concerned, food was number one, conversation came second. Whereupon someone else corrected him: no, no, conversation came third, and the second thing couldn't be mentioned with ladies and children present. Those within earshot rewarded the worn-out joke with hearty laughter.

Ruby clapped her hands: 'Okay, everybody! Dinner is served! Please help yourselves and don't be shy, there is lots of food!' She hovered around to play the host in the time-honoured fashion, repeating regretfully before each guest, 'Please forgive us, we could manage nothing worthy of you.'

'What are you saying, Ruby, it all looks wonderful,' they replied. While helping themselves, they took the opportunity to inquire after her pregnancy and when she was expecting.

Nusswan examined the plates that passed before him, lightheartedly scolding the guests who took too little. 'What's this, Mina, you must be joking. Even my pet sparrow would go hungry with this quantity.' He spooned more biryani for Mina. 'Wait, Hosa, wait, one more kabab, it's delicious, believe me, one more, come on, be a sport,' and deftly plopped two onto the reluctant plate. 'Come back for more, promise?'

When everyone had served themselves, Dina noticed Rustom's Shirin Aunty and Darab Uncle on the verandah, a little secluded from the rest, and went to them. 'Please eat well. Have you taken enough?'

'More than enough, my child, more than enough. The food is delicious.' Shirin Aunty beckoned to bring her closer, and beckoned again, to make her bend till Dina's ear was close to her mouth. 'If you ever need anything – remember, anything at all, you can come to me and Darab.'

And Darab Uncle nodded; his hearing was very sharp. 'Whatever the problem. We are like Rustom's parents. And you are like our daughter.'

'Thank you,' said Dina, understanding that this was more than a customary welcoming speech from the other side. She sat with them while they ate. Near the dining table Nusswan, miming with plate and fork, signalled to her to get some food for herself. Yes, later, she mimed back, and stayed with Shirin Aunty and Darab Uncle, who watched her with adoring eyes as they ate.

A few guests still remained when Nusswan gave the caterer's men the go-ahead for the cleanup. The lingerers got the hint and said their thanks and goodbyes.

On the way out, someone clutched Rustom's lapel and giggled, whispering with whisky breath that the bride and groom were fortunate not to have a mother-in-law on either side. 'Not fair, not fair! No one to question you whether the equipment worked on the first night, you lucky rascal! No one to inspect the bedsheet, hahn!' He prodded Rustom in the stomach with one finger. 'You're getting off very lightly!'

'Good night, everybody,' said Nusswan and Ruby. 'Good night, good night. Thank you very much for coming.'

When the last guest had departed, Rustom said, 'That was a lovely evening. Thank you both for arranging it.'

'Yes, it really was, thank you very much,' added Dina.

'You're welcome – most welcome,' said Nusswan, and Ruby nodded. 'It was our duty.'

Originally, Dina and Rustom had agreed with Nusswan's suggestion to spend the night there. Then they realized that the rooms would have to be put back in order after the party. So it was more convenient to go straight to Rustom's flat.

'Now don't worry about anything, these fellows will clear up, that's what they are paid for,' said Nusswan. 'You two carry on.' He gave them both a hug. It was the second time that day for Dina. The first time had been in the morning, after the dustoorji had finished reciting the wedding benediction; it had also been the first time in seven years.

A small lump came to her throat. She swallowed as Nusswan quickly passed his fingers over his eyes. 'Wish you lots of happiness,' he said.

Dina fetched a valise that was packed and ready for the night. The rest of her things would be delivered later. Nusswan was going to let her have some furniture from their parents' possessions. He accompanied them down the cobbled walkway to a taxi and waved goodbye. She noticed with surprise that his voice quavered as he said, 'All the best! God bless you!'

———

They woke up late the next morning. Rustom had taken a week's leave from work, though they couldn't afford to go anywhere on a honeymoon.

Dina made tea in the gloomy kitchen while he watched anxiously. The kitchen was the dingiest room in the flat, its ceiling and plaster blackened by smoke. Rustom's mother had cooked over coal fires all her life. Her brief acquaintance with kerosene had not been propitious – there had been a spill, and flames, and burns down her thighs; coal was more obedient, she had concluded.

Rustom had wanted to paint the kitchen before the wedding, along with the other rooms, but the money had refused to stretch that far. He began to apologize for the flat's condition. 'You are not used to living like this. Just look at these horrible walls.'

'It doesn't matter, it's fine,' she said happily. 'We'll get it painted later.'

Perhaps it was due to her presence in the flat, unusual at breakfast time, but he began detecting new deficiencies around him. 'After my parents died I got rid of things. Seemed like clutter to me. I was planning to live like a sadhu, you see, with only my violin for company. Instead of a bed of nails, the screeching of catgut to mortify myself.'

'Are the strings really made of cat intestines?'

'Used to be, in the olden days. And in the very olden days, violinists had to go out and hunt down their own strings. There were no music shops then, like L. M. Furtado or Godin & Company. At all the great conservatories of Europe, they taught music as well as animal evisceration.'

'Now don't be silly so early in the morning,' she scolded, but his bizarre humour was what she liked most about him.

'Anyway, I have found my beautiful angel, and the sadhu days are over. The catgut can take a rest.'

'I enjoy your playing. You should practise more.'

'Are you joking? I sound worse than the fellow last week at Patkar Hall. And he played as though his f-holes were blocked.'

'Chhee, how filthy!'

He laughed at the face she made. 'I can't help it – that's what they are called. Come, let me show you my f-holes.' He took the violin case down from top of the cupboard. 'See the shape of the two openings in the soundboard?'

'Oh, it looks just like a running-hand f.' She traced the curves with a finger, and touched the strings gently. 'Play something while you have it open.'

He shut the case and, rising slightly on his toes, slipped it on top of the cupboard. 'Play, play, play – that's what my parents used to say.' He took her hand and pressed it to his lips. 'I wish I had at least kept their double bed.' Then he asked shyly, 'Were you comfortable last night?'

'Oh yes.' She blushed at the fresh memory of the narrow single bed in which they had clung together.

After a breakfast of an omelette and buttered toast, he opened the front door and said there was a surprise for her. 'It was too dark to show you last night.'

'What is it?'

'You have to step outside.'

She saw the new brass nameplate gleaming in sunlight, engraved Mr. & Mrs. Rustom K. Dalal. He basked in the pleasure it gave her. 'Day before yesterday is when I screwed it on.'

'It looks lovely.'

'Changing the nameplate was easy,' he chuckled. 'It's much more difficult to change the name on the rent receipt.'

'What do you mean?'

'The rent is collected in my father's name though he's been dead for nine years. The landlord hopes I will get impatient, offer money to transfer the flat to my name. He keeps hinting.'

'Are you going to?'

'Of course not. There's nothing he can do, the Rent Act protects us. It doesn't matter in whose name the rent receipt is issued. And you are entitled to live here too, as my wife. Even if I were to die tomorrow.'

'Rustom! Don't say such things!'

He laughed. 'When the rent-collector comes with the receipt in my father's name, sometimes I feel like telling him to go up, to heaven, to the renter's new address.'

Dina rested her head against his shoulder. 'For me, heaven is in this flat.'

Rustom drew her close and hugged her. 'For me too.' Then he gave the nameplate another shine with his sleeve. While they were admiring it, two handcarts rolled up and stopped by their door, laden with things from the Shroff residence.

At first, Rustom had arranged for a small lorry because Dina had requested Nusswan to let her have Daddy's huge wardrobe, the one with the carved rosewood canopy of a sunburst and flowers. She would forgo everything else, she said, for this one item. Nusswan promised to consider it but refused in the end. He said that squeezing the wardrobe through the narrow door of Rustom's flat would damage it, the scratches would be unfair to their father's memory, and, besides, its proportions wouldn't suit the tiny rooms.

So he let her have another cupboard, smaller and plainer, a little desk, and twin beds. There was also a large box of kitchen utensils that Ruby had put together after discreetly inquiring whether Rustom's kitchen was properly equipped. To get them started, she included pots and pans, a stove, some cutlery, a board and a rolling pin.

The two handcarts were unloaded and the twin beds assembled. One of the carters offered to buy the old single. Rustom let him have it for thirty rupees, and got ten for the mattress from the other man.

As Dina watched them carry it away, he said, 'I know what you're thinking. But this flat has no space for an extra bed.' She wondered how close they would sleep that night, now that there were twin beds.

But one of the two was as good as unslept in when they woke on their second morning. Reassured, she spent the day getting her new home organized the way she wanted it. First, she gave notice to Seva Sadan, terminating delivery of Rustom's evening meals. And for lunch, she would pack something for him when he returned to work the following week.

'No more nonsense of eating out or not eating at all,' she said, and climbed up on a chair to examine the high shelf in the kitchen. She discovered a series of brass and copper vessels, a kettle, and a set of kitchen knives.

'Those are all gone bad,' said Rustom. 'I've been meaning to sell them for scrap. Tomorrow, I promise.'

'Don't be silly, these are solid old things. They can be repaired and tinned. Nowadays you can't buy such quality.'

The next time a tinker yelled outside their window, she called him to fix the leaking vessels and rivet the broken handle of the kettle. She watched to make sure he did the work properly. As he finished each pot, she took it to the bathroom and tested it with water.

The knife-grinder went by with his wheel slung over his shoulder. The tinker stopped hammering while she clapped twice to get his attention.

The dull blades soon began glinting with sharp edges. She relished the energy, the attention, the pounding and banging that went into getting her household shipshape for decades of wedded bliss with Rustom. A lifetime had to be crafted, just like anything else, she thought, it had to be moulded and beaten and burnished in order to get the most out of it.

The knife-grinder averted his face as sparks flew from the spinning grindstone. Like Divali fireworks, she thought, while the tinker's hammer blows rang gaily in her ears.

Dina and Rustom celebrated their first wedding anniversary by going to the cinema and dining out. They saw *Submarine Command*, starring William Holden, who played an American naval commander in Korea. They held hands during the film and, afterwards, ate chicken biryani at the Wayside Inn.

The following year Dina wanted to see something less grim. So they picked Bing Crosby's *High Society*, a brand-new release. She had bought a new frock for the occasion, blue, with a vivacious peplum that came alive with walking.

'I don't know if you should wear that,' said Rustom, coming up behind her and stroking her hips.

'Why?' she smiled, wiggling to tease him.

'You'll drive the men wild in the streets. Better carry your pointy pagoda parasol to protect yourself.'

'Won't you protect me, and fight them off?'

'Okay. In that case, I'll carry your spear. Better still, I'll bring my violin – the screeching will scare them more.'

They enjoyed the film immensely. The blue frock was their private joke all evening as they imagined envious women and lustful men thirsting to get their hands on it. For dinner they went to Mongini's; the desserts there had a wonderful reputation.

On their third anniversary, they decided to invite Nusswan, Ruby, and the children (there were two now) to dinner. Relations between them had been cordial since the wedding. Dina and Rustom were always asked to the children's birthdays, and also on Navroze and Khordad Sal. Dina, sometimes alone, sometimes with Rustom, had taken to dropping in with sweets for her nephews, or just to say hello. The ill feelings had disappeared so completely that it was hard to remember them with any clarity. One was tempted to conclude that it had all been exaggerated by the imagination.

The little anniversary party proceeded most amicably. Dina could not afford a new outfit, and wore last year's blue frock. Ruby admired it, and praised Dina's cooking. She said that the pulao-dal was really tasty. Dina replied graciously that she had learned a lot from her sister-in-law.

'But I still have a long way to go before reaching your standards.'

For the two boys, who were only six and three, Dina had cooked separately, without spices. But Xerxes and Zarir insisted on having what the adults were eating. Ruby allowed them a taste of it, and they wanted more despite their tongues hanging out.

'Never mind,' said Dina, laughing, 'the ice cream will put out the fire.'

'Can I have it now?' chorused the children.

'Rustom Uncle has yet to go and get it,' said Dina. 'We don't have an icebox like yours to store it. Here, have this for the time being,' and she popped sugar crystals in their mouths from the ceremonial tray of garlands and coconuts.

Later, while she cleared the table with Ruby helping, Rustom decided it was time to go for the Kwality Family Pack. 'In case they don't have strawberry, which one – chocolate or vanilla?'

'Chocolate,' said Xerxes.

'Lanilla,' said Zarir, and everyone laughed.

'Lanilla!' teased Rustom. 'You always have to be different, don't you?'

'I wonder from where he got the trait,' said Nusswan. 'Certainly not his father,' and they all laughed again. He seized the opportunity to add, 'But what about you two, Rustom? Time to start a family, I think. Three years is long enough for a holiday.'

Rustom only smiled, not wanting to encourage a discussion. He opened the door to leave, and Nusswan jumped up. 'Shall I give you company?'

'Oh no, just relax, you're the guest. Besides, if we walk, it will take too long. Alone, I can go on my cycle, return in ten minutes.'

Dina set out clean plates and spoons for the ice cream, and put the kettle on. 'The tea should be nice and ready by the time he is back.'

Fifteen minutes later, they were still waiting. 'Where can he be? The tea is getting so strong. Maybe you two should drink yours now.'

'No, we'll wait for Rustom,' said Ruby.

'There must be a big rush or something at the ice-cream shop,' said Nusswan.

Dina boiled a second kettleful to dilute the infusion. She returned the pot under the tea-cosy. 'Forty-five minutes since he left.'

'Maybe it was sold out at the first place,' said Nusswan. 'Strawberry is very popular, always out of stock. Maybe he went somewhere else, further away.'

'He wouldn't, he knows I would worry.'

'Maybe he got a puncture,' said Ruby.

'Even walking back with a puncture would take only twenty minutes.'

She went to the verandah to see if she could spot him pedalling in the distance. It reminded her of the nights when they would part after the concert recitals, and she would be on the upper deck of the bus, trying to keep his disappearing bicycle in sight.

The memory made her smile, but it quickly faded under the present anxiety. 'I think I'll go and see what's the matter.'

'No, I'll go,' offered Nusswan.

'But you don't know where the shop is, or the road Rustom would take. You might miss each other.'

In the end they both went. Seeing how tense Dina was, he kept repeating, 'Has to be a perfectly simple explanation.' She nodded, walking faster. He had to make an effort to keep up.

It was after nine, and the streets were quiet. In the lane at the end of which stood the ice-cream shop, a knot of people had gathered by the footpath. As they got closer, Nusswan and Dina noticed that the police were also present.

'Wonder what's going on,' said Nusswan, trying to conceal his alarm.

Dina was the first to spot the bicycle. 'It's Rustom's,' she said. Her voice had turned into a stranger's, sounding unfamiliar to her own ears.

'Are you sure?' He knew she was. The bicycle was mangled but the saddle was whole. He pushed his way through the crowd towards the policemen. A roaring storm filled her ears, and their words reached her feebly, as though from a great distance.

'A bastard lorry driver,' said the sub-inspector. 'Hit and run. No chance for the poor man, I think. Head completely crushed. But ambulance has taken him to hospital anyway.'

A stray dog lapped at the thick pink puddle near the bicycle. Strawberry ice cream was in stock, thought Dina numbly. A policeman kicked the sand-coloured mongrel. It yelped and retreated, then returned for more. When he kicked it again, she screamed.

'Stop that! What harm is it doing to you? Let it eat!'

Startled, the policeman said 'Yes madam' and stepped back. The dog slurped hungrily, whimpering with pleasure while keeping a wary eye on the man's foot.

Nusswan obtained the name of the hospital. The sub-inspector took his address, and asked Dina, who was staring at the twisted bicycle, for hers. The bicycle would be retained as evidence for the time being – in case the lorry driver was found, he explained gently. He offered to give them a lift to the hospital.

'Thank you,' said Nusswan. 'But they will be wondering at home what happened.'

'It's okay, I'll send a constable to say not to worry, there's been an accident and you are at the hospital,' said the sub-inspector. 'Then you can explain everything later.'

Thanks to the sub-inspector's help, procedures were expedited at the hospital, and Nusswan and Dina were able to leave quickly. 'Let's take a taxi,' said Nusswan.

'No, I want to walk.'

By the time they reached home, the tears were silently streaming down her cheeks. Nusswan held her and stroked her head. 'My poor sister,' he whispered. 'My poor little sister. I wish I could bring him back for you. Cry now, it's all right, cry all you need to.' He wept a little himself as he told Ruby about the accident, in whispers.

'Oh God!' sobbed Ruby. 'What is the meaning of such misfortune! In a few minutes, Dina's whole world destroyed! How can it be? Why does He allow such things?' She composed herself before waking the children, while Dina went to change out of her blue frock.

'Can we eat the strawberry ice cream now?' asked Xerxes and Zarir sleepily.

'Rustom Uncle is not well, we have to go home,' said Ruby, deciding it was better to explain gradually.

Dina soon emerged from her room, and Nusswan went to her side. 'You must also come home with us, you cannot stay here alone.'

'Of course, absolutely,' said Ruby, taking her hand and squeezing it.

Nodding, Dina went to the kitchen and began making a package of the leftover pulao-dal. Ruby watched curiously, half-fearfully, before asking, 'Can I help?'

Dina shook her head. 'No sense wasting this food. On our way home, we can give it to a beggar at the corner.'

Later, Nusswan would say to whoever he was recounting the events that he was really impressed with the dignified way his sister had behaved on that cruel night. 'No wailing, no beating the chest or tearing the hair like you might expect from a woman who had suffered such a shock, such a loss.' But he also remembered their mother's dignity on a similar occasion, and the disintegration that had followed in its wake. He hoped Dina would not follow the same pattern.

Dina packed her valise with a white sari and other things she would need for the next few days. It was the same one she had brought with her three years ago on her wedding night.

After the funeral and four days of prayers, Dina prepared to return to her flat. 'What's the rush?' said Nusswan. 'Stay here a little longer.'

'Of course,' said Ruby. 'Here you are with family. What will you do there all alone?'

Dina wavered easily, for she did not feel ready to go back. The most difficult hours were the ones before dawn. She slept with one arm over a pillow. Sometimes she nudged the pillow lightly with her elbow, her signal to Rustom that she wanted his arm around her. When the human weight did not materialize, she awakened to emptiness, relearning the loss in the darkness before sunrise. Occasionally, she called out his name, and Ruby or Nusswan, if they heard her, came into the room and held her tight, stroking her hair.

'It's not as though you are going to be a burden on us by staying,' said Nusswan. 'In fact, you will be company for Ruby.'

So Dina stayed. Word got about that she was temporarily at her brother's place, and a stream of relatives arrived on condolence visits. After the formal purpose of the call was dealt with, the conversation took on the hue of a genial get-together, and Nusswan and Ruby enjoyed the socializing. 'It's the best thing possible for Dina,' they agreed.

Rustom's Shirin Aunty and Darab Uncle had attended all four days of prayer at the Towers of Silence, but came again after a week. They sat for a while, had a glass of lemon cordial and said, 'For us, it is like losing a son. But remember, you are still our daughter. If you ever need anything, you can come to us. Remember, anything at all.'

Ruby overheard this and prickled. 'That's very kind of you. But we are here, Nusswan and I, to look after her.'

'Yes, of course, thanks be to God,' said the elderly couple, taken aback by the sharpness in her voice. 'May He give you both a long, healthy life. Dina is very fortunate to have you two.' They left shortly, hoping they had managed to salve Ruby's feelings.

A month passed, and Dina settled into her old routine, assuming her former place in the household. The servant was let go. Dina did not mind, it gave her something to do with her long, empty days. Xerxes and Zarir, of course, were thrilled to have Dina Aunty living with them. Xerxes was in the second standard and Zarir had just started kindergarten. She volunteered to take them to school; it would be easy, on her way to the bazaar in the mornings.

On Sunday evenings Nusswan organized card games. The three adults played rummy for a couple of hours while the children watched.

Sometimes Dina allowed Xerxes and Zarir to hold her cards. At seven, the women started dinner, and Nusswan amused himself by building a house of cards with the children or glancing over the Sunday newspaper a second time.

Once a week Dina went to her empty flat to dust and clean. There she followed the exact habit of housework that she had developed when Rustom was alive. At the end of the cleaning she made tea. There in the privacy of the dingy kitchen she sat with her cup, remembering, sometimes crying softly, and the tea usually went cold. She often poured it away after drinking half a cup.

After following this secret pattern of mourning for some weeks, she began allowing a part of herself to pretend everything was normal, the flat was occupied, the separation temporary. There didn't seem to her any harm in it, and the make-believe was so comforting.

Then one evening, as dusk was falling and the headlights of cars had started to come on, she caught herself gazing out from the verandah to see if Rustom's bicycle was approaching. A shiver ran down her spine. She decided enough was enough. Flirting with madness was one thing; when madness started flirting back, it was time to call the whole thing off.

She renounced the weekly cleaning ritual. If a visit to the flat was necessary, she preferred not to go alone, and took her little nephews with her. Xerxes and Zarir enjoyed exploring the unlived-in space. The familiar rooms suddenly seemed remote and mysterious, filled with furniture yet inexplicably empty. The museum-like stillness baffled them. They shouted and ran and skipped through the flat to see if they could banish the void.

One afternoon, when Dina stopped by to pick up a few of her things, she found an envelope from the landlord. The children began organizing a cross-country race, for which Xerxes mapped out the route. 'We will start from the verandah, and run all the way to the kitchen, then all the way to the wc, and then all the way back, going through all the rooms. Understood, Zarir?'

'Okay,' said Zarir. Dina announced ready, get set, go. She opened the windows in the front room and read the letter. It stated that since the premises were no longer occupied, notice was hereby given for the flat to be emptied of its effects and the keys returned within thirty days.

That night, when she showed the letter to Nusswan, he was livid. 'Look at the shameless rascal of a landlord. Not even three months since poor Rustom passed away, and the snake is ready to strike. Nothing doing. You must keep the flat.'

'Yes, I think I'll go back there from next week,' she agreed.

'That's not what I meant. Stay here for a year, two years – as long as you like. But don't give up your right. Mark my words, the time is not far-off when accommodation will be impossible to find in the city. An old flat like yours will be a gold mine.'

'It's true,' said Ruby. 'I heard that Putli Maasi's son had to pay a pugree of twenty thousand rupees just to get his foot in the door. And the rent is five hundred a month. His flat is even smaller than yours.'

'Yes,' said Dina, 'but my rent –'

'Don't worry, I'll pay it,' said Nusswan. 'And my lawyer will reply to this letter.'

He was thinking ahead: sooner or later Dina would remarry. At that juncture, it would be very unfortunate if the lack of a flat were to pose an impediment. He definitely would not want the couple living with him. That would be a blueprint for friction and strife.

On Rustom's first death anniversary, Nusswan took the morning off from work. The previous day, he had written notes to Xerxes' school and Zarir's kindergarten that they would be 'absent in order to attend their late uncle's prayers at the fire-temple.' Dina was grateful for the entire family's presence.

'Hard to imagine,' said Nusswan when they got back home, 'a whole year has gone by. How time flies.'

A few days later he formally signalled an end to the mourning period by inviting some friends to tea.

Among them were Porus and Solly, two of the many eligible bachelors whom he had strenuously recommended to Dina a few years ago. The two were still single, and still quite eligible, according to Nusswan, if one were willing to forgive minor flaws like incipient potbellies and greying hair.

Priding himself on his subtlety, he said to Dina in private, 'You know, either Porus or Solly would jump at the chance to become your husband. Porus's law practice is flourishing beyond belief. And Solly is now a full partner in the accounting firm. They would have no problem that you are a widow.'

'How kind of them.'

He did not like the sarcasm. It was a reminder of the old Dina – the stubborn, insolent, defiant sister, who he assumed had been transformed into a better person. But he swallowed and continued calmly.

'You know, Dina, I am very impressed with you. No one can accuse you of being frivolous in mourning. You have acted so correctly, so perfectly, this whole year.'

'I was not acting. And it was not difficult.'

'I know, I know,' he said hastily, regretting his choice of words. 'What I meant was, I admire your dignity. But the point is, you are still so young. It has been over a year, and you must think of your future.'

'Don't worry, I understand your concern.'

'Good, that's all I wanted to say. Come on, time for cards. Ruby!' he called to the kitchen. 'Time for rummy!' Now there would be progress, Nusswan was certain.

Over the next few weeks he continued to invite the old assortment of bachelors. 'Come, Dina,' he would say, 'let me introduce you.' Then, pretending a memory lapse, he would exclaim, 'Wait, wait, what am I saying, where is my head? You already know Temton. So let it be a reintroduction.'

All this was enacted in a manner suggesting that a relationship of deep significance was being resumed, a passion rekindled. It irritated Dina intensely, but she tried to keep from frowning while pouring the tea and passing the sandwiches. When the visitors departed, Nusswan resumed with his sledgehammer hints, praising one's looks, commending the merits of another's career, pointing out the inheritance awaiting a third.

After four months of bachelor-entertaining and no sign of cooperation from Dina, Nusswan lost his patience. 'I have been tactful, I have been kind, I have been reasonable. But which raja's son are you waiting for? Every chap I introduce, you turn your face away from him and go to the other side of the room. What is it that you want?'

'Nothing.'

'How can you want nothing? Your whole life will be nothing. Be sensible.'

'I know you are doing it for my own good, but I am just not interested.'

The answer reminded Nusswan once again of the old Dina, the ungrateful little sister. He suspected that she looked down upon his friends. And they were such good fellows, all of them. Never mind, he would not let her anger him.

'Fine. As I said, I am a reasonable person. If you don't like these men, no one is forcing you. Find one yourself. Or we can hire a matchmaker. I hear that Mrs. Ginwalla has the best track record for successful kaaj. Let me know what you prefer.'

'I don't want to get married so soon.'

'Soon? You call this soon? You are twenty-six years old. What are you hoping for? For Rustom to return miraculously? Be careful, or you'll go crazy like Bapsy Aunty – she at least had an excuse, her husband's body was never found after the dock explosion.'

'What a horrible thing to say!' Dina turned away in disgust and left the room.

She had been very young when it happened, but remembered the day clearly, during wartime, when two British ammunition ships had blown up after docking, killing thousands within a large radius of the harbour. Rumours about Nazi spies had begun to spread while the detonations were still in progress. The authorities said that many of those unaccounted for were vaporized during the deadly blasts, but Bapsy Aunty refused to accept this theory. She felt her husband was alive, wandering amnesiac somewhere, and it was only a matter of time before he was located. Alternately, Bapsy Aunty allowed that he might have been hypnotized or fed something by an unscrupulous sadhu and led away into slavery. In either case, she believed her husband would be found. That seventeen years had passed since the calamity did not diminish her faith. She spent her time chatting busily with his photograph, which sat in a heavy silver frame at her bedside, narrating for his benefit each day's news and gossip in detail.

'It's your depressing behaviour which reminds me of Bapsy Aunty,' said Nusswan, following Dina into the next room. 'What excuse do you have? You were at the funeral, you saw Rustom's body, you heard the prayers. He has been dead and digested for more than a year now.' As soon as he said it, he rolled his eyes heavenward to ask forgiveness for this bit of irreverence.

'Do you know how fortunate you are in our community? Among the unenlightened, widows are thrown away like garbage. If you were a Hindu, in the old days you would have had to be a good little sati and leap onto your husband's funeral pyre, be roasted with him.'

'I can always go to the Towers of Silence and let the vultures eat me up, if that will make you happy.'

'Shameless woman! What a loose mouth! Such blasphemy! All I am saying is, appreciate your position. For you it is possible to live a full life, get married again, have children. Or do you prefer to live forever on my charity?'

Dina did not answer. But the next day, while Nusswan was at work, she began moving her belongings back to Rustom's flat.

Ruby tried to stop her, following her from room to room, pleading with her. 'You know how hotheaded your brother is. He does not mean everything he says.'

'Neither does he say everything he means,' she replied, and continued packing.

In the evening Ruby told Nusswan about it. 'Hah!' he scoffed, loud enough for Dina to hear. 'Let her go if she wants. I would just love to see how she supports herself.'

After dinner, while still at the table, he cleared his throat. 'As the head of the family, it's my duty to tell you I don't approve of what you are doing. You are making a big mistake, which you will regret. It's a hard world out there, but I'm not going to beg you to stay. You are welcome here if you will be reasonable.'

'Thank you for the speech,' said Dina.

'Yes, make fun of me. You have done it all your life, why stop now. Remember, this is your decision, no one is kicking you out. None of our relatives will blame me, I have done all I can to help you. And will continue to do so.'

It was not long before the children understood that Dina Aunty was leaving. First they were bewildered, and then angry. Xerxes hid her handbag, screaming, 'No, Aunty! You cannot go!' When she threatened to leave without it, Zarir brought it tearfully from the hiding place.

'You can always visit me,' she tried to pacify the two, hugging them and drying their eyes. 'On Saturday and Sunday. And maybe during the vacation. It will be such fun.' They were excited at the prospect but would have much preferred that she stay with them forever.

The morning after she was back in her flat, Dina went to visit Rustom's Darab Uncle and Shirin Aunty. 'Darab! Look who's here!' Shirin Aunty shouted excitedly. 'Our dear Dina! Come in, my child, come in!'

Darab Uncle emerged, still in his pyjamas, and hugged Dina, saying they had waited a long time for this. 'Excuse my appearance,' he said, sitting down opposite her and smiling broadly.

As always, Dina was touched by their happiness at seeing her. She felt their love pour over her like something palpable. It reminded her of the milk bath she was given as a child on her birthday, by her mother, when half a cup of warm milk, with rose petals afloat, came trickling down her face and neck and chest in tiny white runnels over her light-brown skin.

'The hardest part,' she said, 'is leaving the two little boys. I have become so attached to them.'

'Yes, that's how it is with children,' said Shirin Aunty. 'But you know, Rustom had told us how shabbily your brother treated you in the years before you were married.'

'He is not a bad person,' Dina objected feebly. 'He just has his own ideas about things.'

'Yes, of course,' said Shirin Aunty, sensing the weight of family loyalty. 'Anyway, you can stay with us. We are so happy you came.'

'Oh,' said Dina, anxious to keep the misunderstanding from going further. 'Actually, I have decided to live in Rustom's flat from now on. I came only to ask if you could find me some work.'

Her words made Darab Uncle's mouth begin to move. He laboured to swallow the disappointment suddenly filling it, his soft slurping sounds teasing the quiet while Shirin Aunty played desperately with the hem of her dustercoat. 'Work,' she said, blank, unable to think. 'My dear child . . . yes, work, you must work. What work, Darab? What work for her, do you think?'

Dina waited in guilty silence for his answer. But he was still struggling with his mouthful. 'Go change your clothes,' Shirin Aunty scolded him. 'Almost afternoon, and still loitering in your sleeping suit.'

He rose obediently and went inside. Shirin Aunty relinquished her hem, rubbed her hands over her face and sat up. By the time Darab Uncle returned, having exchanged his blue-striped pyjamas for khaki pants and bush shirt, she had the beginnings of a solution for Dina.

'Tell me, my child, can you sew?'

'Yes, a little. Ruby taught me how to use a sewing-machine.'

'Good. Then there will be work for you. I have an extra Singer you can take. It is quite old, but runs well.'

For years, Shirin Aunty had supplemented her husband's salary from the State Transport Corporation by sewing for a few families. She made simple things like pyjamas, nightgowns, baby blouses, bedsheets, pillowcases, tablecloths. 'You can be my partner,' she said. 'There is lots of work, more than I can manage now with my weak old eyes. We will start tomorrow.'

Dina picked up her handbag and hugged Shirin Aunty and Darab Uncle. They accompanied her to the front door. Then a commotion in the street drew them to the balcony. A huge protest march was surging down the road.

'It's another silly morcha about language,' said Darab Uncle, spotting the banners. 'The fools want to divide the state on linguistic lines.'

'Everyone wants to change things,' said Shirin Aunty. 'Why can't people learn to be happy with things as they are? Anyway, let's go back inside. Dina cannot leave now. All the traffic is stopped.' She sounded quite pleased about it, and enjoyed Dina's company for two more hours, till the streets had returned to normal.

Over the next few days, Dina was taken around and introduced to the customers. At each stop she waited nervously by Shirin Aunty's side, smiling timidly, trying to grasp the barrage of names and the tailoring instructions. Shirin Aunty kept handing over most of the new jobs to her.

At the end of the week, Dina finally protested: 'I cannot accept so much, I cannot deprive you of your income.'

'My dear child, you are not depriving me of anything. Darab's pension is enough for us. I was going to give up the sewing anyway, it was becoming too hard for me. Here, don't forget this new pattern.'

Along with the assignments, Shirin Aunty passed along background material on the customers, information that would help Dina in her dealings with them. 'The Munshi family is the best – always pays promptly. The Parekhs too, except that they like to haggle. You just be firm, tell them I have set the rates. Who else? Oh yes, Mr. Savukshaw. He has a big problem with the bottle. By the end of the month his poor missis has hardly any money left. Make sure you take advance payment.'

With the Surtees, the situation was rather unique. Whenever Mr. and Mrs. Surtee fought, she did not cook any dinner. Instead, she pulled out all his pyjamas from the cupboard and set fire to them, saving the ashes and charred wisps in a dinner plate to set before him when he came home from work.

'The result,' said Shirin Aunty, 'is more business for you. Every two or three months, after they make up, Mrs. Surtee will give you a large order for pyjamas. But you must pretend it's normal, or she will get rid of you.'

Dina's collection of domestic portraits continued to grow as Shirin Aunty rendered descriptions of the Davars and Kotwals, the Mehtas and Pavris, the Vatchas and Seervais, and added them to the portfolio. 'You must be getting fed up with all these details,' she said. 'Just one last thing, and the most important: never measure the misters for their inseam. Ask for a sample to sew from. And if that is not possible, make sure there is someone present when you measure, a wife or mother or sister. Otherwise, before you know it, they move thisway-thatway and thrust something in your hand which you don't want. Believe me, I had a nasty experience when I was young and innocent.'

This last bit of advice was uppermost in Dina's mind when she was taken to meet Fredoon, a bachelor who lived alone. Shirin Aunty warned her not to go alone to his flat. 'Although he is a perfect gentleman, people's tongues are mischievous. They will talk that some funny business is going on. Your name will be spoilt.'

Dina did not care about people's tongues and felt no danger from Fredoon, though she was prepared to bolt if he ever asked her to take his inseam. To reassure Shirin Aunty, she said a friend was always with her. What she did not say was that the friend was Fredoon. For that was what he soon became. His commissions consisted mainly of little frocks and short pants and pinafores; to help Dina, he presented clothing on birthdays to the children of friends and relatives instead of envelopes stuffed with rupees.

Their friendship grew. Dina often accompanied him to textile stores to help him select material for the gifts. After the shopping, they would stop for tea and cakes at Bastani's. Sometimes Fredoon invited her back to his flat for dinner, picking up fried mutton chops or vindaloo on the way. He was always encouraging her to try new frock patterns, assert herself forcefully before her clients, demand higher rates.

Over the next several months, Dina became more confident about her abilities. The sewing was easy, thanks to her sister-in-law's training. And when there was something tricky, she consulted Shirin Aunty. Her visits brought the two old people such pleasure, she went regularly, pretending to be confused by something or other: ruched collars, raglan sleeves, accordion pleats.

The sewing produced snippets of fabric every day, and Shirin Aunty suggested collecting them. 'Waste nothing – remember, there is a purpose for everything. These scraps can be very useful.' She quickly demonstrated by making a lumpy sanitary pad.

'What a good idea,' said Dina. Her budget needed all the help it could get. The textile stuffing was not as absorbent as the pads she used to buy, but the homemade ones could be changed more frequently since they cost nothing. As an added precaution, though, she wore a very dark skirt for the duration.

Work made the hours pass quickly in the little flat. While her eyes and fingers were immersed in the sewing, she acquired a heightened awareness of noises from the flats around her. She collected the sounds, sorted them, replayed them, and created a picture of the lives being lived by her neighbours, the way she transformed measurements into clothes.

Rustom's policy regarding neighbours had been to avoid them as much as possible. A little sahibji-salaam was enough, he said, or it led to gossiping and kaana-sori that got out of hand. But the washing of pots and pans, ringing of doorbells, bargaining with vendors, laundry noises, the flop and slap of clothes thrashed in soapy water, family quarrels, arguments with servants – all this seemed like gossip too. And she realized that the noises from her own flat would narrate her life for the neighbours' ears, if they bothered to listen. There was no such thing as perfect privacy, life was a perpetual concert-hall recital with a captive audience.

Sometimes, the old pastime of attending free concerts tempted her, but she was reluctant to resume it. Anything which seemed like a clutching at bygone days made her wary. The road towards self-reliance could not lie through the past.

By and by, when the tailoring had settled into a comfortable routine for Dina, Shirin Aunty taught her to knit pullovers. 'There is not much demand for woollen things,' she said, 'but some people order them for style, or if they are going to hill-stations for a holiday.' As they progressed towards complicated patterns, Shirin Aunty presented her with her entire collection of design books and knitting needles.

Lastly, she instructed Dina in embroidery, with a warning: 'Needlework on table napkins and tea-cloths is very popular, and pays well. But it's a great strain on the eyes. Don't do too much, or it will catch up with you after forty.'

And so, three years later, when Shirin Aunty passed away, followed by Darab Uncle a few months later, Dina felt confident of managing on her own. She also felt very alone, as though she had lost a second set of parents.

Contrary to Nusswan's conviction that no one would blame him for Dina's leaving, the relatives quickly grouped into two camps. While a few, professing neutrality, felt comfortable on both sides of the line, at least half were staunchly in support of Dina. To show their approval of her independent spirit, they came out with numerous ideas for money-making ventures.

'Butter biscuits. That's where all the cash is.'

'Why don't you start a crèche? Any mother would prefer you to look after her children, instead of an ayah.'

'Make a good rose sherbet and you won't have to look back. People will buy it by the gallon.'

Dina listened with gratitude to everything, inclining her head interestedly as they formulated their schemes. She became an expert at non-committal nodding. When the tailoring was slow, she filled their orders for cakes, bhakras, vasanu, and coomas.

Then her friend Zenobia had a brainwave about in-home haircuts for children. Zenobia had fulfilled her schoolgirl ambition: she was now chief hairstylist at the Venus Beauty Salon. After the shop closed at night, she instructed Dina on a wig glued to a plaster-of-Paris cranium. The comb kept getting caught in the cheap mop's knotted strands.

'Don't worry,' she reassured Dina. 'It's much easier with real hair.' From the surplus in the shop she put together a kit of scissors, hair clippers, brush, comb, talcum powder and powder puff. Then they made a list of friends and relatives with children who could be used as guinea pigs. Xerxes and Zarir's names were left out; though Nusswan would have welcomed the opportunity to save on haircuts, Dina felt uncomfortable now in his house.

'Just go after the brats, one by one, till you have cropped the whole jing-bang lot,' said Zenobia. 'It's only a question of practice.' She monitored the results, and soon declared Dina trained and ready. Now Dina began going door to door.

After a few days, however, the enterprise folded without a single haircut. Neither she nor Zenobia had remembered that most people regarded hair clippings within their dwellings as extreme bad luck. Dina related the misadventures to her friend, how the thought of hair hitting the floor made the prospective clients hit the ceiling. 'Madam, you have no consideration? What have we done to you that you want to bring misfortune within our four walls?'

Some people did offer her their children's heads. 'But only if you do it outside,' they said. Dina refused. There were limits to what she would do. She was an in-home children's stylist, not an open-air pavement barber.

Afterwards, she did not hang up her clippers for good. Her friends' children continued to benefit from her skills. Some of the little boys and girls, remembering the practice haircuts, hid when Dina Aunty arrived. As she got better, they were less afraid.

Through all this, there were lean times when it was difficult to meet the rent or pay the electricity bill. Shirin Aunty and Darab Uncle, while they were still alive, had often tided her over with a loan of forty or fifty rupees. Now the only alternative was Nusswan.

'Of course, it's my duty,' he said piously. 'Are you sure sixty will be enough?'

'Yes, thank you. I will pay it back next month.'

'No rush. So tell me, have you found a sweetheart?'

'No,' she replied, wondering if he suspected something about Fredoon. Could someone have seen them together and reported back to Nusswan?

During the two years since Shirin Aunty's death, the bachelor had progressed from friend to lover. Though the idea of marriage was still difficult for Dina to entertain, she enjoyed Fredoon's company because he was perfectly content to spend time in her presence without feeling compelled to make clever conversation or to participate in the usual social activities of couples. The two were equally happy sitting in his flat or walking in a public garden.

But when they ventured into the private garden of intimacy, it was a troubled relationship. There were certain things she could not bring herself to do. The bed – any bed – was out of bounds, sacred and reserved for married couples only. So they used a chair. Then one day, as she swung a leg over to straddle Fredoon, her action suddenly resurrected the image of Rustom flinging his leg over his bicycle. Now the chair, like the bed, was no longer possible.

'Oh God!' said Fredoon, groaning softly. He put on his trousers and made tea.

A few days later he persuaded her into the standing position, and Dina had no objections. He began to refine the procedure as much as he could, finding a low platform for her to stand on; their heights became more compatible during their embraces. Next he bought a stool, took some personal measurements, and sawed off precisely two and a quarter inches, adjusting it to the proper size for her to rest one leg. Sometimes she raised the left, sometimes the right. He arranged these accessories against the wall and suspended pillows from the ceiling at appropriate heights for her head and back, and under the hips.

'Is it comfortable?' he asked tenderly, and she nodded.

But the ultimate satisfaction of the bed could only be approximated. What should have been the occasional spice to vary the regular menu had become the main course, leaving the appetite often confused or unfulfilled.

The opposite wall of Fredoon's room had a small window in it. Outside the window was a streetlamp. Once, between dusk and nightfall, as they were locked in their vertical lovemaking, it started to rain. A moist garden smell came in through the window. Through her half-open eyes Dina saw the drizzle float like mist around the lamplight. Occasionally, a hand or elbow or shoulder strayed beyond the pillows, onto the bare wall, and the cement felt deliciously cool against their heated flesh.

'Mmm,' she said, enjoying with all her senses, and he was pleased. The rain was heavier now. She could see it slanting in needles past the streetlamp.

She watched it for a while, then stiffened. 'Please stop,' she whispered, but he continued moving.

'Stop, I said! Please, Fredoon, stop it!'

'Why?' he begged. 'Why? Now what's wrong?'

She shivered. 'The rain . . .'

'The rain? I'll shut the window if you like.'

She shook her head. 'I'm sorry, something made me think of Rustom.'

He took her face between his hands, but she pushed them away. She swam out of his embrace and into the memory of that night from long ago: she was wearing Rustom's warm raincoat; her umbrella had broken in the storm. And after the concert, at the bus shelter, they had held hands for the first time ever, their palms moist with the finely falling drizzle.

Remembering the purity of that moment, Dina contrasted it with the present. What Fredoon and she did in this room seemed a sordid, contraption-riddled procedure, filling her with shame and remorse. She shuddered.

Silently, Fredoon handed Dina her brassière and underpants. She shrank towards the pillowed wall while she dressed, turning away from him. He put on his trousers and made tea.

Later, he tried to cheer her up. 'In all the bloody Hindi movies, rain brings the hero and heroine closer together,' he complained. 'But it is, from this moment onwards, the bane of my life.' She smiled, and he was encouraged. 'Never mind, I'll dismantle this and design a new set for our performance.'

And Fredoon kept trying. Despite his creative efforts and secret consultations of sex manuals, however, the past could only be imperfectly distanced. It was a slippery thing, he discovered, slithering into the present at the least excuse, dodging the strongest defences.

But he remained uncomplaining, and Dina liked him for it. She was determined to keep him a secret from Nusswan as long as possible.

'No boyfriend as yet?' said Nusswan, counting out the money from his wallet. 'Remember, you are thirty already. It will be too late for children, once you have dried up. I can still find you a decent husband. For what are you slaving and slogging?'

She put the sixty rupees in her purse and let him have his say. It was the interest he extracted on his loan, she thought philosophically – a bit excessive, but the only currency that she could afford and he would accept.

━━

The violin had sat untouched upon the cupboard for five years. During the biannual flat cleaning, when Dina wrapped a white cloth over her head and swept the walls and ceilings with the long-handled broom, she wiped the top of the cupboard without moving the black case.

For six more years, she continued to employ the same strategy against the violin, barely acknowledging its existence. Now it was the twelfth death anniversary. Time to sell the instrument, she decided. Better that someone use it, make music with it, instead of it gathering dust. She got up on a chair and took down the case. The rusted metal snaps squealed as her fingers flipped them open; then she raised the lid, and gasped.

The soundboard had collapsed completely around the f-holes. The four strings flopped limply between the tailpiece and tuning pegs, while the felt-lining of the case was in shreds, chewed to tatters by marauding insects. Bits of burgundy wool clung to her hands. Her stomach felt queasy. With a trembling hand she drew out the bow from its compartment within the lid. The horsehair hung from one end of it like a thin long ponytail; barely a dozen unbroken strands remained in place. She put everything back and decided to take it to L. M. Furtado & Co.

On the way, she had to duck inside a library while demonstrators rampaged briefly through the street, breaking store windows and shouting slogans against the influx of South Indians into the city who were stealing their jobs. Police jeeps arrived as the demonstrators finished their work and departed. Dina waited a few minutes longer before relinquishing the library.

At L. M. Furtado & Co., Mr. Mascarenhas was supervising the cleanup of the large plate-glass window, its shattered pieces glittering among two guitars, a banjo, bongos, and some sheet music for the latest Cliff Richard songs. Mr. Mascarenhas returned behind the counter as Dina entered the shop with the violin.

'What a shame,' she said, pointing at the window.

'It's just the cost of doing business these days,' he said, and opened the case she put before him. The contents made him pause grimly. 'And how did this happen?' He didn't recognize Dina, for it had been a long time since Rustom had introduced her, when they had dropped in once to buy an E string. 'Doesn't anyone play it?'

'Not for a few years.'

Mr. Mascarenhas scratched his right ear and frowned fiercely around the thick black frames of his spectacles. 'When a violin is in storage, the strings should be loosened, the bow should be slack,' he said severely. 'We human beings loosen our belts when we go home and relax, don't we?'

Dina nodded, feeling ashamed. 'Can it be repaired?'

'Anything can be repaired. The question is, how will it sound after it is repaired?'

'How will it sound?'

'Horrible. Like fighting cats. But we can reline the case with new felt. It's a good hard case.'

She sold the case to Mr. Mascarenhas for fifty rupees, leaving behind the remains of the violin. He said a beginner might buy the repaired instrument at a discount. 'Learners squawk and screech anyway, the tone will make no difference. If it sells, I'll pay you fifty more.'

She was comforted by the thought that an enthusiastic youngster might acquire it. Rustom would have liked that – the idea of his violin continuing to torment the human race.

From time to time, Dina's guilt about the violin returned to anguish her. How stupid, she thought, to ignore it on top of the cupboard for twelve years, leaving it to destruct. She could at least have given it to Xerxes and Zarir, encouraged them to take lessons.

Then, one morning, someone came to the flat and announced that there was a delivery for Mrs. Dalal.

'That's me,' she said.

The youth, wearing fashionably tight pants and a bright yellow shirt with the top three buttons left undone, returned to the van to fetch the item. Dina wondered if it might be the violin. Six months had passed since she had taken it to L. M. Furtado & Co. Perhaps Mr. Mascarenhas was sending it back because it was beyond redemption.

The young fellow appeared at the door again, dragging Rustom's mangled bicycle. 'From the police station,' he said.

Before he could get her to sign and acknowledge receipt of the goods, her hand slid along the door jamb, lowering her gracefully to the floor. She fainted.

'Ma-ji!' the delivery boy panicked. 'Shall I call ambulance? Are you sick?' He fanned her frantically with the delivery roster, waving it at various angles to her face, hoping that one of these airflows might work, might put the breath back into her nostrils.

She stirred, and he fanned harder. Encouraged by the improvement, he took her wrist as though checking for a pulse. He didn't know what exactly to do with the wrist, but had seen the gesture being performed several times in a film where the hero was a doctor and his faithful and bosomy nurse was the heroine.

Dina stirred again, and the delivery boy released the wrist, pleased with his very first medical success. 'Ma-ji! What happened? Shall I get someone?'

She shook her head. 'The heat . . . it's okay now.' The twisted frame and handlebars swam into view again. For a moment she wondered why the police would have painted the bicycle a reddish brown; it used to be black.

Then the haziness passed, and her focus returned to normal. 'It's completely rusted,' she said.

'Completely,' he nodded, then checked the tag inscribed with the file number and date. 'No wonder. Twelve years it has sat in the evidence room, where the windows are broken and the ceiling leaks. Twelve monsoon rains will make human bones rust also.'

Dina's inner turmoil made her rage at the youth. 'Is that any way to treat important evidence? If they caught the criminal, how would they prove it in court – with the evidence damaged?'

'I agree with you. But the whole building leaks. The employees get wet just like the evidence. Important files also, making the ink run. Only the big boss has a dry office.'

His explanation gave her little comfort, and he tried again. 'You know, ma-ji, once we had a bag of wheat in the storage room. Someone had murdered the owner to steal it. There were bloodstains on the jute sacking. By the time the case came to court, rats had chewed through it and eaten up most of the wheat. Judge dismissed the case for lack of evidence.' He laughed carefully as he finished the story, hoping she would see the funny side of it.

'You find that a joking matter?' said Dina angrily. 'The criminal walks free. What happens to justice?'

'It's terrible, just terrible,' he agreed, giving her the roster to sign, then thanked her and departed.

She examined her copy of the receipt. It stated that the file was closed and the property returned to the next-of-kin.

Dina was not a superstitious person. But the bicycle's reappearance, after the fate of the violin, was more than she could bear. She decided there was a message in it for her. She completed Fredoon's last order, a party frock for a niece, delivered it, shook his hand, and said it wouldn't be possible to see him anymore, for she was giving up the sewing business and getting married.

——

From then on, Dina did not meet Fredoon again. To avoid running into him, she even gave up other clients in that building. There was enough work from her remaining sources to support her.

A full five years passed in this manner. Then, right on schedule, Shirin Aunty's prophecy came to pass. At forty-two, Dina's eyes began to trouble her. In twelve months she had to change her spectacles twice. The lenses had grown quite formidable.

'Stop the eye strain or accept blindness,' said the doctor. He was a wiry little man with a funny manner of wiggling his fingers all over the room when checking for peripheral vision. It reminded Dina of children playing at butterflies.

But his suddenly blunt manner made her indignant, and also a little frightened. She did not know what she would do if sewing became impossible.

Fortune, sticking to its own schedule, brought along a solution. Her friend Zenobia told her about the export manager of a large textile company. 'Mrs. Gupta is one of my regular clients. I've done her lots of favours, she can surely find some easy work for you.'

One afternoon that week, at the Venus Beauty Salon, amid the disagreeable odours of hydrogen peroxide and other beautifying chemicals, Dina waited to meet Mrs. Gupta, who was nestled under a hairdryer. 'Just a few more minutes,' whispered Zenobia. 'I'm doing such a wonderful bouffant for her, she'll be in a superb mood.'

Dina watched from a chair in the reception area as Zenobia performed architecturally, even sculpturally, with the export manager's hair, and created a monument. As construction proceeded, Dina glanced sidelong in a mirror, imagining the lofty edifice upon her own head.

Soon, the scaffolding of clips and curlers was carefully dismantled, and the hairdo was complete. The two women came over to the waiting area. Mrs. Gupta was beaming.

'It looks beautiful,' Dina felt compelled to say after introductions were completed.

'Oh, thank you,' said the export manager. 'But all the credit goes to Zenobia, the talent is hers. I only supply raw material.'

They laughed, and Zenobia insisted she had nothing to do with it. 'Mrs. Gupta's facial structure – look at those cheekbones, and also her elegant carriage – they are responsible for the total effect.'

'Stop, stop! You are making me blush!' squeaked Mrs. Gupta.

Discussing the magic of imported shampoos and hairsprays, Zenobia steered the conversation towards the garment industry, as skilfully as she had twirled the whorls and spirals. Mrs. Gupta was quite happy to talk about her achievements at Au Revoir Exports.

'In just one year I have doubled the turnover,' she said. 'Highly prestigious labels from all over the world are asking for my creations.' Her company – she used the possessive throughout – had begun supplying women's clothing to boutiques in America and Europe. The sewing was done locally to foreign specifications, and contracted out in small lots.

'It's more economical for me. Better than having one big factory which could be crippled by a strike. Who wants to deal with union goondas if it can be avoided? Especially these days, with so much trouble in the country. And leaders like that Jay Prakash Narayan encouraging civil disobedience. Simply at all creating problems. Thinks he is Mahatma Gandhi the Second.'

At Zenobia's prompting, Mrs. Gupta agreed Dina would be ideal for the work. 'Yes, you can easily hire tailors and supervise them. You don't have to strain yourself.'

'But I have never handled complicated things or latest fashions,' confessed Dina, and Zenobia frowned at her. 'Only simple clothes. Children's frocks, school uniforms, pyjamas.'

'This is also simple,' assured Mrs. Gupta. 'All you have to do is follow the paper patterns as you follow your nose.'

'Exactly,' said Zenobia, annoyed with Dina's hesitation. 'And no investment is needed, two tailors can easily fit in your back room.'

'What about the landlord?' asked Dina. 'He could make big trouble for me if I start a workshop in the flat.'

'He doesn't have to know,' said Zenobia. 'Just keep it quiet, don't tell your neighbours or anyone.'

The tailors would have to bring their own sewing-machines, for that was the norm, according to Mrs. Gupta. And piecework was better, it created some incentive, whereas a daily wage would be a recipe for wasting time. 'Always remember one thing,' she stressed. 'You are the boss, you must make the rules. Never lose control. Tailors are very strange people – they work with tiny needles but strut about as if they were carrying big swords.'

So Dina was convinced, and set out to look for two tailors, scouring the warren of laneways in the sordid belly of the city. Day after day, she entered dilapidated buildings and shops, each one standing precariously like a house of battered cards. Tailors she saw in plenty – perched in constricted lofts, crouched inside kholis that looked like subterranean burrows, bent over in smelly cubicles, or cross-legged on street corners – all engaged in a variety of tasks ranging from mattress covers to wedding outfits.

The ones who were eager to join her did not seem capable of handling the export work. She saw samples of their sewing: crooked collars, uneven hems, mismatched sleeves. And those who were skilled enough wanted the work delivered to them. But this was Mrs. Gupta's one strict condition: the sewing had to be done under the supervision of the contractor. No exceptions, not even for Zenobia's friend, because Au Revoir's patterns were top secret.

The best Dina could do was to write her address on little squares of paper and leave it at shops where the quality was reasonable. 'If you know someone who does good work like you and needs a job, send them to me,' she said. Many of the owners threw away the paper as soon as she left. Some rolled it into a tight cone to scratch inside their ears before discarding it.

Meanwhile, Zenobia had another suggestion for Dina: to take in a boarder. It would involve no more than providing a few basics like bed, cupboard, bath; and for meals, cooking a bit extra of what she ate.

'You mean, like a paying guest?' said Dina. 'Never. Paying guests are trouble with a capital t. I remember that case in Firozsha Baag. What a horrible time the poor people had.'

'Don't be so paranoid. We are not going to allow crooks or crackpots into the flat. Think of the rent every month – guaranteed income.'

'No baba, I don't want to take the risk. I've heard of lots of old people and single women being harassed.'

But as her meagre savings dwindled, she relented. Zenobia assured her they would only accept someone reliable, preferably a temporary visitor to the city, who had a home to return to. 'You look for tailors,' she said. 'I'll find the boarder.'

So Dina continued to distribute her name and address at tailors' shops, going further afield, taking the train to the northern suburbs, to parts of the city she had never seen in all her forty-two years. Her progress was frequently held up when traffic was blocked by processions and demonstrations against the government. Sometimes, from the upper deck of the bus, she had a good view of the tumultuous crowds. The banners and slogans accused the Prime Minister of misrule and corruption, calling on her to resign in keeping with the court judgment finding her guilty of election malpractice.

And even if the Prime Minister stepped down – would it do any good? wondered Dina.

One evening, while the slow local waited for a signal change, she gazed beyond the railway fence where a stream of black sewer sludge spilled from an underground drain. Men were hauling on a rope that disappeared into the ground. Their arms were dark to the elbows, the black slime dripping from hands and rope. In the slum behind them, cooking fires smouldered, with smoke smudging the air. The workers were trying to unblock the overflowing drain.

Then a boy emerged out of the earth, clinging to the end of the rope. He was covered in the slippery sewer sludge, and when he stood up, he shone and shimmered in the sun with a terrible beauty. His hair, stiffened by the muck, flared from his head like a crown of black flames. Behind him, the slum smoke curled towards the sky, and the hellishness of the place was complete.

Dina stared, shuddering, transfixed by his appearance, covering her nose against the stench till the train had cleared the area. But the underworld vision haunted her for the rest of the day, and for days to come.

The long, depressing trips, the squalid sights, wore her down. Her spirits were lower than ever. Zenobia could see it in her eyes. 'What's this gloomy face for,' she said, pinching Dina's cheek lightly.

'I am fed up with this struggle. I can't do it anymore.'

'You mustn't give up now. Look, more people have contacted me for paying guests. And one of them is Maneck Kohlah – Aban's son. Remember her? She was at school with us. She wrote to me that Maneck hates his college hostel, he is desperate to move. I just want to be sure we pick a good character.'

'All these train fares are a waste of money,' said Dina, not listening. She wanted her friend's approval to abandon the soul-draining journeys.

'But just think – once you find two tailors, how easy your life will be. You want to give up your independence and live with Nusswan or what?'

'Don't even joke about it.' The prospect persuaded her to continue to leave her address at more and more shops. She felt like the lost children in that fairy tale whose title had slipped her mind, leaving a trail of bread, hoping to be rescued. But birds had devoured the bread. Would she ever be saved, she wondered, or would her trail of paper be devoured, by the wind, by the black sewer sludge, by the hungry army of paper-collectors roaming the streets with their sacks?

Tired and discouraged, she entered a lane where a rivulet of waste water flowed down the middle. Vegetable peelings, cigarette butts, eggshells bobbed along the surface. A little further, the lane narrowed and turned almost entirely into a gutter. Children were floating paper boats in the effluent, chasing them down the lethargic current. Planks had been thrown across to form walkways into shops and houses. When a boat sailed under a plank, emerging safely on the other side, the children clapped with glee.

Dina heard the familiar rattle and hum of a sewing-machine from someone's doorway. This would be the last tailor for today, she decided, gingerly crossing the plank, and then she would go straight home.

Halfway across, her foot went through a rotten spot. A brief cry escaped her; she kept her balance but lost a shoe. The children waded in, yelling, groping beneath the dark surface, competing to retrieve it.

She reached the shop entrance and took back her dripping shoe, giving the excited little boy who found it a twenty-five-paisa coin. The sound of the sewing-machine had ceased; its operator stood in the doorway, summoned by the commotion.

'What are you rascals up to again?' he shouted at the children.

'They were helping me,' said Dina. 'I was coming to your shop and my shoe fell in.'

'Oh,' he grunted, a little deflated. 'The thing is, they are always playing bad mischief.' Recognizing a potential customer, he changed his tone. 'Please come in, please.'

Her inquiry about tailors disappointed him. He dismissed it with an indifferent 'Okay, I'll try,' playing with his tape measure while she wrote down her name and address.

Then he brightened suddenly. 'The thing is, you have come to the right place. I have two wonderful tailors for you. I will send them tomorrow.'

'Really?' she asked, sceptical about the change of heart.

'Oh yes, two beautiful tailors, or my name is not Nawaz. The thing is, they don't have their own shop, they go out and work. But they are very skilled. You will be so happy with them.'

'Okay, I'll see them tomorrow.' She departed, nurturing no expectations. There had been several false promises in the past few weeks.

On reaching home, she washed her feet and cleaned her shoes, sickened again at the thought of that lane where the children played with their paper boats. Her hopes would not be raised – neither by the tailor's pledge nor by Zenobia's assurance that a boarder was just round the corner, that their schoolfriend's son, Maneck Kohlah, would drop in any day now to inspect the room.

And so, next morning, when the doorbell rang, Dina welcomed her change of fortune with open arms. The paying guest stood at her door, along with the fruit of yesterday's square of paper: two tailors named Ishvar and Omprakash Darji.

As Zenobia would have put it, the whole jing-bang trio arrived at her flat together.

II For Dreams to Grow

THE OFFICES OF Au Revoir Exports looked and smelled like a warehouse, the floors stacked high with bales of textiles swaddled in hessian. The chemical odour of new fabric was sharp in the air. Scraps of clear plastic, paper, twine, and packing material littered the dusty floor. Dina located the manager at a desk hidden behind metal shelving.

'Hello! Zenobia's friend – Mrs. Dalal! How are you?' said Mrs. Gupta.

They shook hands. Dina reported that she had found two skilled tailors and was ready to start.

'Wonderful, absolutely wonderful!' said Mrs. Gupta, but it was evident that her excellent humour did not flow merely from Dina's announcement. The real reason soon bubbled out: she had another appointment at the Venus Beauty Salon this afternoon. Unruly curls which had slipped the leash during the past week would be tamed and brought back into the fold.

This event alone would have been enough to ensure Mrs. Gupta's happiness, but there were more glad tidings; minor irritants in her life were also being eradicated – the Prime Minister's declaration yesterday of the Internal Emergency had incarcerated most of the parliamentary opposition, along with thousands of trade unionists, students, and social workers. 'Isn't that good news?' she sparkled with joy.

Dina nodded, doubtful. 'I thought the court found her guilty of cheating in the election.'

'No, no, no!' said Mrs.Gupta. 'That is all rubbish, it will be appealed. Now all those troublemakers who accused her falsely have been put in jail. No more strikes and morchas and silly disturbances.'

'Oh good,' said Dina nervously.

The manager opened her order book and selected a pattern for the first assignment. 'Now these thirty-six dresses are a test for you. Test for neatness, accuracy, and consistency. If your two tailors prove themselves, I will keep giving you orders. Much bigger orders,' she promised. 'As I told you before, I prefer to deal with private contractors. Union loafers want to work less and get more money. That's the curse of this country – laziness. And some idiot leaders encouraging them, telling police and army to disobey unlawful orders. Now you tell me, how can the law be unlawful? Ridiculous nonsense. Serves them right, being thrown in jail.'

'Yes, serves them right,' echoed Dina, absorbed in the dress design. She wished the manager would stick to the work and not keep rambling into politics. 'Look, Mrs. Gupta, the hem on the sample dress is three inches wide, but according to the paper pattern it's only two inches.'

The discrepancy was too trivial for Mrs. Gupta's consideration. She nodded and shrugged, which made the sari slip from her shoulder. A hand darted to halt the slide. 'Thank God the Prime Minister has taken firm steps, as she said on the radio. We are lucky to have someone strong at a dangerous time like this.'

She waved aside further queries. 'I have faith in you, Mrs. Dalal, just follow my sample. But did you see the new posters today? They are put up everywhere.'

Dina hadn't; she keenly wanted to measure the fabrics allocated for the thirty-six dresses, in case there was a shortfall. On second thoughts, no, she decided, it would offend the manager.

'"The Need of the Hour Is Discipline" – that's the Prime Minister's message on the poster. And I think she is absolutely right.' Mrs. Gupta leaned closer and confided softly, 'It wouldn't be a bad idea to stick a few posters on the Au Revoir entrance. Look at those two rascals in the corner. Chatting away instead of stacking my shelves.'

Dina clucked sympathetically and shook her head. 'Shall I come back in one week?'

'Please do. And best of luck. Remember, be firm with your tailors or they will sit on your head.'

Dina started to pick up the bundles of cloth but was stopped. The managerial fingers snapped twice to summon a man to load the material in the lift.

'I'll say hello from you to Zenobia this afternoon. Wish me some luck also,' Mrs. Gupta giggled. 'My poor hair is going under the knife again.'

'Yes, of course, good luck.'

Dina brought home the bolts of cloth and made space for the two tailors in the back room. The paying guest wasn't moving in till next month; that would give her time to get used to one thing. She studied the paper patterns and examined the packet of labels: Chantal Boutique, New York. Restless, she decided to start cutting the patterns, have them ready for Monday. She wondered about the Emergency. If there were riots, the tailors might not be able to come. She didn't even know where they lived. It would make a terrible impression in case the delivery date was not met for this trial consignment.

The Darjis arrived promptly on Monday at eight a.m., by taxi, with their sewing-machines. 'On hire purchase,' said Ishvar, proudly patting the Singers. 'In three years, when payments are complete, they will belong to us.'

Everything the tailors could spare must have gone towards the first instalment, for she had to pay the taxi driver. 'Please deduct from what we earn this week,' said Ishvar.

The machines were carried into the back room. They fitted the drive belts, adjusted the various tensions, loaded the bobbins, and ran off seams on waste cloth to test the stitches. Fifteen minutes later they were ready to sew.

And sew they did. Like angels, thought Dina. The treadles of the Singers rocked and the flywheels hummed as the needles danced in neat, narrow rows upon fabric, while the unfurling bolts of cloth were transformed into sleeves, collars, fronts, backs, pleats, and skirts.

I am the supervisor, she had to remind herself constantly, I must not join in the work. She hovered around, inspecting finished pieces, encouraging, advising. She scrutinized the tailors bent over the machines, their brows furrowed. The inch-long nails on their little fingers intrigued her; they used them for folding seams and making creases. Ishvar's disfigured cheek was grotesque, she decided: what might have caused it? He did not look like the type to get into a knife fight. His smile and his funny, undecided moustache tended to soften the damage. She shifted her glance to the silent Omprakash. The skeletal figure, sharp and angular, seemed a mechanical extension of the sewing-machine. Delicate as cut-glass crystal, she thought with a pang of concern. And his oily hair – she hoped he wouldn't smudge the cloth.

Lunchtime came and went, and they continued to work, stopping only to ask for a drink of water. 'Thank you,' said Ishvar, gulping it down. 'Very nice and cool.'

'Don't you eat lunch at this time?'

He shook his head fervently as though the suggestion was preposterous. 'One meal at night is sufficient. More than that is a waste of time and food.' After a pause, he asked, 'Dinabai, what is this Emergency we hear about?'

'Government problems – games played by people in power. It doesn't affect ordinary people like us.'

'That's what I said,' murmured Omprakash. 'My uncle was simply worrying.'

They returned to their Singers, and Dina felt piecework was a brilliant idea. She rinsed the glass and put it in a separate place. From now on it would be the tailors' glass.

As the afternoon deepened, Ishvar seemed uncomfortable at his machine. She noticed him sitting hunched forward, legs tight together, as though he had stomach cramp. His feet began faltering on the treadle.

'What's the matter?' she asked.

'Nothing, nothing,' he smiled embarrassedly.

His nephew came to the rescue, holding up his little finger. 'He needs to go.'

'Why didn't you say it earlier?'

'I was feeling bad to ask,' said Ishvar shyly.

She showed him the wc. The door shut, and she heard the stream hit the toilet. It rose and fell haltingly with the reluctance of an overfull bladder.

Omprakash took his turn when Ishvar returned. 'The flush is out of order,' Dina called after him. 'Throw some water from the bucket.'

The smell in the wc bothered her. Living alone for so long, I've grown too fastidious, she thought. Different diets, different habits – it was only natural their urine left a strange odour.

———

The pile of finished dresses grew without Dina having to do a thing except open the door every morning. Ishvar would have a greeting or a smile for her, but Omprakash's skinny form darted past wordlessly. Perching on his stool like a grouchy little owl, she thought.

The three dozen dresses were completed before the due date. Mrs. Gupta was delighted with the results. She authorized a new assignment, for six dozen garments this time. And safely in Dina's purse was the payment for the first batch. Almost like money for nothing, she felt, experiencing a hint of guilt. How much easier than those tangled days when her fingers and eyes were forever snarled in sewing and embroidery.

The tailors' relief at being approved by the export company was enormous. 'If the first lot is accepted, the rest will be no problem,' brimmed Ishvar with sudden confidence, as she counted out their payment.

'Yes,' cautioned Dina, 'but they will always check the quality, so we cannot get careless. And we have to deliver on time.'

'Hahnji, don't worry,' said Ishvar. 'Always top quality production, on time.' And Dina dared to believe that her days of toil and trouble were ending.

The tailors began taking regular lunch breaks. Dina concluded that the one-meal-a-day formula Ishvar had proclaimed last week was dictated by their pocketbook rather than asceticism or a strict work ethic. But she was pleased because her enterprise was improving their nourishment.

Promptly at one, Omprakash announced, 'I'm hungry, let's go.' They put aside the dresses, returned their treasured pinking shears to the drawer, and departed.

They ate at the Vishram Vegetarian Hotel on the corner. There were no secrets at the Vishram – everything was out in the open: the man chopping vegetables, another frying them in the huge black-bottomed pan, a boy washing up. With only one table in the little shop, Ishvar and Omprakash did not wait for a seat but ate standing with the crowd outside. Then they hurried back to work, past the legless beggar who was rolling back and forth on his platform to the squeal of his rusty castors.

Soon, Dina began to notice that the sewing no longer proceeded at the former breakneck speed. Their recesses became more numerous, during which they stood outside the front door and puffed on beedis. Typical, she thought, they get a little money and they start to slack off.

She remembered the advice that Zenobia and Mrs. Gupta had given: to be a firm boss. She pointed out, in what she presumed was a stern voice, that work was falling behind.

'No no, don't worry,' said Ishvar. 'Everything will finish punctually. But if you like, to save time we can smoke while we sew.'

Dina hated the smell; besides, a stray spark could burn a hole in the cloth. 'You shouldn't smoke anywhere,' she said. 'Inside or outside. Cancer will eat your lungs.'

'We don't have to worry about cancer,' said Omprakash. 'This expensive city will first eat us alive, for sure.'

'What's that? At last I am hearing words from your mouth?'

Ishvar chuckled. 'I told you he speaks only when he disagrees.'

'But why worry about money,' she said. 'Work hard and you will earn lots of it.'

'Not the way you pay us,' muttered Omprakash under his breath.

'What's that?'

'Nothing, nothing,' said Ishvar hastily. 'He was talking to me. He has a headache.'

She asked if he would like to take an Aspro for the pain. Omprakash refused, but from then on, his voice was heard increasingly.

'Do you have to go far to get the work?' he asked.

'Not far,' said Dina. 'Takes about one hour.' She was pleased that he was settling in, making an effort to be agreeable.

'If you need help to carry the dresses there, let us know.'

How nice of him, she thought.

'And what is the name of the company you go to?'

Glad about his grumpy silences having ended, she almost blurted out the name, then pretended not to have heard. He repeated the question.

'Why bother with the name,' she said. 'All that I am concerned with is the work.'

'Very true,' agreed Ishvar. 'That's what interests us also.'

His nephew scowled. After a while he tried again: Was there only one company or several different ones? Was she paid a commission, or a set price for the complete order?

Ishvar was embarrassed. 'Less talk, Omprakash, and more sewing.'

Now Dina longed for the silent nephew. She saw what he was after, and from that day made sure the material from Au Revoir Exports bore no signs of its origin. Labels and tags were torn off the packages if the telltale name was featured. Invoices were kept locked away in the cupboard. Cracks began appearing in her optimism as it tried to keep up with the tailors. She knew the road had turned bumpy.

━━

The Darjis lived far, at the mercy of the railways. Still, Dina worried now if they were late, certain she had been deserted for better-paying jobs. And since she could not afford to let them suspect her fears, she always masked her relief upon their arrival with a show of displeasure.

A day before the due date, they did not come till ten o'clock. 'There was an accident, train was delayed,' explained Ishvar. 'Some poor fellow dead on the tracks again.'

'It's happening too often,' said Omprakash.

The empty-stomach smell floating out their mouths, like a cocoon containing words, was unpleasant. She was not interested in their excuses. The sooner they were at their sewing-machines the better.

But silence on her part could be misconstrued as weakness, so she said, drily, 'Under the Emergency, government says railway runs on time. Strange that your train keeps coming late.'

'If government kept their promises, the gods would come down to garland them,' said Ishvar, laughing with a placating circular nod.

His peace-offering amused her. She smiled, and he was relieved. As far as he was concerned, jeopardizing the steady income would be foolish – Omprakash and he were very fortunate to be working for Dina Dalal.

They pulled out their wooden stools, loaded fresh bobbins, and started to sew while the sky prepared to rain. The gloom of grey clouds infiltrated the back room. Omprakash hinted that the forty-watt bulb was too dim.

'If I exceed the monthly quota, my meter will be disconnected,' she said. 'Then we will be in total darkness.'

Ishvar suggested moving the Singers to the front room which was much brighter.

'Not possible. The machines will be seen from the street, and the landlord will make trouble. It is against the law to have a factory in the flat, even if it is only two sewing-machines. Already he harasses me for other reasons.'

This the tailors understood. They too knew about landlords and harassment. Through the morning they worked steadily, with rumbling bellies, anticipating the midday break. They had eaten nothing since waking.

'Double tea for me today,' said Omprakash. 'And a butter-bun to dip.'

'Pay attention to your machine,' said Ishvar. 'You will end up with double fingers instead of double tea.' They both kept checking the clock. At the hour of deliverance, their feet left the treadles and sought out their sandals.

'Don't go now,' said Dina. 'This job is urgent, and you were late this morning. The manager will be very angry if the dresses are delayed.' She was worried about the due date – what if they came late again tomorrow? Be firm, be strict, she reminded herself.

Ishvar hesitated; his nephew would not take the suggestion kindly. His inquiring glance confirmed it, colliding with an angry glare.

'Let's go,' muttered Omprakash without looking at Dina. 'I'm hungry.'

'Your nephew is always hungry,' she said to Ishvar. 'Has he got worms?'

'No no, Om is all right.'

Dina was not convinced. The suspicion had crawled into her mind during the first week. Apart from Omprakash's skinniness and his constant complaints about headaches and hunger, she frequently spied his fingers relieving an itch in his fundament; and that, she felt, was evidence as conclusive as any.

'You should take him to doctor for checkup. He is so thin – a walking advertisement for Wimco Matches.'

'No no, he is all right. And who has money for doctor?'

'Work hard and there will be plenty. Finish this job quickly,' she coaxed. 'The sooner I deliver it, the sooner you have your money.'

'Five minutes for tea won't make a difference,' snapped Omprakash.

'Your five always become thirty-five. Listen, I will make tea for you later. Special deluxe tea, not the overbrewed, bitter poison you get at the corner. But first finish the work. That way, everybody will be happy – you, me, the manager.'

'Okay,' Ishvar gave in, shaking off his sandals and resuming his place. The cast-iron treadle, warmed all morning by his feet, had not had time to cool.

With the two Singers racing again, Omprakash's angry whispers darted their way through the hammering needles to his uncle's ear. 'You *always* let her bully us. I don't know what the matter is with you. Let *me* do the talking from now on.'

Ishvar nodded mollifyingly. It embarrassed him to argue with Om or scold him within Dina's earshot.

At two o'clock, when the noise of the machines was making her temples throb, Dina decided to deliver what had been completed. She was annoyed with herself. Pleading and bribing with tea was not a good example of a strict boss. It would take more practice, she concluded, to get used to bullying them.

From under the worktable she retrieved the transparent plastic sheet and brown paper in which the bolts of cloth had arrived from Au Revoir. Remembering Shirin Aunty's advice, she wasted nothing. The little snippets of fabric continued to accumulate in great quantities. Enough, she thought, to make sanitary pads for a conventful of nuns. The larger scraps were collecting in a separate pile. She was not yet sure how to use these – for a quilt, perhaps.

She packaged the finished dresses and got her purse ready. To put in an appearance a day ahead of the deadline would impress Mrs. Gupta.

Then, keeping in mind Omprakash's inquisitiveness, she padlocked the door from outside, just in case he decided to follow her.

———

Sore-bottomed and bleary-eyed, the tailors adjourned to the front room. After the morning-long hardness of wooden stools, the old sofa was sweet luxury despite its broken springs, and the pleasure keener because it was stolen. The stiff posture of their profession melted from their bones as they sank into the cushions. Raising their bare feet to the teapoy, they pulled out a packet of Ganesh Beedis and lit up, sucking greedily at the smoke. A torn-off segment of the beedi wrapper served as ashtray.

Omprakash scratched his head and examined the dandruff harvested by his fingertips. With the inch-long nails of his pinkies he cleaned under the others, flicking the oily accretions to the floor. He would not have admitted he was bored – by wasting time he was outsmarting Dina

Dalal. If she thought she could drive them like a pair of dumb oxen harnessed to her plough, she was mistaken. He still had his manhood, he thought bitterly, though his uncle sometimes behaved otherwise.

Ishvar let his nephew idle away the hour. The rock of hunger lay heavy in both their hollow bellies. He watched amusedly as Omprakash squirmed and snuggled in the cushions, determined to pilfer maximum pleasure from Dina Dalal's sofa. He meditatively fingered the cheek that kept half his smile imprisoned in frozen flesh.

Laughing, yawning, stretching, they smoked away the time, temporary kings of the broken sofa, masters of the tiny flat, when their illicit leisure was invaded by a battering at the front door.

'I know you are in there!' shouted the visitor. 'This padlock on the door does not fool me!'

The tailors froze. The pounding continued. 'Paying the rent means nothing! We know what goes on behind the padlock! You and your illegal business will be thrown out on the street!'

The tailors understood – it had to do with the landlord. But what was this about a padlock? The banging at the door ceased. 'Quick, on the floor!' whispered Ishvar, in case the door-banger decided to look through the window.

Something fell through the mail slot, then there was silence. They waited a few moments before venturing to the door. A large envelope addressed to Mrs. Rustom Dalal lay on the floor. Ishvar turned the latch. The door moved half an inch and hit the outside hasp, confirming the padlock's presence.

'She locked us in,' fumed Omprakash. 'That woman. What does she think?'

'Must be a reason for it. Don't get upset.'

'Let's open her letter.'

Ishvar snatched it from his hand and put it aside. They tried to get comfortable again on the cushions, lighting up new beedis, but the intrusion had soured the pleasure. The sofa's sagging comforts hardened into lumps of discontent. Stray threads clinging to their clothes reminded them of the work waiting in the back room. The clock displayed its baleful warning: she would soon be home. Soon, all of this prohibited behaviour would have to cease.

'She cheats us,' grumbled Omprakash. 'We should sew directly for the export company. Why does she have to be in the middle?' His lips made small, careful movements that became words, his smouldering beedi hanging in uneasy equilibrium at one corner of his mouth.

Ishvar smiled indulgently. The insolence of the dangling beedi was aimed, lethal as a toy gun, at Dina Dalal. 'Soon as it's time for her to come, your face looks like you ate a sour lime.'

He continued, his tone more serious, 'She is in the middle because we have no shop. She lets us sew here, she brings the clothes, she gets the orders from the company. And besides, with piecework we have more independence –'

'Leave it, yaar. She treats us like slaves, and you talk of independence. Making money from our sweat without a single stitch from her fingers. Look at her house. With electricity, water, everything. And what do we have? A stinking shack in the slum. We'll never collect enough to go back to our village.'

'Giving up already? That's no way to win in life. Fight and struggle, Om, even if life knocks you around.' He held his beedi between ring and little finger and made a loose fist, raising it to his lips.

'I'll find out where she goes, you watch,' said Omprakash with a defiant toss of his head.

'Your puff moves beautifully when you do that.'

'Just wait, I'll get the address of the company.'

'How? You think she will tell you?'

Omprakash went to the back room and returned with a pair of large pointed scissors. He clutched it with both hands and thrust theatrically into thin air. 'Hold this at her throat and she will tell us whatever we want to know.'

His uncle whacked him on the head. 'What would your father say if he heard you? Stupid words pour from your mouth like stitches from your machine. And just as carelessly.'

Omprakash sheepishly put back the scissors. 'One of these days I'm going to cut her out of the middle – I'll follow her to the company.'

'I didn't know you could walk through padlocked doors like the Great Goghia Pasha. Or is it Omprakash Pasha?' He paused to draw, then whiffed smoke through his nostrils and smiled at the scowling face. 'Listen, my nephew, this is the way the world works. Some people are in the middle, some are on the border. Patience is needed for dreams to grow and give fruit.'

'Patience is good when you want to grow a beard. For what she pays, we couldn't afford the ghee and wood for our funeral pyre.' He gave his hair a ferocious scratching. 'And why do you always talk to her in that silly tone, as though you were an ignorant fellow from the countryside?'

'Isn't that what I am?' said Ishvar. 'People like to feel superior. If my tone helps Dinabai to feel good, what's wrong in that?' Savouring the final delights of his shrinking beedi, he repeated, 'Patience, Om. Some things cannot be changed, you just have to accept them.'

'You want it both ways? First you said struggle, don't give up. Now you are saying just accept it. Swaying from side to side, like a pot without an arse.'

'Your grandmother Roopa used to say that,' laughed Ishvar.

'Make up your mind, yaar, choose one thing.'

'How can I? I'm just a human being,' he replied, laughing again. Halfway, it changed to coughing, shaking him harshly in its racking embrace. He went to the window, moved the curtain aside and spat. Were he close enough to examine it, he would have seen the usual spot of blood.

A taxi approached as he was withdrawing his head from the window. 'Quick, she's back!' he whispered hoarsely.

They began eliminating the traces of their bad behaviour: plumping the cushions, repositioning the teapoy, pocketing the matchsticks and ashes. A spark flew from the beedi in Omprakash's mouth, as though to mock his earlier fire-breathing rage. He fanned it away from the upholstery. Drawing one last time at the beedis while running to the back room, they extinguished the stubs and chucked them out the rear window.

Dina paid the taxi and felt inside her handbag for the key ring. The brass padlock, tarnished, hung grim and ponderous. She turned the key with a twinge of guilt, no jailer at heart.

Omprakash stretched out his arms and relieved her of the package. 'I heard you arrive.'

'There are lots more,' she said, indicating the bundles of fabric piled outside the door. He looked them over, trying to spot the company name or address.

When everything had been brought inside, Ishvar gave her the envelope. 'Someone came banging on the door, saying the padlock did not fool him. He left this for you.'

'Must be the rent-collector.' She put the letter aside without opening it. 'Did he see you?'

'No, we stayed hidden.'

'Good.' She went to put away her purse and exchange her shoes for slippers.

'Did you lock us in when you left?' asked Ishvar.

'Didn't you know? Yes, I had to.'

'Why?' pounced Omprakash. 'You think we are thieves or something? We are going to take your possessions and run away?'

'Don't be silly. What big possessions do I have to worry about? The landlord is the reason. He could barge in while I am gone and throw you out on the street. But if there is a lock, he won't dare. To break a padlock is to break the law.'

'Very true,' said Ishvar. He was eager to see the design for the new dresses. While his nephew glowered, the tablecloth was whipped off the dining table to make way for the paper patterns.

'How much per dress this time?' interrupted Omprakash, fingering the new poplin.

She ignored him while Ishvar moved the sections around. Like a child with a jigsaw puzzle, he was soon absorbed in its complexities. Omprakash tried again, 'Very difficult pattern. Look at all the godets to be inserted for flaring the skirt. We will have to charge more this time, for sure.'

'Stop doing your kutt-kutt,' she scolded. 'Let your elders work. Respect your uncle at least if you cannot respect me.'

Ishvar matched the sections against the sample dress, talking to himself. 'The sleeve, yes. And the back, with a seam in the middle – yes, it's easy.' His nephew frowned at him for that admission.

'Yes, extremely easy,' said Dina. 'Simpler than the ones you just finished. And the good news is, they are still paying five rupees each.'

'Not possible for five rupees,' said Omprakash. 'You said you would bring expensive dresses. This is not worth our time.'

'I have to bring what the company gives. Or they will cancel us from their list.'

'We will do it,' said Ishvar. 'To kick at wages is sinful.'

'You do it, then – I cannot do it for five rupees,' said Omprakash, but Ishvar nodded reassuringly at Dina.

She went to the kitchen to make the tea she had promised. The dissension in their midst was good; the uncle would curb the nephew's rebellion. She squinted at the cups and saucers, at their rose borders. Pink or red? Pink ones for the tailors, she decided, to be set aside with the segregated water glass. Red for myself.

While waiting for the kettle, she checked the chicken wire over the broken windowpanes and found a breach. Those nuisance cats again, she fumed. Sneaking in, prowling for food, or to get out of the rain. And who knew what germs they brought with them from the gutters.

She reinforced the piece, twisting the corners around a nail. The kettle blurted its readiness with a healthy spout of steam. She held back for a vigorous boil, enjoying the thickening haze and the water's steady babble: the illusions of chatter, friendship, bustling life.

Reluctantly she turned down the flame, and the white cloud dissipat-

ed in desultory wisps. She filled three cups and carried in the two with
pink roses.

'Ah,' sighed Ishvar, taking the tea gratefully. Omprakash continued to
sew without looking up, still sulking. She put it down beside him.

'I don't want any,' he muttered. Dina returned wordlessly to the
kitchen for her own cup.

'Delicious,' said Ishvar when she was back. He slurped noisily, making sounds to tempt his nephew. 'Much better than Vishram Vegetarian
Hotel.'

'They must be letting it boil all day,' said Dina. 'That spoils it. Nothing
like fresh tea when you are tired.'

'Very true.' He took another sip and sighed invitingly again.
Omprakash reached for his cup. The other two pretended not to notice.
He gulped down the tea thirstily without displacing his angry pout.

Two hours of sewing were left in the day, and he filled them with
crooked seams and grumbling. Ishvar was grateful to the clock when it
indicated six. Keeping the peace between his nephew and Dinabai was
becoming difficult.

——

Morning was striding towards noon as Ibrahim, the rent-collector, plod-
ding slowly down the pavement, prepared to visit Dina Dalal and
demand a reply to the letter he had delivered yesterday. Dignified in his
maroon fez and black sherwani, he smiled at tenants he met along the
way, saying 'Salaam' and 'How are you?' He was blessed with an automatic smile; it formed whenever he opened his mouth to speak. This
felicitous buccal trick was a liability, though, if the occasion of his message warranted something more in the line of a solemn visage – a touch
of frowning, perhaps, for overdue rents.

Ibrahim was an elderly man but looked old beyond his years. In his
left hand, still sore from pounding the door yesterday, he carried a plastic folder secured by two large rubber bands. It contained rent receipts,
bills, orders for repairs, records of disputes and court cases pertaining to
the six buildings he looked after. Some of those disputes dated back to
when he was a young man of nineteen, just starting in service with the
father of the present landlord. Other cases were more ancient, inherited
from Ibrahim's predecessor.

So thoroughly was everything documented, Ibrahim sometimes felt
he was lugging the very buildings around with him. The folder handed
down almost half a century ago by the retiring rent-collector had not
been of plastic, but rudely fashioned out of two wooden boards bound

by a strip of morocco. It had carried with it the previous owner's smell. A fraying cotton tape, sewn to the leather, went around to secure the contents. The dark, cracked boards had warped badly; when opened, they creaked and released a sweaty tobacco odour.

Young and ambitious as Ibrahim then was, he was ashamed of being seen with this relic. Though it contained nothing but respectable rent receipts, he knew that people would judge it by its cover, which resembled the filthy binders carried by disreputable marketplace jyotshis and fortune-tellers to shelter their quack charts and fake diagrams. That he might be mistaken for one of those odious mountebanks mortified him. He began to harbour grave doubts about this job which forced him to carry around a questionable folder – he felt shortchanged, as though a bazaar vendor had fiddled the weights and tipped the scales unfairly.

Then, on one lucky day, the morocco spine broke. He displayed the wreck at the landlord's office. The clerk examined it, confirmed its demise from natural causes, and filled out the appropriate requisition form. Ibrahim was given a length of string to make do while the paperwork was processed.

After a fortnight's delay, the new folder arrived. It was built of buckramed cardboard, very smart and modern-looking, in colour a dignified umber. Ibrahim was delighted. He began to feel optimistic about his prospects in this job.

With the new folder under his arm, he could hold his head high and strut as importantly as a solicitor while making his rounds. It was far more sophisticated than the old one, with generous pouches and compartments. Briefs, complaints, correspondences could now be organized methodically. Which was just as well, because around this time Ibrahim's duties increased, both at work and domestically.

Ibrahim, the son of ageing parents, became a husband, then a father. And the role of rent-collector began to sprout branches too. He was appointed the landlord's spy, blackmailer, deliverer of threats, and all-round harasser of tenants. His job now included the uncovering of hidden dirt in his six buildings, secrets like extramarital affairs, and he was taught by his employer how to convert adultery into rent increases – the guilty parties would never protest or dare to mention the Rent Act. When the situation demanded, Ibrahim could also play the pleader and cajoler, if the landlord went too far and there was legalistic retaliation. The rent-collector's tears would convince the tenant to back down, to have mercy on the poor beleaguered landlord, a martyr to modern-day housing, who had never meant any harm in the first place.

To sort out the multiple roles in Ibrahim's repertoire, the folder's pouches and compartments were indispensable. At this stage in his career, however, he began to feel the increasing hindrance of his sweet automatic smile. Delivering threats and dire warnings while smiling pleasantly, he discovered, was not a good strategy. If he could have modified it to a menacing smile, that would have been perfect. But the muscles in question were beyond his control. The occasions when he had to express regrets over repairs delayed, or convey condolences for a death in a tenant's family, were equally difficult. Before long, the burdensome dental display earned him an undeserved reputation for being callous, crude, incompetent, retarded, even demonic.

So he smiled his hapless way through three buckram folders, all umber like the first, and added twenty-four years to his own frame. Twenty-four years of drudgery and deprivation during which his youth disappeared, and the bright ambition of his golden season became tainted by bitterness. Desperate, and scarred by the certain knowledge that he no longer had any prospects, he watched his wife, two sons, and two daughters still believing in him and thereby increasing his anguish. He asked himself what it was he had done to deserve a life so stale, so empty of hope. Or was this the way all humans were meant to feel? Did the Master of the Universe take no interest in levelling the scales – was there no such thing as a fair measure?

There no longer seemed any point in going to the masjid as often as he did. His attendance at Friday prayers became irregular. And he began seeking guidance in ways he had once despised as the preserve of the ignorant.

He found the jyotshis and fortune-tellers in the marketplace most comforting. They offered solutions to his money problems, and advice on improving his future, which was becoming his past at an alarming velocity. He discovered their confident pronouncements to be a soothing drug.

Nor did he restrict himself to palmists and astrologers. Seeking stronger drugs, he turned to less orthodox messengers: card-picking doves, chart-reading parrots, communicating cows, diagram-divining snakes. Always worried that an acquaintance would spot him during one of his questionable excursions, he decided, with great reluctance, to leave behind his distinctive fez. It was like abandoning a dear friend. The only other time he had forsaken this fixture of daily wear was during Partition, back in 1947, when communal slaughter at the brand-new border had ignited riots everywhere, and sporting a fez in a Hindu neighbourhood was as fatal as possessing a foreskin in a Muslim one. In certain areas it was wisest to go bareheaded, for choosing incorrectly from among fez, white cap, and turban could mean losing one's head.

Fortunately, his sittings at the avian auguries were relatively private. He could crouch unnoticed on a pavement corner with the creature's keeper, ask the question, and the dove or parrot would hop out of its cage to enlighten him.

The cow session, on the other hand, was a major performance that collected large crowds. The cow, caparisoned in colourful brocaded fabrics, a string of tiny silver bells round her neck, was led into the ring of spectators by a man with a drum. Though the fellow's shirt and turban were bright-hued, he seemed quite drab compared to the richly bedizened cow. The two walked the circle: once, twice, thrice – however long it took him to recite the cow's curriculum vitae, with special emphasis on prophecies and forecasts accurately completed to date. His voice was deafeningly raucous, his eyes bloodshot, his gestures manic, and all this frenzy was calculated as a masterly counterpoint to the cow's calm demeanour. After the brief biography was narrated, the drum that had silently hung from his shoulder came to life. It was a drum meant not for beating but for rubbing. He continued to walk the cow in a circle, rubbing the drumskin with a stick, producing a horrible bleating, a groaning, a wailing. It was a sound to wake the dead and stun the living, it was eldritch, it was a summons to spirits and forces not of this world, a summons to descend, witness, and assist bovine divination.

When the drum ceased, the man shouted the paying customer's question into the cow's ear, loud enough for the entire ring of humans to hear. And she answered with a nod or shake of her intricately made-up head, tinkling the tiny silver bells round her neck. The crowd applauded in wonder and admiration. Then the drum-rubbing resumed while donations were collected.

One day, after Ibrahim's question was bellowed into the soft, brown, unprotected ear, there was no response. The man repeated it, louder. This time the cow reacted. Whether it was the annoying drum that she had put up with for years, or the boorish bellowing in her ear day after day, she gored her keeper with her vermilioned horns.

For a moment, the spectators thought the cow was just responding a bit more energetically than usual to the question. Then she tossed him to the ground, trampling him thoroughly. Now they realized it was not part of the prophecy procedure, especially when the man's blood started to flow.

With cries of mad cow! mad cow! the crowd scattered. But once her tormentor had been dealt with, she stood placidly, blinking her gentle, long-lashed eyes, swishing away the udder-seeking flies with her tail.

The man's bizarre death convinced Ibrahim that this was no longer a reliable method of obtaining divine advice. Some days later a new team of cow and drum-rubber took over the corner, but Ibrahim avoided the performances. There were other, safer systems for procuring preternatural help.

While the mad-cow incident was still fresh in his mind, however, he witnessed another death. This time it was the handler of a sortilegious serpent whose venom ducts had become overdue for milking. Ever after, Ibrahim shivered when picturing the scene: it could have been into him that the cobra sank its fangs, for he had been crouching close to observe its oracular movements.

Shocked by the two fatalities, the rent-collector abandoned all fortune-telling fauna. As though waking from a nightmare, he redonned his forsaken fez and set out to recover his lost self. How much money had been diverted from his family's needs with his blasphemous addiction, he realized, as he sat beside the sea while the setting sun's ocean light bathed the masjid, floating at the end of the long causeway. He gazed out upon the receding tide that lay bare the secrets beneath the waves, and he shuddered. His own dark secrets swam up again from their murky depths of confusion and despair. He tried to push them back, to hold them under, to drown them. But they kept slipping away like eels, resurfacing to haunt him. There was only one way to vanquish them – he returned penitent to the masjid, ready to accept whatever fate had in store for him.

Among other things, it was the plastic folder. Twenty-four years of buckram had passed, and now it was the age of plastic in the landlord's office. Ibrahim no longer cared. He had learned that dignity could not be acquired from accoutrements and accessories; it came unasked, it grew from one's ability to endure. If the office had handed him a coolie's basket to carry the documents around on his head, he would have complied now without complaint.

But the plastic folder did have an advantage – it kept the monsoon at bay. Now he seldom had to recopy documents on which the ink had decided to frolic with the rain in lunatic swirls. At a time when his hands had started to shake, this was a blessing. Also, one pass with a wet rag, and all sneezes and snuff stains, pea green or brown, were wiped clean, no longer embarrassing him during audiences with the landlord.

And at home, too, there were changes he accepted with submission. After all, what other options were there? His older daughter died of tuberculosis, followed by his wife. Then his sons disappeared into the underworld, returning periodically to abuse him. The remaining daughter, just when he was beginning to think she would redeem everything, left to become a prostitute. His life, he thought, had become the plot of a bad Hindi movie minus the happy ending.

Why, he wondered, did he keep working now, making his rounds of the six buildings and collecting rent? Why did he not jump off the top of one of them? Why did he not make a bonfire of the receipts and the cash, and throw himself onto it drenched in kerosene? How was it that his heart kept beating instead of bursting, his sanity intact instead of shattering like a dropped mirror? Was it all made of tough synthetic material, like the indestructible plastic folder? And why was time, the great vandal, now being neglectful?

But plastic, too, had its allotted span of days and years. It could rip and tear and crack like buckram, he discovered. Like skin and bone, he realized with relief. It was simply a matter of patience. Thus the present folder was the third of its kind in twenty-one years.

He examined it from time to time, and saw reflected in its tired covers the furrows inflicted in his brow. The plastic divisions inside were starting to tear, and the neat compartments seemed ready to rebel; within his bodily compartments the rebellion had already begun. Which one would win this ridiculous race between plastic and flesh, he wondered, as he arrived at the flat, wiped the snuff off his nostrils and fingers, and rang the doorbell.

Spotting his maroon fez through the peephole, Dina silenced the tailors. 'Not a sound while he is here,' she whispered.

'How are you?' smiled the rent-collector, baring heavily stained teeth and two gaps: the sweet, innocent smile of an aged angel.

Without acknowledging his greeting, she said, 'Yes? The rent is not yet due.'

He shifted the folder to the other hand. 'No, sister, it isn't. I have come for your reply to the landlord's letter.'

'I see. Wait one minute.' She shut the door and went to look for the unopened envelope. 'Where did I put it?' she whispered to the tailors.

The three searched through the jumble of things on the table. She found herself watching Omprakash, the way his fingers clutched and his hands moved. His bony angularity no longer disturbed her. She was discovering a rare birdlike beauty in him.

Ishvar came upon the envelope under a stack of cloth. She tore it open and read – quickly, the first time, then slowly, to penetrate the legal jargon. The gist of it soon became clear: the running of a business was prohibited on residential premises, she must cease her commercial activities immediately or face eviction.

Cheeks flushing, she raced to the door. 'What kind of nonsense is this?

Tell your landlord his harassment won't work!'

Ibrahim sighed, lifted his shoulders and raised his voice. 'You have been warned, Mrs. Dalal! Breaking the rules will not be tolerated! Next time there will be no nice letter but a notice to vacate! Don't think that –'

She slammed the door. He stopped shouting immediately, relieved to be spared the full speech. Panting, he wiped his brow and left.

Dina read the letter again, dismayed. Barely three weeks with the tailors and trouble already with the landlord. She wondered if she should show it to Nusswan, ask his advice. No, she decided, he would make too much of it. Better to ignore it and continue discreetly.

She had no choice now but to take the tailors further into her confidence, impress on them how essential it was to keep the sewing a secret. She discussed the matter with Ishvar.

They agreed on the fiction to be used if the rent-collector ever confronted the two coming to or going from the flat. They would tell him that they came to do her cooking and cleaning.

Omprakash was insulted. 'I am a tailor, not her maaderchod servant who sweeps and mops,' he said after they left work that evening.

'Don't be childish, Om. It's just a story to prevent trouble with the landlord.'

'Trouble for whom? For her. Why should I worry? We don't even get a fair rate from her. If we are dead tomorrow, she will get two new tailors.'

'Will you forever speak without thinking? If she is kicked out of her flat, we have no place to work. What's the matter with you? This is our first decent job since we came to the city.'

'And I should rejoice for that? Is this job going to make everything all right for us?'

'But it's only been three weeks. Patience, Om. There is lots of opportunity in the city, you can make your dreams come true.'

'I am sick of the city. Nothing but misery ever since we came. I wish I had died in our village. I wish I had also burned to death like the rest of my family.'

Ishvar's face clouded, his disfigured cheek quivering with his nephew's pain. He put his arm around his shoulder. 'It will get better, Om,' he pleaded. 'Believe me, it will get better. And we'll soon go back to our village.'

III In a Village by a River

IN THEIR VILLAGE, the tailors used to be cobblers; that is, their family belonged to the Chamaar caste of tanners and leather-workers. But long ago, long before Omprakash was born, when his father, Narayan, and his uncle, Ishvar, were still young boys of ten and twelve, the two were sent by their father to be apprenticed as tailors.

Their father's friends feared for the family. 'Dukhi Mochi has gone mad,' they lamented. 'With wide-open eyes he is bringing destruction upon his household.' And consternation was general throughout the village: someone had dared to break the timeless chain of caste, retribution was bound to be swift.

Dukhi Mochi's decision to turn his sons into tailors was indeed courageous, considering that the prime of his own life had been spent in obedient compliance with the traditions of the caste system. Like his forefathers before him, he had accepted from childhood the occupation preordained for his present incarnation.

Dukhi Mochi was five years old when he had begun to learn the Chamaar vocation at his father's side. With a very small Muslim population in the area, there was no slaughterhouse nearby where the Chamaars could obtain hides. They had to wait until a cow or buffalo died a natural death in the village. Then the Chamaars would be summoned to remove the carcass. Sometimes the carcass was given free, sometimes they had to pay, depending on whether or not the animal's upper-caste owner had been able to extract enough free labour from the Chamaars during the year.

The Chamaars skinned the carcass, ate the meat, and tanned the hide, which was turned into sandals, whips, harnesses, and waterskins. Dukhi learned to appreciate how dead animals provided his family's livelihood. And as he mastered the skills, imperceptibly but relentlessly Dukhi's own skin became impregnated with the odour that was part of his father's smell, the leather-worker's stink that would not depart even after he had washed and scrubbed in the all-cleansing river.

Dukhi did not realize his pores had imbibed the fumes till his mother, hugging him one day, wrinkled her nose and said, her voice a mix of pride and sorrow, 'You are becoming an adult, my son, I can sniff the change.'

For a while afterwards, he was constantly lifting his forearm to his nose to see if the odour still lingered. He wondered if flaying would get rid of it. Or did it go deeper than skin? He pricked himself to smell his blood but the test was inconclusive, the little ruby at his fingertip being an insufficient sample. And what about muscle and bone, did the stink lurk in them too? Not that he wanted it gone; he was happy then to smell like his father.

Besides tanning and leather-working, Dukhi learned what it was to be a Chamaar, an untouchable in village society. No special instruction was necessary for this part of his education. Like the filth of dead animals which covered him and his father as they worked, the ethos of the caste system was smeared everywhere. And if that was not enough, the talk of adults, the conversations between his mother and father, filled the gaps in his knowledge of the world.

The village was by a small river, and the Chamaars were permitted to live in a section downstream from the Brahmins and landowners. In the evening, Dukhi's father sat with the other Chamaar men under a tree in their part of the settlement, smoking, talking about the day that was ending and the new one that would dawn tomorrow. Bird cries fluttered around their chitchat. Beyond the bank, cooking smoke signalled hungry messages while upper-caste waste floated past on the sluggish river.

Dukhi watched from a distance, waiting for his father to come home. As the dusk deepened, the men's outlines became vague. Soon Dukhi could see only the glowing tips of their beedis, darting around like fireflies with the movement of their hands. Then the burning tips went dark, one by one, and the men dispersed.

While Dukhi's father ate, he repeated for his wife everything he had learned that day. 'The Pandit's cow is not healthy. He is trying to sell it before it dies.'

'Who gets it if it dies? Is it your turn yet?'

'No, it is Bhola's turn. But where he was working, they accused him of stealing. Even if the Pandit lets him have the carcass, he will need my help – they chopped off his left-hand fingers today.'

'Bhola is lucky,' said Dukhi's mother. 'Last year Chhagan lost his hand at the wrist. Same reason.'

Dukhi's father took a drink of water and swirled it around in his mouth before swallowing. He ran the back of his hand across his lips. 'Dosu got a whipping for getting too close to the well. He never learns.' Eating in silence for a while, he listened to the frogs bellowing in the humid night, then asked his wife, 'You are not having anything?'

'It's my fasting day.' In her code, it meant there wasn't enough food.

Dukhi's father nodded, taking another mouthful. 'Have you seen Buddhu's wife recently?'

She shook her head. 'Not since many days.'

'And you won't for many more. She must be hiding in her hut. She refused to go to the field with the zamindar's son, so they shaved her head and walked her naked through the square.'

Thus Dukhi listened every evening to his father relate the unembellished facts about events in the village. During his childhood years, he mastered a full catalogue of the real and imaginary crimes a low-caste person could commit, and the corresponding punishments were engraved upon his memory. By the time he entered his teens, he had acquired all the knowledge he would need to perceive that invisible line of caste he could never cross, to survive in the village like his ancestors, with humiliation and forbearance as his constant companions.

Soon after Dukhi Mochi turned eighteen, his parents married him to a Chamaar girl named Roopa, who was fourteen. She gave birth to three daughters during their first six years together. None survived beyond a few months.

Then they had a son, and the families rejoiced greatly. The child was called Ishvar, and Roopa watched over him with the special ardour and devotion she had learned was reserved for male children. She made sure he always had enough to eat. Going hungry herself was a matter of course – that she often did even to keep Dukhi fed. But for this child she did not hesitate to steal either. And there was not a mother she knew who would not have taken the same risk for her own son.

After her milk went dry, Roopa began nocturnal visits to the cows of various landowners. While Dukhi and the child slept, she crept out of the hut with a small brass haandi, some time between midnight and cock-crow. The pitch-black path she walked without stumbling had been memorized during the day, for a lamp was too dangerous. The darkness brushed her cheeks like a cobweb. Sometimes the cobwebs were real.

She took only a little from each cow; thus, the owner would not sense a decrease in the yield. When Dukhi saw the milk in the morning, he understood. If he awoke in the night as she was leaving, he said nothing, and lay shivering till she returned. He often wondered whether he should offer to go instead.

Soon Ishvar cut his milk teeth, and Roopa began to pay weekly visits to orchards in season and ready for harvest. In the darkness, her fingers felt the fruit for ripeness before plucking it. Again, she restricted herself to a few from each tree, so their absence would not be noticed. Around her, the dark was filled with the sound of her own breathing and little creatures scurrying out of her way to safety.

One night, as she was filling her sack with oranges, a lantern was suddenly raised amid the trees. In a small clearing a man sat on his bamboo-and-string cot, watching her. I'm finished, she thought, dropping her sack and preparing to run.

'Don't be afraid,' said the man. He spoke softly, his hand gripping a heavy stick. 'I don't care if you take some.' She turned around, panting with fear, wondering whether to believe him.

'Go on, pick a few,' he repeated, smiling. 'I have been hired by the owner to watch the grove. But I don't care. He is a rich bastard.'

Roopa retrieved the sack nervously and resumed picking. Her shaking fingers dropped an orange as she tried to slip it past the mouth of the sack. She glanced over her shoulder. His eyes were greedily following her body; it made her uneasy. 'I'm grateful to you,' she said.

He nodded. 'You are lucky I am here, and not some bad man. Go on, take as many as you like.' He hummed something tunelessly. It sounded like a mixture of groans and sighs. He gave up the humming, trying to whistle the tune. The results were equally unmusical. He yawned and fell silent but continued to watch her.

Roopa decided she had enough fruit, it was time to thank him and leave. Reading her movements, he said, 'One shout from me and they will come running.'

'What?' She saw his smile disappear suddenly.

'I only have to shout, and the owner and his sons would be here at once. They would strip you and whip you for stealing.'

She trembled, and the smile returned to his face. 'Don't worry, I won't shout.' She fastened the mouth of the sack, and he continued, 'After whipping you, they would probably show you disrespect, and stain your honour. They would take turns doing shameful things to your lovely soft body.'

Roopa joined her hands in thanks and farewell.

'Don't go yet, take as many as you want,' he said.

'Thank you, I have enough.'

'You are sure? I can easily give you more if you like.' He put down his stick and got up from his cot.

'Thank you, this is enough.'

'Is it? But wait, you cannot go just like that,' he said with a laugh. 'You haven't given me anything in return.' He walked towards her.

Stepping back, she forced a laugh too. 'I don't have anything. That's why I came here in the night, for the sake of my child.'

'You have got something.' He put out his hand and squeezed her left breast. She struck his hand away. 'I only have to shout once,' he warned, and slipped his hand inside her blouse. She shuddered at the touch, doing nothing this time.

He led her cringing to the cot and ripped open her top three buttons. She crossed her arms in front. He pulled them down and buried his mouth in her breasts, laughing softly as she tried to squirm away. 'I gave you so many oranges. You won't even let me taste your sweet mangoes?'

'Please let me go.'

'Soon as I have fed you my Bhojpuri brinjal. Take off your clothes.'

'I beg you, let me go.'

'I only have to shout once.'

She wept softly while undressing, and lay down as he instructed. She continued to weep during the time he moved and panted on top of her. She heard the breeze rustle the leaves in trees that stood like worthless sentinels. A dog howled, setting off others in a chorus. Coconut oil in the man's hair left streaks on her face and neck, and smeared her chest. Its odour was strong in her nostrils.

Minutes later, he rolled off her body. Roopa grabbed her clothes and the sack of oranges and ran naked through the orange grove. When she was certain he wasn't following, she stopped and put her clothes on.

Dukhi pretended to be asleep as she entered the hut. He heard her muffled sobs several times during the night, and knew, from her smell, what had happened to her while she was gone. He felt the urge to go to her, speak to her, comfort her. But he did not know what words to use, and he also felt afraid of learning too much. He wept silently, venting his shame, anger, humiliation in tears; he wished he would die that night.

In the morning Roopa behaved as if nothing had occurred. So Dukhi said nothing, and they ate the oranges.

Two years after Ishvar was born, Roopa and Dukhi had another son. This one was named Narayan. There was a dark-red mark on his chest, and an elderly neighbour who assisted Roopa during the birth said she had seen such a mark before. 'It means he has a brave and generous heart. This child will make you very proud.'

The news of a second son created envy in upper-caste homes where marriages had also taken place around the time Dukhi and Roopa were wed, but where the women were still childless or awaiting a male issue. It was hard for them not to be resentful – the birth of daughters often brought them beatings from their husbands and their husbands' families. Sometimes they were ordered to discreetly get rid of the newborn. Then they had no choice but to strangle the infant with her swaddling clothes, poison her, or let her starve to death.

'What is happening to the world?' they complained. 'Why two sons in an untouchable's house, and not even one in ours?' What could a Chamaar pass on to his sons that the gods should reward him thus? Something was wrong, the Law of Manu had been subverted. Someone in the village had definitely committed an act to offend the deities, surely some special ceremonies were needed to appease the gods and fill these empty vessels with male fruit.

But one of the childless wives had a more down-to-earth theory to explain their unborn sons. It could be, she said, that these two boys were not really Dukhi's. Perhaps the Chamaar had journeyed afar and kidnapped a Brahmin's newborns – this would explain everything.

When the rumours started to spread, Dukhi feared for his family's safety. As a precaution, he went out of his way to be obsequious. Every time he saw high-caste persons on the road, he prostrated abjectly, but at a safe distance – so he couldn't be accused of contaminating them with his shadow. His moustache was shaved off even though its length and shape had conformed to caste rules, its tips humbly drooping downwards unlike proud upper-caste moustaches that flourished skywards. He dressed himself and the children in the filthiest rags he could find among their meagre possessions. To avoid charges of pollution, he told Roopa not to appear anywhere in the vicinity of the village well; her friend Padma fetched their drinking water. Whatever task Dukhi was ordered to do, he did without questioning, without thought of payment, keeping his eyes averted from the high-caste face and fixed safely on the feet. He knew that the least annoyance someone felt towards him could be fanned into flames to devour his family.

Fortunately, the majority of the upper castes were content to wax philosophic about the problem of fallow wombs and leave it at that. They said it was obvious the world was passing through Kaliyug, through the Age of Darkness, and sonless wives were not the only aberration in the cosmic order. 'Witness the recent drought,' they said. 'A drought that came even though we performed all the correct pujas. And when the rains fell, they fell in savage torrents; remember the floods, the huts that were washed away. And what about the two-headed calf in the neighbouring district?'

No one in the village had seen the two-headed calf, for the distance was great, and it was not possible to make the journey and return by nightfall to the safety of their huts. But they had all heard about the monstrous birth. 'Yes, yes,' they agreed. 'The Pandits are absolutely correct. It is Kaliyug that is the cause of our troubles.'

The remedy, the Pandits advised, was to be more vigilant in the observance of the dharmic order. There was a proper place for everyone in the world, and as long as each one minded his place, they would endure and emerge unharmed through the Darkness of Kaliyug. But if there were transgressions – if the order was polluted – then there was no telling what calamities might befall the universe.

After this consensus was reached, the village saw a sharp increase in the number of floggings meted out to members of the untouchable castes, as the Thakurs and Pandits tried to whip the world into shape. The crimes were varied and imaginative: a Bhunghi had dared to let his unclean eyes meet Brahmin eyes; a Chamaar had walked on the wrong side of the temple road and defiled it; another had strayed near a puja that was in progress and allowed his undeserving ears to overhear the sacred shlokas; a Bhunghi child had not erased her footprints cleanly from the dust in a Thakur's courtyard after finishing her duties there – her plea that her broom was worn thin was unacceptable.

Dukhi contributed some of his skin, too, in wrestling the universe out of the clutches of Darkness. He was summoned to graze a herd of goats. The owner was going to be away from the village during the day. 'Watch them carefully,' said the man, 'especially that one with the broken horn and long beard. He is a real devil.' A glass of goat's milk was promised in return for the work.

Dukhi spent the morning minding the herd, dreaming about the pleasure Ishvar and Narayan would get from the milk. But as the day wore on and the afternoon grew hot, he fell asleep. The scrabbling animals strayed onto a neighbour's property. When the owner returned in the evening, instead of a glass of goat's milk, Dukhi got a thrashing.

It was a small price to pay, he felt, considering what the consequence might have been had it taken the man's fancy. That night, Roopa crept out to steal butter to apply to the welts raised on her husband's back and shoulders.

Butter was something Roopa could steal without a second thought. In fact, she did not even consider it stealing. After all, hadn't Lord Krishna himself made a full-time job of it during his adolescence, aeons ago, in Mathura?

At the appropriate age, Dukhi began teaching his sons the skills of the trade to which they were born shackled. Ishvar was seven when he was taken to his first dead animal. Narayan wanted to go as well, but Dukhi said it was not time for him, he was still too young. He promised the child that he would be allowed to help with tasks like salting the skin, scraping off hair and bits of rotten flesh with a dull knife, and collecting the fruit of the myrobalan tree to tan the hide. This cheered Narayan up.

Dukhi and Ishvar arrived with a few other Chamaars at Thakur Premji's farm, and were taken to the field where the buffalo lay. An egret was perched on the dark mound, picking insects from the skin. It flew off when the men approached. Clouds of flies buzzed over the animal.

'Is it dead?' asked Dukhi.

'Of course it's dead,' said the Thakur's man. 'You think we can afford to give away live cattle?' Shaking his head and muttering about the stupidity of these achhoot jatis, he left them to their work.

Dukhi and his friends positioned their cart behind the buffalo; a wooden plank was sloped from the cartbed to the animal. They grabbed its legs and began inching its hulk up the plank, keeping the wood wet so the weight might slide a little more readily.

'Look!' said one of them. 'It's alive, it's breathing!'

'Aray Chhotu, not so loud,' said Dukhi. 'Or they won't let us take it. Anyway, it's almost dead – a few more hours at best.'

They resumed the task, sweating and grunting, while Chhotu cursed the Thakur softly. 'Bastard hypocrite. Making us break our backs. Would be so much easier to kill it, skin the carcass right here, chop it into small hunks.'

'That's true,' said Dukhi. 'But how can Mr. High-Caste Shit permit that? The purity of his land would be spoilt.'

'The only thing high caste about him is his little meat-eating lund,' said Chhotu. 'It feeds on his wife's high-caste choot every night.'

The men chuckled, then renewed their efforts. Someone said, 'He has been seen in the town once a week. Gobbling chicken, mutton, beef, whatever he likes.'

'They are all like that,' said Dukhi. 'Vegetarian in public, meat-eaters in private. Come on, push!'

Ishvar paid close attention to the men's conversation, joining in the effort with his little hands, as the men encouraged him. 'Now we will succeed! Push, Ishvar, push! Harder, harder!'

Amid the joking and cursing and teasing, the buffalo suddenly came alive, raising its head one last time before expiring. The adults shouted in surprise and jumped back to avoid the horns. But the tip caught Ishvar's left cheek, stunning him. He collapsed.

Dukhi grabbed the boy in his arms and began running to his hut. His legs swallowed the distance in urgent gulps. The stunted noonday shadow of their joined figures clung faithfully to his heels. Sweat poured from his brow, sprinkling his son's face. Ishvar stirred then, and his tongue emerged and tasted his father's salt at his lips. Dukhi breathed easier, heartened by the sign of life.

'Hai Bhagwan!' screamed Roopa when she saw her bleeding son. 'Aray father-of-Ishvar, what did you do to my child! What-all was the big rush to take him today? Such a little boy! You couldn't wait till he was older?'

'He is seven,' Dukhi answered quietly. 'My father took me at five.'

'That's a reason? And if you were injured and killed at five, you would do the same to your son?'

'If I were killed at five, I wouldn't have a son,' said Dukhi, even more quietly. He went out to collect the leaves that would heal the wound, and chopped them very fine, till they were almost a paste. Then he returned to work.

Roopa bathed the gash and wrapped the dark-green ointment over it. Afterwards, when she was calmer, her fury at Dukhi subsided. She tied protective amulets to her children's arms, reasoning that it was the evil eye of the Brahmin women that had hurt Ishvar.

And the childless women were also reassured: the universe was returning to normal; the untouchable boy was no longer fair of face but disfigured, which was as it should be.

Dukhi came home in the evening and lowered himself to the floor in the corner which was his eating place. Ishvar and Narayan snuggled close to him, enjoying the smell of the beedi smoke that clung to his breath, temporarily diluting the stench of hides and tannin and offal. The fragrance of the baking dough made them hungry, as Roopa rolled out fresh chapatis.

The wound festered for a few days before starting to heal, and soon there was no cause for worry. The injury, however, left that part of Ishvar's face forever frozen. His father said, trying to make light of it, 'God wants my son to cry only half as much as other mortals.'

He preferred to overlook the fact that Ishvar's smile, too, could only be smiled with half his face.

The year that Ishvar turned ten and Narayan eight, the rainfall was excellent. Dukhi struggled through the monsoon months, scrounging armfuls of thatch to keep the hut from leaking. The fields recovered from the drought and the cattle grew healthy. Dukhi waited in vain for animals to die and yield their hides.

As the fine weather continued, promising a bountiful crop for the zamindars, for the landless untouchables it was a bleak season. There would be work for them when the harvest was ready, but till then they had to depend on charity or the paltry scraps of toil thrown their way at the discretion of the landlords.

After several idle days, Dukhi was grateful to be sent for by Thakur Premji. He was led to the back of the house where a sack of dry red chillies was waiting to be ground into powder. 'Can you finish that by sunset?' asked Thakur Premji. 'Or maybe I should call two men.'

Reluctant to share whatever slim reward was to come his way, Dukhi said, 'Don't worry, Thakurji, it will all be done before the sun disappears.' He filled the massive stone mortar with chillies and selected one of the three long, heavy pestles lying by it. He began pounding vigorously, smiling frequently at the Thakur who stayed to watch for a while.

Dukhi slowed down after he left. The rapid rhythm could only be maintained when there were three people at the mortar, delivering the pestles in succession. By lunchtime he had finished half the sack, and stopped to eat. Looking around to see if anyone was watching, he reached into the mortar and sprinkled a pinch of chilli powder on his chapati. He was just in time, for the Thakur sent his man out with a can of water.

It was late in the afternoon, when the sack was almost empty, that the accident occurred. Without warning, as the pestle landed and rebounded the way it had been doing all day, the mortar split cleanly in two and collapsed. One side landed on Dukhi's left foot and crushed it.

The Thakur's wife was watching from the kitchen window. 'Oiee, my husband! Come quick!' she screamed. 'The Chamaar donkey has destroyed our mortar!'

Her screams roused Thakur Premji, drowsing under the awning at the front of the house, cradling a grandchild in his arms. He passed the sleeping infant to a servant and ran to the back. Dukhi was sprawled on the ground, trying to bandage his bleeding foot with the cloth he normally wrapped around his head like a brief turban.

'What have you done, you witless animal! Is this what I hired you for?'

Dukhi looked up. 'Forgive me, Thakurji, I did not do anything to it. There must have been a flaw in the stone.'

'Liar!' He raised his stick threateningly. 'First breaking it, then lying to me on top! If you did nothing, how can it break? A big thing of solid stone! Is it made of glass to shatter just like that?'

'I swear on the heads of my children,' begged Dukhi, 'I was only pounding chillies, as I have done all day. Look, Thakurji, the sack is almost empty, the work –'

'Get up! Leave my land at once! I never want to see you again!'

'But Thakurji, the work –'

He hit Dukhi across the back with his stick. 'Get up, I said! And get out!'

Dukhi rose to his feet, limping backwards, out of reach. 'Thakurji, have pity, there has been no work for days, I don't –'

The Thakur lashed out wildly. 'Listen, you stinking dog! You have destroyed my property, yet I am letting you off! If I wasn't such a soft-hearted fool, I would hand you to the police for your crime. Now get out!' He continued to swing the stick.

Dukhi dodged, but could not move quickly enough with his injured foot. Several blows found their mark before he had slipped through the gate. He hobbled home, cursing the Thakur and his progeny.

'Leave me alone,' he hissed in response to Roopa's fearful inquiries. When she persisted, clinging to his side, begging to be allowed to examine his damaged foot, he struck her. Angry and humiliated, he sat silent in the hut all evening. Ishvar and Narayan were frightened; they had never seen their father like this.

Afterwards, he let Roopa clean and bandage the wound, and ate the food she brought him, but still he refused to talk. 'You will feel better if you tell me,' she said.

Two days later he told her, his bitterness overflowing like the foul ooze from his foot. He had not minded when he had been beaten that time for the straying goats. It had been his fault, he had fallen asleep. But this time he had done nothing wrong. He had worked hard all day, yet he had been thrashed and cheated of his payment. 'On top of that, my foot is crushed,' he said. 'I could kill that Thakur. Nothing but a low-ly thief. And they are all like that. They treat us like animals. Always have, from the days of our forefathers.'

'Shh,' she said. 'It's not good for the boys to hear such things. It was just bad luck, the mortar breaking, that's all.'

'I spit in their upper-caste faces. I don't need their miserable jobs from now on.'

After his foot had healed, Dukhi turned his back on the village. He left at dawn and arrived in town before noon, getting rides in bullock carts and a lorry. He selected a street corner where there were no other cobblers nearby. With his metal last, awl, hammer, nails, cleats, and leather patches arranged in a semicircle around him, he settled upon the pavement and waited to mend the footwear of town dwellers.

Shoes, moccasins, slippers tramped past in a variety of designs and colours which intrigued and worried him. If one of them chose to stop, would he be capable of doing the repairs? It all seemed more complicated than the simple sandals he was used to.

After a while someone halted before Dukhi, shook the chappal off his right foot, and pointed at its broken cross straps with his big toe. 'How much for fixing that?'

Dukhi picked it up and turned it over. 'Two annas.'

'Two annas? Are you paagal or something? I might as well buy new chappals if I am going to pay a mochi like you two annas.'

'Aray sahab, who will give you new chappals for two annas?' They haggled for a bit, then settled for one anna. Dukhi scraped the soles to expose the groove in which the broken stitches sat. The grime flaked off in large flat crusts. He decided there was no difference between village grime and town grime, it looked and smelled the same.

He inserted the straps in their slits and secured them with a row of new stitches. Before trying on the chappal, the man tugged at the repair work. He took trial steps, wiggled his toes around, grunted his approval and paid.

Six hours and five customers later, it was time to start back. Dukhi made a few purchases with the money – a little flour, three onions, four potatoes, two hot green chillies – then took the homeward road. Traffic was sparser than in the morning. He walked a long time before getting a ride. It was night when he reached the village. Roopa and the children were waiting anxiously for him.

After a few days at the street corner, Dukhi saw striding towards him on the pavement his friend Ashraf. 'I didn't know you were cobbling in my neighbourhood,' said Ashraf, surprised to see him.

Ashraf was the Muslim tailor in town. He was Dukhi's age, and it was to him that Dukhi used to go on the rare occasions when he could afford to get something for Roopa or the children – the Hindu tailor did not sew for untouchables.

Learning about Dukhi's misfortunes in the village, Ashraf asked, 'Would you like to try something different? Something which might pay more?'

'Where?'

'Come with me.'

He gathered up his implements and hurried away with Ashraf. They walked to the other side of town, across the railway line, to the lumberyard. There, Dukhi was introduced to Ashraf's uncle, who managed the place.

From now on, there was always work for him at the yard: loading and unloading lorries, or helping to make deliveries. Dukhi greatly preferred the labour of lifting and carrying, walking up-right among men, instead of crouching all day on the pavement, conducting conversations with strangers' feet. And the fragrance of fresh wood was a welcome respite from the stench of filthy footwear.

One morning, on his way to the lumberyard, Dukhi saw a lot of traffic. The bullock cart he rode in was swallowed by clouds of dust. It had to often pull over to the side, and once, when a large bus passed, ended almost in the ditch.

'What is happening?' he asked the cart-driver. 'Where are they all going?' The man shrugged, concentrating on getting his bullock back on the road. His prod failed to get results, and the two men had to jump off and help the animal.

On arriving in town, Dukhi saw the streets festooned with banners and flags. He learned that some leaders of the Indian National Congress were visiting. He wandered over to Ashraf's shop to tell him, and they decided to join the crowds.

The leaders started their speeches; they said they had come to spread the Mahatma's message regarding the freedom struggle, the struggle for justice. 'We have been slaves in our own country for too long. And the time has come to fight for liberty. In this fight, we do not need guns or swords. We do not need harsh words or hatred. With truth and ahimsa we will convince the British that the moment is right for them to depart.'

The crowd applauded; the speaker continued. 'You will agree that in order to overthrow the yoke of slavery we have to be strong. No one can argue against that. And only the genuinely strong can employ the power of truth and non-violence. But how can we even start to be strong when there is a disease in our midst? First we must be rid of this disease that plagues the body of our motherland.

'What is this disease? you may ask. This disease, brothers and sisters, is the notion of untouchability, ravaging us for centuries, denying dignity to our fellow human beings. This disease must be purged from our society, from our hearts, and from our minds. No one is untouchable, for we are all children of the same God. Remember what Gandhiji says, that untouchability poisons Hinduism as a drop of arsenic poisons milk.'

After this, other speakers addressed the crowd about matters related to the freedom struggle, about those who were spending time honourably in jail for civil disobedience, for refusing to observe unjust laws.

Dukhi and Ashraf stayed till the very end, when the leaders requested the crowd to pledge that they would expunge all caste prejudice from their thoughts, words, and deeds. 'We are taking this message across the nation, and asking people everywhere to unite and fight this ungodly system of bigotry and evil.'

The crowd took the oath that had been enjoined on them by the Mahatma, echoing the words with enthusiasm. The rally was over.

'I wonder,' said Dukhi to Ashraf, 'if the zamindars in our villages would ever clap for a speech about getting rid of the caste system.'

'They would clap, and go on in the same old way,' said Ashraf. 'The devil has stolen their sense of justice, nah – they cannot see or feel. But you should leave your village, bring your family here.'

'And where would we stay? There, at least we have a hut. Besides, that's where my ancestors have always lived. How can I leave that earth? It's not good to go far from your native village. Then you forget who you are.'

'That's true,' said Ashraf. 'But at least send your sons here for a short time. To learn a trade.'

'They would not be allowed to practise it in the village.'

Ashraf was impatient with his pessimism. 'Things will change, nah. You heard those men at the meeting. Send your sons to me, I will teach them tailoring in my shop.'

For a moment, Dukhi's eyes lit up, imagining the promise of the future. 'No,' he said. 'Better to stay where we belong.'

The harvest was ready, and Dukhi stopped going to the lumberyard. His vow to shun the landlords had weakened, for the distance to town was long when the transport was unreliable. He left for the fields before dawn to bring in the crop, returning to his family after dusk with an aching back and all the news from surrounding villages that he had missed in the last few months.

The news was of the same type that Dukhi had heard evening after evening during his childhood; only the names were different. For walking on the upper-caste side of the street, Sita was stoned, though not to death – the stones had ceased at first blood. Gambhir was less fortunate; he had molten lead poured into his ears because he ventured within hearing range of the temple while prayers were in progress. Dayaram, reneging on an agreement to plough a landlord's field, had been forced to eat the landlord's excrement in the village square. Dhiraj tried to negotiate in advance with Pandit Ghanshyam the wages for chopping wood, instead of settling for the few sticks he could expect at the end of the day; the Pandit got upset, accused Dhiraj of poisoning his cows, and had him hanged.

While Dukhi toiled in the fields and leather-work remained scarce, there was no work for his sons. Roopa tried to keep Ishvar and Narayan busy by sending them to search for firewood. Occasionally, they also found stray, unclaimed cowpats overlooked by the cowherds, though this was rare, for the precious commodity was zealously collected by the cows' owners. Roopa did not use the dung for fuel, preferring to daub it level at the entrance to the hut. After it dried, hard and smooth, she enjoyed for a while a threshold as firm as terracotta, like the courtyards of the cattle-keepers.

Despite their chores, the boys had many empty hours to run around by the river or chase wild rabbits. They knew exactly what their caste permitted or prohibited; instinct, and eavesdropping on the conversation of elders, had demarcated the borders in their consciousness as clearly as stone walls. Still, their mother worried that they would get into trouble. She waited anxiously for the threshing and winnowing to finish, when they would be occupied under her eye, sifting the chaff for stray grain.

Sometimes the brothers spent the morning near the village school. They listened to the upper-caste children recite the alphabet, and sing little songs about colours, numbers, the monsoon. The shrill voices flew out the window like flocks of sparrows. Later, in secret among the trees by the river, the two would try to repeat from memory what the children had sung.

If curiosity drew Ishvar and Narayan too close and the teacher spotted them, they were immediately chased away. 'Shameless little donkeys! Off with you or I'll break your bones!' But Ishvar and Narayan were quite skilled at spying on the class; they could creep near enough to hear chalks squeaking on slates.

The chalks and slates fascinated them. They yearned to hold the white sticks in their hands, make little white squiggles like the other children, draw pictures of huts, cows, goats, and flowers. It was like magic, to make things appear out of nowhere.

One morning, when Ishvar and Narayan were hidden behind the bushes, the students were brought into the front yard to practise a dance for the harvest festival. The sky was cloudless, and snatches of song could be heard from the fields in the distance. The labourers' melodies contained the agony of their aching backs, of their skin sizzling under the sun. Ishvar and Narayan listened for their father's voice, but could not separate the strands in the chorus.

The schoolchildren held hands and formed two concentric rings, barefoot, moving in opposite directions. Every now and then, the rings reversed the pattern of movement. This was cause for much mirth because some children were late in turning, and there were mixups and tangles.

After watching for a while, Ishvar and Narayan suddenly realized that the schoolhouse was empty. They went around the yard on all fours till they were behind the hut, and entered through a window.

In one corner, the children's footwear was arranged in neat rows; in another, beside the blackboard, were their lunchboxes. Food odours mingled with chalk dust. The boys headed for the cupboard where the slates and chalks were kept. Grabbing one each, they sat cross-legged on the floor with the slates in their laps, as they had so often watched the children do. But the two were uncertain about what came next. Narayan waited for his older brother to begin.

Ishvar was a little nervous, his chalk poised above the slate, fearful of what might happen. Gingerly he made contact, and drew a line, then another, and another. He grinned at Narayan – how easy it was to make his mark!

Now Narayan, his fingers shaking with excitement, chalked a short white line and displayed it proudly. They grew more adventurous, departing from straight lines, covering the slates with loops and curves and scrawls of all shapes and sizes, stopping only to admire, marvelling at the ease with which they could create, then erase with a sweep of the hand and re-create at will. And the chalk dust on their palms and fingers set them to giggling too – it could make thick funny lines on the forehead just like the caste marks of the Brahmins.

They returned to the cupboard to examine the rest of its contents, unrolling alphabet charts and opening picture books. Lost in the forbidden world, they did not notice that the dancing in the yard had ended, nor did they hear the teacher sneak up behind. He grabbed them by their ears and dragged them outside.

'You Chamaar rascals! Very brave you are getting, daring to enter the school!' He twisted their ears till they yelped with pain and started to cry. The schoolchildren fearfully huddled together.

'Is this what your parents teach you? To defile the tools of learning and knowledge? Answer me! Is it?' He released their ears long enough to deliver stinging blows to the head, then seized them again.

Sobbing, Ishvar said, 'No, masterji, it isn't.'

'Then why were you in there?'

'We only wanted to look –'

'Wanted to look! Well, I will show you now! I will show you the back of my hand!' Holding on to Narayan, he slapped Ishvar six times in quick succession across the face, then delivered the same number to his brother's face. 'And what is this on your foreheads, you shameless creatures? Such blasphemy!' He slapped them again, and by now his hand was sore.

'Get the cane from the cupboard,' he ordered a girl. 'And you two remove your pants. After I am through, not one of you achhoot boys will ever dream of fooling with things you are not supposed to touch.'

The cane was presented, and the teacher asked four older students to hold the trespassers to the ground, face down, by their hands and ankles. He commenced the punishment, alternating strokes between the two. The watching children flinched each time the cane landed on the bare bottoms. A little boy started to cry.

When the two had received a dozen strokes each, the teacher stopped. 'That should teach you,' he panted. 'Now get out, and don't let your unclean faces be seen here ever again.'

Ishvar and Narayan ran off with their pants straggling, stumbling and tripping comically. The other children grabbed the opportunity to laugh; they were grateful for the relief it provided.

Dukhi did not hear till evening about his sons' punishment. He grimly told Roopa to delay baking the chapatis. 'Why?' she asked, alarmed. 'After a whole day in the fields you are not hungry? Where-all are you going?'

'To Pandit Lalluram. He must do something about this.'

'Leave it for now,' she pleaded. 'Don't disturb such an important man at dinnertime.' But Dukhi washed the day's dust off his hands and went.

Pandit Lalluram was not just any Brahmin, he was a Chit-Pavan Brahmin – descended from the purest among the pure, from the keepers of the Sacred Knowledge. He was neither the village headman nor a government official, but his peers said he commanded their unswerving respect for his age, his sense of fairness, and for the Sacred Knowledge locked inside his large, shiny cranium.

Disputes of any sort, over land or water or animals, were presented before him for arbitration. Family quarrels concerning disobedient daughters-in-law, stubborn wives, and philandering husbands also fell within his jurisdiction. Thanks to his impeccable credentials, everyone always went away satisfied: the victim obtained the illusion of justice; the wrongdoer was free to continue in his old ways; and Pandit Lalluram, for his trouble, received gifts of cloth, grain, fruit, and sweets from both sides.

The learned Pandit also enjoyed a reputation for promoting communal harmony. For instance, during the periodic protests against Muslims and cow slaughter, Pandit Lalluram persuaded his co-religionists that it was not right for Hindus to condemn the cow-eaters. He explained that the Muslim, by his religion, was burdened with four wives, poor fellow, and he needed to eat the flesh of animals to heat up his blood and service those four wives – he was carnivorous out of necessity, not out of fondness for cow flesh or to harass Hindus, and, as such, should be pitied and left in peace to satisfy his religious requirements.

With his spotless record, Pandit Lalluram's champions were many. So honest and fair was he, they said, even an untouchable could receive justice at his hands. That no untouchable could verify this claim in living memory was beside the point. People seemed to remember, vaguely, the time a landlord had beaten a Bhunghi to death for arriving late at the house, well after sunrise, to cart away the household's excrement. Pandit Lalluram had ruled – or it might have been his father, or perhaps his grandfather; in any case, someone had ruled – that the offence was serious, but not serious enough to warrant the killing, and that the landlord, in recompense, must provide food, shelter, and clothing for the dead man's wife and children for the next six years. Or was it for six months, or perhaps six weeks?

Relying on this legendary reputation for justice, Dukhi sat at Pandit Lalluram's feet and told him about the beating of Ishvar and Narayan. The learned man was resting in an armchair, having just finished his dinner, and belched loudly several times during his visitor's narration. Dukhi paused politely at each eructation, while Pandit Lalluram murmured 'Hai Ram' in thanks for an alimentary tract blessed with such energetic powers of digestion.

'How much he slapped my sons – you should see their swollen faces, Panditji,' said Dukhi. 'And their backsides look like an angry tiger raked them with his claws.'

'Poor children,' sympathized Pandit Lalluram. He rose and went to a shelf inside. 'Here, put this ointment on their backs. It will soothe the burning pain.'

Dukhi bowed his head. 'Thank you, Panditji, you are truly kind.' He removed the cloth from his head and wrapped the small flat tin in it. 'Panditji, some time ago I was hammered badly by Thakur Premji for no fault of mine. But I did not come to you. I did not want to trouble you.'

Pandit Lalluram raised his eyebrows and rubbed his big toe. Nodding, he kneaded sweat and dirt into black bits that rolled off his fingers.

'That time I suffered silently,' said Dukhi. 'But for my children, I have come to you. They should not have to suffer unjust beatings.'

Still silent, Pandit Lalluram sniffed the fingers which had finished massaging his big toe. He pivoted on one buttock and broke wind. Dukhi leaned back to allow it free passage, wondering what penalty might adhere to the offence of interfering with the waft of brahminical flatus.

'They are only children,' he pleaded, 'and they were doing no harm.' He waited for a response. 'They were doing no harm, Panditji,' he repeated, wanting the learned man to at least agree with him. 'That teacher should be punished for what he has done.'

Pandit Lalluram sighed long and hard. He leaned sideways and blew a thick stream of mucus out of his nose on to the dry earth. The impact of its landing raised a tiny puff of dust. He rubbed his nose and sighed again. 'Dukhi Mochi, you are a good, hardworking man. I have known you for a long time. You always try to do your duty, don't you, according to your caste?'

Dukhi nodded.

'Which is wise,' approved Pandit Lalluram, 'for it is the path to happiness. Otherwise, there would be chaos in the universe. You understand there are four varnas in society: Brahmin, Kshatriya, Vaishya, and Shudra. Each of us belongs to one of these four varnas, and they cannot mix. Correct?'

Dukhi nodded again, hiding his impatience. He had not come to hear a lecture on the caste system.

'Now just as you, a leather-worker, have to do your dharmic duty towards your family and society, the teacher must do his. You would not deny that, would you, Dukhi?'

Dukhi shook his head.

'Punishing your sons for their misdeeds was part of the teacher's duty. He had no choice. Do you understand?'

'Yes, Panditji, punishment is sometimes necessary. But such a terrible beating?'

'It was a terrible offence that they –'

'But they are only children, and curious, like all –'

Pandit Lalluram rolled his eyes at the interruption, pointing heavenward with the index finger of his right hand to silence Dukhi. 'How can I make you understand? You do not have the knowledge that would help you to appreciate these matters.' Now the note of patient suffering in his voice was replaced by something harsher. 'Your children entered the classroom. They polluted the place. They touched instruments of learning. They defiled slates and chalks, which upper-caste children would touch. You are lucky there wasn't a holy book like the Bhagavad

Gita in that cupboard, no sacred texts. Or the punishment would have been more final.'

Dukhi was calm as he touched Pandit Lalluram's sandals to take his leave. 'I understand completely, Panditji, thank you for explaining to me. I am so lucky – you, a Chit-Pavan Brahmin, wasting precious time on an ignorant Chamaar like me.'

Pandit Lalluram absently lifted his hand in farewell. There was a small doubt in his mind as to whether he had been flattered or insulted. Presently, though, another vigorous belch came rumbling upwards, displacing the doubt and putting both mind and belly at ease.

On the way home, Dukhi came across his friends who were still smoking under the tree by the river. 'Oyeh, Dukhi, out so late in that part of the village?'

'Went to see that Chit-Pavan Brahmin,' said Dukhi, and narrated his visit in detail. 'Goo-Khavan Brahmin is what he should be called instead.'

They laughed with delight, and Chhotu agreed that Shit-Eating Brahmin was indeed a more suitable name. 'But how does he have the appetite, after gobbling a pound of ghee and two pounds of sweets at every meal?'

'He gave me this ointment for the children,' said Dukhi. They passed the tin around, examining, sniffing the contents.

'Looks like boot polish to me,' said Chhotu. 'He must apply it to his head every morning. That's why it shines like the sun.'

'Aray bhaiya, you are confusing his head with his arse-hole. That's where he applies the polish – that's where the sun shines from, according to his caste brothers. That's why the shit-eaters all try to lick their way into it.'

'I have a shlokha of advice for all of them,' said Dayaram, and recited in mock Sanskrit, imitating the exalted cadences of a pujari reading scriptures: 'Goluma Ekdama Tajidevum! Chuptum Makkama Jhaptum!'

The men roared at the references to buggery and copulation. Dukhi threw the tin in the river. Leaving his friends to speculate about what exactly, if anything, lay below the rolls of fat that constituted Pandit Lalluram's belly, he went home.

He told Roopa he would be leaving early next morning for town. 'My mind is made up. I am going to talk to Ashraf the tailor.'

She did not ask why. Her mind was busy planning the strategy for another nocturnal assault on someone's butter-churn, this time for her children's backsides.

Ashraf wanted no payment to apprentice Dukhi's sons. 'They will be a help to me,' he said. 'And how much food can two little boys eat? Whatever we cook, they will share with us. That's all right, nah? No restrictions?'

'No restrictions,' said Dukhi.

Two weeks later he returned to the tailor's shop with Ishvar and Narayan. 'Ashraf is like my brother,' he explained to the children. 'So you must always call him Ashraf Chacha.'

The tailor beamed with pleasure, honoured by the title of uncle, as Dukhi continued, 'You will stay with Ashraf Chacha for some time, and learn with him. Listen carefully to everything he says, and treat him with the same respect you have for me.'

The boys had been prepared for the separation in advance by their father. This was only the formal announcement. 'Yes, Bapa,' they answered.

'Ashraf Chacha is going to turn you into tailors like himself. From now on, you are not cobblers – if someone asks your name, don't say Ishvar Mochi or Narayan Mochi. From now on you are Ishvar Darji and Narayan Darji.'

Then Dukhi gave them each a pat on the back, and a slight push, as though to propel them into the other man's keeping. They left their father's side and stepped towards the tailor, who put out his hands to receive them.

Dukhi watched Ashraf's fingers, the warmth with which he gripped the children's shoulders. Ashraf was a good and gentle man, he knew his sons would be well-cared for. All the same, an icy ache was spreading around his heart.

During the journey back to the village, he slumped in the bullock cart, feeling exhausted, barely aware of the wheels jouncing over ruts and bumps, jarring his bones. Simultaneously, he felt crazy surges of energy that made him want to hop out of the cart and run. He knew he had done the best thing possible for his sons, and a weight had lifted. Why, then, did he not feel lighter? What was this other thing pressing down on him?

Late in the afternoon he jumped off the bullock cart by the village road. Roopa was sitting idle in the hut, staring out the entrance, when his shadow appeared in the doorway. He told her everything was settled.

She looked at him accusingly. He had made a hole in her life that nothing could fill. Each time she thought of her two sons – distanced by miles to live with a stranger, and a Muslim at that – then her grief leapt up into her throat, and she felt she would choke, she told her husband. He observed bitterly that at least his Muslim friend treated him better than his Hindu brothers.

Muzaffar Tailoring Company was located on a street of small family businesses. There was a hardware store, coal-merchant, banya, and miller, all in a row, the shops identical in shape and size, distinguished solely by the interior noises and smells. Muzaffar Tailoring Company was the only one that displayed a signboard.

Ashraf's shop was cramped, as were the living quarters over it: one room and kitchen. He had married last year, and had a month-old daughter. His wife, Mumtaz, was less pleased than he to have two more mouths staying with them. It was decided that the apprentices would sleep in the shop.

Ishvar and Narayan were overwhelmed by the sudden change in their lives. Buildings, electric lights, water that flowed from taps – everything so different from the village, and so amazing. On the first day they sat in awe on the stone steps outside the shop, watching the street and seeing a universe of frightening chaos. Gradually, they perceived the river of traffic in the street and, within it, the currents of handcarts, bicycles, bullock carts, buses, and the occasional lorry. Now they learned the wild river's character. They were reassured that it was not all madness and noise, there was a pattern in things.

They observed people come to the banya to purchase salt, spices, coconut, pulses, candles, oil. They saw grain being taken to the miller to be made into flour. The miller's arms slowly became white while he worked; sometimes, his face and eyelashes too. The coal-merchant's arms and face turned black as the hours progressed; his delivery boys ran back and forth all day with baskets of coal. Ishvar and Narayan loved to watch their neighbours when they washed at night, emerging brown from behind their daytime colours.

Ashraf left them alone for two days, till their curiosity turned of its own accord towards the tailoring shop. The centre of their desire was, of course, the sewing-machine. To satisfy them, he let each take a turn at working the treadle while he guided a scrap under the needle. The brothers were thrilled that they could make the machine perform. It was as inspiring as making their mark with chalk upon slate.

Now they were ready to settle down to less exciting things, like threading a needle and hand-stitching. Eager to learn, they impressed Ashraf with their quickness. The next time a customer came to Muzaffar Tailoring Company, he decided to let Ishvar write down the measurements.

The man carried striped material for a shirt. Ashraf opened the order book to a new page, noted the customer's name, then unrolled his measuring tape with a flourish, which the boys simply adored. They had already begun to practise it in private, to Ashraf's amusement.

'Collar, fourteen and half inches,' he dictated. 'Chest, thirty-two.' He glanced at Ishvar, who was bent over the book, his tongue sticking out in grave concentration. Turning to the customer, Ashraf continued, 'Sleeves. Short or long?'

'Has to be long,' said the man. 'I am wearing it to a friend's wedding.' The formalities completed, the customer left, assured that his shirt would be ready in time for the wedding next week.

'Now let's see the measurements,' said Ashraf.

Smiling proudly, Ishvar handed him the book. The page was covered with black scratches and squiggles.

'Ah, yes, I see.' Ashraf controlled his dismay, patting the boy's back. 'Yes, very good.' He quickly jotted down what he could remember of the figures.

After dinner, he began teaching them the alphabet and numbers. Mumtaz was not pleased. 'Now you are becoming their schoolmaster as well. What next? Will you find wives for them also, when they are old enough?'

Next day he finished the wedding-guest's shirt. The man came for it at the end of the week and tried it on. Ashraf had got everything right except the length: it hung closer to the knees than was desirable. The man looked in the mirror, dubious, turning left and right.

'Absolutely perfect,' admired Ashraf. 'This northern Pathani style has become very fashionable these days.' The man left, still a bit uncertain, and the three burst out laughing.

A month after the apprentices had started, Ashraf was wakened in the night by a soft mewling. He sat up to listen, but there was nothing more. He lay down and began to drift.

A few minutes later the sound nudged his sleep again. 'What is it?' asked Mumtaz. 'Why do you keep waking?'

'A noise. Was the baby crying?'

'No, but she will if you keep jumping up.'

Then the soft sobs came again. 'It's downstairs.' He got out of bed and lit the lamp.

'So why do you have to go? Are you their father?'

Her reproaches followed him as he descended the steps into the shop. He entered and held up the lamp. The light caught Narayan's tear-glistened cheeks. Ashraf knelt on the floor beside him, gently rubbing his back.

'What's wrong, Narayan?' he asked, although he knew the answer, having expected an attack of homesickness sooner or later. 'I heard you crying. Is something hurting?'

The boy shook his head. Ashraf put his arm around him. 'When your father is not here, I stand in his place. And Mumtaz Chachi is like your mother, nah? You can tell us anything you like.'

Narayan burst into sobs at that. Now Ishvar awoke as well and rubbed his eyes, shielding them from the lamp.

'Do you know why your brother is crying?' asked Ashraf.

Ishvar nodded gravely. 'He thinks of home every night. I also think of it, but I don't cry.'

'You are a brave boy.'

'I don't want to cry either,' said Narayan. 'But when it gets dark and everybody is sleeping, my father and mother come in my mind.' He sniffed and wiped his eyes. 'I see our hut, and it makes me very sad, and then it makes me cry.'

Ashraf held him on his lap, saying it was all right to think of his parents. 'But don't be sad, your Bapa will arrive in a few weeks to take you home for a visit. And when you have learned all the tailoring, you will open your own shop and earn lots of money. How proud your parents will be, nah?'

He told the boys that whenever they felt sad, they could come and tell him about their village, the river, the fields, their friends. Talking together about it would change the sadness to happiness, he assured them. He lay by their side till they fell asleep, then crept upstairs with the lamp turned low.

Mumtaz was sitting in the dark, waiting for him. 'Are they all right?' she asked anxiously.

He nodded, reassured by her concern. 'They were just feeling lonely.'

'Maybe we should let them sleep upstairs from tomorrow.'

Her offer touched him, and his eyes swam with love. 'They are brave boys. They will learn to sleep alone, it's good for them to become tough,' he said.

It soon became known in Dukhi's village that his children were learning a trade other than leather-working. In the old days, punishment for stepping outside one's caste would have been death. Dukhi was spared his life, but it became a very hard life. He was allowed no more carcasses, and had to travel long distances to find work. Sometimes he obtained a hide secretly from fellow Chamaars; it would have been difficult for them if they were found out. The items he fashioned from this illicit

leather had to be sold in far-off places where they had not heard about
him and his sons.

'Such suffering you have brought upon our heads,' said Roopa almost
daily. 'No work, no food, no sons. What crimes have I committed to be
punished like this? My life has become a permanent shadow.'

But her horizon brightened as the day approached for the children's
visit. She dreamed and made plans, her heartache diverted by the desire
to have some treat waiting for them. And if the treat was unaffordable,
she determined, then it would be obtained moneylessly, in darkness.

For the first time since the children were born, Dukhi acknowledged
that he was aware of her night walks. As she rose stealthily after midnight, he said, 'Listen, mother-of-Narayan, I don't think you should go.'

Roopa jumped. 'O, how you scared me! I thought you were asleep!'

'Taking such a risk is stupid.'

'You never said that before.'

'It was different then. It's not like the boys will starve without butter
or a peach or a bit of jaggery.'

Roopa went anyway, promising herself it was the last time. After all,
her children had been away for three months, she had to give them
something special.

On the long-awaited day, Dukhi left at dawn and brought his sons
back for a week. The two boys sat very close to their father, and couldn't
stop touching him throughout the journey, leaning against him on either
side, Narayan holding on to his knee, Ishvar clutching his arm. They
talked non-stop, then repeated everything for their mother when they
got home in the late afternoon.

'The machine is amazing,' said Ishvar. 'The big wheel is –'

'You do your feet likethis-likethis,' said Narayan, flapping his hands
to mimic the treadle, 'and the needle jumps up and down, it's so good –'

'I can do it very fast, but Ashraf Chacha can do it very-very fast.'

'I like the small needle also, with my fingers, it goes in and out of the
cloth smoothly, it's very pointy, once it poked me in my thumb.'

Their mother immediately asked to see the thumb. Assuring herself
that there was no permanent damage, she let the story proceed. By
dinnertime the boys were exhausted, and started falling asleep over
the food. Roopa wiped their hands and mouths, then Dukhi guided
them to their mats.

For a long while, they gazed at them sleeping before rolling out their
own mats. 'They are looking nice and fit,' she said. 'See their cheeks.'

'I hope it's not an unhealthy swelling,' said Dukhi. 'Like the swollen
bellies that babies get in famine time.'

'What-all rubbish are you talking? With my mother's instinct I would know at once if my children were not well.' But she understood his doubt was prompted by resentment that their children should grow healthier in a stranger's house than when they were living at home; she shared his shame. They went to bed feeling a mixture of gladness and sorrow.

The family's excitement continued the next morning. The boys had brought a tape measure, a blank page, and a pencil from Muzaffar Tailoring, and wanted to measure their parents. Ashraf had taught them a diagrammatic code for the constantly used words like neck, waist, chest, and sleeve.

The boys could not reach high enough, so the two clients had to bend down or sit on the floor for some of the measurements: first their mother, and then their father. While they were recording Dukhi's sizes, Roopa called her friends from nearby huts to watch. Now Ishvar grew self-conscious and smiled shyly, but Narayan flourished the tape and made his gestures more expansive, enjoying the attention.

Everyone clapped with delight when they finished. In the evening, Dukhi borrowed the piece of paper to show to his friends under the tree by the river. He carried it about with him for the rest of the week.

Then it was time for the boys to return to Muzaffar Tailoring. The parents' thoughts turned once again with dread towards the absence looming in their lives, in their hut. Ishvar requested his father for the page with the measurements.

'Can't I keep it?' asked Dukhi. The boys considered their father's request, then rummaged for a scrap of paper and copied the figures so he could have the original.

Three months again passed before the next visit. This time the boys brought presents for their parents. Ishvar and Narayan planned to fool them that they had gone shopping for the gifts in a big store in town, just like rich townspeople.

'What-all is this?' said Roopa uneasily. 'Where did you get the money?'

'We didn't buy them, Ma! We made them ourselves!' said Narayan, forgetting his little joke. Ishvar explained excitedly how Ashraf Chacha had helped them select and match the remnants left over from the fabric for customers' orders. Their father's vest had been easy; there were plenty of white poplin remnants. The choli for their mother had required a bit more planning. A print of red and yellow flowers made up the front of the blouse. The back was a solid red, and the sleeves were fashioned from a swatch of vermilion.

Roopa burst into tears as soon as she put on the choli. Ishvar and

Narayan looked at their father in alarm, who said she was crying because she was happy.

'Yes, I am!' she confirmed his verdict through her sobs. She knelt before them and hugged them in turn, and then hugged them together. She saw Dukhi watching, and led the boys to him. 'Embrace your father also,' she said, 'this is a very special day.'

She left the hut in search of her neighbours. 'Padma! Savitri! Come and look! Amba and Pyari, you come too! See what-all my sons have brought!'

Dukhi grinned at the boys. 'There will be no dinner today. Her new choli will make Ma forget everything, she will spend the whole day showing off.' He patted his front and sides. 'This fits much better than my old one. Material is also nicer.'

'Look, Bapa, there is a pocket as well,' said Narayan.

Roopa and Dukhi wore the new garments all week long. Afterwards, when the boys were back in town, she removed her choli and demanded his vest.

'Why?' he asked.

'To wash.'

But she refused to return it when it was dry. 'What if you tear it or something?' She folded both articles, wrapped them in sacking, and secured the parcel with string. She hung it from the roof of the hut, safe from floodwater and rodents.

Ishvar and Narayan's years of apprenticeship were measured out in three-month intervals, eased somewhat by the week-long visits to their village. They were now eighteen and sixteen, their training was approaching its end, and they would leave Muzaffar Tailoring Company sometime after the monsoon. Ashraf's family had grown – there were four daughters now: the youngest was three, the oldest, eight. Mumtaz took a keen interest in the apprentices' plans. The sooner they came to fruition, the more room there would be for her own children, she thought, though she had grown to like the two young men, quiet and always helpful.

Narayan's preference was to set up in the village and sew for their own people. Ishvar was inclined to stay on in this town or another, become an assistant in someone's shop. 'You cannot earn much in the village,' he said. 'Everyone is so poor. There is more scope in a big place.'

Meanwhile, sporadic riots which had started with the talk of independence were spreading as the country's Partition became a reality. 'Maybe it's better to stay where you are for the time being,' said Ashraf, while Mumtaz glared at him. 'The devil is not doing his evil work in our town. You know all the neighbours, you have lived here for many years. And even if your village is peaceful, it's still the wrong time to start a new business.'

Ishvar and Narayan sent word to their parents with someone passing through that they would remain with Ashraf Chacha till the bad times were over. Roopa was depressed; separated all these long years, and now her sons were further delayed – when would the gods take pity and end her punishment?

Dukhi, too, was disappointed, but accepted the decision as being for the best. Disturbing things were happening around them. Strangers belonging to a Hindu organization that wore white shirts and khaki pants, and trained their members to march about like soldiers, had been visiting the district. They brought with them stories of Muslims attacking Hindus in many parts of the country. 'We must get ready to defend ourselves,' they said. 'And also to avenge ourselves. If they spill the blood of our Hindu brothers, this country shall run red with rivers of Muslim blood.'

In Dukhi's village, the Muslims were too few to pose a threat to anyone, but the landlords saw opportunity in the strangers' warnings. They did their best to galvanize people against the imaginary danger in their midst. 'Better to drive out the Mussulman menace before we are burned alive in our huts. For centuries they have invaded us, destroyed our temples, stolen our wealth.'

The men in white shirts and khaki pants persevered for a few more days but had no luck with the vast majority. The lower castes were not impressed by the rhetoric. They had always lived peacefully with their Muslim neighbours. Besides, they were too exhausted keeping body and soul together.

So the attempt to dispossess the village Muslims fizzled out. Leaving behind sinister threats about dealing with traitors, including the chief traitor, Mohandas Karamchand Gandhi, the men from the Hindu organization moved on. Places with larger populations and shops and commerce offered them more opportunities for success, and the cloak of urban anonymity to hide behind, where hoax and hearsay could find fertile ground to grow.

Dukhi and his friends discussed the developments in the evening, by the river. They were confused by the varying accounts that reached them of events in faraway towns and villages.

'The zamindars have always treated us like animals.'

'Worse than animals.'

'But what if it's true? What if the Mussulman horde sweeps down upon our village, like the khaki pants told us?'

'They have never bothered us before. Why would they do it now? Why should we hurt them because some outsiders come with stories?'

'Yes, it's strange that suddenly we have all become Hindu brothers.'

'The Muslims have behaved more like our brothers than the bastard Brahmins and Thakurs.'

But the stories kept multiplying: someone had been knifed in the bazaar in town; a sadhu hacked to death at the bus station; a settlement razed to the ground. The tension spread through the entire district. And it was all believable because it resembled exactly what people had been seeing in newspapers for the past few days: reports about arson and riots in large towns and cities; about mayhem and massacre on all sides; about the vast and terrible exchange of populations that had commenced across the new border.

—

The killings started in the poorer section of town, and began to spread; the next day the bazaar was empty. There were no fruits or vegetables to be bought, the milkmen did not stir, and the only bakery in town, owned by a Muslim, had already been burned to the ground.

'Bread is become rarer than gold,' said Ashraf. 'What madness. These people have lived together for generations, laughing and crying together. Now they are butchering one another.' He did no work that day, spending the hours gazing out the door at the deserted street, as though waiting for something dreadful to make its appearance.

'Ashraf Chacha, dinner is ready,' said Narayan, responding to Mumtaz's signal. Her husband had not eaten all day. She was hoping he would join them now.

'There is something I have to tell you,' he said to Mumtaz. 'And you as well,' he turned to Ishvar and Narayan.

'Come, food is ready, later we can talk,' she said. 'It is only dal and chapati today, but you must eat a little at least.' She lowered the pot from the stove.

'I am not hungry. You and the little ones eat,' said Ashraf, shepherding the four children towards the food. They were reluctant, having sensed their parents' anxiety. 'Go, boys, you too.'

'I take the trouble to cook and nawab-sahib won't even touch his fingers to the dinner,' said Mumtaz.

In his present mood, her commonplace complaint assumed vicious overtones. He shouted at her, something he rarely did. 'What do you want me to do if I am not hungry? Tie the plate to my belly? Talk sense once in a while, nah!' The youngest two started to cry. One of their elbows overturned a glass of water.

'You must be satisfied now,' said Mumtaz scornfully as she mopped up the spill. 'Trying to scare me with your big shouting. Only the little ones are frightened of that, let me tell you.'

Ashraf took the two weeping children in his arms. 'Okay, okay, no crying. See, we will all eat together.' He fed them from his plate, putting a morsel in his own mouth when they pointed to it. It soon became a new game, and they cheered up.

Dinner finished quickly, and Mumtaz began taking the pot and ladle outside to the tap for washing. Ashraf stopped her. 'I was going to say something before dinner, before your shouting started.'

'I am listening now.'

'It's about this . . . about what's happening everywhere.'

'What?'

'You want me to describe in front of the children?' he whispered fiercely. 'Why are you acting stupid? Sooner or later the trouble will come here. No matter what happens, it will never be the same again between the two communities.'

He noticed Ishvar and Narayan listening with dismay, and added in haste, 'I don't mean us, boys. We will always be like one family, even if we are apart.'

'But Ashraf Chacha, we don't have to be apart,' said Narayan. 'Ishvar and I are not planning to leave yet.'

'Yes, I know. But Mumtaz Chachi and the children and I, we have to leave.'

'My poor, paagal nawab-sahib – gone completely crazy,' said Mumtaz. 'Wants to leave. With four little ones? Where do you want to go?'

'Same place all the others are going. Across the border. What do you want to do? Sit here and wait till the hatred and insanity comes with swords and clubs and kerosene? What I am saying is, tomorrow morning I go to the station and buy our train tickets.'

Mumtaz insisted he was reacting like a foolish old man. But he refused to allow her the temporary comfort of turning her back on danger. He was determined to argue all night, he said, rather than pretend that things were normal.

'I will do whatever is necessary to save my family. How can you be so blind? I will drag you by your hair to the railway station if I have to.' At this threat, the children began crying again.

She dried their tears on her dupatta, and dissolved her opposition to the plan. It was not a case of being blind to danger – the danger could be smelt from miles away, her husband was right. Only, removing the blindfold was difficult because of what she might see.

'It won't be possible to carry much if we are to leave in a hurry,' she said. 'Clothes, a stove, some cooking pots. I'll start packing now.'

'Yes, keep it ready for tomorrow,' said Ashraf. 'The rest we will lock in the shop. Inshallah, someday we will be able to come back and claim it.' He gathered the children for bed. 'Come, we must sleep early tonight. Tomorrow we have to start a long journey.'

Narayan found it unbearable to listen to or watch their troubled preparations. He doubted if anything he said would make a difference. Pretending he was going down to the shop, he slipped out the back to their neighbour and told him of the planned flight.

'Is he serious?' said the hardware-store owner. 'When we talked this morning, he agreed there was nothing to worry about in our neighbourhood.'

'He has changed his mind.'

'Wait, I will come to him right now.'

He collected the coal-merchant, the banya, and the miller, and knocked on Ashraf's door. 'Forgive us for bothering you at this hour. May we come in?'

'Of course. Will you eat something? A drink?'

'Nothing, thank you. We came because we got some news that is causing us great grief.'

'What is it, what?' Ashraf was agitated, wondering if there had been riot casualties in someone's family. 'Can I help?'

'Yes, you can. You can tell us it's not true.'

'What's not true?'

'That you want to leave us, leave the place where you were born and your children were born. This is causing our grief.'

'You are such good people.' Ashraf's eyes began to moisten. 'But I really don't have a choice, nah.'

'Sit down with us and think calmly,' said the hardware-store owner, putting his arm around Ashraf's shoulder. 'The situation is bad, yes, but it would be madness to attempt to leave.'

The others nodded in agreement. The coal-merchant put his hand on Ashraf's knee. 'Every day trains are crossing that new border, carrying nothing but corpses. My agent arrived yesterday from the north, he has seen it with his own eyes. The trains are stopped at the station and everyone is butchered. On both sides of the border.'

'Then what am I to do?'

The desperation in his voice drew the hardware-store owner's hand to his shoulder again. 'Stay here. You are with friends. We will let nothing happen to your family. Where is there any trouble in our neighbourhood? We have always lived here peacefully.'

'But what will happen when those outside troublemakers come?'

'Yours is the only Muslim shop in the street. You think so many of us together cannot protect one shop?' They hugged him, promising he had nothing to fear. 'Any time you want to, day or night, if you feel worried about anything, just come to our house with your wife and children.'

After the neighbours left, Narayan had an idea. 'You know the sign outside – Muzaffar Tailoring Company. We could put another one in its place.'

'Why?' asked Ashraf.

Narayan was hesitant to say. 'A new one . . .'

Then Ashraf saw the point. 'Yes, with a new name. A Hindu name. It's a very good idea.'

'Let's do it right now,' said Ishvar. 'I can get a new board from your uncle's lumberyard. Can I take the cycle?'

'Of course. But be careful, don't go through a Muslim area.'

An hour later Ishvar returned empty-handed without having reached his destination. 'Lots of shops and houses on fire. I kept going – slowly, slowly. Then I saw some people with axes. They were chopping a man. That scared me, I turned back.'

Ashraf sat down weakly. 'You were wise. What will we do now?' He was too frightened to think.

'Why do we need a new board?' said Narayan. 'We can use the back of this old one. All we need is some paint.'

He went next door again, and the hardware-store owner let him have a blue tin that was open. 'It's a good idea,' he said. 'What name are you going to paint?'

'Krishna Tailors, I think,' said Narayan at random.

'The blue will be perfect.' He pointed to the horizon, where smoke and a red glow filled the sky. 'I heard it's the lumberyard. But don't tell Ashraf now.'

Night had fallen by the time they finished painting the letters and remounting the signboard. 'On that old wood the paint looks very new,' said Ashraf.

'I'll rub a handful of ashes over it,' said Ishvar. 'Tomorrow morning, when it's dry.'

'If we are not all reduced to ashes while we sleep,' said Ashraf softly. The fragile sense of security woven out of his neighbours' assurances was starting to fray.

In bed, every noise in the darkness was danger approaching to threaten his family, until he was able to identify it as something innocuous. He relearned the familiar sounds to which he had fallen asleep all his life. The thud of the coal-merchant's charpoy, who liked to sleep in the open, in the back yard (he slammed it down every night to shake out the bedbugs). The crash of the banya's door being locked for the night; swollen and sticking, it needed a firm hand. The clang of someone's pail – Ashraf had never found out whose, and what was being done with it at this late hour.

Sometime after midnight, he awoke with a start, went downstairs to the shop and began removing the three framed Koranic quotations that hung on the wall behind the cutting table. Ishvar and Narayan stirred, roused by his fumbling in the dark, and put on the light.

'It's all right, go to sleep,' he said. 'I suddenly remembered these frames.' The wall paint was darker where the frames had hung. Ashraf tried unsuccessfully to wipe away the difference with a damp rag.

'We have something you can put up instead,' said Narayan. He dragged out their trunk from under the cutting table and found three cardboard-stiffened pictures equipped with little string loops for hanging. 'Ram and Sita, Krishna, and Laxmi.'

'Yes, definitely,' said Ashraf. 'And tomorrow we will burn these Urdu magazines and newspapers.'

At eight-thirty a.m. Ashraf opened the shop as usual, releasing the padlock from the collapsible steel doors on the outside, but without folding them back. The interior wooden door was kept ajar. Like the day before, the street was deserted.

About ten o'clock, the coal-merchant's son called through the grating. 'Father said to ask if you need anything from market, in case it is open. He said it's better if you don't go.'

'God bless you, son,' said Mumtaz, 'yes, a little milk, if possible, for the children. And any kind of vegetables – a few potatoes or onions, anything you can find.'

The boy returned empty-handed in fifteen minutes; the market was bare. Later, the coal-merchant sent a pitcher of milk from his cow. Mumtaz relied on the dwindling flour and lentils in the house to prepare the day's meals. Well before dusk, Ashraf padlocked the grating and bolted the doors.

At dinnertime the youngest ones wanted Ashraf to feed them like yesterday. 'Ah, you are getting fond of that game,' he smiled.

After the meal, Ishvar and Narayan rose to return downstairs, to let the family prepare for bed. 'Stay,' said Ashraf, 'it is still early, nah. Without customers, the devil makes the hours move slowly.'

'It should get better from tomorrow,' said Ishvar. 'They say the soldiers are soon taking charge.'

'Inshallah,' said Ashraf, watching his youngest play with a rag doll he had made for her. The oldest girl was reading a school book. The other two amused themselves with scraps of cloth, pretending to be dressmakers. He signalled to Ishvar and Narayan to observe their exaggerated actions.

'You used to do that when you were new here,' he said. 'And you loved to wave the measure tape, make it snap.' They laughed at the memory, then lapsed into silence again.

The quiet was broken by a hammering at the shop door. Ashraf jumped up, but Ishvar stopped him. 'I'll look,' he said.

From the upstairs window he saw a group of twenty or thirty men on the pavement. They noticed him and shouted, 'Open the door! We want to talk to you!'

'Sure, one moment!' he called back. 'Listen,' he whispered, 'all of you go next door, very quietly, from the upstairs passage. Narayan and I will go down.'

'Ya Allah!' cried Mumtaz softly. 'We should have left when we had the chance! You were right, my husband, and I called you foolish, I am the foolish one who did not –'

'Shut up and come on, quick!' said Ashraf. One of the girls started to sniffle. Mumtaz took the child in her arms and quieted her. Ashraf led them out while Ishvar and Narayan descended to the shop. The banging was furious, directed with hard objects through the grating upon the wooden doors.

'Patience!' shouted Ishvar, 'I first have to undo the locks!'

The crowd fell silent when the two figures became visible through the grating. Most of them had some sort of crude weapon, a stick or a spear; others had swords. A few men were wearing saffron shirts, and carried tridents.

The sight of them made Ishvar tremble. For a brief moment he was tempted to tell them the truth and step out of the way. Ashamed of the thought, he unlocked the grating and pushed it open a bit. 'Namaskaar, brothers.'

'Who are you?' asked the man in front.

'My father owns Krishna Tailors. This is my brother.'

'And where is your father?'

'Gone to our native place – a relative is sick.'

There was some consultation, then the leader said, 'We have information that this is a Muslim shop.'

'What?' said Ishvar and Narayan in unison. 'This has been our father's shop for twenty years!'

From the back of the crowd came complaints. No need for so much talk! Burn it! We know it's a Muslim shop! Burn it! And those who lie to protect it – burn them, too!

'Is it possible that Muslims work in this shop?' asked the leader.

'Business is not good enough to hire anyone,' said Ishvar. 'Barely enough work for my brother and me.' Men shuffled up beside him, trying to look inside the shop. They were breathing hard, and he could smell their sweat. 'Please, see all you want,' he said, moving aside. 'We have nothing to hide.'

The men glanced around quickly, taking in the Hindu deities on the wall behind the cutting table. One of the saffron-shirted men stepped forward. 'Listen, smart boy. If you are lying, I will myself skewer you on the three points of my trishul.'

'Why should I lie?' said Ishvar. 'I'm the same as you. You think I want to die to save a Muslim?'

There was more consultation outside the shop. 'Step on the pavement and remove your pyjamas,' said the leader. 'Both of you.'

'What?'

'Come on, hurry up! Or you won't need pyjamas anymore!'

In the ranks there was impatience. They banged their spears on the ground and shouted to torch the place. Ishvar and Narayan obediently dropped their pyjamas.

'It's too dark to see,' called the leader. 'Give me a lantern.' The light was handed over from behind the group. He bent low, held it close to their naked crotches, and was satisfied. The others crowded round to look as well. There was general agreement that the foreskins were intact.

Now the hardware-store owner opened his upstairs window and shouted, 'What's going on? Why are you harassing Hindu boys? Have you run out of Muslims?'

'And who are you?' they shouted back.

'Who am I? I am your father and your grandfather! That's who I am! And also the owner of this hardware store! If I give the word, the whole street will unite as one to make mincemeat of you! Don't you have somewhere else to go?'

The leader did not think it worthwhile to take up the challenge. His men started to drift away, hurling obscenities to save face. They turned to arguing among themselves about a wasted night and faulty information that had made them look like fools.

'That was beautiful acting,' said the hardware-store owner, patting Ishvar and Narayan heartily on the back. 'I was watching the whole thing from upstairs. You know, if there had been any danger of you getting hurt, I would have called everybody to help. But I thought it's better if there is no confrontation, if you can convince them and they leave quietly.' He looked around to make sure everyone believed him.

Mumtaz fell on her knees before the two apprentices. Her dupatta slid from around her neck and draped their feet. 'Please, Chachi, don't do that,' said Ishvar, shuffling backwards.

'Forever and ever, my life, my children, my husband's life, my home – everything, I owe to you!' she clung to them, weeping. 'There is no repayment possible!'

'Please get up,' begged Ishvar, holding her wrists and trying to make her stand.

'From now on, this home is your home, as long as you will honour us with your presence!'

Ishvar finally succeeded in disentangling his ankles from her hands. 'Chachi, you are like our mother, we have shared your food and home for seven years.'

'Inshallah, you will stay and eat with us for seventy more.' Still sobbing, she replaced the dupatta around her neck, lifting a corner to wipe her eyes.

Ishvar and Narayan returned downstairs. After the children were asleep, Ashraf went downstairs too. The boys had not yet rolled out their sleeping mats. The three sat silently for a few minutes. Then Ashraf said, 'You know, when the banging started, I thought we were finished.'

'I was also scared,' said Narayan.

Their next silence lasted longer. Ashraf cleared his throat. 'I came down to say one thing only.' Tears were rolling down his cheeks; he paused to wipe them. 'The day I met your father – the day I told Dukhi to send me his two sons for tailor-training. That day was the luckiest of my life.' He embraced them, kissed their cheeks three times, and went upstairs.

Ashraf would not hear of the brothers returning to the village, and Mumtaz supported him in this. 'Stay on as my paid assistants,' he said, though he knew very well he could not afford it.

Roopa protested to Dukhi that it was high time she had her two sons back. 'You sent them to apprentice. Now they have learned the trade, so why are they still living with strangers? Are their own mother-father dead or something?'

But no one could predict how two Chamaars-turned-tailors would fare in the village. True, these new times were full of hope, changes were in the air, and the optimism that came with independence was shining bright. Ashraf even felt safe enough to turn over the Krishna Tailors sign and display the Muzaffar Tailoring side again.

Still, it was uncertain if centuries of tradition could be overturned as easily. So they agreed that Ishvar would stay on as Ashraf's assistant, and Narayan would return to test the waters. This suited all sides: Muzaffar Tailoring Company would just barely support one assistant; Dukhi would have the help of wages sent from town; and Roopa would have her younger son back.

She took down the parcel that had hung from the ceiling for seven years. The string knots had shrunk and could not be untied. She cut the string, unwrapped the protective sackcloth, then washed the vest and choli. It was time to wear them again, she told Dukhi, to celebrate the homecoming.

'It hangs a little loose,' he said.

'Mine, too,' said Roopa. 'The fabric must have stretched.'

He liked her explanation. It was easier than contemplating the lean years that had shrunk them both.

In the village, the Chamaar community was quietly proud of Narayan. Gradually, they found the courage to become his customers, though there was not much money in it for Narayan because they could rarely afford to have something new tailored. Garments thrown away by the upper castes clothed their bodies. Mostly, he altered or mended. He used an old hand-cranked sewing-machine that Ashraf had procured for him. It was restricted to a straight lock stitch, but sufficed for the work he did.

Business improved when word spread to neighbouring villages of the one who had done the unthinkable: abandoned leather for cloth. They came as much to see this courageous Chamaar-tailor, this contradiction in terms, as to get their clothes looked after. Many were a little disappointed with their visit. Inside the hut was nothing extraordinary, just a young man with a tape measure around his neck and a pencil behind one ear.

Narayan maintained a record of jobs and transactions as Ashraf had taught him, noting names, dates, and amounts owing. Roopa appointed herself to manage the business, standing around importantly while he measured the client and entered the figures in his book. She kept his pencils sharp with her paring knife. She could not read his register but retained an accurate account in her head. When someone who had yet to settle the balance from a previous job came with more work, she stood behind the client and rubbed her thumb and finger together to remind her son.

One morning, about six months after Narayan's return to the village, a Bhunghi ventured towards the hut. Roopa was heating water over a fire outside, happily listening to the muffled clank of the sewing-machine, when she saw the fellow approach cautiously. 'And where do you think you're going?' she yelled, stopping him in his tracks.

'I am looking for Narayan the tailor,' said the man, timidly holding up some rags.

'What?!' His audacity flabbergasted her. 'Don't give me your tailor-failor nonsense! I'll bathe your filthy skin with this boiling water! My son does not sew for your kind!'

'Ma! What are you doing?' shouted Narayan, emerging from the hut as the man bolted. 'Wait, wait!' he yelled after the fellow. Terrified that retribution was in pursuit, the Bhunghi ran faster.

'Come back, bhai, it's all right!'

'Another time,' called the frightened man. 'Tomorrow, maybe.'

'Okay, I'll wait for you,' said Narayan. 'Please come for sure.' He returned to the hut, shaking his head and ignoring his mother who glared furiously at him.

'Don't you shake your head at me!' she said indignantly. 'What-all nonsense is this, calling him back tomorrow? We are not going to deal with such low-caste people! How can you even think of measuring someone who carts the shit from people's houses?'

Narayan was silent. After working for a few minutes, he went outside to the fire, where she was still stirring her vigorous rage into the pot.

'I think, Ma, that you are wrong,' he said, keeping his voice so soft that it was almost lost in the crackling fire. 'I think I should sew for anybody who comes to me, Brahmin or Bhunghi.'

'You do, do you? Wait till your father comes home, see what he says about it! Brahmin yes, Bhunghi no!'

That evening Roopa told Dukhi about their son's outrageous ideas, and he turned to Narayan. 'I think your mother is right.'

Narayan dropped his hand from the crank and braked the fly wheel. 'Why did you send me to learn tailoring?'

'That's a stupid question. To improve your life – why else?'

'Yes. Because the uppers treat us so badly. And now you are behaving just like them. If that's what you want, then I am going back to town. I cannot live like this anymore.'

Roopa was stunned by the ultimatum, and horrified when Dukhi turned to her and said, 'I think he is right.'

'Father-of-Ishvar, make up your mind! First you say I am right, then you say he is right! From side to side you sway, like a pot without an arse! And this is what comes from sending him to town! Forgetting our village ways! It will only lead to trouble!' Boiling and bubbling, she left the hut, calling Amba, Pyari, Padma, and Savitri to come and hear what-all crazy things were happening in her unfortunate household.

'Toba, toba!' said Savitri. 'Poor Roopa, so upset she is shaking.'

'Children – Hai Ram,' said Pyari, throwing up her hands. 'How easily they forget about a mother's feelings.'

'What to do,' said Amba. 'We feed them milk from our breast when they are babies, but we cannot feed them good sense.'

'Be patient,' said Padma. 'Everything will be all right.'

After bathing in their sympathy, Roopa was calmer. The thought of losing her son a second time made her think carefully. She forgave him his lunatic proposals and agreed to turn a blind eye to them on the basis of a compromise: she would reserve the right to control entry into her hut; some customers would have to conduct their transactions outside.

———

Two years later Narayan could afford to build his own hut, next to his parents'. Roopa wept that he was abandoning them. 'Again and again he breaks his mother's heart,' she complained. 'How will I look after him and his business? Why must he separate?'

'But Ma, it's only thirty feet away,' said Narayan. 'You are welcome there any time to sharpen my pencils.'

'Sharpen pencils, he says! As if that's all I do for him!'

Eventually, though, she got accustomed to the idea and made it a point of pride, speaking of the other hut to her friends as her son's factory. He bought a large worktable, a clothes stand, and a new foot-operated sewing-machine which could do straight and zigzag stitches.

For this last purchase he went to take Ashraf Chacha's advice. The little town had grown since his departure, and Muzaffar Tailoring Company was doing well. Ishvar had rented a room near the shop. From assistant, Ashraf had elevated him to partner. The brothers agreed that their father need not work anymore, between them they would provide for their parents.

'You are such good boys,' said Dukhi, when Narayan told him of the decision. 'We are truly blessed by God.'

Roopa fetched the vest and choli made long ago by their children, and faded by now. 'Remember these?'

'I didn't know you still had them.'

'The day you and Ishvar brought these for us, you were so young, both of you,' she said, starting to cry. 'But even then I knew, in my heart, that everything would be all right in the end.' She went to announce the good tidings to her friends, who hugged her and teased her that she would soon become rich and not have anything to do with them.

'But one thing is certain,' said Padma. 'Time for marriage has come close.'

'You must start looking for two suitable daughters-in-law,' said Savitri.

'Don't delay any longer,' said Pyari.

'We will help you with everything, don't worry,' said Amba.

The happy news spread within their community, and outside it. Among the upper castes, there was still anger and resentment because of what a Chamaar had accomplished. One man in particular, Thakur Dharamsi – who always took charge of the district polls at election time, delivering votes to the political party of his choice – taunted the tailor periodically.

'There is a dead cow waiting for you,' he notified Narayan through a servant. Narayan merely passed on the message to other Chamaars, who were happy to have the carcass. Another time, when a goat perished in one of the drains on Thakur Dharamsi's property, he sent for Narayan to unclog it. Narayan politely sent his reply that he was grateful for the offer but was no longer in this line of work.

Among the Chamaars in the village, he was now looked upon as the spokesman for their caste, their unelected leader. Dukhi wore his son's success modestly, out of sight, indulging himself only sometimes, when he sat smoking with his friends under the tree by the river. Slowly, his son was becoming more prosperous than many upper-caste villagers. Narayan paid to have a new well dug in the untouchable section of the village. He leased the land on which the two huts stood, and replaced them with a pukka house, one of only seven in the village. It was large enough to accommodate his parents and his business. And, thought Roopa fondly, a wife and children before long.

Dukhi and she would have preferred the older son marrying first. But when they offered to find him a wife, Ishvar made it clear he was not interested. By now, Roopa had learned that trying to make her sons do what they did not want to do was a futile endeavour. 'Learning big-town ways,' she grumbled, 'forgetting our old ways,' and left it at that, turning her attention to Narayan.

They made inquiries, and a suitable girl was recommended in another village. A showing-day was fixed, when the boy's family would call on the girl's family. Roopa made certain that Amba, Pyari, Padma, and Savitri were included in plans for the visit – they were like family, she said. Ishvar chose not to go, but arranged a twenty-seven-seater Leyland to transport the bride-viewing party.

The battered little bus arrived in the village at nine in the morning, and stopped in a cloud of dust. The opportunity for a bus ride attracted volunteers for the auspicious event, many more than could be accommodated in that modest conveyance.

'Narayan is like a son to me,' said one. 'It's my duty to come. How can I let him down at this most important time?'

'I will not be able to hold my head up if you don't take me,' pleaded another, refusing to take no for an answer. 'Please don't leave me behind.'

'I have attended every single bride-showing in our community,' bragged a third. 'You need my expertise.'

Many took their going for granted, and climbed aboard without bothering to check with Dukhi or Roopa. When the excursion was ready to commence an hour later, there were thirty-eight people crammed inside, and a dozen sitting cross-legged on the roof. The driver, who had witnessed nasty accidents with low branches along rural roads, refused to proceed. 'Get down from the top! Down, everybody, down!' he yelled at the ones settled serenely in lotus positions. So the dozen from the roof had to be left behind, and the bus set off at a sensible crawl.

They reached their destination two and a half hours later. The girl's parents were impressed by the bus and the size of the visiting delegation, as was the entire village. The thirty-eight visitors stood around uncertainly. There was not room for everyone inside the dwelling. After much agonizing, Dukhi selected a group of seven, including his best friends, Chhotu and Dayaram. Padma and Savitri also made it in, but Amba and Pyari had to wait outside with the unlucky thirty-one, watching the proceedings through the doorway.

Inside, the inner circle had tea with the parents and described the journey. 'Such fine scenery we saw along the way,' said Dukhi to the girl's father.

'Once, all of a sudden, the bus made a big noise and stopped,' said Chhotu. 'It took a while to start again. We were worried about being late.'

By and by, the parents compared genealogies and family histories, while Roopa talked modestly of Narayan's success to the girl's mother. 'So many customers he has. Everybody wants to have clothes made by Narayan only. As if there is no other tailor in the whole country. My poor son works morning till night, sewing, sewing, sewing. But his expensive new machine is so good. What-all wonderful things it can do.'

Then it was time for the bride-viewing moment. 'Come, my daughter,' called the mother casually. 'Bring something sweet for our guests.'

The girl, Radha, sixteen years old, entered with a platter of laddoos. Conversation ceased. Everyone took a good look as she went around with her head modestly lowered and eyes averted. Outside, there was much whispering and jockeying for position as they tried to catch a glimpse.

Narayan kept his eyes on the laddoos when she stopped in front of him. He was nervous about looking – her family was watching for his reaction. The platter had almost reached the end of its circuit. If he didn't see her now, there would be no second chance, she would not return, that was certain, and he would have to make a blind decision. Look, oh look! he persuaded himself – and looked. He caught a profile of her features as she bent before her mother.

'No, daughter,' said the mother, 'none for me,' and with that, Radha disappeared.

Then it was time to go home. During the return journey, those who had been unable to see or hear from outside were fully briefed. Now everyone had the facts, and were able to take part in final discussions back in the village. Opinions were entertained in order of seniority.

'Her size is good, and colour is good.'

'The family also looks honest, hardworking.'

'Maybe horoscopes should be compared before final decision.'

'No horoscopes! Why horoscopes? That is all brahminical nonsense, our community does not do that.'

Thus it continued for a while, and Narayan listened silently. His approval at the end, though not essential, did serve to strengthen the consensus, to his parents' relief and the gathering's applause.

Now the arrangements went ahead. Some of the traditional expenditures were sidestepped at Narayan's insistence; he did not want Radha's family indebted to the moneylender in perpetuity. All he would accept from them were six brass vessels: three round-bottomed, and three flat.

Roopa was furious. 'What-all do you understand about complicated things like dowry? Have you been married before?'

Dukhi was also upset. 'Much more than six vessels is due. It is our right.'

'Since when has our community practised dowry?' asked Narayan quietly.

'If it's okay for the uppers to do it, so can we.'

But Narayan stood firm, with Ishvar's backing. 'Learning big-town ways,' grumbled their mother, foiled again. 'Forgetting our village ways.'

There was a last-minute hitch. Two days before the wedding, under coercion from Thakur Dharamsi and others, the village musicians withdrew their services. They were too frightened to even meet with the family and discuss the problem. So Ishvar arranged for replacements from town. Narayan did not mind the cost of transporting them and their instruments. It was a small price, he felt, for frustrating the landlords.

The new musicians did not know some of the local wedding songs. The elders among the guests were quite concerned – strange anthems and chants could be unpropitious for the marriage. 'Especially for producing children,' said an old woman who used to assist at births before her infirmity. 'The womb doesn't become fertile just like that, without correct procedure.'

'True,' said another. 'I have seen it with my own eyes. When the songs are not sung properly, nothing but unhappiness for husband and wife.' They conferred in worried groups, debating and discussing, trying to determine the antidote that would thwart the impending ill-fortune. They looked disapprovingly at those who were enjoying all that alien music and dancing.

The celebrations lasted three days, during which Chamaar families in the village ate the best meals of their lives. Ashraf and his family, the guests of honour, were lodged and looked after in Narayan's house, which made some people unhappy. There were mutterings about an inauspicious Muslim presence, but the protests were few and muted. And by the third night, to the elders' relief, the musicians were able to pick up many of the local songs.

A son was born to Radha and Narayan; they named him Omprakash.

People came to sing and rejoice with them at the happy occasion. The proud grandfather personally carried sweets to every house in the village.

Later that week, Dukhi's friend Chhotu came with his wife to see the newborn. Taking Dukhi and Narayan aside, he whispered, 'The uppers chucked the sweets in the garbage.'

They did not doubt his word; he would know, for he collected the trash from many of those houses. The news was hurtful but Narayan laughed it away. 'More for the ones who found the packages.'

Visitors continued to arrive, marvelling at how healthy the baby looked, considering it was a Chamaar's child, and how it was always smiling. 'Even when he is hungry there is no puling or mewling,' Radha became fond of boasting. 'Just makes a tiny *kurr-kurr*, which stops as soon as he gets my breast.'

Three daughters were born after Omprakash. Two survived. Their names were Leela and Rekha. No sweets were distributed.

Narayan began teaching his son to read and write, conducting the lessons while sewing. The man sat at the sewing-machine, the child sat with slate and chalk. By the time Omprakash was five, he could also do buttons with great style, imitating the flourish with which his father licked the thread and shot it through the needle's eye, or his flair in stabbing the needle through the cloth.

'All day he spends stuck to his Bapa,' grumbled Radha happily, surveying the adoring father and son.

Her mother-in-law reviewed the scene and drank it in with pleasure. 'Daughters are a mother's responsibility but sons are for the father,' pronounced Roopa, as though she had been granted a brand-new revelation, and Radha received it as such, nodding solemnly.

In the week following Omprakash's fifth birthday, Narayan took him to the tannery, where the Chamaars were busy at work. Since his return to the village, he had continued to join in their labours periodically, helping with whatever stage of skinning, curing, tanning, or dyeing that was in progress. And now he proudly showed his child how it was done.

But Omprakash held back. Narayan did not like this behaviour. He insisted the boy dirty his hands.

'Chhee! It stinks!' shrieked Omprakash.

'I know it stinks. Do it anyway.' He seized the boy's hands and dunked them in the tanning vat, plunging him in to the elbows. He was ashamed of his son's display before his fellow Chamaars.

'I don't want to do this! I want to go home! Please, Bapa, take me home now!'

'Tears or no tears, you will learn this work,' said Narayan grimly.

Omprakash sobbed and wailed, going into convulsions of rage, wrenching his hands away. 'You do that and I will throw your whole body inside,' his father threatened, soaking the arms again and again.

The others tried to persuade Narayan to let it be – the child might have a fit or seizure of some sort, they feared, the way he was screaming hysterically. 'It's his first day,' they said. 'Next week he will do better.' But Narayan forced him to keep at it till he called a halt an hour later.

Omprakash was still crying when they got home. On the porch, Radha was massaging her mother-in-law's scalp with coconut oil. They upset the bottle in their rush to comfort him. Roopa tried to hug her grandson but the thin grey strands hanging greasy and stiff over her forehead made him pull away. He had never seen his grandmother look so frightful.

'What is ailing him? What have you done to him, my poor little laughing-playing child?'

Narayan explained how they had spent the morning, and Dukhi laughed to hear it. The entire episode made Radha furious. 'Why must you torment the boy? There is no need to make my Om do such dirty work!'

'Dirty work? You, a Chamaar's daughter! Saying it is dirty work!'

She was startled by the outburst. It was the first time Narayan had shouted at her. 'But why does he –'

'How will he appreciate what he has if he does not learn what his forefathers did? Once a week he will come with me! Whether he likes it or not!'

Radha silently appealed to her father-in-law and began mopping up the coconut oil. Dukhi acknowledged her by tilting his head. Later, when he and Narayan were alone, he said, 'Son, I agree with you. But no matter what we think, once a week is only a game. It will never be for him like it was for us. And thank God for that.'

Omprakash spent the rest of the day in misery, in the kitchen, clinging to his mother. Radha kept patting his head while doing her work. 'Won't only leave me alone,' she grumbled happily to her mother-in-law. 'I still have to chop the spinach and make the chapatis. God knows when I'll finish.'

Roopa crinkled her forehead. 'When sons are unhappy, they remember their mothers.'

In the evening, while his father was relaxing on the porch, his eyes closed, Omprakash crept out and began massaging his feet, the way he had seen his mother do it. Narayan started, and opened his eyes. He looked down, saw his son and smiled. He held out his arms to him.

Omprakash leapt into them, flinging his hands round his father's neck. They stayed hugging for a few minutes without speaking a word. Then Narayan pried the child's fingers loose and sniffed them. He offered his own to him. 'See? We both have the same smell. It's an honest smell.'

The child nodded. 'Bapa, shall I do some more chumpee for your feet?'

'Okay.' He watched fondly as his son squeezed the heel, rubbed the arch, kneaded the sole, and massaged each toe, copying Radha's methodical manner. Roopa and Radha stood concealed in the doorway, beaming at each other.

The weekly leather-working lessons continued for the next three years. Omprakash was taught how to pack the skins with salt to cure them. He collected the fruit of the myrobalan tree to make tannin solution. He learned to prepare dyes, and how to impress the dye in the leather. This was the filthiest task of them all, and it made him retch.

The ordeal ended when he was eight. He was sent to his uncle Ishvar for exposure to a wider range of sewing skills at Muzaffar Tailoring Company. Besides, the school in town now accepted everyone, high caste or low, while the village school continued to be restricted.

———

Radha and Narayan were not as desolate as Roopa and Dukhi had been when their sons had left to apprentice with Ashraf Chacha. A new road and bus service had shrunk the gap between village and town. They could look forward to frequent visits from Omprakash; besides, they had their two little daughters at home.

Still, Radha felt unjustly deprived of her son's presence. A popular song about a bird that was the singer's constant companion, but which for some inexplicable reason had decided to fly away, became Radha's favourite. She ran to their new Murphy transistor and turned up the volume, shushing everyone when the familiar introduction trickled forth. When her son was home, the song meant nothing to her.

Omprakash's sisters resented his visits. No one paid attention to Leela and Rekha if their brother was in the house. It started as soon as he stepped in the door.

'Look at my child! How thin he has become!' complained Radha. 'Is your uncle feeding you or not?'

'He looks thin because he has grown taller,' was Narayan's explanation.

But she used the excuse to lavish on him special treats like cream, dry fruits, and sweetmeats, bursting with pleasure while he ate. Now and then her fingers swooped into his plate, scooped up a morsel and tenderly transported it to his mouth. No meal was complete unless she had fed him something with her own hands.

Roopa, too, relished the sight of her lunching, munching grandson. She sat like a referee, reaching to wipe away a crumb from the corner of his mouth, refilling his plate, pushing a glass of lussi within his reach. A smile appeared on her wrinkled face, and the sharp light of her memory flickered over those pitch-dark nights from many years ago when she would creep out into enemy territory to gather treats for Ishvar and Narayan.

Omprakash's sisters were silent spectators at the mealtime ritual. Leela and Rekha watched enviously, knowing better than to protest or plead with the adults. During rare moments when no one was around, Omprakash shared the delicacies with them. More often, though, the two girls wept quietly in their beds at night.

Narayan sat on the porch at dusk with his father's aged feet in his lap, massaging the cracked, tired soles. Omprakash, fourteen now, was expected home tomorrow on a week-long visit.

'Ah!' sighed Dukhi with pleasure, then asked if he had checked on the newborn calf.

There was no answer. He repeated his question, nudging Narayan's chest with the big toe. 'Son? Are you listening?'

'Yes Bapa, I was just thinking.' He resumed the massage, staring into the dusk. His fingers worked with extra vigour to make up for his silence.

'What is it, what's bothering you?'

'I was just thinking that . . . thinking how nothing changes. Years pass, and nothing changes.'

Dukhi sighed again but not with pleasure. 'How can you say that? So much has changed. Your life, my life. Your occupation, from leather to cloth. And look at your house, your –'

'Those things, yes. But what about the more important things? Government passes new laws, says no more untouchability, yet everything is the same. The upper-caste bastards still treat us worse than animals.'

'Those kinds of things take time to change.'

'More than twenty years have passed since independence. How much longer? I want to be able to drink from the village well, worship in the temple, walk where I like.'

Dukhi withdrew his foot from Narayan's lap and sat up. He was remembering his own defiance of the caste system, when he had sent his little sons to Ashraf. He felt pride at Narayan's words, but also fear.

'Son, those are dangerous things to want. You changed from Chamaar to tailor. Be satisfied with that.'

Narayan shook his head. 'That was your victory.'

He resumed massaging his father's feet while the dusk deepened around them. Inside, Radha was lost in happy preparations for her son's arrival the next day. By and by, she brought a lamp to the porch. Within seconds it attracted a cluster of midges. Then a brown moth arrived to keep its assignation with the light. Dukhi watched it try to beat its fragile wings through the lamp glass.

That week, parliamentary elections were being conducted, and the district was under siege by politicians, sloganeers, and sycophants. As usual, the assortment of political parties and their campaigning antics assured lively entertainment for the village.

Some people complained that it was difficult to enjoy it all properly, with the air hot enough to sear the lungs – the government should have waited for the rains to come first. Narayan and Dukhi attended the rallies with their friends, taking Omprakash along to see the fun. Roopa and Radha resented the time stolen from the boy's brief visit.

The speeches were crammed with promises of every shape and size: promises of new schools, clean water, and health care; promises of land for landless peasants, through redistribution and stricter enforcement of the Land Ceiling Act; promises of powerful laws to punish any discrimination against, and harassment of, backward castes by upper castes; promises to abolish bonded labour, child labour, sati, dowry system, child marriage.

'There must be a lot of duplication in our country's laws,' said Dukhi. 'Every time there are elections, they talk of passing the same ones passed twenty years ago. Someone should remind them they need to apply the laws.'

'For politicians, passing laws is like passing water,' said Narayan. 'It all ends down the drain.'

On election day the eligible voters in the village lined up outside the polling station. As usual, Thakur Dharamsi took charge of the voting process. His system, with the support of the other landlords, had been working flawlessly for years.

The election officer was presented with gifts and led away to enjoy the day with food and drink. The doors opened and the voters filed through. 'Put out your fingers,' said the attendant monitoring the queue.

The voters complied. The clerk at the desk uncapped a little bottle and marked each extended finger with indelible black ink, to prevent cheating.

'Now put your thumbprints over here,' said the clerk.

They placed their thumbprints on the register to say they had voted, and departed.

Then the blank ballots were filled in by the landlords' men. The election officer returned at closing time to supervise the removal of ballot boxes to the counting station, and to testify that voting had proceeded in a fair and democratic manner.

Sometimes, there was more excitement if rival landlords in the district were unable to sort out their differences and ended up supporting opposing candidates. Then their gangs battled it out. Naturally, whoever captured the most polling booths and stuffed the most ballot boxes got their candidate elected.

This year, however, there were no fights or gun battles. All in all, it was a dreary day, and Omprakash was depressed as he returned home with his father and grandfather. Tomorrow he had to go back to Muzaffar Tailoring Company. The week had passed much too quickly.

They sat on the charpoy outside the house to enjoy the evening air while Omprakash fetched water for them. The trees were loud with frantic birdsong. 'Next time there is an election, I want to mark my own ballot,' said Narayan.

'They won't let you,' said Dukhi 'And why bother? You think it will change anything? Your gesture will be a bucket falling in a well deeper than centuries. The splash won't be seen or heard.'

'It is still my right. And I will exercise it in the next election, I promise you.'

'Lately you are brooding too much about rights. Give up this dangerous habit.' Dukhi paused, brushing away a column of red ants marching towards the foot of the charpoy. The creatures scurried in all directions. 'Suppose you do make the mark yourself. You think they cannot open the box and destroy the votes they don't like?'

'They cannot. The election officer must account for every piece of paper.'

'Give up this idea. It is wasting your time – and your time is your life.'

'Life without dignity is worthless.'

The red ants had regrouped, though it was too dark for Dukhi to see. Radha brought the lamp out to the dusk-devoured porch, instantly populating it with shadows. The fragrance of wood smoke clung to her clothes. She lingered for a moment in the silence, searching her husband's face.

'Government has no sense,' the people complained about the state assembly elections. 'No sense at all. It's the wrong month – with the earth parched and the air on fire, who has time to think about voting? Two years ago they made the same mistake.'

Narayan had not forgotten his promise to his father two years ago. He went off alone to vote that morning. The turnout was poor. A ragged queue meandered by the door of the schoolhouse set up as the polling station. Inside, the smell of chalk dust and stale food made him remember the day when he was a small boy, when he and Ishvar had been beaten by the teacher for touching the slates and books of upper-caste children.

He swallowed his fear and asked for his ballot. 'No, that's okay,' explained the men at the table. 'Just make your thumbprint here, we will do the rest.'

'Thumbprint? I will sign my full name. After you give me my ballot.'

Two men in line behind Narayan were inspired by him. 'Yes, give us our ballots,' they said. 'We also want to make our mark.'

'We cannot do that, we don't have instructions.'

'You don't need instructions. It is our right as voters.'

The attendants whispered among themselves, then said, 'Okay, please wait.' One of them left the polling station.

He returned shortly with a dozen men. Thakur Dharamsi, who, sixteen years ago, had ordered the musicians not to play at Narayan's wedding, was with them. 'What is it, what's the trouble?' he asked loudly from outside.

They pointed at Narayan through the door.

'So,' muttered Thakur Dharamsi. 'I should have known. And who are the other two?'

His assistant did not know their names.

'It doesn't matter,' said Thakur Dharamsi. His men entered with him, and it became very crowded inside. He wiped his brow and held out the wet hand under Narayan's nose. 'On such a hot day you make me leave my house to sweat. Are you trying to humiliate me? Don't you have some clothes to sew? Or a cow to poison and skin?'

'We'll go as soon as we mark our ballots,' said Narayan. 'It is our right.'

Thakur Dharamsi laughed, and his men joined in approvingly. They stopped when he stopped. 'Enough jokes. Make your thumbprint and go.'

'After we vote.'

This time he did not laugh, but raised his hand as though in farewell and left the booth. The men seized Narayan and the other two. They forced their thumbs to the ink pad and completed the registration. Thakur

Dharamsi whispered to his assistant to take the three to his farm.

Throughout the day, at intervals, they were flogged as they hung naked by their ankles from the branches of a banyan tree. Drifting in and out of consciousness, their screams grew faint. Thakur Dharamsi's little grandchildren were kept indoors. 'Do your lessons,' he told them. 'Read your books, or play with your toys. The nice new train set I bought you.'

'But it's a holiday,' they pleaded. 'We want to play outside.'

'Not today. Some bad men are outside.' He shooed them away from the rear windows.

In the distance, in the far field, his men urinated on the three inverted faces. Semiconscious, the parched mouths were grateful for the moisture, licking the trickle with feeble urgency. Thakur Dharamsi warned his employees that for the time being the news should not spread, especially not in the downstream settlement. That might disrupt the voting and force the election commission to countermand the results, wasting weeks of work.

In the evening, after the ballot boxes were taken away, burning coals were held to the three men's genitals, then stuffed into their mouths. Their screams were heard through the village until their lips and tongues melted away. The still, silent bodies were taken down from the tree. When they began to stir, the ropes were transferred from their ankles to their necks, and the three were hanged. The bodies were displayed in the village square.

Thakur Dharamsi's goondas, freed now from their election duties, were turned loose upon the lower castes. 'I want those achhoot jatis to learn a lesson,' he said, distributing liquor to his men before their next assignment. 'I want it to be like the old days, when there was respect and discipline and order in our society. And keep an eye on that Chamaar-tailor's house, make sure no one gets away.'

The goondas began working their way towards the untouchable quarter. They beat up individuals at random in the streets, stripped some women, raped others, burned a few huts. News of the rampage soon spread. People hid, waiting for the storm to blow over.

'Good,' said Thakur Dharamsi, as night fell and reports reached him of his men's success. 'I think they will remember this for a long time.' He ordered that the bodies of the two nameless individuals should be left by the river bank, to be reclaimed by their relations. 'My heart is soft towards those two families, whoever they are,' he said. 'They have suffered enough. Let them mourn their sons and cremate them.'

That was the end of the punishment, but not for Narayan's family. 'He does not deserve a proper cremation,' said Thakur Dharamsi. 'And the father is more to blame than the son. His arrogance went against everything we hold sacred.' What the ages had put together, Dukhi had dared to break asunder; he had turned cobblers into tailors, distorting society's timeless balance. Crossing the line of caste had to be punished with the utmost severity, said the Thakur.

'Catch them all – the parents, wife, children,' he told his men. 'See that no one escapes.'

As the goondas broke into Narayan's house, Amba, Pyari, Savitri, and Padma screamed from the porch to leave their friends alone. 'Why are you harassing them? They have done nothing wrong!'

The women's families pulled them back, terrified for them. Their neighbours did not dare to even look outside, cowering in their huts in shame and fear, praying that the night would pass quickly, without the violence swallowing any more innocents. When Chhotu and Dayaram tried to sneak away for help to the district thanedar, they were chased down and knifed.

Dukhi, Roopa, Radha, and the daughters were bound and dragged into the main room. 'Two are missing,' said Thakur Dharamsi. 'Son and grandson.' Someone checked around, and informed him that they were living in town. 'Well, never mind, these five will do.'

The mutilated body was brought in and set before the captives. The room was dark. Thakur Dharamsi sent for a lamp so the family could see.

The light tore away the benevolent cloak of darkness. The naked corpse's face was a burnt and broken blur. Only by the red birthmark on his chest could they recognize Narayan.

A long howl broke from Radha. But the sound of grief soon mingled with the family's death agony; the house was set alight. The first flames licked at the bound flesh. The dry winds, furiously fanning the fire, showed the only spark of mercy during this night. The blaze swiftly enfolded all six of them.

━━━

By the time Ishvar and Omprakash heard the news in town, the ashes had cooled, and the charred bodies were broken and dispersed into the river. Mumtaz Chachi held Omprakash close to her while Ashraf Chacha accompanied Ishvar to the police station to register a First Information Report.

The sub-inspector, suffering from an earache, kept poking around inside with his little finger. He found it hard to concentrate. 'What name? Spell it again. Slowly.'

To ingratiate themselves with the figure of authority, Ashraf advised him on a home remedy, although he was seething with anger and wanted to slap the fellow across his face to make him attend. 'Warm olive oil will give you relief,' he said. 'My mother used to put it for me.'

'Really? How much? Two or three drops?'

Then, with great reluctance, the police went to the house to verify the allegations in the First Information Report. They reported that nothing was found to support charges of arson and murder.

The sub-inspector was cross with Ishvar. 'What kind of rascality is this? Trying to fill up the F.I.R. with lies? You filthy achhoot castes are always out to make trouble! Get out before we charge you with public mischief!'

Too stunned to speak, Ishvar looked at Ashraf, who tried to intervene. The sub-inspector cut him off rudely: 'This matter doesn't concern your community. We don't interfere when you Muslims and your mullahs discuss problems in your community, do we?'

For the next two days, Ashraf kept the shop closed, crushed by the helplessness he felt. Mumtaz and he did not dare console Omprakash or Ishvar – what words were there for such a loss, and for an injustice so immense? The best they could do was weep with them.

On the third day, Ishvar asked him to open up the shop, and they began sewing again.

'I will gather a small army of Chamaars, provide them with weapons, then march to the landlords' houses,' said Omprakash, his sewing-machine racing. 'It will be easy to find enough men. We'll do it like the Naxalites.' Head bent over his work, he described for Ishvar and Ashraf Chacha the strategies employed by the peasant uprisings in the northeast. 'At the end of it we'll cut off their heads and put them on spikes in the marketplace. Their kind will never dare to oppress our community again.'

Ishvar let him entertain his thoughts of revenge. His own first impulse had been the same; how could he blame his nephew? The hands were easy to divert with sewing, but the tormented mind was difficult to free from turmoil. 'Tell me, Om, how do you know so much of this?'

'I read about it in newspapers. But isn't it common sense? In every low-caste family there is someone mistreated by zamindars. They will be eager to take revenge, for sure. We'll slaughter the Thakurs and their goondas. And those police devils.'

'And afterwards, what?' asked Ishvar gently, when he felt it was time for his nephew to turn his thoughts away from death, towards life. 'They will take you to court and hang you.'

'I don't care. I would be dead anyway if I was living with my parents, instead of safely in this shop.'

'Om, my child,' said Ashraf. 'Vengeance should not be our concern. The murderers will be punished. Inshallah, in this world or the next. Maybe they already have, who knows?'

'Yes, Chachaji, who knows?' echoed Omprakash sarcastically and went to bed.

Since that terrible night six months ago, Ishvar had given up their lodging in the rooming house, at Ashraf's insistence. There was plenty of space in the house, he claimed, now that his daughters had all married and left. He partitioned the room over the shop – one side for Mumtaz and himself, the other for Ishvar and his nephew.

They heard Omprakash moving around upstairs, getting ready for bed. Mumtaz sat at the back of the house, praying. 'This revenge talk is okay if it remains talk,' said Ishvar. 'But what if he goes back to the village, does something foolish.'

They fretted and agonized for hours over the boy's future, then ascended the stairs to retire for the night. Ashraf followed Ishvar around the partition where Omprakash lay sleeping, and they stood together for a while, watching him.

'Poor child,' whispered Ashraf. 'So much he has suffered. How can we help him?'

The answer, in time, was provided by the faltering fortunes of Muzaffar Tailoring Company.

A year had passed since the murders when a ready-made clothing store opened in town. Before long, Ashraf's list of clients began to shrink.

Ishvar said the loss would be temporary. 'A big new shop with stacks of shirts to chose from – that attracts the customers. It makes them feel important, trying on different patterns. But the traitors will return when the novelty wears off and the clothes don't fit.'

Ashraf was not so optimistic. 'Those lower prices will defeat us. They make clothes by the hundreds in big factories, in the city. How can we compete?'

Soon the two tailors and apprentice were lucky to find themselves busy one day a week. 'Strange, isn't it,' said Ashraf. 'Something I've never even seen is ruining the business I have owned for forty years.'

'But you've seen the ready-made shop.'

'No, I mean the factories in the city. How big are they? Who owns them? What do they pay? None of this I know, except that they are beggaring us. Maybe I'll have to go and work for them in my old age.'

'Never,' said Ishvar. 'But perhaps I should go.'

'Nobody is going anywhere,' Ashraf's fist banged the worktable. 'We will share what there is here, I said it only as a joke. You think I would really send away my own children?'

'Don't be upset, Chachaji, I know you didn't mean it.'

Before long, however, the joke turned into a serious consideration as customers continued to flee to the ready-made store. 'If it goes on like this, the three of us will be sitting from morning till night, swatting flies,' said Ashraf. 'For me, it does not matter. I have lived my life – tasted its fruit, both sweet and bitter. But it is so unfair to Om.' He lowered his voice. 'Maybe it would be best for him to try elsewhere.'

'But wherever he goes, I would have to go,' said Ishvar. 'He is still too young, too many foolish ideas clogging his head.'

'Not his fault, the devil encourages him. Of course you have to be with him, you are now his father. What you can both do is, go for a short time. Doesn't have to be permanent. A year or two. Work hard, earn money, and come back.'

'That's true. They say you can make money very quickly in the city, there is so much work and opportunity.'

'Exactly. And with that cash you can open some kind of business here when you return. A paan shop, or a fruit stall, or toys. You can even sell ready-made clothes, who knows.' They laughed at this, but agreed that a couple of years away would be best for Omprakash.

'There is only one difficulty in the way,' said Ishvar. 'I don't know anyone in the city. How to get started?'

'Everything will fall into place. I have a very good friend who will help you find work. His name is Nawaz. He is also a tailor, has his own shop there.'

They sat up past midnight, making plans, imagining the new future in the city by the sea, the city that was filled with big buildings, wide, wonderful roads, beautiful gardens, and millions and millions of people working hard and accumulating wealth.

'Look at me, getting excited as if I was leaving with you,' said Ashraf. 'And if I was younger I would, too. It will be lonely here. My dream was that you and Om would be with me till the end of my days.'

'But we will be,' said Ishvar. 'Om and I will return soon. Isn't that the plan?'

Ashraf wrote to his friend requesting him to put up Ishvar and Omprakash when they arrived, help them settle in the city. Ishvar withdrew his savings from the post office and purchased train tickets.

The night before departure, Ashraf gifted them his treasured pair of dressmaking and pinking shears. Ishvar protested it was too much. 'Our family has already received so many kindnesses from you, for more than thirty years.'

'An eternity of kindness could not repay what you and Narayan did for my family,' said Ashraf, swallowing. 'Come on, put the shears in your trunk, make an old man happy.' He dried his eyes but they grew moist again. 'Remember, you are welcome here at any time if it does not work out.'

Ishvar clasped his hand and held it to his chest. 'Maybe you will visit the city before we come back.'

'Inshallah. I have always wanted to go on haj once before I die. And the big boats all sail from the city. So who knows?'

Mumtaz woke early the next morning to make their tea and prepare a food package for their journey. Ashraf sat silent while they ate, overcome by the moment. He spoke only once, to ask, 'You have Nawaz's address safe in your pocket?'

They drained their cups and Omprakash gathered them for washing. 'Let it be,' a tearful Mumtaz stopped him. 'I'll do it afterwards.'

It was time to leave. They hugged Ashraf and Mumtaz, kissing their cheeks three times. 'Ah, these useless old sockets of mine,' said Ashraf. 'They keep leaking, it's a sickness.'

'And we are catching it from you,' said Ishvar, as he and Omprakash wiped their own eyes. The sun had not yet risen when they picked up the trunk and bedding and walked towards the railway line.

It was night when the tailors arrived in the city. Groaning and clanking, the train pulled into the station while an announcement blared like gibberish from the loudspeakers. Passengers poured out into the sea of waiting friends and families. There were shrieks of recognition, tears of happiness. The platform became a roiling swirl of humanity. Coolies conducted aggressive forays to offer their muscular services.

Ishvar and Omprakash stood frozen on the edge of the commotion. The sense of adventure that had flowered reluctantly during the journey wilted. 'Hai Ram,' said Ishvar, wishing for a familiar face. 'What a huge crowd.'

'Come on,' said Omprakash. He took the trunk, struggling urgently against the barrier of bodies and luggage, as though assured that once they were past it, everything would be all right – the city of promise lay beyond this final obstacle.

They ploughed their way through the platform and emerged in the railway station's gigantic concourse, with its ceilings high as the sky and columns reaching up like impossible trees. They wandered around in a daze, making inquiries, asking for assistance. People fired back hurried answers to their questions, or pointed, and they nodded gratefully but learned nothing. It took them an hour to discover they needed a local train to reach Ashraf's friend. The journey took twenty minutes.

Someone they asked for directions pointed them down the right road. The shop-cum-residence was a ten-minute walk from the station. The pavements were covered with sleeping people. A thin yellow light from the streetlamps fell like tainted rain on the rag-wrapped bodies, and Omprakash shivered. 'They look like corpses,' he whispered. He gazed hard at them, searching for a sign of life – a rising chest, a quivering finger, a fluttering eyelid. But the lamplight was not sufficient for detecting minute movements.

Relief began replacing their fears as they neared the home of Ashraf Chacha's friend. The nightmare of arrival was about to end. To get to the shop they crossed the planks thrown across the open sewer. Omprakash's foot almost went through a rotten patch in the wood. Ishvar grabbed his elbow. They knocked on the door.

'Salaam alaikum,' they greeted Nawaz, gazing upon him with expressions appropriate towards a benefactor.

Nawaz barely reciprocated the greeting. He pretended to know nothing about their coming. After numerous denials he conceded there had been a letter from Ashraf, and grudgingly agreed to let them sleep under the awning behind the kitchen for a few days, till they found accommodation. 'I do this for no one but Ashraf,' he emphasized. 'The thing is, there is hardly room here for my own family.'

'Thank you, Nawazbhai,' said Ishvar. 'Yes, just for a few days, thank you.'

They could smell food cooking, but Nawaz did not invite them to eat. Finding a tap outside the building, they washed their hands and faces, and drank, cupping their palms. Light from the house spilled out through the kitchen window. They sat below it and finished the chapatis Mumtaz Chachi had packed, listening to noises from the buildings around them.

The ground under the awning was littered with leaves, potato peelings, unidentifiable fruit stones, fish bones, and two fish heads with vacant eye sockets. 'How can we sleep here?' said Omprakash. 'It's filthy.'

He looked around, and spied a besom beside Nawaz's back door, propped against the downpipe. He borrowed it to sweep the rubbish aside, while Ishvar brought mugfuls of water and splashed the ground before giving it a second going-over with the besom.

The sound brought Nawaz out to investigate. 'This place not good enough for you? No one is forcing you to stay.'

'No no, it's perfect,' said Ishvar. 'Just cleaning it a little.'

'That's my property you are using,' he pointed to the besom.

'Yes, we were –'

'The thing is, you must ask before you take something,' he snapped and went in.

They waited till it was dry under the awning, then unrolled their sleeping mats and blankets. Noise from the surrounding buildings did not abate. Radios blared. A man yelled at a woman, beating her, stopping for a bit when she screamed for help, then starting again. A drunkard shouted abuse, and there was boisterous laughter at his expense. The grind of the traffic was constant. A flickering glow at one window made Omprakash curious; he rose and peered inside. He beckoned to Ishvar to come, look. 'Doordarshan!' he whispered excitedly. After a minute or two, someone inside spotted them gazing at the television and told them to be off.

They returned to their bedding and slept badly. Once, they were awakened by shrieks that seemed to come from an animal being slaughtered.

There was no offer of morning tea from inside the house, which Omprakash found quite offensive. 'Customs are different in the city,' said Ishvar.

They washed, drank water, and waited around till Nawaz opened his shop. He saw them on the steps, craning, trying to look inside. 'Yes? What do you want?'

'Sorry to trouble you, but do you know we are also tailors?' said Ishvar. 'Can we do sewing for you? In your shop? Ashraf Chacha told us –'

'The thing is, there is not enough work,' said Nawaz, retreating within as he spoke. 'You will have to search elsewhere.'

Ishvar and Om wondered aloud on the steps outside – was this it, the full extent of Nawaz's help? But he came back in a minute with paper and pencil for them, dictating names of tailoring shops and instructions to get there. They thanked him for the advice.

'By the way,' said Ishvar, 'we heard some terrible screams last night. Do you know what happened?'

'It was those pavement-dwellers. One fellow was sleeping in someone else's spot. So they took a brick and bashed his head. Animals, that's what they all are.' He returned to his work, and the tailors left.

After stopping for tea in a stall at the street corner, the two spent a futile, frightening day locating the addresses. The street signs were missing sometimes, or obscured by political posters and advertisements. They had to stop frequently to ask storekeepers and hawkers for directions.

They tried to follow the injunction repeated on several billboards: 'Pedestrians! Walk On Pavement!' But this was difficult because of vendors who had set up shop on the concrete. So they walked on the road with the rest, terrified by the cars and buses, marvelling at the crowds who negotiated the traffic nimbly, with an instinct for skipping out of the way when the situation demanded.

'Just takes practice,' said Om with an experienced air.

'Practice at what? Killing or getting killed? Don't act smart, you'll get run over.'

But the only mishap they witnessed that day involved a man's handcart; the rope securing a stack of boxes snapped, scattering the goods. They helped him to reload the cart.

'What's in them?' asked Om, curious about the rattling.

'Bones,' said the man.

'Bones? From cows and buffaloes?'

'From people like you and me. For export. It's a very big business.'

They were glad when the cart rolled away. 'If I knew what was inside, I would never have stopped to help,' said Ishvar.

By evening, the addresses on the list had been exhausted, yielding neither work nor hope. They tried to make their way back to Nawaz's shop. Though they had walked this route in the morning, nothing seemed familiar now. Or everything looked the same. Either way it was confusing. Approaching darkness made it worse. The cinema billboards they had hoped to use as landmarks led them astray because all of a sudden there seemed to be so many of them. Was it a right turn or left at the *Bobby* advertisement? Was it the lane with the poster of Amitabh Bachchan facing a hail of bullets while kicking a machine-gun-wielding villain in the face, or the one with him flashing a hero-type smile at a demure, rustic maiden?

Famished and tired, they at last found Nawaz's street, and debated whether to buy food before returning to the awning. 'Better not,' decided Ishvar. 'Nawaz and his bibi will be insulted if they are expecting us to eat with them today. Maybe last night they were just unprepared.'

Their host was at his sewing-machine as they passed the shop. They waved but he didn't appear to notice, and they went round to the back. 'I am finished,' said Omprakash, unrolling the bedding and letting himself drop.

Lying on their backs, they listened to Nawaz's wife working in the kitchen. A tap was running, glasses rattled, and something clanged. Presently they heard his voice calling 'Miriam!' She left the kitchen, and her words were too soft for them to hear. Then from the front came his loud, surly tone again, 'No need for all that, I told you already.'

'But it's just a little tea,' said Miriam. Now husband and wife were both in the kitchen.

'Haramzadi! Don't argue with me! No means no!' They heard the sharp sound of a slap, and Omprakash flinched. A cry escaped her lips. 'Let them go to a restaurant! The thing is, you pamper them and they'll never leave!'

Miriam's sobs prevented them outside from picking up what she said, except for fragments: 'But why . . .' and then '. . . Ashraf's family . . .'

'Not my family,' he spat.

The tailors left the awning and went to the stall where they had stopped for morning tea. After devouring a plate of puri-bhaji, Omprakash said, 'What I wonder is, how Ashraf Chacha can have someone so horrible for his friend.'

'All people are not the same. Besides, Nawaz's years in the city must have altered him. Places can change people, you know. For better or worse.'

'Maybe. But Ashraf Chacha would be ashamed to hear him now. If only we had somewhere else to stay.'

'Patience, Om. This is our first day. We'll find something soon.'

But in four weeks of searching, they obtained a mere three days of work, at a place called Advanced Tailoring. The proprietor, a man named Jeevan, hired them to meet a deadline. The work was very simple: dhotis and shirts, a hundred of each.

'Who needs so many?' asked Omprakash in amazement.

Jeevan strummed his pursed lips with one finger, as though checking the instrument for tuning. He did this whenever he was about to make what he thought was a significant utterance. 'Don't repeat it to anyone – the clothes are for bribes.' Ordered by someone running in a by-election, he explained. The candidate was going to distribute them to certain important people in his constituency.

There was room for only one tailor in Advanced Tailoring, but Jeevan had props in the back that quickly converted the place into a workshop for three. At a height of four feet from the floor, he arranged planks horizontally on brackets in the walls, making a temporary loft. The planks were supported below with bamboo poles. Then he rented two sewing-machines, hoisted them into the loft, and sent Ishvar and Om up after them.

They settled gingerly on their stools. 'Don't be scared,' said Jeevan, strumming his lips. 'Nothing will happen to you, I have done this many times before. Look, I am working under you – if you collapse, I also get crushed.'

The structure was shaky, and trembled heavily when the treadles worked. Traffic passing in the street made Ishvar and Om jiggle up and down on the stools. If a door slammed somewhere in the building, their scissors rattled. But they soon got used to the unsteadiness of their existence.

Returning to solid earth after working twenty hours a day for three days, they found the absence of vibrations quite strange. They thanked Jeevan, helped him dismantle the loft, and returned exhausted to their awning.

'Now for some rest,' said Omprakash. 'I want to sleep the whole day.'

Nawaz came repeatedly to register his disapproval while they lay recovering. He posed in the back door, looking disgusted, or muttering to Miriam about useless, lazy people. 'The thing is, work only comes to those who genuinely want it,' he preached. 'These two are wasters.'

Ishvar and Omprakash were too tired to feel indignation, let alone anything stronger. After their day of recuperation, it was back to the routine: asking for directions in the morning and searching for work until evening.

'God knows how much longer we have to suffer those two,' the complaint emerged through the kitchen window. Nawaz did not trouble to lower his voice. 'I told you to refuse Ashraf. But did you listen?'

'They do not bother us,' she whispered. 'They only –'

'Careful, that one hurts, you'll cut my toe!'

Ishvar and Omprakash exchanged questioning looks while Nawaz continued his harangue. 'The thing is, if I wanted people living under my back awning, I would rent it for good money. You know how dangerous it is, keeping them for so long? All they have to do is file a claim for the space, and we'd be stuck in court for – aah! Haramzadi, I said be careful! You'll make a cripple out of me, slashing away with your blade!'

The tailors sat up, startled. 'I have to see what's going on,' whispered Omprakash.

He stretched up on tiptoe and peered through the kitchen window. Nawaz was seated on a chair, his foot upon a low stool. Miriam knelt before it with a safety razor blade, slicing away slivers of tough skin from his corns and calluses.

Omprakash lowered himself from the window and described the sight for his uncle. They chuckled a long time about it. 'What I am wondering is, how that chootia gets corns if he sits at his sewing-machine all day,' said Omprakash.

'Maybe he walks a lot in his dreams,' said Ishvar.

Roughly four months after the tailors' arrival, Nawaz began scolding them one morning when they asked him for advice. 'Every day you pester me while I am working. This is a very big city. You think I know the names of all the tailors in it? Go search for yourself. And if you cannot find tailoring, try other things. Be a coolie at the railway station. Use your heads, carry wheat and rice for ration-shop customers. Do something, anything.'

Omprakash could see his uncle discomposed by the outburst, so he was quick to retort. 'We wouldn't mind that at all. But it would be an insult to Ashraf Chacha who trained us for so many years and gave us his skills.'

Nawaz was embarrassed by the reminder of that name. 'The thing is, I am very busy right now,' he mumbled. 'Please go.'

In the street, Ishvar patted his nephew's back. 'Sabaash, Om. That was a first-class reply you gave him.'

'The thing is,' mimicked Omprakash, 'the thing is, I am such a first-class fellow.' They laughed and toasted their tiny victory with half-glasses of tea at the street corner. The celebration was short-lived, however, extinguished by the reality of their dwindling savings. Out of desperation Ishvar took up work for a fortnight in a cobbler's shop that specialized in custom-made shoes and sandals. His job was to prepare the leather for soles and heels. To induce the hardness required in this type of leather, the shop used vegetable tanning. He was familiar with the process from his village days.

They kept the job a secret, for Ishvar was much ashamed of it. The reek from his hands was strong, and he preserved his distance from Nawaz.

Another month passed, their sixth in the city, with their prospects bleak as ever, when Nawaz opened the back door one evening and said, 'Come in, come in. Have some tea with me. Miriam! Three teas!'

They approached and put their heads around the doorway. Had they heard him correctly, they wondered?

'Don't stand there – come, sit,' he said cheerfully. 'There is good news. The thing is, I have work for you.'

'Oh, thank you!' said Ishvar, instantly bursting with gratitude. 'That's the best news! You won't be sorry, we will sew beautifully for your customers –'

'Not in my shop,' Nawaz rudely snuffed out the exuberance. 'It's somewhere else.' He tried to be pleasant again, smiling and continuing. 'You will enjoy this job, believe me. Let me tell you more about it. Miriam! Three teas, I said! Where are you?'

She entered with three glasses. Ishvar and Omprakash stood up, joining their palms: 'Salaam, bibi.' They had heard her gentle silvery voice often, but it was the first time they found themselves face to face with her. In a manner of speaking, that is, for a black burkha hid her countenance. Her eyes, caged behind the two lace-covered openings, were sparkling.

'Ah, good, tea is ready at last,' said Nawaz. He pointed out the spot where he wanted the glasses set down, then waved his hand at her in a curt dismissal.

After a few sips he got back to business. 'A rich Parsi lady came here this afternoon while you were out. Her shoe fell in the gutter.' He snickered. 'The thing is, she has a very big export company, and is looking for two good tailors. Her name is Dina Dalal and she left her address for you.' He drew it out of his shirt pocket.

'Did she say what kind of sewing?'

'Top quality, latest fashions. But easy to do – she said paper patterns will be provided.' He watched them anxiously. 'You will go, won't you?'

'Yes, of course,' said Ishvar.

'Good, good. The thing is, she said she was handing out these slips at many shops. So lots of tailors will be applying.' On the back of the paper he wrote down directions and the train station where they should get off. 'Now don't get lost on your way there. Go to sleep early tonight, wake up early in the morning. Nice and fresh, clear-headed, so you can win the job from the lady.'

Like a mother bustling her charges on the first day of school, Nawaz opened the back door at dawn and roused them by shaking their shoulders, presenting a big smile to their reluctant eyelids. 'You don't want to be late. Please come in for tea after washing and gargling. Miriam! Two teas for my friends!'

He murmured encouragement, advice, caution while they drank. 'The thing is, you have to impress the lady. But it must not sound like big talk. Answer all her questions politely, and never interrupt her. Don't scratch your head or any other part – fine women like her hate that habit. Speak with confidence, in a medium voice. And take a comb with you, make sure you look neat and tidy before you ring her doorbell. Bad hair makes a very bad impression.'

They listened eagerly, Omprakash making a mental note to buy a new pocket-comb; he had broken his, last week. When the tea was drunk Nawaz sped them on their way. 'Khuda hafiz, and come back soon. Come back successful.'

They returned after three o'clock, explaining sheepishly to an anxious Nawaz that though they had got there on time, finding the train station for the return journey had been difficult.

'But that would be the same station you got off at in the morning.'

'I know,' Ishvar smiled embarrassedly. 'I just cannot tell what happened. The place was so far, we had never been there before, and we –'

'Never mind,' said Nawaz, magnanimous. 'A new destination always seems further away than it really is.'

'Every street looks the same. Even when you ask people, the directions are confusing. Even that nice college boy we met on the train had the same problem.'

'You be careful who you talk to. This is not your village. Nice boy could steal your money, cut your throat and throw you in the gutter.'

'Yes, but he was very kind, he even shared his watermelon sherbet with us and –'

'The thing is, did you get the work?'

'Oh yes, we start from Monday,' said Ishvar.

'That's wonderful. Many, many congratulations and felicitations. Come inside, sit with me, you must be tired. Miriam! Three teas!'

'You are too generous,' said Omprakash. 'Just like Ashraf Chacha.'

The sarcasm was lost on Nawaz. 'Oh, it's my responsibility to help Ashraf's friends. And now that you have found jobs, my next duty is to find you a place to stay.'

'No rush, Nawazbhai,' said Ishvar, mildly alarmed. 'We are happy where we are, your awning is beautiful, very comfortable.'

'Just leave it to me. The thing is, it's almost impossible in this city to find a house. When something becomes available you must grab it. Come on, finish your tea, let's go.'

'Last stop!' called the conductor, clanging his ticket punch against the chrome railing. The bus skirted the gloomy slum lanes, groaned as it turned the corner, and stopped.

'This one is the new colony,' said Nawaz, indicating the field which was in the process of being annexed by the slum. 'Let's find the man in charge.'

They entered between two rows of shacks, and Nawaz asked someone if Navalkar was around. The woman pointed. They found him in a shack that was his office.

'Yes,' said Navalkar, 'we still have a few places for rent.' His straggly moustache fluttered with studied exaggeration in front of his mouth when he spoke. 'Let me show you.'

They returned through the two rows of shacks. 'This corner house,' said Navalkar. 'It's vacant, if you want it. Come, look inside.'

As he opened the door of the shack, a pariah dog departed through a hole in the back. The mud floor was partially covered with planks. 'You can put more pieces of wood if you like,' suggested Navalkar. The walls were a patchwork, part plywood and part sheet metal. The roof was old corrugated iron, waterproofed in corroded areas with transparent plastic.

'The tap is out there, in the middle of the lane. Most convenient. You won't have to go far for water, like they do in other inferior colonies. This is a nice place.' He swept his arm around to take in the field. 'Newly developed, not too crowded. The rent is one hundred rupees per month. In advance.'

Nawaz tapped the walls with his fingers like a doctor examining a chest, then stamped his foot on a floor plank, making it wobble. He made an approving face. 'Well built,' he whispered to the tailors.

Navalkar gave a circular nod. 'We have even better huts. You want to see?'

'No harm in looking,' said Nawaz.

They were led behind the rows of tin-and-plastic jhopadpattis to a set of eight brick-walled huts. The roofs once again were of rusted corrugated metal. 'These are two hundred and fifty rupees per month. But for that money you get a pukka floor, and electric light.' He pointed to the poles that fed wires to the huts, pirated from the street-lighting supply.

Inside, Nawaz inspected the bare bricks and scratched one with his thumb nail. 'Very good quality,' he said. 'You want to know what I think? For the first month, take the cheaper house. Then if your job goes well and you can afford it, move to this one.'

Navalkar kept up his circular nodding. The tailors' silence made Nawaz uneasy. 'What's the matter, you don't like it?'

'No no, it's very nice. But money is the problem.'

'Money is a problem for everyone,' said Navalkar. 'Unless you are a politician or a blackmarketeer.'

When the forced laughter concluded, Ishvar said, 'The advance rent is difficult.'

'Don't you have even a hundred rupees?' asked Nawaz disbelievingly.

'It's because of the tailoring lady. She told us we must bring our own sewing-machines. And we have just enough for the rental deposit. These last few months without work, we have been spending and –'

'You useless people!' Nawaz spat, seeing his plan to be rid of them begin to disintegrate. 'Wasting your money!'

'If we can stay with you a little longer,' pleaded Ishvar, 'we could save enough –'

'You think this house is going to wait for you?' he snarled, and Navalkar shook his head on cue.

Desperate, Nawaz turned to him. 'Can you make an exception, Mr. Navalkar? Twenty-five rupees today, which I will pay. And twenty-five from the tailors each week, for the rest.'

Navalkar curled his lips, gnawing at the moustache with his lower incisors. He brushed back the wet hairs with his knuckles. 'For your sake only. Because I trust you.'

Nawaz counted out the money before any minds could be changed. They returned to the first shack, where Navalkar put a lock on the plywood door and gave the key to Ishvar. 'Your house now. Live well.'

They picked their way through the cracked earth of the field and waited at the bus stop. The tailors looked worried. 'My congratulations and felicitations to you again,' said Nawaz. 'In one day you have found jobs and a new house.'

'Only with your help,' said Ishvar. 'Is Navalkar the landlord?'

Nawaz laughed. 'Navalkar is a little crook working for a big crook. A slumlord called Thokray, who controls everything in this area – country liquor, hashish, bhung. And when there are riots, he decides who gets burned and who survives.'

Seeing the apprehension on Ishvar's face, he added, 'You don't have to deal with him. Just pay your rent regularly, you will be all right.'

'But then, whose land is this?'

'No one's. The city owns it. These fellows bribe the municipality, police, water inspector, electricity officer. And they rent to people like you. No harm in it. Empty land sitting useless – if homeless people can live there, what's wrong?'

On this last night, Nawaz's relief spurred him to greater generosity. 'Please eat with me,' he invited them in. 'Honour me at least once before you go. Miriam! Three dinners!'

He inquired if they were happy under the back awning. 'If you prefer, you can sleep indoors. The thing is, that's where I was going to put you anyway, when you first arrived. But I thought to myself, the house is so cramped and crowded, better outside in the fresh air.'

'Yes yes, much better,' said Ishvar. 'We have to thank you for your kindness for six months.'

'Has it really been that long? How fast the time has flown.'

Miriam brought the food to the table and left. Even obscured by the burkha, Ishvar and Omprakash had been able to see her eyes cloud with embarrassment at her husband's hypocrisy.

iv Small Obstacles

MIRROR, RAZOR, SHAVING BRUSH, plastic cup, loata, copper water pot –
Ishvar arranged them on an upturned cardboard carton in one corner of
the shack. Trunk and bedding took up most of the remaining space. He
hung their clothes from rusted nails protruding through the plywood
walls. 'So everything fits nicely. We have jobs, we have a house, and
soon we'll find a wife for you.'

Om did not smile. 'I hate this place,' he said.

'You want to go back to Nawaz and his awning?'

'No. I want to go back to Ashraf Chacha and his shop.'

'Poor Ashraf Chacha – deserted by his customers.' Ishvar picked up
the copper pot and moved to the door.

'I'll get the water,' offered Om.

He went to the tap in the lane where a grey-haired woman watched
him fumble with the handle to start the flow. Nothing happened. He
kicked the standpipe and rattled the spout, shaking out a few drops.

'Don't you know?' the woman called. 'It only runs in the morning.'

Om turned to see who was speaking. She was standing very short in
her darkened doorway. 'Water only comes in the morning,' she repeated.

'No one told me.'

'Are you a child that you must be told everything?' she scolded, stepping out of her shack. Now he could see she was not short, just badly
stooped. 'Can't you use your own intelligence?'

He tried to decide which would best demonstrate his intelligence:
retorting or walking away. 'Come,' she said, and retreated within. He
glanced in the doorway. She spoke again from the darkness, 'Are you
planning to wait by the tap till dawn?'

Opening the lid of a round-bottomed earthen matka, she transferred
two glassfuls into his copper pot. 'Remember, you have to fill up early.
Wake up late, and you go thirsty. Like the sun and moon, water waits
for no one.'

A long queue had formed at the tap in the morning when the tailors
emerged with toothbrushes and soap to await their turn. From the next

shack a man came out smiling, blocking their way. He was bare above the waist, and his hair hung to his shoulders. 'Namaskaar,' he greeted them. 'But you cannot go like that.'

'Why not?'

'If you stand at the tap, brushing your teeth, soaping and scrubbing and washing, you'll start a big fight. People want to fill up before the water goes.'

'But what to do?' said Ishvar. 'We don't have a bucket.'

'No bucket? That's only a small obstacle.' Their neighbour disappeared inside, and came back with a galvanized pail. 'Use this till you get one.'

'What about you?'

'I have another – one bucketful is enough for me.' He gathered his hair in a tail and tugged it before spreading it out again. 'Now. What else do you need? A small can or something, for toilet?'

'We have a loata,' said Ishvar. 'But where should we go?'

'Come with me, it's not far.' They collected their water, deposited the heavy pail in their shack, then walked towards the railway lines beyond the field with their loata. The water in it sloshed a little as they scrambled over mounds of concrete rubble and broken glass. A foul-smelling stream, greyish yellow, trickled through the mounds, carrying a variety of floating waste in its torpid flux.

'Come to the right side,' he said. 'The left side is for ladies only.' They followed, glad to have a guide; it would have been awkward to have blundered. Women's voices, mothers coaxing their children, rose from that direction, along with the stench. Further down, men were squatting on the tracks or by the ditch to the side, near the prickly scrub and nettles, their backs to the railroad. The ditch was a continuum of the roadside sewer where the hutment colony pitched its garbage.

Past the crouching men, the three found a suitable spot. 'The steel rail is very useful,' said their neighbour. 'Works just like a platform. Puts you higher than the ground, and the shit doesn't tickle your behind when it piles up.'

'You know all the tricks, for sure,' said Om, as they undid their pants and assumed their positions on the rail.

'Takes very little time to learn.' He indicated the men in the scrub. 'Now squatting there can be dangerous. Poisonous centipedes crawl about in there. I wouldn't expose my tender parts to them. Also, if you lose your balance in those bushes, you end up with an arseful of thorns.'

'Are you speaking from experience?' asked Om, teetering on the rail with laughter.

'Yes – the experience of others. Careful with your loata,' he cautioned. 'If you spill the water you'll have to go back with a sticky bum.'

Ishvar wished the fellow would be quiet for a minute. He did not find the jocularity helpful to the task, especially when his bowels were reacting disagreeably to the communal toilet. It had been decades since he used to go outdoors, as a child. With his father, in the morning's half-darkness, he remembered. When the birds were loud and the village was quiet. And afterwards, washing in the river. But the years with Ashraf Chacha taught him big-town ways, made him forget the village ways.

'Only one problem with squatting on the rail,' said their long-haired neighbour. 'You have to get up when the train comes, whether you have finished or not. Railway has no respect for our open-air sundaas.'

'Now you tell us!' Ishvar craned his neck in both directions, searching up and down the track.

'Relax, relax. There's no train for at least ten minutes. And you can always jump off if you hear a rumbling.'

'That's very good advice, as long as one isn't deaf,' said Ishvar peevishly. 'And what's your name?'

'Rajaram.'

'We're very lucky to have you for our guru,' said Om.

'Yes, I'm your Goo Guru,' he chortled.

Ishvar was not amused, but Om roared with laughter. 'Tell me, O great Goo Guruji, do you recommend that we buy a railway timetable, if we are to squat on the tracks every morning?'

'No need for that, my obedient disciple. In a few days your gut will learn the train timings better than the stationmaster.'

The next train was not heard till they had finished, washed, and buttoned their pants. Ishvar decided he would sneak out tomorrow morning before Rajaram awoke. He did not want to squat next to this philosopher of defecation.

Along the line, men and women abandoned the tracks and waited by the ditch for the locomotive interruption to pass; the ones in the bushes stayed put. Rajaram pointed at a train compartment as it glided slowly in front of them.

'Look at those bastards,' he shouted. 'Staring at people shitting, as if they themselves are without bowels. As if a turd emerging from an arsehole is a circus performance.' He flung obscene gestures at the passengers, making some of them turn away. One observer took exception and spat from his window seat, but a favourable wind returned it trainward.

'I wish I could bend over, point, and shoot it like a rocket in their faces,' said Rajaram. 'Make them eat it, since they are so interested in it.'

He shook his head as they walked back to their shacks. 'That kind of shameless behaviour makes me very angry.'

'My grandfather's friend, Dayaram,' said Om, 'he was forced to eat a landlord's shit once, because he was late ploughing his field.'

Rajaram emptied the last drops of water from his can into his palm and slicked back his hair. 'Did that Dayaram develop any magic power afterwards?'

'No, why?'

'I've heard of a caste of sorcerers. They eat human shit, it gives them their black powers.'

'Really?' said Om. 'Then we could start a business – collect all these lumps from the track, package them and sell to that caste. Ready-made lunches, teatime snacks, hot and steaming.' Rajaram and he laughed, but Ishvar strode ahead, disgusted, pretending he hadn't heard.

Om returned to the tap for another bucketful. The line had grown considerably. A few places ahead he saw a girl with a big brass pot balanced against her hip. When she raised her arms to lift it to her head, his eyes were drawn to the swell of her blouse. The weight thrust a fine sharpness into her hips as she passed. Water overbrimmed the pot and sloshed, trickling down her forehead. Glistening drops hung in her hair and eyelashes. Like morning dew, thought Om. Oh, she was lovely. For the rest of the day he felt he would burst with longing and happiness.

By the time the tap went dry, the hutment colony had finished its morning ablutions, leaving the ground charted with little rivulets of foam and froth. As the day wore on, the earth and sun readily swallowed it all. The smell from the railroad-latrine endured longer. The capricious breeze escorted the stench for hours into the shacks before changing direction.

Late in the evening, Rajaram was cooking on a Primus stove outside his door as the tailors returned from exploring the area around the slum. They heard the oil hissing in the frying pan. 'Have you eaten?' he asked.

'At the station.'

'That can be expensive. Get a ration card as soon as possible, cook your own food.'

'We don't even have a stove.'

'That's only a small obstacle. You can borrow mine.' He told them about a woman in the colony who hawked vegetables and fruit in residential neighbourhoods. 'If something remains in her basket at the end of the day – a few tomatoes, peas, brinjal – she sells it cheaply. You should buy from her, like me.'

'Good idea,' said Ishvar.

'Only one thing she won't sell you – bananas.'

Om snickered, expecting a juicy punch line, but there wasn't one. The monkey-man in the colony had a standing agreement with the woman. Her blackened or damaged bananas went to his two main performers. 'The poor dog has to find his own food, though,' said Rajaram.

'Which dog?'

'Monkey-man's dog. He's part of the act – the monkeys ride him. But he is always in the garbage, looking for food. Monkey-man can't afford to feed them all.' The Primus sputtered twice; he pumped it up and stirred the pan. 'Some people say Monkey-man does dirty, unnatural things with the monkeys. I don't believe it. But even if he does, so what? We all need comfort, no? Monkey, prostitute, or your own hand   what difference? Not everyone can have wives.'

He poked the sizzling vegetables to check if they were done, then extinguished the stove and spooned out a helping on a plastic plate for the tailors.

'No, we ate at the station, really.'

'Don't insult me – have one bite at least.'

They accepted the plate. A man with a harmonium slung from his neck overheard them while passing. 'Smells good,' he said. 'Save one bite for me also.'

'Yes, sure, come on.' But the man squeezed out a chord, waved, and continued on his way.

'Have you met him? Lives in the second row.' Rajaram stirred the pan and helped himself. 'He begins work in the evening. Says people are more generous if he sings when they are eating or relaxing. Have some more?'

Their refusal was final this time. Rajaram finished what remained. 'It's very nice for me that you are renting this house. On the other side of me,' he said, lowering to a whisper, 'lives a useless fellow – drunk all the time. Beats his wife and his five-six children if they don't bring back enough from begging.'

They looked at the shack, where all was quiet at present. The children were not in evidence. 'Sleeping it off. To start again tomorrow. And she must be on the streets with the little ones.'

The tailors sat with their neighbour for the rest of the evening, talking about their village, about Muzaffar Tailoring Company, and about the job they were starting on Monday with Dina Dalal. Rajaram nodded at the familiar story. 'Yes, thousands and thousands are coming to the city because of bad times in their native place. I came for the same reason.'

'But we don't want to stay too long.'

'Nobody does,' said Rajaram. 'Who wants to live like this?' His hand moved in a tired semicircle, taking in the squalid hutments, the ragged field, the huge slum across the road wearing its malodorous crown of cooking smoke and industrial effluvium. 'But sometimes people have no choice. Sometimes the city grabs you, sinks its claws into you, and refuses to let go.'

'Not us, for sure. We are here to make some money and hurry back,' said Om.

Ishvar did not want to discuss their plans, fearing contamination by doubts. 'What's your trade?' he asked, changing the subject.

'Barber. But I gave it up some time ago. Got fed up with complaining customers. Too short, too long, puff not big enough, sideburns not wide enough, this, that. Every ugly fellow wants to look like a film actor. So I said, enough. Since then I've done lots of jobs. Right now, I'm a hair-collector.'

'That's good,' said Ishvar tentatively. 'What do you have to do, as a hair-collector?'

'Collect hair.'

'And there is money in that?'

'Oh, very big business. There is a great demand for hair in foreign countries.'

'What do they do with it?' asked Om, sceptical.

'Many different things. Mostly they wear it. Sometimes they paint it in different colours – red, yellow, brown, blue. Foreign women enjoy wearing other people's hair. Men also, especially if they are bald. In foreign countries they fear baldness. They are so rich in foreign countries, they can afford to fear all kinds of silly things.'

'And how do you collect the hair?' asked Om. 'Steal it from people's heads?' There was a sneer in his voice.

Rajaram laughed good-naturedly. 'I go to pavement barbers. They let me take it in exchange for a packet of blades, or soap, or a comb. In hair-cutting saloons they give it free if I sweep the floor myself. Come – come inside my house, I'll show you my stock.'

Rajaram lit a lamp to dispel the early dusk within the shack. The flame flickered, steadied, and blossomed into orange, revealing gunny sacks and plastic bags stacked high against the wall.

'The sacks are from pavement barbers,' he said, opening one under their curious gaze. 'See, short hair.'

They held back from the unappetizing contents, and he plunged in his hand to display a greasy clump. 'Not more than two or three inches long. Fetches twenty-four rupees a kilo from the export agent. It's only good for making chemicals and medicines, he tells me. But look inside this plastic bag.'

He untied the string and drew out a handful of long tresses. 'From a ladies' barber. So beautiful, no? This is the valuable stuff. It's a very lucky day for me when I find this kind of hair. From eight to twelve inches, it brings two hundred rupees a kilo. Longer than twelve, six hundred rupees.' He fingered his own hair and held it out like a violin.

'So that's why you are growing yours.'

'Naturally. God-given harvest will put food in my stomach.'

Om took the tresses and stroked them, not repulsed as he had been by the mounds of short clippings. 'Feels good. Soft and smooth.'

'You know,' said Rajaram, 'when I find hair like this, I always want to meet the woman. I lie awake at night, wondering about her. What does she look like? Why was it cut? For fashion? For punishment? Or did her husband die? The hair is chopped off, but there is a whole life connected to it.'

'This must have been a rich woman's hair,' said Om.

'And why do you think so?' asked Rajaram, with the air of a mentor examining the novice.

'Because of the fragrance. Smells like expensive hair tonic. A poor woman would use raw coconut oil.'

'Perfectly correct,' he tapped Om's shoulder approvingly. 'By their hair shall you know them. Health and sickness, youth and age, wealth and poverty – it's all revealed in the hair.'

'Religion and caste also,' said Om.

'Exactly. You have the makings of a hair-collector. Let me know if you get tired of tailoring.'

'But would I be able to stroke the hair while it's still attached to the woman? All the hair? From top to bottom, and between the legs?'

'He's a clever rascal, isn't he?' said Rajaram to Ishvar, who was threatening to hit his nephew. 'But I am strictly a professional. I admit that sometimes, seeing a woman with long hair, I want to run my fingers through it, twine it around my wrist. But I have to control myself. Till the barber severs it, I can only dream.'

'You would dream a lot about our new employer if you saw her,' said Om. 'Dina Dalal's hair is beautiful. She probably has nothing to do all day but wash it and oil it and brush it and keep it looking perfect.' He held the tresses against his head, clowning. 'How do I look?'

'I was planning to find you a wife,' said his uncle. 'If you prefer, we can find a husband.' Laughing, Rajaram took back the hair and replaced it carefully in the plastic bag.

'But I am thinking,' said Ishvar. 'Wouldn't a hair-collector get more business in a place like Rishikesh? Or a temple town like Hardwar? Where people shave their heads and offer their locks to God?'

'You are correct,' said Rajaram. 'But there's a big obstacle in the way. A friend of mine, also a hair-collector, went south, to Tirupati. Just to check out the production in the temples there. You know what he found? About twenty thousand people a day, coming to sacrifice their hair. Six hundred barbers, working in eight-hour shifts.'

'That must produce a huge hill of hair.'

'Hill? It's a Himalayan mountain of hair. But middlemen like me have no chance to collect it. After the hair is dedicated, the very holy Brahmin priests put it in their very holy warehouse. And every three months they hold an auction, where the export companies buy it directly.'

'You don't have to tell us about Brahmins and priests,' said Ishvar. 'The greed of the upper castes is well known in our village.'

'It's the same everywhere,' agreed Rajaram. 'I'm still waiting to meet one who will treat me as his equal. As a fellow human being – that's all I want, nothing more.'

'From now on you can have our hair,' said Om generously.

'Thank you. I can cut it for you free, if you like, as long as you're not fussy.' He tucked away the sacks of hair and brought out his comb and scissors, offering a crop on the spot.

'Wait,' said Om. 'I should first let it grow long like yours. Then you can get more money for it.'

'Nothing doing,' said Ishvar. 'No long hair. Dina Dalal won't like a tailor with long hair.'

'One thing is certain,' said Rajaram. 'Supply and demand for hair is endless, it will always be big business.' As they returned outside into the evening air, he added, 'Sometimes, it also turns into big trouble.'

'Why trouble?'

'I was thinking about the hair of the beard of the Prophet. When it disappeared from the Hazrat-Bal mosque in Kashmir some years ago. You remember?'

'I do,' said Ishvar. 'But Om was just a baby then, he doesn't know.'

'Tell me, tell me. What happened?'

'Just that,' said Ishvar. 'The sacred hair disappeared one day, and there were big riots. Everyone was saying the government should resign, that the politicians must have something to do with it. To cause trouble, you know, because Kashmiris were asking for independence.'

'What happened was,' added Rajaram, 'after two weeks of riots and curfews, the government investigators announced they had found the sacred hair. But the people were not happy – what if the government is fooling us? they asked. What if they are passing off some ordinary hair for the sacred one? So the government got a group of very learned mullahs and put them in complete charge of inspecting the hair. When they said it was the correct one, only then did calm return to the streets of Srinagar.'

Outside, the smoke of cooking fires had taken control of the air. A voice yelled in the darkness, 'Shanti! Hurry with the wood!' and a girl responded. Om looked: it was her, the one with the big brass pot. Shanti, he repeated silently, losing interest in the hair-collector's story.

Rajaram propped a rock against the door of his shack so the wind wouldn't blow it open, then escorted the tailors on a tour of the neighbourhood. He showed them a shortcut to the train station through a break in the railroad fence. 'Keep walking through that gully, till you see the big advertisements for Amul Butter and Modern Bread. It will save you at least ten minutes when you go to work.'

He also warned them about the slum abutting their field. 'Most of the people in that bustee are decent, but some lanes are very dangerous. Murder and robbery is definitely possible if you walk through there.' In the safe part of the slum, he introduced them to a tea stall whose owner he knew, where they could have tea and snacks on credit, paying at the end of the month.

Late that night, as they sat outside their shack, smoking, they heard the harmonium player. He had returned from work, and was playing for pleasure. The reedy notes of his instrument, in the bleak surroundings, were rich as a golden flute. 'Meri dosti mera pyar,' he sang, and the song about love and friendship took the sting out of the acrid smoke of smouldering fires.

The rations officer was not at his desk. A peon said the boss was on his meditation break. 'You should come back on Monday.'

'But we have to start our new jobs on Monday,' said Ishvar. 'How long is the meditation break?'

The peon shrugged. 'One hour, two hours, three – depends on how much weight is on his mind. Sahab says without the break he would turn into a madman by the end of the week.' The tailors decided to wait in line.

It must have been a relatively easy week for the Rations Officer, for he returned thirty minutes later, looking suitably revitalized, and gave the tailors a ration-card application form. He said there were experts on the pavement outside who, for a small fee, would fill it out for them.

'That's okay, we know how to write.'

'Really?' he said, feeling snubbed. He prided his ability to appraise at a glance the applicants flowing past his desk every day – their place of origin, financial status, education, caste. His face muscles twitched, tightening in defiance of his just-completed meditation. The tailors' literacy was an affront to his omniscience. 'Complete it and bring it back,' he dismissed them with a petulant flutter of fingers.

They took the form into the corridor to fill in the blanks, using a window ledge to write on. It was a rough surface, and the ballpoint went through the paper several times. They tried to nurse the pockmarked sheet back to health by flattening the bumps with their fingernails, then rejoined the line to face their interlocutor.

The Rations Officer scanned the form and smiled. It was a superior smile: they may have learned how to write, but they knew nothing about neatness. He read their answers and stopped in triumph at the address portion. 'What's this rubbish?' he tapped with a nicotine-stained finger.

'It's the place where we live,' said Ishvar. He had entered the name of the road that led to their row of shacks on the north side. The space for building name, flat number, and street number had been left blank.

'And where exactly is your house?'

They offered additional information: the closest intersection, the streets east and west of the slum, the train station, names of neighbourhood cinemas, the big hospital, the popular sweetmeat shop, a fish market.

'Stop, enough,' said the Rations Officer, covering his ears. 'I don't need to hear all this nonsense.' He pulled out a city directory, flipped a few pages, and studied a map. 'Just as I thought. Your house is in a jhopadpatti, right?'

'It's a roof – for the time being.'

'A jhopadpatti is not an address. The law says ration cards can only be issued to people with real addresses.'

'Our house is real,' pleaded Ishvar. 'You can come and see it.'

'My seeing it is irrelevant. The law is what matters. And in the eyes of the law, your jhopdi doesn't count.' He picked up a stack of forms and shuffled them to align the edges. Tossed back to their corner, they landed in disarray, raising dust. 'But there is another way to get the ration card, if you are interested.'

'Yes, please – whatever is necessary.'

'If you let me arrange for your vasectomy, your application can be approved instantly.'

'Vasectomy?'

'You know, for Family Planning. The nussbandhi procedure.'

'Oh, but I already did that,' lied Ishvar.

'Show me your F.P.C.'

'F.P.C.?'

'Family Planning Certificate.'

'Oh, but I don't have that.' Thinking quickly, he said, 'In our native place there was a fire in the hut. Everything was destroyed.'

'That's not a problem. The doctor I send you to will do it again as a special favour, and give you a new certificate.'

'Same operation, two times? Isn't that bad?'

'Lots of people do it twice. Brings more benefits. Two transistor radios.'

'Why would I need two radios?' smiled Ishvar. 'Do I listen to two different stations, one with each ear?'

'Look, if the harmless little operation frightens you, send this young fellow. All I need is one sterilization certificate.'

'But he is only seventeen! He has to marry, have some children, before his nuss is disconnected!'

'It's up to you.'

Ishvar left in a rage, Om hurrying after him to calm him down as he fumed at the shocking, almost blasphemous, suggestion. No one noticed, though, because the corridor was crowded with people like Ishvar, lost and stumbling, trying to negotiate their way through the government offices. They waited around in varying stages of distress. Some were in tears, others laughed hysterically at bureaucratic absurdities, while a few stood facing the wall, muttering ominously to themselves.

'Nussbandhi, he says!' seethed Ishvar. 'Shameless bastard! For a young boy, nussbandhi! Someone should cut off the ugly rascal's pipe while he is meditating!' He fled down the corridor, down the stairs, and out through the building's main door.

A small, clerkish-looking man on the pavement, noticing Ishvar's agitation, rose from his wooden stool to greet them. He wore glasses and a white shirt, with writing material spread before him on a mat. 'You have a problem. Can I help?'

'What help can you give?' said Ishvar dismissively.

The man touched Ishvar's elbow to make him stop and listen. 'I am a facilitator. My job, my speciality, is to assist people in their dealings with government offices.' His runny nose made him sniff several times during the course of his introduction.

'You work for government?' asked Ishvar, suspicious, pointing at the building they had just left.

'No, never, I work for you and me. To help you get what the government people make difficult to get. Hence my title: Facilitator. Birth certificates, death certificates, marriage licence, any types of permits and clearances – I can arrange it all. You just select what information you want on it, and I will have it issued.' He removed his glasses and smiled his most facile smile, then lost it to six violent sneezes. The tailors jumped back to avoid the spray.

'All we wanted was a ration card, Mr. Facilitator. And the fellow wanted our manhood in exchange! What kind of choice is that, between food and manhood?'

'Ah, he wanted the F.P.C.'

'Yes, that's what he called it.'

'You see, since the Emergency started, there's a new rule in the department – every officer has to encourage people to get sterilized. If he doesn't fill his quota, no promotion for him. What to do, poor fellow, he is also trapped, no?'

'But it's not fair to us!'

'That's why I am here, no. Just pick the names you want on the ration card, up to a maximum of six, and whatever address you like. Cost is only two hundred rupees. Hundred now, and hundred when you get the card.'

'But we don't have so much money.'

The Facilitator said they could come back when they did, he would still be here. 'While there is government, there will be work for me.' He blew his nose and returned to his spot on the pavement.

—

Taking Rajaram's shortcut, the tailors trotted down the platform towards the wasteland of track and cinder, watching the train slide out of the station to disappear into the evening. 'The closer he gets to the stable, the faster the tired horse gallops,' said Ishvar, and Om nodded.

Their first day with Dina Dalal was over. Borne along by the homeward-bound flock, exhausted from ten hours of sewing, they shared the sanctity of the hour with the crowd, this time of transition from weariness to hope. Soon it would be night; they would borrow Rajaram's stove, cook something, eat. They would weave their plans and dream the future into favourable patterns, till it was time to take the train tomorrow morning.

The end of the platform sloped downwards to become one with the gravel hugging the rails. Here was the crucial opening in the endless cast-iron fence, where one of its spear-pointed bars had corroded at the hands of the elements, and broken away with a little help from human hands.

The swelling knot of men and women trickled through the gap, far from the exit where the ticket-collector stood. Others, with an agility prompted by their ticketless state, ran farther down the tracks, over cinders and gravel sharp against bare soles and ill-shod feet. They ran between the rails, stretching their strides from worn wooden sleeper to sleeper, vaulting over the fence at a safe distance from the station.

Though he had a ticket, Om yearned to follow them in the heroic dash for freedom. He felt he too could soar if he was alone. Then he glanced sideways at his uncle who was more-than-uncle, whom he could never abandon. The spears of the fence stood in the dusk like the rusting weapons of a phantom army. The ticketless men seemed ancient, breaching the enemy's ranks, soaring over the barbs as if they would never come down to earth.

Suddenly, a posse of tired policemen materialized out of the twilight and surrounded the gap-seeking crowd. A few constables gave half-hearted chase to the railing jumpers in the distance. The only energetic one among them was an inspector brandishing a swagger-stick and shouting orders and encouragement.

'Catch them all! Move, move, move! No one gets away! Back to the platform, all you crooks! You there!' he pointed with the swagger-stick.

'Stop lagging! We'll teach you to travel without tickets!'

The tailors' attempt to inform someone, anyone, that they actually had tickets was drowned in the noise and confusion. 'Please, havaldar, we were only taking a shortcut,' they implored the nearest uniform, but were herded along with the rest. The ticket-collector wagged a reproving finger as the captive column shuffled past him.

Outside, the prisoners were loaded onto a police truck. The last few were levered in with the help of the tailgate. 'We're finished,' said someone. 'I heard that under Emergency law, no ticket means one week in the lockup.'

For an hour they were kept sweating in the truck while the inspector attended to some business in the ticket office. Then the truck started down the station road, followed by the inspector's jeep. They journeyed for ten minutes and turned into a vacant lot, where the tailgate was thrown open.

'Out! Everybody out! Out, out, out!' shouted the inspector with a penchant for triplets, slapping the swagger-stick against the truck tyre. 'Men on this side, women on that side!' He organized the two groups into a formation of rows six deep.

'Attention everyone! Grab hold of your ears! Come on, catch them! Catch, catch, catch! What are you waiting for? Now you will do fifty baithuks! Ready, begin! One! Two! Three!' He prowled among the rows, supervising the knee-bends and counting, performing sudden about-turns to catch them off guard. If he found someone cheating, not doing a full squat or releasing their ears, he let them have it with his stick.

'. . . forty-eight, forty-nine, fifty! That's it! And if you are found again without a ticket, I will make you remember your grandmothers! Now you can go home! Go! What are you waiting for? Go, go, go!'

The crowd dispersed rapidly, making jokes about the punishment and the inspector. 'Stupid Rajaram,' said Om. 'From now on I'm not going to believe anything from his mouth. Get a ration card, he told us, it's very easy. Take the shortcut, you'll save time.'

'Ah, no harm done,' said Ishvar genially. Back at the railway station he had been quite frightened. 'Look, the police spared us some walking, we are almost at the colony.'

They crossed the road and continued towards the hutments. The familiar hoarding loomed into view, but the illustration was different. 'What happened?' said Om. 'Where did Modern Bread and Amul Butter go?'

The advertisements had been replaced by the Prime Minister's picture, proclaiming: 'Iron Will! Hard Work! These will sustain us!' It was a quintessential specimen of the face that was proliferating on posters throughout the city. Her cheeks were executed in the lurid pink of cinema billboards. Other aspects of the portrait had suffered greater infelicities. Her eyes evoked the discomfort of a violent itch somewhere upon the ministerial corpus, begging to be scratched. The artist's ambition of a benignant smile had also gone awry – a cross between a sneer and the vinegary sternness of a drillmistress had crept across the mouth. And that familiar swatch of white hair over her forehead, imposing amid the black, had plopped across the scalp like the strategic droppings of a very large bird.

'Look at it, Om. She is making the sour-lime face, just like yours when you are upset.'

Om obliged by duplicating the expression, then laughed. The towering visage continued to deliver its frozen monition to trains rumbling by on one side, and buses and motorcars scrambling in clouds of exhaust on the other, while the tailors trudged to the hutment colony.

The hair-collector emerged as they were unlocking their shack. 'You naughty children, you are so late,' he complained.

'But –'

'Never mind, it's only a small obstacle. The food will soon get warm again. I put off the stove because vegetables were drying up.' He disappeared inside to return with the frying pan and three plates. 'Bhaji and chapati. And my special masala wada with mango chutney, to celebrate your first day at work.'

'How much trouble you're taking for us,' said Ishvar.

'Oh, it's nothing.'

Rajaram let the food heat for a minute, then handed out the plates with the four items neatly arranged around the circumference. A substantial amount still remained in the pan. 'You cooked too much,' said Ishvar.

'I had a little extra money today, so I bought more vegetables. For them,' he pointed with his elbow at the other shack. 'That drunken fellow's little ones are always hungry.'

While they ate, the tailors described the police action against ticketless travel. The gift of dinner softened the accusing tone Om had planned to use; he told it like a traveller's adventure instead.

Rajaram clapped a dramatic hand to his forehead. 'What foolishness on my part – I completely forgot to warn you. You see, it's been months and months since a raid.' He slapped his forehead again. 'Some people travel all their lives without buying a single ticket. And you two get caught on the first day. Even with tickets,' he chuckled.

Ishvar and Om, appreciating the irony, started laughing too. 'Just bad luck. Must be a new policy because of Emergency.'

'But it was all a big show. Why did the inspector let everyone go, if they are really getting strict?'

Rajaram thought about it while chewing, and fetched glasses of water for everyone. 'Maybe they had no choice. From what I hear, the jails are full with the Prime Minister's enemies – union workers, newspaper people, teachers, students. So maybe there is no more room in the prisons.'

While they were mulling over the incident, cries of joy went up near the water tap. It had started gurgling! And so late in the night! People watched the spout, holding their breath. A few drops dribbled out. Then a little stream. They cheered it like a winning racehorse as it gathered strength, gushing full and strong. A miracle! The hutment dwellers clapped and shouted with excitement.

'It has happened once before,' said Rajaram. 'I think someone made a mistake at the waterworks, opening the wrong valve.'

'They should make such mistakes more often,' said Ishvar.

Women ran to the tap to make the most of the fortuitous flow. Babies in their arms squealed with delight as cool water glided over their sticky skin. Older children skipped about gleefully, bursting into little involuntary dances, looking forward to the generous drenching instead of the meagre mugfuls at dawn.

'Maybe we should also fill up now,' said Om. 'Save time in the morning.'

'No,' said Rajaram. 'Let the little ones enjoy. Who knows when they'll get a chance like this again.'

The festivities lasted less than an hour; the tap went dry as suddenly as it had started. Children soaped in anticipation had to be wiped off and sent to bed disappointed.

Over the next fortnight, the slumlord erected another fifty ramshackle huts in the field, which Navalkar rented out in a day, doubling the population. Now the fetid smell from the ditch hung permanently over the shacks, thicker than smoke. There was nothing to distinguish the small hutment colony from the huge slum across the road; it had been incorporated into the inferno. The rush at the water tap assumed riotous proportions. Accusations of queue-jumping were exchanged every morning, there was pushing and shoving, scuffles broke out, pots were overturned, mothers screamed, children wailed.

The monsoon season started, and on the first night of rain, the tailors were awakened by the roof leaking on their bedding. They sat huddled in the only dry corner. The rain poured down beside them in a steady stream and gradually lulled them into slumber. Then the rain slowed. The leak became an aggravating drip. Om began counting the splashes in his head. He reached a hundred, a thousand, ten thousand, counting, adding, tallying, as though hoping to dry them out by attaining a high enough number.

They ended up sleeping very little. In the morning, Rajaram climbed onto the roof to examine the corrugated iron. He helped them spread a piece of plastic, not quite wide enough, over the leaking area.

Later that week, heartened by the remuneration from Dina Dalal, Ishvar was able to plan a little shopping excursion to buy a large plastic sheet and a few other items. 'What do you say, Om? Now we can make our house more comfortable, hahn?'

His suggestion was greeted with a mournful silence. They stopped at a pavement stall selling polythene bowls, boxes, and assorted tableware. 'So, what colour plates and glasses shall we get?'

'Doesn't matter.'

'A towel? That yellow one with flowers, maybe?'

'Doesn't matter.'

'Would you like new sandals?'

'Doesn't matter' came yet again, and Ishvar finally lost his patience. 'What's wrong with you these days? All the time with Dinabai you make mistakes and argue. You take no interest in tailoring. Anything I ask, you say doesn't matter. Make an effort, Om, make an effort.' He cut the shopping expedition short, and they started back with two red plastic buckets, a Primus stove, five litres of kerosene, and a package of jasmine agarbatti.

Ahead they heard the familiar *dhuk-dhuka dhuk-dhuka* of Monkeyman's little handheld drum. The string-tied rattle bounced upon the skin as he spun his wrist. He was not looking to collect a crowd, merely accompanying his charges home. One of his little brown monkeys had hitched a ride on his shoulder, the other ambled along listlessly. The emaciated dog followed at a distance, sniffing, chewing newspaper in which food had once been wrapped. Monkey-man whistled, and called 'Tikka!' and the mongrel trotted up.

The monkeys started teasing Tikka, tweaking his ears, twisting his tail, pinching his penis. He bore his tormentors with a dignified calm. His reprieve came when the red plastic buckets swinging from Om's hands attracted the monkeys' attention. They decided to investigate, and hopped in.

'Laila! Majnoo! Stop it!' scolded their master, tugging the leashes. They bobbed their heads out over the bucket rims.

'It's okay,' said Om, enjoying their pranks. 'Let them have some fun. They must have worked hard all day.'

They walked together to the hutment colony, the tailors, Monkey-man, and his animals, moving to the drum's hypnotic *dhuk-dhuka*. Laila and Majnoo soon tired of the buckets and began clambering over Om, sitting on his shoulders or his head, hanging from his arms, clinging to his legs. He laughed all the way home, and Ishvar smiled with pleasure.

Om's playfulness vanished when he and the monkeys parted compa-ny. Once again he sank into his gloom, casting a nauseated look in Rajaram's direction, who was sorting his bags of hair outside the shack. The little black mounds looked like a collection of shaggy human heads.

Seeing the two laden with purchases, Rajaram complimented them. 'Makes me happy to see you started on the road to prosperity.'

'You need spectacles if you think this is the road to prosperity,' snapped Om. He went inside and unrolled the bedding.

'What's the matter with him?' asked Rajaram, hurt.

'I think he's just tired. But listen, today you must eat with us. To cele-brate our new stove.'

'How can I refuse such good friends?'

They prepared the food together, and called Om when it was ready. Halfway through the meal, Rajaram asked if he could borrow ten rupees. The request took Ishvar by surprise. He had assumed the hair-collector was doing well in his line of work, judging by his enthusiastic talk during the past fortnight.

The hesitation showed on his face, for Rajaram added, 'I'll return it in a week, don't worry. Business is little slow right now. But a new style is coming into fashion for women. Everyone will start chopping off their plaits. Those long chotelas will fall straight into my lap.'

'Stop talking about hair,' said Om. 'It makes my stomach sick.' After dinner, instead of sitting outside to chat and smoke with them, he said he had a headache and went to bed.

His uncle came in an hour later and stood watching the back of Om's head for a minute. Poor child, what a burden of terrible memories he had to carry. He leaned across and saw his eyes were open. 'Om? Headache gone?'

He groaned and answered no.

'Patience, Om, it will go.' To cheer him up, he added, 'Our stars must be in the proper position at last. Everything is going well, hahn?'

'How can you keep repeating such rubbish? A lousy, stinking house we live in. Our jobs are terrible, that Dinabai watching us like a vulture, harassing us, telling us when to eat and when to belch.'

Ishvar sighed; his nephew was in one of his implacable black moods. He lit two sticks from the jasmine agarbatti package. 'This will make our house smell nice. Sleep well, your headache will be gone in the morning.'

Late at night, after the harmonium player's song was silent and Tikka stopped barking, it was the noises from the hair-collector's shack that continued to keep Om awake. There was a visitor. A woman giggled, then Rajaram laughed. Soon he was panting, and the sounds through the plywood walls tormented Om. He thought of them naked amid those eerie bags of hair, contorting in the erotic poses of cinema posters. He thought of Shanti by the water tap, her lovely shining hair, the tightness of her blouse when she lifted the big brass pot to her head, the things he could do with her in the bushes by the railroad. He looked at his uncle, sound asleep. He got out of bed, went to the side of the shack, and masturbated. The woman next door was just departing. He hid in the shadows till she was gone.

He fell asleep after midnight only to be awakened by piercing screams. This time Ishvar was roused as well. 'Hai Ram! What can that be?'

Outside, they ran into Rajaram, smiling contentedly. Om scowled at him with equal parts of envy and disgust. People were emerging from shacks all down the row. Then word spread that it was a woman in labour, and everyone went back to sleep. The screams ceased after a while.

In the morning, they heard that a girl had been born during the early hours. 'Let's go and give them good wishes,' said Ishvar.

'You go if you like,' said Om gloomily.

'Ah, don't be so unhappy,' he ruffled his hair. 'We will find a wife for you, I promise.'

'Find her for yourself, I don't need one.' He moved out of reach and snatched the comb on the packing case to restore his hair.

'Back in two minutes,' said Ishvar. 'Then off to work.'

Om sat in the doorway, fingering a piece of chiffon he had slipped in his pocket yesterday from the scraps littering Dina Dalal's floor. How comforting it felt, liquid between his fingers – why couldn't life be like that, soft and smooth. He caressed his cheek with it, observing the drunkard's children running about, sprawling in the dust, passing the time till their mother took them out to beg. One of them found a curiously shaped stone, which he showed off to his siblings. Then they chased a crow probing a lump of something rotten. The mettlesome bird refused to fly away, hopping, circling, returning to the putrefying tidbit to provide more fun for the children. How could they be so happy? wondered Om – dirty and naked, ill-fed, sores on their faces, rashes on their skin. What was there for anyone to laugh about in this wretched place?

He slipped the chiffon back into his pocket and wandered to Monkey-man's shack. Laila was grooming Majnoo, and he settled down to watch. A minute later, they had jumped onto his shoulders, combing their delicate infant-sized fingers through his hair.

Seeing that Om did not mind, Monkey-man smiled and let them be. 'They do it to me also,' he said. 'Means they like you. Best way of keeping a clean head.'

Laila found something in Om's hair and held it up to examine. Majnoo grabbed it from her paw and put it in his mouth.

Om chose a black Hercules at the rental shop on the road to Dina Dalal's flat. It had an impressive spring-loaded carrier over the rear wheel and a large shiny bell on the handlebars.

'But why do you need a cycle?' persisted Ishvar. His nephew smiled cunningly while the man used a spanner to adjust the seat height.

'One month has passed since we started working for her,' said Om. 'That's long enough, I've made my plan.' The freshly pumped-up tyres withstood the inspecting squeeze of his fingers. He wheeled it out into the main street. 'Today is her day to go to the export company, right? And I'm going to follow her taxi on my cycle.' Swinging one leg lightly over the saddle, he rolled off.

'Careful,' said Ishvar. 'Traffic is heavy, it's not our village road.' On the kerb he quickened his pace to keep up. 'The plan is good, Om, but you forgot one thing – her padlocked door. How will you get out?'

'Wait and see.'

Freewheeling alongside his uncle, Om was in high spirits. The mud-guards rattled and the brakes were spongy, though the bell worked perfectly. *Tring-tring tring-tring*, his thumb urged it on, *tring-tring*. Brimming with confidence, he plunged into the traffic on his carilloning cycle, on the wheels that would help put the future right.

He returned to the safety of the kerb, and Ishvar breathed easier. The scheme was absurd, but he was happy that his nephew was enjoying himself. He watched him swing the handlebars from side to side and backpedal, to keep from racing ahead. Om on the saddle performed an intricate dance, the dance of balancing-at-slow-speed. Soon, hoped Ishvar, he would forsake his crazy ideas and perform with equal facility the arduous dance of sewing-for-the-employer.

At Om's prompting, Ishvar got on the carrier behind the saddle. He sat sideways, legs straight out. With his feet inches off the ground, sandals grazing the road now and then, they sailed away. Om's optimism pealed in the *tring-tring* showers spouting from the bell. For a while the world was perfect.

Soon, the tailors neared the corner where the beggar was wheeling his platform around. They stopped to toss him a coin. It landed with a clink in the empty can.

They hid the bicycle at a safe distance from Dina Dalal's door, in a cob-webby stairwell that smelled of urine and country liquor. Chaining it to a disused gas pipe, they emerged brushing off the invisible threads clinging to their hands and faces. Ghosts of the webs continued to bother them for some time. Their fingers kept returning to their foreheads and necks to remove strands that were not there.

Dina's fingers flitted like skittish butterflies, folding the dresses for delivery to Au Revoir Exports. She checked the paper patterns to make sure everything was accounted for. The manager had been repeatedly dire about them. 'Guard the patterns with your life,' Mrs. Gupta always said. 'If they fall in the wrong hands my entire company will be ruined.'

Dina thought this was somewhat exaggerated. Nonetheless, she could not help feeling, while sorting through the brown-paper sections of bodice and sleeve and collar, that her own torso and arms and neck were at stake. Of late, she sensed a haughtiness in Mrs. Gupta, as though the manager had discovered they were not social equals. She no longer left her desk to greet her and see her off, nor did she offer tea or a Fanta.

Her fingers returned nervously to the folded garments, picking one up at random, examining its seams and hems. Would this lot pass Mrs. Gupta's inspection? How many rejections? The angelic tailors had fallen from grace; carelessness was rife now in their handiwork.

From his corner, Om watched as Dina completed her weekly perfor-mance of fretfulness. His thoughts were bent on bracing himself; the moment was approaching.

It was now.

She snapped shut her handbag.

He stabbed his left index finger with the scissors.

The pain, sharper than expected, jolted him. He had assumed that because it was anticipated, it would be less intense, the way it was with anticipated pleasure. The blood spurted in bright-red arcs upon the yel-low voile.

'Oh my goodness!' said Dina. 'What have you done!' She grabbed a snippet of cloth from the floor and pressed it over the cut. 'Raise the hand, raise it up or more blood will flow.'

'Hai Ram!' said Ishvar, removing the soiled garment from under the presser foot of the Singer. Just when he thought his nephew was improving, he did this. His obsession to find the export company was not good.

'Quick, soak that dress in the bucket,' said Dina. She got the tincture of benzoin from her first-aid box and applied it liberally. The cut was not as serious as the blood had led her to believe. She indulged in the relief of a scolding.

'Careless boy! What were you trying to do? Where is your mind? A skinny person cannot afford to lose so much blood. But always there is so much anger, so much haste in whatever you do.'

Still stunned by what his scissors had accomplished, a lukewarm scowl was the best Om could reply with. He liked the pungent fragrance of the golden-brown liquid coating his finger. She taped a cotton wad tightly over the cut as the bleeding slowed to a trickle.

'Your finger has made me late. Now the manager will be upset.' She did not mention the cost of the blood-stained garment. Better to see if the voile was salvageable before discussing restitution. She took the bundle of dresses to the door and picked up the padlock.

'It's paining too much,' said Om. 'I want to go to doctor.'

And now Ishvar understood: the encounter of scissors and finger was part of his nephew's foolish plan.

'Doctor for this? Don't be a baby,' she said. 'Rest with your hand up for a while, you will be all right.'

Om screwed his face into caricatures of agony. 'What if my finger rots and falls off because of your advice? It will be on your head, for sure.'

She suspected the act was put on to shirk the afternoon's work, but it planted the seed of unease in her mind. 'What do I care – go if you want,' she said brusquely.

The stress of dealing with these two fellows, their sloppy work, their tardiness, was wearing her out, she felt. Mrs. Gupta was bound to cancel the arrangement sooner or later. The only question was, which would disappear first, the tailors or her health. She envisioned two leaky faucets: one said Money, the other, Sanity. And both were dripping away simultaneously.

Thank goodness that Maneck Kohlah was arriving tomorrow. At least his room and board was one hundred per cent guaranteed income.

Om watched from a distance, holding aloft his punctured finger until

Dina was inside the taxi. Then, spurred by the smell of success, he rushed to his hiding place.

By the time he unlocked the bicycle and wheeled it out from under the stairs, the taxi had disappeared. He raced to the side street and – there it was, waiting at the red traffic light.

He caught up, staying two cars away. Keeping her in sight was as important as keeping himself out of sight. He sped up, slowed down, ducked behind buses, changed lanes like a demon. Cars honked in protest. People shouted at him and made nasty gestures. He was forced to ignore them, the taxi and bicycle requiring all his concentration.

So confident was he now of tracking the destination, he was trembling. It was a curious palpitation, the excitement of the hunter mingling with the trepidation of the hunted.

The street merged into the main road, and the traffic was thicker now, deranged and bad-tempered, worse than anything he had encountered so far. Within minutes he was panting with frustration. The taxi was lost and found half a dozen times, slipping farther away. Scores of identical yellow and black Fiats swarming the street, their bulky meters sticking out on the left side, did not make his task easier.

Confused, Om began to lose his nerve. The brief early-morning ride from the train station was no preparation for the hysteria of midday traffic. It was like seeing wild animals lethargic in zoo cages, then coming upon them in the jungle. Making a final desperate bid, he squeezed between two cars and was knocked off his bicycle. People screamed from the pavement.

'Hai bhagwan! Poor boy is finished!'

'Crushed to death!'

'Careful, his bones might be broken!'

'Catch the chauffeur! Don't let him run! Bash the rascal!'

Feeling bad about generating so much needless concern, Om stood up, dragging the bicycle after him. He had scraped his elbow and bruised one knee, but was otherwise unhurt.

Now it was the chauffeur's turn. He emerged boldly from the car where he had been cowering. 'You have eyes or marbles?' he screamed. 'Can't see where you're going? Causing damage to people's property!'

A policeman arrived and checked most solicitously on the passengers in the car. 'Everybody all right, sahab?' Om looked on, a little dazed, and also frightened. Were people who caused accidents sent to jail? His finger was bleeding again, throbbing madly.

A man in an ochre-coloured safari suit, snuggled in the back of the car, fished out his wallet. He passed the policeman some money, then beckoned his chauffeur to the window. The chauffeur put something in Om's hands. 'Now go! And be more careful or you'll kill somebody! Use your God-given eyes!'

Om looked down at what lay in his shaking hands: fifty rupees.

'Come on, you paagal-ka-batcha!' shouted the policeman. 'Take your cycle and clear the road!' He waved the car through with his smartest VIP salute.

Om wheeled the bicycle to the kerb. The handlebars were askew and the mudguards rattled more resolutely than before. He dusted off his pants, examining the black smears of grease on the cuffs.

'How much did he give you?' asked someone on the pavement.

'Fifty rupees.'

'You got up too fast,' said the man, shaking his head disapprovingly. 'Never get up so fast. Always stay down and make some moaning-groaning noise. Cry for doctor, cry for ambulance, scream, shout, anything. In this type of case, you can pull at least two hundred rupees.' He spoke like a professional; his twisted elbow hung at his side like a qualification.

Om put the money in his pocket. He braced the front wheel between his knees and tugged at the handlebars till they were straight. He walked the bicycle down a side street, leaving the crowd to continue analysing his accident.

Returning to the flat was useless, the padlock would be on the door, hanging dark and heavy, like a bullock's lost scrotum. He was also reluctant to turn in the bicycle early – a day's rent had been paid in advance. He wished he had listened to his uncle in the morning. But the plan seemed so perfect when he had imagined the sequence of events, shining with success, like the sunlight gilding the handlebars. Imagination was a dangerous thing.

He mounted the bicycle where the traffic was less threatening, and took the seaward road. No longer quarry or pursuer, he could enjoy the ride now. The tinkling bell of the candy-floss man outside a school caught his ear. He stopped and squinted into the man's neck-slung glass container, getting a hazy look at the pink, yellow, and blue cottony balls through the side that was cleanest.

'How much?'

'Twenty-five paise for one. Or try a lottery for fifty paise – win from one to ten balls.'

Om paid and dipped a hand into the brown-paper lottery bag. The chit he pulled out had a 2 scrawled on it.

'What colours?'

'One pink, one yellow.'

The man plopped off the round lid and reached inside. 'Not that one, the one next to it,' directed Om.

The sweet fluff melted quickly in his mouth. Got the bigger pink ball for sure, he thought, pleased with himself as he separated a ten-rupee note from the crackling group of five. The man wiped his fingers on the neck-sling before taking it. Om pocketed the change and continued towards the sea.

At the beach he paused to read the chiselled name under a tall black stone statue. The plaque said he was a Guardian of Democracy. Om had studied about the man in his history class, in the story of the Freedom Struggle. The photo in the history book was nicer than the statue, he decided. Letting the bicycle lean against the pedestal, he rested in the statue's shade. The sides of the pedestal were plastered with posters extolling the virtues of the Emergency. The obligatory Prime Ministerial visage was prominent. Small print explained why fundamental rights had been temporarily suspended.

He watched two men making juice at a sugar-cane stall in the sand. One fed the sticks to the crushing wheels while the other swung the handle. The latter was shirtless, his muscles rippling, skin shining with sweat as he heaved mightily at the machine. His job was harder, thought Om, and he hoped they took turns, or it would not be a fair partnership.

The frothing golden juice made Om's mouth water. Despite the money in his pocket, he hesitated. Recently, he had heard stories in the bazaar about a cane stall that had pulped a gecko along with cane. An accident, they said – the thing was probably lurking about the innards of the machine, licking the sugary rods and gears, but many customers had been poisoned.

Liquid lizards kept swimming into Om's thoughts, alternating with glassfuls of golden juice. Eventually the lizards won, squelching all desire for the drink. Instead, he bought a length of sugar cane, peeled and chopped into a dozen pieces. These he munched happily, chewing the juice out of them, one by one. He spat each husky mouthful in a tidy pile at the statue's feet. His jaws tired quickly, but the ache was as satisfying as the sweetness.

The desiccated shreds attracted a curious gull. Next time he spat, he aimed for the bird. It dodged the missile and poked around in the macerated remnants, scattering the neat little hill before turning away disdainfully.

Om tossed it his last piece, unchewed. The gull's interest was renewed. It investigated thoroughly, refusing to believe its beak was not up to tackling sugar cane.

A street urchin shooed away the gull and snatched the prize. She took it to the juice stall and washed off the sand in the bucket where the men were rinsing dirty glasses. Om felt drowsy watching her gnaw the chunk. He wished he could come here with the lovely shiny-haired girl. Shanti. He would buy bhel-puri and sugar cane for both of them. They would sit in the sand and watch the waves. Then the sun would set, the breeze would come up, they would snuggle together. They would sit with their arms around each other, and then, for sure . . .

Dreaming, he fell asleep. When he awoke the sun was still harsh, and shining in his eyes. An hour and a half of rental time remained on the bicycle, but he decided to turn it in anyway.

Ishvar was certain that his nephew had reached his goal, if the grinning insouciance with which he took his place at the Singer was any indication.

Dina, having returned hours ago, began scolding him. 'Wasting time, that's all it is. Were you taking a tour of the whole city? How far away is your doctor – at the southernmost tip of Lanka?'

'Yes, I was carried through the sky by Lord Hanuman,' he replied, wondering if she could have spied him on the bicycle.

'This fellow is getting very sharp.'

'Too sharp,' said Ishvar. 'If he isn't careful, he will cut himself again.'

'And how is the finger that was going to rot?' she inquired. 'Has it fallen off yet?'

'It's better. Doctor checked it.'

'Good. Do some work, then. Start pushing your feet, there are lots of new dresses.'

'Hahnji, right away.'

'My goodness. No more grumbling? Whatever medicine your doctor prescribed, it's working. You should take a dose every morning.'

Unexpectedly, the last hour of the day, usually the most difficult, passed with banter and laughing. Why couldn't it be like this every day, wished Dina. Before they left, she took advantage of their good mood to move part of the furniture from her bedroom into the sewing room.

'Are you rearranging the whole flat?' asked Ishvar.

'Just this room. I have to prepare for my guest.'

'Yes, the college boy,' said Om, remembering. They rolled up the mattress from the bed, carried in the frame and slats, then replaced the mattress. The Singers, stools, worktable were crammed closer together to make space. 'When does he arrive?'

'Tomorrow night.'

She sat alone in the sewing room after they were gone, watching the floc and fibres float in the electric light. The heavily starched cloth from the Au Revoir mills mingled its cloying textile sweetness with the tailors' scent of sweat and tobacco. She liked it while their bustle filled the room. But the smell was depressing during the empty evenings, when something acrid suspired from the bolts, stiffening the air, clouding it with thoughts of dingy factories, tubercular labourers, bleak lives. The emptiness of her own life appeared starkest at this hour.

━━

'So. What's the name of the company?' asked Ishvar.

'I don't know.'

'The address?'

'I don't know.'

'Then why so pleased? Your cunning plan got you nothing.'

'Patience, patience,' he mimicked his uncle. 'It got me something.' He flashed the money and narrated his afternoon's adventures.

Ishvar began to laugh. 'Only to you could such things happen.' Neither of them seemed disappointed – it may have been the money, or relief at the failure: finding the export company would have led to some difficult choices.

A mobile Family Planning Clinic was parked outside the hutment colony when they got home. Most of the slum-dwelling multitudes were giving it a wide berth. The staff were handing out free condoms, distributing leaflets on birth-control procedures, explaining incentives being offered in cash and kind.

'Maybe I should have the operation,' said Om. 'Get a Bush transistor. And then the ration card would also be possible.'

Ishvar whacked him. 'Don't even joke about such things!'

'Why? I'm never getting married. Might as well get a transistor.'

'You will marry when I tell you to. No arguments. And what's so important about a little radio?'

'Everybody has one nowadays.' He was imagining Shanti at the beach, twilight fading, while his transistor serenaded them.

'Everybody jumps in the well, you will also? Learning big-city ways – forgetting our good, humble small-town ways.'

'You get the operation if you don't want me to.'

'Shameless. My manhood for a stupid radio?'

'No, yaar, it's not your manhood they want. The doctor just cuts a tiny little tube inside. You don't even feel it.'

'Nobody is taking a knife to my balls. You want a transistor? Work

193

hard for Dinabai, earn some money.'

Rajaram came up, displaying the condoms he had collected at the clinic. They were handing out four per person, and he wondered if they would get their quota for him if they didn't need it. 'Who knows when the van will come this way again,' he said.

'Are you a frequent fucker or what?' said Om, laughing but envious. 'Not going to keep us awake again tonight, are you?'

'Shameless,' said Ishvar and tried to whack him as he skipped away to visit the monkeys.

━━

Dina reread the letter from Mrs. Kohlah that had arrived with the first rent cheque, postdated to Maneck's moving day. The three pages listed instructions concerning the care and comfort of Aban Kohlah's son. There were tips about his breakfast: fried eggs should be cooked floating in butter because he disliked the leathery edges that got stuck to the pan; scrambled eggs were to be light and fluffy, with milk added during the final phase. 'Having grown up in our healthy mountain air,' continued the letter, 'he has a large appetite. But please don't give him more than two eggs, not even if he asks. He must learn to balance his diet.'

About his studies, Aban Kohlah wrote that 'Maneck is a good, hardworking boy, but gets distracted sometimes, so please remind him to do his lessons every day.' Also, he was very particular about his clothes, the way they were starched and ironed; a good dhobi was indispensable to his sense of well-being. And Dina should feel free to call him Mac because that was what everyone in the family called him.

Dina snorted and put away the letter. Eggs floating in butter, indeed! And a good dhobi, of all things! The nonsense that people foisted on their children. When the boy had visited last month, he seemed nothing like the person described in his mother's letter. But that was always the case – people hardly ever saw their children as they really were.

To prepare the room for his arrival, Dina carried out her clothes, shoes, and knickknacks, making space for them amid the tailoring paraphernalia. Place was found in the trunk on the trestle for her stock of homemade sanitary pads and snippets. The larger leftovers of fabric, with which she had recently started to design a quilt, went into her cupboard's bottom shelf. The pagoda parasol remained hanging from the top of the boarder's cupboard, it wasn't going to bother him there.

Her old bedroom was empty and ready for Maneck Kohlah. Her new bedroom was – horrible. I'll probably lie sleepless, gasping for breath, she thought, hemmed in by the stacks of cloth. But it was out of the question to put the boarder in with the sewing-machines. That would make him run back to his college hostel.

She selected pieces of cloth from the bundle under the bed and settled down to make more patches for the quilt. Concentrating on the work made the anxieties about tomorrow fade. Ridiculous, she felt, to even think of competing with Aban Kohlah and the luxuries of her home in the north. Giving Maneck the bedroom was the only concession she would make.

v Mountains

WHEN MANECK KOHLAH finished moving his belongings from the college hostel to Dina's flat, he was soaking with sweat. Fine strong arms, she thought, watching him carry his suitcase and boxes noiselessly, setting things down with care.

'It's so humid,' he said, wiping his forehead. 'I'll take a bath now, Mrs. Dalal.'

'At this time of the evening? You must be joking. There's no water, you have to wait till morning. And what's this Mrs. Dalal again?'

'Sorry – Dina Aunty.'

Such a good-looking boy, she thought, and dimples when he smiles. But she felt he should get rid of the few hairs at his upper lip that were trying so hard to be a moustache. 'Shall I call you Mac?'

'I hate that name.'

He unpacked, changed his shirt, and they had dinner. He looked up from his plate once, meeting her eye and smiling sadly. He ate little; she asked if the food was all right.

'Oh yes, very tasty, thank you, Aunty.'

'If Nusswan – my brother – saw your plate, he would say that even his pet sparrow would go hungry with that quantity.'

'It's too hot to eat more,' he murmured apologetically.

'Yes, I suppose compared to your healthy mountain air it's boiling here.' She decided he needed putting at ease. 'And how is college?'

'Fine, thank you.'

'But you didn't like the hostel?'

'No, it's a very rowdy place. Impossible to study.'

There was silence again through several morsels, the next attempt at conversation coming from him. 'Those two tailors I met last month – they still work for you?'

'Yes,' she said. 'They'll be here in the morning.'

'Oh good, it will be nice to see them again.'

'Will it?'

He didn't hear the edge in it, and tried to nod pleasantly while she began clearing the table. 'Let me help,' he said, pushing back his chair.

'No, it's okay.'

She soaked the dishes in the kitchen for the morning, and he watched. The flat depressed him, the way it had when he had come to inspect the room. He would be gone in less than a year, he thought, thank God for that. But for Dina Aunty this was home. Everywhere there was evidence of her struggle to stay ahead of squalor, to mitigate with neatness and order the shabbiness of poverty. He saw it in the chicken wire on the broken windowpanes, in the blackened kitchen wall and ceiling, in the flaking plaster, in the repairs on her blouse collar and sleeves.

'If you are tired you can go to bed, don't wait for me,' she said.

Taking it to be a polite dismissal, he withdrew to his room – her room, he thought guiltily – and sat listening to the noises from the back, trying to guess what she was doing.

Before going to bed herself, Dina remembered to turn on the kitchen tap in order to be roused by its patter at first flow. She lay awake for a long while, thinking about her boarder. The first impression was good. He didn't seem fussy at all, polite, with fine manners, and so quiet. But maybe he was just tired today, might be more talkative tomorrow.

Maneck did not sleep well. A window kept banging in the wind, and he felt unsure about rising to investigate, afraid of stumbling in the dark, disturbing Mrs. Dalal. He tossed and turned, haunted by the college hostel. Finally escaped, he thought. But it would have been much better to go straight home . . .

He was up early; the open tap turned out to be his alarm clock as well. After cleaning his teeth he returned to his room and did pushups in his underwear, unaware that Dina, having finished in the kitchen, was watching through the half-open door.

She admired the horseshoe of his triceps as they formed and dissolved with his ascent and descent. I was right last night, she thought, nice strong arms. And such a handsome body. Then she blushed confusedly – Aban in school with me . . . young enough to be my son. She turned away from the door.

'Good morning, Aunty.'

She turned around cautiously, relieved to see he was wearing his clothes. 'Good morning, Maneck. Did you sleep well?'

'Yes, thank you.'

She acquainted him with the bathroom and the working of the immersion water heater, then left. He shut the door to undress, moving carefully in the small, unfamiliar space. Hot water steamed, ebullient in the bucket. He tested it with the fingertips, then plunged his hand past the wrist, exulting in the warmth. He realized it was only the dank monsoon day making the steam threaten and cloud so thick, no more scalding than the dreamy mist that would be hugging the mountains at home now.

If he shut his eyes he could picture it: at this hour it would be swirling fancifully, encircling the snow-covered peaks. Just after dawn was the best time to observe the slow dance, before the sun was strong enough to snatch away the veil. And he would stand at the window, watch the pink and orange of sunrise, imagine the mist tickling the mountain's ear or chucking it under the chin or weaving a cap for it.

Soon he would hear the familiar sounds from downstairs as his father opened up the store and stepped outside to sweep the porch. First, his father would greet the dogs who had spent the night on the porch. There was never any trouble with the strays; Daddy had an arrangement with them: they could sleep here and feed on scraps so long as they left in the morning. And they always went obediently at first light, albeit with reluctance, after nuzzling his ankles. In the kitchen Mummy would stoke the boiler with shiny black coal, fill the tea kettle, slice the bread, and keep an eye on the stove.

At this hour, as the pan hissed and sputtered, the aroma of fried eggs would begin to travel upstairs and to the porch. The appetizing emissary would deliver wordless messages to Maneck and his father. Then Maneck would leave the moving-mist panorama and hurry to breakfast, hugging his parents, whispering good morning to each before sitting down at his place. His father had a special big cup, from which he took great gulps of tea while still standing. He always drank his first cup standing, moving around the kitchen, gazing out the window at the early-morning valley. When Maneck was sick with a cold or had exams at school, he was allowed to drink from his father's cup, with its bowl so huge that Maneck thought he would never finish, never drain its depths, and yet he had to keep drinking if he was to triumph and reveal the star-shaped design at the bottom, changing colour through the final trace of liquid, appearing and disappearing as he sloshed it around . . .

Shaking water off his wet forearm, Maneck tried to shut the leaking tap – a bad washer – and gazed abstractedly at the steamy swirls haloing his bucket of hot water. His homesick imagination made him see the hills float through the fog again, passing from nimbus to nothing. He sighed, stood on the high step enclosing the bathing area, and hung his clothes on the empty nail next to his towel. The third nail was occupied by a brassière, with something else behind it – knitted from strong, rough yarn, like a thumbless glove. Curious, he pulled it out to examine. A bath mitt, he decided, and stepped off the ledge, picking up the mug to splash himself with water from the bucket.

Then he saw the worms. *Phylum Annelida*, he remembered from biology class. They were crawling out of the drain in formidable numbers, stringy and dark red, glistening on the grey stone floor, advancing with their mesmeric glide. Maneck froze for an instant before leaping back to the safety of the ledge.

━━

Weeks earlier, when Dina had first heard that the boarder found for her by Zenobia was the son of a girl who had gone to school with them, her memory could not leap back across the years to pluck out the face in question.

'She had a beauty spot on her chin,' reminded Zenobia, 'and her nose was slightly crooked. Though I think it made her look quite cute.'

Dina shook her head, still unable to remember.

'Do you have the class photo for . . . let's see,' and Zenobia counted on her fingers, '1946, '47, '48, '49 – that's it, 1949.'

'Nusswan would not give me the money to buy it. Have you forgotten how my brother was, after Daddy died?'

'Yes, I know. Such a wretch. Making you wear those ridiculous long uniforms and those heavy, ugly shoes. You poor thing. Makes me mad even after all these years.'

'And because of him I lost touch with everyone. Except you.'

'Yes, I know. He didn't allow you to stay for choir or dramatics or ballet or anything.'

All that evening they enjoyed the pleasures of reminiscing, laughing at the follies and tragedies of their pasts. Very often there was a little sadness in their laughter, for these memories were of their youth. They remembered their favourite teachers, and Miss Lamb, the principal, who was called Lambretta because she was always scooting up and down the halls. They calculated how old they would have been in the sixth standard, when they had started French, and the French teacher, who they had nicknamed Mademoiselle Bouledogue, began terrorizing their lives three times a week. Everyone assumed the name was an example of the cruelty of schoolgirls, but it had been bestowed as much for her heavy jowls as for her pugnacious approach to irregular verbs and conjugations.

After Zenobia left, Dina measured out half a cup of rice, picked out the pebbles from the grain, and boiled the water. The last drop of daylight was used up, and the kitchen light had to be switched on. Through the open window she heard a mother calling her children in from play.

Then the smell of frying onions swooped in. Everywhere the cooking hour had begun.

As the rice cooked, she thought how pleasant it had been to remember her school-days – better than the brooding and daydreaming she had been doing lately about Nusswan and Ruby; her father's house; her nephews, Xerxes and Zarir, grown men now at twenty-two and nineteen, whom she seldom met more than once a year.

After dinner, she sat at the window, watching the balloonman across the road tempt the passing children. Somewhere, a radio began blaring the signature tune for 'Choice of the People.' Eight o'clock, thought Dina, as Vijay Correa's voice introduced the first song. She worked on her quilt for an hour or so. Before going to bed she soaped her clothes and left them in the bucket, ready for the morning wash.

Zenobia stopped by again the next evening on her way home from the Venus Beauty Salon and took a large envelope out of her purse. 'Go on, open it,' she said.

'Oh, it's the class photograph,' Dina exclaimed with delight.

'Look at us all,' said Zenobia wistfully. 'We must have been about fifteen.' She pointed out the girl in the second row.

'Yes, I remember her now. Aban Sodawalla. Though you can't see her beauty spot in this picture.'

'How the girls teased her about it. And that mean poem someone made up, remember? Aban Sodawalla has no grace, needs a soda to clean her face.'

'See the spot upon her chin, pick it out with a pointy pin,' completed Dina. 'How stupid we were then, chanting such nonsense.'

'I know. And by sixteen, the whole jing-bang lot of us was trying to copy the beauty spot. Weren't we silly, trying to paint it on.'

Dina studied the photograph again for a moment. 'I remember her most clearly in the fourth standard. Eight or nine years old. The three of us were always together then. She was the one very good at skipping rope, wasn't she?'

'Yes, exactly.' Zenobia was pleased that at last a firm connection was made. 'Trouble with a capital t, the teacher called us, remember?'

They picked up the trail of nostalgia where they had left it the day before: the games they had played during the short and long recess, and the fun of plaiting one another's hair, comparing ribbons, exchanging hairclips. And when their breasts began to grow, how they would stoop their shoulders to try and reduce the embarrassing protuberances, or wear cardigans to disguise them, even in sweltering heat, and discuss their first periods, walking oddly while they got used to sanitary pads.

And then the teasing about imagined boyfriends and kisses, and fantasies of moonlight walks in romantic gardens.

Most of all, Dina and Zenobia marvelled at how, during those years of their terrible innocence, all the girls had known practically everything about one another's lives. 'Then your father passed away,' said Zenobia. 'And that brother of yours wouldn't allow you to have any friends. But you know, you didn't miss that much – after the final year most of us lost contact with the gang anyway.'

With high school completed, some of their companions had had to go to work because their families were poor; others went on to college, and some were not allowed to, because college could be harmful to the lives of soon-to-be wives and mothers – they were kept home to help in the kitchen. If there were no younger sisters to wear the blouse and pinafore of the school uniform, it was cut into kitchen cloths, to wipe the stoves or carry hot pots and pans. Then the ex-schoolgirls were vague, even secretive, when they chanced to meet. There was an air of embarrassment about how they were spending their days, as though they had colluded in a collective betrayal of their youth and childhood. Most of them knew practically nothing about one another's lives.

'You were the only one I kept in touch with – you and Aban Sodawalla, of course,' said Zenobia.

She continued with the rest of their schoolmate's story: soon after matriculation, Aban had been introduced by family friends to a certain Farokh Kohlah, who was visiting the city, and who had a business in the north, far away, in a hill-station. The Sodawalla family immediately approved of him. How tall and straight stood the young Parsi gentleman, Mr. Sodawalla had said, such a fine bearing, thanks to the healthy life in the mountains. Mrs. Sodawalla was most impressed by the young gentleman's light pigmentation. Not white like a European ghost, she told her friends, but fair and golden.

In view of the possibilities, the Sodawalla family took a tactical vacation the following year at the hill-station. And, in time, the strategy produced the desired results. Aban fell in love with Farokh Kohlah and the natural beauty of the place. Then she married and settled there.

'She still writes to me once a year, without fail,' said Zenobia. 'That's how I knew she was looking for a room for her son.'

'Which was very lucky for me,' said Dina. 'Thanks for all your help.'

'Don't mention it. But God only knows how Aban has managed to live all these years in some tiny hill town. Especially after being born and brought up in our lovely city. To be honest, I would go crazy.'

'If they have their own business, they must be rich people,' said Dina.

Zenobia was doubtful. 'How wealthy can you get these days, with a small shop in some little hill place?'

———

Once, though, Maneck's family had been extremely wealthy. Fields of grain, orchards of apple and peach, a lucrative contract to supply provisions to cantonments along the frontier – all this was among the inheritance of Farokh Kohlah, and he tended it well, making it increase and multiply for the wife he was to marry and the son who would be born.

But long before that eagerly awaited birth, there was another, gorier parturition, when two nations incarnated out of one. A foreigner drew a magic line on a map and called it the new border; it became a river of blood upon the earth. And the orchards, fields, factories, businesses, all on the wrong side of that line, vanished with a wave of the pale conjuror's wand.

Ten years later, when Maneck was born, Farokh Kohlah, trapped by history, was still travelling regularly to courthouses in the capital, snared in the coils of the government's compensation scheme, while files were shuffled and diplomats shuttled from this country to the other. Between journeys he helped his wife to run their old-fashioned general store in town. The shop was all that remained from his vast fortune, having escaped the cartographic changes by being located on the right side of that magic line.

For years the shop had languished, more a hobby or a social club than a business. The real income had come from those other, lost, sources. Now it needed to be nurtured for all it was worth.

Aban Kohlah turned out to be a natural manager in the General Store. 'I can easily handle all this,' she said to her husband. 'You have more important things to do.'

A cradle was set up behind the counter to ensure that she was not separated from her child. She ordered the goods, kept accounts, stocked shelves, served customers, and, in her free moments, revelled in the magnificent view of the valley from the back of the shop. Life in the hills suited her perfectly.

Farokh Kohlah had worried at first that his wife would miss the city and her relatives. He feared that once the novelty of the exotic locale had worn off, the complaining would begin. His worries turned out to be needless; her love for the place only increased with the passage of time.

The cradle was soon outgrown, and Maneck was crawling round and about the counter, then toddling among the shelves. Mrs. Kohlah's vigilance was now strained to the limit. She was afraid that the boy might bring things crashing down on his head. But whenever her back had to be turned, the customers took over, helping to keep him safely busy, playing with him, amusing him with coins and key-rings, or the brilliant hues of their handmade scarves and shawls. 'Hello, baba! Ting-ting! Baba, ak-koo!'

By the time he was five, Maneck was proudly assisting his parents in the shop. He stood behind the counter, his black hair barely visible over the edge, waiting to hear the customer's request. 'I know where it is! I'll get it!' he would say, and run to fetch the item under the fond glances of Mrs. Kohlah and the customer.

After starting school the following year, he continued to help out in the evening. He devised his own system for the regulars, keeping their everyday purchases – three eggs, loaf of bread, small butter packet, biscuits – ready and waiting on the counter at their expected time.

'Look at that son of mine,' said Mr. Kohlah proudly. 'Just six, and what initiative, what organizational skill.' He savoured the pleasure of watching Maneck greet the shoppers and chat with them, describe the aggressive pack of langurs he had seen from the schoolbus that morning, or join in the discussion about a dried-up waterfall. The easygoing manner of the townspeople came naturally to Maneck, having been born and brought up here, and it delighted his father that he mixed so well with everyone.

Sometimes, at dusk, in the bustle of the shop, Mr. Kohlah, surrounded by his wife and son and the customers, who were also friends and neighbours, almost forgot the losses he had suffered. Yes, he would think then, yes, life was still good.

The Kohlahs sold newspapers, several varieties of tea, sugar, bread and butter; also candles and pickles, torches and lightbulbs, biscuits and blankets, brooms and chocolates, scarves and umbrellas; then there were toys, walking-sticks, soap, rope, and more. There was no grand system of inventory selection – just basic groceries, household necessities, and a few luxuries.

The shop's casual approach to commerce made it the favourite with locals as well as with the neighbouring settlements. If someone could not afford a full packet of, say, biscuits, Mrs. Kohlah would think nothing of tearing it open and selling half; she had faith that someone else would come along for the other half. If an item was not in stock, Mr. Kohlah would gladly order it as long as the customer was not particular about the delivery date. Even if the delivery date was crucial, there was not much to be done because deliveries depended on the roads, and roads depended on the weather, and everyone knew weather depended on the One Up Above. The morning newspaper usually arrived by early evening, when the regulars gathered on the porch to smoke or sip tea and discuss the news as they read it, calling out the headlines to Mr. Kohlah if he was pottering around inside the shop.

For all the vast inventory it carried, the shop's backbone, ultimately, was a secret soft-drink formula handed down in the Kohlah family for four generations. There was a little factory in the cellar where the soft drinks were mixed, aerated, and bottled. An assistant washed and prepared the empties, and loaded the crates for delivery. To maintain the formula's secret, Mr. Kohlah did the actual mixing and manufacturing himself; his eyepatch testified to that, covering the hole created by a defective bottle exploding under the pressure of carbonation.

With a handkerchief covering the mess on his face, he had gone upstairs to his wife. Barely a year had passed since their marriage, and it was their first crisis. Would she weep and wail, or faint, or stay composed? He was as curious about her reaction as he was concerned about his eye.

Seven months pregnant, Aban Kohlah was quite in control. 'Farokh, would you first like a peg of brandy?' He said yes. She had a tiny sip herself, then drove him to the hospital down in the valley. The doctor said he was lucky to be alive – his spectacles had broken the impact of the glass projectile, keeping it from reaching his brain. But it was impossible to save the eye.

Mr. Kohlah said that was all right. 'One eye is sufficient for the things I am looking forward to seeing,' he smiled, touching his wife's swollen belly. Whereas, he added, the ugliness of the world would now trouble him only half as much.

He refused to have a glass eye fitted after the socket had healed. An eyepatch became part of his daily attire. He wore it while working in the store, and at social occasions. On his long evening walks through the hillside forest, however, the patch occupied his pocket while he admired for the umpteenth time the beauty of the place and munched on a carrot.

The loss of his eye allowed him to indulge his fondness for carrots. It had been kept in check by Mrs. Kohlah, who said that though carrots were a good thing, any kind of mania was a bad thing. But now she had to allow his passion full play: carrot juice, carrot salad, carrot-ma-gose, carrots in his pocket as walking companions.

'I need carrots,' insisted Mr. Kohlah. 'My one remaining eye must stay fitter than ever, it has to do double duty.'

Their little son, growing quickly, soon learned about his father's craze. When he was scolded for misbehaving, he would steal a carrot from the kitchen and carry it to his father as a peace offering, risking a second scolding from his mother.

After the accident Mr. Kohlah was extra careful in the cellar. He allowed no one in the area while the tired old machines rattled and hissed, filling bottles with the fizz of Kohlah's Cola and the till with the tinkle of much-needed money.

His friends, fearing for his safety, showed their concern by joking about it. 'Careful, Farokh, it can be dangerous when you go underground. Cola mining is as risky as coal mining.' But he laughed with them and ignored their hints.

Sacrificing subtlety, they suggested he should seriously consider replacing the ancient equipment, give some thought to modernizing and expanding the operation. 'Listen, Farokh, look at it rationally,' they urged. 'Kohlah's Cola is so good, it deserves to be known throughout the country, not just in our little corner.'

But modernization and expansion were foreign ideas, incomprehensible to someone who refused even to advertise. Kohlah's Cola (or Kaycee, as it was known) was famous through all the little settlements perched on hillsides for miles around. Word of mouth had been good enough for his forefathers, he said, and it was good enough for him.

From time to time contenders emerged with fanfare, touting rival brands, but soon went out of business, unable to compete with the Kohlah family's product. Nothing could approach Kaycee, claimed the faithful patrons – its delicious flavour was as unique as the air in the mountains. The soft drink and the General Store flourished.

And so, by the time Maneck started school, the business was on a sound footing. Mr. Kohlah carefully guarded the formula that had salvaged their livelihood, waiting for the day when he would reveal it to Maneck, as his father had revealed it to him. An air of contentment surrounded his life, a quiet pride at having survived the ordeal by fire. It surfaced when neighbours gathered in the evening and the talk shifted gently to times gone by, to the stories of their lives; and when Mr. Kohlah's turn came he told of his family's glory days, not from self-pity or notions of false grandeur, nor to sing his own achievement in the present, but as a lesson in living life on the borderline – modern maps could ruin him, but they could not displace his dreams for his family.

Of course, the stories had all been heard before, many times over, yet there was always room for one more telling. And Mr. Kohlah was not the only one guilty of repetition.

Most of his and Mrs. Kohlah's friends were army men and their wives, who, grown used to a lifetime of British-style cantonment living, had chosen to retire here in the hills, unable to countenance a return to dusty plains and smelly cities. They too had oft-told tales to tell, of bygone days, when discipline was discipline and not some watered-down version unworthy of the name. When leaders could lead, when everyone knew their place in the scheme of things, and life proceeded in an orderly fashion, without daily being threatened by chaos.

When these retired brigadiers, majors, and colonels came to tea at the Kohlahs', they arrived suited and booted, as they called it, with watches in their fobs and ties around their necks. These trappings might have seemed comical to a nationalist bent of mind but had talismanic value for their wearers. It was all that stood between them and the disorder knocking at the door. Mr. Kohlah himself was partial to bow ties. Mrs. Kohlah served the tea on Aynsley bone china; the cutlery was Sheffield. If it was a special dinner at Navroze or Khordad Sal, she used the Wedgwood set.

'Such a lovely pattern,' said Mrs. Grewal. 'When will they learn to make such beautiful things in this country?'

Brigadier and Mrs. Grewal were the Kohlahs' closest neighbours, and dropped in fairly often. Mrs. Grewal was also the unchallenged leader of the army wives. Taking the cue from her, someone lightly struck a crystal glass to test the purity of its music; another inverted a plate to gaze lovingly at the manufacturer's monogram. Praise was lavished in equal portions on the food and on the bowls and platters that held it. Chaos was successfully kept at bay for yet another day.

Later, the talk turned, as it had countless times before, to the nightmare that would haunt them to the end of their days – they anatomized the Partition, recited the chronology of events, and mourned the senseless slaughter. Brigadier Grewal wondered if the sundered parts would some day be sewn together again. Mr. Kohlah fingered his patch and said anything was possible. Consolation, as always, was found in muddled criticism of the colonizers who, lacking the stomach for proper conclusions, had departed in a hurry, though the post-mortem was tempered by nostalgia for the old days.

After such evenings, Mr. Kohlah wondered why his air of contentment felt ruffled – not undermined, but as though someone or something was trying to tamper with it. He enjoyed the dinners and tea parties greatly, and would not have absented himself for anything; yet there was a sense of unease, like a smell which should not have been there, of something rotten.

It took a day or two for his equilibrium to return. Then he began to feel again that yes, it had been the right decision not to leave his home in the hills, it was still a good place for his family. 'The air and water is so pure, the mountains so beautiful, and the business is doing very well,' wrote he and Mrs. Kohlah to the relatives who periodically beseeched them to leave. 'Nowhere else can Maneck have better expectations for his future.'

If Maneck had been consulted he would have agreed completely; and never mind the future, the present would have been reason enough for him, for his happy childhood universe. His days were rich and full – school in the morning and afternoon, the General Store after that, followed by a walk with his father, late in the evening, when he would stride manfully alongside to keep up, or else Daddy would tease him that slow coaches got left behind.

But Sundays were the best days. On Sundays a gaddi man called Bhanu came to tidy the garden behind the house. Maneck looked forward all week to being outdoors with Bhanu, wandering around the property and doing chores under his direction. The area beyond the first fifty yards, where it began to slope downhill, wild with shrubs and trees and thick undergrowth, was the most interesting. There, Bhanu taught him the names of strange flowers and herbs, things which did not grow near the front of the house with the roses and lilies and marigolds. He pointed out the deadly datura plant and the one that was its antidote, and leaves that mitigated the poison of certain snakes, others which cured stomach ailments, and the stems whose pulp healed cuts and wounds. He showed Maneck how to squeeze a snapdragon to make its jaws open. Late in the year, when the weather turned chilly, they gathered dead twigs and branches as the afternoon drew to a close, and made a small fire.

Sometimes Bhanu brought along his daughter, Suraiya, who was the same age as Maneck. Then Maneck divided his time between chores and play. At noon, Mrs. Kohlah called the children in for lunch. Suraiya was shy about eating at the table; there were no chairs in her house. It was a few visits before she would run in with Maneck and readily take her place. Bhanu continued to eat his food outside.

One afternoon, Suraiya squatted on the far slope among the bushes. Maneck waited out of sight for a moment, then followed her curiously. She smiled as he approached. He heard the soft hiss, and bent over to look. Her little stream had made a frothy puddle.

He unbuttoned his pants beside her and produced a fluid arc. 'I can do soo-soo standing,' he said.

Laughing, she finished and pulled up her underpants. 'So can my brother, he also has a small soosoti like yours.'

It became a ritual from then on to go in the bushes every time Suraiya came to work with her father. Gradually, their curiosity led them to closer anatomical examinations.

'What is it?' asked Mrs. Kohlah when they came in to tea. 'Why are you two giggling all the time?'

Over the next few Sundays she began watching from the kitchen window, and saw them go repeatedly down the slope, where her eyes could not follow. Her attempt to sneak up on them failed. They heard her footsteps before she was anywhere near, and ran out laughing.

Later, she confided her suspicions to Mr. Kohlah. 'Farokh, I think you need to keep an eye on Maneck. While Suraiya is here.'

'Why, what has he done?'

'Well, they go in the bushes and –' she blushed. 'I haven't actually seen anything, but . . .'

'The little rascal,' smiled Mr. Kohlah. The following Sunday he stayed out in the garden, supervising Bhanu's work and patrolling the periphery of the slope. It became part of his routine for the rest of that year. The children had to exercise all their cunning to evade the adult's watchful eye.

When Maneck completed the fourth standard, Mr. Kohlah began to investigate the possibility of sending him to a boarding school. The quality of instruction available in the local day school had become quite appalling, Brigadier Grewal and everyone else agreed. 'A good education is the most important thing,' they said.

The boarding school they selected was eight hours away by bus. Maneck detested the decision. The thought of leaving the hill-station – his entire universe – brought him to a state of panic. 'I like my school here,' he pleaded. 'And how will I work in the shop in the evening if you send me away?'

'Stop worrying about work, you're only eleven,' laughed Mr. Kohlah. 'You have to enjoy your boyhood first. It will be great fun, living with fellows your own age. You will love the school. And the store will still be here when you come home for holidays.'

Maneck learned to tolerate boarding school but not to love it. He felt an ache of betrayal. Not one day passed without his remembering the house, his parents, the shop, the mountains. He found his classmates very different from the boys he had known. They behaved as though they were better than him. The older boys talked about girls, and touched the younger boys. Someone showed him a deck of playing cards that had pictures of naked women. The dark patches between their legs horrified him. It couldn't be, the pictures had to be fake, he thought, remembering the smooth, sweetly whispering hole of Suraiya.

'That's hair – that's the way it's supposed to be,' said the older boy. 'These are genuine photographs. Look, I'll show you.' He undid his pants to display his pubic hair, also releasing his tumescent penis from its confines.

'But you're a boy, it doesn't prove anything about girls,' said Maneck. He wanted a closer look at the cards. The fellow would not let him unless he did him a favour. He held Maneck very close, rubbing against him and moaning. It was a strange sound, thought Maneck, as though he was trying to do kakka. The cards were handed over after the fellow had spurted.

Maneck returned home for the Divali vacation, let two days pass, then tried to convince his parents not to send him back. He kept it up till Mr. Kohlah got annoyed. 'There will be no more talk on this subject,' he said.

Maneck went to bed without wishing them good night. The omission tormented him for a long time, leaving a hollow that sleep refused to fill. After midnight had struck, he considered going to his parents' room and rectifying his foolish defiance. But pride, and the fear of angering Daddy again, kept him in his own bed.

Up at dawn, he hugged his mother by the stove and murmured good morning, then skirted his father at the kitchen window and slipped into his chair. 'His little lordship is still sulking,' said Mr. Kohlah, smiling.

Maneck looked down at his cup, frowning into it. He did not want to lose control of his mouth and smile back.

It was Sunday, and Bhanu came as usual to work in the garden. Suraiya was not with him. Maneck tagged along for a while before asking about her.

'She is with her mother,' said Bhanu. 'She will be with her from now on.'

Maneck felt another segment of his universe collapse. He did not return to the garden after lunch. Mrs. Kohlah took him aside and said it was not nice to be unkind to Daddy who loved him so much. 'What he is doing, sending you to a fine school, is for your own good. You should not think of it as punishment.'

In the evening, Mr. Kohlah bade his son sit beside him on the sofa. 'Boarding school is not forever,' he said. 'Remember, Mummy and I miss you more than you miss us. But what is the choice? You don't want to be ignorant, unable to read or write, like these poor gaddi people who go through their whole lives cold and hungry, with a few sheep or goats, struggling to survive. Remember, the slow coach gets left behind. Once you obtain the Secondary School Certificate in another six years, nobody is going to send you away. You will take charge of this business.'

Maneck allowed himself a smile as his father continued, 'In fact, the sooner it is, the better for me. I can relax and go hiking all day.'

Next morning at breakfast, Mr. Kohlah gave him the special big cup to drink from. Then he let him sit behind the till to make change for their customers. Maneck cherished that day for the rest of the school year.

Whenever the pain of banishment surfaced, he summoned the happy memory to counterbalance his despair, his dark thoughts of rejection and loneliness.

━━━

Despite his initial dread of the eternity that was six years, time chipped away three of them at its steady pace. Maneck turned fourteen, and came home for the May vacation.

That year, for the first time, his parents were going to leave him on his own for two days while they attended a wedding. Instead of closing down the place and sending him to a neighbour's house, Mr. Kohlah decided, as a special treat, to let him run the shop alone.

'Just do things the way we do when I'm here,' he said. 'Everything will go smoothly. Don't forget to count the soft-drink crates taken by the driver. And phone for tomorrow's milk – very, very important. If there is a problem, call Grewal Uncle. I've told him to check on you later on.' Mr. and Mrs. Kohlah went around the shop one more time with Maneck, reminding and pointing, then departed.

The day passed like any other. There were flurries of activity followed by periods of calm during which he wiped the glass cases, dusted the shelves, cleaned the counter. The regulars inquired about his parents' absence, and praised his ability. 'Look at the boy, keeping the barracks shipshape. Deserves a medal.'

'Farokh and Aban could retire tomorrow if they wanted to,' said Brigadier Grewal. 'Nothing to worry about, with Field Marshal Maneck in charge of General Store.' Everyone present laughed heartily at that.

Late in the evening, quiet descended upon the square as daylight began to fade. Maneck went to switch on the porch lamp, feeling proud of his day's work. It was almost time to close the store. All that remained was to empty the till, count the money, and enter the amount in the book. From the porch he saw the shop's interior, and paused. That big glass case in the centre, with soaps and talcum powders – it would look much nicer in the front. And the old newspaper table near the entrance, scarred and wobbly – wouldn't it be better off pushed to the side?

The idea pursued Maneck and seized his imagination while he warmed his food. The more he thought about it, the more it seemed like a smart rearrangement of the display. He could easily manage it alone, tonight. What a surprise for Mummy and Daddy when they came back.

After eating his dinner, he returned to the darkened shop, switched on the light, and dragged the old table out of the way. The glass case was more difficult, heavy and cumbersome. He emptied the merchandise and pushed it slowly to its new, prominent spot. Then he replaced the cans and cartons, but not in their boring old stacks – he arranged them in interesting pyramids and spirals. Perfect, he thought, standing back to admire the effect, and went to bed.

The next evening, Mr. Kohlah walked in and saw the alterations. Without pausing to greet Maneck or ask how things were, he told him to shut the door, hang out the Closed sign.

'But there's still one hour left,' said Maneck, hungry for his father's praise.

'I know. Shut it anyway.' Then his father ordered him to put everything back the way it was. His voice was barren of emotion.

Maneck would have preferred it if his father had scolded or slapped him, or punished him in any manner he wanted. But this contempt, this refusal to even talk about it, was horrid. The enthusiasm drained from his face, leaving behind a puzzled anguish, and he felt on the verge of tears.

His mother was moved to intervene. 'But Farokh, don't you think it looks nice, what Maneck has done?'

'The looks are irrelevant. What instructions did we give when we trusted him with the shop for two days? This is how he repays the trust. It's a question of discipline and following orders, not of looking nice.'

Maneck returned the displays to their old places, but for the rest of his school vacation he refused to enter the shop. 'Daddy doesn't need me – I don't want to be there,' he said bitterly to his mother. 'He only wants a servant in the shop.'

In bed at night she conveyed to Mr. Kohlah that Maneck's feelings were badly hurt. 'I am aware of that,' he said, facing away from her on the pillow. 'But he must learn to walk before he can run. It's not good for a boy to think he knows everything before his time.'

She persevered, and was successful just before the vacation came to an end. Peace was restored between father and son one morning when Mr. Kohlah started reorganizing one of the glass cases and called Maneck into the shop to ask his opinion. As school reopening day approached, they began working together again in the soft-drink factory in the cellar, Maneck taking down the cleaned empties, then carrying up the crates of freshly bottled Kaycee.

On the last night, Mr. Kohlah said, while switching off the machine, 'I'll miss you when you leave tomorrow.' The motor's dying throbs left his words clutching helplessly at the dank subterranean air. He hugged Maneck as they went up the stairs together.

Boarding school was the cause of Maneck's second unwilling departure from the mountains. The first had come when he was six, when he and his mother went to visit her family in the city, travelling by train for two days. He had been fascinated by the towering buildings and palatial cinema houses, the avalanche of cars and buses and lorries, and the brightness of streets as the lights went on when night had fallen. But after the first few days, he had missed his father terribly. He was thrilled to return home when their holiday was over.

'I am never going to leave the mountains again,' he said. 'Never, ever.'

Mrs. Kohlah whispered something in Mr. Kohlah's ear, who was waiting on the station platform to receive them. He smiled, embraced Maneck, and said neither was he.

But the day soon came when the mountains began to leave them. It started with roads. Engineers in sola topis arrived with their sinister instruments and charted their designs on reams of paper. These were to be modern roads, they promised, roads that would hum with the swift passage of modern traffic. Roads, wide and heavy-duty, to replace scenic mountain paths too narrow for the broad vision of nation-builders and World Bank officials.

One morning, at the worksite, a minister was garlanded as a band played. It was the Bhagatbhai Naankhatai Marching Band: three brass winds, a pair of snares, and a bass drum. Their uniforms were white, with the letters BNMB in gold braid on their backs; on the bass drum, the initials were painted in red. The band's specialty was wedding processions, and the ministerial programme included the paean of the bride's mother, the lament of the bride's mother-in-law, the bridegroom's triumphal progress, an ode to the matchmaker, and a hymn to fertility. But the BNMB expertly adapted the repertoire for the occasion. The drums tattooed away militarily, heralding the march of progress, while the trombone eschewed its mournful matrimonial glissandi in favour of a sunburst staccato.

The audience of unemployed villagers cheered on cue, anxious to earn their attendance money. Speeches were delivered from a makeshift platform. The minister swung a golden pickaxe that missed its mark. He grinned at the crowd and swung again.

After the dignitaries left, the workers moved in. Progress was slow at first, so slow that Mr. Kohlah and all the inhabitants of the hills harboured an irrational hope: the work would never be completed, their little haven would remain unscathed. Meanwhile, Brigadier Grewal and he organized meetings for the townspeople where they condemned the flawed development policy, the shortsightedness, the greed that was sacrificing the country's natural beauty to the demon of progress. They signed petitions, lodged their protest with the authorities, and waited.

But the road continued to inch upwards, swallowing everything in its path. The sides of their beautiful hills were becoming gashed and scarred. From high on the slopes, the advancing tracks looked like rivers of mud defying gravity, as though nature had gone mad. The distant thunder of blasting and the roar of earth-moving machines floated up early in the morning, and the dreaminess of the dawn mist turned to nightmare.

Mr. Kohlah watched helplessly as the asphalting began, changing the brown rivers into black, completing the transmogrification of his beloved birthplace where his forefathers had lived as in paradise. He watched powerlessly while, for the second time, lines on paper ruined the life of the Kohlah family. Only this time it was an indigenous surveyor's cartogram, not a foreigner's imperial map.

When the work was finished, the minister returned to cut the ribbon. In the years since the ground-breaking ceremony, he had grown more corpulent but not less clumsy. He shuffled up to the ribbon and dropped the golden scissors. Seven eager sycophants leapt to the rescue. A tussle ensued; the scissors were wrested away by the strongest of the seven and restored to the minister. He fixed them all with a fierce glare for calling so much attention to a simple slip, then smiled for the crowd and cut the ribbon with a flourish. The crowd applauded, the Bhagatbhai Naankhatai Marching Band struck up, and in the offkey din of the brass winds no one noticed the minister struggling quietly to extricate his pudgy fingers from the scissors.

Then the promised rewards began rolling up the road into the mountains. Lorries big as houses transported goods from the cities and fouled the air with their exhaust. Service stations and eating places sprouted along the routes to provide for the machines and their men. And developers began to build luxury hotels.

That year, when Maneck came home for the holidays, he was puzzled (and later alarmed) to discover his father perpetually irritable. They found it impossible to get through the day without quarrelling, breaking into argument even in the presence of customers.

'What's the matter with him?' Maneck asked his mother. 'When I'm here, he ignores me or fights with me. When I'm at school, he writes letters saying how much he misses me.'

'You have to understand,' said Mrs. Kohlah, 'people change when times change. It does not mean he doesn't love you.'

For Mrs. Kohlah, this unhappy vacation would also be remembered as the one during which Maneck abandoned his habit of hugging his parents and whispering good morning. The first time that he came down and took his place silently, his mother waited with her back to the table till the pang of rejection had passed, before she would trust her hands with the hot frying pan. His father noticed nothing.

Stomach churning, Mr. Kohlah was absorbed in watching the growth of development in the hills. His friends and he agreed it was a malevolent growth. The possibility of increased business at the General Store was no consolation. All his senses were being assaulted by the invasion. The noxious exhaust from lorries was searing his nostrils, he told Mrs. Kohlah, and the ugly throbbing of their engines was ripping his eardrums to shreds.

Wherever he turned, he began to see the spread of shacks and shanties. It reminded him of the rapidity with which the mange had overtaken his favourite dog. The destitute encampments scratched away at the hillsides, the people drawn from every direction by stories of construction and wealth and employment. But the ranks of the jobless always exponentially outnumbered the jobs, and a hungry army sheltered permanently on the slopes. The forests were being devoured for firewood; bald patches materialized upon the body of the hills.

Then the seasons revolted. The rain, which used to make things grow and ripen, descended torrentially on the denuded hills, causing mudslides and avalanches. Snow, which had provided an ample blanket for the hills, turned skimpy. Even at the height of winter the cover was ragged and patchy.

Mr. Kohlah felt a perverse satisfaction at nature's rebellion. It was a vindication of sorts: he was not alone in being appalled by the hideous rape. But when the seasonal disorder continued year after year, he could take no comfort in it. The lighter the snow cover, the heavier was his heart.

Maneck said nothing, though he thought his father was being overly dramatic when he declared, 'Taking a walk is like going into a war zone.'

Mrs. Kohlah had never been one for walking. 'I prefer to enjoy the view from my kitchen,' she said whenever her husband invited her. 'It's less tiring.'

But for Mr. Kohlah, long, solitary rambles were the great pleasure of his life, especially after winter, when every outing was graced by delicious uncertainty – what lay round the next bend? A newborn rivulet, perhaps? Wildflowers he had not noticed yesterday? Among his more awesome memories was a mighty boulder riven by a shrub growing out of it. Sometimes he was the victim of a sweet ambush: a prospect of the valley from a hitherto unseen angle.

Nowadays, every stroll was like a deathwatch, to see what was still standing and what had been felled. Coming upon a favourite tree, he would stop under its branches a while before moving on. He would run his hand along the gnarled trunk, happy that an old friend had survived another day. Many of the rocky ledges that he used to sit on to watch the sunset had been removed by dynamite. When he did find one, he rested for a few minutes and wondered if it would be here for him the next time.

Before long they began talking in town about him. 'Mr. Kohlah's screw is getting a little loose,' they said. 'He speaks to trees and rocks, and pats them like they were his dogs.'

When Maneck heard the gossip, he burned with shame, wishing his father would stop this embarrassing behaviour. He also boiled with anger, wishing to slap some sense into the ignorant, insensitive people.

On the fifth anniversary of the new road, the local punchayet, dominated by a new breed of businessmen and entrepreneurs, organized a small celebration, inviting everyone to participate. Repulsed by the very idea, Mr. Kohlah left the shop early that evening. He pulled off his eyepatch and started on his walk. The rented loudspeakers, from their perches on tree branches in the town square, followed him for some distance with tinny music and the babble of empty speeches.

He must have walked about three miles when the light of day turned towards the promise of sunset. Strains of pink and orange were weaving their ephemeral threads through the sky. He stopped to gaze westwards, eager to savour the moment. At times like these he wished for two eyes again, to get a wider sweep of the landscape.

Then his gaze was pulled downwards, across the treeless hillside. From hundreds of shacks there rose the grey, stinging smoke of frugal cooking fires. The gauze obscured the horizon. Facing upwind, he could smell the acrid haze and, behind it, the stench of human waste that it grimly tried to shroud. He shifted his weight uncertainly. A twig snapped under his feet. He stood still, asking himself what he was waiting for. He heard the stark voices of mothers calling, the shrieks of children, the barking of pariah dogs. He imagined the miserable contents of the pots blackening over the fires while hungry mouths waited around.

Suddenly, he noticed that dusk had fallen: the sunset was forfeited behind the pall. And the entire scene was so mean and squalid by twilight, so utterly beyond his ability to accept or comprehend. He felt lost and frightened. Waves of anger, compassion, disgust, sorrow, failure, betrayal, love – surged and crashed, battering and confusing him. For what? Of whom? And why was it? If only he could . . .

But he could make no sense of his emotions. He felt a tightness in his chest, then his throat constricted as if he were choking. He wept helplessly, silently.

The evening darkened. He took out his handkerchief and wiped his eyes. It was a moment before he realized, dabbing at phantom tears, that only the good eye was wet. Strange, he could have sworn the missing one had cried too.

Returning home through the gloom, he decided there was no meaning in going for walks from now on. If meaning there was, it was too new and terrifying for him to explore.

There was no place of escape. Not for himself, at any rate. His dreams had succumbed, as they must, during their collisions with the passing years. He had struggled, he had won, he had lost. He would keep on struggling – what else was there for him?

But for his son, he began considering other options for the first time.

Between them, relations did not improve when Maneck came home for the two-week break before his final term. Their most frequent arguments concerned the running of the store. Maneck was full of ideas about merchandising and marketing, which his father rejected outright.

'At least let me finish talking,' said Maneck. 'Why are you so stubborn? Why not give it a try?'

'This is not a little hobby that we can try and toy with,' said Mr. Kohlah, his face mournful. 'It's our bread and butter.'

'Are you fighting again, you two?' said Mrs. Kohlah. 'I'm going crazy listening to it.'

'You have no control over your son,' said Mr. Kohlah, even more mournful. 'Can you not do something about his non-stop keech-keech? He contradicts everything I say. He thinks he has a new formula for success – he thinks this is a science experiment.'

He refused to let Maneck order new brands of soap or biscuits which were proving popular elsewhere. Suggestions to improve the lighting in the dingy interior, paint the walls, renovate the shelves and glass cases to make the display more attractive were all received like blasphemy.

Maneck had trouble reconciling this absurdly cautious man with the image that had grown in his head from stories told by his mother, and by his father's friends: of the fearless individual who had descended a rope into the rain-swollen gorge to rescue a puppy; who had shrugged off the loss of his eye to flying glass as though it was no more than a mosquito bite; and who had once thrashed three thieves that had wandered into the store looking for easy prey, tempted by the sight of the lone woman behind the counter, not reckoning on her husband bottling soft drinks in the cellar – like sacks of rice Mr. Kohlah had tossed them around, said his friends.

And now his father was disintegrating all because of the construction of a silly road. Maneck, too, had lately seen the world being remade around him. But with optimism surging through youthful veins, he was certain that things would sort themselves out. He was fifteen: he was immortal, the hills were eternal. And the General Store? It had been there for generations and would be there for generations more, there was no doubt in his mind.

Secretly, Mr. Kohlah also hoped it would be thus – that a miracle would restore the past. But he had read the signs, and the message was unfavourable. Snuggled amid the goods that the loathsome lorries transported up the mountains was a deadly foe: soft drinks, to stock the new shops and hotels.

In the beginning they dribbled into town in small quantities – a few crates that were easily outnumbered by the ever-popular Kaycee. Out of curiosity, people would occasionally sample the newcomers, then shrug and turn their backs; Kohlah's Cola was still number one.

But the giant corporations had targeted the hills; they had Kaycee in their sights. They infiltrated Mr. Kohlah's territory with their board-room arrogance and advertising campaigns and cut-throat techniques. Representatives approached him with a proposition: 'Pack up your machines, sign over all rights to Kohlah's Cola, and be an agent for our brand. Come grow with us, and prosper.'

Of course Mr. Kohlah refused the offer. For him it was not merely a business decision but a question of family name and honour. Besides, he was certain his good neighbours and the people of these settlements were not fickle, they would stay loyal to Kohlah's Cola. He was prepared to put up a fair fight against the competition.

But, like bow ties and watch-chains, fair fights had gone out of style while Mr. Kohlah wasn't looking. The corporations handed out free samples, engaged in price wars, and erected giant billboards showing happy children with smiling parents, or a man and woman tenderly touching foreheads over a bottle out of which two straws penetrated the lovers' lips. The dribble of new soft drinks turned into a deluge. Brands which had been selling for years in the big cities arrived to saturate the town.

'We must strike back,' said Maneck. 'We should also advertise – give out free samples like them. If they want to use hard sell, we do the same.

'Hard sell?' said Mr. Kohlah disdainfully. 'What kind of language is that? Sounds absolutely undignified. Like begging. These big companies from the city can behave like barbarians if they want to. Here we are civilized people.' He gave Maneck his mournful gaze, disappointed with him for even suggesting it.

'Look at him,' Maneck appealed to his mother. 'He's making his long face again. Anything I say, he makes that face at me. He doesn't give my ideas any consideration.'

So Kohlah's Cola never stood a chance. The General Store's backbone was broken, and the secret formula's journey down the generations was nearing its end.

Mr. Kohlah went ahead with the alternate plan for his son, who would soon be obtaining his Secondary School Certificate. He began making inquiries and sending away to various colleges for their prospectuses.

'Are you sure this is necessary, Farokh?' asked Mrs. Kohlah.

'The slow coach gets left behind,' he answered. 'And I don't want the same thing to happen to Maneck.'

'Oh Farokh, how can you say that? Just look at your success – you lost everything during Partition, yet you made such a good life for all of us. How can you call yourself a slow coach?'

'Maybe I'm not – maybe the world is moving too fast. But the end result is the same.'

He would not be distracted from his purpose, and career possibilities were discussed with the faithful family friends. They agreed it was an excellent idea to keep the options open.

'Not that your business is going to fail,' said Brigadier Grewal. 'But it's good to be prepared on all fronts. Nice to have a big gun in reserve.'

'Exactly my thinking,' said Mr. Kohlah.

'Would be so nice if he could be a doctor or lawyer,' said Mrs. Kohlah, plunging straight into the glamour areas.

'Or an engineer.'

'Chartered accountant is also very prestigious,' said Mrs. Grewal.

It was up to the army chaps to steer the discussion into the practical realm. 'We have to deal with the reality on the ground. The choice is limited by Maneck's marks.'

'Which is not to say that he isn't talented.'

'Not at all. Sharp as a bayonet, like his father.'

'And he is good with his hands,' agreed Mr. Kohlah, taking the compliment in stride.

Something technical for Maneck, that much was certain, they all agreed. Preferably in an industry that would grow with the nation's prosperity. The answer, in a country where most of the population lived in tropical or subtropical climates, was obvious and unanimous: 'Refrigeration and air-conditioning.' And the best college granting diplomas in this field, they discovered, was in Mrs. Kohlah's native city by the sea, the one she had forsaken to marry Mr. Kohlah.

When the final term ended, Maneck came home to discover what had been decided for him and protested vehemently. The second betrayal was not received with a slow ache, as the first one had been. It exploded inside him.

'You promised that when I got my S.S.C. I could work with you! You said you wanted me to take over the family business!'

'Calm down – you will, you will,' said Mr. Kohlah, mustering more conviction than he felt. 'This is just in case. You see, in the past it was easier to plan for the future. Nowadays, things are more complicated, too much uncertainty.'

'It's a waste of time,' said Maneck. He was sure that his father was doing this to be rid of him – to be rid of his interference in the General Store, as though he were a rival. 'If you want me to learn a trade or something, I can become a mechanic at Madanlal's Garage. In the valley. Why do I have to go so far away?'

Mr. Kohlah made his mournful face. Brigadier Grewal laughed good-humouredly. 'Young man, if you are planning a second line of defence, make sure it's a strong one. Or don't bother.'

The family friends said Maneck was a very lucky fellow, and should be grateful for the opportunity. 'At your age, we would have been thrilled to spend a year in the most modern, most cosmopolitan city in the whole country.'

So Maneck was enrolled in the college, and preparations were made for his departure. A new suitcase was purchased. His clothes were sorted through, and tickets booked for the various legs of the journey.

'Don't worry,' said his mother. 'Everything will be all right when you come back after a year. Daddy is just concerned about your future. All these changes – they have happened too fast for him. He should be calmer in a year's time.'

She began to assemble the items he would take with him in boxes. Fearful of forgetting something, she frequently consulted the suggested checklist in the college handbook. She kept opening and shutting the suitcase, taking things out and putting them back in, counting and re-arranging. The woman who effortlessly managed the General Store's merchandise began going to pieces over her son's packing.

Time and again, she asked for her husband's advice. 'Farokh, how many towels shall I include? Do you think Maneck will need his good trousers, the grey gabardine ones? How much soap and toothpaste, Farokh? And which medicines shall I pack?

His answer was always the same: 'Don't bother me with silly things. You decide.' He refused even to come near the growing pile of clothes and personal effects, as though denying its existence. If he had to pass by the open suitcase on the table in the upstairs passage, he would avert his eye.

Mrs. Kohlah understood perfectly well the meaning of her husband's behaviour. She had assumed that inviting him to share in the planning and packing might help him, make it easier for him to get through the days that were causing so much pain to all of them.

After his brusque responses, she preferred to leave him alone. In any case, she was the stronger of the two when it came to coping with such matters, though neither of them had experienced this long a separation from Maneck. Distance was a dangerous thing, she knew. Distance changed people. Look at her own case – she could never return now to live with her family in the city. And just going to boarding school had made Maneck shun the good-morning hug that he had never missed, ever, not even on days when he was sick, when he came down so lovingly, put his arms around her, then went back to bed. What else would he shun after this separation? Already he was getting more solitary, harder to talk to and share things with, always looking so depressed. How much more would he change? What things would the city do to her son? Was she losing him now forever?

Musing and worrying, in the midst of serving customers, she wandered absentmindedly from the shop to Maneck's boxes. Mr. Kohlah sensed something amiss upstairs, shut off the soft-drink machines in midflow and came bounding up the cellar steps to apologize to the lingering clientele.

He curbed his annoyance that morning. The next time it happened, however, he burst out, 'Aban! What emergency are you attending to in the bedroom, may I ask?'

Sarcasm was difficult for him, and rare, so it surprised him and hurt her. But she refused to be drawn into an argument, answering mildly, 'I remembered something very important. Had to check it right away.'

'Your mania will drive us crazy. Please understand once and for all – if you forget something we can always mail a parcel.'

But the things she was concerned about could not be contained or sent in parcels, and attempts to explain them also went frustratingly awry, the words coming out all wrong. 'You don't take an interest in Maneck's packing, you don't want the responsibility. And then you say things like mania and crazy to me? Don't you fear for him? What has happened to your feelings?'

Despite his own confused anger, Mr. Kohlah understood the meaning of his wife's behaviour. A week after this exchange, he was awakened in the night by her rising to leave the room. The clock had finished striking twelve a few minutes ago. He pretended to be asleep. He heard the swish and rustle of her feet as she felt about for her slippers. When she had shut the door behind her, he rose softly and followed.

The floorboards felt cold to his bare feet. He padded down the dark passage and, rounding the corner, saw her standing before the suitcase. He retreated a step. She stood motionless, her head bent, her hands immersed in Maneck's clothes. When the cloud-hidden moon emerged, the silver light illuminated her face. An owl hooted, and he was glad that he had stayed silent, had followed her secretly like this, to see her so beautiful, so absorbed, as she stood there, embodying their years together, their three lives fused in her being, vivid in her face and in her eyes.

The owl hooted again. The moonlight wavered, hesitating, letting a cloud slide across. Her hands stirred within Maneck's suitcase. The dogs on the porch barked – at what ghost?

Farokh Kohlah heard the ticking of the clock, and then the single bong of twelve-fifteen. He felt grateful to the night for giving him this opportunity, this vision by moonlight. He returned to bed, and did not disturb her when she slid under the sheet minutes later.

The time for last-minute instructions had arrived. More or less repeating the advice given all along, after Maneck's going away had first become reality, his parents cautioned him against mixing at college with those who gambled or drank or smoked. They told him to be careful with his money, and to cultivate a healthy scepticism, for people were very different in the city. 'All your life here, we never once discouraged your friendly nature. Whether your companions were rich or poor, and whatever caste or religion – those differences were not important. But now you are facing the most crucial difference of all, by leaving here for the city. You must be very, very careful.'

Mr. Kohlah was planning to accompany his son on the bus ride into the valley, and then by auto-rickshaw to the railway station. But the part-time assistant who had promised to arrive early to take over the morning chores did not show up. So Maneck started off alone on the long day-and-a-half trip to the city.

'Be sure to get a coolie at the station,' said his father. 'Don't try to carry everything yourself. And fix the amount before he touches the luggage. Three rupees should be enough.'

'Aren't you going to hug him?' said Mrs. Kohlah, exasperated, as the two shook hands.

'Oh, all right,' said Maneck, and put his arms around his father.

The *Frontier Mail* was in the station when the shuddering auto-rickshaw drew up at the gate. Maneck paid, then followed the coolie over the footbridge to reach the southbound platform. He paused for a moment at the top, the train stretched long and thin underneath him with people scurrying around it. Like ants trying to carry off a dead worm, he thought.

The coolie had walked on, and he ran to catch up. Near the waiting room a vendor was roasting maize, fanning the crepitating coals. Maneck decided to come back for some after finding his seat.

'Fifty rupees from now on,' he overheard the stationmaster, who was collecting his weekly tribute of maize and money. 'You have the best location. That's what others are willing to pay for it.'

'All day the burning smoke blinds my eyes and throttles my lungs,' said the vendor. 'And just look at my fingers – charred black. Have some pity, sahab.' He turned the corncobs deftly to keep them from scorching. 'How to afford fifty rupees? Police also have to be kept happy.'

'Don't pretend,' said the stationmaster, tucking the money into a pocket of his starched white uniform. 'I know how much you earn.'

Now and again a kernel exploded with a sharp burst. The sound and aroma faithfully nudged Maneck's memory of his first train journey: his mother and he, going to visit their relations.

Daddy had come to see them off. 'You're getting too heavy,' he had groaned playfully, lifting Maneck to give him a good view of the steam engine. How huge it was, and the train, like a string of bungalows, stretched so far, in a long, long line. Daddy carried him down to the end of the platform, close to the hissing, clanking monster, while Maneck busily tackled his corncob. He bit into it, and milk-white juice spotted Daddy's spectacles.

Daddy made a yanking gesture, which the engine driver understood; he gave a smart tap to his cap visor and sounded the whistle for Maneck. The piercing shriek, so close it seemed to spring from his own heart, startled him into dropping the cob. 'Never mind,' said Daddy. 'Mummy will buy you another.'

He bundled Maneck through the window into his seat, next to

Mummy, as the final announcement was made. The train moved, and the station began to float past them. Daddy waved his hand, smiling, blowing kisses. He walked beside the compartment, then ran a bit, but was soon left behind to disappear like the fallen corncob lying on the station platform. Everything familiar swept out of sight . . .

Maneck found his compartment and paid the coolie after the luggage was stowed away. The bungalow on wheels from his childhood had shrunk. Time had turned the magical to mundane. The whistle sounded. No time to buy the maize. He sank into the seat beside his fellow passenger.

The man did not encourage Maneck's efforts at conversation, answering with nods and grunts, or vague hand movements. He was neatly dressed, his hair parted on the left. His shirt pocket bristled with pens and markers in a special clip-on plastic case. The two seats facing them were occupied by a young woman and her father. She was busy knitting. By the fragment hanging from the needles, Maneck tried to decipher what it might be – scarf, pullover sleeve, sock?

The father rose to go to the lavatory. 'Wait, Papaji, I'll help you,' said the daughter, as he limped into the aisle on one crutch. Good, thought Maneck, she would have to take the upper berth. The view would be better, from his own upper berth.

In the evening, Maneck offered his neatly dressed neighbour a Gluco biscuit. He whispered thank you. 'You're welcome,' Maneck whispered back, assuming the man had a preference for speaking softly. In return for the biscuit he received a banana. Its skin was blackened in the heat, but he ate it all the same.

The attendant began making the rounds with blankets and sheets, readying the berths for sleep. After he left, the neatly dressed man took a chain and padlock from the bag that held his bananas and shackled his trunk to a bracket under the seat. Leaning towards Maneck's ear, he explained confidentially, 'Because of thieves – they enter the compartments when passengers fall asleep.'

'Oh,' said Maneck, a little perturbed. No one had warned him about this. But maybe the chap was just a nervous type. 'You know, some years ago my mother and I took this same train, and nothing was stolen.'

'Sadly, now the world is much changed.' The man took off his shirt and hung it neatly on a hook by the window. Then he removed the plastic case from the pocket and clipped it to his vest, careful not to snare his chest hair in the formidable spring. Seeing Maneck watching, he whispered with a smile, 'I am very fond of my pens. I don't like separating from them, not even in sleep.'

Maneck smiled back, whispering, 'Yes, I also have a favourite pen. I don't lend it to anyone – it spoils the angle of the nib.'

The father and daughter did not take kindly to these whispers which excluded them. 'What can we do, Papaji, some people are just born rude,' she said, handing him his crutch. They went off again to the bathroom, hurling a frosty glance at the opposite seats.

It went unnoticed, for Maneck had begun to worry about his suitcase. The pen-lover's soft words about thieves ruined his night, and he forgot all about the woman in the upper berth. By the time he remembered, she was under cover from prying eyes, Papaji having tucked in the sheet around her neck.

Before climbing into his own berth, Maneck positioned his suitcase so that one corner would be visible from above. He lay awake, peering at it every now and then. The young woman's father caught him looking a few times, and eyed him suspiciously. Towards dawn, slumber overpowered Maneck's vigilance. The last thing he saw while surrendering to sleep was Papaji balanced on one crutch, curtaining off his daughter with a bedsheet as she descended without exposing so much as a calf or an ankle.

He did not awake till the attendant came to collect the bedclothes. The young woman was already busy with her knitting, the inscrutable woollen segment dancing below her fingers. Tea was served. Now the neatly dressed pen-lover was more talkative. The cluster of pens was back in his shirt pocket. Maneck learned that yesterday's reticence had been due to a throat ailment.

'Thankfully, it has eased a little this morning,' said the man, as he coughed and threatened to hawk.

Remembering how he had returned the man's hoarse whispers by whispering back dramatically, Maneck felt a little embarrassed. He wondered if he should apologize or explain, but the pen-lover did not appear to bear any resentment.

'It's a very serious condition,' he explained. 'And I am travelling to seek specialist treatment.' He cleared his throat again. 'I could never have imagined, long, long ago, when I started my career, that this was what it would do to me. But how can you fight your destiny?'

Maneck shook his head in sympathy. 'Was it a factory job? Toxic fumes?'

The man laughed scornfully at the suggestion. 'I'm an LL.B., a fully qualified lawyer.'

'Oh, I see. So the lengthy speeches in dusty courtrooms strained and ruined your vocal cords.'

'Not at all – quite the contrary.' He hesitated, 'It's such a long story.'

'But we have lots of time,' encouraged Maneck. 'It's such a long journey.'

Papaji and daughter had had enough of them exchanging comments in low voices. Papaji was certain that their soft laughter contained a leering note, aimed directly at his innocent daughter. He scowled, picked up his crutch, took his daughter by the hand and stomped one-leggedly down the aisle. 'What to do, Papaji,' she said. 'Some people just have no manners.'

'I wonder what's wrong with those two,' said the pen-lover, watching the precise, machinelike movement of the crutch. He uncorked a small green bottle, sipped, and put it aside. Fingering his pens affectionately, he tried out the freshly medicated larynx with the opening sentence of the story of his throat.

'My law career, which was my first, my best-loved career, started a very long time ago. In the year of our independence.'

Maneck counted rapidly. 'From 1947 to 1975 – twenty-eight years. That's a lot of legal experience.'

'Not really. Within two years I changed careers. I couldn't stand it, performing before a courtroom audience day after day. Too much stress for a shy person like me. I would lie in bed at night, sweating and shivering, scared of the next morning. I needed a job where I would be left to myself. Where I could work *in camera*.'

'Photography?'

'No, that's Latin, it means in private.' He scratched his pens as though relieving an itch for them, and looked rueful. 'It's a bad habit I have, because of my law training – using these silly phrases instead of good English words. Anyway, seeking privacy, I became a proofreader for *The Times of India*.'

How would proofreading ravage the throat? wondered Maneck. But he had already interrupted twice and made a fool of himself. Better to keep quiet and listen.

'I was the best they had, the absolute best. The most difficult and important things were saved for my inspection. The editorial page, court proceedings, legal texts, stockmarket figures. Politicians' speeches, too – so boring they could make you drowsy, send you to sleep. And drowsiness is the one great enemy of the proofreader. I have seen it destroy several promising reputations.

'But nothing was too tricky for me. The letters sailed before my eyes, line after line, orderly fleets upon an ocean of newsprint. Sometimes I felt like a Lord High Admiral, in supreme command of the printer's navy. And within months I was promoted to Chief Proofreader.

'My night sweats disappeared, I slept well. For twenty-four years I held the position. I was happy in my little cubicle – my kingdom with my desk, my chair, and my reading light. What more could anyone want?'

'Nothing,' said Maneck.

'Exactly. But kingdoms don't last for ever – not even modest little cubicle kingdoms. One day it happened, without warning.'

'What?'

'Disaster. I was checking an editorial about a State Assembly member who made a personal fortune out of the Drought Relief Project. My eyes began to itch and water. Thinking nothing of it, I rubbed them, wiped them dry, and resumed my work. Within seconds they were wet again. I dried them once more. But it kept on happening, on and on. And it was no longer a tear or two which could be ignored, but a continuous stream.

'Soon, my concerned colleagues were gathered around me. They crowded my little cubicle, pouring comfort upon what they thought was grief. They presumed that reading about the sorry state of the nation, day after day – about the corruption, the natural calamities, the economic crises – had finally broken me. That I was dissolving in a fit of sorrow and despair.

'They were wrong, of course. I would never let emotions stand in the way of my professional duties. Mind you, I'm not saying a proofreader must be heartless. I'm not denying that I often felt like weeping at what I read – stories of misery, caste violence, government callousness, official arrogance, police brutality. I'm certain many of us felt that way, and an emotional outburst would be quite normal. But too long a sacrifice can make a stone of the heart, as my favourite poet has written.'

'Who's that?'

'W. B. Yeats. And I think that sometimes normal behaviour has to be suppressed, in order to carry on.'

'I'm not sure,' said Maneck. 'Wouldn't it be better to respond honestly instead of hiding it? Maybe if everyone in the country was angry or upset, it might change things, force the politicians to behave properly.'

The man's eyes lit up at the challenge, relishing the opportunity to argue. 'In theory, yes, I would agree with you. But in practice, it might lead to the onset of more major disasters. Just try to imagine six hundred million raging, howling, sobbing humans. Everyone in the country – including airline pilots, engine drivers, bus and tram conductors – all losing control of themselves. What a catastrophe. Aeroplanes falling from the skies, trains going off the tracks, boats sinking, buses and lorries and cars crashing. Chaos. Complete chaos.'

He paused to give Maneck's imagination time to fill in the details of the anarchy he had unleashed. 'And please also remember: scientists haven't done any research on the effects of mass hysteria and mass suicide upon the environment. Not on this subcontinental scale. If a butterfly's wings can create atmospheric disturbances halfway round the world, who knows what might happen in our case. Storms? Cyclones? Tidal waves? What about the land mass, would it quake in empathy? Would the mountains explode? What about rivers, would the tears from twelve hundred million eyes cause them to rise and flood?'

He took another sip from the green bottle. 'No, it's too dangerous. Better to carry on in the usual way.' He corked the bottle and wiped his lips. 'To get back to the facts. There I was with the day's proofs before me, and my eyes leaking copiously. Not one word was readable. The text, the disciplined rows and columns, were suddenly in mutiny, the letters pitching and tossing, disintegrating in a sea of stormy paper.'

He passed his hand across his eyes, reliving that fateful day, then stroked his pens comfortingly, as though they too might be upset by the evocation of those painful events. Maneck took the opportunity to slip in a bit of praise, to ensure that the story continued. 'You know, you're the first proofreader I've met. I would have guessed they'd be very dull people, but you speak so . . . with such . . . so differently. Almost like a poet.'

'And why shouldn't I? For twenty-four years, the triumphs and tragedies of our country quickened my breath, making my pulse sing with joy or quiver with sorrow. In twenty-four years of proofreading, flocks of words flew into my head through the windows of my soul. Some of them stayed on and built nests in there. Why should I not speak like a poet, with a commonwealth of language at my disposal, constantly invigorated by new arrivals?' He gave a mighty sigh. 'Until that wet day, of course, when it was all over. When the windows were slammed shut. And the ophthalmologist sentenced me to impotence, saying that my proofreading days were behind me.'

'Couldn't he give you new spectacles or something?'

'That wouldn't have helped. The trouble was, my eyes had become virulently allergic to printing ink.' He spread his hands in a gesture of emptiness. 'The nectar that nurtured me had turned to poison.'

'Then what did you do?'

'What can anyone do in such circumstances? Accept it, and go on. Please always remember, the secret of survival is to embrace change, and to adapt. To quote: "All things fall and are built again, and those that build them again are gay."'

'Yeats?' guessed Maneck.

The proofreader nodded, 'You see, you cannot draw lines and compartments, and refuse to budge beyond them. Sometimes you have to use your failures as stepping-stones to success. You have to maintain a fine balance between hope and despair.' He paused, considering what he had just said. 'Yes,' he repeated. 'In the end, it's all a question ot balance.'

Maneck nodded. 'All the same, you must have missed your work very much.'

'Well, not really,' he dismissed the sympathy. 'Not the work itself. Most of the stuff in the newspaper was pure garbage. A great quantity of that which entered through the windows of my soul was quickly evacuated by the trapdoor.'

This seemed to Maneck to contradict what the man had said earlier. Perhaps the lawyer behind the proofreader was still active, able to argue both sides of the question.

'A few good things I kept, and I still have them.' The proofreader tapped audibly, first on his forehead, then on his plastic pen case. 'No rubbish or bats in my belfry – no dried-up pens in my pocket-case.'

The thump of the single crutch signalled the return down the aisle of Papaji and daughter. Maneck and the proofreader greeted them with pleasant smiles. But they were not to be so easily placated. While passing through to his seat, Papaji lunged with his crutch at the proofreader's foot. He would have successfully speared it had the proofreader not anticipated the attack.

'Sorry,' said Papaji, gruff with disappointment. 'What to do, clumsy mistakes happen when you have only one good leg in a world of two legs.'

'Please don't worry,' said the proofreader. 'No harm has been done.'

The daughter resumed knitting, and Papaji concentrated his grim look outside the window, startling the occasional farmer working his field who happened to catch the angry eye. Maneck wanted the proofreader to continue. 'So are you retired now?'

He shook his head. 'Can't afford to. No, luckily for me, my editor was very kind, and got me a new job.'

'But what about your throat trouble?' Maneck assumed that the point of the entire narration had somehow been overlooked.

'That happened in the new job. Because of his position, the editor-in-chief was friendly with many politicians and was able to set me up for freelancing, in morcha production.' Seeing the question on Maneck's face, he explained, 'You know, to make up slogans, hire crowds, and produce rallies or demonstrations for different political parties. It seemed simple enough when he presented me with the opportunity.'

'And was it?'

'There was no problem on the creative front. Writing speeches, designing banners – all that was easy. With years of proofreading under my belt, I knew exactly the blather and bluster favoured by professional politicians. My *modus operandi* was simple. I made up three lists: Candidate's Accomplishments (real and imaginary), Accusations Against Opponent (including rumours, allegations, innuendoes, and lies), and Empty Promises (the more improbable the better). Then it was merely a matter of taking various combinations of items from the three lists, throwing in some bombast, tossing in a few local references, and there it was – a brand-new speech. I was a real hit with my clients.' A smile played on his face as he remembered his successes.

'My difficulties lay in the final phase, out on the street. You see, I had spent my working life in an office, in silence, and my throat was unexercised. Now suddenly I was yelling instructions, shouting slogans, exhorting the crowds to repeat after me. This was *terra incognita* for a person of my background. It became too much. Much too much for my underused larynx. My vocal cords suffered such injuries, the doctors tell me they will never fully recover.'

'That's terrible,' said Maneck. 'You should have let the others scream and yell. After all, that's what the crowds are hired for, aren't they?'

'Correct. But the habit of my old job – doing everything myself, down to the smallest detail – was a hard habit to break. I could not leave it to the rented crowd to do the shouting. After all, the success of a demonstration is measured in decibels. Clever slogans and smart banners alone will not do it. So I felt I must lead by example, employ my voice enthusiastically, volley and thunder, beseech the heavens, curse the forces of evil, shriek the praises of the benefactor – bellow and clamour and cry and cheer till victory was mine!'

Excited by his remembrances, the proofreader forgot his limitations and began raising his voice. He plucked a pen from his pocket and gesticulated with it like a conductor's baton. Then his symphonic descriptions were cut short by a violent fit of hacking and choking and gasping.

Papaji and daughter cringed, shrinking backwards into their seats, fearing contagion from the vile-sounding cough. 'What to do, Papaji,' sniffed the daughter, covering her nose and mouth with her sari. 'Some people just have no concern for those around them. So shamelessly spreading their germs.'

The proofreader caught his breath and said, 'You see? You see the extent of my suffering? This is the result of the morcha profession. A second impotence.' He lifted his hands and clutched himself round the neck. 'You could say that I have cut my own throat.'

Maneck laughed appreciatively, but the proofreader had not intended to be humorous. 'I have learned from my experience,' he said with gravity. 'Now I keep a strong-throated assistant at my side, to whom I whisper my instructions. I teach him the phrasing, the cadence, the stressed and unstressed syllables. Then he leads the shouting brigades on my behalf.'

'And his throat is okay, no problems?'

'Yes, quite okay, on the whole. He used to be a sergeant-major before he left the army. Still, I have to keep him supplied with mentholated throat lozenges. In fact, he is meeting me at the station. There is always a lot of demand in the city for morchas. Various groups are in a state of perpetual agitation – for more food, less taxes, higher wages, lower prices. So we will also do some business while I get my medical treatment.'

Towards the end of the story, his voice sank to the feeble whisper that he had struggled to produce last night, and Maneck asked him to please not strain himself any further.

'You're quite right,' said the proofreader. 'I should have stopped talking ages ago. By the way, my name is Vasantrao Valmik,' and he held out his hand.

'Maneck Kohlah,' he replied, shaking it, while Papaji and daughter looked the other way, wanting to take no part in an introduction with these two ill-mannered individuals.

It was thirty-six hours after leaving home that Maneck arrived in the city, clothes covered in dust and eyes smarting. His nose ached, and his throat felt raw. He wondered what additional damage the journey had inflicted on the poor proofreader's ravaged vocal cords.

'Bye-bye, Mr. Valmik – all the best,' he said, struggling outside with his suitcase and boxes.

Standing woebegone on the platform, looking around for his retired sergeant-major, Vasantrao Valmik was hardly able to croak a reply. He raised a hand in farewell, which stroked his pens on the way down.

Maneck's taxi from the train station to the college hostel made a small detour around an accident. An old man had been hit by a bus. The conductor flagged down passing buses, transferring his passengers while waiting for the police and ambulance.

'Have to be young and quick to cross the street,' mused the taxi driver.

'True,' said Maneck.

'Bastard bus drivers, they buy their licence with bribes, without passing the test,' the driver took an angrier tone, moving into the opposing lane of traffic to overtake. 'Should all be sent to jail.'

'You're right,' said Maneck, only half-listening. Filtered through his exhaustion, the city seemed to roll past the taxi window like the frames of a film reel. On the pavement, children were pelting pebbles at a dog and bitch joined in copulation. Someone emptied a bucket over the animals to separate them. The taxi narrowly missed hitting the dog as it darted into traffic.

At the next signal light, police were arresting a man who had been beaten up by a gang of six or seven young fellows. The mohulla's residents had spilled into the road to witness the culmination of the drama. 'What happened?' the taxi driver leaned out his window to ask an onlooker.

'Threw acid in his wife's face.'

The signal changed before they found out why. The driver speculated that maybe she was fooling around with another man; or she may have burnt the husband's dinner. 'Some people are cracked enough to do anything.'

'Could have been a dowry quarrel,' said Maneck.

'Maybe. But in those cases they usually use kerosene, in the kitchen.'

It was late evening when Maneck reached the hostel. At the warden's office he was given his room number, keys, and a list of rules: Please always keep room locked. Please do not write or scratch on walls with sharp instruments. Please do not bring female visitors of the opposite sex into rooms. Please do not throw rubbish from windows. Please observe silence at night time . . .

He crumpled the cyclostyled list and tossed it on the little desk. Too enervated to eat or wash, he unpacked a white bedsheet and went to sleep.

Something crawling along his calf woke him. He rose on one elbow to deliver a furious swat below the knee. It was dark outside. He shivered, and his heart thumped wildly with the panic of not being able to remember where he was. Why had his bedroom window shrunk? And where was the valley that should lie beyond it, with pinpoints of light dancing in the night, and the mountains looming darkly in the distance? Why had everything vanished?

Relief covered him like a blanket as his eyes were able to trace the outline of his luggage on the floor. He had travelled. By train. Travelling made everything familiar vanish. How long had he slept – hours or minutes? He peered at his watch to unravel the puzzle, pondering the glowing numbers.

He started, suddenly remembering what it was that had woken him. The crawling thing on his leg. He jumped out of bed, kicked the suitcase, knocked into the chair, and felt around frantically on the wall. The switch. Click. His finger gave life to the naked ceiling bulb, and the bedsheet gleamed like a fresh, dazzling snowfield. Except for the side where he had slept, smudged by the dust from his face and clothes.

Then he saw it on the edge of the white expanse. Under the glare of the light it scuttled towards the gap between bed and wall. He grabbed a shoe and smacked wildly in its general direction.

It was a very poor shot; the cockroach disappeared. Chagrined, he fought off his fatigue and tackled the problem with more determination. He pulled the bed away from the wall, slowly, not to alarm the fugitive, till there was a space for him to squeeze in.

The exposed bit of floor revealed a conference of cockroaches. He crouched stealthily, raised his arm, and unleashed a flurry of blows. Three succumbed to his shoe, the rest disappeared under the bed. He got down on his hands and knees, resolved that they would not escape to haunt him later. Meanwhile, his ankle began to itch, and his scratching fingers felt a red swelling. He discovered similar itchy bumps on his arms.

There was a knock on the door. He hesitated, loath to leave his prey – if they managed to hide, he would be at their mercy for the rest of the night.

A voice called, 'Hi! Everything okay?'

Maneck crawled out from under the bed and opened the door. 'Hi,' said the visitor. 'I'm Avinash. From the next room.' He put out his right hand; the left held a spray pump.

'I'm Maneck.' He dropped the shoe and shook hands, then glanced quickly over his shoulder in case the enemy was trying to flee.

'Heard the banging,' said Avinash. 'Cockroaches, right?'

Maneck nodded, picking up his shoe again.

'Relax, I got you some advanced technology.' Grinning, he held up the spray pump.

'Thanks, but it's okay,' said Maneck, vigorously scratching the red trophies on his arms. 'I killed three and –'

'You don't know this place. Kill three, and three dozen will arrive marching in single file, to take revenge. It's like a Hitchcock movie.' He laughed and came closer, lightly touching the red bumps on Maneck's arms. 'Bedbugs.'

His advice was to fumigate the room and wait outside for forty-five minutes. 'It's the only way you'll be able to sleep tonight, believe me. This is my third year in the hostel.'

They removed the sheet, lifted the mattress, and treated the frame and slats. The rest of the room was also sprayed – along the window ledge, in the corners, inside the cupboard. The suitcase and boxes were moved to Avinash's room, to keep the bugs and cockroaches from seeking refuge in them.

'I feel bad using up so much of your spray,' said Maneck.

'Don't worry, you'll have to buy your own can of Flit. You can do mine later. The rooms need spraying at least once a week.'

They settled down to wait for the insects to die, Maneck on the only chair, Avinash on the bed. 'So,' he said, leaning back upon his elbows.

'Thanks for your help.'

'It's okay, yaar, no big deal.' There was a pause, to see which way the conversation would go. It didn't. 'You want to play chess, or draughts or something, to pass the time?'

'Okay, draughts.' Maneck liked his eyes, the way they looked directly into his.

It was easier to start talking once they began the game, their heads bowed over the board. 'So where are you from?' asked Avinash, obtaining his first king.

The account of the hill-station, the settlements, the mountains, the langurs, the snow fascinated Avinash. He confessed, as he won the game and set up the board again, that he had never travelled anywhere.

'The house was built by my great-grandfather, on a hill,' continued Maneck. 'And because of the steep slope, we have steel cables to keep it tied in place.'

'Wait a sec – you think I was born yesterday?'

'No, really. There was an earthquake, and the foundation shifted downhill. That's why the cables were connected.' He explained how the repair work had been done, and described technical details.

His earnestness convinced Avinash. The idea of a house on a leash, tethered to mountain rock, amused him. 'Sounds like a house with suicidal tendencies.'

They laughed. Avinash moved up one of his men and said, 'Crown me.' A few moves later, he won again. 'So what does your father do?'

'We have a shop.'

'Ah, a businessman. Must be making solid money, sending you all the way here to study.'

The slight jeer in his voice offended Maneck. 'It's just a small store, and very hard work for my parents. They sent me to study because the business is going downhill and –'

They looked up at the same instant, laughing at his chosen word. Maneck decided he had answered enough questions. 'What about you? You're also studying here, your father must be well off to afford it.'

'Sorry to disappoint you. I got a scholarship.'

'Congratulations.' Maneck contemplated his next move. 'And what does your father do?'

'Employed in a textile mill.'

'He's the manager?'

Avinash shook his head.

'Accountant?'

'He operates the machinery. He's been running a fucking loom for thirty years, okay?' His voice shook on the brink of a rage, then he calmed down.

'I'm sorry,' said Maneck, 'I didn't mean to . . .'

'Why sorry? I'm not ashamed of the truth. I should be sorry, that I have no more interesting story than this. No mountains, no snow, no runaway houses – just a father who has given his years to the mill, and got TB in exchange.'

They turned their faces to the board again, and Avinash kept talking. After winning the scholarship, he had been looking forward to his own room in the hostel. All his life he had lived with his parents and three sisters in a one room-and-kitchen rented to them by the mill. His father had had tuberculosis for a few years now, but was forced to keep working amid the dust and fibres to support the family. Besides, if he were to quit, they would have to vacate the mill's quarters, and there was nowhere else to go.

The hostel had been a big disappointment when Avinash had arrived, filthy, with rats and cockroaches everywhere. 'Our home may be one room and kitchen, but at least we keep it clean.' Then there were the frustrations of being President of the Student Union and Chairman of the Hostel Committee. 'I regret getting elected. There is nothing in the college prospectus to prepare you for hostel life.'

'What do you mean?'

'I don't want to spoil your first day by describing it. What you've seen so far is nothing. But if students took an interest, demanded improvement, the bathrooms and toilets would easily be repaired. The money for maintenance is all going into someone's pocket. Just like the canteen. The caterer has a fat contract, and provides garbage for the students. But you get to choose your garbage – veg or non-veg.'

'I'm not fussy about food,' said Maneck bravely.

Avinash laughed. 'We'll see. Actually, it's not much of a choice. I think the veg food is the same as non-veg, but minus the gristle and bone.'

Maneck concentrated; he thought one of his men was at last going to breach the defences.

'The trouble is,' said Avinash, devouring the hopeful piece, 'most of the students in the hostel are from poor families. They are afraid to complain, all they want is to finish their studies and find a job so they can look after their parents and brothers and sisters.'

Foiled again, Maneck crowned another king for Avinash and lost the game two moves later. He didn't mind that he kept losing, because his opponent did not gloat.

'You look sleepy,' said Avinash. 'No wonder you can't focus on the game.'

'It's okay, let's play one more. But you know, you are different from the other students.'

Avinash laughed. 'How can you tell? You've just arrived.'

Maneck considered, running a finger around the concentric grooves that embellished the surface of the draughtsmen. 'Because . . . because of everything you just said. Because you became the president, to improve things.'

Avinash shrugged. 'I don't think so. I'm planning to resign. I should be spending my time and energy on studies. I was the first one ever to finish high school in our family. Everyone's relying on me. My three young sisters, too. I must collect money for their dowries, or they won't be able to get married.' He paused, smiling. 'When they were small they used to bite my fingers, when I helped my mother to feed them.' He laughed at the memory. 'My father says that all the blood he spits will not be in vain if I get my degree and a good job.'

They raised their faces from the board, and Avinash fell silent. It had been easy to keep talking while their eyes were glued to the pieces. The logic of the checkered board had been in control, towing both the game and the conversation. Now the thread was broken. Embarrassment and awkwardness came tumbling out.

'I must unpack.'

'Your room should be fine now. Let's check.'

They carried back the suitcase and boxes, swept up the dead cockroaches, and made the bed. 'Don't push it to the wall again,' said Avinash. 'Safer to leave at least a foot.' He also suggested immersing the bed's legs in cans of water, to discourage things from climbing up. 'We can do that tomorrow. You'll be okay for tonight.'

Maneck complained to the warden's office that nothing happened when he pulled the chain in the toilet.

'That's because there is no water supply for the flush tank,' said the clerk, looking up from scotchtaping some torn documents. 'The building contractor did not connect the pipes, to save money. College has taken him to court. But don't worry, the sweeper who cleans the bathrooms is looking after the problem.'

'How?'

'With buckets of water.'

'What time does the sweeper come?'

'Before the hostel awakes – four a.m., sometimes five a.m.'

Maneck immediately made a firm resolution: to be first in the toilet every morning, no matter how early he had to rise for that privilege.

The next day, hearing him up before dawn, Avinash came to check. 'What's wrong? Are you sick or something?'

'No, I'm fine – why?'

'Do you know what time it is? Five-fifteen.'

'I know. But I hate someone's shit staring me in the face when I go to the toilet.'

Avinash was annoyed that he had dragged himself out of bed for no reason, then laughed. 'You rich boys. When will you get used to reality?'

'I told you I'm not rich. The bathroom at home is plain, just like this. But there's water in the flush. And not such a stink.'

'The problem with you is, you see too much and smell too much. This is big-city life – no more beautiful snow-covered mountains. You have to learn to curb your sissy eyes and nose. And another thing you better be prepared for is ragging.'

'Oh no,' said Maneck, remembering his boarding school. 'Haven't these fellows grown up yet? What do they do? Pour water in the bed? Salt in the tea?'

'Something like that.'

In his letter home at the end of the week, Maneck was hard-pressed to find things to say that would not be mistaken for whining. He didn't want Brigadier and Mrs. Grewal, and all the others who would share the letter, to think he was a softie who couldn't manage by himself.

After the first fortnight, however, when Avinash and he had become good friends, he could almost believe what he had been told before leaving home: that he would have an enjoyable time in college.

One evening, over draughts, Maneck confessed his ignorance of chess. Avinash said he could teach him in three days. 'That is, if you're seriously interested in learning the game.'

Since they were both non-vegetarian and sat in the same section of the dining hall, the chess lesson began during dinner, with paper and pencil. Maneck said the diversion made the canteen swill easier to swallow.

'Now you're learning,' said Avinash. 'That's the secret – to distract your senses. Have I told you my theory about them? I think that our sight, smell, taste, touch, hearing are all calibrated for the enjoyment of a perfect world. But since the world is imperfect, we must put blinders on the senses.'

'The world of the hostel is more than just imperfect. It's a gigantic deformity.'

After eating, they adjourned to the common room, where it was still quiet. A few students were gathered around the carrom board. Each time the striker slammed into the ledge and rebounded, the spectators followed with a murmur of approval or commiseration. Another group came in, laughing and boisterous, and started a game of capping-the-fan: tossing a pen cap at the slow ceiling fan and trying to land it on one of the three blades. After several attempts, the game's originator climbed onto a chair, arrested the fan and placed the pen cap on it. They turned up the speed to raucous cheers as the cap came flying off. Next, they grabbed one among them and raised him towards the fan, threatening to shove him into the blades. He shrieked and howled – out of fear, and also because it was expected of him.

Maneck and Avinash watched their antics for a while, then went upstairs to continue the chess lesson. Avinash's chessmen were waiting on his desk, in a plywood box with a maroon, high-gloss varnish. Removing the sliding lid, he emptied the box onto the board.

The plastic pieces that tumbled out were crudely moulded; green felt lined their bases. Maneck noticed a sheet of paper face-down in the bottom of the box, and flipped it over.

'Hey, that's private,' said Avinash.

'Solid,' said Maneck, reading the certificate in admiration: the set had been awarded as first prize in the 1972 Interclass Chess Tournament. 'I never knew my teacher was a champion.'

'I didn't want to make you nervous,' said Avinash. 'Come on now, pay attention.'

By the third day Maneck had learned the basics of the game. They were in the dining hall, pondering a problem Avinash had sketched out, with white to play and mate in three moves. Suddenly, there was a commotion in the vegetarian section. Students leapt from their places, tables were overturned, plates and glasses smashed, and chairs flung at the kitchen door. It was not long before the reason for the uproar was learned by the entire dining hall: a vegetarian student had discovered a sliver of meat floating in a supposedly vegetarian gravy of lentils.

The news spread, about the bastard caterer who was toying with their religious sentiments, trampling on their beliefs, polluting their beings, all for the sake of fattening his miserable wallet. Within minutes, every vegetarian living in the hostel had descended on the canteen, raging about the duplicity. Some of them seemed on the verge of a breakdown, screaming incoherently, going into convulsions, poking fingers down their throats to regurgitate the forbidden substance. Several succeeded in vomiting up their dinners.

But there were no fingers long enough to reach the meals digested since the beginning of term. That vile stuff was already absorbed to become part of their own marrow, and the cause of their anguish. They retched and spat and groaned, and spun in circles, holding their heads, crying about the calamity, unwilling to acknowledge that their stomachs were empty, there was nothing left to bring up.

The hysteria found a more satisfying focus when the kitchen workers were dragged out. Smelling of rancid oil and sweat and hot stoves, the six men trembled before their accusers. Their white uniforms carried stains from their labours with the evening's menu – brown splashes of lentils, dark green streaks of spinach.

The prospect of vengeance acted like an antacid on the violated vegetarian innards. Nausea retreated; the outpouring of bile and vomit and greenish-yellow effluent was replaced by a torrent of verbal violence.

'Smash the fucking rascals!'

'Break their faces!'

'Make them eat meat!'

The threats did not immediately become blows because the six wisely fell to their knees, setting up a loud wailing. Their snivelling and begging for mercy was as hysterically incoherent as the vegetarians' emetic exertions had been.

Avinash observed the drama unfold for a minute, then pushed back his chair. 'I have an idea. Will you look after my chess board?'

'You'll simply get hurt,' said Maneck. 'Why are you interfering?'

'Don't worry, I'll be okay.'

Maneck returned the chessmen to the box, watching from his corner. The kitchen workers and students were still locked in their respective poses: discovered Crime cowering for clemency at the feet of implacable Retribution. It would have been funny were it not for the real danger of the workers being pounded to a pulp. But so far, the invisible line was holding, separating the potential from its realization. Strange, that invisible lines could be so powerful, thought Maneck – strong as brick walls.

'Stop! Wait a sec!' shouted Avinash, putting himself between the frightened kitchen workers and the students.

'What?' they asked impatiently, recognizing their Hostel Committee Chairman and Student Union President.

'Hang on for a minute. What's the point of thrashing these guys? The crooked caterer is the one to blame.'

'He'll get the message if we give his workers a pasting. Won't dare to show his face here again.'

'You're wrong. He'll just come with police protection.'

A great opening gambit, thought Maneck – the invisible line reinforced.

Avinash pleaded with the vegetarians, and everyone else disgusted with the food, to join him in lodging a complaint with the college administration. 'Let's do this democratically, let's not behave like goondas on the street. It's bad enough that the bloody politicians do.'

Check, thought Maneck. Cleverly manoeuvred.

Some were in favour and some against the suggestion. There was a fresh volley of vegetarian threats, while the kitchen workers responded with a broadside of grovelling and whimpering. But the intensity was starting to diminish in both camps. More voices were raised in support of Avinash's appeal. The vegetarian offensive gradually fell silent, and the kitchen workers ceased their salvos of weeping, though they maintained their knees in readiness for a swift descent should the need arise again.

Plans were made to organize a large protest outside the Principal's office next morning. Enthusiasm for the chosen course of action was general by now. Even the strictest vegetarians stopped puking, composed themselves, and went off to undertake their pollution-cleansing ablutions, promising to gather with the others in the morning.

Checkmate, thought Maneck. The invisible line was impregnable.

'I guess you're what is called a born leader,' he said to Avinash later that night, half-teasing, half-admiring

'Not really. A born fool. I should stick to my decision – to give up all this and pay attention to my studies. Come on, let's go upstairs.'

The canteen agitation's success astonished Avinash and his followers. The Principal dictated a letter of termination addressed to the caterer. The Hostel Committee was authorized to select a replacement.

Now the jubilant students held a victory celebration and grew more ambitious. Their President promised that, one by one, they would weed out all the evils of the campus: nepotism in staff hiring, bribery for admissions, sale of examination papers, special privileges for politicians' families, government interference in the syllabus, intimidation of faculty members. The list was long, for the rot went deep.

The mood was euphoric. The students fervently believed their example would inspire universities across the country to undertake radical reforms, which would complement the grass-roots movement of Jay Prakash Narayan that was rousing the nation with a call to return to Gandhian principles. The changes would invigorate all of society, transform it from a corrupt, moribund creature into a healthy organism that would, with its heritage of a rich and ancient civilization, and the wisdom of the Vedas and Upanishads, awaken the world and lead the way towards enlightenment for all humanity.

It was easy to dream noble dreams for those few days after the canteen protest. With so much determination and good intention circulating within the student body, numerous subcommittees were created, agenda adopted, minutes recorded, and resolutions passed. The canteen meals improved. Optimism reigned.

Maneck, however, had had enough of it. He wanted his life, and Avinash's, to return now to their earlier routine. This business of endless agitation was tiresome. He tried to wean Avinash from his new passion, making what he thought was a crafty move: he invoked his friend's family. 'I think you were right. What you said before, you know, about focusing completely on studies, for the sake of your parents, and for your sisters' dowries. You really should.'

The reminder troubled Avinash, glooming his brow. 'I often feel guilty about that. I'll give up my chairmanship. Soon as these few remaining problems are fixed.'

'What problems?' Maneck was impatient. 'In all your meetings you haven't once mentioned the filthy toilets and bathrooms. Cockroaches and bedbugs should be on the agenda. Mahatma Gandhi wouldn't have liked your approach, he believed firmly in cleanliness – physical purity precedes mental purity precedes spiritual purity.'

The objection cheered Avinash, and he laughed, throwing his arm over Maneck's shoulders as they crossed the quadrangle. 'I didn't know you were an expert in Gandhian philosophy. Tell me, would you like to chair the cockroach subcommittee? I'll second the motion.'

Maneck attended a few rallies and protests, only in order to support his friend. After a while, even that wasn't a sufficient reason. The process was so tediously repetitious, he stopped going.

Avinash did not have time for chess in the evenings anymore. They still ate together but were seldom alone, and Maneck resented it. A crowd hung around his friend, discussing and arguing about things he did not understand and was not interested in understanding. Their talk was filled with words like democratization, constitution, alienation, degeneration, decentralization, collectivization, nationalism, capitalism, materialism, feudalism, imperialism, communalism, socialism, fascism, relativism, determinism, proletarianism – ism, ism, ism, ism, the words flying around him like buzzing insects.

Why couldn't these fellows talk normally? wondered Maneck. To amuse himself he began counting their various isms, and stopped when he reached twenty. Sometimes, dogs came into their debates – imperialist dogs, running dogs of capitalism. Sometimes the dogs were pigs, capitalist pigs. Money-lending hyenas and landowning jackals also put in occasional appearances. And lately, besides the isms, there was this Emergency that they kept going on about, behaving as if the sky had fallen.

Feeling ignored, Maneck went to his room as soon as he finished his meal. He still had the plastic chessmen, and he set them up to play against himself. He made a move, then turned the board around. After a while it became boring. He tried the book Avinash had lent him, containing a series of endgame problems in increasing degrees of difficulty.

Hard though it was, Maneck continued to shun his friend's company. Then, just as he was weakening after a few days of loneliness, deciding to give him a second chance, Avinash knocked on the door.

'Hi, what's new?' he slapped Maneck's back affectionately.

'This game.'

'Playing alone?'

'No, with me.' Maneck toppled his own king.

'Haven't seen you much lately. Aren't you curious about what's been happening?'

'You mean in college?'

'Yes – and everywhere else, since the Emergency was declared.'

'Oh, that ' Maneck made an indifferent face. 'I don't know much about those things.'

'Don't you read the newspapers?'

'Only the comics. All the political stuff is too boring.'

'Okay, I'll make it simple and quick for you, so you don't fall asleep.'

'Good. I'll time you.' Maneck checked his watch. 'Ready, begin.'

Avinash took a deep breath. 'Three weeks ago the High Court found the Prime Minister guilty of cheating in the last elections. Which meant she had to step down. But she began stalling. So the opposition parties, student organizations, trade unions – they started mass demonstrations across the country. All calling for her resignation. Then, to hold on to power, she claimed that the country's security was threatened by internal disturbances, and declared a State of Emergency.'

'Twenty-nine seconds,' said Maneck.

'Wait, there's a bit more. Under the pretext of Emergency, fundamental rights have been suspended, most of the opposition is under arrest, union leaders are in jail, and even some student leaders.'

'You better be careful.'

'Oh, don't worry, our college is not that important. But the worst thing is, the press is being censored –'

'Not much point then in reading newspapers, is there?'

'And she has retroactively changed the election laws, turning her guilt into innocence.'

'And you don't have time to play chess because of this.'

'I'm playing it all the time. Everything I do is chess. Come on, let's see how much you've learned.' He set up the board, then concealed a white and a black pawn behind his back. Maneck guessed correctly and started the game by advancing the king's pawn. Half an hour later he had won, much to his surprise.

'Serves me right, for teaching you so well,' said Avinash. 'But we'll have to have a return match soon.'

Now it would be like before, thought Maneck. Once again he would have Avinash to himself. His secret wish was that the Principal would ban the bloody Student Union because of the Emergency, as other universities were doing. Then there would be nothing to distract his friend.

But Maneck remained disappointed; their chess games did not resume. He knocked at Avinash's door on several evenings, and there was no answer. Twice he slipped a note under the door: 'Hi. Where have you been hiding? Afraid to face me over the chessboard or what? See you soon – Maneck.'

After the second note, when he saw him in the dining hall, Avinash only had time for a quick wave. 'Got your message,' he said. 'Free tomorrow?'

'Sure.'

And next night Maneck waited in his room, but his friend did not turn up. Angry and hurt, he went to bed promising himself this was it. If Avinash wanted to see him, he could chase after him for a change.

He missed Avinash. Strange, he thought, how a friendship could spring up suddenly one evening, facilitated by cockroaches and bedbugs. And then fizzle out just as suddenly, for reasons equally ludicrous. Maybe it was silly to have assumed it was a friendship in the first place.

Everything disgusting about the hostel that Maneck had learned to live with began to nauseate him with a renewed vengeance. As an antidote, he developed a morning waking routine: when his eyes opened, he shut them again and, head still on the pillow, imagined the mountains, swirling mist, birdsong, dogs' paws pattering on the porch, the cool dawn air on his skin, the excited chatter of langurs, breakfast cooking in the kitchen, toast and fried eggs upon his tongue. When all his senses were thus anointed by home imaginings, he reopened his eyes and got out of bed.

On campus, a new group, Students For Democracy, which had surfaced soon after declaration of the Emergency, was now in the ascendant. Its sister organization, Students Against Fascism, maintained the integrity of both groups by silencing those who spoke against them or criticized the Emergency. Threats and assaults became so commonplace, they might have been part of the university curriculum. The police were now a permanent presence, helping to maintain the new and sinister brand of law and order.

Two professors who chose to denounce the campus goon squads were taken away by plainclothesmen for anti-government activities, under the Maintenance of Internal Security Act. Their colleagues did not interfere on their behalf because MISA allowed imprisonment without trial, and it was a well-known fact that those who questioned MISA sooner or later answered to MISA; it was safer not to tangle with something so pernicious.

Maneck worried about Avinash; as President of the original Student Union, surely he was in grave danger from the new groups on campus. At night, he listened for sounds from the room next to his. The door shutting softly, the clatter of the metal cupboard, the wheeze of the spray pump, the thunk of the bed revealed that his friend was fine, that he had not been assaulted or taken away into secret detention.

Maneck hurried between hostel and college without stopping to watch the daily farces of bullying, toadying, and submission. The office of the campus newspaper was attacked, the writers and editors roughed up and sent packing. The paper used to indulge in light satire and occasionally poke fun at the government or university administration, although satire had become increasingly difficult in recent times, for the government was practising the art in its own reports to the censored media, better than the campus paper had ever done.

After taking over, Students For Democracy released a statement in the next issue that the publication's new voice would be more representative of the college population. The rest of the paper was filled with a model code of conduct for students and teachers.

One morning, classes were cancelled and a flag-raising ceremony was organized in the quadrangle. Attendance was compulsory, enforced by Students Against Fascism. The president of Students For Democracy took the microphone. He appealed to the figures of authority to come forward, prove their love for the country, set an example of patriotic behaviour.

On cue, lecturers, associate professors, full professors, and department heads approached the dais, en masse, in a feeble show of spontaneity. The organizers tried furtively to slow them down, to make it look like a genuine outpouring of support. But it was too late to improve the choreography. The entire teaching staff had already lined up at the table, like customers at a ration shop. They obediently signed statements saying they were behind the Prime Minister, her declaration of Emergency, and her goal of fighting the anti-democratic forces threatening the country from within.

As much as fear, Maneck felt a loathing for the entire place. But for his teachers he had only pity. They slipped away from the flag-raising ceremony, looking guilty and ashamed.

That night, the hostel room next to his own remained silent. The familiar sounds refused to rise and signal Avinash's well-being. Maneck lay awake, worrying into the early hours of the morning. Should he report to the warden's office that his friend was missing? But what if he had gone to visit his family, or something innocent like that? Better to wait a day or two.

At dinnertime he looked about the dining hall for a glimpse of Avinash, in vain. He asked someone at his table, casually, 'What's the Managing Committee of the Student Union up to these days?'

'Those fellows have all split the scene, yaar. Gone underground. It's too risky for them to hang around here.'

The reply reassured Maneck. He was convinced now that Avinash was just lying low somewhere, hiding in his parents' flat in the mill tenements, perhaps. And he would return soon – after all, how long could this Emergency and goondaism go on? Besides, he would not be caught easily. Not the way he played chess.

The former canteen caterer was back on the job, wreaking his gastric revenge. Maneck felt vindicated as he remembered the vegetarian incident that had started it all – he had told Avinash not to interfere, that it would end badly.

Nowadays, when the meal was particularly ghastly, he got himself sandwiches or samosas at a stall in the lane outside the college. He was luckier than most because he got a bit of pocket money from home. It was comforting to watch tomatoes being sliced and bread being buttered, and to hear the roar of the stove, the hot hiss of frying in oil.

One evening, as he returned to the hostel from his roadside snack, the cry of Rag-ging! Rag-ging! Rag-ging! went up in the corridor, like a hunting call. He watched in the games room as two first-year automotive students were cornered, surrounded by twelve others. They stripped the pants off one, held him bent over the ping-pong table, and handed an empty soft-drink bottle to the other. He was ordered to demonstrate what had been learnt about pistons and cylinders in the class on internal combustion engines. They overcame his reluctance by threatening to make him the cylinder if he refused to cooperate.

Maneck slunk away in terror. From then on, he went straight to his room after dinner and locked himself in. He made sure that he had whatever he needed – newspaper, library books, glass of water – so he would not have to leave his sanctuary when the raggers were on the prowl.

One night, after he had changed into his pyjamas, his stomach began rumbling in a nasty way. Must be the samosa chutney at the roadside stall, he assumed. Shouldn't have eaten it, there had been something peculiar about the taste.

He badly needed the toilet, filthy as it would be at this hour. He opened the door cautiously. The corridor was empty. He walked rapidly, looking over his shoulder. Halfway down the hall they pounced out of a storage room and caught him. He fought back. 'Please! I have to go to the toilet! Very badly!'

'Later,' they said, twisting his arms behind him to make him stop struggling.

'Ahhhh!' he screamed.

'Listen, it's just a game,' they reasoned with him. 'Why turn it into a fight? You'll simply get hurt.'

He stopped resisting, and they eased up on his arms. 'Good boy. Now tell us, what subject are you taking?'

'Refrigeration and air-conditioning.'

'Okay, we'll just give you a little test. To see if you've been studying like a good boy.'

'Sure. But can I go to the toilet first?'

'Later.' They led him to the workshop where there was a large working model of a freezer, and asked him to take off his clothes. He did not move. They closed in to undress him.

'Please!' he begged, kicking and pulling away. 'Please don't! No, please!' He prayed that Avinash would appear miraculously and save him, as he had saved the kitchen workers from the vegetarians.

The raggers were very efficient, taking less than a minute to hold Maneck down and strip him. 'Now listen carefully,' they said. 'The first part of the test is simple. We are refrigerating you for ten minutes. Don't panic.' They tumbled him into the freezer, doubled over to fit the confined space, and heaved the door shut. The darkness of a coffin closed in around him.

They waited to be amused by his reaction. For a while there was nothing. Then a banging commenced, and continued for the next two minutes, followed by a brief silence. His hammering started again – weaker now, and sporadic, faltering, picking up, fading.

The blows became alarmingly feeble before dying out altogether. They looked at their watches; only seven minutes of the promised ten had elapsed. They decided to open the door.

'Aagh! Chhee!' They fell back as the stench hit them. 'Bastard shat in the freezer!'

Maneck was stiff and could not emerge. They pulled him out moulded in a stoop and slammed the door to seal away the smell. He looked around dazed, unable to straighten.

They offered mock applause. 'Very good. Full marks for the first test. Bonus marks for the shit. Well done. Now comes the second part.'

His blue lips trembled as he tried to speak. His hands reached stiffly for the pyjamas. Someone snatched them away. 'Not yet. For the second part, you must demonstrate that your thermostat is working.'

Numb, he gaped uncomprehendingly.

'You said you're taking refrigeration and air-conditioning. What's the matter, don't you know what a thermostat is?'

Maneck shook his head and made another pathetic slow-motion grab for his pyjamas.

'*This* is your thermostat, you idiot,' said one of them, slapping the frigid penis. 'Now show us if it's working.'

Maneck looked down at himself as if he was seeing it for the first time, and they clapped again. 'Very good! Thermostat correctly identified! But is it working?'

He nodded.

'Prove it.' He was not sure what they wanted. 'Come on, make it work. Shake it up.' They took up the chant. 'Shake-it-up! Shake-it-up! Shake-it-up!'

Maneck understood, and discovered his lips had thawed enough to speak. 'Please, I cannot. Please, let me go now?'

'The second part of the test must be completed. Or we'll have to repeat the first part, freeze you with your shit this time. Thermostat checkup is compulsory.'

Maneck held his penis weakly, moved his hand to and fro a few times and let go.

'It's not working! Try harder! Shake-it-up! Shake-it-up!'

He started to sniffle, working his foreskin back and forth while they chanted. Desperate to end the humiliation, he laboured hard, his wrist aching, feeling nothing in the penis, worried that something was wrong, that the freezer had damaged it. After much effort he ejaculated without a proper erection.

They broke into cheers, whistling and hooting. Someone returned his pyjamas, and they dispersed. To avoid walking back with them, he stayed in the workshop until it was quiet outside the building.

He washed his thighs and legs where he had soiled himself, then returned to his room. He got into bed and lay on his back in the dark, shivering, staring at the ceiling. He wondered what would happen the next time the instructor opened the freezer.

An hour later the trembling was still in his limbs, and he fetched the blanket from the cupboard. He knew what he was going to do – as soon as he felt warmer, he would get up and pack. In the morning he would take a taxi to the railway station and go home on the *Frontier Mail*.

What would his parents say, though? He could guess Daddy's reaction – that he had run away like a coward. And Mummy would first take his side, then she would listen to Daddy and change, as always. Change, always. That's what the proofreader had said on the train – cannot avoid change, have to adapt to it. But surely that did not mean accepting a change for the worse.

For half the night Maneck struggled with his thoughts, slowly packing his boxes and suitcase. The other half of the night he spent unpacking, and writing to his parents. He wrote that so far he had not been truthful with them, and was sorry, but he had wanted to spare them the worry: 'The hostel is such a horrible place, I cannot stay here anymore. Not only is it dirty and stinking, which I can tolerate, but the people are disgusting. Many of them are not even students, and I don't know how these goondas are allowed to live in a student hostel. They take hashish and ganja, get drunk, fight. Gambling goes on openly, and they sell drugs to the students.' He thought a bit, then added, 'One of them even tried to sell to me.' That should make them think twice. 'It is all absolutely horrible, and I want to return as soon as possible. I'll work in the shop without interfering, and do as you tell me, I promise.'

Surely this was drastic enough, he felt, to make his parents act. There was no need to reveal the real shame.

—

Secretly, Mr. and Mrs. Kohlah were both delighted that Maneck wanted to come home. They missed him intensely but had never dared talk about it, not even to each other. They preferred to pretend, especially in company, how proud and happy they were that their son was away getting a worthwhile education.

And Maneck's urgent letter did nothing to change this. They carefully controlled their responses to keep up appearances. 'What a pity if he comes back so soon,' said Mr. Kohlah.

'Yes,' said Mrs. Kohlah. 'He will lose his only chance for a good career. What do you think, Farokh? What should we do?'

Mr. Kohlah knew in his heart that if his son was unhappy he should return home immediately. But perhaps there ought to be some effort made, however halfhearted, at finding another solution – it would surely be expected by everyone, including their friends. Or he might be accused of being too soft a father.

'Seems to me there is definitely a problem at the college hostel,' he said cautiously.

'Of course there is! My son does not lie! And he simply cannot be allowed to remain in such a wicked place, full of vice and rogues and ruffians, just for the sake of a college diploma! What kind of parents would we be?'

'Yes, yes, calm down, I am trying to think.' He massaged his forehead. 'If the hostel is not suitable, maybe we should find him some other lodging. Privately, in someone's home. That would solve the problem.'

'That's a good idea,' said Mrs. Kohlah, playing along. She did not want to carry the lifelong label of the possessive mother who had ruined her son's future. 'What about asking my relatives?'

'No, they live too far from the college, remember?' Besides, who could tell what kind of namby-pamby thoughts they would fill Maneck's head with. After twenty years they still hadn't got used to the idea of Aban living away from them.

'If only we can find him a nice safe room somewhere,' she said. 'Somewhere that we can afford.' Which was next to impossible, she imagined cheerfully, in a city where millions were living in slums and on the pavements. And not just beggars – even people with jobs who had the money to pay rent. Only, there was nothing to rent. No, there was no chance for Maneck, he would be home soon. And she broke into a smile at that happy thought.

'What are you smiling for when we have such a big problem on our hands?' said Mr. Kohlah.

'Was I smiling? No, nothing, just thinking of Maneck.'

'Hmm,' he grunted, finding it difficult to contain his own pleasure. 'You can try writing to that friend of yours. She might know of some place.'

'Yes, good idea. After dinner tonight I'll write to Zenobia,' agreed Mrs. Kohlah, joyful in the knowledge that it would be a waste of a stamp.

They returned to their chores. The ordeal of masking delight with disappointment was over. Now it was just a question of waiting till their lukewarm efforts failed and their son came home.

In a few days, however, they had to pretend all over again, but in reverse, when, to their bitter surprise, accommodation was swiftly arranged for Maneck. Now they had to force a display of satisfaction that his education was going ahead, and sweep away the remains of their short-lived hopes.

Mrs. Kohlah resentfully wrote a thank-you letter to Mrs. Dalal, at the address Zenobia had sent. 'I wonder if Dina is still as beautiful as she was in high school,' she said, relishing the sound as she tore the page from the writing pad. The rip was in harmony with her present mood.

'You can ask Maneck. He will soon be able to give you a full report from her flat,' said Mr. Kohlah. 'Even send you an up-to-date photo if you like.' He could not help feeling, as he watched her at the desk, that the busybodies from his wife's past were interfering in his family life, conniving to keep his son away from him.

Immediately afterwards, he realized he was being silly. He brought out his bank book and wrote a cheque for the first month's rent. Mrs. Kohlah enclosed it with her letter to Mrs. Dalal.

═══

Dina listened closely for sounds of life from the silent bathroom. What was he up to, why was there no splashing of water? 'Maneck! Is everything all right? Is the water hot enough?'

'Yes, thank you.'

'You found the mug? Should be next to the bucket. And you can sit on the wooden stool if you like.'

'Yes, Aunty.' Maneck felt awkward about mentioning the worms, which were advancing in battalions from the drain. He hoped they would soon return to their underground home of their own accord. But maybe I should have returned home on the train, of my own accord, he thought bitterly. How stupid of me to write a letter. Hoping Daddy would allow me to come back.

Dina kept waiting to hear the mug's clatter and the splash of water. The silence outlasted her patience. 'What's wrong, Maneck? Can you please hurry up? I have to bathe too, before the tailors come.'

She hoped there would be some time today to cash the rent cheque. First, however, she had to see Maneck off to college and start things on the right footing. He wouldn't be a problem once he became used to her routine. And learned to use modern gadgets, like the immersion heater. Poor boy had no idea what it was. And when she'd asked him what they did at home for hot water, he described the boiler stoked with coal every morning. How primitive. But he had made his own bed, folding everything neatly – that was impressive.

She went to the bathroom door and asked again, 'Are you managing all right?'

'Yes, Aunty. But some worms are crawling out of the gutter.'

'Oh, them! Just throw a little water and they will go away.'

There was a splash, and then silence again.

'Well?'

'They're still coming.'

'Okay, let me take a look.'

He started to put on his clothes, and she knocked. 'Come on, please wrap your towel and open the door. I don't have time to stand here all morning.'

He dressed fully before letting her in.

'Shy boy. I'm as old as your mother. What was I going to see? Now. Where are those worms that frightened you?'

'I was not frightened. They just look so disgusting. And there are so many of them.'

'Naturally. It's the season for worms. The monsoon always brings them. I thought you would be used to such things, where you live. In the mountains, with wild animals.'

'But certainly not in the bathroom, Aunty.'

'In my bathroom you'll have to get used to it. All you can do is push the worms back by throwing water. Cold water – don't use up the hot.' She demonstrated, brushing past him to reach the bucket, hurling mugfuls that sent the creatures sliding towards the drain. 'See? There they go, into the gutter.'

The soft lines of her outstretched upper arm did more to reassure him than the water technique. Bent over the parapet, her back pulled the nightgown taut against her hips, revealing the underwear outline. His eyes lingered, turning away when she straightened.

'Well? Are you going to bathe now? Or do you want me to stay with you, stand on guard against the worms?' He blushed, and she, worried about the tailors arriving, said, 'Listen, because this is your first morning, I will do something special for you.'

She fetched the bottle of phenol from the shelf outside the WC, uncorked it, and trickled the white fluid onto the worms. It worked instantaneously, transforming them into a writhing red mass, and then into little lifeless coils.

'There. But remember, phenol is very expensive, I cannot waste it every day. You will have to learn to bathe with them.'

He shut the door and undressed again. The picture of her beside him, bending, reaching, pulsated through his limbs. But the antiseptic odour of phenol hanging in the air tugged in the opposite direction.

VI Day at the Circus, Night in the Slum

THE EARLY-MORNING gathering of red double-deckers outside the slum was noticed first by a child from the drunk's family. The little girl came running in to tell her mother. She saw Ishvar and Om awake outside their shack, and told them too. Her father was adrift in his alcoholic slumber.

The drivers honked flurries of greetings to one another as they parked; twenty-two buses lined up in two perfect rows. The tailors collected their water and proceeded towards the train tracks. Rain had fallen during the night. The ground was soft, the mud sucking at their feet like a many-mouthed creature.

'Let's go early to Dinabai today,' said Om.

'Why?'

'Maneck will have arrived.'

They found a spot that was to Ishvar's liking, and squatted. He was glad that the hair-collector with his pointless chatter was not in sight. He hated conversations at toilet, even sensible ones.

His luck did not last; Rajaram materialized along the curve in the tracks, spotting them at the far end of the ditch. He squatted beside them and began speculating about the buses.

'Maybe they are starting a new terminal,' said Om.

'Would be convenient for us.'

'But wouldn't they first build a station office or something?'

They washed up and went to the mud-spattered vehicles to investigate. Khaki-uniformed drivers leaned in the doorways or rested on their haunches along the kerb, reading newspapers, smoking, or chewing paan.

'Namaskaar,' called out Rajaram to no one in particular. 'Where are you taking your red chariots today?'

One of them shrugged. 'Who knows. Supervisor said to bring the buses, wait for special assignment.'

The rain started again. Drops rang out on the roofs of the empty buses. The drivers withdrew inside their vehicles and shut the grimy windows.

Soon, the twenty-third bus arrived, its windshield wiper swinging ineffectively, loose and slow, like a wet pendulum. This one was packed full, the upper deck devoted to uniformed policemen who stayed on board while the lower deck spewed out men with briefcases and pamphlets.

They stretched, eased their pants riding high at the crotch, and entered the slum. To save their leather sandals in the rain-muddied field, some walked tiptoe with heels aloft, balancing under open umbrellas. Others squelched along on their heels to favour the soles, scrutinizing the ground for grass tufts, stones, broken bricks – anything that might provide a less mucky step.

Their performance on the tightrope of mud soon collected a crowd. A puff of wind caught the umbrellas; the men wobbled. A stronger gust pulled them off balance. The audience began to laugh. Some children imitated the funny walk. The visitors abandoned their sandals to the mud and, mustering dignity, walked towards the water-tap queue.

The one with the finest footwear said they were party-workers with a message from the Prime Minister. 'She sends her greetings and wants you all to know that she is holding a big meeting today. Everyone is invited to attend.'

A woman placed her empty bucket under the tap. The drumroll of water blurred the man's words, and he modified his pitch. 'The Prime Minister especially wants to talk to honest, hardworking people like you. These buses will take you to the meeting, free of charge.'

The water queue moved forward disinterestedly. A few whispered among themselves, and there was laughter. The party-worker tried again. 'The Prime Minister's message is that she is your servant, and wants to help you. She wants to hear about things from your own lips.'

'Tell her yourself!' someone shouted. 'You can see in what prosperity we live!'

'Yes! Tell her how happy we are! Why do we need to come?

'If she is our servant, tell her to come here!'

'Ask your men with the cameras to pull some photos of our lovely houses, our healthy children! Show that to the Prime Minister!'

There was more scornful laughing, and murmurings about unpleasant things that could be done to party-workers who bothered poor people at watertime. The visitors retreated for a brief consultation.

Then the leader spoke again. 'There will be a payment of five rupees for each person. Also, free tea and snack. Please line up outside at seven-thirty. Buses will leave at eight.'

'Go push the five rupees up your arse!'

'And set fire to the money!'

But the insults tapered off quickly, for the new offer was creating interest.

The party-workers fanned out through the slum to spread the message.

A ragpicker asked if his wife and six children could come too. 'Yes,' said the organizer, 'but they won't get five rupees each. Only you.' The hopeful father turned away, crestfallen, and was tempted again when the offer of free tea and snack was extended to the whole family.

'It sounds like fun for sure,' said Om. 'Let's go.'

'Are you crazy? Waste a day of sewing?'

'Not worth it,' Rajaram agreed with Ishvar. 'These people are giving us bogus talk.'

'How do you know? Have you been to such a meeting?'

'Yes, they are always the same. If you were jobless, I would say go, take their five rupees. It's fun the first time to see the government's tamasha. But to give up a day of tailoring or hair-collecting? No.'

At seven-thirty the queue by the buses was barely long enough to fill one double-decker. There were unemployed day-labourers, some women and children, and a handful of injured dockyard mathadis. The party-workers discussed the situation and agreed to put into motion their alternate plan.

Shortly, Sergeant Kesar, who was in charge of the constables, gave his men the order to alight. A dozen were instructed to block the slum exits, the rest followed him inside. He tried to move with a slow swaggering walk, but his flat feet in the mud made it more of a slippery waddle. He had a megaphone, which he raised to his mouth with both hands, holding it like a trumpet.

'Attention, attention! Two people from each jhopdi must get on the bus! In five minutes – no delay. Otherwise, you will be arrested for trespassing on municipal property!'

People protested: how could they be trespassing when rent had been paid in full? The hutment dwellers went in search of Navalkar, the one who collected the rent, but his shack was empty.

'I wonder if the Prime Minister knows they are forcing us,' said Ishvar.

'She only knows important things,' said Rajaram. 'Things her friends want her to know.'

The policemen began rounding up the busloads. The double-deckers filled slowly, looking redder now with the dust and mud washed off by rain. Arguments in some shacks were easily settled when the policemen raised their lathis to emphasize the importance of complying.

Monkey-man was willing to go, but wanted to take his monkeys too. 'They will enjoy the ride, they have such a good time on the train when we go to work,' he explained to a party-worker. 'And I won't ask for extra tea or snack, I'll share mine with them.'

'Don't you understand plain language? No monkeys. It's not a circus or something.'

Behind him, Rajaram whispered to his friends, 'That's exactly what it is.'

'Please, sahab,' implored Monkey-man. 'The dog can stay alone. But not Laila and Majnoo, they will cry all day without me.'

Sergeant Kesar was called to arbitrate. 'Are your monkeys properly trained?' he asked.

'Police-sahab, my Laila and Majnoo are beautifully trained! They are my obedient children! Look, they will give you a salaam!' He signalled; the monkeys raised their paws to their heads in unison.

Sergeant Kesar was greatly amused, and returned the salute, laughing. Monkey-man slapped the leashes against the ground, and the monkeys genuflected. Sergeant Kesar's delight overflowed.

'Actually speaking, I see no harm in allowing the monkeys,' he said to the party-worker.

'Excuse me, Sergeant,' said the party-worker, taking him aside. 'The problem is, the monkeys might be seen as some kind of political comment, and the enemies of the party could use it to ridicule us.'

'It's possible,' said Sergeant Kesar, swinging his megaphone. 'But it could also be seen as proof of the Prime Minister's power to communicate not only with humans but with animals too.'

The party-worker rolled his eyes. 'Do you want to take responsibility for it in writing? With a memorandum in triplicate?'

'Actually speaking, that is not part of my jurisdiction.'

Sergeant Kesar returned sadly to Monkey-man and broke the news. 'I'm sorry, this is an important meeting for the Prime Minister. No monkeys allowed.'

'Wait and see,' said Rajaram softly to the people in line. 'The stage will be full of them.'

Monkey-man thanked Sergeant Kesar for trying. He locked Laila and Majnoo in the shack with Tikka and returned looking miserable. The buses were almost full now, and the convoy was ready for departure as soon as the few remaining stubborn cases were persuaded with caning and slapping to climb aboard.

'I have seen nothing so unfair,' said Ishvar. 'And what will Dinabai be thinking?'

'We cannot help it,' said Om. 'Just enjoy the free ride.'

'Right,' said Rajaram. 'If we have to go, might as well have fun. You know, last year they took us in lorries. Packed like sheep. This bus is more comfortable.'

'At least a hundred people in each one,' said Ishvar. 'Over two thousand altogether. What a big meeting it will be.'

'That's only from our colony,' said Rajaram. 'Buses must have been sent everywhere. The meeting will have fifteen or twenty thousand people in all, wait and see.'

After travelling for an hour, the buses reached the outskirts of the city. Om announced that he was hungry. 'I hope they give us our tea and snack when we arrive. And the five rupees.'

'You're always hungry,' said Ishvar in a falsetto. 'Do you have worms?' They laughed, explaining the joke about Dina Dalal to Rajaram.

Soon they were on rural roads. It had stopped raining. They passed villages where people stood and stared at the buses. 'I don't understand,' said Ishvar. 'Why drag us all the way here? Why not just take these villagers to the meeting?'

'Too complicated, I think,' said Rajaram. 'They would have to visit so many villages, with people scattered all over – two hundred here, four hundred there. Much easier to get them wholesale in the city jhopadpattis.' He broke off excitedly, pointing. 'Look! Look at that woman – at the well! What beautiful long hair!' He sighed. 'If only I could wander the countryside with my scissors, harvesting what I need. I'd soon be rich.'

They knew they were nearing their destination when the traffic increased and other vehicles passed them, also ferrying the Prime Minister's made-to-measure audience. Occasionally, the buses moved over to allow a flag-flying car filled with VIPs to sweep past in an orgy of blaring horns.

They stopped near a vast open field. As the passengers alighted, an organizer told them to memorize their bus number for the return journey. He directed people to their seating area, repeating applause instructions for each batch. 'Please watch the dignitaries on stage. Whenever they begin to clap, you must also clap.'

'What about the money?'

'You will get it when the rally is finished. We know your tricks. If we pay you first, you crooks run off halfway in the speech.'

'Keep moving! Keep moving!' called an usher, helping the new arrivals along with a pat on the back.

'Don't push!' snarled Om, sweeping the hand off his back.

'Aray Om, stay calm,' said Ishvar.

Bamboo posts and railings divided the field into several enclosures, the main one being at the far end, containing a covered stage at an elevation of thirty feet. In front of the stage was the area for prominent personages. This was the sole section furnished with chairs, and arguments were in progress to determine their allocation. The chairs were of three types: padded, with arms, for VVIPs; padded, but without arms, for VIPs; and bare metal, folding, for the mere IPs. Invitees were bickering and wrangling with the ushers, pressuring them to add a V to their status.

'Try to stay near the edge of the field, near that tent,' said Rajaram. 'That's where they must have the tea and snacks.' But volunteers wearing round tricolour cloth badges herded the arrivals into the next available enclosure.

'Look at that, yaar!' said Om in awe, pointing at the eighty-foot cutout of the Prime Minister to the right of the stage. The cardboard-and-plywood figure stood with arms outstretched, waiting as though to embrace the audience. An outline map of the country hung suspended behind the head, a battered halo.

'And look at that arch of flowers!' said Ishvar. 'Like a rainbow around the stage. Beautiful, hahn? You can smell them from here.'

'See, I told you you'd enjoy it,' said Rajaram. 'First time, it's always fun.'

They made themselves comfortable on the ground and examined the faces in their vicinity. People smiled and nodded. The soundman went on stage to check the microphones, making the loudspeakers screech. A hush of anticipation descended on the audience and dissipated almost instantly. Buses continued to disgorge passengers by the thousands. The sun was hot now, but Ishvar said that at least it wasn't raining.

Two hours later the enclosures were full, the field was packed, and the first casualties to fall to the sun were carried away to be revived under the shade of nearby trees. People questioned the wisdom of holding a rally at the hottest time of the day. An organizer explained there was no choice, the Prime Minister's astrologer had charted the celestial bodies and selected the hour.

Eighteen dignitaries began taking their places on stage. At twelve o'clock there was a roar in the sky and twenty-five thousand heads turned upwards. A helicopter circled the field thrice, then began its descent to land behind the stage.

A few minutes later, the Prime Minister, in a white sari, was escorted up to the stage by someone in a white kurta and Gandhi cap. The eighteen notable personages took turns garlanding their leader, bowing, touching her toes. One dignitary outdid the rest by prostrating full length before her. He would stay at her feet, he said, till she forgave him.

The Prime Minister was baffled, though no one could see her look of puzzlement because of the eighteen garlands engulfing her face. An aide reminded her of some minor disloyalty on the man's part.

'Madamji, he is repenting, he says he is sorry, most sincerely.'

The live microphones ensured that the sun-scorched audience was at least able to enjoy the onstage buffoonery. 'Yes, okay,' she said impatiently. 'Now get up and stop making a fool of yourself.' Chastened, the man jumped up like a gymnast completing a somersault.

'See?' said Rajaram. 'I told you it's going to be a day at the circus – we have clowns, monkeys, acrobats, everything.'

When the storm of manufactured adulation had passed, the Prime Minister tossed her garlands, one by one, out into the audience. The VIP seats and dignitaries cheered wildly at this grand gesture.

'Her father also used to do that, when he was Prime Minister,' said Ishvar.

'Yes,' said Rajaram. 'I saw it once. But when he did it, he looked humble.'

'She looks like she is throwing rubbish at us,' said Om.

Rajaram laughed. 'Isn't that the politician's speciality?'

The member of parliament for the district started the welcome address, thanking the Prime Minister for showing such favour to this poor, undeserving place. 'This audience is small,' he said, sweeping his hand to indicate the captive crowd of twenty-five thousand. 'But it is a warm and appreciative audience, possessing a great love for the Prime Minister who has done so much to improve our lives. We are simple people, from simple villages. But we understand the truth, and we have come today to listen to our leader . . .'

Ishvar rolled up his sleeves, undoing two buttons and blowing down his shirt. 'How long will it last, I wonder.'

'Two, three, four hours – depends on how many speeches,' said Rajaram.

'. . . and take note, all you journalists who will write tomorrow's newspapers. Especially the foreign journalists. For grave mischief has been done by irresponsible scribbling. Lots of lies have been spread about this Emergency, which has been declared specially for the people's benefit. Observe: wherever the Prime Minister goes, thousands gather from miles around, to see her and hear her. Surely this is the mark of a truly great leader.'

Rajaram took out a coin and began playing Heads or Tails with Om. Around them, people were making new friends, chatting, discussing the monsoon. Children invented games and drew pictures in the dust. Some slept. A mother stretched out her sari-draped legs, nestled her baby in the valley of her thighs, and began exercising it while singing softly, spreading the arms, crossing them over the chest, raising the tiny feet as far as they would go.

The minders and volunteers patrolled the enclosures, keeping an eye on things. They did not care so long as people amused themselves discreetly. The only prohibited activity was standing up or leaving the enclosure. Besides, this was just a warm-up speech.

'. . . and yet there are people who say she must step down, that her rule is illegal! Who are these people uttering such falsehoods? Brothers and sisters, they are the pampered few, living in big cities and enjoying comforts that you and I cannot even dream about. They do not like the changes the Prime Minister is making because their unfair privileges will be taken away. But it is clear that in the villages, where seventy-five per cent of our people live, there is nothing but complete support for our beloved Prime Minister.'

Near the end of his speech he gave a hand signal to someone waiting in the wings with a walkie-talkie. Seconds later, coloured lights hidden in the floral proscenium arch began to flash powerfully enough to compete with the midday sun. The audience was impressed. The feeble mandatory clapping for the member of parliament's speech now became genuine applause for the visual display.

While the flashing lights still dazzled, the noise of a helicopter filled the sky again, its *whup-whup-whup* approaching from behind the stage. Something dropped from the belly of the turbulent machine. Out of the package floated – rose petals!

The crowd cheered, but the pilot had mistimed it. Instead of showering the Prime Minister and dignitaries, the petals fell in a pasture behind the stage. A goatherd who was grazing his animals thanked the heavens for the honour, then hurried home to tell his family about the miracle.

The second package, intended for the VIP enclosure, landed on target but failed to open. Someone was carried away on a stretcher. By the time the third package was released over the general audience, the pilot had mastered the technique, and it was a perfect drop. An obliging breeze came up, scattering the petals generously. Children in the crowd had a lovely time chasing them down.

On stage there was more bowing and scraping, then the Prime Minister approached the cluster of microphones. One hand maintaining the sari at her neck, she began speaking. Every sentence was followed by thunderous applause from the stage and the VIP enclosure, which, in turn, set off the conscientious ones in the audience. Her speech seemed in danger of being strangled by an excess of clapping. Finally, she stepped away from the podium and whispered something to an aide, who gave instructions to the dignitaries. The effect was immediate. From now on, the clapping was more sensibly apportioned.

She adjusted the white sari that was slipping off her head and continued. 'There is nothing to worry about just because the Emergency is declared. It is a necessary measure to fight the forces of evil. It will make things better for ordinary people. Only the crooks, the smugglers, the blackmarketeers need to worry, for we will soon put them behind bars. And we will succeed in this despite the despicable conspiracy, which has been brewing since I began introducing programmes of benefit for the common man and woman. There is a foreign hand involved against us – the hand of enemies who would not wish to see us prosper.'

Rajaram took out a deck of cards and began shuffling, to Om's delight. 'You came prepared, for sure,' he said.

'Of course. Sounds like it's going to be a long one. Playing?' he asked Ishvar, and dealt him in. The people near them perked up, grateful for the distraction. They shifted around and formed a circle to watch the game.

'. . . but no matter, for we are determined that disruptive forces will be put down. The government will continue to fight back until there is no more danger to democracy in our country.'

Om refused to clap now, he said his hands were aching. He played his card, and someone near him blurted: Mistake, mistake. Om realized his error, took back the card and played another, while the features of the new Twenty-Point Programme were outlined.

'What we want to do is provide houses for the people. Enough food, so no one goes hungry. Cloth at controlled prices. We want to build schools for our children and hospitals to look after the sick. Birth control will also be available to everyone. And the government will no longer tolerate a situation where people increase the population recklessly, draining the resources that belong to all. We promise that we will eliminate poverty from our cities and towns and villages.'

The card game had gradually become quite boisterous. Om was smacking his cards down with gusto, accompanied by fanfares. 'Tantan-tana-nana!' he sang at his next turn.

'Is that all?' said Rajaram. 'So much noise for that? Only a small obstacle! Beat this if you have the strength!'

'Hoi-hoi – wait for my chance,' said Ishvar, trumping the hand and making the other two groan. The onlookers provided a chorus of approval for his smart play.

Before long, an audience-monitor came over to investigate. 'What is this nonsense? Show some respect for the Prime Minister.' He threatened to withhold their money and snack if they did not behave themselves and pay attention to the speech. The cards were ordered put away.

'. . . And our newly-formed flying squads will catch the gold smugglers, uncover corruption and black money, and punish the tax evaders who keep our country poor. You can trust your government to fulfil the task. Your part in this is very simple: to support the government, support the Emergency. The need of the hour is discipline – discipline in every aspect of life, if we are to reinvigorate the nation. Shun all superstitions, don't believe in horoscopes and holy men, only in yourself and in hard work. Avoid rumours and loose talk if you love your country. Do your duty, above all else! This, my brothers and sisters, is my appeal to you! Jai Hind!'

The eighteen on stage rose as one to congratulate the Prime Minister on a most inspiring speech. Another brisk round of fawning commenced. At the end of it, the party official who would officially thank the Prime Minister went smirking and simpering to the microphone.

'Oh, no!' said Om. 'One more speech? When do we get our snack?'

After the stock acknowledgements and hackneyed tributes were exhausted, the speaker pointed dramatically at the sky towards the far end of the field. 'Behold! Yonder in the clouds! Oh, we are truly blessed!'

The audience looked up and around for the source of his rapturous seizure. There was no whirring helicopter this time. But on the horizon, floating towards the field, was a huge hot-air balloon. The canopy of orange, white, and green drifted across the cloudless blue sky in the silence of a dream. It lost some height as it neared the crowds, and now the sharp of sight could recognize the high-hovering face behind dark glasses. The figure raised a white-clad arm and waved.

'Oh, we are twice blessed today in this meeting!' the man sang into the microphone. 'The Prime Minister on stage with us, and her son in the sky above us! What more could we ask for!'

The son in the sky, meanwhile, had started throwing leaflets overboard. With a flair for the theatric, he first released a single sheet to tantalize the audience. All eyes were riveted on it as it swooped and circled lazily. He followed this with two more leaflets, and waited, before getting rid of the lot in fluttering handfuls.

'Yes, my brothers and sisters, Mother India sits on stage with us, and the Son of India shines from the sky upon us! The glorious present, here, now, and the golden future, up there, waiting to descend and embrace our lives! What a blessed nation we are!'

Down to earth floated the first few leaflets, containing the Prime Minister's picture and the Twenty-Point Programme. Once again, the children had fun running after them to see who could capture the most. The hot-air balloon cleared the airspace, leaving the field to the helicopter for a final assault.

This time it was flying much lower than before. The risk paid off in accuracy: a grand finale of rose petals showered the stage. But the Prime Minister's eighty-foot cutout began to sway in the tempest of the helicopter's blades. The crowd shouted in alarm. The figure with outstretched arms groaned, and the ropes strained at their moorings. Security men waved frantically at the helicopter while struggling to hold on to the ropes and braces. But the whirlwind was much too strong to withstand. The cutout started to topple slowly, face forward. Those in the vicinity of the cardboard-and-plywood giant ran for their lives.

'Nobody wants to be caught in the Prime Minister's embrace,' said Rajaram.

'But she tries to get on top of everyone,' said Om.

'Shameless boy,' said his uncle.

They hurried to the refreshments, where an endless line was being kept in order by security men. A shortage of cups prevented it from moving faster. The snack – one pakora per head – had run out. The servers' hands grew ungenerous with the diminishing supply of tea. They began doling out half-cups. 'It's not less tea,' they explained to those who protested the stinginess. 'It's just more concentrated.'

While the queue crawled forward, ambulances swept past the edge of the field, sirens blaring, come to collect the casualties of the eighty-foot Prime Minister's collapse. After an hour of waiting, Ishvar, Om, and Rajaram were still at the back of the line when the tea was depleted. Simultaneously, there was an announcement: the buses would be leaving in ten minutes. Frantic about being stranded, everyone abandoned the quarrel with the tea-dispensers and rushed to the departure area. They were paid four rupees each as they boarded the bus.

'Why four?' asked Ishvar. 'They told us five when we came.'

'One rupee for bus fare, tea and snack.'

'We didn't even get tea and snack!' Om thrust his face furiously before the other's. 'And they said the bus was free!'

'Heh? You want free bus ride? Your father's Divali or what?'

Om tensed. 'I'm warning you, don't take my father's name.'

Ishvar and Rajaram coaxed him onto the bus. The man laughed about someone looking like an insect and talking like a tiger.

They sat glumly through the return journey, thirsty and tired. 'What a waste of a day,' said Ishvar. 'We could have stitched six dresses. Thirty rupees lost.'

'And how much hair I would have collected by now.'

'Maybe I should visit Dinabai when we get back,' said Ishvar. 'Just to explain. Promise her we'll come tomorrow.'

Two hours later, the bus stopped in unfamiliar surroundings. The driver ordered everyone off. He had his instructions, he said. As a precaution, he rolled up his window and locked himself in the cabin.

The hutment dwellers rattled the door, spat on it, kicked the sides a few times. 'You indecent people!' shouted the driver. 'Damaging public property!'

A few more blows were rained on the bus before the crowd moved on. Ishvar and Om had no idea where they were, but Rajaram knew the way. There was thunder, and it began raining again. They walked for an hour. It was night in the slum when they arrived.

'Let's eat something quickly,' said Ishvar. 'Then I'll go and pacify Dinabai.'

While he pumped up the Primus stove and struck a match, the darkness was torn to shreds by a terrifying shriek. It seemed neither human nor animal. The tailors grabbed their hurricane-lamp and ran with Rajaram towards the noise, towards Monkey-man.

They found him behind his shack, trying to strangle his dog. Tikka was on his side, his eyes bulging, with Monkey-man's knees upon him. The dog's legs pawed the air, seeking a purchase to help him flee the inexplicable pain around his neck.

Monkey-man's fingers squeezed harder. His insane screams mingled with Tikka's fearful howling. The terrible harmony of human and animal cries continued to rend the night.

Ishvar and Rajaram succeeded in prying loose Monkey-man's fingers. Tikka struggled to stand. He did not run, waiting faithfully nearby, coughing, pawing at his face. Monkey-man tried to grab him again but was foiled by others who had gathered.

'Calm down,' said Rajaram. 'Tell us what's wrong.'

'Laila and Majnoo!' he wept, pointing to the shack, unable to explain. He tried to lure back the dog, making kissing sounds. 'Tikka, Tikka, come my Tikka!'

Seeking pardon, the beast approached trustingly. Monkey-man got in a kick to his ribs before the others pulled him back. They raised the lantern and looked inside the shack.

The hissing light fell on the walls, then found the floor. They saw the monkeys' corpses lying in a corner. Laila and Majnoo's long brown tails, exuberant in life, seemed strangely shrunken. Like frayed old rope, the tails draggled on the earthen floor. One of the creatures had been partially eaten, the viscera hanging out, dark brown and stringy.

'Hai Ram,' said Ishvar, covering his mouth. 'What a tragedy.'

'Let me look,' said someone trying to push through the crowd.

It was the old woman who had shared her water with Om on the first day, when the tap was dry. The harmonium player said she should be let through immediately, she could read entrails as fluently as a swami could read the Bhagavad Gita.

The crowd parted, and the old woman entered. She asked that the lantern be brought closer. With her foot she nudged the corpse till the entrails were better exposed. Bending, she stirred in them with a twig.

'The loss of two monkeys is not the worst loss he will suffer,' she pronounced. 'The murder of the dog is not the worst murder he will commit.'

'But the dog,' started Rajaram, 'we saved him, he is –'

'The murder of the dog is not the worst murder he will commit,' she repeated with grim forcefulness, and left. Her audience shrugged, assuming that the old woman, despite her fierce demeanour, was a little disoriented and upset by the event.

'I'll kill him!' Monkey-man began wailing again. 'My babies are dead! I'll kill that shameless dog!'

Someone led Tikka to safety while others tried to talk sense into Monkey-man. 'The dog is a dumb animal. When animals get hungry, they want to eat. What's the point of killing him? It's your fault for locking them in together.'

'He played with them like brother and sister,' he wept. 'All three were like my children. And now this. I'll kill him.'

Ishvar and Rajaram led Monkey-man away from his shack. Comforting him would be easier if the gory little bodies were out of sight. They entered Rajaram's shack, then quickly marched out again. The bundles of hair all over the place, like macabre hairy little corpses, were not something Monkey-man could tolerate in his present condition. So they went into the tailors' shack, and gave him a drink of water. He sat with the glass in his hands, whimpering, shaking, muttering to himself.

Ishvar decided that dropping in on Dinabai now was out of the question, it was too late. 'What a day it's been,' he whispered to Om. 'We'll explain to her tomorrow.'

They stayed with Monkey-man past midnight, letting him grieve for as long as he liked. A burial was planned for Laila and Majnoo, and they convinced him to forgive the dog. The question of livelihood was raised by Rajaram: 'How long will it take you to train new monkeys?'

'They were my friends – my children! I don't want any talk of replacing them!'

He was silent for a while, then, oddly enough, broached the subject himself. 'I have other talents, you know. Gymnastics, tightrope walking, juggling, balancing. A new act without monkeys is possible. I'll think later about what to do. First, I must finish mourning.'

Dina displayed her displeasure when Maneck returned late from college. And this on his very first day, she thought. Nobody believed in punctuality anymore. Perhaps Mrs. Gupta was right, the Emergency wasn't such a bad thing if it taught people to observe the time.

'Your tea was ready over an hour ago,' she said, pouring him a cup and buttering a slice of Britannia Bread. 'What kept you?'

'Sorry, Aunty. Very long wait at the bus stop. I was late for class in the morning as well. Everybody is grumbling that the buses seem to have disappeared from the road.'

'People are always grumbling.'

'The tailors – they finished work already?'

'They didn't come at all.'

'What happened?'

'If I knew, would I look so worried? Coming late is like a religion for them, but it's the first time they've been absent for the whole day.'

Maneck bolted the tea and went to his room. Kicking off his shoes, he sniffed the socks – a slight smell – and put on his slippers. There were some boxes left to unpack. Might as well do it now. Clothes, towels, toothpaste, soap went into the cupboard. A nice odour came from the shelf. He breathed deeply: reminded of Dina Aunty, she was lovely – beautiful hair, kind face.

The unpacking finished, he was at a loss for things to do. The umbrella hanging from the cupboard caught his eye. He opened it, admired the pagoda shape, and pictured Dina Aunty walking down the street with it. Like the women at the racecourse in *My Fair Lady*. She looked much younger than Mummy, though Mummy had written they were the same age, forty-two this year. And that she had had a hard life, many misfortunes, her husband dying young, so Maneck was to be kind to her even if she was difficult to get along with.

That would explain Dina Aunty's tone, he thought, the hard life. The way she talked, her voice sounding old, having endured a vast range of weather. Her words always sharp – the words of a tired, cynical person. He wished he could cheer her up, make her laugh once in a while.

The little room was getting on his nerves. What a bore this was, and the rest of the academic year was going to just drag on and on. He picked up a book, flipped through it, tossed it back on the desk. The chessmen. He arranged the board and made a few mechanical moves. For him, the joy had seeped out of the plastic shapes. He tumbled them back into the maroon box with its sliding top – from the prison of their squares into the prison of the coffin.

But he, at least, had escaped his prison, he thought, had seen the last of that bloody hostel. His only regret was not being able to say goodbye to Avinash, whose room remained locked and silent. Probably still hiding at his parents' – it would be foolhardy to return while the Emergency regime governed the campus and people continued to disappear.

Maneck remembered the early days with him, when their friendship was new. Everything I do is chess, Avinash had once said. Now he was under a serious check. Had he castled in time, protected by three pawns and a rook? And Dina Aunty, playing against her tailors, making her moves between front room and back room. And Daddy, attempting to take on the soft-drink opponents who did not observe the rules of the game, who played draughts using chess pieces.

Evening deepened the shadows in the room, but Maneck did not bother with the light. His whimsical thoughts about chess suddenly acquired a dark, depressing hue in the dusk. Everything was under threat, and so complicated. The game was pitiless. The carnage upon the chessboard of life left wounded human beings in its wake. Avinash's father with tuberculosis, his three sisters waiting for their dowries, Dina Aunty struggling to survive her misfortunes, Daddy crushed and brokenhearted while Mummy pretended he was going to be his strong, smiling self again, and their son would return after a year of college, start bottling Kohlah's Cola in the cellar, and their lives would be full of hope and happiness once more, like the time before he was sent away to boarding school. But pretending only worked in the world of childhood, things would never be the same again. Life seemed so hopeless, with nothing but misery for everyone . . .

He slapped shut the folding chessboard: a puff of air kissed his face. Where his cheeks were wet with tears, the kiss felt cold. He dried his eyes and slapped the two sides together again, like bellows, then fanned himself with the board.

Dina Aunty's call of 'Dinnertime,' when it finally came, was like a release from jail. He was at the table instantly, hovering about, not sitting till his place was indicated.

'Have you got a cold?' she asked. 'Your eyes look watery.'

'No, I was resting.' She didn't miss much, he thought.

'I forgot to ask yesterday – do you prefer knife and fork, or fingers?'

'Anything, it doesn't matter.'

'What do you do at home?'

'We use cutlery.'

She set a knife, fork, and spoon around his plate, leaving hers unadorned, and brought the food to the table.

'I can also eat with fingers,' he protested. 'You don't have to give me special treatment.'

'Don't flatter yourself, cheap stainless steel is not special.' She filled his plate and sat opposite him. 'When I was young, we always had proper place settings. Sterling silver. My father was very particular about such matters. After he died our habits changed. Especially when my brother Nusswan married Ruby. She got rid of it. She said we didn't need to ape foreigners while God had given us perfectly good fingers. Which is true in a way. But I think she was just lazy about cleaning all the cutlery.'

Halfway through the meal Dina washed her hands and fetched a knife and fork for herself. 'You've inspired me,' she smiled. 'It's been twenty-five years since I used these things.'

He looked away, trying not to make her fingers nervous. 'Will the tailors come tomorrow?'

'I hope so,' she said, dismissing the topic briefly.

Then her anxiety drew her back to it. 'Unless they've found better jobs, and disappeared. But what else can I expect from such people? Ever since I started this tailoring business, they've made my life a misery. Day after day, they drive me mad with worry about finishing the dresses on time.'

'Maybe they are sick or something.'

'Both together? Maybe it's the sickness that comes out of a booze bottle – I did pay them yesterday. No discipline at all, no sense of responsibility. Anyway, I don't know why I'm bothering you with my problems.'

'That's okay.' He helped her carry the dirty dishes to the kitchen. The stray cats were mewing outside. He had heard them last night while falling asleep, and dreamt of the pariah dogs congregating on the front porch of the General Store, and Daddy feeding them, making his usual joke, that he would soon have to open a new branch for his canine customers.

'Not through the window, Maneck – in the garbage pail,' said Dina, as he tossed out the scraps.

'But I want to feed the cats, Aunty.'

'No, don't encourage them.'

'They're hungry – see how they're waiting.'

'Nonsense. Nuisances outside my window, that's what they are. And they break in to make a mess in the kitchen. Only good thing about them is their intestines. To make violin strings, my husband used to say.'

Maneck was sure she would see it his way if he talked about the cats every day as though they were human; that was the trick Daddy used. When her back was turned he threw out the remainder. Already he knew which was his favourite: the brown and white tabby with a misshapen ear who was saying, Hurry with the food, I haven't got all day.

After clearing up, Dina invited him to sit with her in the front room, read or study, do whatever he liked. 'You don't have to lock yourself away in there. Treat this as your home. And if you need something, don't be shy to ask.'

'Thank you, Aunty.' He had been dreading the return to his jail cell before bedtime. He took the armchair across from her and riffled a magazine.

'Have you been to see your mummy's family yet?'

He shook his head. 'I hardly know them. And we have never got along with them. Daddy always says they are so dull, they are in danger of boring themselves to death.'

'Tch-tch-tch,' she frowned and smiled simultaneously, sorting her fabric remnants and patches. The half-dozen squares she was shaping to fit together were spread out on the sofa.

Maneck came closer. 'What are these?'

'My cloth collection.'

'Really? What for?'

'Does there have to be a reason? People collect all kinds of things. Stamps, coins, postcards. I have cloth, instead of a photo album or scrapbook.'

'Yes,' he said, nodding doubtfully.

She let him watch for a while, then said, 'Don't worry, I'm not going crazy. These pieces are to make a quilt. A nice counterpane for my bed.'

'Oh, now I see.' He began looking through the heap, making suggestions, picking out fragments which he thought would go well together. Some, like the swatches of chiffon and tusser, felt gorgeous between his fingers. 'Too many different colours and designs,' he said.

'Are you trying to be a critic or what?'

'No, I mean it's going to be very difficult to match them properly.'

'Difficult, yes, but that's where taste and skill come in. What to select, what to leave out – and which goes next to which.'

She snipped off some jagged edges and temporarily tacked the six selections together, to obtain a better perspective. 'What do you think?' she asked.

'So far so good.'

A nice friendly boy, she felt. Her fears about a spoilt brat could not have been more unfounded. And it was good to have someone to talk to. Someone besides the tailors, who were always mistrustful of her – not that she trusted them either.

Next afternoon she intercepted Maneck on the verandah when he returned from college and whispered that the tailors had turned up. 'But don't say a word about how upset I was yesterday.'

'Okay.' The queen's gambit, he thought, tossing his books on the bed. He went into the front room as the tailors emerged for their tea break.

'Ah, there he is, there he is!' said Ishvar. 'After a whole month we meet again, hahn?'

He put out his hand and asked Maneck how he was, while Om stood by grinning. Maneck said he was fine, and Ishvar said they were both first class, thanks mainly to the regular work provided by Dinabai, who was such a good employer. He smiled at her to include her in the conversation.

Throughout the afternoon, she watched the three disapprovingly – behaving as if they were long-lost friends. And to think they had met just once before, on the train, trying to find her flat.

In the evening, when the tailors were getting ready to put away the skirts, she gave them some parting advice: 'Better tell the Prime Minister your jobs are in danger if she takes you again to a meeting. There are two more tailors begging me for work.'

'No no,' said Ishvar. 'We definitely want to work for you. We are very happy working for you.'

Dina sat alone in the back room after the tailors left. The space still seemed to vibrate with the Singers. Soon the evening gloom would materialize, infect the fibre-filled air, drape itself over her bed, depress her from now till morning.

But as dusk fell and the streetlamps came on, her spirit remained buoyant. Like magic, she thought, the difference made by another human presence in the flat. She returned to the front room to have her little planned talk with Maneck.

Queen to king's knight, he thought.

'You realize why I have to be strict with them,' she said. 'If they know I'm desperate, they'll sit on my head.'

'Yes, I understand. By the way, Aunty, do you play chess?'

'No. And I should tell you right now – I don't like your chatting so much with them. They are my employees, you are Aban Kohlah's son. A distance has to be kept. All this familiarity is not good.'

Things were worse the following afternoon. She could not believe her ears – the impudence of that Omprakash, boldly asking Maneck, 'You want to come with us for tea?' And worst of all, on Maneck's face glimmered the inclination to say yes. Time to step in, she decided.

'He has his tea here. With me.' There was ice in Dina's voice.

'Yes, but maybe . . . maybe just for today I can go out, Aunty?'

She said if he wanted to waste his parents' payment for boarding and lodging, it was fine with her.

At the Vishram Vegetarian Hotel the air was alive with hearty cooking smells. Maneck felt he had only to stick out his tongue to sample the menu. His stomach rumbled hungrily.

They sat at the solitary table and ordered three teas. The spills from countless spicy meals had imparted a pungent varnish to the wood. Ishvar took the packet of beedis from his pocket and offered it to Maneck.

'No, thanks. I don't smoke.'

The tailors lit up. 'She won't let us smoke at our machines,' said Om. 'And now the room is so crowded with her bed also in there. Place is like a dingy godown.'

'So what?' said Ishvar. 'It's not as if you have to run around in it catching goats or something.'

The cook in one corner of the restaurant was working within a circle of pots and pans. They could see their tea simmering in an open kettle. Three roaring stoves sent clouds of greasy smoke to the ceiling. Flames licked the black bottom of a huge karai full of boiling oil, bubbling dangerously and ready for frying. A drop of sweat from the cook's shining brow fell into the oil; it spat viciously.

'You like your room?' asked Ishvar.

'Oh yes. Much better than the hostel.'

'We also found a place,' said Om. 'At first I hated it, but now it's all right. There are some nice people living near us.'

'You must come visit one day,' said Ishvar.

'Sure. Is it far?'

'Not very. Takes about forty-five minutes by train.' The teas arrived with a splash, the cups sitting in little brown-puddled saucers. Ishvar slurped from the saucer. Om poured his puddle back into the cup and sipped. Maneck followed his example.

'And how is college?'

Maneck made a wry face. 'Hopeless. But I'll have to finish it somehow, to please my parents. Then home I go, on the first train.'

'Soon as we collect some money, we're also going back,' said Ishvar, coughing and hawking. 'To find a wife for Om. Hahn, my nephew?'

'I don't want marriage,' he scowled. 'How many times to tell you.'

'Look at that sour-lime face. Come on, finish your tea, time's up.' Ishvar got up to leave. The boys swallowed the last draughts and tumbled out of the little tea shop after him. They hurried back to Dina's flat, past the beggar on his rolling platform.

'Remember him?' said Om to Maneck. 'We saw him on the first day. He's become our friend now. We pass him every day, and he waves to us.'

'O babu!' sang the beggar. 'Aray babu! O big paisawalla babu!' He smiled at the trio, rattling his begging tin. Maneck tinkled into it the small change from the Vishram.

'What's that smell?' Dina leaned forward angrily to sniff Maneck's shirt. 'Were you smoking with those two?'

'No,' he whispered, embarrassed that they would hear in the back room.

'Be honest. I stand in your parents' place.'

'No, Aunty! They were smoking, and I was sitting next to them, that's all.'

'If I ever catch you, I will write straight to your mummy, I'm warning you. Now tell me, did they say anything else about yesterday? The real reason they were absent?'

'No.'

'What did you talk about?'

He resented the cross-examination. 'Nothing much. This and that.'

She did not pursue it, snubbed by his taciturnity. 'There's another thing you better be warned about. Omprakash has lice.'

'Really?' he asked interestedly. 'You've seen them?'

'Do I put my hand in the fire to check if it's hot? All day long he scratches. And not just his head. Problems at both ends – worms at one, lice at the other. So take my advice, stay away if you know what's good for you. His uncle is safe, he's almost bald, but you have a nice thick thatch, the lice will love it.'

Dina's advice went unheeded. As the days turned to weeks, the afternoon break at the Vishram Vegetarian Hotel became a regular affair for the three. Once, Maneck was delayed in returning from college, and Om whispered to Ishvar that they should wait for him.

'My, my,' said Dina, overhearing. 'Postponing your tea. Are you feeling well? Are you sure you will survive that long?'

Ishvar reflected upon why it annoyed Dinabai so much, their going off together. When Maneck arrived and Om leapt up from his Singer, he decided to stay behind. 'You boys go, I want to finish this skirt.'

Dina was all praise for him. 'Listen to your uncle, learn from his example,' she said to Om as the two left. She poured Maneck's tea into the segregated pink roses cup and brought it to Ishvar. 'You might as well drink it.'

He thanked her for her trouble. He took a sip and remarked that Maneck and Om were getting on well, enjoying each other's company. 'They are both the same age. Om must be fed up being with his old uncle all the time. Night and day we are together.'

'Nonsense.' She said that in her opinion, if it weren't for the uncle's steadying presence, Om would turn into a wastrel. 'I only hope he is not a poor influence on Maneck.'

'No no, don't worry. Om is not a bad boy. If sometimes he is disobedient or bad-tempered, it's only because he is frustrated and unhappy. He has had a very unfortunate life.'

'Mine has not been easy either. But we must make the best of what we have.'

'There is no other way,' he agreed.

From that day, he stayed behind more and more while Dina continued to make tea in Maneck's name but poured it in Ishvar's cup. They chatted about matters both tailoring and non-tailoring. His half-smile of gratitude was always something she looked forward to, with the frozen half straining to catch up as his face beamed at the pink roses along the rim of the saucer.

'Om's sewing is improving, hahn, Dinabai?'

'He makes fewer mistakes.'

'Yes yes. He is much happier since Maneck came.'

'I am worried about Maneck, though. I hope he is studying properly – his parents are relying on it. They have a small shop, and it's not doing well.'

'Everybody has troubles. Don't worry, I will talk to him, remind him to work hard. That's what these two young fellows have to do, work hard.'

Ishvar noted that the tea breaks upset Dinabai no more. It confirmed his suspicion, that she was longing for company.

The boys' conversation inevitably took a different turn when they were on their own. Om was curious about the hostel Maneck had abandoned. 'Were there any college girls living there?'

'You think I would leave if there were? They have a separate hostel.

Boys are not allowed inside.'

From the Vishram they could see a cinema advertisement on a roof across the road, for a film called *Revolver Rani*. The billboard was a diptych. The first panel showed four men tearing off a woman's clothes. An enormous bra-clad bosom was exposed, while the men's lips, parted in lewd laughter, revealed carnivorous teeth and bright-red tongues. The second panel depicted the same woman, her clothes in tatters, mowing down the four men with automatic gunfire.

'Why is it called *Revolver Rani*?' said Om. 'That's a machine-gun in her hands.'

'They could have called it *Machine-Gun Maharani*. But that doesn't sound as good.'

'Should be fun to see it.'

'Let's go next week.'

'No money. Ishvar says we must save.'

'That's okay, I'll pay.'

Om searched Maneck's face while drawing on the beedi, trying to decide if he meant it. 'No, I can't let you do that.'

'It's okay, I don't mind.'

'I'll ask my uncle.' His beedi went out and he reached for the matches. 'You know, there's a girl who lives near our house. Her breasts look like that.'

'Impossible.'

The outright dismissal made Om study the poster again. 'Maybe you're right,' he yielded. 'Not exactly that big. They always paint them gigantic. But this girl has a solid pair, same beautiful shape as that. Sometimes she lets me touch them.'

'Go, yaar, I wasn't born yesterday.'

'I swear she does. Her name is Shanti. She opens her blouse and lets me squeeze them whenever I like,' he said, giving his imagination free rein. Seeing Maneck laugh and slap his knee, he inquired innocently, 'You mean you've never done that to a girl?'

'Of course I have,' Maneck answered hastily. 'But you said you live with your uncle in a small house. How would you get the chance?'

'Easy. There is a ditch at the side of the colony, and lots of bushes behind it. We go there after dark. But for a few minutes only. If she's away longer, someone would come looking for her.' He puffed airily at the beedi as he fabricated explorations that involved Shanti's hair and limbs, and complicated excursions into her skirt and blouse.

'Good thing you're a tailor,' said Maneck. 'You know all the ins and outs of clothing.'

But Om continued undiscouraged, stopping short only of the final for-ay. 'Once, I was on top of her, and we almost did it. Then there was a noise in the bushes so she got scared.' He drained his saucer and poured more from the cup. 'What about you? Ever done it?'

'Almost. On a railway train.'

It was Om's turn to laugh. 'You're a champion fakeologist, for sure. On a train!'

'No, really. A few months ago, when I left home to come to college.' Catalysed by Om's fantasies, Maneck's inventiveness took the field at a gallop. 'There was a woman in the upper berth opposite mine, very beautiful.'

'More beautiful than Dinabai?'

The question made him pause. He had to think for a moment. 'No,' he said loyally. 'But the minute I got on the train, she kept staring at me, smil-ing when no one was watching. The problem was, her father was travel-ling with her. Finally night came, and people began going to sleep. She and I kept awake. When everyone had fallen asleep, including her father, she pushed aside the sheet and pulled one breast out from her choli.'

'Then what?' asked Om, happy to enjoy the imaginary fruits.

'She began massaging her breast, and signalled for me to come over. I was scared to climb down from my berth. Someone could wake up, you know. But then she put her hand between her legs and began rubbing herself. So I decided I had to go to her.'

'Of course. You'd be a fool not to,' Om breathed hard.

'I got down without disturbing anyone, and in a second I was stroking her breast. She grabbed my hand, begging me to climb in with her. I wondered what was the best way to get up there. I didn't want to jolt her father's berth underneath. Suddenly there was a movement. He turned over, groaning. She was so frightened that she pushed me away and started snoring loudly. I pretended I was on my way to the bathroom.'

'If only the bastard had kept sleeping.'

'I know. It's so sad. I'll never meet that woman again.' Maneck felt suddenly desolate, as though the loss was real. 'You're lucky Shanti lives near you.'

'You can see her one day,' said Om generously. 'When you visit me and Ishvar. But you won't be able to talk to her, just look at her from far. She's very shy, and meets me secretly, as I said.'

They gulped their tea and ran all the way back, for they had exceeded the time.

Batata wada, bhel puri, pakora, bhajia, sherbet – Maneck paid for all the snacks and drinks at the Vishram because Om got just enough from Ishvar for one cup of tea. The allowance from Maneck's parents was sufficient for the treats, since he no longer needed to supplement canteen food. The following week he kept his word and took Om to see *Revolver Rani* after the day's sewing was done. He offered to pay for Ishvar too, who refused, saying his time would be better spent finishing one more dress.

'How about you, Aunty? Want to come?'

'I wouldn't see such rubbish if you paid me,' said Dina. 'And if your money weighs too much in your pocket, let me know. I can tell your mummy to stop sending it.'

'Bilkool correct,' said Ishvar. 'You young people don't understand the value of money.'

Undeterred by the reproaches, they set off for the cinema. She reminded Maneck to come straight home after the film, his dinner would be waiting. He agreed, grumbling to himself that Dina Aunty was taking her self-appointed role of guardian too seriously.

'The old woman's prophecy came true,' said Om, as they started towards the train station. 'Half of it, anyway – Monkey-man finally took his revenge.'

'What did he do?'

'A terrible thing. It happened last night.' Tikka had been back living with Monkey-man, and his neighbours assumed the two were friends again. But after the hutment dwellers had gone to sleep, Monkey-man put a wooden crate outside his shack and adorned it with flowers and an oil lamp. A photograph of Laila and Majnoo riding on Tikka's back was propped up in the centre. It was a Polaroid shot taken long ago by an American tourist charmed by the act. The altar was ready. Monkey-man led Tikka before it, made the dog lie down, and slit his throat. Then he went around letting people know he had fulfilled his duty.

'It was horrible,' said Om. 'We got there and saw poor Tikka floating in his blood. He was still twitching a little. I almost vomited.'

'If my father was there, he would have killed Monkey-man,' said Maneck.

'Are you boasting or complaining?'

'Both, I guess.' He kicked a stone from the footpath into the road. 'My father cares more about stray dogs than his own son.'

'Don't talk rubbish, yaar.'

'Why rubbish? Look, he feeds the dogs every day on the porch. But me he sent away. All the time I was there, he kept fighting with me, didn't want me around.'

'Don't talk rubbish, your father sent you here to study because he cares for your future.'

'You're an expert on fathers or what?'

'Yes.'

'What makes you?'

'Because my father is dead. That quickly makes you an expert. You better believe me – stop talking rubbish about your father.'

'Okay, my father is a saint. But what happened to Monkey-man?'

'People in the colony were angry, they said we should tell the police, because ever since the monkeys died, Monkey-man has two small children living with him, three-four years old. They are his sister's son and daughter, training for his new act. And if he went mad, it would be dangerous for the children. But then others in the colony said there was no point putting crooks in charge of the insane. Anyway, Monkey-man loves the children. He has been taking very good care of them.'

They alighted from the train, pushing their way through the crowd waiting to climb on. Outside the platform, a woman sat in the sun with a small basket of vegetables beside her. She was drying her laundered sari, one half at a time. One end was wound wet round her waist and over her shrunken breasts, as far as it would go. The drying half was stretched along the railway fence, flowing from her body like a prayer in the evening sun. She waved to Om as the two passed by.

'She lives in our colony,' he said, weaving through the traffic to cross the lane towards the cinema. 'She sells vegetables. She has only one sari.'

Revolver Rani ended later than they had expected. While the credits rolled, they began inching down the aisles, lingering, not wanting to miss the reprise of the soundtrack. Then the fluttering national flag appeared on the screen, 'Jana Gana Mana' started to play, and there was a rush for the exits.

But the outward-bound audience ran into an obstacle. A squad of Shiv Sena volunteers guarding the doors blocked their way. People at the back, unaware of the reason for the bottleneck, began shouting. 'Side please! Aray bhai, side please! Move on, mister! Filmshow finished!'

The crowd in the front couldn't go forward, however, threatened by the Shiv Sena's waving sticks and an assortment of signs: RESPECT THE NATIONAL ANTHEM! YOUR MOTHERLAND NEEDS YOU DURING THE EMERGENCY! PATRIOTISM IS A SCARED DUTY! No one was allowed to leave till the flag faded on the screen and the lights came on.

'Why is patriotism a scared duty?' laughed Om. 'They need to frighten people to be patriotic?'

'These idiots can't even spell sacred, and they are telling us what to do,' said Maneck.

Om observed that the protesters were about fifty in all, whereas the audience was over eight hundred strong. 'We could have easily overpowered them. Dhishoom! Dhishoom! Like that fellow in the film,' he said, clenching his fists before his chest.

In high spirits, they began repeating some of the more dramatic lines they remembered from *Revolver Rani*. 'Blood can only be avenged by blood!' growled Maneck, with a swordfighting flourish.

'Standing on this consecrated earth, I swear with the sky as my witness that you will not see another dawn!' proclaimed Om.

'That's because I wake up late every day, yaar,' said Maneck. The sudden departure from the script made Om lose his pose with laughing.

Outside the railway station, the woman was still sitting with her vegetable basket. The dry half of the sari was now wrapped around her, with the wet stretch taking its turn along the fence. The basket was almost empty. 'Amma, time to go home,' said Om, and she smiled.

On the station platform, they decided to try the machine that said Weight & Fortune 25P. Maneck went first. The red and white wheel spun, lightbulbs flashed, there was a chime, and a little cardboard rectangle slid out into the curved receptacle.

'Sixty-one kilos,' said Maneck, and read the fortune on the reverse. '"A happy reunion awaits you in the near future." That sounds right – I'll be going home when this college year is finished.'

'Or it means you will meet that woman on the train again. You can finish her breast massage. Come on, my turn.' He climbed on, and Maneck fished in his pocket for another twenty-five-paise coin.

'Forty-six kilos,' said Om, and turned it over. '"You will soon be visiting many new and exciting places." That doesn't make sense. Going back to our village – that's not a new place.'

'I think it means the places in Shanti's blouse and skirt.'

Om struck a stance and raised his hand, reverting to the film dialogue. 'Until these fingers are wrapped around your neck, squeezing out your wretched life, there shall be no rest for me!'

'Not when you weigh only forty-six kilos,' said Maneck. 'You will have to first practise on a chicken's neck.'

The train arrived, and they ran from the ticket window to get on. 'These train tickets look exactly like the weight cards,' said Om.

'I could have saved the fare,' said Maneck.

'No, it's too risky. They've become very strict because of Emergency.'

He described the time when Ishvar and he had been trapped in a raid on ticketless travellers.

The rush hour was over, and the compartment was sparsely occupied. They put up their feet on the empty seat. Maneck unlaced his shoes and pulled them off, flexing his toes. 'We walked a lot today.'

'You shouldn't wear those tight shoes, yaar. My chappals are much more comfortable.'

'My parents would get very upset if I went out in chappals.' He kneaded the toes and soles, then pulled up his socks and put on the shoes.

'I used to massage my father's feet,' said Om. 'And he would massage my grandfather's feet.'

'Did you have to do it every day?'

'I didn't have to, but it was a custom. We sat outside in the evenings, on the charpoy. There would be a cool breeze, and birds singing in the trees. I enjoyed doing it for my father. It pleased him so much.' They swayed slightly in their seats as the train rocked along. 'There was a callus under the big toe of his right foot – from treadling his sewing-machine. When I was small, that callus used to make me laugh if he wiggled the toe, it looked like a man's face.'

Om was silent for the rest of the way, gazing pensively out the window. Maneck tried to distract him by imitating the characters in *Revolver Rani*, but a weak smile was all he could get out of him, so he lapsed into silence as well.

'You should have come with us,' said Maneck. 'It was fun. What thrilling fights.'

'No, thank you, I've seen enough fighting in my life,' said Ishvar. 'But when are you visiting our house?' Maneck's spending regularly on Om was creating too much obligation, he felt, it was time to reciprocate in some small way. 'You must have dinner with us soon.'

'Sure, any time,' answered Maneck, reluctant to make a commitment. It would upset Dina Aunty – the cinema trip had been bad enough.

Fortunately, Ishvar did not press for a firm date right then. He put the cover over his Singer and left with Om.

'Well, I hope you enjoyed yourself,' said Dina. 'Going against my wishes, mixing more and more with him in spite of what I told you.'

'It was just one film show, Aunty. For the first time Om went to a big theatre. He was so thrilled.'

'I hope he is able to sew tomorrow, and you can concentrate on your studies. These films about fighting and killing can only have a bad effect on the brain. In the old days the cinema was so sweet. A little dancing and singing, some comedy, or a romance. Now it's all just guns and knives.'

Next day, as though to vindicate Dina's theory, Om joined the bodice of a size-seven dress to the skirt of a size eleven, squeezing the excess into the gather at the waist. The mistakes were repeated in three garments and not discovered till the afternoon.

'Leave everything else, fix this first,' said Dina, but he ignored her.

'It's all right, Dinabai,' said Ishvar. 'I will separate the seams and stitch them again.'

'No, he made the mistakes and he should correct them.'

'You do them,' scowled Om, scratching his scalp. 'I have a headache. You gave me the wrong pieces so it's your mistake.'

'Listen to him! Lying shamelessly! And take your fingers out of your hair before you get oil on the cloth! Scratch-scratch-scratch the whole day!'

The argument was still going when Maneck returned from college. The tailors did not break for tea. He went to his room and shut himself in, wishing they would stop. For the rest of the afternoon the squabble kept dribbling under his door, creating a pool of distress around him.

At six, Dina knocked and asked him to come out. 'Those two have left. I need the company of a sane person.'

'Why were you fighting, Aunty?'

'I was fighting? How dare you! Do you know the whole story, to say who was fighting?'

'I'm sorry, Aunty. I meant, what was the fight about?'

'Same reason as always. Mistakes and shoddy work. But thank God for Ishvar. I don't know what I would do without him. One angel and one devil. Trouble is, when the angel keeps company with the devil, neither can be trusted.'

'Maybe Om behaves this way because something is upsetting him – maybe it's because you lock them in when you go out.'

'Ah! So he's told you that, has he? And did he say why I do it?'

'The landlord. But he thinks it's just an excuse. He says you make them feel like criminals.'

'His guilty conscience makes him feel that way. The landlord's threat is real, you remember it too. Don't let the rent-collector's sweet smile fool you into admitting anything. Always pretend you are my nephew.' She began tidying the room, picking up the scraps, stuffing the fragments in the bottom shelf. 'That Ibrahim's eyeballs can see the whole flat right from the front door, the way they wander, round and round. Faster than

Buster Keaton's. But you are too young to know Buster Keaton.'

'I've heard Mummy mention the name. She said he was funnier than Laurel and Hardy.'

'Never mind that – there is also a second reason. The tailors will put me out of business if I don't lock them in. Do you know Om tried to follow me to the export company? Did he tell you that? No, of course not. My tiny commission sticks in their throats. As it is, I can barely manage.'

'Shall I tell Mummy to send more money? For my rent and food?'

'Absolutely not! I am charging a fair price and she is paying it. You think I am telling you all this because I want charity?'

'No, I just thought –'

'My problems are not a beggar's wounds! Only a beggar removes his cloth to shock you with his mutilation. No, Mr. Mac Kohlah, I'm telling you all this so you understand your beloved Omprakash Darji a little better.'

━━

The next time she went to Au Revoir Exports, Dina decided to take Maneck further into her confidence. 'Listen, I'm not padlocking the door today. Since you are home, I'll leave you in charge.' The responsibility would draw him over to her side, she was sure; besides, Om wouldn't attempt the bicycle caper twice.

After Dina had departed, Ishvar continued sewing, uncomfortable about taking his customary rest on her sofa with Maneck present. But Om stopped immediately, and escaped to the front room. 'Two hours of freedom,' he announced, stretching and letting himself drop on the sofa next to Maneck.

While he smoked, they browsed through Dina's old knitting books. Models wearing various styles of sweaters adorned the inside pages. Luscious red lips, creamy skin, and luxuriant hairdos dazzled them from the dog-eared glossy paper. 'Look at those two,' said Om, indicating a blonde and a redhead. 'You think the hair between their legs is the same colour?'

'Why don't you write a letter to the magazine and ask? "Dear Sir, We wish to make an inquiry regarding the colour of your models' choot hair – specifically, if it matches the hair on their heads. The models in question appear on page forty-seven of your issue dated"' – he flipped to the cover – '"July 1961." Forget it, yaar, that's fourteen years ago. Whatever colour it was then, it must be grey or white by now.'

'I should ask Rajaram the hair-collector,' said Om. 'He's an expert on hair.'

The boys restored the knitting books to their corner and went into Maneck's room. The pagoda parasol amused them for a while, then they explored the kitchen, calling to the cats, who refused to approach the window since it was not dinnertime. Om wanted to throw water at them, make them yowl, but Maneck wouldn't let him.

In the back room they examined the collection of cloth pieces, the beginnings of the quilt. 'You boys don't meddle with Dinabai's things,' warned Ishvar, glancing up from the machine.

'Just look at all this cloth,' said Om. 'She steals from us, not paying us properly, and also from the company.'

'You are talking nonsense, Omprakash,' his uncle said. 'Those are little garbage pieces that she puts to good use. Come on, get back to your machine, stop wasting time.'

Om replaced the makings of the quilt and pointed to the trunk on the trestle in the corner. Maneck raised his eyebrows at the daring suggestion. They opened it, and discovered her supply of homemade sanitary pads.

'You know what those are for?' whispered Om.

'Little pillows,' said Maneck, grinning, picking up a couple of the lumpy pads. 'Little pillows for little people.'

'My little man can rest his head on it.' Om slung one between his legs.

'Stop fooling with the trunk there,' said Ishvar.

'Okay, okay.' They took a handful of pads into the front room and continued clowning.

'What's this?' said Maneck, holding two above his head.

'Horns?'

'No,' he waggled them. 'Donkey's ears.'

Om held one behind him. 'Rabbit's tail.'

They held them at their crotches like phalluses and pranced around the room, making large masturbatory gestures. The knot at the end of Maneck's pad came undone. The stuffing fell out, leaving the casing flopping in his hand.

'Look at that!' laughed Om. 'Your lund has already gone to sleep, yaar!'

Maneck took a firm new pad and struck Om's with it. A duel ensued but the weapons collapsed quickly, scattering fabric snippets around the room. They picked up two more and began rushing at each other in a gallop, like jousters on horseback, their sanitary lances sticking out at their flies.

'Tan-tanna tan-tanna tan-tanna!' they trumpeted and attacked. Backing up to their corners, they adjusted the pads at their crotches while Om reared and neighed like a charger champing at the bit.

Just as they were ready to tilt again, Dina opened the front door and entered through the verandah. The fanfare died in mid-flourish. She got as far as the sofa, then froze. The scene left her speechless: the floor littered with the scraps of her carefully prepared sanitary pads, the two boys standing guiltily, clutching their embarrassing toys.

They dropped their hands and started to hide the pads behind their backs, then realized the gesture was as futile as it was silly. They lowered their heads.

'You shameless boys!' she managed to utter. 'You shameless boys!'

She ran to the back room where Ishvar was still ploughing away at his machine, blissfully unaware of the goings-on in the front room. 'Stop!' she said, her voice trembling. 'Come and see what those two have been doing!'

Om and Maneck had put aside the pads, but Dina thrust one each into their hands. 'Go on!' she said. 'Do it for him, let him see your shameless behaviour!'

Ishvar did not need to see. He gathered that something filthy had been going on, especially if she was so upset. He went to Om and slapped him across the face. 'You I cannot slap,' he said to Maneck. 'But someone should. For your own good.'

He led Om into the back room and flung him upon his stool. 'I don't want another word from you, now or ever. Just do your work quietly till it's time to leave.'

Dinner was a silent meal; only the knives and forks spoke. Dina cleared up quickly, then went into the sewing room and bolted her door.

As if I was a sex maniac or something, thought Maneck, feeling miserable. He waited for a while in the front room, hoping she would come out, give him a chance to apologize. His ears picked up the opening and closing of a drawer. The creaking of her bed. A clatter that could be her hairbrush. The thud of the tailors' stools being pushed aside. He heard the sound of the trunk lid, and his face burned with shame. Then the bright line under her door went dark, and his wretchedness engulfed him.

Would she write to his parents and complain? Surely he deserved it. For almost two months now, she had treated him so well in her flat, and he had behaved disgustingly. For the first time since leaving home, he had felt at peace, unthreatened, thanks to Dina Aunty. Rescued from the hostel that had made him ill, with that tightness in the chest, that nauseated feeling every morning.

Now he had brought it all back, through his own doing. He switched off the light beside the sofa and dragged himself to his room.

Morning could not alleviate Maneck's shame from last night. To help keep it burning, Dina slammed the plate of two fried eggs before him at breakfast. When it was time to leave for college and he called out 'Bye, Aunty,' she would not come to wave. Woefully, he shut the door upon the empty, accusing verandah.

The first hint of forgiveness quivered in the air after dinner. Like the night before, she retreated to the back room instead of bringing the quilt to the sofa; however, she kept her door ajar.

Waiting hopefully in the front room, he passed the time listening to the neighbours. Someone screamed retributive warnings – at a daughter, he presumed. 'Mui bitch!' came a man's voice. 'Behaving like a slut, staying out so late at night! You think eighteen years is too old to get a thrashing? I'll show you! When we say back by ten o'clock, we mean ten o'clock!'

Maneck glanced at his watch: ten-twenty. Still Dina Aunty did not emerge. Neither did the light go off. At their usual bedtime of ten-thirty, he decided to peek in and say good night.

She was in her nightgown, her back to the door. He changed his mind and tried to retreat, but she saw him through the crack. Oh God, he thought, panicking – now she would assume he was spying.

'Yes?' she said sharply.

'Excuse me, Aunty, I was just coming to say good night.'

'Yes. Good night.' Her stiffness persisted.

He re-echoed the words and began edging away, then stopped. He cleared his throat. 'Also . . .'

'Also what?'

'Also, I wanted to say sorry . . . for yesterday . . .'

'Don't mumble from outside the room. Come in and say what you have to say.'

He entered shyly. Her bare arms in the nightgown looked so lovely, and through the light cotton, the shape of . . . but he dared not let his eyes linger. Mummy's friend was the unsummoned thought that terrified him as he finished his apology.

'I want you to understand,' she said. 'I was not angry with your shameful act because of any harm to me. I was ashamed for you, to see you behaving like a loafer. Like a roadside mavali. From Omprakash I cannot expect better. But you, from a good Parsi family. And I left you to watch after them, I trusted you.'

'I'm sorry,' he hung his head. She raised her hands to her hair, reinserting a clip that had become ineffective. He found the fuzz in her armpits extremely erotic.

'Go to bed now,' she said. 'Next time, use better judgement.'

As he fell asleep, thinking of Dina Aunty in the nightgown, she began to merge with the woman on the train, in the upper berth.

AFTER THE INCIDENT with the sanitary pads, Dina was certain that neither Ishvar nor Om would dare follow through with a dinner for Maneck at their house. And even if they did, he would refuse, for fear of offending her.

In a few days, however, the invitation was indeed renewed, and acceptance seemed to linger close at hand. 'I don't believe it,' she whispered angrily to Maneck. 'After what you did that day, isn't it enough? Haven't you upset me enough?'

'But I apologized for that, Aunty. And Om was also very sorry. What's the connection between the two things?'

'You think sorry makes it all right. You don't understand the problem. I have nothing against them, but they are tailors – my employees. A distance has to be maintained. You are the son of Farokh and Aban Kohlah. There is a difference, and you cannot pretend there isn't – their community, their background.'

'But Mummy and Daddy wouldn't mind,' he said, trying to explain he hadn't been brought up to think this way, that his parents encouraged him to mix with everyone.

'So you are saying I am narrow-minded, and your parents are broad-minded, modern people?'

He grew tired of arguing. Sometimes she seemed to him on the verge of being reasonable, only to make another absurd statement: 'If you are so fond of them, why don't you pack your things and move in with them? I can easily write to your mummy, tell her where to send the rent next month.'

'I just want to visit once. It feels rude to keep refusing. They think I'm too big to go to their house.'

'And have you thought of the consequences of one visit? Good manners is all very well, but what about health and hygiene? How do they prepare their food? Can they afford proper cooking oil? Or do they buy cheap adulterated vanaspati, like most poor people?'

'I don't know. They haven't fallen sick and died as yet.'

'Because their stomachs are accustomed to it, you foolish boy, and yours is not.'

Maneck pictured the hideous canteen food his own stomach had endured, and the roadside snacks devoured for weeks on end. He wondered if mentioning that would make her modify her culinary theories.

'And what about water?' she continued. 'Is there a clean supply in their neighbourhood, or is it contaminated?'

'I'll be careful, I won't drink any water.' His mind was made up, he was going. She was getting too bossy. Even Mummy never controlled his life the way Dina Aunty was trying to.

'Fine, do as you please. But if you catch something, don't think I'll be your nurse for one moment. You'll be sent back by express delivery to your parents.'

'That's all right with me.'

The next time Ishvar and Om asked him, he said yes. She flushed, and ground her teeth. Maneck smiled innocently.

'Tomorrow then, okay?' said Ishvar with delight. 'We'll leave together at six o'clock.' He inquired what he would like to eat. 'Rice or chapati? And which is your favourite vegetable, hahn?'

'Anything,' answered Maneck to all questions. The tailors spent the rest of the afternoon discussing the menu, planning their humble feast.

———

Ishvar was first to notice that the smoke from cooking fires did not linger over the hutment colony. He tripped on the crumbling pavement, his eyes searching the horizon. At this hour the haze should have been clouding thick. 'Everyone fasting or what?'

'Forget worrying about everyone – I'm starving.'

'You're always starving. Do you have worms?'

Om did not laugh; the joke was growing stale. The absence of smoke bothered Ishvar. In its place a dull roar, as of heavy machinery, hung in the distance. 'Repairing the roads at night?' he wondered, as the noise rose with their approach. Then, thinking about Maneck's dinner, he said, 'Tomorrow we will shop in the morning, keep everything ready. We shouldn't waste time after work. Now if you were married, your wife would have the food cooked and waiting for our guest.'

'Why don't *you* get married?'

'I'm too old.' But, he thought, teasing aside, it really was high time for Om – not wise to delay these things.

'But I've even selected a wife for you,' said Om.

'Who?'

'Dinabai. I know you like her, you're always taking her side. You should give her a poke.'

'Shameless boy,' said Ishvar, thumping him lightly as they turned the corner into the slum lane.

The rumbling ball of sound that had been rolling towards them, slow and placid in the dusk, grew larger, louder. Then it detonated. The air was suddenly filled with noises of pain and terror and anger.

'Hai Ram! What's going on?' They ran the final distance and came upon a battle in progress.

The hutment dwellers were massed on the road, fighting to return to their shacks, their cries mingling with the sirens of ambulances that couldn't get through. The police had lost control for the moment. The residents surged forward, gaining the advantage. Then the police rallied and beat them back. People fell, were trampled, and the ambulances supplemented their siren skirls with blaring horns while children screamed, terrified at being separated from their parents.

The hutment dwellers straggled back from the pulse of the assault, spent, venting their anguish in helpless outrage. 'Heartless animals! For the poor there is no justice, ever! We had next to nothing, now it's less than nothing! What is our crime, where are we to go?'

During the lull, Ishvar and Om found Rajaram. 'I was there when it all started,' he said, panting. 'They went in and – just destroyed it. And just smashed – everything. Such crooks, such liars –'

'Who did it?' they tried to make him talk slowly.

'The men, the ones who said they were safety inspectors. They tricked us. Sent by the government, they said, to check the colony. At first the people were pleased, the authorities were taking some interest. Maybe improvements were coming – water, latrines, lights, like they kept promising at voting time. So we did as they told us, came out of the shacks. But once the colony was empty, the big machines went in.'

Most of the bulldozers were old jeeps and trucks, with steel plates and short wooden beams like battering rams affixed to the front bumpers. They had begun tearing into the structures of plywood, corrugated metal, and plastic. 'And when we saw that, we rushed in to stop them. But the drivers kept going. People were crushed. Blood everywhere. And the police are protecting those murderers. Or the bastards would be dead by now.'

'But how can they destroy our homes, just like that?'

'They said it's a new Emergency law. If shacks are illegal, they can remove them. The new law says the city must be made beautiful.'

'What about Navalkar? And his boss, Thokray? They collected this month's rent only two days ago.'

'They are here.'

'And they're not complaining to the police?'

'Complaining? Thokray is the one in charge of this. He is wearing a badge: Controller of Slums. And Navalkar is Assistant Controller. They won't talk to anyone. If we try to go near them, their goondas threaten to beat us.'

'And all our property in the shacks?'

'Lost, looks like. We begged them to let us remove it, but they refused.'

Ishvar suddenly felt very tired. He moved away from the crowd and crossed the lane, where he sank to his haunches. Rajaram hitched up his pants and sat down beside him. 'No sense crying for those rotten jhopdis. We'll find somewhere else, it's only a small obstacle. Right, Om? We'll search together for a new house.'

Om nodded. 'I'm going to take a closer look inside.'

'Don't, it's dangerous,' said Ishvar. 'Stay here, with me.'

'I'm here only, yaar,' said Om, and wandered off to examine the demolition.

The evening was on the edge of darkness. A vigorous lathi-charge had finally cleared the area near the front of the colony. Slippers and sandals lost by the fleeing crowd littered the ground, strewn like the flotsam of a limbless human tide. The police cordon, now firmly in place, kept the rage of the residents smouldering at a safe distance.

The bulldozers finished flattening the rows of flimsy shacks and tackled the high-rental ones, reversing and crunching into the brick walls. Om felt nothing – the shack had meant nothing to him, he decided. Maybe now his uncle would agree to go back to Ashraf Chacha. He remembered Maneck, coming to visit tomorrow. He laughed mirthlessly about telling him the dinner was off – cancelled due to the unexpected disappearance of their house.

Sergeant Kesar's megaphone blared in the dusk: 'Work will be stopping for thirty minutes. Actually speaking, this is simply to give you a chance to collect your personal belongings. Then the machines will start again.'

In the crowd, the announcement was received with some scorn – a goodwill gesture from the police to avoid more trouble. But most were grateful for the opportunity to retrieve their few possessions. A desperate scramble commenced in the wreckage. It reminded Om of children on garbage heaps. He saw them every morning from the train. He rejoined his uncle to become part of the bustle among the ruins.

The machines had transformed the familiar field with its carefully ordered community into an alien place. There was much confusion amid the people rooting for their belongings. Which piece of ground had supported whose shelter? And which pile of scantlings and metal was theirs to comb through? Others were turning the turmoil to advantage, grabbing what they could, and fights broke out over pieces of splintered plywood, torn rexine sheets, clear plastic. Someone tried to seize the harmonium player's damaged instrument while he was burrowing for his clothes. He fought off the thief with an iron rod. The tussle inflicted more wounds on the harmonium, ripping its bellows.

'My neighbours have become robbers,' he said tearfully. 'Once, I sang for them, and they clapped for me.'

Ishvar offered him perfunctory solace, anxious about his own possessions. 'At least our sewing-machines have a safe home with Dinabai,' he said to Om. 'That's our good fortune.'

They dragged aside the corrugated sheet that used to be the roof, and uncovered the trunk. The lid had sustained several deep dents. It swung open with a protesting squeal. Om aimed a kick at the biggest depression and the lid moved less stubbornly. They cleared more debris and came upon the small mirror they used for shaving. It was intact: the aluminium frying pan had fallen over it like a helmet.

'No bad luck for us,' said Om, stuffing both items into the trunk. The Primus stove was crushed beyond repair, and he tossed it back. Ishvar found a pencil, a candle, two enamel plates, and a polythene glass. Om found their razor, but not the packet of blades. By shifting more pieces of plywood they unearthed the copper water pot. Someone else spied it at the same moment, grabbed it, and ran.

'Thief!' shouted Om. Nobody paid attention. His uncle stopped him from chasing the man.

They pulled out their wicker mat, sheets, blankets, and the two towels used for pillows. Shaking out clouds of dust, Ishvar rolled it all into one neat bedding bundle and wrapped it with sackcloth.

Rajaram's concern was solely for his hoard of hair. The stock was ravaged, the plastic sacks ripped, their contents spilled. 'One month's precious collection,' he grieved. 'All scattered in the mud.' The allotted thirty minutes were running out. Ishvar and Om helped him gather what they could, concentrating on retrieving the longest specimens.

'It's hopeless,' said Rajaram bitterly. 'The bastards have ruined me. The locks and plaits have broken up, it's impossible to join them together. Like trying to recover grains of sugar out of a cup of tea.'

The three made their way through the police barricade, where the Controller of Slums was giving instructions to his workers. 'Levelled smooth – that's how I want this field. Empty and clean, the way it was before all these illegal structures were built.' The debris was to be dumped in the ditch by the railway tracks.

The dispossessed lingered outside, watching numbly. The workers flattened walls and corners that had survived the first assault, then stopped, claiming it was too dark for the equipment to shift the rubble without tumbling into the ditch. The Controller of Slums could not risk that, there was much work ahead for his machines, many unlawful encroachments to be razed. He agreed to postpone the final phase till the morning, and the workers departed.

'I'll spend the night here,' said Rajaram. 'I might find something valuable in the field. What about you?'

'We should go to Nawaz,' said Ishvar. 'Maybe he'll let us sleep under his back awning again.'

'But he was so mean to us.'

'Still – he might help us find a house, like he did last time.'

'Yes, it's worth trying,' said Rajaram. 'And I'll check what happens here. Who knows, some other gang boss might be planning to build new shacks.'

They agreed to meet next evening and exchange information. 'Can you do me a favour in the meantime?' asked Rajaram. 'Keep these few plaits for me? They are very light. I have nowhere for them.'

Ishvar agreed, and put them in the trunk.

———

There were strangers living in Nawaz's house. The man who answered the door claimed to know nothing about him.

'It's very urgent for us to find Nawazbhai,' said Ishvar. 'Maybe your landlord has some information. Can you give me his name and address?'

'It's none of your business.' Someone shouted from inside, 'Stop pestering us so late at night!'

'Sorry to disturb you,' said Ishvar, rehoisting the bedding bundle and retreating down the steps.

'Now what?' panted Om, his face showing the weight of the trunk.

'Your breath has leaked out already?'

He nodded. 'Like a broken balloon.'

'Okay, let's have tea.' They went to the stall at the corner, the one they had frequented during their months on the back porch. The owner remembered them as friends of Nawaz.

'Haven't seen you for some time,' he said. 'Any news of Nawaz since the police took him?'

'Police? For what?'

'Smuggling gold from the Gulf.'

'Really? Was he?'

'Of course not. He was just a tailor, like you.' But Nawaz had quarrelled with somebody whose daughter was getting married. The man, well-connected, had given him a large assignment – wedding clothes for the entire family. After the wedding he refused to pay, claiming that the clothes fit badly. Nawaz kept asking for his money to no avail, then found out where the man's office was. He showed up there, to embarrass him among his colleagues. 'And that was a big mistake. The bastard took his revenge. That same night the police came for Nawaz.'

'Just like that? How can they put an innocent man in jail? The other fellow is the crook.'

'With the Emergency, everything is upside-down. Black can be made white, day turned into night. With the right influence and a little cash, sending people to jail is very easy. There's even a new law called MISA to simplify the whole procedure.'

'What's MISA?'

'Maintenance of . . . something, and Security . . . something, I'm not sure.'

The tailors finished the tea and departed with their loads. 'Poor Nawaz,' said Ishvar. 'Wonder if he was really up to something crooked.'

'Must have,' said Om. 'They don't send people to jail for nothing. I never liked him. But now what?'

'Maybe we can sleep at the railway station.'

The platform was thick with beggars and itinerants bedding down for the night. The tailors picked a corner and cleaned it, whisking away the dust with a newspaper.

'Oiee, careful! It's coming in my face!' screamed someone.

'Sorry bhai,' said Ishvar, abandoning the sweeping. The urge to talk about tomorrow dawning homeless, about what to do next, was strong, but each wanted the other to broach the subject. 'Hungry?' he asked.

'No.'

Ishvar wandered down anyway to the railway snack shop. He bought a spicy mix of fried onions, potatoes, peas, chillies, and coriander, stuffed into two small buns. Carrying it back to Om, a little guilt accompanied his passage through the gauntlet of hungry eyes ranged along the platform. 'Pao-bhaji. One for you and one for me.'

The glossy magazine page the bun was served on felt soggy. Little circles of warm grease were starting to appear. Om ate hungrily, finishing first, and Ishvar slowed down to save him a piece of his. 'I'm full, you have it.'

They took turns visiting the drinking fountain; the trunk and bedding needed guarding. After this, no further distractions were available. 'Maybe Rajaram will have good news tomorrow evening,' Om started tentatively.

'Yes, who knows. We could even build something ourselves, once the tamasha dies down. With plywood and sticks and plastic sheets. Rajaram is a smart fellow, he will know what to do. The three of us could live together in one big hut.'

They visited the wasteland beyond the station to urinate, and had another drink of water before untying the bedding. The frequency of trains diminished as the night deepened. They lay down with their feet resting protectively on the trunk.

After midnight, they were awakened by a railway policeman kicking at the trunk. He said sleeping on the platform was prohibited.

'We are waiting for the train,' said Ishvar.

'This is not that kind of station. No waiting room. Come back in the morning.'

'But these other people are sleeping.'

'They have special permission.' The policeman jingled the coins in his pocket.

'Okay, we won't sleep on the platform, we will just sit.'

The policeman left, shrugging. They sat up and rolled away the bedding.

'Ssst,' called a woman lying next to them. 'Ssst. You have to pay him.' The plastic sheet she lay upon rustled loudly at her slightest movement. Her feet were wrapped in bandages blotched by a dark-yellow ooze.

'Pay him for what? It's not his father's platform.'

She smiled, cracking the grime on her face. 'Cinema, cinema!' she pointed excitedly at the film posters lining the platform wall. 'One rupee per beggar. Fifty paise for child. Cinema every night.'

Ishvar secretly raised a hand to his forehead and gave the loose-screw sign, but Om insisted on explaining. 'We're not beggars, we're tailors. And what will he do if we don't pay? Can't take us to jail for it.'

The woman turned on her side, observing them closely, silent except for the random giggling. A half-hour passed, and there was no sign of the policeman.

'I think it's safe now,' said Om. He unrolled the bedding and they lay down again. She was still watching them amusedly. A faint smell of rot came from her bandaged feet.

'Are you going to look at us all night?' said Om. She shook her head but kept staring. Ishvar quietened his nephew, and they closed their eyes.

Within minutes of their dozing off, the policeman returned with a bucket of cold water and emptied it over the sleeping tailors. They howled and jumped off their bedding. The policeman walked away wordlessly, giving his empty bucket a jaunty swing. The woman on the plastic sheet was shaking with laughter.

'Animal from somewhere!' hissed Om, and Ishvar shushed him. He need not have bothered; the woman's hysterical laughter drowned the words. She slapped her hands with delight on the plastic sheet, making it flap.

'Cinema! Cinema! Johnnie Walker comedy!' she managed to get out between laughs.

'She knew! The crazy witch knew and didn't tell us, yaar!'

Thoroughly soaked, they picked up everything and moved to the only remaining spot, at the end of the platform, where the urine smell was strong. The dry clothes in the trunk were a precious treasure. They took turns changing. Their wet things were spread out on the trunk's open lid. The sheets and blanket were hung on a broken sign fixture protruding from the platform wall.

The wicker mat dried quickly but they were afraid to lie down. Shivering, they sat guarding their belongings, swaying with sleep, nodding off occasionally. Due to the drenching, they needed to visit the wasteland several times. After the station was asleep, walking down to the tracks was not necessary. They emptied their bladders off the edge of the platform.

The railway snack shop crashed open its steel shutters at four a.m. Cups and saucers started clinking, pots and pans banged. Ishvar and Om gargled at the drinking fountain, then bought two teas and a loaf of crusty bread. The hot liquid cleared their sleep-logged heads. The plan for the day began falling into place: at a suitable hour they would take the train to work, sew till six as usual, then return to meet Rajaram.

'We'll leave the trunk with Dinabai, just for tonight,' said Ishvar. 'But we won't say our house is destroyed. People are scared of the homeless.'

'I'll give you anything if she lets us leave it there.'

They spent two more hours on the platform, smoking, watching the early-morning commuters who were mainly vendors waiting with baskets of pumpkin, onions, pomfret, salt, eggs, flowers balanced on their heads. An umbrella repairer was preparing for work, anatomizing broken umbrellas, salvaging the good ribs and handles. A contractor with his band of painters and masons, armed with ladders, pails, brushes, trowels, and hods, went by smelling like a freshly painted house.

The tailors got on a train at six-thirty. They were at Dina's flat by seven. She flung a dustercoat over her nightgown and opened the door.

'So early?' Trust them to be inconsiderate, she thought – the sun barely up, the washing to do, Maneck's breakfast still to make, and here they were, expecting attention.

'The trains are at last running on time. Because of the Emergency,' said Om, feeling rather clever.

She concluded that the brazen excuse was designed to infuriate her. Then Ishvar added placatingly, 'Longer day means more dresses, hahn, Dinabai?'

True enough. 'But what's all this big fat luggage?'

'We have to take it to a friend in the evening. Oh, Maneck. Before I forget. You must forgive us, dinner is not possible today. Something very urgent has come up.'

'That's okay,' said Maneck. 'Another time.'

She made them leave the trunk and bedding by the door. It could be crawling with bugs, for all she knew. And their behaviour was very suspicious. If it was urgent, they could have gone to their friend now. Especially since they were so early. But at least Maneck's dinner invitation was cancelled, which was a relief.

All that day, Ishvar was not his usual steady self, and once, he almost joined a skirt and bodice back to front. 'Stop!' she cried as the needle drove in the first line of stitches. 'You, Ishvar? If Omprakash did this it would be no surprise. But you?' Smiling sheepishly, he severed the delinquent stitches with a safety razor blade.

At four o'clock they wanted to leave, two hours earlier than usual. So much for the extra dresses they were going to sew, she thought, but was glad to see them go, taking with them the weight that hung in the air.

Before she realized the trunk was left behind, they had shut the door and hurried away to the station.

Heavy rain had fallen during the day, submerging much of last night's debris in muddy little ponds. Pieces of plywood or metal rose through the water like sails and shipwrecks. Seagulls screeched over the transfigured slum. Some former residents were wandering outside, gazing at the land, but Rajaram was nowhere to be seen.

'Maybe he found out there is no chance of building here again,' said Ishvar.

The portly Sergeant Kesar was not in evidence at the moment. Six constables from his new enforcement squad were guarding the field. They approached the tailors and the others hanging around, and warned them, 'If you try to put up any new jhopdis, we'll have to take you straight to jail.'

'Why?'

'It's our assignment – slum prevention and city beautification.' The constables returned to their post at the corner.

'I think we should go back and tell Dinabai the truth,' said Ishvar.

'Why?'

'She might help us.'

'In your dreams,' said Om.

A work crew was erecting two new hoardings, one on each side of the road. They pasted the Prime Minister's face over the boards, then debated about the accompanying message. There was a variety to choose from. They unrolled the banners and spread them out over the pavement for consideration, using stones to hold down the corners.

The workers were unanimous concerning the first slogan: THE CITY BELONGS TO YOU! KEEP IT BEAUTIFUL! The second was posing some difficulty. The supervisor wanted to use FOOD FOR THE HUNGRY! HOMES FOR THE HOMELESS! His subordinates advised him that something else would be more appropriate; they recommended THE NATION IS ON THE MOVE!

The tailors waited around till the displays were completed. The crowd clapped as the huge frames were raised. The posts were embedded in holes, buttressed with diagonal braces, and the earth tamped down. Someone asked Om if he could please read what the two boards were saying. Om translated for him. The man contemplated the meaning for a moment, then went away shaking his head, muttering that this time the government had gone completely mad.

'I knew you would come back,' said Dina. 'You forgot your trunk.' They shook their heads, and she saw how scared and exhausted they were. 'What's wrong?'

'A terrible misfortune has fallen on our heads,' said Ishvar.

'Come inside. Would you like some water?'

'Hahnji, please.' Maneck fetched it in their segregated glass. They drank and wiped their lips.

'Dinabai, we've had very bad luck. We need your help'

'Times are such, I don't know how much help I can be to anyone. But tell me anyway.'

'Our home . . . it's gone,' said Ishvar timidly.

'You mean your landlord kicked you out?' She sympathized. 'Landlords are such rascals.'

He shook his head. 'I mean . . . gone completely,' and he swept his palm through the air. 'It has been destroyed by big-big machines. All the houses in the field.'

'They said it was illegal to live there,' added Om.

'Are you serious?' said Maneck. 'How can they do that?'

'They are the government,' said Ishvar. 'They can do anything they want. Police said it's a new law.'

Dina nodded, remembering that as recently as last week, there had been ringing praise from Mrs. Gupta for the proposed slum clearance programme. How unfortunate for the tailors, though. Poor people. And she was right about one thing – they did live in an unhygienic place. Thank goodness Maneck was spared from eating with them. 'It's terrible,' she said. 'Government makes laws without thinking.'

'Now you know why we had to cancel dinner,' said Om to Maneck. 'We felt bad to tell you in the morning.'

'You shouldn't have,' said Maneck. 'It would have given us more time to think of some way to help and –' He broke off, silenced by Dina knitting her brow fiercely in his direction.

'Rent was already paid for this month,' said Ishvar. 'Now we have no house or money. Can we sleep on your verandah . . . for a few nights?'

Maneck turned, appealing to Dina as she weighed her response. 'Myself, I have no objection,' she said. 'But if the rent-collector sees, there will be trouble. He will use it as an excuse to say I have made this an illegal guest house. Then you and Maneck and me, and your sewing-machines – everything will land on the street, roofless.'

'I understand,' said Ishvar. His pride would not let him push against the rejection. 'We'll try elsewhere.'

'Don't forget to take your trunk,' said Dina.

'Can we leave it for tonight?'

'Leave it where? There's no room to even move in this flat.'

Disgusted by her answer, Om passed the bedding to his uncle and picked up the trunk. They nodded and left.

Dina followed them to the door, locked it, and walked back into the glare of Maneck's reproach. 'Don't look at me like that,' she said. 'I had no choice.'

'You could have let them stay at least tonight. They could have slept in my room.'

'That would be trouble with a capital t. One night is enough for the landlord to bring a case against me.'

'And what about the trunk? Why can't you keep it for them?'

'What's this, a police interrogation? You've lived such a sheltered life, you've no idea what kind of crookedness exists in a city like this. A trunk, a bag, or even a satchel with just two pyjamas and a shirt is the first step into a flat. Personal items stored on the premises – that's the most common way of staking a claim. And the court system takes years to settle the case, years during which the crooks are allowed to stay in the flat. Now I'm not saying Ishvar and Om came tonight with this plan in their heads. But how can I take the risk? What if they get the idea later from some rascal? Any trouble with the landlord means I have to ask for Nusswan's help. My brother is absolutely unbearable. He would crow and crow about it.'

Maneck looked out the window, trying to sort out the degree of Dina Aunty's suspicion. He imagined the invasion of dirty laundry that she feared, the fabricated occupation force.

'Don't worry so much about the tailors,' she said. 'They'll find somewhere to stay. People like them have relatives all over the place.'

'They don't. They came just a few months ago from a faraway village.' He was pleased to see a trace of worry in slow migration across her face.

Then she was annoyed. 'It's amazing. Just amazing how much you know about them, isn't it?'

They ignored each other for most of the evening, but while working on the quilt after dinner, she spread out the squares and tried to get him to talk. 'Well, Maneck? How does it look now?'

'Looks terrible.' He was not ready to forgive her while the tailors remained unaccommodated in the night.

━━

The sign read 'Sagar Darshan – Ocean View Hotel.' The only sea in sight was the rectangle of blue painted on the weather-beaten board, with a little sailboat perched upon a wave.

Inside, a youth in a frayed white uniform sat on the floor by an umbrella stand, staring at pictures in *Filmfare*. He did not look up as the tailors came in. A grey-haired man, eating busily behind the counter, broke pieces from a loaf of bread and dipped them in quick succession into a series of four stainless steel saucers. 'Thirty rupees per night,' he mumbled through an overloaded mouth, revealing a gold tooth in the process. Masticated fragments of his dinner flew past the moist lips onto the counter. He swept them to the floor, then polished away the smudge with his sleeved elbow.

'See? I told you, we cannot afford a hotel,' said Ishvar as they retreated. 'Let's try another one.'

They checked place after place: Paradise Lodge, at twenty rupees a night, located over a bakery with a badly insulated ceiling, so that the searing heat of oven flames could be felt upstairs; Ram Nivas, the sign-board stating that all castes were welcome, whose rooms reeked with a horrible stench, courtesy of a small chemical factory next door; Aram Hotel, where their luggage was almost stolen while they inquired, the would-be thief bolting as they retraced their steps down the hallway.

'Had enough?' said Ishvar, and Om nodded.

They lifted their loads and started towards the train station, pausing to inspect every doorway, awning, and façade that might offer shelter. But wherever shelter was possible, the place was already taken. To discourage pavement-dwellers, one shop had laid down in its entrance an iron framework covered with spikes, on hinges that could be unlocked and folded away in the morning. This bed of nails was being used by an enterprising individual – first, a rectangle of plywood over the spikes, and then his blanket.

'We will have to learn things like that,' said Ishvar, watching admiringly.

They passed the beggar on his platform, who greeted them with the usual rattle of his tin. Intent in their search, they didn't acknowledge him. He gazed forlornly after them. There were a few empty places outside a furniture store that was still open. 'We could try there,' said Om.

'Are you crazy? You want to get killed for taking someone's spot? Have you forgotten what happened on the pavement near Nawaz's shop?'

They passed the store that never closed, the twenty-four-hour chemist's. The lights were going out in the main section as the sales clerks left. The dispensing side stayed bright, with a compounder on duty.

'Let's wait here,' said Ishvar. 'See what happens.'

Someone put a wooden stool outside, in the entrance way that was shared by the chemist's and the antique shop next door. Steel shutters descended like eyelids on the two windows. Soaps, talcum powders, cough syrups on one side, and bronze Natarajas, Mughal miniatures, inlaid jewel boxes on the other, all vanished from view. The two managers locked up and handed over the keys to the nightwatchman.

The tailors waited till the nightwatchman loosened his belt, pulled off his shoes, and got comfortable on the wooden stool. Then they approached with their packet of beedis. 'Matches?' asked Ishvar, making the striking gesture with his hand.

The nightwatchman stopped rubbing his calves to dig in his pocket. The tailors shared a match. They offered the beedis to the nightwatchman. He shook his head, producing a pack of Panama cigarettes. The three puffed silently for a while.

'So,' said Ishvar. 'You sit here all night?'

'That's my job.' He reached for the night stick that leaned against the door and tapped it twice. The tailors smiled, nodding.

'Anyone sleeps in this entrance?'

'No one.'

'Sometimes you must feel like taking a rest.'

The nightwatchman shook his head. 'Not allowed. I have to watch two shops.' He leaned towards them and confided, pointing inside to the night compounder, 'But he. He takes a rest. He takes a long sleep, inside, on a mat on the floor, every night. For that, the rascal gets paid, and much more than me.'

'We have no place to sleep,' said Ishvar. 'The colony where we lived – it was destroyed by the government yesterday. With their machines.'

'That's happening often these days,' said the nightwatchman. He continued his complaint about the compounder. 'That fellow has very little work at night. Sometimes a customer comes for medicine. Then I unlock the door and wake the rascal to mix the prescription. But if he has been sleeping his mind is cloudy. He has trouble reading the labels.' He leaned closer again. 'Once, he put wrong things in the medicine mixture. Customer died, and police came to investigate. Manager and police talked. Manager offered money, police took money, and everybody was happy.'

'Crooks, all of them,' said Ishvar, and they nodded in agreement. 'Can you let us sleep here?'

'It's not allowed.'

'We could pay you.'

'Even if you pay, where's the space?'

'Space is enough. We can put our bedding near the door if you move your stool just two feet.'

'And what about other things? There is no storage place.'

'What things – just one trunk. We will take it with us in the morning.'

They shifted the stool and unrolled the bedding. It fit exactly. 'How much can you pay?' asked the nightwatchman.

'Two rupees each night.'

'Four.'

'We are poor tailors. Take three, and we will do some free tailoring also for you. We can repair your uniform.' He pointed to the worn knees and fraying cuffs.

'Okay. But I'm warning you, sometimes the nights are very noisy here. If a customer comes for medicine you will have to move. Then don't say I spoiled your sleep. No refund for spoiled sleep.' And if the night compounder should ask, they were to say two rupees, because the rascal would demand a cut from it.

'Bilkool,' agreed the tailors to all his conditions. After another beedi, they took needles and thread out of the trunk and got to work. The nightwatchman sat in his underwear while they fixed his uniform.

'First class,' he said, slipping on his trousers.

The compliment gratified Ishvar, and he said they would be pleased to mend other things for him and his family. 'We can do everything. Salwar-kameez, ghaghra-choli, baby-baba clothes.'

The nightwatchman shook his head sadly. 'You are kind. But wife and children are living in my native place. I came here alone, looking for work.'

Later, as the tailors slept, he watched them from his wooden stool. When Omprakash twitched in his sleep, it reminded him of his children: those special nights with the family still together, and he present at his babies' dreamings.

The street awoke early to rouse the tailors before dawn. In fact, the street never slumbered, explained the nightwatchman, only drowsed lightly between two a.m. and five a.m. – after the insomniac gambling and drinking ended, and before the newspapers, bread, and milk arrived. 'But your sleep was beautiful,' he smiled proprietorially.

'It was two nights' sleep poured into one,' said Ishvar.

'Look, the rascal is still snoring inside.' As they peered through the window, the compounder's eyes opened suddenly. He scowled at the three faces flattened against the glass, turned over, and went back to sleep.

They smoked in the entranceway, observing the streetsweeper at work, collecting the previous night's cigarette and beedi stubs. His broom made neat designs in the dust. Later, they rolled up the bedding, paid three rupees and departed with their loads, promising to be back in the evening.

Om's left shoulder and arm were aching from the trunk, but he refused to let his uncle take it. 'Use your right hand,' said Ishvar. 'Give them both equal exercise, they will grow strong.'

'Then both will be useless. How will I sew?'

They stopped at the railway station and washed before proceeding to the Vishram Vegetarian Hotel for tea and a bun. 'You didn't come yesterday,' said the cashier-cum-waiter.

'We were busy – looking for a place to rent.'

'Now that is something you could spend your whole life searching for,' put in the cook from his corner, shouting over the roaring, blue-flamed stoves.

In the window Om noticed a large picture of the Prime Minister that hadn't been there before, along with a poster of the Twenty-Point Programme. 'You have a new customer or what?'

'That's no customer,' said the cashier. 'That's the goddess of protection. Her blessing is a business necessity. Compulsory puja.'

'How do you mean?'

'Her presence keeps my windows from being smashed and my shop from being burned. You follow?'

The tailors nodded. They told the cashier and the cook about the Prime Minister's meeting into which they had been dragooned. Their stories of the helicopter, the rose petals, the hot-air balloon, and the huge cutout had them laughing.

After the first night of sound sleep, the nightwatchman's forecast about nocturnal disturbances proved accurate. He apologized each time he had to shake the tailors awake. In his system of beliefs, nothing was more despicable than depriving a fellow human being of either food or sleep. He helped move the bedding to unlock the door, comforting them as they stumbled around in the dark, Om's drowsy head on one shoulder, Ishvar leaning heavily on the other.

They kept muttering while the customers waited for their medicine. 'Why do all these people have to fall sick at night only?' grumbled Ishvar. 'Why are they harassing us?'

'What a headache I have,' moaned Om.

The nightwatchman gently rubbed his brow. 'Not long now. Only two minutes more, okay? Then you can sleep very, very peacefully. I promise, I won't let any more customers disturb you.' But he had to break his promise over and over.

Later they learned about an outbreak of dysentery – bad milk had been sold in the neighbourhood. If the tailors had stayed around during the day, they would have discovered that illness was an impartial thief who struck in sunshine and darkness. Fifty-five adults and eighty-three children dead, the nightwatchman told them, having heard the official figure from the compounder, who explained that fortunately it was bacillary dysentery, and not the more serious amoebic variety.

Lugging the trunk and bedding, the tailors arrived at work ready to collapse, dark circles around their red-streaked eyes. Work fell further behind. Ishvar's impeccable seams strayed often. Om with his stiff arm had trouble doing anything right. The Singers' rhythms turned sour; the stitches were no longer articulated gracefully in long, elegant sentences but spat out fitfully, like phlegm from congested lungs.

Dina read the deterioration in their haggard faces. She feared for their health and the approaching delivery date – the two were joined like Siamese twins. The trunk's weight hung heavy on her conscience.

That evening, the sight of Om straining to lift his load yanked her to the verge of saying the trunk could stay. Maneck watched her from the doorway, anxious to hear it. But the other fears made her leave the words unspoken.

'Wait, I'll come with you,' said Maneck, hastening to the verandah. Om protested feebly, then surrendered the trunk to him.

Dina was relieved – and angry and hurt. Nice of him to help, she thought. But the way he did it. Walking out without a word, making her seem like a heartless person.

'Here it is, our new sleeping place,' said Om, and introduced the nightwatchman: 'Our new landlord.'

The latter laughed, beckoning them into the entrance. They huddled together on the steps to smoke and watch the road. 'Ah, what kind of landlord am I? I cannot even guarantee a good night's sleep.'

'Not your fault,' said Om. 'It's all this sickness. And on top of that, I keep having bad dreams.'

'So do I,' said Ishvar. 'The nights are full of noises and shapes and shadows. Too scary.'

'I am sitting here with my stick,' said the nightwatchman. 'What's there to be scared of?'

'It's hard to give it a name,' said Ishvar, coughing and extinguishing his beedi.

'We should just go back to our village,' said Om. 'I'm fed up of living like this, crawling from one trouble to another.'

'You prefer to run towards it?' Ishvar squeezed the tip of the beedi to make sure it was out, then reinserted it in the packet. 'Patience, my nephew. When the time comes, we will go back.'

'If time were a bolt of cloth,' said Om, 'I would cut out all the bad parts. Snip out the scary nights and stitch together the good parts, to make time bearable. Then I could wear it like a coat, always live happily.'

'I'd also like a coat like that,' said Maneck. 'But which parts would you cut out?'

'The government destroying our house, for sure,' said Om. 'And working for Dinabai.'

'Hoi-hoi,' cautioned Ishvar. 'Without her, where would the money come from?'

'Okay, let's keep the paydays and throw out the rest.'

'What else?' asked Maneck.

'Depends how far back you want to go.'

'All the way. Back to when you were born.'

'That's too much, yaar. So many things to cut, the scissors would go blunt. And there would be very little cloth left.'

'How much nonsense you boys are talking,' said Ishvar. 'Been smoking ganja or what?'

The evening sky darkened, summoning the streetlights. A torn black kite swooped down from the roof like an aggressive crow, startling them. Om grabbed it, saw that it was badly damaged, and let it go.

'Some things are very complicated to separate with scissors,' said Maneck. 'Good and bad are joined like that.' He laced his fingers tight together.

'Such as?'

'My mountains. They are beautiful but they also produce avalanches.'

'That's true. Like our teatime at Vishram, which is good. But the Prime Minister sitting in the window gives me a stomach-ache.'

'Living in the colony was also good,' suggested Ishvar. 'Rajaram next door was fun.'

'Yes,' said Om. 'But jumping up in the middle of a shit because of a fast train – that was horrible.'

They laughed, Ishvar too, though he insisted that that had happened just once. 'It was a new train, even Rajaram didn't know about it.' He cleared his throat and spat. 'Wonder what happened to Rajaram?'

Pavement-dwellers began emerging through the gathering dusk. Cardboard, plastic, newspaper, blankets materialized across the footpaths. Within minutes, huddled bodies had laid claim to all the concrete. Pedestrians now adapted to the new topography, picking their way carefully through the field of arms and legs and faces.

'My father complains at home that it's become very crowded and dirty,' said Maneck. 'He should come and see this.'

'He would get used to it,' said the nightwatchman. 'Just like I did. You watch it day after day, then you stop noticing. Especially if you have no choice.'

'Not my father, he would keep grumbling.'

Ishvar's cough came back, and the nightwatchman suggested asking the compounder for medicine.

'Can't afford it.'

'Just go and ask. He has a special system for poor people.' He unlocked the door to let him in.

For those who could not pay the price of a full bottle, the compounder sold medicine by the spoonful or by the tablet. The poor were grateful for this special dispensation, and the compounder made up to six times the original price, pocketing the difference. 'Open your mouth,' he instructed Ishvar, and deftly poured in a spoonful of Glycodin Terp Vasaka.

'Tastes nice,' said Ishvar, licking his lips.

'Come tomorrow night for another spoonful.'

The nightwatchman inquired how much he had been charged for the dose. 'Fifty paise,' said Ishvar, and the nightwatchman made a mental note to demand his cut.

For three more days the trunk hung from Om's arm during the march between the nightwatchman and Dina Dalal. The distance was short but the weight made it long. He was sore from shoulder to wrist, the hand useless for guiding the fabric through the machine. To feed the cloth accurately to the voracious needle took two hands: the right in front of the presser foot, and the left behind.

'The trunk has paralysed me,' he said, giving up.

Dina watched him, her compassion muted but not dead. My spirited little sparrow is really not well today, dragging his injured wing, she thought. No more hopping and chirping, no more arrogance and argument.

In the midst of a morning filled with tangled threads and twisted seams, the doorbell rang. She went to the verandah to look, and returned very annoyed. 'It's someone asking for you. Disturbing our work in the middle of the day.'

Surprised and apologetic, Ishvar hurried to the front door. 'You!' he said. 'What happened? We went to the colony that evening. Where were you?'

'Namaskaar,' said Rajaram, joining his hands. 'I feel very bad about it, what to do. I got a new job, they needed me right away, I had to go. But look, my employer has more jobs to fill, you should apply.'

Ishvar could sense Dina trying to listen in the background. 'We'll have to meet later,' he said, and gave him the address of the chemist's.

'Okay, I'll come there tonight. And look, can you lend me ten rupees? Just till I get paid?'

'Only have five.' Ishvar handed it over, wondering if Rajaram's habit of borrowing money was going to become a nuisance. The earlier loan was still unpaid. Should never have let him know where we work, he thought. He returned to his Singer and told Om about their visitor.

'Who cares about Rajaram, I'm dying here.' He extended his sore left arm, the limb delicate as porcelain.

The gesture finally melted Dina. She brought out her bottle of Amrutanjan Balm. 'Come, this will make it better,' she said.

He shook his head.

'Dinabai is right,' said Ishvar. 'I'll rub it for you.'

'You keep sewing, I'll do it,' said Dina. 'Or the balm smell from your fingers will fill the dress.' Besides, she thought, if he starts wasting time, I might as well start begging for next month's rent.

'I'll apply it myself,' said Om.

She uncapped the bottle. 'Come on, take off your shirt. What are you shy about? I'm old enough to be your mother.'

He unbuttoned reluctantly, revealing a vest with many holes. Like Swiss cheese, she thought. A salty-sour odour tarried about him. She dug a dark-green blob out of the bottle and started at the shoulder, spreading the cold unguent down towards the elbow in frigid one-finger lines. He shuddered. The chill of it made his skin horripilate. Then she began to massage, and the salve released its heat, causing his arm, her hand, to tingle. The goose flesh dwindled and vanished.

'How is it?' she asked, kneading the muscles.

'Cold one minute, hot the next.'

'That's the beauty of balm. Nice zhumzhum feeling. Just wait, the pain will soon be gone.'

The odour from his flesh had disappeared, drowned in the balm's pungency. How smooth the skin, she thought. Like a child's. And almost no hair, even on his shoulder.

'How does it feel now?'

'Good.' He had enjoyed the rub.

'Anything else hurting?'

He pointed from elbow to wrist. 'All this.'

Dina hooked out another blob and rubbed his forearm. 'Take some of it with you tonight, apply it when you go to bed. Tomorrow your arm will be good as new.'

Before washing her hands she went to the kitchen, to the dusty shelf by the window. Standing on tiptoe and still unable to see, she felt around. The blind hand dislodged a pivotal box. Things came sliding down: board and rolling pin, the coconut grater with its circular serrated blade, mortar and pestle.

She dodged the avalanche, letting the kitchen implements crash to the floor. The tailors came running. 'Dinabai! Are you okay?' She nodded, a bit shaken but pleased to glimpse the look of concern on Om's face before he erased it.

'Maybe we could fix the shelf a little lower,' said Ishvar, helping her replace the fallen items. 'So you can reach it.'

'No, just leave it. I haven't used these things in fifteen years.' She found what her fingers had been groping for: the roll of wax paper in which she used to wrap Rustom's lunch. She blew off the dust and tore out a hanky-sized square, transferring green daubs of Amrutanjan onto it.

'Here,' she said, folding the piece into a little triangular packet. 'Don't forget to take it with you – your balm samosa.'

'Thank you,' laughed Ishvar, trying to prompt Om into showing his appreciation. And against Om's wishes, a sliver of gratitude pushed a weak smile across his face.

In the evening, as they were leaving, she mentioned the trunk. 'Why don't you leave it where you sleep?'

'There's no room for it there.'

'Then you might as well keep it here. No sense carrying this burden morning and night.'

Ishvar was overcome by the offer. 'Such kindness, Dinabai! We are so grateful!' He thanked her half a dozen times between the back room and verandah, joining his hands, beaming and nodding. Om, once again, was more careful in spending his gratitude. He slipped out a softly murmured 'thank you' while the door was shutting.

'See? She is not as bad as you think.'

'She did it because she wants money from my sweat.'

'Don't forget, she applied the balm for you.'

'Let her pay us properly, then we can buy our own balm.'

'It's not the buying, Omprakash – it's the applying I want you to remember.'

Rajaram came to the chemist's on a bicycle, which impressed Om. 'It's not exactly mine,' said the hair-collector. 'The employers have provided it for the job.'

'What is this job?'

'I must thank my stars for it. That night, after the colony was destroyed, I met a man from my village. He works for the Controller of Slums, driving one of the machines for breaking down houses. He told me about the new job, and took me next morning to the government office. They hired me straight away.'

'And your work is also to destroy homes?'

'No, never. My title is Motivator, for Family Planning. The office gives me leaflets to distribute.'

'That's all? And the pay is good?'

'It depends. They give me one meal, a place to sleep, and the cycle. As Motivator, I have to go around explaining the birth-control procedures. For each man or woman I can persuade to get the operation, I am paid a commission.'

He said he was happy with the arrangement. Gathering just two vasectomies or one tubectomy each day would equal his takings as a hair-collector. His responsibility ended once the candidates signed the forms and were shepherded to the clinic. There were no restrictions, anyone qualified for the operation, young or old, married or unmarried. The doctors were not fussy.

'In the end, everybody is satisfied,' said Rajaram. 'Patients get gifts, I get paid, doctors fill their quotas. And it's also a service to the nation – small families are happy families, population control is most important.'

'How many operations have you collected so far?' asked Ishvar.

'So far, none. But it's only been four days. My talking style is still developing force and conviction. I'm not worried, I'm sure I'll succeed.'

'You know,' said Om, 'with this new job, you could continue the old one side by side.'

'How? There isn't enough time for hair-collecting.'

'When you take patients to the clinic, does the doctor shave the beards between their legs?'

'I don't know.'

'He must,' said Om. 'They always shave before the operation. So you can collect all that hair and sell it.'

'But there is no demand for such short, curly hair.'

Om sniggered at the answer, and Rajaram caught on. 'Rascal, making fun of me,' he laughed. 'But listen, the office is hiring more Motivators. You should apply right away.'

'We are happy with tailoring,' said Ishvar.

'But you told me the woman was difficult, and cheating you.'

'Still, it's the profession we trained for with Ashraf Chacha. Motivator – now that's something we know nothing about.'

'That's just a small obstacle. They will teach you the job at the Family Planning Centre. Don't be afraid to change, it's a great opportunity. Millions of eligible customers. Birth control is a growth industry, I'm telling you.'

But Rajaram's efforts to persuade the tailors and the nightwatchman were unsuccessful. He picked up his bicycle and got ready to leave.

'Any one of you interested in vasectomy? I can use my influence and give you special treatment, double gifts.'

They declined the offer.

'By the way, what about your hair in our trunk?' asked Ishvar.

'Can you keep it a little longer? Once I finish my probation period as Motivator, I can get rid of those plaits.'

He waved and disappeared down the road, ringing his bicycle bell in farewell. Om said the job did sound interesting, in a way. 'And the cycle would be wonderful to have.'

Ishvar's opinion was that only someone like Rajaram, speaking with his long, dangerous tongue, could succeed as a Motivator. 'Telling us we are afraid to change. What does he know? Would we have left our native place and come all the way here if we were afraid of change?'

The nightwatchman agreed. 'In any case, no human being has a choice in that matter. Everything changes, whether we like it or not.'

———

During the evening, Dina went repeatedly to look at the tailors' dented trunk. Maneck watched her with amusement, wondering how long she would keep it up. 'I hope you are happy,' she said after dinner. 'Now pray that my kindness does not come back to hurt me.'

'Stop worrying so much, Aunty. How can it hurt you?'

'Do I have to explain everything again? I only did this because that poor skinny tailor is starting to look like his battered trunk. You think I am unkind to them, that I don't care about their problems. You will think it strange if I tell you this, but after they leave in the evening I miss them – their talking and sewing and joking.'

Maneck did not think it strange at all. 'I hope Om's arm is better tomorrow,' he said.

'One thing is certain, he wasn't pretending. The way his muscles felt while applying the balm, I knew he was in pain. I have experience in massaging. My husband had chronic backaches.'

She used Sloane's Liniment in those days, she said, more efficacious than Amrutanjan Balm, making his knotted muscles ease under her very fingers. 'Rustom would say there was magic in my hands that worked better than the doctor's antispasmodic intramuscular injection.'

She examined her hand wistfully, holding it before her. 'They have a long memory, these fingers. They still remember that feeling, of Rustom's muscles relaxing.' She lowered her hand. 'And in spite of his aching back he loved to cycle. Every chance he got, he jumped on it and pedalled off.'

Till bedtime came, Dina kept talking about Rustom: how they had met, and how her jackass of a brother had reacted, and then the wedding. Her eyes shone, and Maneck was touched by the stories. But he couldn't understand why listening to her was making him bend once again under the familiar weight of despair, while she was delighting in her memories.

VIII Beautification

IN ABOUT A WEEK, the alchemy of time had translated the noisy nocturnal street outside the chemist's shop into a lulling background for the tailors. Now their sleep was no longer poisoned by nightmares. The shadows and disturbances – bookies yelling out the midnight Matka numbers, winners hooting with delight, dogs howling, drunks locked in mortal combat with their demons, the crash of milk-bottle racks, doors slamming on bakery vans – all these became, for Ishvar and Om, the bonging of hours by a faithful clock.

'I told you the street was nothing to be frightened of,' said the night-watchman.

'True,' said Ishvar. 'Noises are like people. Once you get to know them, they become friendly.'

The rings around their eyes began to fade, their work improved, and their sleep grew pleasant. Ishvar dreamt a wedding celebration in the village; Om's bride was beautiful. And Om dreamt about the deserted slum. Shanti and he, holding hands, fetched water from the tap, then romped through the wasted field, now transformed into a garden teeming with flowers and butterflies. They sang, danced around trees, made love while flying aboard a magic carpet of clouds, machine-gunned Sergeant Kesar and his evil policemen as well as the Controller of Slums, and restored the hutment dwellers to their rightful place.

The chemist's shop was the centre of the tailors' new routine. They picked out a change of clothing from the trunk when leaving Dina's flat at the end of the day. Soap and toothbrushes went back and forth with them. After dinner at the Vishram, they washed their clothes in the railway station bathroom and dried them in the chemist's entrance. Electrical wiring that had lost its moorings hung like a clothesline for the laundry. Pants and shirts floated like truncated sentries while they slept. On windy nights the garments danced on the wire, friendly funambulating ghosts.

Then came the night of noises that were strangers on the street. Police jeeps and a truck roared down the road and parked across from the chemist's. Sergeant Kesar barked short, sharp instructions to his men; the constables' sticks thudded hollowly on cardboard boxes sheltering

sleepers along the pavement; heavy steps in regulation footwear pounded the footpath.

The noises, like menacing interlopers, barged their way into the tailors' slumber. Ishvar and Om awoke trembling as though from a bad
dream, and crouched fearfully behind the nightwatchman. 'What's happening? What do you see?' they asked him.

He peered around the entrance. 'Looks like they are waking all the
beggars. They are beating them, pushing them into a truck.'

The tailors shook off their sleep and saw for themselves. 'That really is
Sergeant Kesar,' said Om, rubbing his eyes. 'I thought I was dreaming
about our jhopadpatti again.'

'And that other chap, the one next to Sergeant Kesar – he also seems
familiar,' said Ishvar.

The small, clerkish-looking man was hopping along like a rabbit, snif-
fling with a heavy cold. He periodically snorted back the mucus and
gulped it. Om edged forward. 'It's that fellow who wanted to sell us a
ration card for two hundred rupees – the Facilitator.'

'You're right. And he is still coughing and sneezing. Come on back,
better stay hidden, it's safer.'

The Facilitator was making notes on a clipboard, keeping count as the
truck was loaded. 'Wait a second, Sergeant,' he protested. 'Look at that
one – completely crippled. Leave her out, no.'

'You do your work,' said Sergeant Kesar, 'I'll do mine. And if you
have extra time, look after your spectacles.'

'Thank you,' said the Facilitator, his hand shooting up to halt the slide
of his glasses. On the way down, the fingers collected the pearl dangling
at his nose. It was a smooth combination of gestures. 'But please listen to
me, no,' he sniffed. 'This beggar is useless in her condition.'

'Actually speaking, that's not my concern. I have to follow orders.'
Tonight, Sergeant Kesar had decided he was going to tolerate no nonsense, his job was getting harder by the day. Gathering crowds for political rallies wasn't bad. Rounding up MISA suspects was also okay. But
demolishing hutment colonies, vendors' stalls, jhopadpattis was playing
havoc with his peace of mind. And prior to his superiors formulating
this progressive new strategy for the beggary problem, he had had to
dump pavement-dwellers in waste land outside the city. He used to
return miserable from those assignments, get drunk, abuse his wife, beat
his children. Now that his conscience was recuperating, he was not
about to let this nose-dripping idiot complicate matters.

'But what good is she to me?' objected the Facilitator. 'What kind of
labourer will such a cripple be?'

'With you it's always the same complaint,' said Sergeant Kesar, sticking his thumbs in the black leather belt that followed the generous curve below his belly. He was a fan of cowboy films and Clint Eastwood. 'Don't forget, they will all work for free.'

'Hardly free, Sergeant. You're charging enough per head.'

'If you don't want them, others will. Actually speaking, I am sick and tired of listening to your moaning every night. I cannot pick and choose healthy specimens for you – this isn't a cattle market. My orders are to clear the streets. So you want them or not?'

'Yes, okay. But at least tell your men to hit carefully, not to make them bleed. Or it becomes very difficult for me to find places for them.'

'Now there I agree with you,' said Sergeant Kesar. 'But you don't need to worry, my constables are well trained. They know the importance of inflicting hidden injuries only.'

The sweep continued, the policemen performing their task efficiently, prodding, poking, kicking. No obstacle slowed them down, not shrieks nor wails nor the comical threats of drunks and lunatics.

The policemen's detached manner reminded Ishvar of the streetsweeper who came for the garbage at five a.m. 'Oh no,' he shuddered, as the team reached the street corner. 'They're after the poor little fellow on wheels.'

The legless beggar made a break for it. Pushing the ground with his palms, he propelled the platform forward. The policemen were amused and cheered him on, wanting to see how fast his castors could go. The escape attempt ran out of energy outside the chemist's. Two constables carried him to the truck, platform and all.

'Just look at this one!' cried the agitated Facilitator. 'No fingers, no feet, no legs – a great worker he will be!'

'You can do what you like with him,' said one constable.

'Let him out beyond the city limits if you don't need him,' said the other. A slight push, and the platform rolled till it came to rest at the front end of the truck bed.

'What are you saying, how can I do that? I have to account for all of them,' said the Facilitator. Remembering Sergeant Kesar's ultimatum, he looked over his shoulder cautiously, biting the cap of his ballpoint – had he heard? To make up, he voiced agreement for a change. 'Those blind ones are fine. Blindness is no problem, they can do things with their hands. Children also, many little jobs for them.'

The constables ignored him as they pursued their quarry. Once the initial panic had subsided, the beggars went meekly. Most of them had endured such roundups outside businesses or residences that persuaded the police, with a little baksheesh, to remove the eyesores. Sometimes the policemen themselves stationed the beggars there, then eagerly awaited the lucrative removal request.

Lined up by the truck, the pavement-dwellers were counted off and asked to give their names, which the Facilitator noted on his clipboard along with sex, age, and physical condition. One old man remained silent, his name locked away in his head, the key misplaced. A policeman slapped him and asked again. The grizzled head rolled from side to side with each blow.

His friends tried to help, calling out the various names they used for him. 'Burfi! Bevda! Four-Twenty!' The Facilitator selected Burfi, and entered it on the roster. For the age column he used a rough estimate by appearance.

The drunks and the mentally disturbed were a little more difficult to deal with, refusing to move, screaming abuse, most of it incoherent, and making the police laugh. Then one drunk began swinging his fists wildly. 'Rabid dogs!' he shouted. 'Born of diseased whores!' The constables stopped laughing and set on him with their sticks; when he fell, they used their feet.

'Stop, please stop!' beseeched the Facilitator. 'How will he work if you break his bones?'

'Don't worry, these fellows are tough. Our sticks will break, they won't.' The unconscious drunk was thrown into the truck. On the pavement, discussion was adjourned with truncheons in the kidneys and, in extremely voluble cases, a crack on the skull.

'These are not hidden injuries!' the Facilitator protested to Sergeant Kesar. 'Look at all that blood!'

'Sometimes it's necessary,' said Sergeant Kesar, but he did remind his men to curb their zeal or it would stretch out the night's work by involving doctors and bandages and medical reports.

Still concealed within the chemist's entrance, the tailors wondered what was happening now. 'Are they leaving? They finished?'

'Looks like it,' said the nightwatchman, and the sound of engines starting confirmed it. 'Good, you can go to sleep again.'

Sergeant Kesar and the Facilitator checked the roster. 'Ninety-four,' said the latter. 'Need two more to complete the quota.'

'Actually speaking, when I said eight dozen I was giving an approximate number. One truckload. Don't you understand? How can I predict in advance exactly how many we are going to catch?'

'But I told my contractor eight dozen. He will think I am cheating him, no. Can't you look for two more?'

'Okay,' said Sergeant Kesar wearily, 'let's find two more.' Never again would he deal with this fellow. Whining and whimpering non-stop, like a whipped dog. If it weren't a question of paying for his daughter's sitar lessons, he would chuck these overtime assignments without a second thought. Not only did he have to deal with scum like the Facilitator; the late nights also kept him from rising before dawn and putting in an hour of yoga as he used to. No wonder he was so short-tempered these days, he reflected. And suffering all this stomach acidity. But what choice? It was his duty to improve his child's marriage prospects.

The tailors and the nightwatchman heard the approach of thumping feet and sticks. Two silhouettes, faceless as their shadows, looked inside the entrance. 'Who's there?'

'It's all right, don't worry, I am the nightwatchman and –'

'Shut up and come out! All of you!' Sergeant Kesar's patience had been devoured by the Facilitator.

The nightwatchman rose from his stool, decided it would be prudent to leave his night-stick behind, and stepped onto the pavement. 'Don't worry,' he beckoned the tailors forward. 'I will explain to them.'

'We have done nothing wrong,' said Ishvar, buttoning his shirt.

'Actually speaking, sleeping on the street is breaking the law. Get your things and into the truck.'

'But police-sahab, we are sleeping here only because your men came with machines and destroyed our jhopadpatti.'

'What? You lived in a jhopadpatti? Two wrongs don't make a right. You could get double punishment.'

'But police-sahab,' interrupted the nightwatchman, 'you cannot arrest them, they were not sleeping on the street, they were inside this –'

'You understand what shut up means?' warned Sergeant Kesar. 'Or you want to find out what lockup means? Sleeping in any non-sleeping place is illegal. This is an entranceway, not a sleeping place. And who said they are being arrested? The government is not crazy that it would go around jailing beggars.' He stopped abruptly, wondering why he was making a speech when his men's lathis would get quicker results.

'But we are not beggars!' said Om. 'We are tailors, look, these long fin-gernails to fold straight seams, and we work at –'

'If you are tailors then sew up your mouths! Enough, into the truck!'

'*He* knows us,' Ishvar pointed at the Facilitator. 'He said he could sell us a ration card for two hundred rupees, payable in instalments and –'

'What's this about ration cards?' demanded Sergeant Kesar, turning.

The Facilitator shook his head. 'They're confusing me with some crooked tout, it looks like.'

'It *was* you!' said Om. 'You were sneezing and coughing, snot coming from your nose just like it is now!'

Sergeant Kesar motioned to a constable. The stick came down across Om's calves. He yelped.

'No, please, no beating,' pleaded the nightwatchman. 'It's all right, they will listen to you.' He patted the tailors' shoulders. 'Don't worry, this is definitely a mistake, just explain to the people in charge and they will let you go.'

The constable lifted his stick again, but Ishvar and Om began rolling up the bedding. The nightwatchman embraced them before they were led off. 'Come back soon, I'll keep this place for you.'

Ishvar tried one last time. 'We really have jobs, we don't beg –'

'Shut up.' Sergeant Kesar was in the midst of calculating his proceeds for the night's haul, and arithmetic was not his strong point. The interruption forced him to start the sum over again.

The tailors climbed onto the truckbed, then the tailboard was slammed shut and the bolt shot into place. The men assigned to escort the transport took their seats in the police jeep. The Facilitator settled the final amount with Sergeant Kesar and got in beside the truck driver.

The truck, recently used for construction work, had clods of clay stuck to its insides. Underfoot, stray gravel stabbed the human cargo. Some who were standing tumbled in a heap as the driver threw the gears into reverse to turn around and return the way he had come. The police jeep followed closely behind.

They travelled through what remained of the night, the bumps and potholes making their bodies collide ceaselessly. The beggar on castors had the worst of it, shoved back each time he skidded into someone. He smiled nervously at the tailors. 'I see you often on my pavement. You've given me many coins.'

Ishvar moved his hand in a think-nothing-of-it gesture. 'Why don't you get off your gaadi?' he suggested, and with Om's help the beggar removed the platform from under him. His neighbours were relieved. Inert as a sack of cement, he clutched the board to his chest with his fingerless hands, then cradled it in his abbreviated lap, shivering in the warm night.

'Where are they taking us?' he yelled above the engine's roar. 'I'm so scared! What's going to happen?'

'Don't worry, we'll soon find out,' said Ishvar. 'Where did you get this nice gaadi of yours?'

'My Beggarmaster gave it to me. Gift. He is such a kind man.' Fear made his shrill voice sharper. 'How will I find Beggarmaster again? He will think I have run away when he comes tomorrow for the money!'

'If he asks around, someone will tell him about the police.'

'That's what I cannot understand. Why did police take me? Beggarmaster pays them every week – all his beggars are allowed to work without harassment.'

'These are different police,' said Ishvar. 'The beautification police – there's a new law to make the city beautiful. Maybe they don't know your Beggarmaster.'

He shook his head at the absurdity of the suggestion. 'Aray babu, everybody knows Beggarmaster.' He began fidgeting with the castors, finding comfort in spinning the wheels. 'This gaadi here, it's a new one he gave me recently. The old one broke.'

'How?' asked Om.

'Accident. There was a slope, I crashed off the pavement. Almost damaged somebody's motorcar.' He giggled, remembering the event. 'This new one is much better.' He invited Om to inspect the castors.

'Very smooth,' said Om, trying one with his thumb. 'What happened to your legs and hands?'

'Don't know exactly. Always been like this. But I'm not complaining, I get enough to eat, plus a reserved place on the pavement. Beggarmaster looks after everything.' He examined the bandages on his hands and unravelled them using his mouth, which silenced him for a few minutes. It was a slow, laborious procedure, involving a lot of neck and jaw movement.

The palms revealed, he scratched them by rubbing against the tailors' bedding. The sackcloth's delicious roughness relieved the itch. Then he began retying the bandages, the arduous process of neck and jaw in reverse. Om moved his own head in sympathy – up, and down, around, carefully, yes, around again – stopping when, feeling a little foolish, he realized what he was doing.

'The bandage protects my skin. I push with my hands to roll the gaadi. Without bandages they would start bleeding against the ground.'

The casually offered fact made Om uncomfortable. But the beggar kept talking, easing his own fear and anxiety. 'I did not always have a gaadi. When I was little, too little to beg on my own, they carried me around. Beggarmaster used to rent me out each day. He was the father of the one who looks after me now. I was in great demand. Beggar-master would say I earned him the highest profits.'

The panic in his voice had been routed by the memory of happier days. He recalled how well the renters would care for him and feed him, because if they were neglectful, Beggarmaster would thrash them and never do business with them again. Luckily, due to his reduced size, he resembled a baby till he was twelve. 'A child, a suckling cripple, earns a lot of money from the public. There were so many different breasts I drank milk from during those years.'

He smiled mischievously. 'Wish I could still be carried around in women's arms, their sweet nipples in my mouth. More fun than bumping along all day on this platform, banging my balls and wearing out my buttocks.'

Ishvar and Om were surprised, then laughed with relief. Passing him by on the pavement with a wave or a coin was one thing; sitting beside him, dwelling on his mutilations was another – and quite distressing. They were happy that he was capable of laughter too.

'At last my baby face and baby size left me. I became too heavy to carry. That's when Beggarmaster sent me out on my own. I had to drag my self around. On my back.'

He wanted to demonstrate, but there was no room in the crammed truck. He described how Beggarmaster had trained him in the technique, as he trained all his beggars, with a personal touch, teaching them different styles – whatever would work best in each case. 'Beggarmaster likes to joke that he would issue diplomas if we had walls to hang them on.'

The tailors laughed again, and the beggar glowed with pleasure. He was discovering a new talent in himself. 'So I learned to crawl on my back, using my head and elbows. It was slow going. First I would push my begging tin forward, then wriggle after it. It was very effective. People watched with pity and curiosity. Sometimes little children thought it was a game and tried to imitate me. Two gamblers placed bets every day on how long I would take to reach the end of the pavement. I pretended not to know what they were doing. The winner always dropped money in my can.

'But it took me very long to get to the different spots which Beggarmaster reserved for me. Morning, noon, and night – office crowd, lunch crowd, shopping crowd. So then he decided to get me the platform. Such a nice man, I cannot praise him enough. On my birthday he brings sweetmeats for me. Sometimes he takes me to a prostitute. He has many, many beggars in his team, but I'm his favourite. His work is not easy, there is so much to do. He pays the police, finds the best place to beg, makes sure no one takes away that place. And when there is a good Beggarmaster looking after you, no one dare steal your money. That's the biggest problem, stealing.'

A man in the truck grumbled and gave the beggar a shove. 'Simply screeching like a cat on fire. No one's interested in listening to your lies.'

The beggar was silent for a few minutes, adjusting his bandages and toying with the castors. The tailors' drowsy heads started to loll, alarming him. If his friends fell asleep he would be left alone in the dark rush of this terrifying night. He resumed his story to drive away their sleep.

'Also, Beggarmaster has to be very imaginative. If all beggars have the same injury, public gets used to it and feels no pity. Public likes to see variety. Some wounds are so common, they don't work anymore. For example, putting out a baby's eyes will not automatically earn money. Blind beggars are everywhere. But blind, with eyeballs missing, face showing empty sockets, plus nose chopped off – now anyone will give money for that. Diseases are also useful. A big growth on the neck or face, oozing yellow pus. That works well.

'Sometimes, normal people become beggars if they cannot find work, or if they fall sick. But they are hopeless, they stand no chance against professionals. Just think – if you have one coin to give, and you have to choose between me and another beggar with a complete body.'

The man who had shoved him earlier spoke again. 'Shut up, you monkey, I'm warning you! Or I'll throw you over the side! At a time like this we don't want to listen to your nonsense! Why don't you do an honest job like us?'

'What work do you do?' inquired Ishvar politely, to calm him down.

'Scrap metal. Collecting and selling by weight. And even my poor sick wife has her own work. Rags.'

'That's very good,' said Ishvar. 'And we have a friend who is a hair-collector, although he recently changed to Family Planning Motivator.'

'Yes babu, all very good,' said the beggar. 'But tell me, metal-collector, without legs or fingers, what could I do?'

'Don't make excuses. In a huge city like this there is work even for a corpse. But you have to want it, and look for it seriously. You beggars create nuisance on the streets, then police make trouble for everyone. Even for us hardworking people.'

'O babu, without beggars how will people wash away their sins?'

'Who cares? We worry about finding water to wash our skins!'

The discussion got louder, the beggar yelling shrilly, the metal-collector bellowing back at him. The other passengers began taking sides. The drunks awoke and shouted abuse at everyone. 'Goat-fucking idiots! Offspring of lunatic donkeys! Shameless eunuchs from somewhere!'

Eventually, the commotion made the truck driver pull over to the edge of the road. 'I cannot drive with so much disturbance,' he complained. 'There will be an accident or something.'

His headlights revealed a stony verge and tussocks of grass. A hush descended over the truck. The darkness was deep on both sides, betraying nothing – beyond the road's narrow shoulders, the night could be hiding hills, empty fields, a thick forest, or demon-monsters.

A policeman came through the beam of light to warn them. 'If there is any more noise, you will be thrashed and thrown out right here, in the jungle, instead of being taken to your nice new homes.'

The silenced truckload started moving. The beggar began to weep. 'O babu, I'm feeling so frightened again.' He fell into a stupor of exhausted sleep after a while.

The tailors were wide awake now. Ishvar wondered what would happen when they didn't turn up for work in the morning. 'Dresses will be late again. Second time in two months. What will Dinabai do?'

'Find new tailors, and forget about us,' said Om. 'What else?'

Dawn turned the night to grey, and then pink, as the truck and jeep left the highway for a dirt road to stop outside a small village. The tailboard swung open. The passengers were told to attend to calls of nature. For some, the halt had come too late.

The beggar tilted on one buttock while Om slid the platform under him. He paddled himself to the edge of the truck and waved a bandaged palm at two policemen. They turned their backs, lighting cigarettes. The tailors jumped off and lowered him to the ground, surprised at how little he weighed.

The men used one side of the road, the women squatted on the other; children were everywhere. The babies were hungry and crying. Parents fed them from packages of half-rotten bananas and oranges and scraps scavenged the night before.

The Facilitator went on ahead to arrange for tea. The village chaiwalla set up a temporary kitchen near the truck, building a fire to heat a cauldron of water, milk, sugar, and tea leaves. Everyone watched him thirstily. The early sun dabbled through the trees, catching the liquid. Boiling and ready in a few minutes, it was served in little earthen bowls.

Meanwhile, word of the visitors percolated swiftly through the little village, and its population gathered round to watch. They took pride in the pleasure the travellers obtained from sipping the tea. The headman greeted the Facilitator and asked the usual friendly, villager questions about who, where, why, ready to offer help and advice.

The Facilitator told him to mind his business, take his people back to their huts, or the police would disperse them. Hurt by the rude behaviour, the crowd left.

The tea was consumed and the little earthen bowls were returned to the chaiwalla. He proceeded to shatter them in the customary way, whereupon some pavement-dwellers instinctively rushed to save them. 'Wait, wait! We'll keep them if you don't want them!'

But the Facilitator forbade it. 'Where you are going, you will be given everything that you need.' They were ordered back into the truck. During the halt, the sun had cleared the tree tops. Morning heat was rapidly gaining the upper hand. The engine's starting roar frightened the birds, lifting them from the trees in a fluttering cloud.

Late in the day the truck arrived at an irrigation project where the Facilitator unloaded the ninety-six individuals. The project manager counted them before signing the delivery receipt. The worksite had its own security men, and the police jeep departed.

The security captain ordered the ninety-six to empty their pockets, open up their parcels, place everything on the ground. Two of his men moved down the line, passing hands over their clothes in a body search and examining the pile of objects. This need not have taken long, since half of them were near-naked beggars and the possessions were meagre. But there were women too, so it was a while before the guards finished the frisking.

They seized screwdrivers, cooking spoons, a twelve-inch steel rod, knives, a roll of copper wire, tongs, and a comb of bone with teeth deemed too large and sharp. A guard gave Om's plastic comb the bending test. It broke in two. He was allowed to keep the pieces. 'We're not supposed to be here, my uncle and I,' he said.

The guard pushed him back in line. 'Talk to the foreman if you have a complaint.'

The extremely ragged were issued half-pants and vests, or petticoats and blouses. The beggar on castors got only a vest, there being nothing suitable to fit his cloth-swaddled amputated lower half. Ishvar and Om did not get new clothes, nor did the ragpicker and the metal-collector. The latter, whose many sharp-edged items had been confiscated, was chagrined, considering it most unfair. But the tailors felt the new clothes were poorly stitched, and preferred what they were wearing.

The group was shown to a row of tin huts, to be occupied twelve to a hut. Everyone rushed in a frenzy to the nearest of the identical shelters and fought to get inside. The guard drove them back, allocating places at random. A stack of rolled-up straw mats stood within each hut. Some

331

people spread them out and lay down, but had to get up again. They were told to store their belongings and reassemble for the foreman.

The foreman was a harried-looking individual, sweating profusely, who welcomed them to their new houses. He took a few minutes to describe the generous scheme the government had introduced for the uplift of the poor and homeless. 'So we hope you will take advantage of this plan. Now there are still two hours of working-time left, but you can rest today. Tomorrow morning you will start your new jobs.'

Someone asked how much the salary was, and if it would be paid daily or weekly.

The foreman wiped the sweat from his face, sighed, and tried again. 'You didn't understand what I said? You will get food, shelter, and clothing. That is your salary.'

The tailors edged forward, anxious to explain their accidental presence in the irrigation project. But two officials got to the foreman first and led him away for a meeting. Ishvar decided against running after him. 'Better to wait till morning,' he whispered to Om. 'He's very busy now, it might make him angry. But it's clear that the police made a mistake with us. This place is for unemployed people. They will let us go once they know we have tailoring jobs.'

Some people ventured to lie down inside the huts. Others chose to spread their mats outside. Blazing under the daylong sun, the tin walls enclosed a savage heat. The shade cast by the corrugated metal was cooler.

A whistle blew at dusk and workers returned from their tasks. After thirty minutes it blew again, and they made their way to the camp's eating area. The newcomers were told to go with them. They lined up outside the kitchen to receive their dinner: dal and chapati, with a green chilli on the side.

'The dal is almost water,' said Om.

The server overheard him and took it personally. 'What do you think this is, your father's palace?'

'Don't take my father's name,' said Om.

'Come on, let's go,' said Ishvar, pulling him away. 'Tomorrow we'll tell the top man about the policeman's mistake.'

They finished eating in silence, concentrating like everyone else on the food's hidden perils. The chapatis were made from gritty flour. The meal was punctuated by the diners spitting out small pebbles and other foreign bodies. Tinier fragments which could not be caught in time were triturated with the food.

'They should have been here more than an hour ago,' Dina said to Maneck when breakfast was done.

She's after the poor chaps again, he thought, gathering the books he needed for the day's classes. 'Does it matter that much, if it's piecework?'

'What do you know about running a business? Your mummy and daddy pay your fees and send you pocket money. Wait till you start earning your living.'

When he returned in the afternoon, she was pacing by the door. The instant his slightly bent key rattled in the keyhole, she turned the knob. 'No sign of them all day,' she complained to him. 'I wonder what excuse they'll have this time. Another meeting with the Prime Minister?'

As the afternoon meandered towards evening, her sarcastic tone was elbowed aside by anxiety. 'The electricity bill is due, and the water bill. Rations to be bought. And Ibrahim will arrive next week to collect the rent. You've no idea how harassing he can be.'

Her worries continued to bubble like indigestion after dinner. What would happen if the tailors did not come tomorrow even? How could she get two new ones quickly enough? And it wasn't just a question of these dresses being late – a second delay would seriously displease the high and mighty empress of Au Revoir Exports. This time the manager would place the black mark of 'unreliable' next to her name. Dina felt that perhaps she should go to the Venus Beauty Salon, talk to Zenobia, request her to again use her influence with Mrs. Gupta.

'Ishvar and Om wouldn't stay absent just like that,' said Maneck. 'Something urgent must have come up.'

'Rubbish. What could be so urgent that they cannot take a few minutes to stop by?'

'Maybe they went to see a room for rent or something. Don't worry, Aunty, they'll probably be here tomorrow.'

'Probably? Probably is not good enough. I cannot *probably* deliver the dresses and *probably* pay the rent. You, without any responsibilities, probably don't understand that.'

He thought the outburst was unfair. 'If they don't come tomorrow, I'll go and ask what's wrong.'

'Yes,' she brightened. 'It's a good thing you know where they live.' Her anxiety seemed to diminish. Then she said, 'Let's visit them right now. Why spend the whole night worrying?'

'But you always say you don't want them thinking you are desperate. If you run there at night, they'll see you are helpless without them.'

'I am not helpless,' she said emphatically. 'Just one more difficulty in life, that's all it is.' But she decided to wait till morning, agreeing that he should check on them before going to college. She was too distracted to continue working on the quilt; the squares and scraps sat in a pile on the sofa, hiding their designs.

Maneck ran back from the chemist's shop, frantic. Near the Vishram Vegetarian Hotel he slowed down for a quick look inside, hoping that Ishvar and Om might be sipping their morning tea. Empty. He reached the flat, panting, and repeated the nightwatchman's account for Dina.

'It's terrible! He thinks they were mistaken for beggars – dragged into the police truck – and God knows where they are now!'

'Hmm, I see,' she said, weighing the story for truth and substance. 'And how long is their jail sentence? One week, two weeks?' If those rascals were trying a new job somewhere, playing for time, this would be the way to do it.

'I don't know.' Distraught, he did not detect her question's cynicism. 'It's not just them – everyone from the street, all the beggars and pavement-dwellers were taken away by the police.'

'Don't make me laugh, there's no law for doing that.'

'It's a new policy – city beautification plan or something, under the Emergency.'

'What Emergency? I am sick and tired of that stupid word.' Still sceptical, she took a deep breath and decided to be direct. 'Maneck, look at me. Straight in my eyes.' She brought her face closer to his. 'Maneck, you would not be lying to me, would you? Because Ishvar and Om are your friends, and they asked you to?'

'I swear on my parents' name, Aunty!' he drew away from her, shocked. Then the accusation made him angry. 'You don't have to believe me, think what you like. Next time don't ask me to do your work.' He left the room.

She followed him. 'Maneck.' He ignored her. 'Maneck, I'm sorry. You know how worried I am about the sewing – I said it without thinking.'

A moment's silence was all he could maintain before forgiving her. 'It's all right.'

Such a sweet boy, she thought, he just cannot stay upset. 'How long have they been sleeping outside the – what is it, chemist's shop?'

'Since the day their home was destroyed. Don't you remember, Aunty? When you wouldn't let them sleep on your verandah?'

She bristled at the tone. 'You know very well why I had to refuse. But if you were aware of it, why didn't you tell me? Before something like this happened?'

'Suppose I had. What difference? Would you have let them stay here?'

She avoided the question. 'I still find it hard to believe this story. Maybe that watchman is lying – covering up for them. And in the meantime I will have to go begging to my brother for the rent.'

Maneck could sense the things she was trying to juggle, conceal, keep in proportion: concern, guilt, fear. 'We could check with the police,' he suggested.

'And what good will that do? Even if they have the tailors, you think they will unlock the jail on my say-so?'

'At least we'd know where they are.'

'Right now I'm more worried about these dresses.'

'I knew it! You're so selfish, you don't think about anyone but yourself! You just don't –'

'How dare you! How dare you talk to me like that!'

'They could be dead, for all you care!' He went to his room and slammed the door.

'If you damage my door, I'll write to your parents! For compensation, remember!'

He kicked off his shoes and fell in bed with a thump. It was half past nine, he was late for college. To hell with it – to hell with her. Enough of trying to be nice. He jumped off the bed and exchanged his shirt for an old wear-at-home one from the cupboard. The door clattered off the lower hinge. He jiggled it into the bracket and banged it shut.

He flopped on the mattress once more, his finger angrily tracing the floral design carved in the teak headboard. The bed was the identical twin of the one in the sewing room. Dina Aunty's and her husband's – they must have slept side by side on them. A long time ago. When her life was filled with happiness, and the flat with the sounds of love and laughter. Before it went silent and dingy.

He could hear her pacing in the next room, could sense her distress in the footsteps. And barely a week ago the work had been going so well, after she gave the Amrutanjan Balm to Om. Massaging his arm had put her in a good mood, she had started reminiscing about her husband's back, about their lives.

All the things she told Maneck came back now to crowd his room:

those enchanted evenings of music recitals, and emerging with Rustom from the concert hall into the fragrant night when the streets were quiet – yes, she said, in those days the city was still beautiful, the footpaths were clean, not yet taken over by pavement-dwellers, and yes, the stars were visible in the sky in those days, when Rustom and she walked along the sea, listening to the endless exchange of the waves, or in the Hanging Gardens, among the whispering trees, planning their wedding and their lives, planning and plotting in full ignorance of destiny's plans for them.

How much Dina Aunty relished her memories. Mummy and Daddy were the same, talking about their yesterdays and smiling in that sad-happy way while selecting each picture, each frame from the past, examining it lovingly before it vanished again in the mist. But nobody ever forgot anything, not really, though sometimes they pretended, when it suited them. Memories were permanent. Sorrowful ones remained sad even with the passing of time, yet happy ones could never be recreated – not with the same joy. Remembering bred its own peculiar sorrow. It seemed so unfair: that time should render both sadness and happiness into a source of pain.

So what was the point of possessing memory? It didn't help anything. In the end it was all hopeless. Look at Mummy and Daddy, and the General Store; or Dina Aunty's life; or the hostel and Avinash; and now poor Ishvar and Om. No amount of remembering happy days, no amount of yearning or nostalgia could change a thing about the misery and suffering – love and concern and caring and sharing come to nothing, nothing.

Maneck began to weep, his chest heaving as he laboured to keep silent. Everything ended badly. And memory only made it worse, tormenting and taunting. Unless. Unless you lost your mind. Or committed suicide. The slate wiped clean. No more remembering, no more suffering.

Poor Dina Aunty, how much of the past she was still carrying around with her, although she deceived herself that these were happy memories she was dwelling upon. And now the problems with the sewing, the rent, the rations . . .

He felt ashamed of his earlier tantrum. He got out of bed, tucked in his shirt, dried his eyes, and went to the back room where she was pacing the prison of her incomplete dresses.

'When do you have to deliver them?' he asked gruffly.

'Oh, you're back? Day after tomorrow. By twelve o'clock.' She smiled to herself, having expected him to sulk for an hour; he had emerged in thirty minutes. 'Your eyes look watery. Have you got a cold?'

He shook his head. 'Just tired. Day after tomorrow – that's two whole days. Lots of time.'

'For two expert tailors, yes. Not for me alone.'

'I'll help you.'

'Don't make me laugh. You, sewing? And me with my eyes. I can't see to put my finger through a wedding ring, let alone thread the eye of a needle.'

'I'm serious, Aunty.'

'But there are sixty dresses, six-zero. Only the hems and buttons are left, true, but it's still a lot of work.' She picked one up. 'See the waist, all puckered? That's called 'gather.' Now it measures' – she stretched the tape – 'just twenty-six inches. But because of the gather, the hemline of the skirt is, let's see, sixty-five inches, to be done by hand. That takes a lot of –'

'How will they know if you do it by machine?'

'The difference is like night and day. And then eight buttons on each dress. Six in the front, one on each sleeve. An hour's work per dress for someone like me. Sixty hours altogether.'

'We have forty-eight till delivery time.'

'If we don't eat or sleep or go to the bathroom, yes.'

'We can at least try. You can deliver what we finish, and make an excuse that the tailors fell sick or something.'

'If you're really willing to help . . .'

'I am.'

She started to get things ready. 'You're a good boy, you know? Your parents are very fortunate to have a son like you.' Then she turned abruptly. 'Wait a minute – what about college?'

'No lectures today.'

'Hmm,' she said dubiously, selecting the thread. They took the dresses into the front room where the light was better. 'I'll teach you buttons. Easier than hems.'

'Anything. I learn quickly.'

'Yes, we'll see. First you measure and mark the places with chalk, in a straight line. It's the most important step, or the front will look crooked. Thank goodness these are plain poplin dresses, not slippery chiffon like last month.' She took him through the paces, emphasizing that the stitches in the four-holed button should be parallel and not crisscross.

He tried the next one. 'Oh, to have young eyes again,' she sighed, as he moistened the thread between his lips and passed it through the needle. Finding the holes in the button from the blind side took a bit of poking around with the needle. But he managed to finish in fair time, and snipped the threads, triumphant.

Two hours later, between them they had finished sixteen buttons and three hemlines. 'See how long it takes?' she said. 'And now I must stop to make lunch.'

'I'm not hungry.'

'Not hungry today, no lectures today. Very strange.'

'But it's true, Aunty. Forget lunch, I'm really not hungry.'

'And what about me? Worrying all yesterday, I didn't eat a single bite. Today at least may I have the pleasure?'

'Work before pleasure,' he smiled down at the button, looking up from the corner of his eye.

'Planning to be my boss, are you?' she said with mock sternness. 'If I don't eat, there will be no work and no pleasure. Only me fainting over needle and thread.'

'Okay, I'll take care of lunch. You keep on hemming.'

'Proper housewife you are becoming. What will it be? Bread and butter? Tea and toast?'

'A surprise. I'll be back soon.'

Before leaving the flat he readied six needles with thread, to spare her pitting her eyes in contest with the little silvery ones.

'Wasting money like that,' scolded Dina. 'Your parents already pay me for your food.'

Maneck emptied the alayti-palayti from A-1 Restaurant into a bowl and brought it to the table. 'It's out of my pocket money. I can spend it any way I like.'

Chunks of chicken liver and gizzard floated tantalizingly in the thick, spicy sauce. Bending over the bowl, she sniffed. 'Mmm, the same wonderful fragrance that made it a favourite of Rustom's. Only A-1 makes it in rich gravy – other places cook it too dry.' She dipped a spoon, raised it to her lips, and nodded. 'Delicious. We could easily add a little water without harming the taste. Then it will be enough for lunch and dinner.'

'Okay. And this is specially for you,' he handed her a bag.

She felt inside and withdrew a bunch of carrots. 'You want me to cook these for us?

'Not for us, Aunty – for you, to eat raw. Good for your eyes. Especially since they'll be very busy now.'

'Thank you, but I prefer not to.'

'No alayti-palayti without carrot. You must have at least one with your lunch.'

'You're crazy if you think I will eat raw carrots. Even my mother could not make me.' While she got the table ready, he scraped a medium-sized specimen, lopped off the ends, and placed it next to her plate.

'I hope that's yours,' she said.

'No carrot, no alayti-palayti.' He refused to pass her the bowl. 'I make the rules. For your own good.'

She laughed but her mouth started to water while he ate. She picked up the vegetable by the thin end as though to hit him over the head with it, and bit into it with a vengeance. Grinning, he passed her the bowl. 'My father says his one eye is equal to most people's two because he eats carrots regularly. A carrot a day keeps blindness away, he claims.'

Throughout the meal, she grimaced each time she crunched into it. 'Thank goodness for the delicious alayti-palayti. Without the gravy this raw roughage would stick in my throat.'

'Now tell me, Aunty,' he said when they finished eating. 'Are your eyes any better?'

'Good enough to see you for the devil that you are.'

The sewing picked up speed after lunch, but late in the afternoon Dina's eyelids grew heavy. 'I have to stop now for tea. Okay, boss?'

'Fifteen minutes only, remember. And one cup for me too, please.'

She went to the kitchen, smiling and shaking her head.

Seven o'clock, and her mind turned to dinner duties. 'That alayti-palayti sitting in the kitchen is making me hungry earlier than usual. What about you? Now, or wait till eight?'

'Whenever you like,' he mumbled through lips clutching an empty needle. He unrolled a length of thread from the spool.

'Look at that! First time sewing, and already acting like a crazy tailor! Take it out of your mouth! At once! Before you swallow it!'

He removed the needle, a little sheepish. She had hit the mark – he was trying to copy Om's jaunty way of sticking things between his lips: pins, needles, blades, scissors, the daredevilry of juxtaposing sharp, dangerous objects with soft, defenceless flesh.

'How will I explain to your mother if I return her son with a needle stuck in his craw?'

'You never shouted at Om for doing it.'

'That's different. He's trained, he grew up with tailors.'

'No, he didn't. His family used to be cobblers.'

'Same thing – they know how to use tools, to cut and sew. And besides, I should have stopped him. His mouth can bleed just like yours.' She went to the kitchen, and he kept working till dinner was on the table.

Halfway through the meal, she remembered what he had said about the tailors. 'They were cobblers? Why did they change?'

'They requested me not to tell anyone. It's to do with their caste, they are afraid of being treated badly.'

'You can tell me. I don't believe in all those stupid customs.'

So he briefly related the story Ishvar and Om had shared with him in bits and pieces, over weeks, over cups of tea in the Vishram Vegetarian Hotel, about their village, about the landlords who had mistreated the Chamaars all their lives, the whippings, the beatings, the rules that the untouchable castes were forced to observe.

She stopped eating, toying with her fork. She rested an elbow on the table and balanced her chin on the fist. As he continued, the fork slipped from her fingers, clattering outside the plate. He concluded quickly when he came to the murders of the parents and children and grandparents.

Dina retrieved her fork. 'I never knew . . . I never thought . . . all those newspaper stories about upper- and lower-caste madness, suddenly so close to me. In my own flat. It's the first time I actually know the people. My God – such horrible, horrible suffering.' She shook her head as though in disbelief.

She tried to resume eating, then gave up. 'Compared to theirs, my life is nothing but comfort and happiness. And now they are in more trouble. I hope they come back all right. People keep saying God is great, God is just, but I'm not sure.'

'God is dead,' said Maneck. 'That's what a German philosopher wrote.'

She was shocked. 'Trust the Germans to say such things,' she frowned. 'And do you believe it?'

'I used to. But now I prefer to think that God is a giant quiltmaker. With an infinite variety of designs. And the quilt is grown so big and confusing, the pattern is impossible to see, the squares and diamonds and triangles don't fit well together anymore, it's all become meaningless. So He has abandoned it.'

'What nonsense you talk sometimes, Maneck.'

While she cleared the table he opened the kitchen window and miaowed. Out went bits of bread and alayti-palayti. Hoping it was not too pungent for the cats, he returned to the sewing room and picked up another dress, reminding Dina Aunty to hurry.

'This boy is going crazy. Not letting me rest even five minutes after dinner. I'm an old woman, not a young puppy like you.'

'You're not old at all, Aunty. In fact, you're quite young. And beautiful,' he added daringly.

'And you, Mr. Mac, are getting too smart,' she said, unable to hide her pleasure.

'There's only one thing that puzzles me.'

'What?'

'Why someone who looks so young should sound so elderly, grumpy all the time.'

'You rascal. First you flatter me, then you insult me.' She laughed as she folded and pinned the hem, holding up the dress to check if the border was even. Adjusting the edges, she said, 'Now I can appreciate the long nails on the tailors' fingers. You really became friends with them, didn't you? And them telling you all about their life in the village.'

He looked up briefly, and shrugged.

'Day after day they sat here working, and wouldn't say anything to me. Why?'

He shrugged again.

'Stop speaking with your shoulders. Your quiltmaking God has sewn a tongue inside your mouth. Why did they talk to you but not to me?'

'Maybe they were afraid of you.'

'*Afraid* of me? What nonsense. If anything, I was afraid of them. That they would find the export company and cut me out. Or that they would get better jobs. Sometimes I was afraid even to point out their errors – I would correct the mistakes myself at night, after they left. For what reason could they be afraid of me?'

'They thought you'd find better tailors and get rid of them.'

She considered it in silence for a moment. 'I wish you had told me before. I could have reassured them.'

He shrugged again. 'That wouldn't change anything, Aunty. You could have saved them only by giving them a place to sleep.'

She flung down the sewing. 'You keep on saying that! Keep on, don't worry about my feelings! Repeat it till I am blinded by guilt!'

Maneck pricked himself as the needle surfaced through the button. 'Ouch!' he sucked the thumb.

'Go on, you callous boy! Tell me I am responsible, tell me I left them out on the street because I am heartless!'

He wished he could cancel the hurt of his words. She fumbled with the hem, beginning to cough as though something was stuck. It sounded like an attention-getting cough to him, and he brought her a glass of water.

She said, after drinking, 'You were right about carrots. I can see much better.'

'It's a miracle!' he raised his hands theatrically, bringing a smile to her face. 'Now I am incarnated as Maharishi Carrot Baba, and all the opticians will lose their business!'

'Oh stop being silly,' she said, draining the glass. 'Let me tell you what I can see better. When I was twelve my father decided to go and work in an area of epidemic. It worried my mother very much. She wanted me to change his mind – you see, I was his favourite. Then my father died while working there. And my mother said if I had followed her advice I might have saved him.'

'That wasn't fair.'

'It was and it wasn't. Just like what you said.'

He understood.

Dina rose, lifted the glass hen squatting on the worktable, and put away the thimble, scissors, and needle in its porcelain bowels.

'Where are you going, Aunty?'

'Where do you think – to a Lalya's wedding? It's ten o'clock, I'm going to bed.'

'But we only finished sixteen dresses. Today's quota is twenty-two.'

'Listen to the senior manager.'

'My plan is to do twenty-two today, thirty tomorrow, and eight the day after, so everything can be delivered by noon.'

'Wait a minute, mister. What about college, tomorrow and the day after – what about studies? I don't think they give a refrigeration diploma for sewing buttons.'

'Lectures are cancelled for the next two days.'

'Right. And I'm winning the State Lottery on the third day.'

'Forget it, Aunty. You're always doubting me.' He continued to sew, exhaling injury and martyrdom in his sighs, dragging the needle as though its thread was an iron chain. 'It's okay, I'll keep working, you go to bed.'

'And miss your Oscar-winning performance?'

He dropped a button, groaned, and bent to find it, feeling about with his fingers like an old man. 'Go, Aunty, go and rest, don't worry about me,' he waved a trembling hand.

'You said you were good at acting, but I didn't think you were this good. Okay, let's finish one more dress.'

The bidding was open; he sat up briskly. 'We need six more for today's quota.'

'Forget your quota. I said one.'

'At least three, then.'

'Two is my final offer. And no more argument. But first I need something from the kitchen.'

She returned shortly, a steaming mug hooked in the fingers of each hand, and set one down beside him. 'Horlicks. To refresh us.' As proof, she took a swallow and sat tall in her chair, shoulders back, face beaming.

'You sound like an advertisement,' he said. 'And it doesn't even need a professional model, you look so pretty.

'Don't think flattery will get you a cup every day. I cannot afford that.'

Blowing and sipping, they joked their way through two more dresses. Near midnight, Dina's was the only light left on in the building. The lateness of the hour, the streets fallen silent outside the window, the flat enveloped in darkness, all lent a conspiratorial air to their innocent activity.

'That makes eighteen,' she said, as they finished after midnight. 'And not a single stitch left in these fingers. Now can we go to sleep, boss?'

'Soon as they are properly folded.'

'Yes, Mr. Mac Kohlah.'

'Please – I hate that name.'

While passing through to their rooms she hugged him, whispering, 'Good night. And thank you for helping.'

'Good night, Aunty,' he said, and floated happily to bed.

An hour before sunrise the whistle blast ended the night, snatching back the labourers from its dark, comforting bosom. They spilled out from the tin huts in a trickle towards the food area. Two pariah dogs sniffed at dusty feet, lost interest and slunk away around the kitchen. Tea was served with last night's chapatis. Then the whistle blew again to commence work.

The newcomers were assembled separately and assigned their chores by the foreman. There were jobs for everyone with the exception of the beggar on the rolling platform. 'You stay here,' said the foreman. 'I will decide later for you.'

Om was teamed with a group of six to start a new ditch. Ishvar's task was to carry gravel where concrete was being mixed. The foreman came to the end of the list, and the scraggy army dispersed to their locations as directed by the overseers. The tailors waited till everyone had gone.

'There is a mistake, sahab,' said Ishvar, approaching the foreman with his palms together.

'Name?'

'Ishvar Darji and Omprakash Darji.'

The foreman read off their assignments again. 'No mistake.'

'The mistake is that we should not be here, we –'

'All you lazy rascals think you should not be here. The government will no longer tolerate it. You *will* work. In return you will get food and a place to sleep.'

'We *have* work, we are tailors, and the policeman said to speak to you –'

'My duty is to give you jobs and shelter. You say no, and the security men will take you away.'

'But why are we being punished? What is our crime?'

'You are using the wrong word. It's not a question of crime and punishment – it's problem and solution.' He beckoned to two khaki-uniformed men patrolling with sticks. 'We have no trouble here, all the people are happy to work. Now you decide.'

'Okay,' said Ishvar. 'But we would like to talk to the top man.'

'The project manager will come later. He is busy with his morning prayers.'

The foreman personally escorted the tailors to the worksite. He handed them over to their respective supervisors with instructions to watch them carefully, to make sure they worked without slacking. The beggar rolled alongside them on his platform. Where the path ended, the rough terrain was impossible for his castors. He turned back, waving to the tailors, promising to wait by their hut in the evening.

The hillside was alive with a flock of tiny crouching figures. At first the children seemed frozen by sunlight; then the sound of their hammers revealed the movement of their hands. Pounding rock, making gravel. Clumps of dead grass pocked the sere slope. The greening hand of rain had yet to touch this earth. Occasionally, a boulder got away and crashed somewhere below. In the distance, the rumbling of earth movers, cranes, and cement mixers rose like a wall upon which the steady ring of stone-chipping hammers carved a pattern. From the sky, the sledge of heat pounded relentlessly.

A woman filled Ishvar's gravel basket and helped him hoist it to his head. The effort made her hands tremble, quivering the wrinkled skin pouches under her arms. He staggered beneath the weight. When she let go, he felt the load start to unbalance. He clawed the sides desperately, tilting his head the other way, but the falling basket fell, jerking his neck sharply.

'I have never done this kind of work,' he said, embarrassed by the heavy shower of gravel that stung their feet.

Wordlessly she slanted the basket against her shins and bent over to fill it again. Her skimpy grey plait slid forward over the shoulder. Wouldn't be much use to Rajaram the hair-collector, thought Ishvar absently. With each pull of the hoe her plastic bangles made dull clinks. Soft echoes of the stone-hammering children. He watched her forearms glisten with sweat, the powerful back and forth movement. Then he noticed, behind him, others in the backed-up gravel chain. He knelt to assist her, anxious to make up for his clumsiness. He scooped gravel into the basket with his hands.

'Filling is my task, carrying is yours,' she said.

'It's okay, I don't mind.'

'You don't, but the overseer will.'

Ishvar desisted, and asked if she had done this work a long time.

'Since I was a child.'

'Pay is good?'

'Enough to keep from starving.' She showed him how to hold his head and shoulders to carry the weight, and they raised the load. He staggered again but managed to retain the basket.

'See, it's easy once you learn to balance,' she encouraged, and pointed him on his way towards the men mixing concrete. Tottering, faltering several times, he reached his destination and dumped the gravel. Then it was back with the empty basket to the woman who filled it. Again, and again, and again.

A few trips, and the sweat was streaming down his face; the ground spun; he asked if he could go for a drink of water. The overseer refused. 'The bhistee will come when it's time for water.'

With the man watching, the woman filled the basket as slowly as she dared. Ishvar was grateful for the restful seconds she stole for him. He shut his eyes and took deep breaths.

'Pile it to the brim!' the overseer screamed, 'You are not paid for filling half-baskets!' She pulled in four additional hoefuls. While lifting the load she tipped it slightly to get rid of the extra weight.

Ishvar stumbled back and forth, fighting dizziness as the morning ground him down. His mind was emptied of all thought. The blasting at the other end of the site sent dust clouds rolling through the gravel area, and women pulled their saris over their noses. He felt that were it not for the pounding hammers to guide him, he would lose his way in the fog. The feeling of sightlessness persisted even when the air cleared. Clinging to the rope of sound, he hovered between the gravel and the concrete mixers.

It seemed an age before the water-carrier arrived. The stone-breaking hammers fell silent. Ishvar heard the slurp of thirsty tongues before he saw the man. The swollen waterskin hung from the bhistee's shoulder like a dark-brown animal, its leather strap cutting deep into him. His steps unsteady under the heavy bulge of water, the blind man passed among the labourers. Whoever was thirsty touched his hand to stop him. He sang softly, a song he had made up:

> O call to me and I
> Will quench your thirst for water.
> But who, on earth, can grant
> My parched eyes' desire?

Ishvar fell on his knees before the bhistee, positioned his mouth under the leather spout and drank. Then he moved his mouth, and cold water splashed over his grateful face. The overseer shouted, 'Careful, don't waste! That's for drinking only!' Ishvar rose hurriedly and returned to his gravel basket.

By the time the bhistee reached the place where Om was working, the waterskin had grown lighter. So had the bhistee's steps. The six ditch-diggers drank first, and then the women who were assigned to carry away the loosened earth. Their babies played near the ditch. The women scooped water in their palms to let the children slurp it.

Om wet his fingers and slicked back his hair. He pulled out his half-comb and whipped it through. 'Aray, hero-ka-batcha!' yelled the overseer. 'Get back to work!'

Om put away the comb, returning his ragged attention to the digging. He enjoyed the moment when the women bent over to gather up the rubble, their breasts hanging forward in their cholis. With the load on their heads, they repositioned their saris and walked away, tall and stately, their limbs flowing with liquid smoothness. Like Shanti at the tap, he thought, with the brass pot that made her hips sway.

As the hours strained to pass, the women were not enough to distract him from the torment of the work. Bent double at the ditch, the pickaxe unwieldy in hands accustomed to scissors and needle and thread, he struggled with the hard ground. The shame of seeming weak in the women's eyes kept him going. Blisters which had flared within minutes of commencing the job were now in full eruption. He could barely straighten his back, and his shoulders were on fire.

One of the babies by the ditch started to cry. The mother dropped her basket and went to it. 'Saali lazy woman,' said the overseer. 'Get back to work.'

'But baby is crying.' She picked up the child. Its tears were tracing glistening paths down the dust-coated cheeks.

'It's natural for babies to cry. They cry and then they stop. Don't give me excuses.' He moved towards her as though to take it from her arms. She returned it gently to the rubble, to amuse itself.

When the whistle sounded for lunch, Om, like Ishvar, felt he was too exhausted to eat the watery mix of vegetables. But they knew they must, if they were to survive the rest of the day. They swallowed the food quickly and slipped into the shadow of their tin hut to rest a little.

The whistle ended the lunch break. Within minutes of returning to the site they started retching; a gush of vomit followed. Emptying their bellies took a fraction of the time spent in filling them. Fighting dizziness, they hunkered down, refusing to move. Close to the ground they felt safe.

The overseer whacked their heads a couple of times, pulled at their collars, and shook them by the shoulders. The tailors moaned to be excused. The foreman was sent for.

'What's the matter now? You are determined to make trouble or what?' asked the foreman.

'We are sick,' said Ishvar. As proof, he pointed to the two pools of vomit being investigated by a crow. 'We are not used to this kind of work.'

'You will get used to it.'

'We want to meet the manager.'

'He is not here.' The foreman put a hand under Ishvar's arm and pulled. Ishvar rose, swaying from side to side, his mouth vomit-streaked, and lurched towards the foreman. The latter pushed him back hastily, afraid of getting vomit on himself. 'Okay, go. Sleep for some time. I will see you later.'

No one bothered them for the rest of the day in the tin hut. At dusk they heard people proceeding towards the kitchen area. Ishvar asked Om if he wanted to eat. 'Yes, I'm hungry,' he said, and they sat up. Feeling dizzy again, they lay down. They did not resist the returning drowsiness.

Some time later the beggar rolled in on his platform, with food. He paddled very slowly, taking care not to spill the dinner balanced upon his stumps. 'I saw you becoming sick. Eat, it will give you strength. But chew properly, no rushing.'

The tailors thanked him for the food. He watched with satisfaction as they took the first bite, refusing to share. 'I've already eaten.'

Ishvar emptied the water mug, and the beggar started rolling to fetch more. 'Wait, I'll get it,' said Om. 'I'm all right now.'

The beggar was having none of that, and soon returned with a full mug. He inquired if they wanted extra chapatis. 'I made friends with someone in the kitchen, I can get as many as I like.'

'No no, bas, we are full, thank you,' said Ishvar, then asked him his name.

'Everybody calls me Worm.'

'Why?'

'I told you, babu. Before my Beggarmaster gave me the gaadi, I used to crawl around.'

'But now you have the gaadi. What's your real name?'

'Shankar.'

He stayed with them for another half-hour, chatting, describing the irrigation project where he had been wandering all day. Then he suggested they try to sleep and wake up strong for tomorrow's work. In a few minutes, when they were snoring lightly, he rowed away on his platform, smiling happily to himself.

ix What Law There Is

OUT OF A DOORWAY a woman beckoned to Dina, and furtively displayed a basket. 'Tamaater, bai?' the woman whispered. 'Big, fresh tamaater?'

Dina shook her head. She, as always, was searching for tailors, not tomatoes. Further ahead, someone stood concealed in an alcove with a box of leather wallets; another half-hidden man balanced a stack of bananas in his arms. Everyone was on the lookout for the police and ready to run. The rubble of broken stalls littered the ground.

She wandered through several bleak streets where pavement life had been sucked away by the Emergency. But perhaps her chances of finding replacements for Ishvar and Om were better now, she comforted herself. Perhaps the tailors who used to ply their trade from roadside stalls would seek alternate work.

Delivering the final dresses to Au Revoir Exports, she had casually advised Mrs. Gupta that her employees were going on a two-week vacation. As the tailorless fortnight drew to a close, however, she realized her optimism was misplaced. The manager had to be informed that resumption of work was being further postponed.

Dina started by praising Mrs. Gupta's hair. 'It looks lovely. Did you just come from Venus Beauty Salon?'

'No,' said Mrs. Gupta grouchily. 'I had to go to a strange place. Zenobia has let me down.'

'What happened?'

'I needed an urgent appointment, and she said to me she was all booked up. To me – her most faithful client.'

Oh no, thought Dina, wrong topic. 'By the way, my tailors have been delayed.'

'That's very inconvenient. For how long?'

'I'm not sure, maybe two more weeks. They have fallen sick in their village.'

'That's what they all say. Too many production days are lost to such excuses. Probably drinking and dancing in their village. We are Third World in development, but first class in absenteeism and strikes.'

Stupid woman, thought Dina. If she only knew how hard poor Ishvar and Om worked, and how much they had suffered.

'Never mind,' said Mrs. Gupta. 'The Emergency is good medicine for the nation. It will soon cure everyone of their bad habits.'

Wishing the manager's head could be cured of its chronic brainlessness, she agreed. 'Yes, that would be a great improvement.'

'Two more weeks, then – and no more delays, Mrs. Dalal. Delays are the by-products of disorder. Remember, strict rules and firm supervision lead to success. Indiscipline is the mother of chaos, but the fruits of discipline are sweet.'

Dina listened in disbelief, and said goodbye. She wondered if Mrs. Gupta had taken up writing slogans for the Emergency, as a sideline or hobby. Or perhaps she had suffered an overdose of the government's banners and posters, and lost the capacity for normal speech.

While the manager's words hung like an ultimatum over Dina and the second fortnight commenced, the rent-collector arrived on his appointed day. He lifted his right hand towards the maroon fez as if to raise it. Stiffness in his shoulder kept the greeting incomplete. The hand dropped to the collar of his black sherwani, tugging it in a surrogate salutation.

'Oh, rent-collector,' she sniffed. 'Wait. I'll bring the money.'

'Thank you, sister,' smiled Ibrahim winsomely, as the door shut in his face. He relinquished the collar to rub his snuff-streaked nostrils. His fingers missed the light shower of brown dust that had rained on his clean-shaven upper lip, stark amid the full white beard.

He felt under the sherwani, got hold of the tip of his handkerchief, and pulled. He mopped his brow, then thrust it back into the trouser pocket, pushing repeatedly till all but a dangling corner disappeared.

Sighing, he leaned against the wall. Midday, and he was exhausted. Even if he finished his rounds early, there was nowhere to go – from nine a.m. to nine p.m. he had rented his room to a mill-worker on night shift. Doomed to roam the streets, Ibrahim occupied park benches, sat on bus-shelter stiles, sipped a glass of tea at a corner stall till it was time to return home and sleep in the mill-worker's smell. This was life? Or a cruel joke? He no longer believed that the scales would ever balance fairly. If his pan was not empty, if there was some little sustenance in it for his days and nights, it was enough for him. Now he expected nothing better from the Maker of the Universe.

He decided to find Dina's receipt while waiting outside her door. Cautiously, the rubber band was pulled upwards. He brought it safely as far as the edge of the folder, then it snapped, stinging his nose and making him drop the folder.

The contents scattered. He went down on his knees to recover the precious pieces of paper. His hands fluttered methodlessly among them. For every two he picked up, one slipped from his fingers. A slight breeze rustled the pages ominously, and he panicked. He swept with his palms to gather them together, not caring that the sheets were being crumpled.

Dina opened the door with the rent money in her hand. For a second she thought the old man had fallen. She bent to help. Then, realizing what had happened, she straightened away from the landlord's emissary, watching the enemy's discomfort.

'Sorry,' he smiled upwards. 'Old hands are clumsy hands, what to do.' He managed to cram everything back inside the plastic folder. The large rubber band was slipped around a wrist for safekeeping. He rose to his feet, and staggered. Dina's hand shot out to steady him.

'Heh, heh, don't worry. Legs are still working, I think.'

'Please count it,' she sternly presented the money.

With both hands clutching the unsecured folder, the money remained unaccepted. He listened intently for the chatter of the sewing-machines. Nothing. 'Please, sister, can I sit for a minute to find your receipt? Or everything will fall again to the ground. Hands are shaking too much.'

The need for a chair was real, she knew, and he would exploit it, without question. 'Sure, come in,' she opened wide the door. There was nothing to lose today.

Excitement augmented Ibrahim's tremors of fatigue. At last, after months of trying, he was inside. 'All the papers are mixed up,' he said apologetically, 'but I'll find your receipt, don't worry, sister.' He listened again for sounds from the back room. Ah, but they were quiet as mice, of course.

'Yes, here it is, sister.' The name and address were already entered. He filled in the amount received and the date. A signature writhed its way across the revenue stamp at the bottom, and the money was taken.

'Count it, please.'

'No need, sister. A twenty years' tenant like you – if I cannot trust you, who can I trust?' Then he began counting it all the same. 'Only to make you happy.' From an inside pocket of the sherwani he withdrew a thick wad of notes and thickened it further with Dina's contribution. Like the plastic folder, the money was secured by a rubber band.

'Now,' he said, 'what else can I do for you while I am here? Taps leaking? Anything broken? Plaster all right in the back room?'

'I'm not sure.' The cheek of it, she thought indignantly. Tenants could complain till they were exhausted, and here this crook was pretending with his automatic smile. 'Better check for yourself.'

'Whatever is your wish, sister.'

In the back room he rapped the walls with his knuckles. 'Plaster is fine,' he muttered, unable to hide his disappointment at the silent sewing-machines. Then, as though noticing the Singers for the first time, he said, 'You have *two* machines in this room.'

'There is no law against two machines, is there?'

'Not at all, I was just asking. Although these days, with this crazy Emergency, you can never tell what law there is. The government surprises us daily.' His laugh was hollow, and she wondered if a threat was concealed in the words.

'One has a light needle, the other heavy,' she improvised. 'Presser feet and tensions are also different. I do a lot of sewing – my curtains, bedsheets, dresses. You need special machines for all that.'

'They look exactly the same to me, but what do I know about sewing?' They went into Maneck's room, and Ibrahim decided to put subtlety aside. 'So this must be where the young man lives.'

'What?'

'The young man, sister. Your paying guest.'

'How dare you! How dare you suggest I keep young men in my flat! Is that the kind of woman you think I am? Just because –'

'Please, no, that's not –'

'Don't you dare insult me, and then interrupt me! Just because I am a poor defenceless widow, people think they can get away with saying filthy things! Such courage you have, such bravery, when it comes to abusing a weak and lonely woman!'

'But sister, I –'

'What has happened to manhood today? Instead of protecting the honour of women, they indulge in smearing and defiling the innocent. And you! You, with your beard so white, saying such nasty, shameful things! Have you no mother, no daughter? You should be ashamed of yourself!'

'Please forgive me, I meant no harm, I only –'

'Meant no harm is easy to say, after the damage is done!'

'No sister, what damage? A foolish old man like me repeats a silly rumour, and begs your forgiveness.'

Ibrahim made his escape clutching the plastic folder. The attempt to raise his fez in farewell was, like the earlier greeting, short-circuited. He substituted again with a yank at the sherwani's collar. 'Thank you, sister, thank you. I will come next month, with your permission. Your humble servant.'

She played with the idea of taking him to task for using 'sister' so hypocritically. He had been let off too lightly towards the end, she felt. Still, he was an old man. She would have preferred to scold a younger hireling of the landlord's.

In the afternoon she re-enacted the scene for Maneck, some sections twice at his urging. He enjoyed it the most when she came to the slandered-woman bit. 'Did I show you my pose for the harassed and helpless woman?' She crossed her arms with hands on shoulders, shielding her bosom. 'I stood like this. As if he was going to attack me. Poor fellow actually looked away in shame. I was so mean. But he deserved it.'

Their laughter acquired a touch of brave desperation after a while, like slicing a loaf very thin and pretending that bread was plentiful. Then the quiet in the room was sudden. The last crumb of fun had been yielded by the rent-collector's visit.

'The play is acted and the money digested,' she said.

'At least the rent is paid up, and water and electricity too.'

'We cannot eat electricity.'

'You can have my pocket money, I don't need it this month,' he said, reaching for his wallet.

She leaned forward and touched his cheek.

Another fortnight flew by, as swiftly, it seemed to Dina, as the rows of stitches that used to spill merrily from the Singers during happier days. She did not notice that already, in her memory, those months with Ishvar and Om, of fretting and tardiness, quarrels and crooked seams, had been transmuted into something precious, to be remembered with yearning.

Towards the end of the month, the hire-purchase man came to inquire about the sewing-machines. The instalment was overdue. She showed him the Singers to prove they were safe, and talked him into a grace period. 'Don't worry, bhai, the tailors can cover your payment three times over. But an urgent family matter has delayed them in their native place.'

Her daylong searches for new tailors continued to yield nothing. Maneck sometimes went with her, and she was grateful for his company. He made the dreary wanderings less dispiriting. Happy to skip college, he would have gone more often were it not for her threats to write to his parents. 'Don't create extra problems for me,' she said. 'As it is, if I don't have two tailors by next week, I will have to borrow from Nusswan for the rent.' She shuddered at the prospect. 'I'll have to listen to all his rubbish again – I told you so, get married again, stubbornness breeds unhappiness.'

'I'll come with you if you like.'

'That would be nice.'

At night, they busied themselves with the quilt. The stack of remnants was shrinking in the absence of new material, making her resort to pieces she had avoided so far, like the flimsy chiffon, not really suitable for her design. They sewed it into little rectangular pouches and stuffed in fragments of more substantial cloth. When the chiffon ran out, the quilt ceased to grow.

'Welcome,' the foreman greeted the Facilitator, as he delivered a fresh truckload of pavement-dwellers at the work camp.

The Facilitator bowed and presented an enormous cellophane-wrapped box of dry fruits. He was making a tidy profit between what he paid Sergeant Kesar and what he collected from the foreman; the wheels had to be kept oiled.

Cashews, pistachios, almonds, raisins, apricots were visible through the windows in the lid. 'For your wife and children,' said the Facilitator, adding, 'Please, please take it, no,' as the foreman made a show of refusing. 'It's nothing, just a small token of appreciation.'

The project manager, too, was delighted with the arrival of new pavement-dwellers. The scheme allowed him great liberties in manipulating the payroll. What the free labour lacked in efficiency, it made up in numbers. The expanding irrigation project no longer needed to hire extra paid workers.

In fact, a few were laid off; and the remaining day-labourers began to feel threatened. In their view, this influx of starving, shrivelled, skeletal beings was turning into an enemy army. Regarded at first with pity or amusement as they struggled with puny little tasks, the beggars and pavement-dwellers now seemed like invaders bent on taking away their livelihood. The paid workers began directing their resentment at them.

Harassment of the newcomers was constant. Abuse, pushing, shoving became commonplace. A spade handle would emerge out of a ditch to trip somebody. From scaffoldings and raised platforms, spit descended like bird droppings but with greater accuracy. At mealtimes a flurry of suddenly clumsy elbows overturned their plates, and since the rules denied a second serving, the beggars and pavement-dwellers often ate off the ground. Most of them were used to foraging in garbage, but the water-thin dal soaked quickly into dry earth. Only solids like chapati or bits of vegetable could be salvaged.

Their supplications to the foreman were ignored. The view from the top showed a smooth, economical operation with little need for managerial intervention.

By the end of the first week, Ishvar and Om felt they had spent an eternity in this hell. They were barely able to rise for the dawn whistle. Dizzy spells made the world dance around them when they got out of bed. Their morning steadied somewhat after their glass of strong, over-boiled tea. They staggered through the day, listening to the bewildering threats and insults of overseers and paid workers. They fell asleep early in the evening, cradled in the scrawny lap of exhaustion.

One night their chappals were stolen while they slept. They wondered if it was one of the men who shared the tin hut with them. They went barefoot to complain to the foreman, hoping he would issue replace-ments for them.

'You should have been more careful,' said the foreman, stooping to buckle his sandals. 'How can I guard everybody's chappals? Anyway, it's not a big problem. Sadhus and fakirs all travel with naked feet. And so does M. F. Husain.'

'Who is M. F. Husain, sahab?' asked Ishvar humbly. 'Government minister?'

'He is a very famous artist in our country. He never covers his feet because he does not want to lose contact with Mother Earth. So why do you need chappals?'

There was no footwear available in the camp supplies. The tailors looked inside their hut one more time in case someone had taken the chappals by mistake. Then they walked carefully to the worksite, trying to avoid sharp stones.

'I will soon get back the feet of my childhood,' said Ishvar. 'You know, your grandfather Dukhi never wore chappals. And your father and I could not afford our first pair till we had finished apprenticing with Ashraf Chacha. By then our feet had become like leather – as though the Chamaars had tanned them, tough as cowhide.'

In the evening Ishvar claimed that his soles were already hardening. He examined the dust-caked skin with satisfaction, enjoying the rough-ness under his fingers. But it was excruciating for Om. He had never gone with unprotected feet.

At the start of the second week, Ishvar's dizziness persisted past the morning glass of tea, getting worse under the burgeoning dome of heat. The sun battered his head like a giant fist. Towards noon, he stumbled and fell into a ditch with his load of gravel.

'Take him to Doctor sahab,' the overseer ordered two men. Ishvar put his arms over their shoulders and hopped on one foot to the work camp's dispensary.

Before Ishvar could tell Doctor sahab what had happened, the white-coated man turned away towards an array of tubes and bottles. Most were empty; nevertheless, the display looked impressive. He selected an ointment while Ishvar, balancing on one leg, held up his injured ankle to encourage an examination. 'Doctor sahab, it's paining over there.'

He was told to put his foot down. 'Nothing broken, don't worry. This ointment will cure your pain.'

The white-coated man gave him permission to rest for the remainder of the day. Shankar spent a lot of time with Ishvar in the hut, leaving at intervals on his rolling platform to fetch food and tea. 'No, babu, don't get up, tell me what you want.'

'But I have to make water.'

Shankar slipped off his platform and motioned to him to get on. 'You shouldn't put weight upon your injured foot,' he said.

Ishvar was touched that he who had no feet should care so much about another's. He seated himself gingerly on the platform, crossed his legs, and began rolling, using his hands the way Shankar did. It was not as easy as it looked, he discovered. The trip to the latrine and back exhausted his arms.

'Did you like my gaadi?' asked Shankar.

'Very comfortable.'

The next day Ishvar had to leave his bedding and hobble to the gravel area, though his ankle was swollen and painful. The overseer told him to fill baskets with the women instead of transporting them. 'You can do that job sitting down,' he said.

There were other accidents too, more severe than Ishvar's. A blind woman, set to crushing rocks, had, after several successful days, smashed her fingers with the hammer. A child fell from a scaffolding and broke both legs. An armless man, carrying sand in panniers on a shoulder yoke, suffered neck injuries when he lost his balance and the yoke slipped.

By week's end, scores of newcomers were classified as useless by the foreman. Doctor sahab treated them with his favourite ointment. In his more inspired moments he even used splints and bandages. Shankar was assigned to ferrying the patients' meals. He enjoyed the task, looking forward eagerly to mealtimes, paddling his platform from the hot kitchen to the groaning huts with a newfound sense of purpose. At every stop he was showered with the invalids' grateful thanks and blessings.

What he really wanted, though, was to nurse their injuries and alleviate their pain, which Doctor sahab seemed unable to do. 'I don't think he is a very clever doctor,' he confided to Ishvar and Om. 'He keeps using the same medicine for everyone.'

The patients cried out for help through the long, hot days, and

Shankar talked to them, moistened their brows with water, gave them assurances of better times to come. When the workers returned in the evening, hungry and exhausted, the ceaseless moaning irritated them. It continued deep into the night, and they could not sleep. After a few nights, someone finally went to complain.

Annoyed at being awakened, the foreman admonished the injured. 'Doctor sahab is looking after you so well. What more do you people want? If we took you to a hospital, you think you'd be better off than here? Hospitals are so overcrowded, so badly run, the nurses will throw you in filthy corridors and leave you to rot. Here at least you have a clean place to rest.'

Over the next few days, the foreman, shorthanded, was forced to rehire the laid-off paid workers. They quickly realized this was the answer to their problem: incapacitate the free labour, and the jobs would return.

Animosity towards the beggars and pavement-dwellers reached dangerous proportions. The day-labourers began pushing them off ledges and scaffoldings, swung carelessly with pickaxes, let boulders accidentally roll down hillsides. The number of casualties increased sharply. Shankar welcomed his new charges. He poured his entire soul into the added responsibility.

Now the project manager took a different view of the victims' complaints. Security staff was increased, and ordered to patrol the worksite at all times, not just at night. Day-labourers were warned that negligence on the job would be punished by dismissal. The attacks decreased, but the irrigation project began to look like an armed camp.

The next time the Facilitator arrived with a fresh load of pavement-dwellers, the foreman complained that his free labour was a bad investment. He pretended the injuries had been sustained prior to their arrival. 'You have stuck me with feeding and housing too many unproductive cripples.'

The Facilitator opened his register to the delivery date in question, and showed him details pertaining to the detainees' physical condition. 'I admit there were a few bad ones. But that's not my fault. The police shoves everybody, living and half-dead, into my truck.'

'In that case, I don't want any more.'

The Facilitator tried to pacify the foreman and rescue the deal. 'Give me a few days, no, I'll sort something out. I'll make sure you won't suffer a total loss.'

In the meantime, the latest consignment waiting to be unloaded from the truck included various types of street performers. There were jugglers, musicians, acrobats, and magicians. The foreman decided to give them a choice – join the labour force like the other pavement-dwellers, or entertain the camp in return for boarding and lodging.

The entertainers chose the latter option, as the foreman had expected. They were housed separately from the rest, and told to prepare for a performance that night. The project manager agreed with the foreman's proposal. The diversion would be good for the morale of the labourers, and would help relieve the tension and bad blood threatening the work camp.

The show was held after dinner, under the lights of the eating area. The security captain agreed to be master of ceremonies. Tumbling tricks, a man juggling wooden clubs, and a tightrope walker started the proceedings. Then there was a musical interlude with patriotic songs, which elicited a standing ovation from the project manager. Next, a husband-and-wife contortionist team proved very popular, followed by card tricks and more jugglers.

Shankar, who sat with Ishvar and Om to watch the entertainment, was having a splendid time, bouncing on the platform with excitement, clapping heartily, though his bandaged palms only produced muffled reports. 'I wish the others could also enjoy,' he said from time to time, thinking of his patients in the tin huts. He could hear their groans during the moments of quiet when the audience became silent, tense with anxiety, as a performer did something particularly daring with knives and swords or on the tightrope.

The project manager kept nodding approvingly at the foreman; the decision had been a good one. The last entertainer was waiting in the kitchen's shadow. The props of the previous act were cleared away. The security captain announced that for the finale they would witness an amazing display of balancing. The performer stepped into the light.

'It's Monkey-man!' said Om.

'And his sister's two children,' said Ishvar. 'Must be the new act he told us he was planning.'

The children were not included in Monkey-man's opening move, some brief juggling of the sort already seen. It was received poorly. Now he introduced the little girl and boy, lifting them in the air, one in the palm of each hand. Both had colds, and sneezed. He proceeded to tie them to the ends of a fifteen-foot pole. Then he lowered himself to the ground, rolled onto his back, and balanced the pole horizontally on the soles of his bare feet. When it was steady, he began spinning it with his toes. The children revolved on the rudimentary merry-go-round, slowly at first, while he assayed the equilibrium and the rhythm, then faster and faster. They hung limply, making no sound, their bodies a blur.

The cheering was scattered, the audience anxious and uncertain. Then the clapping became urgent, as though they hoped the hazardous feat would end if they gave the man his due, or, at the very least, the applause would somehow sustain the balance, keep the children safe.

The pole began to slow down, and stopped. Monkey-man untied the children and wiped their mouths; centrifugal force had drawn a stream of mucus from their runny noses. Next he laid them face to face on the ground. This time they were both tied to the same end of the pole, their feet resting on a little crossbar. He tested the bindings and erected the pole.

The children were lifted high above the ground. Their faces disappeared into the night, beyond the reach of the kitchen lights. The audience gasped. He raised the pole higher, gave it a little toss, and caught the end upon his palm. His stringy arm muscles quivered. He moved the pole to and fro, making the top end sway like a treetop in a breeze. Then another little toss, and the pole was balanced on his thumb.

A cascade of protest spilled from the spectators. Doubt and reproach swirled in the area of darkness around Monkey-man. In the deafness of his concentration he heard nothing. He started walking back and forth within the circle of light, then running, tossing the pole from thumb to thumb.

'It's too dangerous,' said Ishvar. 'I don't find it enjoyable.' Shankar shook his head too, mesmerized on his platform, swaying his trunk to the swaying of the pole.

'Would have been better if he stuck to monkeys,' said Om, his eyes fixed on the tiny figures in the sky.

Then Monkey-man threw his head back and balanced the pole on his brow. People rose angrily to their feet. 'Stop it!' yelled someone. 'Stop it before you kill them!'

Others joined in, 'Saala shameless budmaas! Torturing innocent children!'

'Saala gandoo! Save it for the mohallas of the heartless rich! We are not interested in watching!'

The shouting dislocated Monkey-man's focus. He could hear again. He hurriedly lowered the pole and untied the children. 'What's wrong? I'm not mistreating them. Ask them yourself, they enjoy it. Everybody has to make a living.'

But the uproar did not give him much of a chance to defend himself. Even more than Monkey-man, people were upset with the foreman who had arranged this cruel entertainment, and they screamed at him to let him know. 'Monster from somewhere! Worse than Ravan!'

The security guards quickly dispersed the audience to their huts for the night, while the project manager's former approval turned to censure. He shook his finger in the foreman's face. 'It was an error in judgement on your part. These people neither need nor appreciate kindness. If you are nice to them, they sit on your head. Hard work is the only formula.'

No more performances were scheduled. Next day the street entertainers were apportioned among various work crews. Monkey-man became the most unpopular person in the irrigation project, and before the week was out he joined the casualties with severe head injuries. Ishvar and Om felt sorry for him because they knew he was really so tenderhearted.

'Remember the old woman's prophecy?' said Om. 'The night his monkeys died?'

'Yes,' said Ishvar. 'About killing his dog and committing an even worse murder. Right now, the poor fellow looks as though he himself has been murdered.'

The Facilitator returned to the irrigation project a fortnight later with someone he introduced to the foreman as 'the man who will solve your crippling labour problems.'

The foreman and the Facilitator laughed at the joke. The new man's face remained deadly serious, acquiring a hint of displeasure.

They went to the tin huts where the injured were prostrate, forty-two in all. Shankar was trundling back and forth among them, stroking one's forehead, patting another's back, whispering, comforting. The smell of festering wounds and unwashed bodies wafted through the doors, nauseating the foreman.

'I'll be in my office if you need me,' he excused himself.

The visitor said he would prefer to take a quick look at the injuries and estimate their potential. 'Only then can I make a reasonable offer.'

They stepped inside the first hut, temporarily blinded by the move from harsh sunlight into semidarkness. Shankar wheeled his platform around to see who it was. Craning his neck, he let out a shriek of recognition.

'Who's that?' said the visitor. 'Worm?' His eyes had not adjusted to the interior, but he knew the familiar rumble of rolling castors. 'So this is where you are. All these weeks I wondered what happened to you.'

Shankar paddled his platform towards the man's feet, his palms flailing the ground excitedly. 'Beggarmaster! The police took me away! I did not want to go!' Relief and anxiety merged in his sobs as he clutched the man's shins. 'Beggarmaster, please help me, I want to go home!'

The distraction in the hut prompted the injured to start moaning and coughing, pleading for attention, hoping that this stranger, whoever he was, had at long last brought them deliverance. The Facilitator moved closer to the door for fresh air.

'Don't worry, Worm, of course I'll take you back,' said Beggarmaster. 'How can I do without my best beggar?' He completed a quick inspection of the disabled and turned to leave. Shankar wanted to accompany him right then, but was told to wait. 'First I have to make some arrangements.'

Outside, Beggarmaster asked the Facilitator, 'Is Worm included in the lot?'

'Of course he is.'

'I won't pay you for what is already mine. I inherited him from my father. And my father had him since he was a child.'

'But see it from my side, no,' bargained the Facilitator. 'I had to pay the police for him.'

'Forget all that. I am willing to give two thousand rupees for the lot. Worm included.'

The amount was higher than the Facilitator had expected. Taking into account the rebate promised to the foreman, he would still make a nice profit. 'We have much business ahead of us,' he said, concealing his delight. 'I don't want to haggle. Two thousand is okay, you can take your Worm.' He chuckled. 'And any bugs or centipedes that you like.'

A look of disapproval darkened Beggarmaster's face. This time he sharply rebuked the Facilitator. 'I don't like people making fun of my beggars.'

'I meant no harm.'

'One more thing. Your truck must take them back to the city – that's part of the price.'

The Facilitator agreed. He led Beggarmaster to the kitchen and brought him a glass of tea to make up for offending him. Then he went to find the foreman, whose cut was still to be negotiated.

Rowing full tilt, Shankar sped to tell his two friends the happy news, but was intercepted by the overseer, who refused to let the rhythm of the work be interrupted. He shooed him away, stamping his foot, pretending to pick up a stone. Shankar retreated.

He waited till the lunch whistle blew, and caught up with Ishvar and Om near the eating area. 'Beggarmaster has found me! I'm going home!'

Om bent to pat his shoulder, and Ishvar comforted him, 'Yes, it's okay, Shankar, don't worry. One day we'll all go home, when the work is finished.'

'No, I am going home tomorrow, really! My Beggarmaster is here!' They continued to disbelieve till he explained in more detail.

'But why are you so happy to go?' asked Ishvar. 'You are not suffering like us slaves. Free meals, a little fetching and carrying on your gaadi.

Don't you prefer this to begging?'

'I did enjoy it for a while, especially looking after you, and the other sick ones. But now I miss the city.'

'You're lucky,' said Om. 'This work is going to kill us, for sure. Wish we could go back with you.'

'I can ask Beggarmaster to take you. Let's talk with him.'

'Yes, but we . . . okay, ask him.'

They found Beggarmaster sipping tea on a bench near the kitchen. Shankar rolled up and tugged at his trouser cuff. 'What's the matter, Worm? I asked you to wait in the hut.' But he left his tea to kneel beside him, listening, nodding, then tousling his hair and laughing. He came over to the tailors.

'Worm says you are his friends. He wants me to help you.'

'Hahnji, please, we will be very grateful.'

He sized them up doubtfully. 'Do you have any experience?'

'Oh yes. Many years' experience,' said Ishvar.

Beggarmaster was sceptical. 'It doesn't look to me like you could be successful.'

Om was indignant. 'I can tell you we are very successful.' He held up his two little fingers like votive candles. 'Our long nails have broken in all this rough work, but they will grow back. We are fully trained, we can even take measurements straight from the customer's body.'

Beggarmaster began to laugh. 'Measurements from the body?'

'Of course. We are skilled tailors, not hacks who –'

'Forget it. I thought you wanted to work for me as beggars. I have no need for tailors.'

Their hopes crashed. 'We are no good here, we keep falling sick,' they pleaded. 'Can you not take us? We can pay you for your trouble.' Shankar added his appeal to theirs, that they had been so kind to him from the moment the police had thrown him in the truck that terrible night, almost two months ago.

Beggarmaster and the Facilitator discussed the deal in low voices. The latter wanted two hundred rupees per tailor, because, he said, he would have to make it attractive for the foreman to release two able-bodied specimens: Ishvar's sprained ankle did not qualify.

Gripping his tea glass, Beggarmaster returned to the tailors. 'You can come if the foreman agrees. But it will cost you.'

'How much?'

'Usually, when I look after a beggar, I charge one hundred rupees per week. That includes begging space, food, clothes, and protection. Also, special things like bandages or crutches.'

'Yes, Shankar – Worm – told us about it. He praised you and said you are a very kind Beggarmaster. What luck for him that you came here.'

Pleased as he was with the compliment, he clarified the matter without undue modesty. 'Luck has little to do with it. I am the most famous Beggarmaster in the city. Naturally, the Facilitator contacted me. Anyway, your case is different, you don't need looking after in the same way. Besides, you've been good to Worm. Just pay me fifty a week per person, for one year. That will be enough.'

They were staggered. 'That means almost two thousand five hundred each!'

'Yes, it's minimum for what I am offering.'

The tailors calculated the payments between them. 'Three days' worth of sewing each week will go to him,' whispered Ishvar. 'That's too much, we won't be able to afford it.'

'What choice?' said Om. 'You want to toil to death, in this Narak of heartless devils? Just say yes.'

'Wait, I'll bring him down a bit.' Ishvar approached the man with a worldly expression on his face. 'Listen, fifty is too much – we'll give you twenty-five a week.'

'Get one thing straight,' said Beggarmaster coldly. 'I'm not selling onions and potatoes in the bazaar. My business is looking after human lives. Don't try to bargain with me.' He turned away disdainfully to go back to the kitchen bench.

'Now look what you've done!' said Om, panicking. 'Our only chance is finished!'

Ishvar waited a moment and shuffled back to Beggarmaster. 'We talked it over. It's expensive, but we'll take it.'

'You're sure you can afford it?'

'Oh yes, we have good jobs, regular work.'

Beggarmaster nibbled his thumbnail and spat. 'Sometimes, one of my clients will vanish without paying, after enjoying my hospitality. But I always manage to find him. And then there is big trouble for him. Please remember that.' He finished his tea and accompanied the Facilitator to make a renewed offer to the foreman.

When the lunch hour ended, the tailors were reluctant to rejoin the gravel gang and ditch-diggers. With the promise of rescue so close, their resignation to the back-breaking labour vaporized; fatigue overwhelmed them.

'Aray babu, just be a little patient,' said Shankar. 'It's only one more day, don't cause any trouble. You don't want them to beat you. Stop worrying now, the foreman will agree, my Beggarmaster is very influential.'

Bolstered by Shankar's encouragement, they found the strength to return to the overseer. In the late afternoon, they listened anxiously for the bhistee's song. His arrival signalled the last two hours of work. They drank from his waterskin and got through the remainder of the day.

At dusk, when they stumbled back to their hut, Shankar was waiting, squirming excitedly on his platform. 'It's all decided. They are taking us tomorrow morning. Stay ready with your bedding, don't miss the truck. Now I must make my preparations.'

He went to find the mechanic in charge of heavy machinery, who gave him oil for his castors. The grit and dust of the construction site was beginning to slow them down. Shankar wanted the platform in prime condition for his return to the pavement. He brought back the can cradled against his stomach. Om helped to lubricate the sluggish wheels.

Early next morning, a security guard ordered Shankar, the tailors, and the injured to assemble at the gate with their things. Those unable to walk were carried by men seconded from a work detail. They did it resentfully, grudging the invalids their imminent freedom. It was the tailors, however, who bore the brunt of the embittered glances.

'See how lucky we are, Om,' said Ishvar, gazing upon the damaged bodies accumulating in the truck. 'We could be lying here with broken bones if our stars were not in the proper position.'

Monkey-man was still comatose from his head injury, and Beggarmaster refused to take him. But he wanted the children; they had real potential, he said. The little boy and girl resisted removal, weeping and clinging to their motionless uncle. They had to be dragged away when the truck was ready to leave.

The Facilitator and foreman balanced the debits and credits with a rebate towards the next delivery. Then there was a short delay. The foreman insisted that clothing issued on arrival be removed before departure – he had to account for every article to his superiors.

'Take what you want,' said Beggarmaster. 'But please hurry, I have to get back in time for a temple ceremony.'

The ones who had been carried to the truck were incapable of undressing themselves. The workers, about to return to their regular tasks, were ordered to assist them. They vented their frustration by tugging the garments roughly off the injured bodies. Beggarmaster did not pay attention to it. When Shankar's turn came, however, he made sure they were gentle with his vest.

Now the pavement-dwellers were as naked, or half-naked, as the day they had entered the labour camp; the gate opened and the truck was allowed to leave.

Dressing up to visit Nusswan's office was Maneck's idea. 'We should go there looking tiptop. He'll give you more respect. Appearances are very important to some people.'

In Dina's present state, anything that sounded like half-sensible advice was welcome. She touched up his grey gabardine trousers with the iron. For herself, she selected her most effective frock, the blue one from her second wedding anniversary, with the vivacious peplum that came alive with walking. Would it still fit? she wondered. Shutting the adjoining door, she tried it on, pleased to discover that a little squeezing was all it took to fasten the zipper. She went into the front room.

'How about some makeup, Aunty?'

Unused for years, the lipstick poked up its head reluctantly as she rotated the base. She made a false start and smudged the lip line, but the labial acrobatics soon came back to her, the pursing and puckering and tautening, the simian contortions that seemed so absurd in the mirror.

The rouge was caked stiff, but under the discoloured crust there was enough to blush her cheeks. The round velvet pad had desiccated into a leathery scab. Once, Rustom had teased her while she was making up, and she retaliated by rouging his nose with the pad. Soft as a rose petal, he had said.

If Nusswan mentioned marriage today, she didn't know what she would do – overturn his desk, perhaps. She surveyed herself in the mirror. Her reflection nodded approvingly. She hoped that Maneck's theory linking appearance and respect was correct.

'Are you ready?' she called into his room.

'Wow! You look absolutely beautiful.'

'That's enough from you,' she scolded, inspecting him from head to toe. He passed muster except for his shoes. She made him shine them before they left.

The office peon made the two wait in the corridor while he disappeared to check with the boss. 'Just watch, Nusswan will be busy,' she predicted.

The man returned to announce in a regretful voice, 'Sahab is busy.' The peon had worked here for many years, but it always embarrassed

him to have to abet his employer's charade. 'Please sit for a few minutes.' He lowered his head and withdrew.

'Goodness knows why Nusswan still tries to impress me in these silly
ways,' said Dina. 'His busyness will end in exactly fifteen minutes.'

But in her second prediction she was proved wrong, for the peon had
mentioned to Nusswan that his sister was beautifully dressed today and
accompanied by someone.

'Who?' said Nusswan. 'Have we seen her before?'

'Not her, sahab. Him.'

Very curious, thought Nusswan, feeling his chin where he had nicked
it that morning. 'Young? Old?'

'Young,' said the peon. 'Very young.'

Even more curious, decided Nusswan, his imagination wandering
wishfully. Boyfriend, maybe? Dina was very attractive at forty-two.
Almost as beautiful as she was twenty years ago, when she married that
poor, unfortunate Rustom. Unfortunate from beginning to end. In looks,
in money, in his life span . . .

Nusswan paused in his thoughts, gazed ceilingward, and patted his
cheeks alternately, reverently, with his right fingertips, to ensure that
his brother-in-law rested in peace. He had no desire to speak ill of the
departed. So sad, his death. But also a God-given second chance for
Dina to set things right, find a more suitable husband. If only she had
grabbed the chance.

Such a terrible thing her pride was, and her strange idea of independence. Working like a slave to earn a pittance, humiliating the whole
family. And now this latest fiasco with the export company. Slowly, he
had learned to let his skin grow thick. But shaking off embarrassment
was easier than discarding his sense of duty. She was still his little sister,
he had to do his best for her.

What a waste, he thought, what a waste of a life. Like watching a tragic play. Only, instead of three hours it had lasted almost three decades –
a family estranged, Xerxes and Zarir growing up deprived of the love
and attention of their Dina Aunty, she hardly knowing her two
nephews. So much sadness and misery.

But perhaps there was still a chance of a joyful ending. There could be
nothing better than becoming one happy, united family again. Soon it
would be time for grandchildren in his own life. If Dina had abdicated
as aunty, she could be a grand-aunty.

And this young man with her today, her boyfriend. If they were serious and got married, how wonderful. Even if the chap was only thirty,
he should consider himself lucky to have Dina – so attractive that she

could put women half her age in the shade.

Yes, that was it – she wanted to introduce the fellow and get her older brother's approval. Or why bring him along? As to their age difference, there could be no objection, Nusswan decided reluctantly. One had to be broad-minded, in these modern times. Yes, he would give them his blessing, even pay for this second wedding. As long as the expenses were reasonable – one hundred guests, modest flower arrangements, a small band . . .

Reviewing a lifetime, brooding, regretting, revising, it seemed like ages to Nusswan since their arrival had been announced. He checked his watch – it had been less than five minutes. He put the dial to his ear: it was working. Astonishing, how time and mind conspired in their tricks.

He told the peon to send in the visitors immediately. He wanted to continue in reality the celebration he had begun in imagination.

'What?' said Dina to the peon. 'So soon?' She whispered to Maneck, 'See, already you have brought us good luck – he never calls me in so fast.'

Nusswan rose and shot his cuffs, ready to extend a warm greeting to the man who would be brother-in-law. When he saw Maneck's youth enter the office, his knees almost gave way. His crazy sister had done it again! He clenched the edge of the desk, pale with visions of shame and scandal in the community.

'Are you turning into a European, Nusswan? Or are you sick?' asked Dina.

'I'm fine, thank you,' he answered stiffly.

'How are Ruby and the boys?'

'They are well.'

'Good. I'm sorry to trouble you when you are so busy.'

'It's all right.' Not two seconds in his office, and she was at him. Stupid to have raised his hopes. Where Dina was concerned, it was wiser to despair. Not one paisa would he spend on this wedding. If child marriage was a terrible ancient scourge, child-and-adult marriage was a modern madness. He wanted no part of it. And the doctor telling him to watch his blood pressure, to curtail his activities on the Share Bazaar – while here was his own sister, doing her share to shorten his life.

'But where are my manners,' said Dina. 'Talking on without introductions. Maneck, this is my brother, Nusswan.'

'How do you do?' said Maneck.

'Plea . . . pleased to meet you.' Nusswan fell back in his chair after shaking hands. A typewriter pounded away in the next room. The ceiling fan hiccuped discreetly. Under a paperweight, a sheaf of papers fluttered like a bird in trouble.

'Maneck has heard a lot about you from me,' said Dina, 'and I wanted the two of you to meet. He came to live with me a few months ago.'

'*Live* with you?' His sister had gone mad! Where did she think she was, in Hollywood?

'Yes, live with me. What else would a paying guest do?'

'Oh yes! Of course! What else?' The relief was so keen, it was unbearable. He wanted to fall to his knees. Oh, thank God! Saved! Thank God Almighty!

Then, hiding behind the sunshine and rainbow that had burst on the horizon, Nusswan discovered his pot of sludge: there would be no wedding. He felt cheated. Just like her. Cruel, unfeeling, leading him on with false hopes. To think how genuinely happy he had been for her a few minutes ago. Once again she had mocked him.

'The prices keep going up,' she said. 'I couldn't manage, I had to take a boarder. And I was so lucky to find a wonderful boy like Maneck.'

'Yes, of course. Very nice to meet you, Maneck. And where do you work?'

'Work?' said Dina indignantly. 'He is just seventeen, he goes to college.'

'And what are you studying?'

'Refrigeration and air-conditioning.'

'Very wise choice,' said Nusswan. 'These days only a technical education will get you ahead. The future lies with technology and modernization.' Filling the silence with words was a way of dealing with the tumult of emotions his sister had exploded in him. Empty words, to carry away the foolishness he felt.

'Yes, the country has been held back for too long by outdated ideologies. But our time has come. Magnificent changes are taking place. And the credit goes to our Prime Minister. A true spirit of renaissance.'

Dina didn't mind his rambling, relieved that at least the matrimonial topic had not been revived. 'I have a boarder, but I have lost my tailors,' she said.

'What a pity,' said Nusswan, slightly confused by her interruption. 'The main thing is, now we have pragmatic policies instead of irrelevant theories. For example, poverty is being tackled head-on. All the ugly bustees and filthy jhopadpattis are being erased. Young man, you are not old enough to remember how wonderful this city once was. But thanks to our visionary leader and the Beautification Programme, it will be restored to its former glory. Then you will see and appreciate.'

'I was able to finish the last dresses only because Maneck helped,' put in Dina. 'He worked so hard, side by side with me.'

'That's very good,' said Nusswan. 'Very good indeed.' The sound of his own voice had made him loquacious as usual. 'Hardworking, educated people like Maneck is what we need. Not lazy, ignorant millions. And we also need strict family planning. All these rumours of forced sterilization are not helping. You must have heard that nonsense.'

Dina and Maneck shook their heads in unison.

'Probably started by the CIA – saying people in remote villages are being dragged from their huts for compulsory sterilization. Such lies. But my point is, even if the rumour is true, what is wrong in that, with such a huge population problem?'

'Wouldn't it be undemocratic to mutilate people against their will?' asked Maneck, in a tone that suggested total agreement rather than a challenge.

'Mutilate. Ha ha ha,' said Nusswan, avuncular and willing to pretend it was a clever joke. 'It's all relative. At the best of times, democracy is a seesaw between complete chaos and tolerable confusion. You see, to make a democratic omelette you have to break a few democratic eggs. To fight fascism and other evil forces threatening our country, there is nothing wrong in taking strong measures. Especially when the foreign hand is always interfering to destabilize us. Did you know the CIA is trying to sabotage the Family Planning Programme?'

Maneck and Dina shook their heads again, again in perfect unison and with straight faces. There was the subtlest touch of burlesque about it.

Nusswan eyed them suspiciously before continuing. 'What's happening is, CIA agents are tampering with consignments of birth-control devices and stirring up trouble among religious groups. Now don't you agree that Emergency measures are necessary against such dangers?'

'Maybe,' said Dina. 'But I think the government should let homeless people sleep on the pavements. Then my tailors wouldn't have disappeared and I wouldn't have come here to bother you.'

Nusswan lifted his index finger and waggled it like a hyperactive windshield wiper. 'People sleeping on pavements gives industry a bad name. My friend was saying last week – he's the director of a multi-national, mind you, not some small, two-paisa business – he was saying that at least two hundred million people are surplus to requirements, they should be eliminated.'

'Eliminated?'

'Yes. You know – got rid of. Counting them as unemployment statistics year after year gets us nowhere, just makes the numbers look bad. What kind of lives do they have anyway? They sit in the gutter and look like corpses. Death would be a mercy.'

'But how would they be eliminated?' inquired Maneck in his most likeable, most deferential tone.

'That's easy. One way would be to feed them a free meal containing arsenic or cyanide, whichever is cost-effective. Lorries could go around to the temples and places where they gather to beg.'

'Do many business people think like this?' asked Dina curiously.

'A lot of us think like this, but until now we did not have the courage to say so. With the Emergency, people can freely speak their minds. That's another good thing about it.'

'But the newspapers are censored,' said Maneck.

'Ah yes, yes,' said Nusswan, at last betraying impatience. 'And what's so terrible about that? It's only because the government does not want anything published which will alarm the public. It's temporary – so lies can be suppressed and people can regain confidence. Such steps are necessary to preserve the democratic structure. You cannot sweep clean without making the new broom dirty.'

'I see,' said Maneck. The bizarre aphorisms were starting to grate on him, but he did not possess the ammunition to launch even a modest counterattack. If only Avinash were here. He would straighten out this idiot. He wished he had paid more attention when Avinash talked politics.

Still struggling with the earlier maxim, about breaking democratic eggs to make a democratic omelette, Maneck tried to formulate a variation by juggling democracy, tyranny, frying pan, fire, hen, hard-boiled eggs, cooking oil. He thought he had one: A democratic omelette is not possible from eggs bearing democratic labels but laid by the tyrannical hen. No, too cumbersome. And anyway, the moment was past.

'The important thing,' said Nusswan, 'is to consider the concrete achievements of the Emergency. Punctuality has been restored to the railway system. And as my director friend was saying, there's also a great improvement in industrial relations. Nowadays, he can call the police in just one second, to take away the union troublemakers. A few good saltings at the police station, and they are soft as butter. My friend says production has improved tremendously. And who benefits from all this? The workers. The common people. Even the World Bank and the IMF approve of the changes. Now they are offering more loans.'

Keeping her expression as grave as she could, Dina said, 'Nusswan, can I make a request please?'

'Yes, of course.' He wondered how much it would be this time – two hundred rupees or three?

'About the plan to eliminate two hundred million. Can you please tell your business friends and directors not to poison any tailors? Because tailors are already hard to find.'

Maneck smothered a laugh before it broke. Nusswan spied the facial effort as he said to her disgustedly, 'It's useless talking to you about serious things. I don't know why I even bother.'

'I enjoyed listening,' said Maneck gravely.

Nusswan felt betrayed – first her, now him. He wondered what sort of mockery and ridicule took place at his expense when the two were alone.

'I had fun too,' said Dina. 'Coming to your office is the only entertainment I can afford, you know that.'

Glowering, he began moving papers on his desk. 'Tell me what you need and leave me alone. There's a lot of work to do.'

'Be careful, Nusswan, your eyebrows are doing funny exercises.' She decided not to press her luck further, and got down to business. 'I haven't given up the export work. It's just a matter of time before I find new tailors. But till then I cannot accept more orders.'

The moment of asking, the moment she hated, did not become less unpalatable with the brisk matter-of-fact explanation or the levity leading up to it. 'Two hundred and fifty will be enough to get me through this month.'

Nusswan rang for the peon, and filled out a cash voucher. Dina and Maneck were treated to a vehement display of penmanship, the ballpoint scratching savagely across the form. He crossed his t's and dotted his i's with heavy blows, as though competing with the typewriter being battered in the next room.

The peon carried the voucher to the cashier across the corridor. The run-down ceiling fan laboured like a noisy little factory. So much money, thought Dina, and he still hadn't air-conditioned the office. She lowered her eyes, fixing them on a sandalwood paper-knife stuck strategically inside a half-opened envelope. The peon delivered the money and retreated.

Nusswan began, 'None of this would be necessary if only –' He glanced at Dina, unable to reach her downcast eyes, then at Maneck, and abandoned the thought. 'Here,' he held out the notes.

'Thank you,' she accepted, eyes still averted.

'Don't mention it.'

'I'll return it as soon as possible.'

He nodded, picking up the paper-knife, and opened the rest of the envelope.

'At least he spared me his favourite speech today, thanks to the Emergency,' said Dina when they got off the bus. 'That's something to be grateful for. "And what is so terrible about marrying again?"' she imitated in a sanctimonious voice. '"You are still good-looking, I guarantee I can find you a good husband." You won't believe the number of times he has said this to me.'

'But I do, Aunty,' said Maneck. 'It's the one thing on which I agree with your brother. You *are* good-looking.'

She smacked his shoulder. 'Whose side are you on?'

'On the side of truth and beauty,' he pronounced grandly. 'But it must be quite funny when Nusswan and his business friends get together and talk their nonsense.'

'You know what I was remembering, in his office? When he was a young boy. He would talk about becoming a big-game hunter, about killing leopards and lions. And wrestling crocodiles, like Tarzan. One day, a little mouse came into our room, and our ayah said to him, Baba look, there is a fierce tiger, you can be the hunter. And Nusswan ran away screaming for Mummy.'

She turned the key in the lock. 'Now he wants to eliminate two hundred million. His big talk never stops.'

They entered the flat and were confronted by the silent sewing-machines. Their laughter now seemed out of place; it dwindled rapidly and died.

THE TRUCK GROWLED into the city after midnight along the airport road. Sleeping shanty towns pullulated on both sides of the highway, ready to spread onto the asphalt artery. Only the threat of the many-wheeled juggernauts thundering up and down restrained the tattered lives behind the verges. Headlights picked out late-shift workers, tired ghosts tracing a careful path between the traffic and the open sewer.

'Police had orders to remove all jhopadpattis,' said Ishvar. 'Why are these still standing?'

Beggarmaster explained it was not so simple; everything depended on the long-term arrangements each slumlord had made with the police.

'That's not fair,' said Om, his eyes trying to penetrate the rancid night. Splotches of pale moonlight revealed an endless stretch of patchwork shacks, the sordid quiltings of plastic and cardboard and paper and sackcloth, like scabs and blisters creeping in a dermatological nightmare across the rotting body of the metropolis. When the moon was blotted by clouds, the slum disappeared from sight. The stench continued to vouch for its presence.

After a few kilometres the truck entered the city's innards. Lampposts and neon fixtures washed the pavements in a sea of yellow watery light, where slumbered the shrunken, hollow-eyed statuary of the night, the Galateas and Gangabehns and Gokhales and Gopals, soon to be stirred to life by dawn's chaos, to haul and carry and lift and build, to strain their sinew for the city that was desperately seeking beautification.

'Look,' said Om. 'People are sleeping peacefully – no police to bother them. Maybe the Emergency law has been cancelled.'

'No, it hasn't,' said Beggarmaster. 'But it's become a game, like all other laws. Easy to play, once you know the rules.'

The tailors asked to be let off near the chemist's. 'Maybe the nightwatchman will let us live in the entrance again.'

Beggarmaster insisted, however, on first seeing their place of work. The truck travelled for a few more minutes and stopped outside Dina's building, where they indicated her flat.

'Okay,' said Beggarmaster, jumping out. 'Let's verify your jobs with your employer.' He asked the driver to wait, and strode rapidly to the door.

'It's too late to wake Dinabai,' pleaded Ishvar, wincing as he hurried on his bad ankle. 'She's very quick-tempered. We'll bring you here tomorrow, I promise – I swear upon my dead mother's name.'

The beggars and injured workers in the truck shivered, yearning for the comforting arms of motion that had cradled them through the journey. The idling engine's rumbles endowed the night with a menacing maw. They began to cry.

Beggarmaster paused at the front door to study the nameplate, and made a note in his diary. Then he shot out his index finger and rang the doorbell.

'Hai Ram!' Ishvar clutched his head in despair. 'How angry she will be, pulled out of bed this late!'

'It's late for me also,' said Beggarmaster. 'I missed my temple puja, but I'm not complaining, am I?' He pressed the bell again and again when there was no answer. The truck driver sounded his horn to hurry him up.

'Stop, please!' begged Om. 'At this rate we'll surely lose our jobs!' Beggarmaster smiled patiently and continued his jottings. Writing in the dark posed no difficulty for him.

Inside, the doorbell agitated Dina as much as it did the tailors. She rushed to Maneck's room. 'Wake up, quick!' He needed a few good shakes before he stirred. 'Looks like an angel but snores like a buffalo! Wake up, come on! Are you listening? Someone's at the door!'

'Who?'

'I glanced through the peephole, but you know my eyes. All I can tell is, there are three fellows. I want you to look.'

She had not yet switched on the light, hoping the uninvited visitors would go away. Cautioning him to walk softly, she led the way to the door and held the latch. He took a peek and turned excitedly.

'Open it, Aunty! It's Ishvar and Om, with someone!'

Outside they heard his voice and called, 'Hahnji, it is us, Dinabai, very sorry to disturb you. Please forgive us, it won't take long . . .' Their voices trailed off in a timorous question mark.

She clicked the switch for the verandah light, still cautious, and opened the door a bit – and then wide. 'It is you! Where have you been? What happened?'

She made no attempt to disguise her relief. It surprised her: she relished the wholeness of it, her feelings rising straight to her tongue, without twisting in deception.

'Come inside, come!' she said. 'My goodness, we worried about you all these weeks!'

Beggarmaster stood back as Ishvar limped over the threshold and forced a smile. From his ankle trailed Doctor sahab's filthy strips of cloth. Om followed close behind him, stepping on the bandage in his haste. Through the darkened doorway they crept shamefacedly into the verandah's revealing light.

'My goodness! Look at your condition!' said Dina, overcome by the haggard faces, dirty clothes, matted hair. Neither she nor Maneck spoke for a few moments. They stared. Then the questions rushed out, tripping one over the other, and the fragmented answers were equally frantic.

Still waiting at the door, Beggarmaster interrupted Ishvar and Om's confused explanations. 'I just want to check – these two tailors work for you?'

'Yes. Why?'

'That's fine. It's so nice to see everybody happy and reunited.' The truck honked again, and he turned to leave.

'Wait,' said Ishvar. 'Where to make the weekly payment?'

'I'll come to collect it.' He added that if they wanted to get in touch with him at any time, they should tell Worm, whose new beat would be outside the Vishram Vegetarian Hotel.

'What payment, what worm?' asked Dina when the door had shut. 'And who is that man?'

The tailors digressed from the main story to explain, starting with Beggarmaster's arrival at the work camp, then backing up to Shankar's account, racing forward again, getting confused, confusing their listeners. The harrowing stretch of time in hell was over; exhaustion was flooding the place vacated by fear. Ishvar fumbled with the bandage to wrap it properly round his ankle. His hands shook, and Om tucked in the loose end for him.

'It was the foreman's fault, he . . .'

'But that was before the Facilitator came . . .'

'Anyway, after my ankle was hurt, it was impossible . . .'

The thread of events eluded their grasp, Ishvar picking up a piece of it here, Om grabbing something there. Then they lost track of the narrative altogether. Ishvar's voice faded. He pressed his head with both hands, trying to squeeze out the words. Om stammered and started to cry.

'It was terrible, the way they treated us,' he sobbed, clawing at his hair. 'I thought my uncle and I were going to die there . . .'

Maneck patted his back, saying they were safe now, and Dina insisted the best thing to do was to have a good rest, then talk in the morning. 'You still have your bedding. Just spread it here on the verandah and go to sleep.'

Now it was Ishvar's turn to break. He fell on his knees before her and touched her feet. 'O Dinabai, how to thank you! Such kindness! We are very afraid of the outside . . . this Emergency, the police . . .'

His display embarrassed her. She pulled her toes out of his reach. So urgent was his grasp, her left slipper stayed behind between his clutching fingers. He reached forward and gently restored it to her foot.

'Please get up – at once,' she said with a confused sternness. 'Listen to me, I will say this one time only. Fall on your knees before no human being.'

'Okayji,' he rose obediently. 'Forgive me, I should have known better. But what to do, Dinabai, I just can't think of how to thank you.'

Still embarrassed, she said there had been enough thanks for one night. Om unrolled the bedding after wiping his eyes on his sleeve. He asked if they could wash the dust from their hands and faces before sleeping.

'There's not much water, just what's in the bucket, so be frugal. If you are thirsty, take from the drinking pot in the kitchen.' She locked the verandah door and went inside with Maneck.

'I'm so proud of you, Aunty,' he whispered.

'Are you, now? Thank you, Grandpa.'

Morning light did not bring answers to the questions Dina had wrestled with all night. She could not risk losing the tailors again. But how firm to stand, how much to bend? Where was the line between compassion and foolishness, kindness and weakness? And that was from her position. From theirs, it might be a line between mercy and cruelty, consideration and callousness. She could draw it on this side, but they might see it on that side.

The tailors awoke at seven, and packed up their bedding. 'We slept so well,' said Ishvar. 'It was peaceful as paradise on your verandah.'

They took a change of clothes from the trunk and prepared to leave for the railway bathroom. 'We'll have tea at Vishram, then come back straight – if it's all right.

'You mean, to start sewing?'

'Yes, for sure,' said Om with a weak smile.

She turned to Ishvar. 'What about your ankle?'

'Still hurts, but I can push the treadle with one foot. No need to delay.'

She noticed their cracked and bruised feet. 'Where are your chappals?'

'Stolen.'

'Sometimes there is broken glass on the street. Drunks smashing their bottles. You cannot gamble with your three remaining feet.' She found an old pair of slippers which fitted Om; Maneck gave Ishvar his tennis shoes.

'So comfortable,' said Ishvar. 'Thank you.' Then he inquired timidly if they could borrow five rupees for tea and food.

'There is much more than five rupees coming to you from the last order,' she said.

'Hahnji? Really?' They were overjoyed, having presumed that leaving the work incomplete meant forfeiting the right to any payment, and said as much.

'It may be the practice with some employers. I believe in honest pay for honest work.' She added jokingly, 'Maybe you can share it with Maneck, he deserves something.'

'No, I only helped with a few buttons. Dina Aunty did it all.'

'Forget your college, yaar,' said Om. 'Become a partner with us.'

'Right. And we'll open our own shop,' said Maneck.

'Don't give bad advice,' she scolded Om. 'Everyone should be educated. I hope when you have children you will send them to school.'

'Oh yes, he will,' said Ishvar. 'But first we must find him a wife.'

After Maneck left reluctantly for college and Dina went to Au Revoir Exports for new cloth, the tailors idled away the time at the Vishram Vegetarian Hotel. The cashier-cum-waiter welcomed back his regulars with delight. He finished attending to the customers at the front counter – a tumbler of milk, six pakoras, a scoop of curds – and soon joined them at the solitary table.

'You two have lost weight,' he observed. 'Where have you been so long?'

'Special government diet,' said Ishvar, and told him about their misfortune.

'You fellows are amazing,' the sweaty cook roared over the stoves. 'Everything happens to you only. Each time you come here, you have a new adventure story to entertain us.'

'It's not us, it's this city,' said Om. 'A story factory, that's what it is, a spinning mill.'

'Call it what you will, if all our customers were like you, we would be able to produce a modern *Mahabharat* – the Vishram edition.'

'Please, bhai, no more adventures for us,' said Ishvar. 'Stories of suffering are no fun when we are the main characters.'

The cashier-waiter brought them their tea and bun-muska, then went to serve more customers at the counter. The milk in the tea had formed a creamy skin. Om spooned it into his mouth, licking his lips. Ishvar offered him his own cup, and he skimmed that off too. They separated the halves of the bun-muska to check if both sides were buttered. They were, lavishly.

During a pedestrian lull on the pavement, Shankar, who was already begging outside when they had arrived, rolled up by the door to greet them. Ishvar waved. 'So, Shankar. Happy to be back and working hard, hahn?'

'Aray babu, what to do, Beggarmaster said it's the first day, relax, sleep. So I fell asleep here. Then coins began falling into my can. A terrible clanging sound – right beside my head. Every time I close my eyes, they fly open in fright. The public just won't let me rest.'

His routine this morning was simple. He rattled the coins and made a whining noise, or coughed hoarsely at intervals till tears ran down his cheeks. For visual interest, sometimes he paddled the platform a few feet to the left, then back to the right. 'You know, I specially asked Beggarmaster to move me here from the railway station,' he confided. 'Now we can meet more often.'

'That's good,' said Om, waving goodbye. 'We'll see you again soon.'

The flat was padlocked, and they waited by the door. 'Hope that crazy rent-collector is not prowling around the building,' said Om. It was an anxious ten minutes before the taxi drove up. They helped Dina unload the bolts of cloth and carry them to the back room.

'Not too much weight, careful with your ankle,' she cautioned Ishvar. 'By the way, there's going to be a strike in the mill. No more cloth till it's over.'

'Hai Ram, trouble never ends.' Suddenly, Ishvar's mind returned to what he had done the night before, and he apologized again for having fallen at her feet. 'I should have known better.'

'That's what you said last night. But why?' asked Dina.

'Because someone did it to me once. And it made me feel very bad.'

'Who was it?'

'It's a very long story,' said Ishvar, unwilling to tell her everything about their lives, but eager to share a little. 'When my brother – Om's father – and I were apprenticed to a tailor, we gave him some help.'

'What did you do?'

'Well,' he hesitated. 'Ashraf Chacha is Muslim, and it was the time of Hindu–Muslim riots. At independence, you know. There was trouble in the town, and – we were able to help him.'

'So he touched your feet, this Ashraf?'

'No.' The memory embarrassed Ishvar, even after twenty-eight years. 'No, his wife did, Mumtaz Chachi did. And it made me feel very bad. As though I was taking advantage in some way of her misfortune.'

'That's exactly how I felt last night. Let's forget about it now.' She had a dozen more questions to ask, but respected his reluctance. If they wanted to, they would tell her more some day when they were ready.

For now, she added the pieces to what Maneck had already revealed about their life in the village. Like her quilt, the tailors' chronicle was gradually gathering shape.

Throughout that first day, Dina continued to struggle with words to construct the crucial question. How would she phrase it when the time came? What about: Sleep on the verandah till you find a place. No, it seemed like she was anxious to have them there. Start with a question: Do you have a place for tonight? But that sounded hypocritical, it was plain they didn't. A different question: Where will you sleep tonight? Yes, not bad. She tried it again. No, it expressed too much concern – much too open. Last night had been so easy, the words had sprung of their own accord, simple and true.

She watched the tailors work all afternoon, their feet welded to the treadles, till Maneck came home and reminded them of the tea break. No, they said, not today, and she approved. 'Don't make them waste money. They have lost enough in these last few weeks.'

'But I was going to pay.'

'Yours is not to waste either. What's wrong with my tea?' She put the water on for everyone and set out the cups, keeping the pink rose borders separate. Waiting for the kettle to start chattering, she mulled her word-puzzle. What if she started with: Was the verandah comfortable? No, it sounded hopelessly false.

At quitting time the tailors placed the covers mournfully over the sewing-machines. They rose heavily, sighed, and walked towards the door.

For a moment Dina felt like a magician. She could make everything become shining and golden, depending on her words – the utterance was all.

'What time will you return?'

'Whenever you wish,' said Om. 'As early as you like.' Ishvar nodded in silence.

She took the opening; the pieces fell into place. 'Well, no need to rush. Have your dinner, then come back. Maneck and I will also finish eating by then.'

'You mean we can . . .?'

'On the verandah?'

'Only till you find yourselves a place,' she said, pleased at how neutral her statements were – the line drawn precisely.

Their gratitude warmed her, but she cut short the offer of payment. 'No. Absolutely no rent. I am not renting anything, just keeping you out of those crooked police hands.'

And she made it clear that their comings and goings had to be reduced, the risk with the landlord was too great. The washing trip to the railway station every morning, for one, could be eliminated. 'You can bathe and have tea here. As long as you wake up early, before the water goes. Keep in mind, I have only one bathroom.' Which made Om wonder why anybody would be silly enough to have more than one, but he didn't ask.

'And remember, I don't want a mess in there.'

They agreed to all her conditions and swore they would be no bother. 'But we really feel bad staying for free,' said Ishvar.

'If you mention money once more, you'll have to find somewhere else.'

They thanked her again and left for dinner, promising to be back by eight and sew for an hour before bedtime.

'But Aunty, why refuse their offer of rent? They'll feel good if you take a little money. And it will also help you with the expenses.'

'Don't you understand anything? If I accept money, it means a tenancy on my verandah.'

Stooped over the basin, Dina brushed her teeth with Kolynos. Ishvar watched the foam drip from her mouth. 'I've always wondered if that's good for the teeth,' he said.

She spat and gargled before answering, 'As good as any other toothpaste, I think. Which one do you use?'

'We use charcoal powder. And sometimes neem sticks.'

Maneck said that Ishvar and Om's teeth were better than his. 'Show me,' she said, and he bared them. 'And yours?' she asked the tailors.

The three lined up before the mirror and curled their lips, exposing their incisors. She compared her own. 'Maneck is right, yours are whiter.'

Ishvar offered her a bit of charcoal powder to try, and she squeezed half an inch of Kolynos on his finger. He shared it with Om. 'Taste is delicious,' they concurred.

'That's all very well,' she said. 'But paying for taste is a waste, unless you are talking about food. I think I will switch to charcoal and save money.' Maneck decided to follow suit.

The enlarged household turned the wheel of morning with minimal friction. Dina was the first to rise, Maneck the last. When she had finished in the bathroom the tailors took their turns. They were in and out so fast, she suspected a deficiency in matters of personal hygiene, till she saw their well-scrubbed faces and wet hair. A deep breath in their proximity confirmed the clean odour of freshly bathed skin.

Though the bathroom was unimaginable luxury, the tailors did not linger. High-speed washing came naturally to them. Over the last several months they had honed their skills in public places, where time was critical. The faucet in the alley near Nawaz's awning; the single tap at the centre of the hutment colony; the crumbling toilets in the overcrowded railway bathroom; the trickling spout at the irrigation project: all these had helped to perfect their technique to the point where each could finish within three minutes. They never operated Dina's immersion heater, preferring cold water, and their tidy habits left everything neat.

But the thought of their bodies in her bathroom still made Dina uncomfortable. She was watchful, waiting to pounce if she found evidence that her soap or towel had been used. If they were to live here for a few days, it would be on her terms, there would be no slackening of the reins.

What she disliked most was Ishvar's morning ritual of plunging his fingers down his throat to retch. The procedure was accompanied by a primal yowling, something she had often heard emanating from other flats, but never at such close quarters. It made her skin crawl.

'Goodness, you frightened me,' she said when the series of yips and yelps rang out.

He smiled. 'Very good for the stomach. Gets rid of stale, excess bile.'

'Careful, yaar,' said Om, siding with Dina. 'Sounds like your liver is coming out with the bile.' He had never approved of his uncle's practice; Ishvar had tried to teach him its therapeutic effects and had given up, faced with a lack of cooperation.

'What you need is a plumber,' said Maneck. 'To install a little tap in your side. Then all you do is turn it on and release the excess bile.' He and Om began baying an accompanying chorus when Ishvar started howling again.

After a few days of their combined teasing, Ishvar moderated his habit. The yowls were more restrained, and his fingers no longer explored his gullet to quite the same daredevil depths.

Om sniffed Maneck's skin. 'Your smell is better than mine. Must be your soap.'

'I use powder as well.'

'Show me.'

Maneck got the can from his room.

'And where do you put it? All over?'

'I just take a little in my palm and spread it in the armpits and chest.'

On the next payment day, Om purchased a cake of Cinthol Soap and a can of Lakmé Talcum Powder.

The pattern of each day, thought Dina at the end of the first week, was like the pattern of a well-cut dress, the four of them fitting together without having to tug or pull to make the edges meet. The seams were straight and neat.

Ishvar, however, was still troubled that he and his nephew were taking advantage of Dina's goodness. 'You won't accept any rent from us,' he said. 'You let us use your verandah and bathroom. You give us tea. This is too much, it makes us feel bad.'

His declaration reminded her of her own guilt. She knew that everything she did was done from self-preservation – to keep the tailors from being picked up again by the police, and to have them out of sight of nosey neighbours and the rent-collector. Now Ishvar and Om were wrapping her in the mantle of kindness and generosity. Deceit, hypocrisy, manipulation were more the fabrics of her garment, she thought.

'So what is your plan?' she said brusquely. 'To insult me with fifty paise for tea? You want to treat me like a roadside chaiwalla?'

'No no, never. But is there not something we can do for you in return?'

She said she would let them know.

At the end of the second week, Ishvar was still waiting to hear. Then he took matters into his own hand. While she was bathing, he fetched the broom and dustpan from the kitchen and swept the verandah, the front room, Maneck's room, and the sewing room. As he finished in each, Om got busy with the bucket and cloth, mopping the floors.

They were still at it when Dina emerged from the bathroom. 'What's going on here?'

'Forgive me, but I have decided,' said Ishvar firmly. 'We are going to share the daily cleaning from now on.'

'That does not seem right,' she said.

'Seems just fine,' said Om, briskly squeezing out the mop.

Deeply moved, she poured the tea while they were finishing up. They came into the kitchen to replace the cleaning things, and she handed two cups to Om.

Noticing the red rose borders, he started to point out her error, 'The pink ones for us,' then stopped. Her face told him she was aware of it.

'What?' she asked, taking the pink cup for herself. 'Is something wrong?'

'Nothing,' his voice caught. He turned away, hoping she did not see the film of water glaze his eyes.

═══

'Someone at the door for you,' said Dina. 'The same long-haired fellow who came once before.'

Ishvar and Om exchanged glances – what did he want now? Apologizing for the interruption, they went to the verandah.

'Namaskaar,' said Rajaram, putting his hands together. 'Sorry to bother you at work, but the nightwatchman said you didn't sleep there anymore.'

'Yes, we have another place.'

'Where?'

'Nearby.'

'Hope it's nice. Listen, can I meet you later to talk? Any time today, anywhere, your convenience.' He sounded desperate.

'Okay,' said Ishvar. 'Come to Vishram at one o'clock. You know where it is?'

'Yes, I'll be there. And listen, can you please bring my hair from your trunk?'

After Rajaram had left, Dina asked the tailors if something was wrong. 'He's not connected with that other man, I hope – the one who's squeezing you for money every week.'

'No no, he does not work for Beggarmaster,' said Ishvar. 'He's a friend, probably just wants a loan.'

'Well, you be careful,' said Dina. 'These days, friends and foes look alike.'

The Vishram was crowded, and Rajaram was waiting nervously on the pavement when they arrived. 'Here's your hair,' Ishvar handed him the package. 'So. What will you eat?'

'Nothing, my stomach is full,' said Rajaram, but his mouth betrayed his hunger, masticating phantom food in response to aromas from the Vishram.

'Have something,' said Ishvar, feeling sorry for him. 'Try something, it's our treat.'

'Okay, whatever you two are eating.' He forced a laugh. 'A full stomach is only a small obstacle.'

'Three pao-bhajis and three bananas,' Ishvar told the cashier-waiter.

They carried their food to the site of a collapsed building, just down the road, and chose a window ledge in the shade of a half-crumpled wall. A horizontal door served as their table. Its hinges and knobs had been scavenged; the collapse was several weeks old. Four children with gunny sacks were clambering in the rubble, sifting and searching.

'So how's your work as a Family Planning Motivator?'

Rajaram shook his head, wolfing a large mouthful. 'Not good.' He ate as though he hadn't seen food for days. 'They asked me to leave two weeks ago.'

'What happened?'

'They said I wasn't producing results.'

'Suddenly? After two months?'

'Yes,' he hesitated. 'I mean, no, there were problems from the very beginning. After the training course, I was following the procedure they showed me. I visited different neighbourhoods every day. I carefully repeated the things they taught me, using the correct tone, sounding kind and knowledgeable, so no one would get scared. And usually people listened patiently, took the leaflets; sometimes they laughed, and young fellows made dirty jokes. But no one would sign up for the operation.

'A few weeks later, my supervisor called me into his office. He said I wasn't pursuing the right customers. He said it was a waste of time trying to sell a wedding suit to a naked fakir. I asked him exactly what he meant.'

Rajaram repeated for the tailors the supervisor's reply – that people in the city were too cynical, they doubted everything, it was difficult to motivate them. Suburban slums were the places to tackle. After all, there lived the ignorant people most in need of the government's help. The programme, with its free gifts and incentives, was specifically designed for them.

'So I took his advice and went outside the city. And would you believe it? On the very first day my cycle got a puncture.'

'A bad beginning,' said Ishvar, shaking his head.

'Puncture was only a small problem. The real trouble came later.' While the tyre was being fixed at a cycle shop, said Rajaram, he got to talking with an elderly man waiting in a bus shelter, not far from a fire hydrant. The elderly man needed a wash, and was hoping that street urchins would come along and turn on the hydrant.

For the sake of practice, and to see how long he could hold the fellow's attention, Rajaram began telling him he was a Motivator involved in the good works of the Family Planning Centre. He described the birth-control devices, named the sterilization operations, and the cash inducement for each: a tubectomy was awarded more free gifts than a vasectomy, he explained, because the government preferred intervention that was final and irreversible.

That's the one I want, interrupted the old man, the expensive one, the tube-whatever one. Rajaram almost fell off his perch on the bus-shelter railing. No no, grandfather, it's not for you, I was just talking about it for the sake of talking, he said. I insist, said the old man, it's my right. But tubectomy can only be performed on a woman's parts, explained Rajaram, for a man's parts there is vasectomy, and at your age even that is unnecessary. I don't care about age, I'll take it, whichever is meant for my parts, persisted the old man.

'Maybe he badly wanted a transistor radio,' said Om.

'That's exactly what I assumed,' said Rajaram. 'I thought to myself, if this grandfather desires it so much, who am I to argue? If music makes him happy, why deny him?'

So he got out the proper form, took a thumbprint, paid the tyre-repairer, and escorted his patient to the clinic. That evening, he received the money for his commission, his very first.

Now he regarded the puncture as the harbinger of good fortune: the pointed finger of fate, flattening his tyre and his bad fortune. The badge of Motivator clung with more honesty to his shirt. Brimming with confidence, he returned to the suburban area, certain that he could round up vasectomies and tubectomies by the score.

A week passed, and his peregrinations took him to his first customer's neighbourhood. He cycled among the shacks, seeking to motivate the masses, his head overflowing with various ways of saying the same thing, formulating phrases to make sterility acceptable, even desirable, when someone from the old man's family recognized him and began shouting for help: Motorwaiter is here! Aray, the rascal Motorwaiter has come again!

Rajaram was soon surrounded by an angry crowd threatening to break every bone in his body. In response to his pleas for mercy and his terror-stricken cries of why? why? he learned that something had gone wrong with the operation. The old man's groin had filled up with pus. When the rot began to spread, the clinic was no help, and the old man died.

Ishvar nodded in sympathy as he peeled his banana. He had always felt that the hair-collector's new job was fraught with danger. 'Did they beat you badly?'

Rajaram unbuttoned his shirt and showed them the purple bruises on his back. Across the chest was a gouge, starting to heal, made by some sharp tool. He lowered his head to point out the torn patch of scalp where an attacker had pulled out a clump of hair. 'But I was lucky to escape with my life. They told me I should have known better, the only reason their grandfather went for the operation was because of the cash bonus and gifts. The old man had wanted to help with his granddaughter's dowry.

'I returned straight to my supervisor and made a complaint. How could I produce results, I said, if the doctors killed the patients? But he said the man died because he was old, and the family was simply at all blaming the Family Planning Centre.'

'Goat-fucking bastard,' said Om.

'Exactly. But guess what else the supervisor told me. From now on my job would be easier, he said, because of a policy change.' The new scheme had been explained to Rajaram – it was no longer necessary to sign up individuals for the operation. Instead, they were to be offered a free medical checkup. And it wasn't to be viewed as lying, just a step towards helping people improve their lives. Once inside the clinic, isolated from the primitive influence of families and friends, they would quickly see the benefits of sterilization.

Rajaram picked the crumbs from his pao-bhaji wrapper, then tossed it in the rubble. 'Even though I didn't like the new system, I agreed to try it. By now, everyone realized that Motivators were giving bogus talk to people. Wherever I went, city or suburb, they insulted me, called me a threat to manhood, a dispenser of napusakta, a castrator, a procurer of eunuchs. And here I was, just doing a government job, trying to make a living. How can you function like this day after day? No, I said, this is not for me.'

He told his employers he was willing to work in the old way, distribute leaflets and explain procedures, but no more deception. They said the old way was no longer an option – quotas had fallen behind badly. Concrete results were needed to justify each Motivator's food, shelter, and bicycle.

'So last week I lost all three when they threw me out. Now I am desperate. There is nothing to do but go back to my old profession.'

'Hair-collecting?'

'Yes, I'm going to sell these plaits right away,' he indicated the package the tailors had brought from their trunk. 'And I am also starting my original trade. Barbering. I'll have to do both because without storage space, hair-collecting will be limited. But I need eighty-five rupees. For combs, scissors, clippers, razor. Can you lend me the money?'

'Let me think it over,' said Ishvar. 'Meet us tomorrow.'

'We would really like to do something for him, Dinabai,' said Ishvar. 'He was our neighbour in the hutment colony, and very good to us.'

'I don't have enough to advance you the amount.' But she offered an alternate solution. From the back of her cupboard she dug out the hair-cutting tools Zenobia had set her up with, years ago.

'Aray wah,' said Om, impressed. 'You are also a barber?'

'Used to be – children's hairdresser.'

Maneck fitted his hand around the clippers and pretended to tackle Om's puff. 'That's a nice shrub to practise on.'

'Are you exchanging air-conditioning for barbering?' said Dina. She placed the kit before Ishvar. 'It's old, but still works. Your friend can have it if he likes.'

'Are you sure? What if you need it again?'

'Not likely. My haircutting days are over.' She said that with her eyes and forgotten skills, children's ears would be in danger.

'There is one more problem,' said Rajaram, gratefully receiving the instruments when they met the next day.

'Now what?'

'My hair agent visits the city only once a month. And sleeping on the street, I have nowhere to store what I collect. Will you keep it in your trunk? For me? Your good friend?'

'A month's supply won't fit in the trunk,' objected Ishvar, not anxious to accumulate the unappetizing parcels.

'But it will. I'm going to specialize in long hair – in a month there will be ten plaits at the most, if I'm lucky. Won't take up more than a corner of your trunk. And at month's end I'll sell them to the agent.'

'Your coming to the flat so often – it will annoy our employer.' He wished Rajaram would give up; he felt awkward making excuses to block him. 'It isn't our home, you know, we cannot keep receiving visitors.'

'That's only a small obstacle. I can meet you outside. Here, at Vishram, if you like.'

'We rarely come here,' said Ishvar, then caved in. 'Okay, what you can do is, leave the packet with Shankar, the beggar outside, the one on wheels. He knows us. We'll introduce you.'

'That beggar is your friend? Strange friends you make.'

'Yes, very strange,' said Ishvar, but the hair-collector, absorbed in smoothing the knots and tangles of his life, missed the irony.

—

If with Ishvar it was the bile-seeking fingers that bothered Dina, with Om it was the itchy scalp. She had tolerated the scratching in the old days, knowing it would end at six o'clock. Now, apart from the annoying sight and the constant, irritating rasp, she feared that the itch would migrate to her own hair.

She spoke privately to Ishvar: lice was as bad as any other kind of sickness, and his nephew's health would improve if the parasite was eradicated.

'But problem is money,' said Ishvar. 'I cannot afford to take him to doctor.'

'You don't need a doctor for lice. There's a perfectly good home remedy.' And when she explained the procedure, he remembered his mother using it too.

While topping up the stove, she filled an empty hair-oil bottle with kerosene. 'Do it after tea,' she said. 'Massage it properly and leave for twenty-four hours. It can be washed off tomorrow.'

'Only twenty-four? I thought the remedy said forty-eight. That's how long my mother used to leave it on.'

'Then your mother was a brave woman. Anything can happen in forty-eight hours. We don't want your nephew turning into a human torch.'

'What are you talking about?' puzzled Om. He took the bottle and unscrewed the cap. 'Chhee! It's kerosene!'

'You expected rose water? You want to pamper the lice or kill them?'

'That's right,' said Ishvar. 'Don't fuss, your Roopa Daadi used to do it for your father and me when we were children.'

Grumbling and cringing, Om bent over the basin, complaining that people didn't have enough kerosene to cook their food and here they were, wasting it on hair. Ishvar took a few drops at a time in his palm and worked it in. Under the lightbulb, the oil-streaked black hair turned iridescent. 'Beautiful as a peacock,' he said.

'Dig your fingers in,' instructed Dina. 'Spread it well.' His energetic hands heeded her, rocking the protesting Om back and forth.

'Stop it, yaar! You'll poison me if it enters my blood!'

When he was done she gave him a broken spoon to scratch with. 'Don't use your fingers, or you'll get it on the dresses.'

He sat at the machine, miserable, wrinkling his nose, exhaling forcefully to blow out the smell. Relieving the itch with the spoon was not as satisfying as using fingernails. Now and again, he shook his head like a wet dog while they teased him.

'Would you like to smoke a beedi? Take your mind off?' asked Ishvar. 'I'm sure Dinabai will make an exception today.'

'Of course I will. Shall I bring the matches?'

'Go ahead, laugh,' said Om darkly, 'while I choke to death on these fumes.'

At lunchtime he told his uncle he was not going to the Vishram, he couldn't possibly eat with the stink in his nose. So Ishvar stayed back as well.

Later in the afternoon, Maneck came home and started sniffing around. 'Smells like a kitchen in here.' Keeping his nose low like a bloodhound, he followed the scent to Om. 'Are you starting a new career as a stove?'

'Yes, he is,' said Dina. 'Tonight we'll cook our meal on top of his head. He has always been a hot-headed fellow.'

It was her own joke that first made Dina consider giving the tailors dinner in the flat that night. Other factors reinforced the idea. It would throw off that rascal Ibrahim completely; the tailors hadn't gone for lunch, and they wouldn't emerge for dinner. And besides, Om sitting patiently all day wearing kerosene deserved a reward.

So she chopped another onion and boiled three more potatoes to include them. The breadman arrived at dusk. Instead of two small loaves she bought four. 'Maneck, come here,' she called from the kitchen, and took him into her confidence.

'Really? That's great, Aunty! They'll be thrilled to eat with us!'

'Who said anything about eating with us? I'm going to put their plates on the verandah.'

'Are you trying to be nice or offensive?'

'What's offensive about it? It's a good, clean verandah.'

'Fine. In that case, I'll also eat on the verandah. I cannot take part in such an insult. My father feeds only stray dogs on the porch.'

She grimaced, and he knew he had won.

Dina remembered the last time all sides of the table had been occupied: on her third wedding anniversary, the night Rustom had been killed, eighteen years ago. She set out four plates and called in the tailors. Their faces plainly showed what an immense honour they considered it.

'You have taken your cure like a good boy,' she said to Om, 'and now you get your dinner.' She brought the pot to the table, and a scraped carrot for herself. The tailors regarded her curiously as she bit into it. 'You are not the only one taking a home remedy. This is medicine for my eyes. Right, Dr. Mac?'

'Yes, it's a prescription for improving vision.'

'You know, I've grown to like raw carrots. But I hope Om doesn't get fond of his medicine. Or we'll have to suffer the kerosene stink every day.'

'But how does it work? Does it poison the lice in my hair?'

'I can tell you,' said Maneck.

'You are a champion fakeologist,' said Om.

'No, listen. First, every little louse soaks itself in the kerosene. Then, in the middle of the night, after you are asleep, Dina Aunty gives each one a tiny matchstick. At the count of three they commit suicide in bursts of tiny flames without hurting you. There'll be a beautiful halo round your head when it happens.'

'That's not funny,' said Dina.

'Suicide isn't supposed to be, Aunty.'

'I don't want such a subject at dinnertime. Not even as a joke. You shouldn't even say the word.'

She started eating, and Maneck picked up his fork, winking at Om. The tailors sat motionless, watching the food. When she looked up, they smiled nervously. Exchanging glances, they touched the cutlery, uncertain, hesitating to pick it up.

Dina understood.

How stupid of me, she thought, to set it out tonight. Abandoning her own knife and fork, she used fingers to convey a piece of potato to her mouth. Maneck caught on as well, and the tailors started their meal.

'Very tasty,' said Ishvar, and Om nodded agreement with his mouth full. 'You eat bread every day?'

'Yes,' said Dina. 'Don't you like it?'

'Oh, it's very good,' said Ishvar. 'No, I was just thinking, must be expensive to buy ready-made bread every day. You don't get wheat on your ration card?'

'It's available. But taking it to the mill for grinding, mixing flour, making chapati – that's too much for me to do. I used to when my husband was alive. Afterwards, I didn't care. Nothing worse than cooking for just one.' She broke a piece of her loaf to soak up some gravy. 'Must be expensive for you also, eating at Vishram.'

Ishvar said yes, it was difficult, especially with having to pay Beggarmaster weekly. 'When we had our own place in the colony and a Primus stove, we spent much less, even without the benefit of a ration card. We made chapatis every day.'

'You can buy wheat on my card if you like. I only take rice and sugar.'

'Problem is, where to cook?'

The question was rhetorical, but Maneck had an answer. He let the silence linger over the table for a few moments, then spoke up brightly. 'I have a great idea. Ishvar and Om are used to making chapatis, right? And Dina Aunty has all that grain quota on the ration card, right? So you can share the cost of food, and we can eat together. Both sides will save money.'

More than money, it would save trouble with the landlord, thought Dina, by defeating Ibrahim. He could wait twenty-four hours outside the flat and see no one. Nosey neighbours too, if they were planning to snitch to him, get into his good books to solve their own problems. And besides, fresh puris and chapatis were absolutely delicious.

But was this reason enough to get more familiar with the tailors? Was it wise to tamper with the line she had drawn so carefully? 'I don't know,' she said. 'Ishvar and Om might not like to have my food every day.'

'Not like? It's so tasty!' said Om.

She chewed slowly, giving herself time to think. 'Well, we can try it for a week.'

'That will be very good,' said Ishvar.

'I'll make the chapatis,' said Om. 'I'm the chapati champion.'

The government truck was delivering fresh stock at the ration shop. Dina and the tailors joined the queue while two coolies unloaded fifty-kilo gunnies upon their backs. Sunlight flashed from the large steel hooks they swung to claw a grip into the burlap. Their dripping sweat, when it chanced to fall upon the beige jute sacking, created dark-brown dots. Inside the shop, the sacks of grain landed neatly in a row, like dead bodies in a morgue, beside the scales hanging from the ceiling by a heavy chain.

'These fellows are taking too long,' said Ishvar, 'carrying one at a time. Go on, Om, show them how to carry two.'

'Don't tease the poor boy,' said Dina, as he pretended to roll up his sleeves. 'Why is he so thin anyway? Are you sure he does not have worms?'

'No no, Dinabai, no worms, trust me. Bas, I'll soon get him married, and his wife's cooking will put weight on him.'

'He's too young for marriage.'

'Almost eighteen – that's not young.'

'Dinabai is right, forget your crazy idea,' scowled Om.

'Sour-lime face.'

The line was growing longer. Someone shouted from the back to hurry up, and the banya emerged belligerently, ready to take on the heckler. 'Use your sense when you speak! If the truck is not allowed to unload, what am I going to give you? Rocks and sand?'

'That's what you usually sell us!' the heckler yelled back, and people laughed. 'Have you ever tasted your own stock?' He was a small man with a large goitre, which drew the stares of the people in line.

'Aray saala, go! Nobody is forcing you to buy!'

Those near the heckler tried to prevent the argument from overheating. They reminded him it wasn't wise to fight at a ration shop, it was impossible to win when you depended on them for your food. Someone said the swelling on his neck might burst if he got too excited.

'This swelling is also caused by rascal banyas!' he raged. 'They sell bad salt – salt without iodine! These fat, greedy banyas are responsible for all our suffering! Blackmarketeers, food-adulterers, poisoners!'

The grain truck rolled away. A sprinkle of wheat from leaking sacks marked the place where it had stood. A barefoot man in a vest and short pants quickly collected the spilled grain in an empty vanaspati tin, then ran after the truck to its next destination; tonight he would eat well.

The attendant engaged the scales, and the shop began serving again. The appropriate entries were made in Dina's ration card. Besides the usual sugar and rice, she bought, under the tailors' guidance, her full quota of red and white wheat as well as the allotment of jowar and bajri, which they said was very tasty, very nourishing, and, best of all, not expensive.

They watched the scales while each item was weighed, gazing up at the pointer till the beam came to rest. A cloud of dust rose when the man tipped the pan into Dina's cloth bags. The grain cascaded with the sound of a soft waterfall. Afterwards, the tailors took the bags to the mill.

In the evening Om grew a little anxious about his chapati reputation. He mixed the flour and kneaded the dough more strenuously than he normally would have, concentrating hard while rolling out the chapatis, trying to make them perfectly round. A wayward arc meant that the dough was squished into a ball and rolled out again.

At dinner, everyone complimented his success. The praise was also delivered in the speed with which the eight he had made vanished. Pleased, he decided to make twelve from now on.

The cats came miaowing as soon as the window opened. Maneck told Ishvar and Om the names he had given to some: John Wayne, who liked to swagger about, implying he had the alley under control; Vijayanthimala, his favourite, the brown and white tabby, prancing as though in a film-song dance sequence; Raquel Welch, sitting languidly, stretching, never deigning to rush to the food; and Shatrughan Sinha, bully and villain, from whom the scraps had to be thrown far, to give others a chance.

'Who is John Wayne?' asked Om.

'American actor. Hero type – sort of like Amitabh Bachchan. Walks as though he has piles, and onions under his arms. Always wins in the end.'

'And Raquel Welch?'

'American actress.' He leaned closer. 'Big breasts,' he whispered, while the miaowing continued below the window.

Om grinned. 'Good thing I made extra chapatis today. Looks like she's enjoying them.'

'What's going on?' said Dina. 'Now you are teaching my tailors your bad habits. Please shut that window.' She wondered if something uncontrollable had been started here, with all this cooking together and eating together. Too much intimacy. She hoped she wouldn't regret it.

Ishvar stood aside while the two boys carried on. 'They say it's a blessed deed, Dinabai, to feed dumb animals.'

'Won't be so blessed if they come inside in search of food. They could kill us with filthy germs from the gutter.'

In the WC, the tailors' urine smell that used to flutter like a flag in the air, and in Dina's nose, grew unnoticeable. Strange, she thought, how one gets accustomed to things.

Then it struck her: the scent was unobtrusive now because it was the same for everyone. They were all eating the same food, drinking the same water. Sailing under one flag.

'Let's have masala wada today,' proposed Ishvar. 'Rajaram's recipe.'

'I don't know how to make that.'

'That's okay, I can do it, Dinabai, you relax today.' He took charge, sending Om and Maneck to buy a fresh half-coconut, green chillies, mint leaves, and a small bunch of coriander. The remaining ingredients: dry red chillies, cumin seed, and tamarind were in the spice cabinet. 'Now you two hurry back,' he said. 'There's more work for you.'

'Shall I do something?' asked Dina.

'We need one cup of gram dal.'

She measured out the pulse and immersed it in water, then put the pot on the stove. 'If we had soaked it overnight it wouldn't need boiling,' he said. 'But this is fine too.'

When the boys returned, he assigned Om to grate the coconut and

Maneck to slice two onions, while he chopped four green and six red chillies, the coriander, and the mint leaves.

'These onions are hot, yaar,' said Maneck, sniffing and wiping his eyes on his sleeve.

'It's good practice for you,' said Ishvar. 'Everyone has to cry at some time in life.' He glanced across the table and saw the fat white rings falling from the knife. 'Hoi-hoi, slice it thinner.'

The dal was ready. He drained the water and emptied the pot into the mortar. He added half a teaspoon of cumin seed and the chopped chillies, then began mashing it all together. The drumming pestle prompted Maneck to add cymbals with his knife upon the pot.

'Aray bandmaster, are your onions ready?' said Ishvar. The medley in the mortar was turning into a rough paste, yellow with specks of green and red and brown. He mixed in the remaining ingredients and raised a bit to his nose, sampling the aroma. 'Perfect. Now it's time to make the frying pan sing. While I do the wadas, Om will make the chutney. Come on, grind the remaining copra and kothmeer-mirchi.'

The frying pan hissed and sizzled as Ishvar gently slid ping-pong sized balls into the glistening oil. He pushed them around with a spoon, keeping them swimming for an even colour. Meanwhile, Om dragged the round masala stone back and forth across the flat slab. Maneck took over after a while. Drop by precious drop, the green chutney emerged from their effort.

Dina stood savouring the fragrance of the wadas that were slowly turning mouth-watering brown in bubbling oil. She watched as the cleanup commenced with laughter and teasing, Ishvar warning the boys that if the grinding stone was not spotless he would make them lick it clean, like cats. What a change, she thought – from the saddest, dingiest room in the flat, the kitchen was transformed into a bright place of mirth and energy.

Thirty minutes later the treat was ready. 'Let's eat while it's hot,' said Ishvar. 'Come on, Om, get water for us.'

Everyone took a wada apiece and spread chutney over it. Ishvar waited for the verdict, beaming proudly.

'Superb!' said Maneck.

Dina pretended to be upset, saying he had never praised her meals with superlatives. He tried to wriggle out of it. 'Your food is also superb, Aunty, but it's similar to my mother's Parsi cooking. That's the only reason my tastebuds didn't go crazy.'

Ishvar and Om were modest about their efforts. 'It's nothing. Very simple to make.'

'It's delicious,' affirmed Dina. 'Maneck's idea of eating together was very good. If I knew from the beginning your food was so tasty, I would have hired you as cooks, not tailors.'

'Sorry,' Ishvar smiled at the compliment, 'we don't cook for money – only for ourselves and for friends.'

His words stirred her familiar residue of guilt. There was still a gulf between them, she did not see them as they saw her.

Over the weeks, the tailors expanded their contribution from chapatis, puris, and wadas to vegetarian dishes like paneer masala, shak-bhaji, aloo masala. There were always four people, or at least two, bustling about the kitchen in the evening. My bleakest hour, thought Dina, has now become the happiest.

On days that she made a rice dish, the tailors had a break from chapatis but went to the kitchen to help, if they were not out searching for a room to rent. 'When I was a little boy in the village,' said Ishvar, cleaning the rice, picking out pebbles, 'I used to do this for my mother. But in reverse. We used to go to the fields after the harvest and search for grain left from threshing and winnowing.'

They were trusting her with bits of their past, she realized, and nothing could be as precious. More pieces, to join to the growing story of the tailors.

'In those days,' continued Ishvar, 'it seemed to me that that was all one could expect in life. A harsh road strewn with sharp stones and, if you were lucky, a little grain.'

'And later?'

'Later I discovered there were different types of roads. And a different way of walking on each.'

She liked his way of putting it. 'You describe it well.'

He chuckled. 'Must be my tailor training. Tailors are practised in examining patterns, reading the outlines.'

'And what about you, Om? Did you also help your mother to collect grain?'

'No.'

'He didn't need to,' added Ishvar. 'By the time he was born, his father – my brother – was doing well in tailoring.'

'But he still sent me to learn about the stinking leather,' said Om.

'You didn't tell me that,' said Maneck.

'There are many things I haven't told you. Have you told me everything?'

'Learning about leather was to build character,' explained Ishvar. 'And to teach Om his history, remind him of his own community.'

'But why did he need reminding?'

'It's a long story.'

'Tell us,' said Dina and Maneck, in unintentional unison, which made them laugh.

'In our village we used to be cobblers,' began Ishvar.

'What he means is,' interrupted Om, 'our family belonged to the Chamaar caste of tanners and leather-workers.'

'Yes,' said Ishvar, taking the reins again, 'a long time ago, long before Omprakash was born, when his father, Narayan, and I were young boys of ten and twelve, we were sent by our father, whose name was Dukhi, to be apprenticed as tailors . . .'

'Teach me how to use them,' said Om.

'What?'

'The knife and fork.'

'Okay,' said Maneck. 'First lesson. Elbows off the table.'

Ishvar nodded approvingly. He commented that it would impress everyone and increase Om's worth when they went back to the village to find him a wife. 'Eating with fancy tools – that's a great skill, like playing a musical instrument.'

Dina's quilt started to grow again. With the tailors sailing vigorously through Au Revoir's export orders, remnants piled up like the alluvial deposits of a healthy river. She sat with the patches after dinner, selecting and blending the best of the recent acquisitions.

'These new pieces are completely different in style from the old ones,' said Maneck. 'You think they will look all right?'

'The counterpane critic is starting again,' she groaned.

'Squares and triangles and polygons,' said Om. 'They are a bit confusing, for sure.'

'It will look beautiful,' said Ishvar with authority. 'Just keep connecting patiently, Dinabai – that's the secret. Ji-hahn, it all seems meaningless bits and rags, till you piece it together.'

'Exactly,' she said. 'These boys don't understand. By the way, there is lots of cloth in the cupboard, if you also want to make something.'

Ishvar thought of Shankar – it would be nice to present him with a new vest. He described the problem to Dina: the amputated lower half, where nothing would stay put, neither a loincloth nor underwear nor pants, because of his constant squirming and manoeuvring on the platform. And once the garment had slipped off his waist, he was helpless until Beggarmaster came on his rounds.

'I think I have the answer,' said Dina. She found her old school bathing-costume, a one-piece, and explained its design. Copying it would be easy, with a few modifications such as adding sleeves, a collar, and buttons along the front.

'Your idea is bilkool first class,' said Ishvar.

He set aside sections of light-brown poplin, and next afternoon took his tape measure to the Vishram. Blowing on their tea saucers, Om and he watched through the window. Shankar was trying out a new routine on the pavement.

The ever-innovative Beggarmaster had lengthened the platform by attaching an extension. Shankar lay flat on his back, waving his thigh stumps in the air. His testicles dribbled out of the swaddling cloth during the turbulence. He kept tucking them back, but it required an arduous stretch to accomplish, and after a while he let the scrotum hang.

'O babu ek paisa day-ray,' he sang, rattling the begging tin on the first and third beats. It rested on his forehead between his fingerless palms. When he got tired he set it beside his head, leaving the hands free to wave like the thigh stumps.

He was sitting up by the time the tailors finished their tea. The view from the supine position was new for him, and he could only take it in small doses, spending the minutes in dread, afraid that somebody would step on him. Rush hour, when the hordes swept over the pavement, was a period of sheer terror.

Seeing Ishvar and Om emerge, he rowed his platform in from the kerb to chat with them.

'New improved gaadi, hahn Shankar?'

'What to do, have to keep the public satisfied. Beggarmaster thought it was time for variety. He has been very kind since we came back from that horrible place. Even nicer than before. And he does not call me Worm anymore, uses my real name, just like you.'

He was excited by their plans to design a vest uniquely for him. The three moved into the privacy of the Vishram's back alley where Ishvar could take some measurements.

'Must be nice for you,' said Om. 'Being able to sleep on the job now.'

'You have no idea what a paradise it is,' said Shankar slyly. 'It's been only three days, and the things I've seen. Especially when the skirts go floating over my head.'

'Really?' Om was envious. 'What do you see?'

'Words are too weak to describe the ripeness, the juiciness, of what my eyes have feasted on.'

'Maybe my nephew would like to take your place on the gaadi for a day or two,' said Ishvar drily.

'First he would have to do something about his legs,' said Shankar, relishing his touch of black humour. 'I know – just stop paying Beggarmaster. That will automatically produce broken limbs.'

The gift was ready the next day, and when the tailors went out in the evening to continue their search for accommodation, they stopped by Shankar's pavement. They wanted to take him to the alley and help him into the vest to check the fit, but he was a little doubtful. 'Beggarmaster would not like that,' he said.

'Why?'

'The new cloth looks too good.' He preferred not to wear it till it had been approved.

They went away disappointed, taking with them the parcel of hair from under Shankar's platform. For quite some time there had been nothing from the hair-collector, but in the last few days his deliveries had become regular. Their trunk was filling up.

'If long hair is very rare, how is Rajaram suddenly collecting so much of it?' wondered Om.

'I'm not going to bother my head with that fellow's hair.'

The following week, the tailors finally saw the beggar dressed in their gift. It was hard to recognize at first, for Beggarmaster had modified the brown poplin. Soiled all over, with a hole torn into the front, the garment was now suitable for Shankar.

'That bastard Beggarmaster,' said Om. 'Wrecking our creation.'

'Don't judge him by your clothes,' said Ishvar. 'You wouldn't go to work for Dinabai wearing a tie-collar or a big wedding turban, would you?'

XI The Bright Future Clouded

AFTER THE VERANDAH'S security and comfort had blunted the urgency for new accommodation, the tailors' evening excursions in search of a room to rent became a halfhearted exercise. Ishvar felt a little guilty about this, felt they were taking advantage of Dina's hospitality, now entering its third month. To assuage his conscience, he got into the habit of describing the failures for her in minute detail: the places they visited, the chawls and kholis and sheds they inspected, and how narrowly they missed out.

'So disappointing,' he said, on more evenings than one. 'Just ten minutes before we got there, someone took the room. And such a nice room too.'

But time had tranquillized Dina's worries about the landlord. She was quite content to let the tailors continue sleeping on the verandah. No one could have told her otherwise, not even Zenobia, who was horrified to discover their trunk and bedding there when she dropped in one evening.

'This is dangerous,' she warned. 'You are playing with fire.'

'Oh, nothing will happen,' said Dina confidently. She had repaid Nusswan's loan, there had been no more bother from the rent-collector, and the sewing was proceeding faster than ever.

The fearfully anticipated strike at Au Revoir Exports was also averted, which Mrs. Gupta celebrated as a triumph of good over evil. 'The corporation has its own musclemen now,' she explained to Dina. 'It's a case of our goondas versus their goondas. They deal with the union crooks before they can start trouble or lead the poor workers astray. Mind you, even the police support us. Everybody is fed up with the nuisance of unions.'

The tailors rejoiced when Dina brought home the good news. 'Our stars are in the proper position,' said Ishvar.

'Yes,' she said. 'But it's more important that your stitches be in the proper position.'

Ishvar and Om usually set off on their housing hunt after dinner, and sometimes before, if they were not cooking that day. She wished them good luck, but always added 'See you back soon,' and meant it. Maneck frequently went along. Left alone, her eyes kept turning to the clock as she awaited their return.

And when the evening's wanderings were later reported to her, her advice was: 'Don't rush into anything.' It would be foolish, she said, to pay a premium for a place which might be demolished again because it was illegally constructed. 'Better to save your money and get a proper room that no one can throw you out of. Take your time.'

'But you don't accept rent from us. How long can we burden you like this?'

'I don't feel any burden. And neither does Maneck. Do you, Maneck?'

'Oh yes, I have a big burden. My exams are coming.'

'The other problem is,' continued Ishvar, 'my dear nephew cannot get married until we have our own place.'

'Now that's something I can't help you with,' said Dina.

'Who said I wanted to marry?' scowled Om, while she and Ishvar exchanged parental smiles.

A tip about a possible half-room in the northern suburbs led them to the neighbourhood where they had searched for work on first arriving in the city. By the time they reached the location, the place had already been rented. They happened to be passing Advanced Tailoring Company, and decided to say hello to Jeevan.

'Ah, my old friends are back,' Jeevan greeted them. 'With a new friend. Is he also a tailor?'

Maneck smiled and shook his head.

'Ah, never mind, we'll soon turn you into one.' Then Jeevan waxed nostalgic about the time the three tailors had worked round the clock to meet the by-election deadline. 'Remember, we made a hundred shirts and hundred dhotis, for that fellow's bribes?'

'Felt like a thousand,' said Om.

'I found later that he had parcelled out work to more than two dozen tailors. He gave away five thousand shirts and dhotis.'

'Where do these rascal politicians get the money?'

'Black money, what else – from businessmen needing favours. That's how the whole licence-permit-quota raj works.'

It turned out, however, that the candidate was defeated, despite distributing the garments among his most important constituents, because the opposition kept making clever speeches: that there was no crime in using empty hands to accept fine gifts, as long as wise heads prevailed at voting time.

'He tried to blame me for losing. That the voters rejected him because the clothes were badly stitched. I said, bring it and show me. I never saw him again.' Jeevan cleared his work from the counter and brushed fluff off his shirt front. 'Come, sit, drink a little tea with me.'

The invitation to sit was only a figure of speech. The clutter in the tiny shop made it difficult to take literally. Renovations had been performed since the tailors were last here, and the rear had been partitioned to include a curtained booth for trial fittings. Ishvar accepted a saucer of tea at the counter; Jeevan sipped from the cup. The boys took theirs to the outside steps, to share.

It turned out to be a busy evening for Advanced Tailoring. 'You have brought me good luck,' said Jeevan. A family came to order outfits for their three little daughters, the mother proudly carrying the bundle of fabric under her arm, the father frowning fiercely. They wanted a blouse and long skirt for each child, in time for Divali.

Strumming his lips with one finger, Jeevan pretended to study his order book. 'That's only a month away,' he complained. 'Everybody is in a hurry.' He hummed and hawed, produced dentilingual clicks, then said it was possible, but only just.

The little girls hopped on their toes with relief and excitement. The fierce father snapped at them to stand still or he would break their heads. His family paid no attention to the excessive threat. They were used to this paternal aberration of speech.

Jeevan measured the cloth, a polyester design of peacocks. He frowned grimly, measured again, and pronounced, strumming his lips, that it was insufficient for three blouses and three long skirts. The children were ready to cry.

'The bowlegged bastard is lying,' whispered Om to Maneck. 'Watch now.'

He measured a third time and said, with the air of a philanthropist, that there was another option. 'It will be very difficult, but I can make knee-length frocks.'

The parents desperately seized the alternative, requesting Jeevan to go ahead. He flapped his tape in the air and invited the children forward for measurements. They stood stiffly, like a puppeteer's dolls, turning, raising their heads, lifting their arms with frozen joints.

'The crook will swipe at least three yards from it, maybe four,' murmured Om, vacating the steps to let the family depart. The three little girls complained softly that they wanted long skirts so, so much. Their father hugged them affectionately, threatening to knock their teeth out if they didn't behave themselves, and the happy family disappeared down the footpath.

Jeevan folded the cloth and tucked the page with the children's measurements inside it. 'We tailors have to make a living, no?' he sought approval for his performance.

Ishvar nodded in a non-committal manner.

'These customers – always expecting too much from us,' Jeevan tried again, hiding poorly behind banalities.

He was plucked out of his awkward moment by the appearance of another client. The woman, scheduled for a trial fitting, was handed the preliminary framework of her silk choli. She disappeared into the booth, drawing the curtain shut.

Maneck nudged Om, and they turned to watch. The swaying curtain settled a few inches from the floor, where the woman's sari could be seen caressing her sandalled feet. Jeevan wagged a finger at them, then leered at the booth himself.

'A thinner curtain would put spice in my life,' said Om. They could hear the gentle tinkling of her bangles.

'Shoosh!' warned Jeevan, snickering. 'You will cost me a regular customer.'

The woman's reappearance made them stumble into a guilty silence. They examined her surreptitiously, glancing sideways with heads lowered. Her sari had been left off the shoulders to permit Jeevan to review the blouse-in-progress. 'Arms raised a little, please,' he said, slipping his tape measure under them. Now his tone was clinical, like a doctor asking to see the patient's tongue.

Between the choli and the waistline her midriff was bare. She was wearing a hipster sari, in the modern fashion, showing her navel. Maneck and Om stared as Jeevan recommended two tucks at the back and a slightly deeper plunge for the neckline. She returned behind the curtain.

Om whispered to Maneck that this was the part he missed the most in working for Dinabai from paper patterns. 'It gives me no chance to measure women.'

'As if you could do anything while measuring.'

'You don't know how much is possible, yaar.' Doing a blouse, especially a tight choli like this one, he said, was heaven, because the tape went over the cups. Passing it around and reaching with the other hand to bring it to the front, you had to stand very close to her. This alone was exciting. Then your fingers held the tape in the hollow between the two breasts – so you didn't touch her – but it was always possible to graze a little. You had to be careful, and know when to press on. If she shrank as soon as the tape touched, it was dangerous to try anything. But some of them did not mind, and you could tell from their eyes and their nipples whether it was safe to move your fingers about.

'Have you ever done it?'

'Many times. At Muzaffar Tailoring, with Ashraf Chacha.'

'Maybe I really should give up college and become a tailor.'

'You should. It's more fun.'

Maneck smiled. 'Actually, I'm thinking of continuing college after my year is up.'

'Why? I thought you hated it.'

Maneck was silent for a moment, piano-playing on his knuckles. 'I got a letter from my parents. Saying how much they are waiting for this year to finish, how lonely they are without me – same old rubbish. When I was there, they said go, go, go. So I've decided to write that I want to stay for three more years, do the degree course instead of the one-year diploma.'

'You're stupid, yaar. In your place, I would return to my parents as early as possible.'

'What's the point? To argue and fight again with my father? Besides, I'm having fun here now.'

Om inspected his nails and ran a hand through his puff. 'If you're planning to stay, you should change your subject to tailoring, for sure. Because you cannot measure women for refrigerators.' He chuckled. 'What are you going to say? "Madam, how deep are your shelves?"'

Maneck laughed. 'I could ask "Madam, may I examine your compressors?" Or "Madam, you need a new thermostat in your thermostat cavity."'

'Madam, your temperature control knobs require adjustment.'

'Madam, your meat drawer is not opening properly.'

The customer left as they were getting uproarious, and Ishvar said, 'Come on, you two, time to go. What are you laughing so much about, hahn?'

'As if we don't know,' grinned Jeevan, bidding them good luck and farewell. 'Hope you soon find a room.'

During reading week, prior to Manek's exams, the rent-collector paid an unscheduled afternoon call. The tailors silenced the sewing-machines at the sound of the doorbell.

'How are you, sister?' said Ibrahim, his hand rising fezwards.

'What is it now?' said Dina, barring his way. 'Rent is already paid this month.'

'Rent is not the problem, sister.' Shrinking as he spoke, he blurted in one sentence that the office had sent him to deliver a final notice to vacate in thirty days because they had proof that she was using the flat for commercial purposes despite the warning months ago.

'Nonsense! What proof do they have?'

'Why get upset with me, sister,' he pleaded, tapping the notebook in his pocket. 'It's all here – dates, times, coming-going, taxi, dresses. And more proof is sitting in the back room.'

'Back room? You want to show me?' She stood aside and gestured him in.

The outright challenge startled him. He had no choice but to accept. Entering with his head bowed, he made for the sewing room. The tailors, frozen at the Singers, waited nervously, while Maneck watched from his room.

'This is the problem, sister. You cannot hire tailors and run a business here.' He moved his anguished hands to include the other bedroom. 'And a paying guest, on top of that. Such insanity, sister. The office will throw you out for sure.'

'You are talking rubbish!' she started the counterattack. 'This man,' she said, pointing to Ishvar, 'he is my husband. The two boys are our sons. And the dresses are all mine. Part of my new 1975 wardrobe. Go, tell your landlord he has no case.'

It was difficult to say who she shocked more with the apocryphal revelation: Ishvar, blushing and playing with his scissors, or Ibrahim, wringing his hands and sighing.

Pressing home her advantage, she demanded, 'You have anything else to say?'

Ibrahim hunched his shoulders till they looked sufficiently supplicatory. 'Marriage licence, please? Birth certificates? Can I see, please?'

'My slipper across your mouth is what you will see! How dare you insult me! Tell your landlord, if he does not stop harassing my family, I'll take him straight to court!'

He retreated, muttering that he would have to make a full report to the office, why abuse him for doing his job, he did not enjoy it any more than the tenants did.

'If you don't enjoy it, leave it. At your age you shouldn't have to work anyway. Your children can look after you.'

'I have to work, I am all alone,' he said as the door shut.

The sweetness of her victory faded. She waited, hearing him panting outside, catching his breath before he could set off. In the moment of his brief words, her own life's lonely, troubled years came rushing back, reminding her how recent and unreliable was the happiness discovered in these last few months.

In the back room Ishvar had recovered from the matrimonial surprise. The boys were chortling away, teasing him about the look on his face. 'You keep talking about a wife for me,' said Om. 'Instead you got one for yourself.'

'That was an amazing idea, Aunty. Did you plan it in advance?'

'Never mind that, you better plan for your exams.'

College closed for the three-week Divali vacation, and Dina encouraged Maneck to be a tourist. 'All this time it's been home to class and class to home. But there is so much sightseeing in this city. The museum and aquarium and the sculpted caves will fascinate you. Victoria Garden and the Hanging Gardens are also worth visiting, believe me.'

'But I've seen them before.'

'When? Years ago, with your mummy? You were just a little baba then, you cannot remember anything. You must go again. And you must also visit your Sodawalla relatives – they are your mummy's family.'

'Okay,' he said indifferently, and did not stir from the flat.

That week, the first fireworks of Divali were heard. 'Hai Ram,' said Ishvar. 'What a bombardment.'

'This is nothing,' said Dina. 'Wait till the actual date gets closer.'

The noise delayed bedtime by roughly two hours each night, making Maneck's empty vacation days longer and emptier. To compensate he tried rising late, but the clamorous dawn, filled with clanging milkmen and argumentative crows, was always victorious.

Dina wrote down bus numbers and directions for him. 'It's very easy to find these tourist attractions, you won't get lost,' she said, thinking that perhaps that was what scared him. But Maneck did not budge.

Fed up with his moping about the house, she began scolding him. 'All the time indoors, like a glum grandpa. It's not natural for a young man. And you're driving us crazy with your pacing up and down the whole day.'

His idle presence now began to distract Om, who was once again taking extended tea breaks with him at the Vishram, or playing cards on the verandah, showing a general disinclination to work. Ishvar reproached his nephew, and Dina reprimanded him as well, to no avail.

At the end of the week they took a different approach; they decided it would be best to let Om have a vacation too. Expecting him to slog at the Singer while his friend waited around was unrealistic. After all, it was bad enough having to earn his living at an age when he should have been going to college like Maneck.

So Om was told he could reduce his hours and sew from eight to eleven in the morning. 'You have worked very hard these last few months,' said Dina. 'You deserve a holiday.'

Now there was no keeping them at home. The minute Om finished his short shift, the two were not seen again till dinnertime. Then it was non-stop talk through the meal and until bedtime, for they were full of the things they had done.

'The sea was so rough, the launch was jumping like a wild horse,' said Om. 'It was scary, yaar.'

'I'm telling you, Aunty, your paying guest and half your tailoring factory almost drowned at the jetty.'

'Don't say inauspicious things,' said Ishvar.

'After that launch ride, even the aquarium made me dizzy – all that water around us.'

'But the fish were beautiful, yaar. And such stylish ways they have of swimming. As if they were out for a walk, or shopping in the bazaar, squeezing the tomatoes, or like police running after a thief.'

'Some of them were so colourful, like the cloth from Au Revoir,' said Maneck. 'And the nose of the sawfish looked exactly like a real saw, I swear.'

'Tomorrow, I want to get a massage at the beach,' said Om. 'We saw them today, with their oils and lotions and towels.'

'Be very careful,' warned Dina. 'Those massagewallas are crooks. They give you beautiful chumpee till you are so relaxed, you fall asleep. Then they pick your pocket.'

The next three days, however, were spent at the museum. Om came home and said that the builders must have modelled the domed roof after his uncle's stomach. 'If only I could honestly claim such prosperity,' said Ishvar. For three evenings he and Dina heard all about the Chinese gallery, Tibetan gallery, Nepalese gallery, samovars, tea urns, ivory carvings, jade snuff boxes, tapestries.

Particularly transfixing had been the armour collection – the suits of mail, jade-handled daggers, scimitars, swords with serrated edges ('like the coconut grater on the kitchen shelf,' said Om), bejewelled ceremonial swords, bows and arrows, cudgels, pikes, lances, and spiked maces.

'They looked like the weapons in that old film, *Mughal-e-Azam*,' said Maneck, and Om added they would be useful to arm all the Chamaars in the villages, conduct a massacre of the landlords and upper castes, which made Ishvar frown disapprovingly till the boys' laughter reassured him.

And so they devoured their holidays with youthful appetites. The wonders of the city tumbled from their tongues for Ishvar, who enjoyed their sightseeing vicariously, and for Dina, who, in the tide of their enthusiasm, rediscovered something of her own school-days.

Halfway through the vacation a late monsoon surge darkened the skies. Heavy rain kept the boys indoors. Bored and restless, Maneck remembered the chessmen. Om had never seen a set, and the plastic figures captivated his imagination. He demanded to learn the game.

Maneck began naming the pieces for him: 'King, queen, bishop, knight, rook, pawn.' The sculpted words fell with a familiar caress upon his own ears. He took pleasure in feeling the pieces between his fingers again after so long, resurrecting them from their maroon plywood coffin in their customary squares, ready for battle.

Then, abruptly, the sound of his voice became the faraway echo of another – a voice that had once named the chessmen thus, for him, in the college hostel. He stopped, unable to proceed with explaining the game. The voice began disinterring the bones of his recent past, the ones he was trying to forget, had half-forgotten, had never wanted to see again. Now they were suddenly surfacing with grotesque alacrity.

He stared at the chessboard, where every piece harboured a ghost within its square. Thirty-two ghosts began their own moves, a dancing, colliding, taunting army of memories willing to do battle with his will to forget. Then the dancing chessmen changed partners, and it was the face of Avinash smiling at him from all sixty-four squares.

With an effort, Maneck abandoned the board and went to the window. Rain was pounding the street. Someone's motorcycle lay covered under a loudly thrumming tarpaulin. The puddles around it were muddy and uninviting. There were no children playing or splashing, the street joyless in this rain that had stayed too long and was too torrential. He wished he had never opened the box of chessmen.

'What's wrong?' asked Om.

'Nothing.'

'Come on, then. Stop wasting time, show me how to play.'

'It's a stupid game. Forget it.'

'Why do you have it, if it's stupid?'

'Someone lent it to me. I have to return it soon.' He watched the sewer's whirlpool swallow empty cigarette packs and soft-drink bottlecaps. Kohlah's Cola would not be among them. Not while Daddy continued in his stubborn ways. What a success the business could have been. And he would never have had to come to this bloody college. Must have made a wrong move somewhere in life, he thought, to walk into this check.

'You just don't want to teach me,' said Om, sweeping the pieces into the box. They fell with an accusing clatter. Maneck looked, and opened his mouth as though he would speak. Om did not notice, sliding on the lid.

Maneck lingered at the window a little longer before returning to the chessboard. 'I don't want to give you any trouble,' said Om sarcastically. 'Are you sure you want to teach me?'

He said nothing, set the board up and began to explain the rules. The rain was beating hard on the motorcycle's tarpaulin.

Over the next two days, Om learned how the pieces were moved and captured but the concept of checkmate continued to elude him. If Maneck constructed an example on the board, he grasped it perfectly, feeling the trapped king's helplessness with a visceral anguish. But to reach a similar dénouement on his own during play was beyond him, and he became impatient.

Maneck felt the failure was his – he was just not as good a teacher as Avinash. The corollaries of stalemate and draw were equally difficult. 'Sometimes there aren't enough pieces left on either side, so the king keeps endlessly moving out of check,' he explained over and over.

Again, Om understood when it was illustrated on the board; but the metaphor of kings and armies was not sustained to his satisfaction, and he refused to proceed beyond it. 'Makes no sense,' he argued. 'Look, your army and my army are battling, and all our men are dead. That leaves the two of us. Now one of us has to win, the stronger will kill the other, right?'

'Maybe. But the rules are different in chess.'

'The rules should always allow someone to win,' Om insisted. The logical breakdown troubled him.

'Sometimes, no one wins,' said Maneck.

'You were right, it *is* a stupid game,' said Om.

After five days of rain the skies did not let up, and the two were a thorough nuisance in the flat. They amused themselves watching Ishvar and Dina at work. 'Look,' whispered Maneck. 'His tongue always pokes into his cheek when he starts the machine.' And they found hilarious her habit of hiding both lips between her teeth when measuring something.

'That's too slow, yaar,' observed Om, as his uncle paused to load a bobbin from the spool. 'I can wind it in thirty seconds.'

'You are young, I am old,' said Ishvar good-humouredly. He slipped the fresh bobbin into the shuttle and slid the metal plate over it.

'I always keep six bobbins ready,' said Om. 'Then I can change them phuta-phut, without stopping in the middle of a dress.'

'Aunty, you should also grow long nails on your little fingers, like Ishvar. It will look great.'

Her patience quickly ran out. 'You two are becoming trouble with a capital t. Just because you have a vacation doesn't mean you sit and eat up our heads with your nonsense. Either go out or start working.'

'But it's raining, Aunty. You don't want us to get wet, do you?'

'You think the whole city pulls a blanket over its head because of a little rain? Take the umbrella, it's hanging from the cupboard in your room.'

'That's a ladies' umbrella.'

'Then get wet. But stop bothering us.'

'Okay,' said Om. 'We'll go somewhere in the afternoon.'

They removed themselves to the verandah, and Maneck suggested a second visit to the aquarium. Om said he had a better idea: 'Jeevan's shop.'

'Boring, yaar – there's nothing to do there.'

Om revealed his plan: to convince Jeevan to let them measure female customers.

'Okay, let's go,' grinned Maneck.

'I'll teach you this game,' said Om. 'Measuring the chest is easier than playing chess. And much more fun, for sure.'

The shop was quiet when they arrived. Jeevan was taking a nap, stretched out on the floor behind the counter. On a stool by his head a transistor radio played soft sarangi music. Om turned up the volume, and Jeevan awoke with a start.

He sat gulping air for a minute, his eyes bulging. 'Why did you do that? It's a joke or what? Now I'll have a headache the whole afternoon.'

He refused to even consider Om's offer of free help. 'Measure my customers? Forget it. I know what you are up to. That swelling between your legs will drag my shop's good name through the mud.'

Om promised to behave professionally and not let his fingers wander. He declared that his skills were rusting due to working from paper patterns. 'I just want to keep in touch with real tailoring.'

'Tits are what you want to keep in touch with. You can't fool me. Stay away from my lady customers, I'm warning you.'

Maneck wandered into the changing booth behind the curtain. 'Wouldn't it be fun to hide in here when they came for a trial.'

Om inspected the interior too. He found three clothes hooks and a mirror, but nowhere to conceal oneself. 'It's impossible,' he concluded.

'You think so, do you?' said Jeevan. 'Now let me show you smart boys something.' He led them behind the counter, to the rear of the partition that formed the back of the booth. 'Put your eye to that,' he said, indicating a crack in one corner.

Om gasped. 'You can see everything from here!'

'Let me look,' said Maneck, pushing him. 'It's perfect, yaar!'

Jeevan strummed his lips and smirked. 'Yes, but don't get any ideas. I will be in a madhouse before I let you in here.'

'Aray, please!' said Om. 'It's such a perfect top-to-bottom free show!'

'Perfect, yes. Free, no. Everything has a price. You go for cinema, there is a ticket to buy. Take the train, and there is the fare to pay.'

'How much?' asked Om.

'Never mind how much. I cannot risk my shop's honour.'

'Please, yaar, Jeevan, please!'

He began to relent. 'You'll behave yourselves? No going crazy at the sight of flesh?'

'We'll do whatever you say.'

'Okay. Two rupees each.'

Om watched Maneck check his pocket. 'Yes, we have enough.'

'But I want only one at a time back here. And no noise, not even breathing, understand?' They nodded. Jeevan examined the order book. Two women were due that evening, one for a blouse and one for pants. 'Who wants which?'

Maneck suggested tossing a coin. 'Heads,' said Om, and won. He closed his eyes, smiling, trying to decide, and selected pants. Jeevan said they had at least an hour to wait, the customers would be coming after five. Since the rain had eased up, the two decided to go for a stroll.

It was a tense, silent walk, the air heavy with expectation. They spoke just once, to concur that they should be getting back in case the women were early. Barely fifteen minutes had elapsed.

They waited on edge in the shop, getting on Jeevan's nerves. There were four false alarms – people collecting repairs and alterations. At a quarter to six, their patience was rewarded.

'Yes, madam, your blouse is ready for trial,' said Jeevan, giving the boys a discreet nod. He browsed through a stack of clothes to allow Maneck time to slide behind the counter into the dark space. Then, retrieving the blouse, he indicated the curtain to the woman. 'In there, madam, thank you very much.'

Maneck thought the pounding of his heart would knock down the partition. High heels tapping sharply on the stone floor, she entered, hung the new blouse on a hook, and drew the curtain. She pulled her neatly tucked top out of her skirt and unbuttoned it, her back towards him. He watched her reflection in the mirror.

He held his breath as the top came away. She was wearing a white brassière. Her thumbs travelled under the straps, shifting their position. Two red lines upon the skin of her shoulders marked the place. Then she moved her hands behind and unhooked the brassière.

For one insane moment he thought it was coming off. He clenched his fist. But the hook was merely moved to the next loop on the fraying elastic band. She rolled her shoulders a couple of times and adjusted the cups, pushing them higher till they settled snugly, and put on the new blouse.

Beads of perspiration rolled down Maneck's forehead and stung his eyes. She left the booth. He took the opportunity to inhale deeply. Through the crack, past the open curtain, he could see Jeevan checking the fit. Om turned suddenly and winked at the crack, putting his hands on his chest and squeezing.

The blouse was satisfactory. She returned to change, and exited in less than a minute. Maneck waited; he could hear Jeevan thanking her and providing a final delivery date. Then the high heels tapped their way down the steps, and he emerged from the hiding place.

He wiped his brow on his sleeve, shaking out the shirt underneath his armpits. 'It's so hot behind the partition.'

'Don't blame the partition. Your heat rises from your lower part,' laughed Jeevan. He gestured for the money, and Maneck paid up.

'How was it?' asked Om. 'What did you see?'

'It was great. But she was wearing a bra.'

'What did you expect?' said Jeevan. 'My customers are not low-class village women. They work in big offices – secretaries, receptionists, typists. They apply lipstick and rouge, and wear top-quality underwear.'

Om had to wait another half-hour before his customer arrived. He sidled nonchalantly past the counter, disappearing before Jeevan found the garment and directed the woman into the booth.

When she stepped out Maneck wished he could have opted for this one. The way the new pants hugged her thighs and gripped her crotch brought a lump to his throat. Jeevan knelt before her to verify the inseam, and Maneck swallowed hard.

She returned behind the curtain. Seconds later, there was a muffled thud and a scream.

Jeevan jumped. 'Madam! Is everything all right?'

'I heard a noise! From the back!'

'Please madam, it's all right, I promise you,' he grovelled with masterful calm and speed. 'It's only rats. Please don't worry.'

She came out flustered, flinging the pants on the counter. He reverently restored them to their hanger. 'I'm very sorry you were frightened, madam. Rats are such a problem wherever you go in the city.'

'You should do something about it,' she said angrily. 'It's not nice for your customers.'

'Yes, madam. Sometimes it hides in the boxes behind the partition and makes a noise. I'll have to spread more poison for it.' He apologized again and saw her off.

Om emerged wearing a sheepish smile, quite ready to be teased about his trouser-rat. Jeevan clipped him viciously over the head. 'Saala idiot! Such huge trouble you could have made for me! What caused the noise?'

'Sorry, I slipped.'

'Slipped! What filthy things were you doing that you slipped? Get out, both of you! I don't want to see you again in my shop!'

Maneck tried to placate Jeevan by offering the two rupees for Om's viewing, but that only aggravated him further. He swept the hand aside and looked ready to strike him. 'Keep your money! And keep this troublesome boy out of my shop!' He pushed them through the door and down the steps.

They were subdued as they walked up the lane to the main road. A crow shrieked from a window ledge. The sobering effect of Jeevan's rage was deepened by the evening light lapping at the hem of darkness. Streetlamps started to flicker tentatively – yellow buds, intimating the arrival of the full glow. Something scampered across their path into an alley.

'Look,' said Maneck. 'There goes madam's rat.' They caught a flash of pink skin through the rodent's diseased fur, patchy and mange-eaten.

'It's searching for Advanced Tailoring,' said Om. 'Wants to order a new suit.' They laughed. The rat disappeared into the alley's darker recesses where a gutter gurgled. There were sharp squeaks, and sounds of splashing. They headed for the bus stop.

'So tell me,' Maneck nudged with an elbow. 'What were you doing in there?'

Smiling wryly, Om made a fist and moved it up and down. A short laugh that was more like a cough broke from Maneck.

Ahead, something spattered onto the crowded pavement from an upper-storey window. Pedestrians who had been soiled screamed at the building. They reached the entrance steps and raced upstairs, though it was impossible to know which window was hiding the culprit.

'Did you see much?' asked Maneck.

'Everything. Her new pants were so tight, when she pulled them down her knickers went down as well.'

Maneck kicked a stone into the gutter. 'You saw the hair?'

Om nodded. 'It was a real bush.' He used both hands to describe it, wriggling his fingers to emphasize a rich thicket. 'Have you ever seen one?'

'Only once. A long time ago. We used to have an ayah when I was small. I climbed on a chair while she was bathing and looked through the ventilator over the door. It scared me. It seemed fierce, as though it was going to bite.'

Om laughed. 'It wouldn't scare you now, for sure. You'd jump right into it.'

'Just give me a chance.'

They waited for the signal change to cross the road. At the edge of the footpath two policemen held up a rope, taut between them, keeping the crowds from spilling into traffic. People surged against the barrier like waves testing the shoreline. The policemen dug in their heels, straining, shouting, containing the impatient homeward-bound flock.

'You know, it's a good thing the rat wasn't really behind the partition,' said Maneck. 'It would have chewed off your little soosoti in one second.'

'What do you mean by little?' said Om. 'It stands up like this.' And he brandished his forearm energetically.

The proscriptive red hand on the traffic light disappeared, and a green stick-figure illuminated the round glass. The policemen skipped aside nimbly with the rope; the crowd swarmed across.

Fireworks reached their climax on the night before Divali, and sleep was difficult till well after midnight. At each detonation, especially of the red cubes called Atom Bombs, Ishvar sighed 'Hai Ram' and put his hands over his ears.

'What's the point in covering your ears after the bang?' said Om.

'What else can I do. Bilkool crazy, a time of light and celebration turning into pain and earache. Is this any way to welcome Lord Ram back to Ayodhya from his exile in the forest?'

'The problem is too much wealth in the city,' said Dina. 'If people must make smoke of their money, I wish they would do it prettily.' She flinched as another Atom Bomb exploded. 'If I was in charge, only sparklers, fountains, and chakardees would be allowed.'

'Hahnji, but the great religious experts will tell you that it wouldn't be enough to frighten away the evil spirits,' said Ishvar sarcastically.

'These Atom Bombs will scare the gods as well,' she said, retreating from the verandah. 'In Lord Ram's place, I would run straight back to the forest rather than face the explosions of these fanatics.'

With a plug of cotton wool in each ear she started to work on the quilt. Ishvar followed her in a few minutes, sitting with his hands over his ears, and she got cotton wool for him too. At the next boom he beamed, to say it was working.

Maneck and Om refused to relinquish the verandah, though they stuck fingers in their ears if a reveller began preparing a string of red cubes. 'Too bad we're watching,' said Om. 'Or they'd be in bed – jumping, for sure.'

'Who?'

'Dinabai and my uncle, who else?'

'You have a dirty mind.'

'Yes, I do,' said Om. 'Listen, a riddle for you: to make it stiff and stand up straight, she rubs it; to make it slick and slide it in, she licks it. What is she doing?' He was laughing before he had finished reciting the question, while Maneck hushed him with a finger to his lips.

'Come on, answer. What's she doing?'

'Fucking, what else?'

'Wrong. Give up? She's threading a needle,' said Om smugly, as Maneck clapped a hand to his forehead. 'Now whose mind is dirty?'

There were six days of vacation left before college reopened, and Om had an idea for more fun. He knew that age and moisture had distorted the bathroom door and its frame, leaving a sizeable gap when shut. He said they could take turns peeking while Dina bathed. The other would keep watch, to make sure Ishvar didn't catch them at it.

'Your story about the bathing ayah gave me the inspiration. So what do you think?'

'You're mad,' said Maneck. 'I'm not going to.'

'What are you scared of? She won't know, yaar.'

'I just don't want to.'

'Okay, then I will.' He got up.

'No, you won't.' Maneck grabbed his arm.

'Aray go! Who are you to tell me?' He wrenched his arm away, whereupon Maneck gripped his shoulders and pushed him back in the chair. They grappled in earnest. Om lashed out with his feet but Maneck worked his way behind the chair and pinned him to it. Om gave up, unable to move.

'You're a selfish bastard,' he said softly. 'I know you. All those months you lived alone with her, you must have watched her naked every morning in the bathroom. Now you won't let me have the same fun.'

'It's not true,' said Maneck vehemently from behind the chair. 'I never have.'

'You're lying. At least admit it. Come on, describe her for me if you won't let me look. What about her tits? Are the nipples nice and pointy? And the –'

'Stop it.'

'– and the brown circles around the nipples, how big are they?'

'Shut up, I'm warning you.'

'And the cunt? Is it big and juicy with lots of –'

Maneck moved in front of the chair and slapped him across the mouth. Shocked, Om clutched his face silently for a few seconds. The pain filled his eyes. 'You lousy fucker!' he came to life then, and sprang at him, swinging his fists wildly.

The chair fell over. Maneck caught one blow on the head, the rest landing harmlessly on his arms. To subdue Om without hurting him, he grabbed his shirt and pulled him into a close embrace; now the fists had no room to travel. There was the sound of something tearing. The pocket came away in his hand, and a rent appeared below the shoulder.

'Bastard!' screamed Om, redoubling his efforts. 'You tore my shirt!'

The commotion grew loud enough for Ishvar to hear over the sound of his machine, bringing him to the verandah. 'Hoi-hoi! What is this goonda-giri?'

In his presence their desire to fight suddenly evaporated. It was easy for him to separate them. Now the violence was all in the looks. They glared at each other for a moment before turning away.

'He tore my shirt!' cried Om, staring down at the disembowelled pocket.

'Such things happen if you fight. But why were you behaving like that?'

'He tore my shirt,' anguished Om again.

Meanwhile, Dina had heard the shouting and cut short her bath. 'I can't believe it,' she said, when Ishvar told her. 'I thought it was ruffians on the street. You two? Why?'

'Ask him,' they each muttered.

'He tore my shirt,' added Om, 'look,' and flapped the torn pocket before her.

'Shirt, shirt, shirt! Is that all you can say?' scolded Ishvar. 'Shirt can be repaired. Why were you fighting?'

425

'I'm not rich like him, I only have two shirts. And he tore one.'

Maneck rushed to his room, grabbed the first shirt in sight, and returned to fling it at Om. He caught it and threw it back. Maneck let it lie where it fell.

'You are acting like two little babas,' said Dina. 'Come on, Ishvarbhai, let's get to work.' She felt they would reconcile faster if left to themselves, without the burden of saving face.

Maneck stayed in his room all day, and Om sat on the verandah. Ishvar's attempts to joke about the sour-lime face or hero number zero were stillborn. Dina felt sorry that the vacation was winding down on a bitter note.

'Look at them,' she said, 'two mournful owls nesting in my house,' and she made an owlish face at the boys. Ishvar laughed alone.

Next morning, Om announced with the air of a martyr that he wanted to work full days again. 'This holiday has lasted much too long for my taste.' Maneck pretended not to have heard.

The sewing started badly, and developed into a full-blown disaster. Dina had to warn Om: 'The company will not tolerate this. You must keep your bad humour out of the stitches.'

As a badge of his martyrdom he continued to wear the torn shirt, pocket hanging loose, though it would have taken less than ten minutes to fix. At mealtimes, he pointedly avoided the knife and fork, which he had mastered by now, and used his fingers. In the absence of speech, a war of noises broke out. Maneck's cutlery clattered against the plate, sawing a potato as if it were a deodar log. Om replied by slurping from his fingers, his tongue sucking and licking like a floor mop sloshing industriously. Maneck speared meat like a gladiator lunging at a lion. Om retaliated by involving his palm as well, suctioning food off it with little gurgles.

Their extravagant performances might have been amusing were it not for the palpable misery around the table. Dina felt cheated of the happy family atmosphere she had come to rely on. Instead, this wretched gloom sat uninvited at dinner, residing unwanted in her home.

For a fortnight after Divali, sporadic firecrackers kept puncturing holes in the night before dying out altogether. 'Peace and quiet at last,' said Ishvar, throwing away the cotton-wool plugs he had saved carefully beside his bedding.

Maneck got his marks for the first-term exams, and they were not very good. Dina said it was due to his neglecting his studies. 'From now on, I want to see you with your books for at least two hours. Every night, after dinner.'

'Even my mother is not so strict,' he grumbled.

'She would be if she saw these marks.'

Prodding him into the study routine turned out to be easier than she expected. His resistance was nominal, for there was little else to occupy him. Since the fight with Om, they barely spoke, though Ishvar kept trying valiantly to rekindle their friendship. He also supported Dina's attempt to make Maneck work harder.

'Think how happy your parents will be,' he said.

'Never mind your parents – study for your own sake, you foolish boy,' she said. 'You listen, too, Om. When you have children, make sure you send them to school and college. Look how I have to slave now because I was denied an education. Nothing is more important than learning.'

'Bilkool correct,' said Ishvar. 'But why were you denied an education, Dinabai?'

'It's a very long story.'

'Tell us,' said Ishvar, Maneck, and Om together. It made her smile, especially when the boys frowned to disown the coincidence.

She began. 'I never like to look back at my life, my childhood, with regret or bitterness.'

Ishvar nodded.

'But sometimes, against my will, the thoughts about the past come into my head. Then I question why things turned out the way they have, clouding the bright future everyone predicted for me when I was in school, when my name was still Dina Shroff . . .'

Sounds on the verandah announced the tailors' preparation for sleep. The bedding was unrolled and shaken out. Soon, Om began massaging his uncle's feet. Maneck could tell from the soft sighs of pleasure. Then Ishvar said, 'Yes, that one, harder, the heel aches a lot,' and inside, bent over his textbook, Maneck envied their closeness.

He yawned and looked at his watch – everyone in neutral corners. He missed their company, the walks, the after-dinner gatherings in the front room with Dina Aunty working on the quilt while they watched, chatting, planning next day's work, or what to cook for tomorrow's dinner: the simple routines that gave a secure, meaningful shape to all their lives.

In the sewing room the light was still on. Dina was maintaining her vigil till Maneck closed his books, making sure he did not shave a few minutes off the end of his study shift.

The doorbell rang.

The tailors bolted upright on the bedding and reached for their shirts. Dina came to the verandah and demanded through the door, 'Who's there?'

'Sorry for the trouble, sister.'

She recognized the rent-collector's voice. Absurd, she thought, for him to come at this hour. 'What is it, so late?'

'Sorry to bother you sister, but the office has sent me.'

'Now? Couldn't wait till morning?'

'They said it was urgent, sister. I do as I am told.'

She shrugged at the tailors and opened the door, holding on to the knob. The next moment, two men behind Ibrahim shoved the door aside, and her with it, charging in as though expecting to meet heavy opposition.

One of them was nearly bald and the other had a mop of black hair, but their straggly moustaches, cold eyes, and slouching, bulky torsos made menacing twins of them. They seemed to have fashioned their mannerisms on cinema villains, thought Maneck.

'Sorry, sister,' Ibrahim smiled his automatic smile. 'Office has sent me to deliver final notice – orally. Please listen very carefully. You must vacate in forty-eight hours. For violating tenancy terms and regulations.'

Fear brushed Dina's face lightly, like a feather, before she blew it aside. 'I'm calling the police right now if you don't take your goondas and leave! The landlord has a problem? Tell him to go to court, I will see him there!'

The bald man spoke, soft and soothing. 'Why insult us by saying goondas? We are the landlord's employees. Like these tailors are your employees.'

The other one said, 'We are acting in the place of courts and lawyers. They are a waste of time and money. These days we can produce faster results.' He had a mouthful of paan, and spoke with difficulty, dark-red trickles escaping the corners of his lips.

'Ishvarbhai, run to the corner!' said Dina. 'Fetch the police!'

The bald man blocked the door. Trying to get past him, Ishvar was sent reeling to the other end of the verandah.

'Please, please! No fighting,' said Ibrahim, his white beard trembling with his words.

'If you don't leave I'm going to start screaming for help,' said Dina.

'If you scream, we'll make you stop,' said the bald partner in a re-assuring tone. He continued to guard the front door while the paan-chewing man sauntered into the back room. Ibrahim, Dina, and the tailors followed helplessly. Maneck watched from his room.

The man stood motionless, looking around as though admiring the place. Then he exploded. He picked up one of the stools and began battering the sewing-machines with it. When its wooden legs fell apart, he continued with the second stool till it, too, had shattered.

He tossed it aside, kicked over the Singers, and started to rip the finished frocks stacked on the table, pulling them apart at the seams. He was struggling now – new cloth and fresh stitches did not give easily. 'Tear, maaderchod, tear!' he muttered, addressing the dresses.

Ishvar and Om, paralysed up to now, rediscovered movement and rushed to rescue the products of their labour. They were both flung back like bundles of cloth.

'Stop him!' said Dina to Ibrahim, grabbing his arm and pulling, pushing him towards the fray. 'You brought these goondas! Do something!'

Ibrahim wrung his hands nervously and decided to gather the wrecked frocks. As fast as the paan-chewing man could scatter them, he picked them up, folded the torn pieces, and placed them carefully on the table.

'Need any help?' called the partner from the door.

'No, everything's fine.' Finished with ripping the dresses, he started on the bolts of cloth, but this time the fabric, in its abundance, refused to tear.

'Set fire to it,' was the bald man's advice, and he offered his cigarette lighter.

'No!' panicked Ibrahim. 'Whole building might burn! Landlord won't like that!'

The paan-chewing man conceded the point. Unfurling the cloth in a heap upon the floor, he sprayed it with the paan juice his mouth had worked up. 'There,' he grinned at Ibrahim. 'My red nectar is as fiery as flames.'

Pausing to survey the room, he spied the pinking shears that Ashraf Chacha had gifted to the tailors. He examined them. 'Nice,' he said appreciatively, and lifted his hand to fling them out the window.

'No!' screamed Om.

The goonda laughed and released the tailors' dearest possession. The crash of the shears landing on the pavement came through the window as Om rushed at him. The puny attack amused the man before he decided to end it, slapping Om twice, then punching him in the stomach.

'You bastard,' said Maneck. He grabbed the pagoda umbrella hanging from the cupboard and went after Om's assailant.

'Please! No fighting!' begged Ibrahim. 'There is no need for fighting!'

The man took a whack on his shoulder, noticed the steel shaft's formidable point, and dodged around the fallen sewing-machines. Maneck feinted, relishing his superiority, while the man jerked backwards. He feinted again, and whacked him twice over the head.

The bald man entered the room quietly. Standing behind them, he pulled out a flick-knife and held it open, pointing to the ceiling. Like a film actor, thought Maneck, starting to tremble.

'Okay, batcha,' said the bald man in his soft voice. 'Your little fun is over.'

The others turned to look. Dina screamed when she saw the knife, and Ibrahim was furious now. 'Put that away! And get out, both of you! Your work is done, I am in charge!'

'Shut up,' said the bald man. 'We know our job.' His partner snatched away the umbrella and drove his fist into Maneck's face. Maneck fell against the wall. Blood trickled from his mouth in a painful reflection of the paan juice oozing from the other's lips.

'Stop it! I was present when you got your orders! There was nothing about beatings and knives!' The rent-collector stamped his foot and shook his fist.

The impotent rage entertained the bald man. 'Are you killing cockroaches with your shoe?' he laughed, feeling the blade with his finger before retracting it. Then he snapped it open again and slashed Dina's pillows and mattress. He threw them about, watching the stuffing scatter. The sofa cushions in the front room were treated similarly.

'There,' he said. 'Now the rest is in your hands, madam. You don't want us to return with a second notice, do you?'

The other fellow kicked Maneck's shins in passing. Giving his paan a final workout, he spat on the bed and around it, emptying his mouth over as much of the room as possible. 'Are you coming or not?' he asked Ibrahim.

'Later,' he said, frowning angrily at them. 'I have not finished.'

The front door closed. Dina regarded the rent-collector with loathing and went to Maneck, where Ishvar was cradling him, holding his head, asking if he was all right. Ibrahim followed close behind, whispering repeatedly, 'Forgive me, sister,' like a secret prayer.

Maneck's nose was bleeding and the upper lip was cut. He checked with his tongue – no teeth were broken. They wiped the blood with scraps lying around the sewing-machines. He tried to mumble something and rose groggily.

'Don't talk,' said Om, who had got back his wind, 'it will bleed more.'

'Thank God the knife wasn't used,' said Dina.

The sound of shattering glass came from the front room. Ibrahim ran to the verandah. 'Stop it, you fools!' he yelled. 'What's the idea? That will only cost the landlord!' A few more stones broke the remaining windowpanes, then there was silence.

They helped Maneck to the basin to wash his face. 'I can walk by myself,' he muttered. After cleaning up a bit, they led him to the sofa with a cloth pressed to his nose.

'What that lip needs is ice,' said Dina.

'I'll buy some from Vishram,' volunteered Om.

'Not necessary,' said Maneck, but was overruled by the others. A ten-paisa lump would be enough, they decided. Ibrahim quickly fished a coin out of his sherwani and offered it to Om.

'Don't touch his money!' ordered Dina, fetching her purse. The rent-collector pleaded for its acceptance before dropping the coin back in his pocket.

Waiting for Om to return, they contemplated the damage. Fluff from the shredded cushions floated around, settling slowly to the floor. Dina picked up the slashed casings; she felt dirty, as though the goondas' hands had molested her own being. The ripped dresses and paan-soiled bolts began bearing down heavily on her. How would she explain to Au

Revoir? What could she possibly tell Mrs. Gupta?

'I am finished,' she said, on the verge of tears.

'Maybe the frocks can be repaired, Dinabai,' said Ishvar, making an effort to console her. 'And we can wash off the red stuff.'

But his words sounded so hopeless, even to himself, that instead he turned on Ibrahim. 'You have no shame? Why are you trying to destroy this poor lady? What kind of monster are you?'

Ibrahim stood contritely, ready to listen. He welcomed the revilement, desired an excess of it, to salve his guilt.

'Your beard is pure white but your heart is rotten,' said Ishvar.

'You wicked, sinful man!' hissed Dina. 'A disgrace to old age!'

'Please, sister! I did not know they –'

'You did this! You brought those goondas!' She shook with fear and rage.

Ibrahim could control himself no longer. Putting his hands over his face, he made a peculiar sound. It was not immediately apparent that he was trying to cry noiselessly. 'It's no use,' his voice broke. 'I cannot do this job, I hate it! Oh, what has my life become!' He felt under the sherwani and pulled out his kerchief to blow his nose.

'Forgive me, sister,' he sobbed. 'I did not know, when I brought them, that they would do such damage. For years I have followed the landlord's orders. Like a helpless child. He tells me to threaten somebody, I threaten. He tells me to plead, I plead. If he raves that a tenant must be evicted, I have to repeat the raving at the tenant's door. I am his creature. Everybody thinks I am an evil person, but I am not, I want to see justice done, for myself, for yourself, for everyone. But the world is controlled by wicked people, we have no chance, we have nothing but trouble and sorrow . . .'

He dissolved completely. Ishvar took his arm and led him to a chair, his resentment softening. 'Here, sit down and don't cry. Doesn't look nice.'

'What else can I do but cry? These tears are all I have to offer. Forgive me, sister. I have harmed you. Now the goondas will return after forty-eight hours. They will throw your furniture and belongings on the pavement. Poor sister, where will you go?'

'I won't open the door for them, that's all.'

Her childish assertion touched Ibrahim, and he began weeping again. 'It won't stop them. They will bring policemen to break the lock.'

'As if the police will help them.'

'These Emergency times are terrible, sister. Money can buy the necessary police order. Justice is sold to the highest bidder.'

'But what is it to the landlord if my tailors and I sew here?' Her voice rose uncontrollably. 'Who am I harming with my work?'

'The landlord needs an excuse, sister. These flats are worth a fortune, the Rent Act lets him charge only the old worthless rent, so he –'

Ibrahim broke off and wiped his eyes. 'But you know all that, sister. It's not you alone, he is doing the same with other tenants, the ones who are weak and without influence.'

Om returned with a lump of ice that was too big to hold comfortably against the lip. He covered it in cloth and struck the floor with it. 'You came like a real hero to save me,' he grinned, trying to cheer up Maneck, who looked very pale. 'You jumped in just like Amitabh Bachchan.'

He unwrapped the fragments of ice and turned to the others. 'Did you see it? For a minute that fucker was really scared by Maneck's umbrella.'

'Language,' said Dina.

Maneck smiled, which stretched the cut lip. He restrained himself and took a piece of ice.

'That's it – that's your new name,' said Om. 'Umbrella Bachchan.'

'What are you waiting for?' Dina turned angrily to the rent-collector again. 'You tell your landlord, I am not leaving, I won't give up this flat.'

'I don't think it will help, sister,' said Ibrahim sorrowfully, 'but I wish you best of luck,' and he left.

Maneck said he did not want to create trouble for Dina Aunty with his presence. 'Don't worry about me,' he uttered with minimum lip movement. 'I can always return home.'

'Don't talk like that,' she said. 'After all these months, more than halfway to your diploma, how can you disappoint your parents?'

'No no, he is right,' said Ishvar. 'It's not fair, all this suffering for you because of us. We will go back to the nightwatchman.'

'Stop talking nonsense, all of you,' snapped Dina. 'Let me think for a minute.' She said they were missing the point. 'You heard Ibrahim's words – the landlord just wants an excuse. Your going away will not save my flat.'

The only thing she could count on, in her opinion, was her brother's ability to straighten out the dispute – with money, smooth words, or whatever it was that he was so good at using in his business dealings. 'Once again, I'll have to swallow my pride and ask for his help, that's all.'

XII Trace of Destiny

THEY MOVED MECHANICALLY through their morning acts of washing and cleaning and tea-making. Om's stomach was sore where he had been punched, but he did not tell his uncle. They crept into Maneck's room to check on him. He was still asleep. There were stains on his pillow; his lip and nose had bled again during the night. They called Dina to see it.

She was mentally rehearsing her meeting with Nusswan, imagining his smug face, the expression proclaiming his indispensability. She bent over Maneck – how innocent is his sleep, she thought, and felt like stroking his forehead. The lip was black where the blood had clotted. The final trickle from the nose had also congealed. They backed softly out of the room. 'He's all right,' she whispered. 'The cut is dry, let him sleep.'

As she was readying to leave for her brother's office, Beggarmaster arrived at the door, briefcase chained to his left wrist. It was his scheduled collection day. Ishvar had the money put aside from the previous week's earnings, safe in Dina's cupboard.

She urged him to level with the man that the next instalment would be difficult. 'Better to tell him now than to have him come looking for you with a stick.'

Beggarmaster listened sceptically. Measured against his own experiences, the account of the goondas' nocturnal assault sounded too theatrical to be true. He suspected his clients were concocting the story, preparing to renege on their contract.

Then they took him inside, showed him the shattered windows, battered sewing-machines, torn dresses and soiled fabrics, and he was convinced. 'This is bad,' he said. 'Very bad. Such amateurs they must be, to behave like this.'

'I'm ruined,' said Dina. 'And it's not the tailors' fault that they won't be able to pay you next week.'

'Believe me, they will,' he said grimly.

'But how?' implored Ishvar. 'If we are thrown out and cannot work? Have mercy on us!'

Taking no notice of him, Beggarmaster walked around the room, inspecting, rapping his knuckles on the table, jotting in his little notepad. 'Tell me how much it will cost to fix all the damage.'

'What good is that going to do?' cried Dina. 'Those goondas will return tomorrow if we don't vacate! And you want to waste time on an account? I have more urgent things on my mind, making sure I have shelter!'

Beggarmaster looked up from his notepad, slightly surprised. 'You already have shelter. Right here. This *is* your flat, isn't it?'

She nodded impatiently at the silly question.

'Those goondas committed a big mistake,' he continued, 'and I am going to correct it for them.'

'And when they come back?'

'They won't. You tailors have made your payments regularly, so you don't have to worry – you are under my protection. Everything will be taken care of. But unless I know the amount of damage, how will I reimburse you? You want to start your sewing business again or not?'

Now it was Dina's turn to look sceptical. 'What are you, an insurance company?'

He smiled modestly in reply.

There was nothing to lose, she decided, and started multiplying the mutilated length of Au Revoir fabric by the price per yard. The loss totalled nine hundred and fifty rupees plus tax. Ishvar estimated the charge for repairing the sewing-machines to be approximately six hundred. The belts and needles were broken; and the flywheels and treadles would have to be realigned or replaced, besides a general overhaul.

Beggarmaster wrote it down, totting up the cost of the slashed mattress, pillows, wooden stools, sofa, cushions, and windows. 'Anything else?'

'The umbrella,' said Maneck, awakened by their voices. 'They broke some ribs.'

Beggarmaster added it to the list, then recorded the landlord's office address and descriptions of the two men. 'Good,' he said. 'That's all I need. If your landlord doesn't know you're my clients, he'll soon find out. He'll settle the damages, once I pay him a little visit. Now don't worry, just wait for me, I'll be back this evening.'

'Should I make a complaint to the police?' asked Dina.

He gave her a weary look. 'If you like. But you might as well complain to that crow on your window.' The bird cawed and flew away; he felt vindicated.

Beggarmaster's assurances could not fully assuage Dina's doubts. She went to Nusswan's office in order to inform him of the situation. In case his help was required later, she decided, or he would say: Digging a well when the house is on fire.

The peon informed her sadly that Nusswan sahab was out of town for a meeting; he always felt sad about sahab's sister. 'He won't be back till tomorrow night.'

Dina left the office, tempted to stop at the Venus Beauty Salon and talk with Zenobia. But to what purpose? Empty consolation would solve nothing; besides, it would be accompanied by Zenobia's infuriating 'I warned you but you wouldn't listen.'

She returned to the flat, praying that Beggarmaster would come through. A stench followed her inside the door, and she puzzled about it. 'Can you smell it?' she asked Ishvar.

They went around room by room, checking the kitchen and WC as well. The malodour trailed them everywhere without revealing itself. 'Maybe it's from outside, from the gutter,' said Om. But when they stuck their heads out through the window, the smell seemed to diminish.

'Those stinking goondas must have left it behind,' she said, and Ishvar agreed. Then Om, who was kneeling on the floor, picking up the last bits of broken glass, discovered the smell was coming from her shoe. She had stepped in something on the pavement. She went outside, scraped off the brown mess from the sole, and washed it.

For most of the day Maneck stayed in bed with a thundering headache. Dina and the tailors attempted to restore some order to the shambles of the flat. They swept up the cotton fill, stuffed it back in, and sewed up the slashes, but the cushions still looked deflated. Plumping and patting could not take away their limpness. Next they tackled the paan stains, which were everywhere.

'God knows why we are wasting our energy,' she said. 'Tomorrow night we could be thrown out, if your Beggarmaster is just big talk.'

'I think it will be all right,' said Ishvar. 'Shankar always says Beggarmaster is very influential.'

When he had repeated this for the fourth time late in the day, Dina was irritated. 'So now a poor legless beggar is your fountain of wisdom and advice, is he?'

'No,' said Ishvar, taken aback. 'But he has known Beggarmaster a long time. I mean . . . in the work camp he helped us.'

'Then why isn't he here yet? The evening is almost over.'

'Beggarmaster has betrayed us,' said Om. His uncle did not contradict him.

Their hopes of rescue faded with the twilight. As the night deepened, the four sat in silence, attempting to discern the face of tomorrow. So this was it, thought Dina, the end of the independence she had struggled so long to preserve. There was no use raising her hopes about Nusswan.

Even his lawyer couldn't do much if the landlord's goondas put her furniture on the pavement. What was it that lawyers said – possession is nine-tenths of the law. And, in any case, the idea of independence was a fantasy. Everyone depended on someone. If not on Nusswan, she would have to continue relying on the tailors, and on Au Revoir Exports – which came to the same thing . . . and Nusswan could arrange for a lorry to remove her things, take them to her parents' house – which he liked to call his house. Always saying it was his duty to look after his sister. Now he could, as long as he wanted.

A cat screeched outside the kitchen window, and they sat up, startled. More cats took up the cry. 'Wonder what's scaring them,' said Ishvar uneasily.

'They just like to scream sometimes,' said Maneck. But he went to look, and the others followed. There was no sign of anything unusual in the alley.

'You think the goondas will come back tonight?' said Om.

'Ibrahim gave us forty-eight hours' notice,' said Dina. 'So maybe tomorrow night. Listen, even though I am going to ask my brother's help, our chances are not very good. The time is so short. And who knows what will happen? I don't want more fighting here. Tomorrow morning, you must take your belongings and leave. Later, if everything is fine, you can return.'

'I was thinking the same,' said Ishvar. 'We will go to the nightwatchman. And Maneck can try at the hostel.'

'But we must keep in touch,' said Om. 'Maybe we can sew in your brother's house. Other companies will give you business, even if this one cancels.'

'Yes, we'll do something,' she said, not having the heart to tell them Nusswan would forbid it. 'But you shouldn't depend only on me, you must also look for work elsewhere.'

Maneck was silent as they persevered to rescue the shreds of their livelihood. Not all their skills with needle and thread could sew it together again, he thought. Did life treat everyone so wantonly, ripping the good things to pieces while letting bad things fester and grow like fungus on unrefrigerated food? Vasantrao Valmik the proofreader would say it was all part of living, that the secret of survival was to balance hope and despair, to embrace change. But embrace misery and destruction? No. If there were a large enough refrigerator, he would be able to preserve the happy times in this flat, keep them from ever spoiling; and Avinash and chess, which soured so soon, he would save that too; and the mountains of snow, and the General Store, before it all went gloomy, before Daddy became unrecognizable, and Mummy his willing slave.

But it was an unrefrigerated world. And everything ended badly. What could he do now? The thought of the hostel was more nauseating than ever. And if he went home, the fighting would start with Daddy. There was no way out, it was checkmate for him.

'Listen, the cats have stopped screaming,' said Ishvar. 'So quiet now.' They strained to hear. The silence was as perturbing as the screeching had been.

The tailors had a quick early-morning wash before the tap went dry. There was no telling when they would have again the luxury of a bathroom. In their immediate future they could only see alleyways and standpipes.

Maneck was not in a hurry. His lip was better today, the swelling reduced, and his headache was gone. He sat around listlessly, or moved from room to room as though searching for something.

'Come on Maneck,' said Dina, 'it's getting late. Do something, pack your boxes. Or go to the hostel first, see if they have a place for you.'

He returned to his room, pulled the suitcase out from under the bed and opened it. When she looked in a few minutes later, he had the chessboard set up, and was staring at the pieces.

'Are you crazy?' she yelled at him. 'Time is running out, you have still so much to do!'

'I'll do it when I feel like it. I'm an independent person, even if you are giving up.' He deliberately picked the word she used when talking about herself.

It stung, but she ignored it. 'Big talk is easy. We'll see how independent you are when the goondas come back and break your head open. One beating wasn't enough for you, it looks like.'

'Why should you care? You are packing up and leaving, not even showing a little regret.'

'Regret is a luxury I can't afford. And why should you make such a long face? You would have gone anyway, when you finished your diploma. If not now, then six months later.' She left the room angrily.

Ishvar left the trunk he was packing on the verandah, and came in. He sat on the bed, putting his arm around him. 'You know, Maneck, the human face has limited space. My mother used to say, if you fill your face with laughing, there will be no room for crying.'

'What a nice saying,' he answered bitterly.

'Right now, Dinabai's face, and Om's, and mine are all occupied.

Worrying about work and money, and where to sleep tonight. But that does not mean we are not sad. It may not show on the face, but it's sitting inside here.' He placed his hand over his heart. 'In here, there is limitless room – happiness, kindness, sorrow, anger, friendship – everything fits in here.'

'I know, I know,' said Maneck, and began putting away the chess pieces. 'Are you going to meet the nightwatchman now?'

'Yes, we'll fix up with him and return. To help Dinabai pack her things.'

'Don't forget to give us your hostel address before leaving,' said Om. 'We'll come see you there.'

Maneck emptied out the cupboard and folded his clothes into the suitcase. Dina looked in with a word of praise for his quickness. 'Can you do me a favour, Maneck?'

He nodded.

'You know the nameplate on the door? Can you get the screwdriver from the kitchen shelf and remove it? I want to take it with me.'

He nodded again.

Ishvar and Om returned with bad news. The nightwatchman had been replaced, and the new man wanted to have nothing to do with the tailors' old arrangement. In fact, he thought they were trying to take advantage of his inexperience.

'Now I don't know what to do,' said Ishvar wearily. 'We'll have to go searching street by street.'

'And I'll have to carry the trunk,' said Om.

'No, you mustn't,' said Dina. 'You'll hurt your arm again.' She offered to take the trunk with her to Nusswan's house, pretend it was part of her belongings. The tailors could come to the back door whenever they needed clothes. It was a big house, she said, Nusswan would see nothing, he never went to the kitchen unless he was on one of his inspection and economy rampages.

'Listen, I know where you two can sleep,' said Maneck.

'Where?'

'In my hostel room. You can sneak in at night, and sneak out early every morning. Your trunk can also stay there.'

While they were considering the feasibility of his idea, the doorbell rang. It was Beggarmaster.

'Thank God you've come!' Ishvar and Dina rushed to welcome him like a saviour.

It reminded Om of the way Shankar, whimpering on his rolling platform, had fawned over the man when he had appeared at the irrigation project. He squirmed at the memory. How proudly Ishvar and he had proclaimed then to Beggarmaster: We are tailors, not beggars.

'What happened?' asked Dina. 'You said you would return yesterday evening.'

'Sorry, I was delayed by an emergency,' he replied, enjoying the attention. He was accustomed to being apotheosized by beggars, but the veneration of normal people was far sweeter.

'This wretched Emergency – creating trouble for everyone.'

'No, not that Emergency,' said Beggarmaster. 'I mean a business problem. You see, after I left you yesterday morning, I got a message that two of my beggars, a husband-and-wife team, were found murdered. So I had to rush there.'

'Murdered!' said Dina. 'What evil person would kill poor beggars?'

'Oh, it happens. They are killed for their beggings. But this case is very peculiar – money was not touched. Must be some kind of maniac. Only their hair was taken.'

Ishvar and Om started visibly, gulping.

'Hair?' said Dina. 'You mean from their heads?'

'Yes,' said Beggarmaster. 'Cropped right off. Husband and wife both had lovely long hair. Which was very unusual. The lovely part, I mean – most beggars do have long hair, they cannot afford haircuts, but it's always dirty. These two were different. They used to spend hours cleaning it for each other, picking out the nits, combing it, washing it every time it rained or a water pipe burst on their pavement.'

'How sweet,' said Dina, nodding in empathy with Beggarmaster's tender description of the loving couple.

'You'd be surprised how much beggars are like ordinary human beings. The result of all their grooming was, of course, this beautiful hair. And it was not good for business. I often told them to mess it up, make it look pathetic. But they would say they had nothing in the world to be proud of except their hair, and was I going to deny them even that?'

He paused, considering the question afresh. 'What could I do? I'm softhearted, I gave in. Now those beautiful tresses have cost them their lives. And deprived me of two good beggars.'

He turned to the tailors. 'What's the matter? You both look very upset.'

'No – not upset,' stammered Ishvar. 'Just very surprised.'

'Yes,' said Beggarmaster. 'That's what the police were as well – surprised. They had been receiving a few complaints, that long plaits and ponytails were disappearing mysteriously. Women would go to the bazaar, do their shopping, go home, look in the mirror and find their hair missing. But never anything like this, no one was ever killed or injured. So the detectives are very interested in my beggars' case. They love variety. They are calling it the Case of the Hair-Hungry Homicide.'

He opened the briefcase secured to his wrist and took out a thick wad of rupees. The chain jangled as he counted the notes. 'Getting back to business – here's the money to cover your damage. You can start working again.'

Ishvar deferred the responsibility of accepting the cash to Dina; his hands were shaking violently.

Clasping two thousand rupees, she still found it hard to believe Beggarmaster had defeated the landlord. 'You mean we can stay? It's really safe?'

'Of course you can stay. I told you there would be no trouble. Those men made a mistake.'

The tailors nodded rapidly to transfer their conviction to Dina. 'Only one problem,' said Ishvar. 'What if the landlord sends new goondas?'

'While you pay me, the landlord won't find a single man to come here. I have seen to that.'

'And when the instalments are paid up?'

'That's up to you. Our contract can always be renewed. I'll give you good rates, you're Shankar's friends. And – oh yes, Shankar sends you his greetings. Says he hasn't seen you recently.'

'With all this landlord trouble, we haven't gone to Vishram for a few days,' said Ishvar. 'We'll meet him tomorrow. And, I was wondering, how are Monkey-man and his two children?'

'Good, good – the children I mean. They're learning fast. Monkey-man I haven't seen again. I haven't been back to the work camp. But he was beaten up too badly, probably dead by now.'

'The old woman's prophecy has almost come true, then,' said Om.

'What prophecy?' asked Beggarmaster.

The tailors described the night in the hutment colony, when Monkey-man had discovered his little monkeys slain by his dog, when the old woman uttered her cryptic words. 'I remember exactly what she told us,' said Om. '"The loss of two monkeys is not the worst loss he will suffer; the murder of the dog is not the worst murder he will commit." And later, he did kill Tikka to avenge Laila and Majnoo.'

'What a horrible story,' said Dina.

'Pure coincidence,' said Beggarmaster, 'I don't believe in prophecies or superstitions.'

Ishvar nodded. 'And are the two children happy without Monkey-man?'

Beggarmaster flipped his unchained hand in a who-knows gesture.

'They will have to get used to it. Life does not guarantee happiness.' He raised the same hand in farewell and began walking out the door, then stopped.

'There is something you can do for me. I need two new beggars. If you see someone who qualifies, will you let me know?'

'Sure,' said Ishvar. 'We'll keep our eyes open.'

'But there has to be a unique feature about the candidates. Let me show you.' From the briefcase, he removed a large sketchbook containing his notes and diagrams relating to the dramaturgy of begging. The binding was well-worn, the corners of the pages curling.

He opened the book to an old pencil drawing titled Spirit of Collaboration. 'Here's what I have been trying to create for a long time.'

They crowded around to look at the sketch: two figures, one sitting aloft on the shoulders of the other. 'For this, I need a lame beggar and a blind beggar. The blind man will carry the cripple on his shoulders. A living, breathing image of the ancient story about friendship and coop-eration. And it will produce a fortune in coins, I am absolutely certain, because people will give not only from pity or piety but also from admi-ration.' The hitch was in finding a blind beggar who was strong enough or a lame beggar who was light enough.

'Wouldn't Shankar be suitable?' asked Maneck.

'Without legs, and only quarter thighs, he could never balance upon someone's shoulders – he would slide right down the back. I need a cripple whose legs are not amputated, but lifeless and mutilated, so they can dangle nicely over the carrier's chest. In any case, Shankar is very successful with his rolling platform. We don't want to spoil that.'

They promised to watch out for Beggarmaster's requirements. He said he would appreciate any suggestions. 'By the way, you know the two goondas who came with your rent-collector?'

'Yes?'

'They have sent their apologies for not being here to clean up the mess they made.'

'Really?'

'Yes. They had an unfortunate accident – broke all their fingers. Who knows, if they have a few more accidents they may even qualify to join my team of beggars.' He was pleased at his own wit, and they returned weak smiles.

'Now you really must excuse me,' he said. 'I have to go and look after my two murdered beggars.'

'Will you cremate them today?'

'No, that's too expensive. When the morgue releases the corpses, I'll sell them to my agent.' Seeing their shocked expressions, Beggarmaster felt obliged to justify his action. 'With rising prices and inflation, I have no choice. Besides, it's much better than leaving the bodies in the street for the municipal workers, like in the old days.'

'Yes, of course,' agreed Dina, as though she bought and sold cadavers on a daily basis. 'And what does your agent do with the – bodies?'

'He sells some to colleges, to teach students who want to become doctors. Just imagine, my beggars might participate in the pursuit of knowledge.' His face took on a visionary aspect, gazing out the window to a limitless horizon. 'Some bodies are also bought by practitioners of black magic. And a lot of bones are exported. For fertilizer, I think. I can find out more if you are interested.'

Dina shook her head to decline the offer.

Beggarmaster left a chill in the air as he departed. 'We must be careful with that man,' she said. 'What a peculiar fellow. And that briefcase chained to his wrist – a slave to money. He looks capable of selling our bones before we're finished with them.'

'He's just a thoroughly modern businessman, with his eye on the bottom line,' said Maneck. 'I saw many like him in the cola business, when they came to meet Daddy, pressuring him to sell off Kohlah's Cola.'

Ishvar shook his head sadly. 'Why are business people so heartless? With all their money, they still look unhappy.'

'It's a disease without a cure,' said Dina. 'Like cancer. And they don't even know they have it.'

'Anyway,' said Maneck, his spirits rising again, 'Om is the only one who needs to fear Beggarmaster. There could be a genuine mistake about a walking skeleton.'

'You better be careful too,' retaliated Om. 'Your healthy mountain-grown bones, watered by the pure melting Himalayan snows, will fetch more by the kilo than mine.'

'Enough of this ghoulishness,' said Dina.

But Maneck was unable to curb his silly talk, relieved that the household was preserved. 'Just think, Aunty. Now that we have gleaming teeth cleaned with charcoal powder, they must be worth a lot. We could sell them individually or by the dozen. Maybe as a necklace.'

'Enough, I said. Laughing aside, this fellow is someone to be careful of, remember.'

'As long as he is paid on time, there is nothing to worry about,' said Ishvar.

'I hope so. From now on I will pay half the instalment, since he is protecting me as well.'

'Never,' said Ishvar indignantly. 'That's not why I mentioned it. You don't take any rent, so this is our share.' He refused to be budged on the matter.

They went to the sewing room to calculate how much restitution was due to Au Revoir Exports. He whispered that it was good to see Maneck and Om laughing and joking again.

'Yes, these last two days have been miserable for all of us,' she agreed, then requested the boys to screw back the nameplate on the front door.

'We will never see Rajaram again, for sure,' said Om that night while spreading out the bedding. 'If he's the killer.'

'Of course he is,' said his uncle. He gazed at the streetlamp from the verandah window, thinking of their erstwhile friend. 'It's unbelievable. Someone who seemed such a nice person, murdering two beggars. We should have been more careful, that very first morning in the hutment colony – with all his dirty toilet talk on the train tracks. And what sane person makes a living by collecting hair?'

'That's not the point, yaar. People collect and sell all kinds of things. Rags, paper, plastic, glass. Even bones.'

'But aren't you glad now that I wouldn't let you grow your hair long? That murderer would have slaughtered you for it while you slept next door to him.'

Om shrugged. 'I am worried about Dinabai. Suppose the police find the haircutting kit that she gave Rajaram? Her fingerprints and ours will be on it. We will all be arrested and hanged.'

'You've been seeing too many crazy films with Maneck. That sort of thing only happens in the cinema. What worries me is him coming to us again for help. Then what to do? Call the police?'

Ishvar lay awake for a long time, unable to get Rajaram out of his mind. They had lived beside this murderer in the hutment colony, eaten his food and shared theirs with him. The thought made him shudder.

Om knew that his uncle was having trouble sleeping. He raised himself on one elbow and chuckled in the dark: 'You know the cook and waiter at Vishram who enjoy our stories? Wouldn't they just love to hear this one.'

'Don't even joke about it,' warned Ishvar, 'or we'll be trapped in unending police problems.'

═══

The pavement was crowded with the morning rush of domestics, schoolchildren, officegoers, hawkers. The tailors waited for a lull when

Shankar could paddle over to the Vishram's back alley. He kept waving to them, which made Ishvar jittery – the less attention drawn the better, considering the gruesome cargo on his platform.

After a few minutes, Shankar grew impatient and ventured across the pavement, steering his transport through the thick of the pedestrian throng. 'O babu! Careful!' he called, dodging and being dodged by an endless flurry of legs and feet.

The platform collided with someone's shin. Curses rained down on Shankar, and he looked up timidly. The man threatened to kick his head off. 'Saala bhikhari thinks he owns the pavement! Stay in one place!'

Shankar begged forgiveness and sped away. In his haste the package fell from the platform. The tailors watched worriedly, not daring to go to his help. Shankar grappled and wheeled and spun, somehow managing to rescue the package and bring it over.

'Well done,' said Ishvar. He imagined the traffic policeman regarding them with suspicion from the busy intersection – what if he came over and demanded to open the bag? 'So,' he said, keeping his voice as steady as he could. 'When did our long-haired friend deliver this?'

'Two days ago,' he answered, and Ishvar almost flung the parcel away. 'No, I am wrong,' Shankar changed his mind, rubbing his forehead with a bandaged palm. 'Not two days. It was the day after I last saw you – four days ago.'

Ishvar nodded with relief at Om. The parcel did not contain *that* hair. 'Our friend won't be coming to see you from now on.'

'No?' Shankar was disappointed. 'I used to enjoy playing with his packages. Such lovely hair.'

'You mean you looked inside?'

'Did I do wrong?' he asked anxiously. 'Aray babu, I didn't damage anything, I just touched it to my cheek because it made me feel good. It was so soft and nice.'

'That it was, for sure,' said Om. 'Our friend only collects the best quality hair.'

The gibe was lost on Shankar. 'I wish I had one bunch for myself,' he sighed. 'I could put it on my platform at night and sleep with my face resting against it. How it would soothe me, after the meanness of people all day. Even the ones who throw coins, they look at me as though I was robbing them. What a comfort the hair would be.'

'Why not?' said Om, on an impulse. 'Here, keep this packet – our friend doesn't need it.'

Ishvar was about to protest, then let it go. Om was right, what did it matter now?

With Shankar's gratitude thawing the chill of Rajaram's deed, they walked back to the flat. 'I want to throw away all his rubbish from our trunk,' said Ishvar. 'God knows where it's from, how many others he killed.'

That night, when Dina and Maneck were asleep, Ishvar removed the plaits from the trunk and placed them in a small cardboard carton for ultimate disposal. He felt better afterwards, for their clothes were no longer polluted by the madman's collection.

Noises from the kitchen woke Dina early, well before water time, when the sky was still dark as night. Two months had passed in peace since Beggarmaster had proven his worth, and the flat was back to normal. But drifting half-awake, she was convinced the rattle of pots and pans meant only one thing: the landlord's goondas were back. Heart pounding, hands heavy with sleep, her fingers pecked at the sheet in a bid to uncover herself.

Then again, maybe it was just a nightmare that would play itself out – if she lay still . . . kept her eyes closed . . .

The noises subsided. Good, the strategy was working, no goondas, only a dream, yes, and Beggarmaster was protecting the flat. Nothing to worry about, she felt, floating back and forth over the threshold of slumber.

Eventually, a persistent miaowing pushed her into full wakefulness, and she sat up with a start. Nuisance of a cat! Disentangling herself from the sheet, she got out of bed and blundered into the wooden stools. One fell over with a thud, waking Maneck in the next room, succeeding where the pots and pans had failed.

'Are you all right, Aunty?'

'Yes, it's a rascal cat in the kitchen. I'm going to break its head. You go back to sleep.'

He found his slippers and followed Dina, as much to make sure she would not really hurt the cat as out of curiosity. She switched on the light, and they saw it dart out the window: his favourite, Vijayanthimala, the brown and white tabby.

'The wicked animal,' she fumed. 'God knows what it has been licking with its filthy mouth.'

Maneck examined the chicken wire ripped off the broken windowpane. 'It must have been really desperate to do this. Hope it didn't injure itself.'

'You're more worried about the dirty beast than the trouble it creates for me.' She began picking up the utensils that had been tumbled from their place and would have to be thoroughly scrubbed.

'Wait,' she stopped. 'What's that sound?'

Hearing nothing, they continued to tidy the kitchen. Moments later she froze again, and this time a feeble whimper threaded its way through the silence. There was no mistaking it, it was in the kitchen.

In the corner, in the hollow where coal fires used to burn for cooking in the old days, lay three brown and white kittens. A chorus of tiny miaows greeted Dina and Maneck as they bent over to look.

'Oh my!' she gasped. 'How sweet!'

'No wonder Vijayanthimala was looking fat lately,' he grinned.

The kittens struggled to get to their feet, and she felt she had never seen anything so helpless. 'I wonder if she gave birth to them right here.'

He shook his head. 'They seem a few days old to me. She must have brought them in during the night.'

'I wonder why. Oh, they are so sweet.'

'Would you still like to make violin strings out of them, Aunty?'

She gave him a reproachful look. But when he stroked them gently she pulled him back. 'Don't touch. How do you know what germs they have?'

'They are only babies.'

'So? They can still carry disease.' She spread open a page from an old newspaper and grasped it in the middle.

'What are you doing?' he asked in alarm.

'Protecting my hands. I'll place all three right outside the window, where the cat can see them.'

'You can't do that!' He argued that if the mother had abandoned the kittens they would starve to death. That is, if crows and rats didn't attack them first, peck out their tiny eyes, tear open the little bodies, rip out their entrails, and gnaw at the delicate bones.

'There's no need for so many details,' she said. The kittens kept up a pitiful wailing in concurrence with his gruesome scenario. 'What do you want to do?'

'Feed them.'

'Out of the question,' she declared – once they were fed, they would never leave. And the mother, even if she were contemplating a return, would shirk her duties. 'I cannot be responsible for all the homeless creatures in the world.'

He finally managed to win a reprieve for the kittens. She agreed not to move them for the time being, to give Vijayanthimala a chance to hear her litter calling. Perhaps their cries would persuade her to come back.

'Look,' he pointed outside. 'It's dawn.'

'What a beautiful sky,' she paused, staring dreamily through the window.

The taps began to flow, interrupting her reverie. She hurried to the bathroom while he examined the yard for sleeping cats. He gazed beyond, where the warren of alleys began. In that optimistic first light, the promise of transformation shone down upon the sleeping city. He knew the feeling wouldn't stay more than a few minutes – he had experienced it before, it always faded under stronger light.

Still, he was grateful while it lasted. When the tailors awoke he told them the news and took them to the kitchen. Their approach caused the steady whimpers to increase in volume.

Dina hustled them out. 'With such a big crowd watching, that cat will never return.' Then she went in herself, ostensibly to make tea, and stood in the corner smiling, sighing, watching the kittens wobbling around inside the coal fireplace, clambering over one another, collapsing in a heap. Their mother had chosen the spot well, she thought, the hollow deep enough to keep them from climbing out and wandering.

Not much work was done that morning. Maneck claimed he had no classes till noon. 'How convenient,' said Dina, as he kept up his vigil at the kitchen door and reported back with fresh bulletins. The tailors silenced their machines frequently to listen for the kittens.

Time passed, and their wails grew loud enough to be heard over the Singers. 'How much they are crying,' said Om. 'Must be hungry.'

'Just like human babies,' said Maneck. 'They need to be fed regularly.' He watched Dina from the corner of his eye. He knew the whimpering was starting to bother her. She inquired casually if such tiny creatures could tolerate cow's milk.

'Yes,' he answered promptly. 'But diluted with water, or it's too heavy for them. After a few days they can also eat pieces of bread soaked in it. That's what my father feeds the puppies and kittens at home.'

For another hour she refused to give in, fending off the pleas from the kitchen. Then, 'Oh, it's hopeless,' she said. 'Come on, Mr. Mac, you're the expert.'

They warmed the mixture of milk and water before pouring it in an aluminium saucer. The squirming kittens were lifted out of the coal fireplace onto newspaper spread upon the floor. 'Let me also carry them,' demanded Om, and Maneck let him take the last one.

The three cowered on the paper, unable to stop shivering. Gradually, the smell of milk drew them closer, and they gave a few tentative licks along the rim. Soon they crowded the saucer, lapping furiously. When it was empty they stood with their paws in it and looked up. Maneck refilled it, let them drink again, then removed it.

'Why so stingy?' said Dina. 'Give them more.'

'After two hours. They'll be sick if they overeat.' From his room he fetched an empty cardboard box and lined the bottom with fresh news-paper.

'I won't have them in the kitchen,' she objected. 'It's unhygienic.'

Om volunteered to keep the box on the verandah.

'Fine,' she said. At night, though, she wanted the kittens returned to the hollow of the fireplace. She was still hoping the mother would retrieve her offspring. The broken windowpane was left unrepaired to welcome back the cat.

For seven nights Dina cleared the kitchen of pots and pans, secured the cabinet, and shut the kitchen door. Seven dawns she went to the coal fireplace as soon as she rose, wishing it to be empty, and the kittens greeted her happily, eager for their breakfast.

She began to look forward to the morning reunion. By the end of the week she found herself worrying when she went to bed – what if it was tonight, what if the cat took them away? She ran to the kitchen on wak-ing and – ah, relief! They had not disappeared!

The nightly ritual of transfer from box to fireplace was discontinued. The tailors were happy to share their quarters with the kittens. Growing fast, the three took to exploring the verandah, and the adjoining doors had to be kept shut to stop them wandering into the sewing room and messing up the fabric. Soon they were making brief outdoor forays through the bars on the verandah window.

'You know, Dinabai,' said Ishvar one night after dinner. 'The cat paid you a great tribute. By leaving her babies here she was saying she trust-ed this house – which is an honour to you.'

'What complete nonsense.' She was having none of this sentimental rubbish. 'Naturally the cat came here with her kittens. This was the window from which three softhearted fools regularly tossed food for her.'

But Ishvar was determined to wring some moral, some kind of higher truth out of the situation. 'No matter what you say, this house is blessed. It brings good fortune. Even the wicked landlord couldn't hurt us in here. And the kittens are a good omen. It means Om will also have lots of healthy children.'

'First he must have a wife,' she said drily.

'Bilkool correct,' he said earnestly. 'I have been thinking hard about it, and we mustn't wait much longer.'

'How can you talk so foolishly?' she said, a little annoyed. 'Om is just starting in life, money is short, you don't have a place for yourselves. And you think about a wife for him?'

'Everything will come in time. We must have faith. The important point is, he must marry soon and start a family.'

'You hear that, Om?' she called to the verandah. 'Your uncle wants you to marry soon and start a family. Just make sure it's not in my kitchen again.'

'You must forgive him,' said Om, putting on a paternalistic tone. 'Sometimes, my poor uncle's screw comes a little loose, and he says crazy things.'

'Whatever you do, don't rely on me for accommodation,' said Maneck. 'I have no more cardboard boxes to spare.'

'What, yaar,' complained Om. 'I was hoping you would stack two boxes for me, make me a two-storey bungalow.'

'It's not nice to make fun of auspicious events,' said Ishvar, a little offended. He didn't think his proposal warranted ridicule.

The kittens returned from their wanderings punctually at mealtimes, through the bars on the verandah window. 'Look at them,' said Dina fondly. 'Coming and going like this was a hotel.'

Then the absences grew longer as they learned to forage for food, haunting the alleys with their kin. The gutters and garbage heaps beckoned with irresistible smells, and the kittens answered the call.

Their random disappearances saddened everyone. Maneck and Om kept saving tidbits carefully piled high in one plate. Each day they hoped that the kittens would deign to put in an appearance. After waiting till late at night they got rid of the scraps, before it attracted vermin; they fed whatever was prowling outside the kitchen window, eyes gleaming anonymously in the dark.

When the kittens did show up, it became an occasion for rejoicing. If there were no suitable leftovers, Maneck or Om would dash out to buy bread and milk from the Vishram. Sometimes the kittens lingered after the snack, ready to play a little, worrying the snippets of cloth near the sewing-machines. More often, they departed immediately.

'Eating and running,' said Dina, 'as though they owned the place.'

By and by, the visits grew less frequent and briefer in duration. The kittenish curiosity displayed at every little thing was outgrown; the milk and bread was completely ignored. Outdoor scrounging had evidently endowed them with a more adventurous palate.

To draw their attention, Om and Maneck got down on all fours beside the bowl. 'Miaow!' they chorused. 'Mii-aooow!' Om sniffed loudly along the rim, and Maneck let his tongue flap in and out in a manic display of lapping. The kittens were not impressed. They watched the performance detachedly, yawned, and began cleaning themselves.

Three months after they were discovered in the coal fireplace, the kittens disappeared altogether. When a fortnight passed without a sign of them, Dina was convinced they had been run over. Maneck said they could equally well have been attacked by a crazy pariah dog.

'Or those big rats,' said Om. 'Even full-grown cats are scared of them.'

Considering these gloomy possibilities, they grew morose, though Ishvar continued to believe the kittens were all right. They were smart, tough little creatures, he reminded the others, and used to life on the streets. No one shared his optimism. They became annoyed with him, as though he had suggested something morbid.

Into their grief and dejection arrived Beggarmaster to collect his instalment. The dusk seemed darker than usual because the streetlights had not come on. 'What's the matter?' he asked. 'Is the landlord bothering you again?'

'No,' said Dina. 'But our sweet little kittens have disappeared.'

Beggarmaster began to laugh. The sound startled them, for it was the first time they had heard it from him. 'Look at your gloomy faces,' he said. 'You did not seem so upset even about those goondas.' He laughed again. 'I'm sorry I can't help you – I'm not Kittenmaster. But I do have some happy news, maybe it will cheer you up.'

'What?' asked Ishvar.

'It's about Shankar.' He smiled from ear to ear. 'I cannot tell *him* the news right now, for his own good. But I simply have to share it – it's so wonderful – and you are his only friends. You must swear not to mention anything to him.'

They all gave him their word.

'It happened a few weeks after I took Shankar and you from that irrigation project. One of my beggarwomen, who was very sick, began telling me things about her childhood, and about Shankar's youth. Every time I came for collection, she would start reminiscing. She was old, very old for a beggar, about forty. Last week she finally died. But just before her death, she told me she was Shankar's mother.'

Now this in itself had not been a surprise, explained Beggarmaster, for he had always suspected it. As a small boy, when he used to accompany his father on rounds, he would often see her suckling a baby. Everyone called her Nosey because of her noseless face. She was young then, about fifteen, with a perfect body that would have fetched a decent price, the brothel-keepers had agreed, had it not been for the disfigured face. It was said that when she was born, her drunken father had slashed off her nose in his rage, disappointed with the mother for producing a daughter instead of a son. The mother had nursed the wound and saved the newborn's life, though the father kept saying let her die, her ugly face was the only dowry in store for her, let her die. Because of his continuing harassment and persecution, the child was sold into the begging profession.

'I don't know exactly at what age my father acquired Nosey,' said Beggarmaster. 'I only remember seeing her with her little baby.' Then, a few months later, the infant who was called Shankar was separated from her and sent for professional modifications.

The child was not returned to the mother. It was more profitable to circulate him among beggarwomen in various neighbourhoods. Also, strangers giving him suck found it easier to display the utter despair in their faces that made for successful begging, whereas if Nosey had had the pleasure of clasping her little son to her bosom all day, it would have been impossible to keep a spark of joy, however tiny, out of her eyes, which would have adversely affected the takings.

'So Shankar grew up, branched out on his own, and got the rolling platform, never knowing his mother,' said Beggarmaster. 'And by the time I took over the business, I had forgotten my childhood suspicion that he was Nosey's son. Till recently.'

It was Nosey who had reminded him, as she lay dying on the pavement. Not only that, she claimed that Beggarmaster's father was also Shankar's father. At first, Beggarmaster was stunned that she would have the temerity to suggest something so offensive. He threatened to remove her from his list of clients if she did not apologize. She said it was all the same to her, this close to death she couldn't care.

Still refusing to believe her, he wondered why she would utter such a pointless falsehood. What was she hoping to gain by it? He watched in a daze of anger as pedestrians continued to throw coins in Nosey's tin can. Unaware of the drama taking place, some of them stopped and began eyeing him suspiciously.

'They probably thought you were waiting to steal from her,' said Maneck.

'You are right. And I was so upset, I felt like yelling at them to go fuck themselves.'

Dina flinched, almost admonishing him for his language. The front room had grown dark, and she switched on the light. It made everyone blink and shade their eyes for a moment.

'But I controlled myself,' said Beggarmaster. 'In my profession, we have a saying – the almsgiver is always right.'

So, ignoring the inquisitive rabble, he focused on Nosey's claim. After the outrage came the uncertainty. He accused her of a cheap lie, of playing a vicious trick on him while passing through death's door, leaving him forever in doubt.

Be quiet and listen, she said to Beggarmaster, I am your stepmother, whether you like it or not. And I have proof. Did you ever massage your father's back and shoulders?

Yes, he answered, I have been a good son. I regularly massaged my father whenever he summoned me, right till the day of his passing.

In that case, said Nosey, you would have been familiar with a larger-than-normal bump, a big swelling at the nape of your father's neck, just where the backbone began.

'I wondered how in the world she knew about it,' said Beggarmaster. 'But she insisted on an answer, did he or didn't he have a lump in that place? She would not say another word until I admitted, reluctantly, that yes, my father possessed the feature she had described. Then she was anxious to continue.'

It had happened long, long ago, when Nosey was young and her body had just learned to bleed. Beggarmaster's father had come to her corner of the pavement late one night, when he was drunk, too drunk to be repulsed by her physiognomy, and had slept with her. The liquor-stinking mouth made her want to refuse, but she averted her face and controlled the impulse. She lay inert, as though dead under him, letting him do what he wanted. After he finished she sat and threw up beside his snoring, rumbling body. During the night he awoke and enlarged her little splash with a torrent of bilious vomit. Later, she heard a slurping and opened her eyes; rats were supping at their mingled effluent.

Nosey assumed he must have enjoyed her body, for he kept returning on other nights, even when he was not drunk. Now she hated it less. When he lay on top of her and looked at her face without the armour of alcohol, she started to like it. She let her flesh come alive, and enjoyed melting with him. Her hands explored his body then, discovering the large knob at the nape. She giggled, and asked him about it. He joked that he had grown it for her pleasure – so she would have not one but two big bones to play with.

And thus it was that the man who could look upon her hideous face and still love her found a place in her heart. He explained what the doctor had told him about his special bone. He had been born with thirty-four vertebrae instead of the normal thirty-three, the extra one having fused at the top of the column, and responsible for his chronic pain.

Is it not your father I am describing, said Nosey, is there any doubt remaining now?

Beggarmaster agreed that all this was true. But it was only evidence of his father's drunken fornications, and nothing else.

Not only drunken, she corrected him with pride, but sober as well. This distinction was the dearest thing in her life, and of the utmost importance to her even at death's door.

Grudgingly he admitted it. But it was still not proof, he maintained, that Shankar was his father's son and his own half-brother. Yes, it was, said Nosey, because Shankar had the identical protuberance at the nape of his neck, and it would take only a moment to verify it. Beggarmaster could, of course, pretend it was a coincidence, she said, but he would know the truth in his heart.

'And she was right, the truth was in my heart. Also in my heart was a great, hopeless mixture of feelings. I was angry and frightened and confused. But also happy. For I realized that I, an only child, left in the world without parents, without any relatives, was suddenly blessed with a brother. And a stepmother, even if she was close to my own age, and close to death.'

So, having accepted the truth, all his rage and resentment towards the dying woman was replaced by gratitude. He asked why she had not told him earlier. She said out of fear of what he might have done if the secret angered or shamed him – maybe killed her and Shankar, or sold them to a less pleasant owner in a far-off place where they would have been strangers. Her greatest terror was to lose the familiar pavements of her youth.

But now it did not matter, she would be dead in a short while, and he would be the sole keeper of the knowledge, to do with it as he wished. It would be up to him to tell or not tell Shankar.

He reassured her that her confidences had brought him nothing but happiness. The urgent matter was to get her to a good hospital. He wanted to make her comfortable for whatever time was left to her, and went to hail a taxi.

The first few to stop refused the fare when they saw the sick beggarwoman, concerned about the car's interior. Finally, he flagged one down by waving a thick wad of rupees at the driver. The taxi had a broken headlight and a clanking bumper. In the back seat, with Nosey cradled in his arms through the journey, Beggarmaster heard the driver's hard-luck story about a policeman who had maliciously damaged the vehicle because the driver had been late that week in slipping him the envelope with his parking hafta.

At the hospital there was a long delay. Nosey was left on the floor in a corridor crowded with destitutes awaiting treatment. The antiseptic odour of phenol from the stone tiles penetrated faintly through the human fetor. Beggarmaster did his best to motivate the people in charge, and spoke to a kind-looking doctor. His white coat was torn at the large lower pocket into which he had squeezed his stethoscope. Beggarmaster asked him to please hurry and attend his mother, he would make it worth his while. The doctor said in a gentle voice not to worry, everyone would be looked after. Then he rushed away with his hand in the torn pocket.

Beggarmaster assumed that medical people, dedicated to their noble calling, were not impressed by his sweat-soaked roll of rupees like most of society. But he was unable to sample more doctors and nurses to arrive at an actuarially valid conclusion. Before his stepmother could be treated, her life had ended. He consoled himself by paying for a good funeral instead of a hospital bill.

'And when all this was dealt with, I went to see Shankar,' sighed Beggarmaster. 'Of course, I did not mention the main news right away, because I first wanted to think in peace and quiet about what Nosey had told me.'

He asked Shankar how the begging was going, if the platform was working well, if the castors needed oiling – the usual chitchat of inspection rounds. Shankar complained that almsgiving was drying up in this neighbourhood of misers, people were so bad-tempered. Beggarmaster knelt by his side and put a hand on his shoulder. He said it was the same trouble everywhere – it was a real crisis of human nature, a revolution was needed in people's hearts. But he would look into it, maybe assign him a new location. He patted Shankar's back and said not to worry, then let his fingers slip under the collar to feel the nape of his neck.

'And there, beneath my fingertips, was my father's backbone. The same large bump. My hand was trembling with emotion. My whole body shook with excitement, I could barely keep my balance as I knelt. There was my brother before me, and there, also, my father, living in that spinal column. It was all I could do to keep from embracing Shankar, pressing him to my chest, and confessing everything.'

With a superhuman effort he had restrained himself. Premature divulgence could have caused untold anguish. First, he had to decide on the best course for Shankar. It was all very well to imagine he could take his brother home, keep him in comfort for the rest of his life, and live happily together. Such dreams were cheap, people had them all the time. But what if Shankar could not adjust to the new life? Suppose it seemed purposeless, or worse than purposeless? A prison, where his inadequacies were highlighted instead of being put to use as they were in begging on the pavement? And more important, what if the horrific story of the early years became an ulcer on Shankar's spirit, eating him from within, turning the remainder of his life into one bitter and ravaging accusation of Beggarmaster and his father? After such knowledge, could there be forgiveness?

'I felt it was better for me to wrestle with my own soul, contain within its bounds the truth imparted by Nosey. To involve my poor unfortunate brother in the misery, just for my own comfort – that would have been too selfish.' He reasoned that Shankar's life had already been wrecked once, in infancy. But Shankar had learned to inhabit that wreckage. To wreak a second destruction upon him would be unforgivable.

'So I have decided to wait. To wait, and talk to him about his childhood. Perhaps I will share little things, and watch his reaction. By and by, I will know which is the best course for us. And here is where I need your help.'

'What can we do?' asked Ishvar.

'Ask Shankar questions, make him speak about his past. See what kind of memories he has. He is still a little scared of me, he probably tells you more. Will you keep me informed?'

'Sure, we can do that.'

'Thank you. Meanwhile, I want to make his life on the pavement as pleasant as possible. I have begun to buy him his favourite sweetmeats every day – laddoo and jalebi. And on Sundays, ras-malai. I have also improved his platform with cushioning, and got him a better place to sleep at night.'

'Now it makes sense,' said Ishvar. 'He keeps telling us how nice you have been to him.'

'It's the least I can do. I am also planning to send him my personal barber, to provide the full deluxe treatment – hair trim, shave, facial massage, manicure, everything. And if people give fewer alms because of good grooming, then fuck them.'

Again Dina curbed the urge to say: Language. But this time it wasn't as great a shock to her ears. 'The news you have brought is wonderful,' she said. 'How happy Shankar will be when you finally tell him.'

'Not when, but if. Will I ever have the courage? Do I have the wisdom to make the right decision?'

The weight of these questions suddenly plunged him into despair. The news which was to have cheered everyone became cloud across the sun.

'I'm sure it will be clear to you in time,' said Ishvar.

'What has become clear is a fine line between Shankar and me. Finer than the silken hair of my poor murdered beggars. I did not draw it – it is the trace of destiny. But now I have the power to rub it out.' He sighed. 'Such an awesome, frightening power. Do I dare? For once that line is erased, it can never be redrawn.' He shivered. 'What a legacy my stepmother left me.'

He opened his briefcase, took out his sketchbook and showed them his latest drawing. 'I did it last night, when I was very depressed and could not sleep.'

The picture consisted of three figures. The first was seated on a platform with tiny wheels. He had no legs or fingers, and the thigh stumps jutted like hollow bamboo. The second was an emaciated woman without a nose, the face with a gaping hole at its centre. But the third figure was the most grotesque. A man with a briefcase chained to his wrist was standing on four spidery legs. His four feet were splayed towards the four points of the compass, as though in a permanent dispute about which was the right direction. His two hands each had ten fingers, useless bananas sprouting from the palms. And on his face were two noses, adjacent yet bizarrely turned away, as though neither could bear the smell of the other.

They stared at the drawing, uncertain how to respond to Beggarmaster's creation. He saved them the embarrassment by offering his own interpretation. 'Freaks, that's what we are – all of us.'

Ishvar was about to say he was being too hard on himself, that he should not take Shankar's and Nosey's fates entirely upon his own person, when Beggarmaster clarified himself. 'I mean, every single human being. And who can blame us? What chance do we have, when our beginnings and endings are so freakish? Birth and death – what could be more monstrous than that? We like to deceive ourselves and call it wondrous and beautiful and majestic, but it's freakish, let's face it.'

He shut his sketchbook and returned it to the briefcase with a certain snappiness, indicating that his saga of happiness and misery and doubt and discovery was over, the human emotions were being packed away, and now it was back to business. 'Your year will be up in another four months. I need to know in advance – are you planning to renew the contract with me?'

'Oh yes,' said Ishvar. 'Most definitely. Or the landlord will again start his harassment.'

They followed Beggarmaster to the verandah to see him off. Outside, the night remained unbroken by streetlights. There appeared to be a power outage, for the entire line of lamps was unlit.

'I hope Shankar's lamppost is working,' said Beggarmaster. 'I better hurry and check on him, he gets frightened if the pavement is dark.'

He strode across the black asphalt in his white shirt and trousers, like chalk across a blank slate. He turned once to wave, then gradually became invisible.

'What a weird story,' said Om. 'Our friends at Vishram would really enjoy this one. It's got everything – tragedy, romance, violence, and a suspenseful unresolved ending.'

'But you heard what Beggarmaster told us,' said Ishvar. 'It must be kept secret, for Shankar's sake. It's one more story that cannot be included in the cook's *Mahabharat*.'

XIII Wedding, Worms, and Sanyas

THE KITTENS' REAPPEARANCE outside the kitchen window a month later was not an occasion for rejoicing. The creatures treated it as no more than a scrounging stop. Om and Maneck would have been happy with some sign of recognition – a loud miaow, perhaps, or a look, a purr, an arching of the back. Instead, the kittens grabbed a fish head and ran off to enjoy it in seclusion

'Why are you surprised by that?' said Dina. 'Ingratitude is not uncommon in the world. One day, you too will forget me – all of you. When you go your own way and settle down, you will not know me.' She pointed at Maneck. 'In two months you'll sit for your final exam, pack your things, then disappear.'

'Not me, Aunty,' he protested. 'I will always remember you, and visit you, and write to you wherever I am.'

'Yes, we'll see,' she said. 'And you tailors will some day start on your own and leave as well. Not that I won't be happy for you when it happens.'

'Dinabai, I'll bless your mouth with sugar if that ever happens,' said Ishvar. 'But before there can be homes or shops for people like us, politicians will have to become honest.' He held up his index finger, crooked it, then extended it. 'The bent stick may straighten, but not the government.' In fact, he said, this was his biggest worry – how would Om take a wife if they couldn't find a place to live?

'Surely something will turn up by the time he's ready to marry,' said Dina.

'I think he is ready now,' said Ishvar.

'I think he is not,' snapped Om. 'Why do you keep talking about marriage? Look at Maneck, same age as me, and no one's hurrying to fix his wedding. Are your parents in a rush, Maneck? Come on, speak, yaar, teach my uncle some sense.'

Maneck shrugged his shoulders and said no, they weren't in a rush.

'Go on, tell him the other part. That your parents will wait till you meet someone you like. And if you decide to marry, only then will they make the arrangements. That's how I want it to be for me also.'

'Omprakash, you are speaking nonsense,' his uncle seethed beneath

465

the absurd suggestion. 'We are from different communities, with different customs. Because your parents are not with us, it's my duty to find you a wife.'

Om scowled.

'Sour-lime face,' said Maneck, trying to head off the battle that was brewing. 'Anyway, let me warn you, Aunty. You may not be rid of me in two months.'

'What does that mean?'

'I've decided to go to college for three more years, get a proper degree instead of the technician's certificate.'

Her delight leapt to her face; she pushed it into a less public place. 'That's a wise decision. A degree is more valuable.'

'So can I stay on with you? After going home for my vacation, I mean.'

'What do you think, you two? Should we let Maneck come back?'

Ishvar smiled. 'On one condition. That he does not plant his wild ideas in my nephew's head.'

The question of his nephew's marriage continued to haunt Ishvar. He brought it up at every opportunity, while Dina discouraged him gently. 'Work is plentiful, and at last you are managing to save some money. Why go jumping into a new responsibility? Just when things are improving?'

'All the more reason,' said Ishvar. 'In case things become worse again.'

'They are bound to, whether Om marries or not,' said Maneck. 'Everything ends badly. It's the law of the universe.'

Ishvar looked as though his face had been slapped. 'I thought you were our friend,' he said, his voice shrinking with pain.

'But I am. I'm not saying it out of spite. Just look at the world around you. Things seem promising at times, but in the end every –'

'That's enough philosophy from you,' said Dina. 'If you can't say something nice, don't say anything. Keep your black thoughts to yourself. I disagree with Ishvar too, but that's no reason to utter such inauspicious words.'

'But I don't disagree, it's just that –'

'Enough! You have hurt Ishvar enough!'

The hurt did not keep Ishvar's fixation from growing. Two days later he announced, in a voice dripping uncertainty, that his mind was made up. 'The best way is to write a letter to Ashraf Chacha, ask him to spread the word in our community.'

Om stopped sewing and looked scornfully at his uncle. 'First you kept dreaming we would save, go back to our village and buy a little shop. Now you have a new dream. Why don't you wake up for a change?'

'What's wrong in exchanging an impossible dream for a possible one? A shop will take very long. But marriage cannot be postponed. Bas, I'm writing to Chachaji.'

'I'm warning you, write to him only if *you* want a wife.'

'Did you hear that? My *nephew* is warning *me*.' He gave up the pretence of calm; the damaged left cheek eclipsed his face. 'You will do as you are told, understood? I have been too lenient with you, Omprakash – hahn, too lenient. Somebody else in my place would have softened your bones over the years.'

'Leave it, yaar, I'm not scared of your threats.'

'Listen to him. Just a few months ago, at the work camp, you were weeping in my arms each night. Scared and sick, vomiting like a baby. Now you are all strong and defiant. And why? Because I want what's best for you?'

'Nobody is denying that,' Dina broke in, hoping Ishvar would see sense if she added her voice in opposition. 'But such blind haste is unwise. If Om was longing for a wife, it would be different. What is *your* rush?'

He felt they were ganging up on him. 'It is my duty,' he murmured with the irritating air of a sage and, in effect, declared himself the winner. Then he got back to work. Reaching absently for a length of cloth, he made the entire stack collapse.

'Wonderful!' she pounced. 'Well done! Bring down the whole ceiling, go ahead. See how your urgent duty is affecting you? Mania is what it is – mania, not duty.' She helped him pick up the fallen clothes. 'If only that rascal cat had not left her babies in my kitchen. She put this whole crazy idea in your head.'

Over the next few days, Ishvar's fretting was transformed into clumsiness at the Singer. Errors kept popping up in his sewing like wrong cards in a magic trick, giving Dina occasion to point out the danger of his ways. 'Your marriage mania will destroy our business. You will make the food vanish from our plates.'

'I'm sorry, there is much on my mind,' said Ishvar. 'But don't worry, it's only a passing phase.'

'What do you mean, don't worry? How can it pass? Once there is a wife, there will be children. Then there will be even more on your mind. Where will they all stay? And all those mouths to feed. How many lives do you want to ruin?'

'It may seem like ruining to you. What I am doing is building the foundation for Om's happiness. A marriage does not happen in a month or two. It will take at least a year before we get anywhere. If the girl is too young, the parents may wish to wait longer. All I want is to find the right one and reserve her for my nephew.'

'Like a train ticket,' put in Maneck, and Om laughed.

'You have a very bad habit,' said Ishvar. 'Always making fun of things you don't understand.'

What other choice was there, thought Maneck. But the risk of further upsetting Ishvar kept him silent.

Ashraf's reply came in an envelope bearing black cancellations across the postage stamp. It featured the date, postal district, and a slogan: AN ERA OF DISCIPLINE, followed by a menacing exclamation mark shaped like a cudgel.

They waited impatiently for Ishvar to tear it open and share the news. His eyes travelled across the page with the uncertainty of one unused to reading, stumbling over Ashraf's shaky hand. He smiled broadly once, then looked puzzled, and frowned towards the end, all of which made Om very nervous.

'Chachaji is in good health,' began Ishvar. 'He has missed us. He says the devil must have held time captive, it has been so long in passing. He is happy that Om will marry. He also agrees it should not be delayed.'

'What else?'

Ishvar sighed. 'He has spoken to people in our community.'

'And?'

'There are four Chamaar families interested.' He sighed again.

'Hurray,' said Maneck, thumping Om on the back. 'You're in big demand.' Om pushed away his hand.

'But Ishvarbhai, the news should please you,' said Dina. 'Why so worried? Isn't it what you wanted?'

He shuffled the two pages as though wishing there were more. 'This part pleases me. Difficulty is in the other part.' ·

They waited. 'Are you planning to tell us today or tomorrow?' asked Om.

Ishvar fingered his frozen cheek. 'The four interested families are in a hurry. You see, there are other parties with marriageable sons. Luckily, Chachaji has improved our standing – that Om is working for a big export company in the city, a good match for any girl. So the families want us to select and finalize in the next eight weeks.'

'That's too fast,' said Dina. 'You'll have to refuse them.'

During the year that he and his nephew had worked for Dina, Ishvar had never once raised his voice. When he did it now, it startled every-one, including himself.

'Who are you to say! Who are you to tell me what is best for my nephew in this, the most important decision of his life! What do you know about us, about his upbringing, about my duty, that you think you can advise on such matters!'

Ishvar the peacemaker, gentle and soft-spoken, raged and waved his hands. 'You think you own my nephew and me? We are not your slaves, we only work for you! Or would you like to tell us how to live, and when to die?'

And then, because he had no practice with the emotion of anger, and did not know how a tantrum should conclude, he burst into tears, flee-ing to the verandah.

'Fine!' she called after him, finding her voice. 'Do what you like! But don't expect me to provide shelter for wife and children and grand-children!'

'I don't expect anything from you!' he shouted back, his voice cracking.

Dina escaped to the front room to be alone; she did not trust herself or her tongue. Shaking, she sat on the sofa beside Maneck.

'Calm down, Aunty, he doesn't really mean it.'

'I don't care what he means,' her voice trembled. 'But you see this? You heard with your own ears. After all I've done – taken them into my home, treated them like family – he shouts at me like a dog. I should throw them out right now.'

'Throw, throw!' shouted Ishvar from the verandah. 'What do I care!' He snorted to clear his runny nose, and tasted salt.

With a finger to his lips, Maneck signalled to her to ignore him. 'He is completely illogical about this marriage business,' he whispered. 'Why argue with him?'

'Only because I feel sorry for Om. But you're right, it's between him and his uncle. They can do what they like. This thing has become trou-ble with a capital t.'

Om heard them in the back room, and buried his face in his hands.

The hours dredged the stagnant afternoon in vain, revealing nothing. Ashraf's abandoned letter lay on the dining table. The clock's big hand fell from mark to mark like a stone. No one made tea, no one went out for tea. Ishvar on the verandah, Om in the back, Maneck and Dina in the front room: the household was frozen.

The sun dropped towards the horizon, and the light started to change. A breeze visited each window, rustling the letter on the table. Soon it would be dinnertime – time to make chapatis. Om was hungry.

He walked around with his chappals flopping purposefully. He drank water, letting his glass clatter against the pot. He wanted his noises to touch the others; friendly noises could melt hostility. He sat down, drummed on the Singer's bench, rattled the scissors, filled six bobbins. Then he went to the front room.

They were relieved he had come. Maneck winked. 'That was something else, yaar. He exploded like a Divali Atom Bomb.'

Om forced a short laugh. 'I just don't know what to do with my uncle,' he confided, his voice hushed. 'I'm worried about him.'

His words amused Dina, for they echoed the ones that Ishvar the conciliator would use in the old days when Om was rude, sewed badly, or misbehaved in general. 'Be patient,' she said.

'What is it about marriages and weddings that turns people crazy. On this one topic he becomes a madman.'

'Yes, he does, doesn't he,' grimaced Dina. 'Reminds me of my brother.'

'Just wait, I'll straighten out my uncle.' He went to the verandah, where Ishvar sat cross-legged on the floor beside the bedding roll.

'Are you crazy, speaking like that to someone who has been so good to us?' Om began scolding, arms folded across his chest.

Ishvar looked up, smiling weakly. He heard the same echo in his nephew's words that Dina had detected. After his freak outburst of anger, he felt confused, foolish, ready to make amends.

'You go at once and tell Dinabai you are sorry. Tell her you lost your head, you didn't mean the nasty things. Go right now. Say that you respect her opinions, you realize what she says is out of concern for us. Now get up, go.'

His uncle held out a hand; Om grabbed it, leaned back, hoisted him up. Ishvar shuffled into the front room and stood sheepishly before the sofa to apologize. For Dina it was a reprise: the sermon on the verandah had been audible inside. But she remained stiff, scrutinizing the wall to her right.

Having almost run out of words, Ishvar sighed. 'Dinabai, to thank you for your kindness and beg forgiveness for my rudeness, I fall at your feet.' He started to bend, and the threat worked.

'Don't you dare,' she broke her silence. 'You know how I feel about that. We will speak no more about all this.'

'Okayji. It's my problem, I agree to work it out in my head.'

'Fine. He is your nephew, and the fatherly duties are yours.'

The agreement was broken by Ishvar the following evening. The correspondence he had initiated was yet to be dealt with, and the ordeal was putting him through bouts of excruciating doubt. Sighs of 'Hai Ram' steamed from his lips at intervals. The real cause of yesterday's explosion was now clear to everyone.

'The opportunity is perfect,' he brooded. 'Only, it comes before we are ready for it.'

'Om is a handsome fellow,' said Maneck. 'Look at his chikna hairstyle. He does not need a marriage reservation. Top-notch girls will line up for him by the dozen.'

Ishvar whirled around and pointed, his finger an inch from Maneck's face. 'You stop mocking such a serious matter.'

For a moment it seemed he might strike Maneck; then he dropped his hand. 'Like a son I look on you — like a brother to Om. And this is how you treat me? Jeering and making fun of what is so important to me?'

Maneck was nonplussed; he thought he saw tears starting in Ishvar's eyes. But before he could come up with something to reassure him, Om intervened, 'You've gone crazy for sure, you can't even take a joke anymore. All you do is drama and naatak every chance you get.'

His uncle nodded meekly. 'What to do, I am so worried about this. Bas, I'll keep my mouth shut from now on and think quietly.'

But he badly wanted their opinions, wanted a proper discussion, a favourable consensus to cloak his obsession. And within minutes he started again. 'Who can tell when a golden chance like this will reappear? Four good families to choose from. Some people go through life without finding even one suitable match.'

'It's too soon for me to get married,' Om repeated wearily.

'Better too soon than too late.'

'What if our tailoring goes phuss because of a strike or something?' said Dina. 'These are bad times, you cannot take anything for granted.'

'All the more reason to marry. A new wife's kismat will change all our lives for the better.'

'Even if that's true, where is the space for her in this tiny flat?'

'I would not dream of asking for more space. The verandah is enough.'

'For you and Om, *and* his wife? All three on the verandah?' The idea sounded preposterous. 'Are you ridiculing me?'

'No, Dinabai, I am not. Next time I go searching for accommodation, you should come with me, see how families live. Eight, nine, or ten people in a small room. Sleeping one over the other on big shelves, from floor to ceiling, like third-class railway berths. Or in cupboards, or in the bathroom. Surviving like goods in a warehouse.'

471

'I know all that. You don't have to lecture me, I have lived my whole life in this city.'

'Compared to such misery, three people on the verandah is a deluxe lodging,' he said fervently. 'But I am not insisting on it. If it's not your wish, we'll just go back to our village. The important thing is Om's marriage. Once that is done, my duty is done. The rest does not matter.'

A week after Ashraf Chacha's letter, Ishvar found the courage to proceed with the viewing of the four brides-to-be. He wrote back, laboriously forming the words, that Om and he would arrive in a month. 'Which will give us time to complete the dresses you brought yesterday,' he told Dina. With his response in the mail, the old calm returned to him, slipping like a shirt upon his person.

Dina found it baffling: a sensible man like Ishvar, suddenly turned irrational. Could he be conducting a form of blackmail? Could he be hoping that her need for their skills would force her to take in Om's wife?

Her suspicion waxed and waned. It was stronger at times when he kept emphasizing how Dina's fortune would change if the bride resided in this flat. 'You will see the difference the minute she crosses your threshold, Dinabai. Daughters-in-law have been known to transform the destiny of entire households.'

'She will be neither my daughter-in-law nor yours,' Dina pointed out.

But he was not to be put off by a trifling technicality. 'Daughter-in-law is just a word. Call her anything you like. The hand of good fortune is not fussy about words.'

She shook her head in frustration and amusement. Ishvar and deceit – the two just did not go together. His inability to dissemble was well known. If his mind was in turmoil, his fingers were never far behind in manifesting the confusion; when he was pleased about something, his half-smile radiated uncontrollably, his arms ready to embrace the world. Cunning strategies did not proceed from such an open nature.

She dismissed her suspicion about blackmail. It would have made more sense in dealing with someone like Nusswan. Now he – he was capable of every devious twist and turn. A person could go crazy trying to predict his actions. She wondered how it would be when the time came for the children to get married. Not children anymore – Xerxes and Zarir were grown men. And Nusswan trying to select wives for them, putting to use all the practice he got when he was set on finding her a husband.

She remembered the years when her nephews were small. What a time of fun it had been, but so brief. And how miserable they were when Nusswan and Ruby and she argued, and there was screaming and shouting. Not knowing whose side to take, whether to run to Daddy or to Aunty to plead for peace. In the end, she had missed out on so much. Their school years, report cards, prize distribution days, cricket matches, their first long trousers. Independence came at a high price: a debt with a payment schedule of hurt and regret. But the other option – under Nusswan's thumb – was inconceivable.

As always, on looking back, Dina was convinced she was better off on her own. She tried to imagine Om a married man, tried to imagine a wife beside him, a woman with a small delicate figure like his. A wedding photo. Om in stiff new starched clothes and an extravagant wedding turban. Wife in a red sari. A modest necklace, nose-ring, earrings, bangles – and the moneylender waiting in the wings, happy to put the noose around their necks. And what would she be like? And what would it be like to finally have another woman living in this flat?

A picture began to form, and Dina let it develop for two days, adding depth and detail, colour and texture. Om's wife, standing in the front door. Her head demurely lowered. Her eyes sparkling when she looks up, her mouth smiling shyly, lips covered with her fingers. The days pass. Sometimes the young woman sits alone at the window, and remembers forsaken places. Dina sits beside her and encourages her to talk, to tell her things about the life left behind. And Om's wife begins at last to speak. More pictures, more stories . . .

On the third day Dina said to Ishvar, 'If you seriously think the verandah is big enough for three people, we can try it out.'

He heard her through the Singer's hammer and hum, and braked the flywheel, slamming his palm upon it.

'Good thing you drive a sewing-machine and not a motorcar,' she said. 'Your passengers would be chauffeured straight into the next world.'

Laughing, he leapt from the stool. 'Om! Om, listen!' he called to the verandah. 'Dinabai says yes! Come here – come and thank her!' Then he realized he himself still hadn't done that. 'Thank you, Dinabai!' he joined his hands. 'Once again you are helping us in ways beyond repayment!'

'It's only a trial. Thank me later, if it works out.'

'It will, I promise! I was right about the cat . . . the kittens coming back . . . and I will be right about this, too, believe me,' he said, breathless in his joy. 'The main thing is, you are willing to help. That's like receiving your good wishes and blessings. It's the most important thing – the most important.'

The mood in the flat changed, and Ishvar couldn't stop beaming at the seams he was running off. 'It will be perfect, Dinabai, believe me. For all of us. She will be useful to you also. She can clean the house, go to the bazaar, cook for –'

'Are you getting a wife for Om, or a servant?' she inquired, her tone caustic.

'No no, not servant,' he said reproachfully. 'Why does it make her a servant if she does her duties as a wife? How else do people find happiness except in fulfilling their duty?'

'There can be no happiness without fairness,' she said. 'Remember that, Om – don't let anyone tell you otherwise.'

'Exactly,' said Maneck, concealing the inexplicable sadness that came over him. 'And if you misbehave, Umbrella Bachchan and his pagoda parasol will straighten you out.'

Dina felt that granting consent for the verandah had legitimized a role for herself in Om's marriage, and given her certain rights. He had come along quite nicely in these past few months, she thought. The scalp itch was gone and his hair was healthy, no longer dripping with smelly coconut oil. For this last, the credit went to Maneck and his distaste of greasy stuff in the hair.

Slowly but surely, Om had reinvented himself in Maneck's image, from hairstyle to sparse moustache to clothes. Most recently, he had made flared trousers for himself, borrowing Maneck's to trace the pattern. He even smelled like Maneck, thanks to Cinthol Soap and Lakmé Talcum Powder. And Maneck had learned from Om as well – instead of always wearing shoes and socks in the heat, which made his feet smell by the end of the day, he now wore chappals.

But imitation only underscored the difference between the two: Maneck sturdy and big-boned, Om with his delicate birdlike frame. If anyone was to become a husband, she thought, Maneck seemed more ready, not Om, the skinny boy of eighteen.

Once more, she was acutely aware of the painful thinness flitting and darting about the flat, especially in the kitchen, in the evenings, when it charmed her to watch his flour-coated fingers fly, kneading the dough and rolling out the chapatis. The rolling pin moved like magic under his hands. His skill, and the delight he took in it, had a mesmerizing effect. It made her want to cease her own chores, just stand and stare.

She reflected on the time Om had been living with her. She had observed him devouring hearty meals, quantities that were anything but birdlike. Which removed one possibility – he was not underweight because he ate poorly. And her original suspicion of a year ago wriggled out again.

'It just won't do,' she said, discussing the matter with Ishvar. 'Thanks to you, the boy is going to take on a big responsibility. But what kind of husband and father will he make with a stomachful of worms?'

'How can you be so sure, Dinabai?'

'He complains about headaches, and itches in private places. He eats a lot but continues to be skin and bones. Those are definite signs.'

Next day, she showed Ishvar the dark-brown bottle of vermifuge she had purchased at the chemist's. 'It's the best wedding gift I can give the boy.'

The pink liquid was to be ingested in a single dose. He examined it, unscrewing the top to sniff: not a pleasant smell. How good it would be if Om were cured before the wedding, he thought. 'But what if it's something else, not worms?'

'That's okay, the medicine won't do any harm. It just acts like a purge. He must fast this evening, and take it late at night. Look, it explains on the label here.'

But the directions were quite complex for his rudimentary English, lost when it strayed too far beyond chest, sleeve, collar, waist. He promised to make his nephew swallow the dose before going to bed.

The more difficult part was to persuade Om to miss dinner. 'Such injustice,' he complained. 'Starving the cook who makes your chapatis.'

'If you eat, the worms eat. They need to be kept waiting hungrily inside your stomach, with their mouths wide open. So when you take the medicine, they swallow it eagerly and die.'

Maneck said he had once seen a film about a doctor who became very tiny, in order to go inside the patient's body and fight the disease. 'I could take a tiny gun and shoot dead all your worms.'

'Sure,' said Om. 'Or a tiny umbrella, to stab them. Then I won't need to drink this foul stuff.'

'One thing you are forgetting,' said Ishvar. 'If you are very tiny in the stomach, the worms will be like giant cobras and pythons. Hahnji, mister, hundreds of them swarming, seething, hissing around you.'

'I hadn't thought of that,' said Maneck. 'Forget it. I'm cancelling my voyage.'

Dina lost count after Om's first seven trips to the toilet next morning. 'I am dead,' he moaned. 'Nothing left of me.'

Then late in the afternoon he burst out of the WC, shaken but triumphant. 'It fell! It looked like a small snake!'

'Was it wriggling or lifeless?'

'Wriggling madly.'

'That means the medicine couldn't sedate it. What a powerful para-site. How big was it?'

He thought for a moment and held out his hand. 'From here to here,' he pointed from fingertips to wrist. 'About eight inches.'

'Now you know why you are so thin. That wicked creature and its children were eating up your nourishment. Hundreds of stomachs with-in your stomach. And none of you believed me when I said worms. Never mind, it won't be long now before you put on weight. Soon you'll be as well built as Maneck.'

'Yes,' said Maneck, 'we have three weeks to make a strong husband out of you.'

'And the father of half a dozen boys,' added Ishvar.

'Don't give bad advice,' said Dina. 'Two children only. At the most, three. Haven't you been listening to the family planning people? Remember, Om, treat your wife with respect. No shouting or screaming or beating. And one thing is certain, I will not allow any kerosene stoves on my verandah.'

Ishvar understood her allusion, veiled though it was. He protested that bride burnings and dowry deaths happened among the greedy upper castes, his community did not do such things.

'Really? And what does your community say about male and female children? Any preferences?'

'We cannot determine these things,' he declared. 'It's all in God's hands.'

Maneck nudged Om and whispered, 'It's not in God's hands, it's in your pants.'

Om took a day to recover from the vermifuge. Next evening Maneck made plans to celebrate the return of the appetite with bhel-puri and coconut water at the beach.

'You are spoiling my nephew,' said Ishvar.

'Not really. It's the first time I'm treating him. Previously his pet worm did the eating.'

Ishvar stared at the man in the doorway, trying to place him, for the voice was familiar but not the face. Then he recoiled, recognizing the greatly transformed hair-collector. His scalp was smooth and shining, and he had shaved off his moustache.

'You! Where did you come from?' He wondered whether to tell him to get lost or threaten to call the police.

Shoulders drooping, head bowed, Rajaram would not meet his gaze. 'I took a chance,' he said. 'It's been so many months, I didn't know if you still worked here.'

'What happened to your long hair?' asked Om, and Ishvar clicked his tongue disapprovingly. He didn't want his nephew to get familiar again with this murderer.

'It's okay to ask about my hair,' said Rajaram, raising his head. The expression in his eyes was empty, the fire of relentless enterprise extinguished. 'You are my only friends. And I need your help. But I feel so bad . . . still haven't returned your last loan.'

Ishvar withheld his disgust. To get involved in police business, with just days left before the wedding trip, would be most inauspicious. If a few rupees could get rid of the killer, he would do it. He stepped backwards to allow Rajaram to enter the verandah. 'So what's wrong this time?'

'Terrible trouble. Nothing but trouble. Ever since our shacks were destroyed, my life has been filled with immense obstacles. I am ready to renounce the world.'

Good riddance, thought Ishvar.

'Excuse me,' said Dina. 'I don't know you very well, but as a Parsi, my belief makes me say this: suicide is wrong, human beings are not meant to select their time of death. For then they would also be allowed to pick the moment of birth.'

Rajaram stared at her hair, letting moments elapse before responding. 'Choosing the ending has nothing to do with choosing the beginning. The two are independent. Anyway, you misunderstand me. All I meant was, I want to reject the material world, become a sanyasi, spend my life meditating in a cave.'

She regarded this as much an evasion as suicide. 'It's all the same thing.'

'I don't agree,' said Maneck.

'Please don't interrupt me, Maneck,' she said, turning to Rajaram again. 'And how is my old haircutting kit? Does it still work? It is a Made In England set, mind you.'

He blanched. 'Yes, it's working first class.'

Then he would speak no more of himself in the presence of Maneck and Dina. 'Can I buy my two old friends a cup of tea? What's that restaurant you go to – Aram?'

'Vishram,' said Ishvar, and checked if he had enough money in his pocket for tea. Although the invitation was the hair-collector's, chances were, he would end up paying.

They walked silently to the corner, and settled around the solitary table. The cook waved an oily hand from his corner. 'Story time!' he shouted happily. 'And what is today's topic?'

The tailors laughed, shaking their heads. 'The story is, our friend is thirsty for your special tea,' said Ishvar. 'He has come very far to meet us.'

Rajaram looked about him awkwardly; he had forgotten how tiny and exposed the Vishram was. But he was grateful for the privacy afforded by the din of the roaring stoves.

'So what's all this fakeology about sanyasi?' asked Om.

'No, I'm serious, I want to renounce the world.'

'What happened to barbering?'

'That's where the whole problem started. I was a failure right from the first day. My hair-collecting years had left me useless for barbering.'

Ishvar was unwilling to believe a single word from the mouth of this killer. 'You mean you forgot how to do haircuts?'

'Much worse than that. Whenever a customer sat on the pavement and asked for a trim, he ended up almost a baldie.'

'And how did that happen?'

'Something would come over me. Instead of clipping and pruning, shaping the hair, I hacked off everything. In a way it was funny – some of them so nice and polite, when I held up the mirror they would say, 'Good, very good, thank you.' They probably didn't want to hurt my feelings and tell me I was a lousy barber. But most customers were not kind. They shouted angrily, refused to pay, threatened to beat me up. And I just couldn't stop my clippers or scissors. My hair-collecting instinct had become too powerful, I was like a monster.'

Word got around of the maniac with scissors, and no one stopped anymore at his pavement stall. Soon he was left without a choice. It had to be full-time hair-collecting again. But there was a problem: he had no place to store the bags of low-value clippings, which were his stock in trade. 'And you could not have kept it in your trunk either. You need a small warehouse for that. You saw my hut in the colony, how it was stacked from floor to ceiling.'

Rajaram wrung his hands and shook his head. 'If I could have obtained even one set of twelve- or fourteen-inch hair every week, I would have survived. It would have paid for one daily meal. But there was no long hair in my horoscope.'

'What about the packets you left with Shankar?' interrupted Om. 'They contained long hair.'

'That came later,' he said. 'Be patient, I am making a full confession.' He gazed wistfully in the distance, as though at a parade of long-haired lovelies. 'I will never understand why women hang on forever to their long hair. It's beautiful to look at, yes, but so much trouble to take care of.'

He took a sip of tea and licked his lips. 'I wasn't ready to give up. Not yet. Now I started offering free haircuts to beggars, vagrants, and drunks.' Late at night, after the hustling and drinking was done, he would approach the ones with long hair. A few needed tempting with a small coin. If they were comatose, or too impaired to know what was happening, he just helped himself.

But the venture failed. The quality of his harvest was very poor. The agent said this type of long hair, knotted and dirty, was worth no more than the snippets of pavement barbers. Besides, the supply became erratic when the police started their Emergency roundups under the Beautification Law.

Hungry and homeless, Rajaram would stare ravenously at women who passed with their tantalizing dangling plaits, taunting him with the wealth they carried on their heads. Sometimes he picked one to follow, a well-dressed society lady, a likely candidate for a visit to the hairdresser, who just might be planning to have her tresses lopped off. The women he pursued led him to their friends' homes, doctors' offices, astrologers, faith healers, restaurants, sari shops, but never to a hair salon.

He scrutinized long-haired men, too: hippies, foreign and local, in their beads and beards – foreign ones gone native in chappals, kurtas, and pyjamas, local ones slouching in sneakers, bell-bottoms, and T-shirts, and all of them equally smelly. He wondered how much a head of blond or red hair might fetch, but did not bother following them, for he knew they would never get a haircut.

It was a pity, he began to muse, that hair was so firmly fastened to the owner's head, making it so difficult to steal. Firmer than the most tightly clutched purse, snugger than a fat wallet in skin-tight trousers. Beyond the fingers of the most skilful pickpocket. Or pickhead. To think that something as fine and light as hair could cling so tenaciously was truly an amazing thing. The way its roots clutched the scalp, it might have been a powerful banyan tree anchored to the earth. Unless, of course, alopecia set in and the hair fell out.

To pass the time, Rajaram told the tailors, he dreamt of being the first pickhead to go into business. He dreamt of developing a system that would overcome healthy hair's natural reluctance to relinquish the head. Perhaps invent a chemical which, when sprayed on the victim's scalp, would melt the roots but leave the hair untarnished. Or a magic mantra that would hypnotize the individual and make the hair jump off, the way ancient Vedic shlokas recited by sadhus could inspire flames to leap from logs or clouds to pour rain.

Dreaming away the hungry hours, he concluded that in reality a pickhead needed no new invention or supernatural power: the existing techniques of pickpockets, with a few modifications, would suffice. In crowded places it would be easy, using roughly (and smoothly) the same procedure as cutpurses. They were known to employ a sharp blade to ease a restrictive pocket; he still had his razor-keen scissors. One snip and the hair could be his.

At some point, Rajaram's fanciful notions took on a serious aspect. Now he began to believe there was no ethical connection between picking pockets and administering unwelcome haircuts. One was a crime, which deprived the victims of their money. The other was a good deed, the alleviation of an encumbrance, the eradication of a lice-breeding pasture, which would save the victims time and effort and itchy scalps, not to mention the frivolous expenses of shampoo and hair lotions. And 'victim' was hardly the correct word in this case, he felt. Surely 'beneficiary' would be more accurate. Surely it was vanity that kept people from realizing their own good, and a helping hand was necessary. In any case, the loss would be temporary, the hair would grow back.

'I began training earnestly,' he said, stroking his bald head while the tailors shifted on the bench in the Vishram, rendered speechless by the hair-collector's story thus far. 'I travelled through the suburbs till I found a place in the barren countryside where I could rehearse.'

There, removed from the gaze of human eyes, he stuffed a bag with newspaper to produce a ball the size of a human head, but much lighter, light enough to sway at the least disturbance when suspended with twine from a branch. To the bag he tied lush clusters of string. Then he practised severing them close to the head, without shaking the bag. For variation he would weave the strings into plaits, or hang them in a thick ponytail, or spread them loose like cascading curls.

As his skills advanced, the setup was modified to simulate real-life situations. He held a cloth bag beneath the plait to catch it as it fell, dropped in the scissors, and drew the bag shut – all in one smooth movement. He performed this drill in very tight places, to discipline his hands to work within crowds. And when they were trained, he returned to the city's jostling streets and bazaars.

'But why did you go through all this madness?' asked Ishvar. 'If your hair business collapsed, wouldn't it have been easier to collect something else? Newspapers, dabba, bottles?'

'I have been asking myself the same question. The answer is yes. There were dozens of possibilities. At the very worst, I could have become a beggar. Even that would have been preferable to the horrible road I was starting on. It's easy to see now. But a blindness had come over me. The more difficult it was to collect long hair, the more desperately I wanted to succeed, as though my life depended on it. And so my scheme did not seem at all crazy.'

In fact, when it was put to work, he realized he had developed a brilliant system. With his cloth bag and scissors he would elbow himself into a crowd, selecting the victim (or beneficiary) with care, never impatient and never greedy. A head with two plaits could not tempt him to go for both – he was happy with one. And he always resisted the urge to cut too close to the nape – the extra inch or two could be his undoing.

In the bazaar, Rajaram stayed clear of the shoppers who came with servants, no matter how luxuriant the hair. Similarly, matrons with children in tow were avoided – youngsters were unpredictable. The woman he singled out to receive the grace of his scissors would be alone, preferably someone poorly dressed, engrossed in buying vegetables for her family, agitated by the high prices, bargaining tenaciously, or absorbed in watching the vendor's weights and scales to make sure she wasn't short-changed.

Soon, though, she would be short-haired. Amid the milling shoppers, Rajaram's sharp instrument emerged unnoticed. It went snip, once, quickly and cleanly. The plait dropped into the cloth bag, and he disappeared, having delivered one more fellow human of the hindrance that, unbeknown to her, was weighing her down.

At bus stops, Rajaram chose the woman most anxious about her purse, clamped tight under her arm, its leather or plastic hot against her sweltering skin. Semicircles of sweat would be travelling like an epidemic across her blouse. He would join the commuters, another weary worker returning home. And when the bus's arrival converted the queue into a charging horde, the nervous woman hesitated at the periphery long enough for the scissors to do their work.

He never operated twice in the same marketplace or at the same bus stop. That would be too risky. Often, though, he returned empty-handed to the scene of his crime (or beneficence) to listen to the bazaar talk.

For the first little while there was nothing. Probably as he suspected, the women were too embarrassed to make a fuss. Or maybe no one believed them, or thought the matter not serious enough.

Eventually, however, quips and wisecracks about lost, stolen, or misplaced hair started to sprout. One joke making the rounds of the paan shops was that under the Emergency, with the slums cleaned up, a new breed of urban rodents had evolved, with a taste not for rotting garbage but feminine hair. At the docks, mathadis unloading ships cheered the exploits of the mysterious hair-hunter, convinced that it was the work of a lower-caste brother extracting revenge for centuries of upper-caste oppression, of strippings and rapes and head-shavings of their womenfolk. In tea stalls and Irani restaurants, the intelligentsia wryly commented that the Slum Clearance Programme had been given a larger mandate due to bureaucratic bungling: a typo in a top-level memorandum had the Beautification Police down as the Beautician Police, and now they were tackling hair as crudely as they had tackled slums. The inevitable foreign hand also put in its appearance, in the form of female CIA agents spreading stories about missing coiffures in order to demoralize the nation.

'Since everyone was joking about it, I wasn't worried,' said Rajaram. 'My confidence grew, and I thought about expansion.'

The hippies, whom he had long regarded as perfect but impossible beneficiaries, became the focus of his ministrations. He discovered that in the early hours of the morning they lay in drug-filled slumber around the dealer's addaa where they bought their hashish.

Relieving catatonic foreigners of their locks was child's play. If someone among them happened to open his eyes and see a companion being sheared, he assumed it was a hallucination; he giggled stupidly, or whispered something like 'groovy, man' or 'wow, real cool' and went back to sleep after scratching his crotch. Once Rajaram even cropped a fornicating couple. First the man, who was on top, and then the woman when, halfway through, she mounted him. The rocking and pumping posed no problem for the hair-collector's expert hand. 'Oh man!' said the man, excited by his vision. 'Far out! I see Kama, grooming you for nirvana!' And the woman murmured, 'Like, baby, it's instant karma!'

Rajaram felt things were finally looking up for him. He welcomed the invasion of foreigners, unlike the conservative section of the citizenry that complained about degenerate Americans and Europeans passing on filthy habits and decadent manners to the impressionable youth. As long as the aliens possessed hair down to there, shoulder-length or longer, Rajaram was happy to see them pouring into the city.

Around this time, beggars reoccupied their places on the pavements, as the Beautification Law ran its schizophrenic course and grew moribund. The hair-collector's professional eye noticed immediately. Of course, with his business flourishing, he no longer went after the beggars' dirty, knotted hair. Some, recognizing him, would call out to him, requesting their free haircuts, but he ignored them.

'And if only I had continued to ignore them,' said Rajaram, sighing heavily, 'my life would have been so different today. But our destinies are engraved on our foreheads at birth. And it was beggars that brought about my downfall. Not the beautiful women in bazaars, whom I was so scared to approach. Not the hashish-smoking hippies, who I thought would beat me up one day. No – it had to be two helpless beggars.'

Rajaram paused, eyeing the cashier-waiter who was smiling at them from the counter, still hoping to be invited to share the story. The tailors did not acknowledge him. 'We know all about the beggars,' said Ishvar quietly. 'Why did you have to kill them?'

'You know!' exclaimed Rajaram, horrified. 'But of course! Your Beggarmaster – but I didn't! I mean, I did . . . I mean – it was all a mistake!' He hid his head in his hands upon the table, unable to look at his friends. Then he sat up, rubbing his nose. 'This table stinks. But please help me! Please! Don't let –!'

'Calm down, it's okay,' said Ishvar. 'Beggarmaster doesn't know about you. He only mentioned that two of his beggars were murdered and their hair stolen. We at once thought of you.'

Now Rajaram looked injured. 'It could have been another hair-collector, you know. There are hundreds in the city. You didn't have to think of me straight away.' He swallowed. 'So you didn't say anything to him?'

'It was none of our business.'

'Thank God. I meant the beggars no harm, it was such a terrible mistake the way it happened, believe me.'

One night, while he had been out on his rounds, he came upon two mendicants, a man and a woman, asleep under a portico, their knees drawn up to their hollow stomachs. He would have walked right past them, except that the streetlight revealed their hair. And it was beautiful. Both heads glimmered with a full-bodied lustre, a radiance he had rarely seen during his extensive travels. Hair such as this was the stuff that advertising executives' dreams were made of. Clients would have fought to feature it – its brilliance could have promoted products like Shikakai Soap or Tata's Perfumed Coconut Hair Oil to new heights of profitability.

But how strange, thought Rajaram, that such a treasure should adorn the heads of two shrivelled beggars. He knelt beside them and gently touched the shimmering tresses with his fingertips; they felt silken. Unable to resist, he heaped them in his hand and revelled in their texture. His fingers stiffened in sensual agony, as though they would steal the secret of the shine and softness.

The beggars stirred, breaking the spell. Rajaram remembered his professional duty. He took out his scissors and set to work, starting with the woman. For the first time in his career he felt regret. It was a crime, he thought, to separate hair this gorgeous from its roots – its magic glow would fade, as surely as the blush of a plucked flower.

The locks came away in his hand. He twisted the tresses together and packed them in his cloth bag. Then he worked on the man's hair. It was virtually indistinguishable from the woman's.

Just as the hair-collector finished, she awakened and saw him crouched beside her, the scissors glinting in the dark like a murderous weapon. She let out a heart-stopping shriek. It woke the man, who released his own bloodcurdling yells.

'Those screams,' said Rajaram, shuddering as though they still rang in his ears. 'They frightened me so much. I was sure the police would come and beat me to death. I begged the beggars to stop the noise. It was all right, I said, I was not going to hurt them. I clipped a lock of my own hair to show that what I was doing was harmless. I pleaded, I pulled notes and coins out of my pocket, and showered money on them. But they kept on screaming. On and on and on! It drove me crazy!'

He panicked, raised the scissors and struck. First the woman, then the man. In the throat and chest and stomach: in all the wretched places that were pumping the breath and quickening the organs to create those terrible screams. Again and again and again he stabbed, till there was silence.

No one came to investigate. The streets were accustomed to the caterwauling of lonely lunatics and the howling of disillusioned dipsomaniacs.

Across the road someone laughed hysterically; dogs barked; a temple bell clanged. Rajaram fled the place, walking as fast as he dared without attracting attention.

Later he threw away his scissors, his bloodstained clothes, and the hair. The first chance he got, he shaved his head and moustache, for when the police questioned the people in the area, the beggars would be sure to describe the fellow who used to come around regularly, cutting and collecting hair.

'But I am not safe,' said Rajaram. 'Though it has been months, the CID is still looking for me. God knows why my case fascinates them – there are hundreds of other crimes taking place every day.' The tea in his cup had gone cold. He made a face as he swallowed it. 'So now you know every unfortunate thing that has happened. Will you help me?'

'But how?' said Ishvar. 'Maybe it is best to give yourself up. It seems hopeless for you.'

'There is hope.' Rajaram paused and leaned closer, fixing his eyes on them. They were shining a little now. 'As I first told you, I want to renounce this world of trouble and sorrow. I want the simple existence of a sanyasi. I want to meditate for long hours in a cold, dark Himalayan cave. I will sleep on hard surfaces. Rise with the sun and retire with the stars. Rain and wind, no matter how strong, will be of little consequence to my mortified flesh. I will throw away my comb, and my hair and beard will grow long and knotted. Tiny creatures will find peaceful refuge in them, digging and burrowing as they choose, for I will not disturb them.'

Ishvar raised his eyebrows and Om rolled his eyes, but Rajaram did not notice either of them. He pushed aside his teacup slowly, deliberately, as though performing his first act of abnegation. The wild, romantic vision of an ascetic was a stimulant to his imagination, giving it a graphic turn.

'I will go with bare feet, my soles and heels cracked, torn, bleeding from a dozen lesions and lacerations to which shall be applied no salve or ointment. Snakes wandering across my path in dark jungles will not frighten me. Stray dogs will nip at my ankles as I roam through strange towns and remote villages. I will beg for my food. Children, and sometimes even adults, will mock me and throw stones at me, scared of my strange countenance and my frenzied inward-gazing eyes. I will go hungry and naked when necessary. I will stumble across rocky plains and down steep hills. I will never complain.'

His eyes had drifted from his audience, focusing wistfully in the distance, having already started their travels across the subcontinent. He seemed to be rather enjoying himself, as though it were a holiday itinerary he was planning. In the cook's corner, the stove ran out of fuel. Without its roar the place was hushed.

The silence dragged Rajaram away from his daydream, back to the Vishram's solitary and smelly table. The cook went to the rear to fetch the kerosene can. They watched him insert the funnel and fill the stove.

'Worldly life has led me to disaster,' said Rajaram. 'It always does, for all of us. Only, it's not always obvious, as was in my case. And now I am at your mercy.'

'But we don't know anything about becoming a sanyasi,' said Ishvar. 'What do you want from us?'

'Money. I need train fare to reach the Himalayas. There is hope of redeeming myself – if I can get away from the police and CID.'

They returned to the flat. Rajaram waited at the door while Ishvar went inside and asked Dina to let him have, out of their savings, the price of a third-class *Frontier Mail* ticket.

'It's your money, and it's not for me to say how you spend it,' she said. 'But if he is renouncing the world, why does he need train fare? He can get there on foot, begging his way like other sadhus.'

'That's true,' said Ishvar. 'But that would take a lot of time. He is in a hurry for salvation.'

He took the money out to Rajaram on the verandah, who counted it, then hesitated. 'Could I possibly have another ten rupees?'

'For what?'

'Sleeping berth surcharge. It's very uncomfortable to sit all night through such a long train journey.'

'Sorry,' said Ishvar, almost ready to snatch back the notes. 'We can't spare any more than this. But please visit us if you are in the city sometime, we can have tea together.'

'I doubt it,' said Rajaram. 'Sanyasis don't take vacations.' Then he laughed mirthlessly and was gone.

Om wondered if they would ever see him again. 'His habit of borrowing money was a nuisance, but he was an interesting fellow. He brought us news of the world.'

'Don't worry,' said Ishvar. 'With Rajaram's luck, all the caves will be occupied when he gets there. He'll come back with a story about how there was a No Vacancy sign in the Himalayas.'

XIV Return of Solitude

DUST AND FLECKS of fibre made Dina sneeze as she cleaned out the sewing room and sorted the leftovers. The rush of breath lifted bits of fabric. The last dresses had been delivered to Au Revoir, and Mrs. Gupta was informed about the six-week break.

Now Dina regarded the approaching emptiness of time with curiosity. Like a refresher course in solitude, she thought. It would be good practice. Without tailors, without a paying guest, alone with her memories, to go through them one by one, examine like a coin collection, their shines and tarnishes and embossments. If she forgot how to live with loneliness, one day it would be hard for her.

She set aside the best swatches for the quilt, stuffing the remainder in the bottom shelf. The Singers were pushed into a corner and the stools stacked on top, which provided more room around the bed. The tailors' trunk, packed and ready, stood on the verandah. The things they were not taking were stored in cardboard boxes.

With two days to departure and nothing to do, the passing hours had a strangeness to them, loose and unstructured, as though the stitches were broken, the tent of time sagging one moment, billowing the next.

After dinner Dina resumed work on the quilt. Except for a two-square-foot gap at one end, it had grown to the size she wanted, seven by six. Om sat on the floor, massaging his uncle's feet. Watching them, Maneck wondered what it might be like to massage Daddy's feet.

'That counterpane looks good, for sure,' said Om. 'Should be complete by the time we return.'

'Could be, if I add more pieces from old jobs,' she said. 'But repetition is tedious. I'll wait till there is new material.' They took opposite ends of the quilt and spread it out. The neat stitches crisscrossed like symmetrical columns of ants.

'How beautiful,' said Ishvar.

'Oh, anyone can make a quilt,' she said modestly. 'It's just scraps, from the clothes you've sewn.'

'Yes, but the talent is in joining the pieces, the way you have.'

'Look,' Om pointed, 'look at that – the poplin from our first job.'

'You remember,' said Dina, pleased. 'And how fast you finished those first dresses. I thought I had found two geniuses.'

'Hungry stomachs were driving our fingers,' chuckled Ishvar.

'Then came that yellow calico with orange stripes. And what a hard time this young fellow gave me. Fighting and arguing about everything.'

'Me? Argue? Never.'

'I recognize these blue and white flowers,' said Maneck. 'From the skirts you were making on the day I moved in.'

'Are you sure?'

'Yes, it was the day Ishvar and Om did not come to work – they had been kidnapped for the Prime Minister's compulsory meeting.'

'Oh, that's right. And do you recall this lovely voile, Om?'

He coloured and pretended he didn't. 'Come on, think,' she encouraged. 'How can you forget? It's the one on which you spilled your blood, when you cut your thumb with the scissors.'

'I don't remember that,' said Maneck.

'It was in the month before you came. And the chiffon was fun, it made Om lose his temper. The pattern was difficult to match, so slippery.'

Ishvar leaned over to indicate a cambric square. 'See this? Our house was destroyed by the government, the day we started on this cloth. Makes me feel sad whenever I look at it.'

'Get me the scissors,' she joked. 'I'll cut it out and throw it away.'

'No no, Dinabai, let it be, it looks very nice in there.' His fingers stroked the cambric texture, recapturing the time. 'Calling one piece sad is meaningless. See, it is connected to a happy piece – sleeping on the verandah. And the next square – chapatis. Then that violet tusser, when we made masala wada and started cooking together. And don't forget this georgette patch, where Beggarmaster saved us from the landlord's goondas.'

He stepped back, pleased with himself, as though he had elucidated an intricate theorem. 'So that's the rule to remember, the whole quilt is much more important than any single square.'

'Vah, vah!' exclaimed the boys with a round of applause.

'That sounds very wise,' said Dina.

'But is it philosophy or fakeology?'

Ishvar rumpled his nephew's hair in retaliation.

'Stop it, yaar, I've got to look good for my wedding.' Om pulled out his comb and restored the parting and puff.

'My mother collects string in a ball,' said Maneck. 'We used to play a game when I was little, unravelling it and trying to remember where each piece of string came from.'

'Let's try that game with the quilt,' said Om. He and Maneck located the oldest piece of fabric and moved chronologically, patch by patch, reconstructing the chain of their mishaps and triumphs, till they reached the uncompleted corner.

'We're stuck in this gap,' said Om. 'End of the road.'

'You'll just have to wait,' said Dina. 'It depends on what material we get with the next order.'

'Hahnji, mister, you must be patient. Before you can name that corner, our future must become past.'

Ishvar's lighthearted words washed over Maneck like cold rain; his joy went out like a lamp. The future *was* becoming past, everything vanished into the void, and reaching back to grasp for something, one came out clutching – what? A bit of string, scraps of cloth, shadows of the golden time. If one could only reverse it, turn the past into future, and catch it on the wing, on its journey across the always shifting line of the present . . .

'Are you listening?' asked Dina. 'How strong is your memory? Can you remember everything about this one year without looking at my quilt?'

'Seems much longer than one year to me,' said Om.

'Don't be stupid,' said Maneck. 'It's just the opposite.'

'Hoi-hoi,' said Ishvar. 'How can time be long or short? Time is without length or breadth. The question is, what happened during its passing. And what happened is, our lives have been joined together.'

'Like these patches,' said Om.

Maneck said the quilt did not have to end when the corner was filled in. 'You could keep adding, Aunty, let it grow bigger.'

'Here you go again, talking foolishly,' said Dina. 'What would I do with a monster quilt like that? Don't confuse me with your quiltmaker God.'

In the midst of the morning Dina was becalmed. The water chores were done, last night's dishes were scrubbed, clothes were washed. Without the chatter and hammer of the Singers, the rest of the day stretched emptily. She sat and watched Maneck eat a late breakfast.

'You should have gone with Ishvar and Om,' he tried to cheer her up. 'You could have helped to choose the wife.'

'Are you being smart again?'

'No, I'm sure they'd have been happy to take you. You could have joined the Bride Selection Committee.' He choked on his toast, retaining the morsel with difficulty.

She patted his back till the fit passed. 'Weren't you taught not to speak with your mouth full?'

'It's Ishvar in my throat,' he grinned. 'Taking revenge because I am making fun of his auspicious event.'

'Poor man. I just hope he knows what he is doing. And I hope that whoever they pick, she tries to fit in, get along with all of us.'

'I'm sure she will, Aunty. Om is not going to get a bad-tempered or unfriendly wife.'

'Oh, I know. But he may not have a choice. In these arranged marriages, astrologers and families decide everything. Then the woman becomes the property of the husband's family, to be abused and bullied. It's a terrible system, turns the nicest girls into witches. But one thing she will have to understand it's my house, and follow my ways, like you and Ishvar and Om. Or it will be impossible to get along.'

She stopped, realizing she was sounding like a mother-in-law. 'Come on, finish that egg,' she changed the subject. 'Your final exams begin tomorrow?'

He nodded, chewing. She began to clear the breakfast things. 'And five days later you leave. Have you made your reservation?'

'Yes, it's all done,' he said, gathering his books for the library. 'And I'll be back soon, don't give away my room to anyone, Aunty.'

The mail arrived, with an envelope from Maneck's parents. He opened it, handed the rent cheque to Dina, then read the letter.

'Mummy-Daddy are all right, I hope?' she said, watching his face start to cloud.

'Oh yes, everything is normal. Same as always. Now their complaints are starting again. They say: "Why are you going to college for three more years? Your fees are not the problem, but we will miss you. And there is so much work in the shop, we cannot manage alone, you should take over."' He put the letter down. 'If I do decide to go back, it will be fighting and shouting with Daddy every day.'

She saw his fist clench, and she squeezed his shoulder. 'Parents are as confused by life as anyone else. But they try very hard.'

He gave her the letter, and she read the rest of it. 'Maneck, I really think you should do what your mummy is requesting – visit the Sodawalla family. You haven't seen them even once in this whole year.'

Shrugging, he made a face and went to his room. When he emerged, she noticed the box under his arm. 'Are you taking your chess set to college?'

'It's not mine. Belongs to a friend. I'm going to return it today.'

On the way to the bus stop he deliberated about the letter – Daddy's turmoil, Mummy's anguish, their doubts and fears writhing through the words. What if they really meant it? Maybe it would work out fine this time, maybe the year's absence really had helped Daddy come to terms with the changes in his life.

He made a little detour past the Vishram in order to wave to Shankar. The beggar did not notice him, distracted, craning and staring down the pavement towards the corner. Maneck bent over, waving again, and Shankar acknowledged him by tapping his tin against the platform. 'O babu, are you fine? My friends departed safely?'

'Yesterday,' said Maneck.

'How exciting for them. And today is an exciting day for me also. Beggarmaster's barber is coming to shave me. But I wish Ishvar and Om were here. How they would enjoy seeing my face afterwards.'

'I'll be here, don't worry. I'll see you tomorrow,' said Maneck, and continued to the bus stop.

Shankar's eyes followed Maneck until he disappeared around the corner, then resumed their vigil for the barber. The platform stood motionless by the kerb. The begging tin remained empty, the begging song unheard. Shankar did nothing to attract the attention of almsgivers. All he could think of was the sumptuous grooming, the full luxury treatment that awaited him at the hands of Beggarmaster's personal barber.

Shankar did not know that earlier in the morning the personal barber had declined the commission. Pavement work was something he did not do, he had told Beggarmaster. Instead, he had presented someone else for the job. 'This is Rajaram. He is very good and very cheap, and does pavement work.'

'Namaskaar,' said Rajaram.

'Listen,' said Beggarmaster, 'Shankar may be just a beggar but I love him dearly – I want the very best for him. No offence to you, but I cannot help questioning your skills. How much can a bald man know about hair?'

'That's not a fair question,' said Rajaram. 'Does a beggar possess a lot of money? No. Yet he knows how to handle it.'

Beggarmaster had liked the answer, and given his approval. So it was Rajaram who arrived outside the Vishram, armed with his barber's kit.

Shankar thought he recognized the man from somewhere. 'Babu, have I met you before?'

'Never seen you in my life,' said Rajaram, haunted by their hair connection, and anxious to disown it. Staying on in the city was risky, he knew, but he had decided it would be safer to commence his journey to the Himalayas in a sanyasi's outfit. Saffron robes and beads and a hand-carved wooden bhiksha bowl didn't come cheap, however; Beggarmaster's bonus for this special job would certainly help.

He tied a white sheet round the beggar's neck and whipped up a cup of lather with the shaving brush. Shankar bowed his head towards it to catch the fragrance, almost losing his balance. Rajaram pushed him back. 'Sit still,' he said, his tone surly to discourage conversation.

Surliness was regular fare for Shankar, and could not diminish his good cheer. 'Looks like a cream puff,' he said, when the froth rose in the cup.

'Why don't you eat a bowlful?' Rajaram moistened the jowls and slapped on the soap. The careless brush strokes pushed some lather into Shankar's open mouth. Rusty as Rajaram was, he also forgot to pinch the nostrils shut while lathering the upper lip. He opened the razor and began to strop the gleaming blade.

Shankar loved the swishing sound. 'Do you ever make a mistake with your razor?' he asked.

'Lots of times. Some people's throats are such weird shapes, they cut easily. And police cannot arrest barbers for occupational accidents, it's the law.'

'You better not make a mistake on my throat, it's the proper shape! And Beggarmaster would punish you!'

Despite the bravado Shankar kept very still, tense till the blade had finished its dangerous tour of his map. Rajaram mopped up bits of lather missed by the razor, then glided an alum block over the shaved areas. The callow skin had been badly nicked in places.

'Show me the mirror,' demanded Shankar, feeling the smart and worrying that the razor had erred after all.

Rajaram held up the glass. The beggar's anxious face peered back, but the styptic had checked the bleeding and there were no drops of red.

'Okay, next is face massage. That's what Beggarmaster instructed.' From a bottle in his box he scooped out a dab of cream and spread it over the jowls.

Shankar went stiff, not sure what those muscular hands were up to. Then he allowed his head to roll with the rubbing, stroking movements. He began oohing and aahing with pleasure as the fingers kneaded his cheeks, worked under the eyes, around and over the nose, forehead and temples, massaging away a lifetime of pain and suffering.

'A little more,' he pleaded when the barber stopped and wiped his hands. 'One extra minute, I beg you, babu, it feels so wonderful.'

'It's all done,' said Rajaram, wrinkling his nose. He had never enjoyed giving face massages, not even to middle-class faces in the heyday of his career. He flexed his fingers before taking up the scissors and comb. 'Now your haircut,' he said.

'No, that I don't want.'

'Beggarmaster has told me what to do.' He jerked the head down to trim around the nape, anxious to finish and get away.

'Aray babu, I don't want it!' Shankar started screaming. 'I said I don't want it! I like long hair!' He shook his tin to make noise, but it had been a slow morning, the tin remained silent. He banged it on the pavement.

Passersby slowed to examine the duo curiously, and Rajaram ceased to press him, worried about attracting more attention. 'Don't be scared, I will cut your hair very carefully, very handsomely.'

'I don't care how handsome! I don't want a haircut!'

'Please don't shout. Tell me what you want, I'll do it for you. Scalp massage? Dandruff treatment?'

Shankar reached under his platform and took out a package. 'You are the hair expert, right?'

He nodded.

'I want you to fix this to my hair.' He pushed the package towards him.

Rajaram opened it, and quailed as two lovely ponytails slid out. 'You want me to tie these to your hair?'

'Not just tie. I want it permanent. It must grow from my own head.'

Rajaram was at a loss. He had, in his time as a barber, had his share of unusual assignments: grooming a circus's bearded lady; shaping a gigolo's private hair into little plaits; designing artistic pubic coiffures for a brothel moving upmarket to target ministers and corporate executives; shaving (blindfolded in the interest of modesty) the crotch of a caste-conscious man's wife because the husband didn't want her polluted by performing the lowly task herself. With these and other challenges, Rajaram had dealt with a barber's professional aplomb. But Shankar's request was beyond his skills.

'It's not possible,' he said flatly.

'You must, you must, you must!' screamed Shankar. Of late, Beggarmaster's attentions, sudden and excessive, had had a spoiling effect on the gentle, accepting beggar. He refused to listen to the barber's explanation. 'A rose can be grafted!' he yelled. 'So graft my hair! You're the expert! Or I'll complain to Beggarmaster about you!'

Rajaram begged him to speak softly, to put away the ponytails for now, he would come back tomorrow with special equipment for the complicated job.

'I want it today!' shouted Shankar. 'I want my long hair right now!'

The cashier-waiter of the Vishram Vegetarian Hotel watched from the doorway, and so did the cook. More passersby stopped, expecting something interesting to develop. Then a lottery-ticket vendor brought up the case of the beggars who had been killed many months ago for their hair. What a coincidence, he said, that two thick tails of hair should be in this beggar's possession.

Speculation flourished. Perhaps there was a connection – a ritual of beggars that involved human sacrifice. Or maybe this beggar was a psychopath. Someone mentioned the gruesome Raman Raghav serial killings a few years ago; the beggars' murders suggested a similar bloodthirsty pattern.

Trembling with fear, Rajaram tried to dissociate himself from Shankar. He packed up his kit and edged backwards till he became part of the crowd confronting the beggar. At the first opportunity he slipped away.

People moved in closer around Shankar. It frightened him. Now he was sorry he had made a fuss with the barber. He regretted forgetting the cardinal rule of all good almsmen: beggars could be seen, and also heard, but not too loudly – especially not on non-begging matters.

He felt claustrophobic as the crowd towering over him blotted out the sun. His pavement went dark. He tried to appease them by singing the begging song, 'O babu ek paisa day-ray,' his bandaged palm repeatedly touching his forehead. It didn't work. Opinion continued to churn menacingly.

'Where did you steal that hair, you crook?' shouted someone.

'My friends gave it to me,' whined Shankar, frightened yet indignant about the accusation.

'Saala murderer!'

'What a monster he is!' marvelled another, torn between repulsion and admiration. 'Such dexterity! Even without fingers or legs, he can commit these violent crimes!'

'Maybe he is just hiding his fingers and legs. These people have ways to modify their body.'

Shankar wept that he had not committed any bad acts, he was a good beggar who did not harass anyone and stayed in his proper place. 'May God watch over you forever! O babu, please listen, I always give a salaam to the people who pass by! Even when I am in pain I smile for you! Some beggars curse if the amount is insulting, but I always give a blessing, whether the coin is big or small! Ask anyone who walks by here!'

A policeman approached to see what the commotion was about. He bent down, and Shankar spied his face outside the forest of legs. The crowd parted to let the constable take a better look. Shankar decided it was now or never. He pushed off on his platform and shot through the opening.

The crowd laughed to see him crouch low, paddling with his arms for all he was worth. '*Chalti Ka Naam Gaadi*!' said someone, eliciting more laughter from those who remembered the old film.

'The beggars' Grand Prix!' said another.

A hundred yards past the Vishram, Shankar found himself in unexplored territory. Here, the pavement sloped quite steeply, and the castors began to spin faster. Turning the corner at high speed was going to be impossible. But Shankar had not thought so far ahead. The terrifying crowd had to be escaped, that was all.

He reached the end of the pavement and screamed. The platform took flight, sailing out into the busy intersection.

Maneck stayed in the centre of the stairway, away from the paan-stained banisters and the ugly daubs of God-knows-what on the wall. The old revulsion returned as he climbed the hostel stairs. Empty cigarette packs, a shattered lightbulb, a blackened banana peel, chapati in newspaper, orange rind littered the corridors. Was the jharoowalla late, or had the garbage descended since the morning sweep? he wondered.

He did not expect to find Avinash in, but decided he would leave the box with someone, maybe at the counter in the lobby. Reaching his floor, he held his breath while passing the toilets. The stench confirmed their continuing state of disrepair, the stink so deep it could be tasted in the throat.

His old room was vacant, the door unlocked. No one had occupied it since his departure, it was exactly the way he had left it. Eerie to look at, as though he were split in two – one half still living here, the other half with Dina Aunty. And the bed, a foot away from the wall, its four legs in cans of water. Avinash's method, to discourage crawling things – it had worked really well. Avinash used to joke that what he didn't know about cockroaches and bedbugs after being raised in the mill tenements wasn't worth knowing.

Maneck went closer, half-expecting to see water in the cans. They were dry, empty except for brown cockroach eggs, a dead moth, and a drowsy spider. The water had left rings on the wooden legs. His watermark: Maneck Was Here. Desk and chair, the faithful witnesses to so many games of chess, were near the window, where they had been shifted to catch a better light. Seemed so long ago.

He withdrew and shut the door gently on the past. To his surprise, there were sounds coming from the next room. What would Avinash say when he saw him? What would he say to Avinash? He collected himself, he didn't want to look anxious or uncertain.

He knocked.

The door opened, and a middle-aged couple gazed at him questioningly. They both had grey hair, the man hollow-cheeked and coughing terribly, the woman red-eyed. Must be the parents, he decided.

'Hello, I'm Avinash's friend.' Perhaps they were expecting him back soon, he could be around somewhere in the building. 'Are you waiting for him?'

'No,' the man spoke in a small voice. 'The waiting is over. Everything is over.' They moved back slowly, weighed down by invisible burdens, and beckoned him inside. 'We are his mother and father. Today we cremated him.'

'Pardon? Today what?'

'Cremated today, yes. And after a very long delay. For months and months we have been searching for our son. Going to all different police stations, begging for help. Nobody would help us.'

His voice quavered, and he stopped, making an effort to control it. 'Four days ago they told us there was a body in the morgue. They sent us to check.'

The mother began to cry, and hid her face in a corner of her sari. The father's coughing stabbed the air as he tried to comfort her; he touched her arm lightly with his fingers. A door slammed somewhere in the corridor.

'But what – I mean . . . nothing, no one . . .' stammered Maneck. The father put a hand on his shoulder.

Maneck cleared his throat and tried again. 'We were friends.' And the parents nodded, seeming to take comfort in the feeble fact. 'But I didn't know . . . what happened?'

The mother spoke now, her words fluttering away almost unheard. 'We don't know either. We came here straight from the cremation ceremony. It went well, thanks to God's grace. No rain, and the pyre flamed brilliantly. We stayed with it all night.'

The father nodded. 'They told us the body was found many months ago, on the railway tracks, no identification. They said he died because he fell off a fast train. They said he must have been hanging from the door or sitting on the roof. But Avinash was careful, he never did such things.' His eyes were watering again, he paused to wipe them. The mother touched his arm lightly with her fingers.

He was able to continue. 'At last, after such a long time, we saw our son. We saw burns on many shameful parts of his body, and when his mother picked up his hand to press it to her forehead, we could see that his fingernails were gone. So we asked them in the morgue, how can this happen in falling from a train? They said anything can happen. Nobody would help us.'

'You must report it!' said Maneck, angrily fighting his tears. 'You must! To . . . to the minister – I mean, the governor. Or the police commissioner!'

'We did, we made a complaint. The police wrote it all down in their book.'

They resumed the task of gathering Avinash's belongings. Maneck watched helplessly as they carried clothes, textbooks, papers, and placed them in the trunk with reverence, now and then putting their lips to some object before packing it. The room was silent except for their soft footsteps.

'Did he tell you about his three sisters?' said the mother suddenly. 'When they were small, he used to help me look after them. He very much enjoyed feeding them. Sometimes they bit his fingers and made him laugh. Did he ever tell you that?'

'He told me everything.'

In a few minutes they were ready to leave. He insisted on carrying the trunk downstairs for them, glad for the exertion that kept his eyes from overflowing. The parents' gratitude reminded him how little he could do to help with the weight of their grief. All he could think of was that first day, when Avinash had appeared at the door with the Flit pump. They had killed cockroaches. They had played draughts. They had told each other their life stories. And now he was dead.

He said goodbye, and proceeded to the technical building. Then he remembered that he still had the chessmen and board. He hurried to the gate. There was no sign of the parents. How stupid of me, he thought, it would have meant so much to them, the remembrance, Avinash's high-school prize for winning the tournament.

He started walking back aimlessly, and found himself in the hostel lobby again. Then he stopped, and decided: the chess set – somehow he had to give it back to the parents. He felt like a thief, robbing them of a source of comfort. He was adding to their grief, the longer he kept it.

The task of returning the set assumed an overriding urgency, a matter of life and death. He was weeping silently now as he climbed the stairs, watched by a handful of curious students. Someone hooted and shouted something he couldn't catch. They began chanting: 'Baby, baby, don't cry, Mummy making chilli-fry, Daddy catching butterfly . . .'

He slipped into his old room and sat down on the musty bed. Maybe there was something in Avinash's room, in the wastepaper basket, an old envelope or letter with the address. He went to look. Nothing. Not a scrap of paper. The address, he had to find the parents' address, to send them the set. He could ask around on this floor. But those bastards in the corridor would start their juvenile teasing again, watching him stumbling in and out of rooms, making a fool of himself.

Clutching the box against his chest, he closed his eyes, trying to think calmly. The address. The answer was simple – the warden's office. Yes, they would have the address. He could mail it to Avinash's parents.

He opened his eyes and gazed at the maroon plywood box as it swam through his tears. He remembered that day in the canteen: white to play and mate in three – and then the vegetarians vomited. The memory made him smile. Revolution through regurgitation, Avinash had said. And he had asked him to look after the chess set.

And he never asked for it back. His gift. The game of life. To send it back would be wrong. He would keep it. He would keep it now forever.

—

Dina urged Maneck to stay calm, to mentally recite one Ashem Vahu before reading the exam paper and one more before beginning to write the answers. 'I am not a very religious person myself,' she said. 'But think of it as insurance. I find it helps. And good luck.'

'Thanks, Aunty.' He opened the door to leave and almost stumbled into Beggarmaster on the other side, his index finger poised to ring the bell.

'Excuse me,' said Beggarmaster. 'I have come with very bad news.' He was utterly exhausted, his eyes strained from weeping. 'May I please see the tailors?'

'But they left two days ago.'

'Oh, of course. I forgot – the wedding.' He looked as though he would collapse.

'Come in,' said Dina.

He stepped onto the verandah and, choking back a sob, revealed that Shankar was dead.

Disbelief, the sort that allowed time to deal with shock, was what Maneck reached for. 'But we talked to him three days ago – Ishvar and Om and I, when we went for tea. And yesterday morning he spoke to me about the barber coming. He was hale and hearty, rolling as usual.'

'Yes, till yesterday morning.'

'What happened then?'

'Terrible accident. He lost control of his gaadi. Flew off the pavement . . . straight into a double-decker bus.' He swallowed and said he hadn't witnessed it himself but had identified the remains. 'With all my years in this profession, my eyes have seen much that is gruesome. But never anything this horrible. Both Shankar and the gaadi were crushed completely – not possible to separate the two. Removing the wood and castors embedded in his flesh would have meant mutilating his poor body still more. It will have to be cremated with him.'

They coped in silence with the grisly picture. Beggarmaster broke down and wept uncontrollably. Attempts to muffle the sobs made him tremble. 'I should have told him we were brothers. I waited too long. And now it's too late. If only he had brakes for his platform . . . I thought about it once, but the idea seemed silly. He could barely drag it around . . . not a fast car or something. Maybe I should have taken him off the street.'

'You mustn't blame yourself,' said Dina. 'You were trying to do the best for him, as you said.'

'Was I? Did I? How can I be sure?'

'He was such a nice person,' said Maneck. 'Ishvar and Om told us how he nursed them when they were sick in that work camp. You never met him, Aunty, but in most ways he was like everyone else. He even made funny jokes sometimes.'

'I feel like I knew him. Ishvar and Om brought his measurements and described him for me, remember? And the special vest I designed for him?'

'That was very kind of you,' said Beggarmaster, in tears again at the thought of how he had lovingly ripped and soiled the garment, customizing it for Shankar's requirements.

'Would you like a glass of water?' she asked. He nodded, and Maneck fetched it.

Beggarmaster regained his composure after the drink. 'I wanted to invite the tailors to Shankar's cremation. Tomorrow at four o'clock. They were his only friends. There will be plenty of beggars there, but Ishvar and Om would have been special.' He returned the empty glass.

'I'll go,' said Maneck.

Beggarmaster's surprise shone through his sorrow. 'Will you really? I will be so grateful.' He took Maneck's hand and shook it. 'The funeral procession begins outside Vishram. I thought it a suitable place for everyone to gather – out of respect for Shankar. Don't you think? His last location?'

'Yes, I'll meet you there.'

'What about your exam?' asked Dina.

'It finishes at three.'

'Yes, but what about the exam the day after?' she tried to discourage him. The idea of his attending a beggar's funeral made her uneasy. 'Shouldn't you come straight home and study for it?'

'I will, after going to the cremation.'

'Excuse me for a minute,' she said to Beggarmaster, and retreated inside. 'Maneck!' she called from the back room. He shrugged and followed.

'What is this nonsense? Why do you have to go?'

'Because I want to.'

'Don't give smart answers! You know how that man scares me. The only reason I put up with him is because he protects the flat. No need to get more familiar.'

'I don't want to argue, Aunty. I am going to the cremation.' His voice was soft, emphasizing each word.

It puzzled Dina that he should feel so intensely about the beggar's funeral. She attributed his behaviour to the pressure of his final exams.

'Fine. I cannot stop you. But if you go, I go with you.' To keep an eye on him if nothing else, she decided.

They returned to the verandah. 'We were discussing about tomorrow afternoon,' she said. 'Both of us will come.'

'Oh, that is wonderful,' said Beggarmaster. 'How shall I ever thank you? You know, I was just thinking, in a way it's good that Ishvar and Om left two days ago. The grief would have ruined the wedding. And marriage is like death, only happens once.'

'How true,' she said. 'I wish more people would understand this.' She was surprised that his words so perfectly fitted her feelings on the matter.

Beggarmaster gave everyone the afternoon off to attend the cremation ceremony. The assembly of crippled, blinded, armless, legless, diseased, and faceless individuals on the pavement soon attracted an audience. Onlookers inquired whether some hospital, for lack of space, was conducting an outdoor clinic.

Dina and Maneck joined Beggarmaster having tea inside the Vishram. 'Look at that crowd,' he said disgustedly. 'They think it's a circus.'

'And not a single coin are they donating,' said Dina.

'That's not surprising. Pity can only be shown in small doses. When so many beggars are in one place, the public goes like this' – he put his fists to his eyes, like binoculars. 'It's a freak show. People forget how vulnerable they are despite their shirts and shoes and briefcases, how this hungry and cruel world could strip them, put them in the same position as my beggars.'

Maneck studied Beggarmaster's excessive chatter, his attempt to hide his heartache. Why did humans do that to their feelings? Whether it was anger or love or sadness, they always tried to put something else forward in its place. And then there were those who pretended their emotions were bigger and grander than anyone else's. A little annoyance they acted out like a gigantic rage; where a smile or chuckle would do, they laughed hysterically. Either way, it was dishonest.

'Also,' said Beggarmaster, 'the public apathy you are witnessing illustrates an important point. In this business, as in others, the three most crucial things are location, location, and location. Right now, if I move these beggars from Vishram to a major temple or a place of pilgrimage, the money would come flowing in.'

Shankar's body lay on a fresh bamboo bier outside the Vishram's back door, next to a storage shed containing plates, utensils, spare stoves, and fuel. Beggarmaster explained that the face was not left uncovered for the mourners to see because the sight was unbearable. A sheet concealed the mutilated corpse, and over the sheet, a blanket of fresh flowers: roses and lilies.

Gazing at the bier, Maneck wondered if Avinash's parents had started his funeral procession from the morgue. Or was it permitted to take the body home for prayers? Probably depended on the state of decomposition, and how long it would keep at room temperature. In the unrefrigerated world. Where everything ended badly.

'It's nice of the Vishram Vegetarian Hotel to let Shankar lie here before the funeral,' said Dina.

'Nice nothing. I paid the cook and waiter handsomely.' Beggarmaster craned to look through the window, and waved at four men who had just arrived. 'Good, we can start now.'

The four men were porters from the railway station hired to carry the bier. 'I had no choice,' he explained regretfully. 'I'm the only relative. Of course I will shoulder my brother from time to time, to honour him, but I cannot allow any of the beggars. They're not strong enough. Whole thing might come crashing down.'

He had spared no expense for Shankar, purchasing the best ghee and incense, and mountains of sandalwood. It was all waiting at the cremation site, along with a well-qualified mahapaatra to perform the funeral rites. There were baskets of rose petals for the mourners to shower the bier during the long walk. And after the death ceremonies, Beggarmaster would make a donation to the temple in Shankar's name.

'There's only one thing worrying me,' he said. 'I hope the other beggars don't assume this is standard procedure, that they will each get the same lavish farewell.'

The slowest-moving procession ever to wind its way through city streets started towards the cremation grounds just after four. The great number of cripples kept it at a snail's pace. The deformities of some had atrophied their bodies, reducing them to a froglike squat: they swung along using their arms as levers. A few could only manage the sideways shuffle of a crab. Others, doubled over, crawled forward on their hands and feet, their behinds raised in the air like camels' humps. By a tacit consensus, the cortège proceeded at the lowest common velocity, but their spirits were high as they laughed and chatted among themselves, enjoying a new experience, so that it seemed more a festival than a funeral.

'It's very sad,' said Dina disapprovingly. 'There is a death but no mourning. And Beggarmaster is not even telling them to behave properly.'

'What do you expect, Aunty,' said Maneck. 'They are probably envying Shankar.' And anyway, he thought, what sense did mourning make? It could be himself on that bier and the world would be no different.

Beggarmaster drifted up and down the length of the column like a line monitor, making sure there were no avoidable delays. Dina beckoned to him as he approached the tail end of the procession. 'Neither Maneck nor I have ever been to a Hindu funeral,' she confessed. 'What should we do when we get there?'

'Nothing,' said Beggarmaster. 'You are honouring Shankar by just being there. The pujari will perform the prayers. And I will have to light the pyre and break the skull at the end, since Shankar does not have a son.'

'Is it hard to watch? Someone told me there is a very strong smell. Can you actually see the flesh burning?'

'Yes, but don't worry, it's a beautiful sight. You will come away feeling good, feeling that Shankar has been properly seen off on his continuing journey. And, I hope, not needing a platform anymore. That's the way I always feel after watching a burning pyre – a completeness, a calmness, a perfect balance between life and death. In fact, for that reason I even go to strangers' cremations. Whenever I have some free time, if I see a funeral procession, I just join it.'

He hurried now to the front of the column to placate some disgruntled policemen. The sluggish funeral march was annoying the traffic constables, who felt the tempo was all wrong. 'Keep Moving' was their one credo in life, and they had a phobia about anything in slow motion, whether it was cars, handcarts, pariah dogs, or people. If they made an occasional exception, it was for cows. Anxious to get the mourners through at a healthy clip, they waved their arms, tooted their whistles, shouted and pleaded, gesticulated, grimaced, clutched their foreheads, and shook their fists. But these tried-and-true methods were employed in vain: absent limbs could not respond, no matter how piercing the whistle or vigorous the wave.

The railway porters, accustomed to fast trotting with heavy luggage, also had trouble adjusting to the unorthodox pace. Whenever the chants of 'Ram naam satya hai!' began to fade behind them, they realized they had raced too far ahead, and called a halt till the gap was closed.

Halfway to the cremation grounds, after an hour's inching along, a small contingent of helmeted riot police charged the cortège without warning, swinging their sticks. Shankar's corpse rolled off the bier as the porters swerved to avoid the blows. Screaming in terror, the beggars tumbled to the ground. Rose petals scattered from half a dozen baskets, and a delicate puddle of pink spread across the road.

'See? This is why I was afraid to let you go,' said Dina, panting as she and Maneck ran to the safety of the pavement. 'These are bad times – trouble can come without warning. But what is wrong with the stupid police? Why are they beating up the beggars?'

'Maybe they are grabbing people for another work camp. Like they took Ishvar and Om.'

Then, just as abruptly, the troops withdrew. Their commanding officer sought out Beggarmaster and apologized profusely for violating the sanctity of the occasion. 'I myself am a prayerful man, and most sensitive to religious matters. This is a very unfortunate mistake. All due to faulty intelligence.'

He said a report had been received on the wireless that a mock funeral was underway, intended to make some kind of political statement, which would most definitely have contravened Emergency regulations. Suspicion had been aroused, in particular, by the assembly of so many beggars, he explained. 'They were mistaken for political activists in fancy dress – troublemakers indulging in street theatre, portraying government figures as crooks and criminals embarked on beggaring the nation. You know the sort of thing.'

'An understandable mistake,' said Beggarmaster, accepting the explanation. He was more upset with the people who had prepared the bier – they must have been very careless while tying down Shankar's body, for it to slide off so easily. At the same time, he reasoned, it was not entirely their fault, they probably had little experience in readying remains as segmented as Shankar's.

Still squirming with embarrassment, the commanding officer continued to apologize. 'Soon as we saw that the corpse was not a symbolic dummy, we realized our error. It's all very regrettable.' He took off his black-visored cap. 'May I offer my condolences?'

'Thank you,' said Beggarmaster, shaking hands.

'Trust me, heads will roll for this blunder,' promised the commanding officer, while his men hurried to retrieve the one which already had: off the bier and into the road, along with a few other body parts.

To make up for the debacle, he insisted on providing an official entourage for the rest of the way. The riot squad was ordered to reassemble the bier and refill the beggars' baskets with the rose petals strewing the asphalt. 'Don't worry,' he assured Beggarmaster. 'We'll soon have everyone marching shipshape to the cremation grounds.'

As the procession cleared the scene of the ambush, a car stopped by the kerb and honked. 'Oh no,' said Dina. 'It's my brother. He's probably on his way home from the office.'

Nusswan waved from the back seat and rolled down the window. 'Are you part of the procession? I didn't know you had any Hindu friends.'

'I do,' said Dina.

'Whose funeral is it?'

'A beggar's.'

He began to laugh, then stopped and came out of the car. 'Don't make jokes about serious matters.' Must be a fairly important person, he imagined, to have a police escort. Some high-up from the Au Revoir corporation, maybe – chairman or managing director. 'Come on, stop teasing, who is it?'

'I told you. It's a beggar.'

Nusswan opened and shut his mouth: opened, in exasperation, then shut, in horror, becoming aware of the procession's character. He realized she was not joking.

Now the mouth was open again, in speechlessness, and Dina said, 'Shut it, Nusswan, or a fly will get in.'

He shut it. He couldn't believe this was happening to him. 'I see,' he said slowly. 'And all these beggars are – friends of the deceased?'

She nodded.

A dozen questions crossed his mind: Why a funeral for a beggar? With a police escort? And why was she attending, and Maneck? Who was paying for it? But the answers could wait till later. 'Get in,' he ordered, opening the car door.

'What do you mean, get in?'

'Come on, don't argue. Get in, both of you. I'm taking you back to your flat.' His list of grievances, compiled over thirty years, flashed through his mind. And now this. 'You're not walking another step in the procession! Of all things – going to a beggar's funeral! How low can you sink? What will people say if they see my sister –'

Beggarmaster and the commanding officer approached them. 'Is this man bothering you?'

'Not at all,' said Dina. 'He's my brother. He is just offering condolences for Shankar's death.'

'Thank you,' said Beggarmaster. 'May I invite you to join us?'

Nusswan faltered. 'Uh . . . I'm very busy. Sorry, another time.' He slipped inside the car, hurriedly pulling the door shut.

They waved and went to regain their places, not that there was much catching up to do; the column had barely moved another dozen metres. Beggarmaster went to the front and reshouldered the bier from one of the railway porters.

'That was fun,' said Dina to Maneck. 'He'll be having bad dreams tonight, I think. Nightmares of funeral pyres – his reputation going up in smoke.'

Maneck smiled, but his thoughts were of the other cremation, three days ago. Where he should have been. Where the generational order of dying was out of joint. Avinash's hollow-cheeked father would have lit the pyre. Crackle of kindling. Smoke smarting the eyes. And fingers of fire teasing, playing, tickling the corpse. Causing it to arch, as though trying to sit up . . . a sign, they said, the spirit protesting. Avinash used to often arch like that when playing chess, lying back, almost flat on the bed, turning his head sideways, contemplating the board. Rising on his elbow to reach the piece, to make his move.

Checkmate. And then the flames.

Time passed slowly, as though it had lost interest in the world. Dina dusted the furniture and the Singers in the corner of the room. Nothing so lifeless as silent sewing-machines, she thought.

She busied herself with the quilt again. Straightening a seam, trimming a patch, adjusting what did not look right to her eye. The afternoon sun through the ventilator glass dappled the squares in her lap.

'Move it a little to your left, Aunty,' said Maneck.

'Why?'

'I want to see how the yellow bit looks with circles of sunlight.'

Clicking her tongue, she obliged.

'Beautiful,' he said.

'Remember how doubtful you were the first time you saw it?'

He laughed self-deprecatingly. 'I had no experience with colours and designs in those days.'

'And now you are a big expert, right?' She hauled the opposite corner into her lap.

'Will you spread it on your bed when it's done?'

'No.'

'Are you planning to sell it then, Aunty?'

She shook her head. 'Can you keep a secret? It's going to be Om's wedding gift.'

He couldn't have been more pleased if he had thought of it himself. His face went soft, touched by her intention.

'Don't look so hurt,' she said. 'I'll make one for your wedding as well.'

'I'm not hurt, I think it's a superb idea.'

'But don't go blabbing to Ishvar and Om the minute you see them again. I'll finish it when tailoring resumes, after we get new cloth from Au Revoir. Not a word till then.'

Maneck's exams concluded; he felt he had done quite badly on most of them. He prayed that the marks would at least be good enough to get him into the three-year degree programme.

Dina asked how he had fared, and he answered 'Fine.'

She heard the lack of conviction in his voice. 'We'll have to wait for the results, to see how fine.'

On the last evening, goaded by Dina, he surrendered to the pleas in his mother's letter and finally went to visit his relatives. He spent two hours enduring the gushing Sodawalla family and fending off a dozen different types of snacks and cold drinks. 'Thank you, but I've already eaten.'

'Next time, you must come with an empty stomach,' they said. 'We want the pleasure of feeding you.' They put away the snacks and tried to make him join them for a cinema show and late dinner, inviting him to stay the night.

'Please excuse me, I should leave now,' said Maneck when he felt he had done his time. 'I have to start early tomorrow.'

Back in Dina's flat, he accused her of ruining his evening. 'I'm never going again, Aunty. They talk non-stop, and behave like silly children.'

'Don't be mean, they are your mother's family.'

She helped to take down his empty suitcase from the top of the cupboard, then dusted it for him. Watching him pack, she interrupted often with advice, reminders, instructions: don't forget, take this, do that. 'And most of all, be nice to your parents, don't get into any arguments with them. They have missed you so much this year. Enjoy your vacation.'

'Thank you, Aunty. And please don't forget to feed the cats.'

'Oh yes, I'll feed them. I'll even cook their favourite dishes. Shall I serve with cutlery, or do they eat with fingers?'

'No, Aunty, save the cutlery for your daughter-in-law. She'll be here in three weeks.'

She threatened to spank him. 'Trouble is, your mother didn't do it often enough when you were small.'

Early next morning he hugged her and was gone.

The return of solitude was not quite as Dina expected it to be. These many years I made a virtue of inescapable reality, she thought, calling it peace and quiet. Still, how was it possible to feel lonely again after living alone most of her life? Didn't the heart and mind learn anything? Could one year do so much damage to her resilience?

For the umpteenth time she consulted the dates on the calendar: three weeks before Ishvar and Om returned; and then three more, for Maneck.

The days shuffled along unhurriedly. She decided this was a good opportunity to give the flat a thorough going-over. In every room she heard the echoes of the tailors' tireless banter, haunting her while she scoured the kitchen, swept the ceilings with the long-handled broom, cleaned the windows and ventilators, washed all the floors.

In Maneck's room she found his friend's chess set in the cupboard. To be returned when college reopens, she assumed.

Next, her own cupboard was emptied out, all but the bottommost shelf. She wiped the interior, stacked the Au Revoir remnants, and sorted her clothes. The things she did not wear anymore went in a separate pile. To offer to Om's wife. Depending, of course, on her size. And what type of person she turned out to be.

Then Dina tackled the bottommost shelf, crammed with a year's worth of the snippets from each sewing day, the tiny bits, useless for anything except stuffing the homemade sanitary pads. She dug her arms in and out tumbled the mountain of fragments, making her laugh aloud. Not even another fifty years of periods would use up so much cotton filling. She stocked a bag with a reasonable amount and prepared to get rid of the rest.

Then she thought of Om's wife again. Surely her youth and vitality could use a healthy lot of it. Better save it for now, she thought, happily pushing the shreds back onto the shelf.

The spate of cleaning eased the passage of many days. She turned her mind to the verandah, soon to be home for the married couple and the uncle. The tailors' one bedding roll was insufficient, she decided, and set to making extra sheets and covers out of Au Revoir's bounty.

The foot treadle of Ishvar's Singer was hard going for her. She had never worked on this type of model during her sewing years. She switched to Shirin Aunty's little hand-cranked machine, and it was fun. With every seam she ran off, she said to herself: how fortunate, to have all this cloth for all our needs.

The picture of Ishvar, Om and his wife sleeping on the verandah bothered her. Just imagine, she thought, if on my wedding night Darab Uncle and Shirin Aunty had slept in the same room with Rustom and me.

The only solution she could come up with was to string a curtain down the middle of the verandah. She measured the distance, then stitched together the thickest fabrics from the hoard of remnants. Better a token wall than nothing.

She hoped Ishvar and Om would be pleased with her efforts. She had done what she could. If the new wife tried half as hard, she was certain they would get along well.

Two nails plus a length of twine, and the symbolic partition was erected. She stood back, examining each side of the curtain. The lives of the poor were rich in symbols, she decided.

xv Family Planning

A GAUNT, BEARDED figure hurried towards the tailors as they wrestled their trunk out of the compartment and onto the platform. 'At last,' he clapped for joy. 'Here you are.'

'Ashraf Chacha! We were going to surprise you at the shop!' They dragged their belongings to the side, shaking hands, hugging, laughing with no reason other than the pleasure of being together again.

Ishvar and Om were the sole passengers to alight. Two coolies resting by the water tap remained on their haunches; instinct told them their services were not required. The sleepy little station awakened gradually under the engine's pulse. Vendors with fruit, cold drinks, tea, pakora, ice gola, sunglasses, magazines besieged the train, embellishing the air with their cries.

'Come,' said Ashraf. 'Let's go home, you must be tired. We'll eat first, then you can tell me what wonders you have been up to in the city.'

A woman with a small basket of figs sang at their side: 'Unjir!' The shrill call started out in a plea, sliding into a rebuke as they passed her by. The cry went unrepeated. She tried the passengers on the train, framed by windows like a travelling gallery of portraits. Jogging alongside the compartments, she supported the basket at her hip; it bounced like a baby. The guard blew the warning whistle and startled a cream-coloured mongrel drowsing near the siding tracks. It scratched languidly behind an ear, face screwed up like a man shaving.

'Chachaji, you're a genius,' said Om. 'We don't write you the arrival date and yet you meet the train. How did you know we were coming today?'

'I didn't,' he smiled. 'But I knew it would be this week. And the train rolls in at the same hour every day.'

'So you waited here every day? And what about the shop, hahn?'

'It's not that busy.' He reached to help with the luggage. His hand, corded by prominent veins, shook uncontrollably. The whistle blew again, and the train rumbled past. The vendors disappeared. Like a house abandoned, the railway station sank from sleepy to forlorn.

But the emptiness was transitory. Slowly, more than a dozen figures materialized from the shadows of the sheds and storehouses. Lapped in rags, wrapped in hunger, they lowered their brittle bodies over the edge of the platform onto the rails and began moving systematically down the tracks from sleeper to sleeper, searching for the flotsam of railway journeys, bending now and then, collecting the garbage of travellers. When two hands grabbed the same prize, there was a tussle. The wood and gravel underneath where the WC had halted was wet, stinking, buzzing with flies. The tattered army retrieved paper, food scraps, plastic bags, bottle tops, broken glass, every precious bit jettisoned by the departing train. They tucked it away in their gunny sacks, then melted into the shadows of the station, to sort their collections and await the next train.

'So the city has been good to you, nah?' said Ashraf, as they took the level-crossing to the other side. 'Both of you look prosperous.'

'Chachaji, your eyes are generous,' said Ishvar. The trembling of Ashraf's hands distressed him. And age, taking advantage of the tailors' absence, had finally taught his shoulders to stoop. 'We have no complaints. But how are you?'

'First class, for my years.' Ashraf straightened, patting his chest, though the stoop returned almost immediately. 'And what about you, Om? You were so reluctant to go. Look at you now, a healthy shine upon your face.'

'That's because my worms have vacated the premises.' He explained with gusto how the parasites had been vanquished by the vermifuge.

'You meet Chachaji after a year and a half, and all you can talk about is your worms?'

'Why not?' said Ashraf. 'Health is the most important thing. See, you could never have got such good medicine over here. One more reason to be happy you went, nah?'

Ishvar and Om slowed at the corner near the rooming house, but Ashraf steered them on towards his shop. 'Why waste money for a bed filled with bugs? Stay with me.'

'That's too much trouble for you.'

'But I insist – you must use my house to entertain for the wedding. Do me that favour. It's been so lonely this last year.'

'Mumtaz Chachi won't be pleased to hear you say that,' said Om. 'Doesn't her company count?'

Puzzlement clouded Ashraf's smile. 'You didn't receive the letter? My Mumtaz passed away, about six months after you left.'

'What?' They stopped and let the luggage slip from their hands. The trunk hit the ground hard.

'Careful!' Ashraf bent to lift it. 'But I wrote to you, care of Nawaz.'

'He didn't give it to us,' said Om indignantly.

'Maybe the letter came late – after we moved to the hutment colony.'

'He could have brought it to us.'

'Yes, but who knows if he received it.'

They dropped their speculating and took turns hugging Ashraf Chacha; they kissed his cheeks three times, as much for their own comfort as his.

'I was worried when there was no reply,' he said. 'I thought you must be very busy, trying to find work.'

'No matter how busy, we would have written if we knew,' said Ishvar. 'We would have come to you. This is terrible – we should have been here for the funeral, she was like my mother, we should never have left . . .'

'Now that is foolish talk. Nobody can see into the future.'

They resumed walking, and Ashraf told them about the illness that had overtaken, and then taken, Mumtaz Chachi. As he spoke about his loss, it became clear why he had waited at the station platform every day to meet their train: he was matching his wits with time the great tormentor.

'It's a strange thing. When my Mumtaz was alive, I would sit alone all day, sewing or reading. And she would be by herself in the back, busy cooking and cleaning and praying. But there was no loneliness, the days passed easily. Just knowing she was there was enough. And now I miss her so much. What an unreliable thing is time – when I want it to fly, the hours stick to me like glue. And what a changeable thing, too. Time is the twine to tie our lives into parcels of years and months. Or a rubber band stretched to suit our fancy. Time can be the pretty ribbon in a little girl's hair. Or the lines in your face, stealing your youthful colour and your hair.' He sighed and smiled sadly. 'But in the end, time is a noose around the neck, strangling slowly.'

A clutter of troublesome feelings filled Ishvar – guilt, sorrow, the foreboding of old age waiting to waylay his own future. He wished he could assure Ashraf Chacha that they would not leave him alone again. Instead he said, 'We would like to visit Mumtaz Chachi's grave.'

The request pleased Ashraf greatly. 'Her anniversary date is next week. We can go together. But you have come a long way for a joyous occasion. Let us talk about that now.'

He was determined not to let the sad news dampen their spirits. He explained that preliminary meetings with each of the four families were three days away. 'Some of them were worried at first. I, a Muslim, making arrangements for you, nah.'

'How dare they,' said Ishvar indignantly. 'Didn't they know we are one family?'

'Not at first,' said Ashraf. But others who were aware of the long-standing ties between them had explained there was no cause for concern. 'So it's fixed now. The bridegroom must be anxious,' he prodded Om's stomach playfully. 'You will have to be patient a little longer. Inshallah, everything will go well.'

'I'm not worried,' said Om. 'So tell me what's new. Anything in town?'

'Not much. A Family Planning Centre has opened. I don't think you would be interested in that,' he chuckled. 'And everything else, good or bad, has remained the same.'

A surge of excitement quickened Om's steps as their street came into view, and then the signboard of Muzaffar Tailoring. He walked ahead, greeting the hardware-store owner, the banya, the miller, the coal-merchant, who leaned out from their doorways and bubbled good wishes and blessings for the auspicious event.

—

'Let me know when you are hungry,' said Ashraf. 'I have cooked some dal and rice. I also have your favourite mango achaar.'

Om licked his lips. 'It's such fun to be back.'

'It's good to have you back.'

'Yes,' said Ishvar. 'You know, Chachaji, Dinabai is very nice, and we get along very well now, but here it's different. This is home. Here I can relax more. In the city, every time I go out anywhere, I feel a little scared.'

'What, yaar, you're simply letting all those troubles haunt you. Forget them now, it was a long time ago.'

'Troubles?'

'Nothing much,' said Ishvar. 'We'll tell you later. Come, let's eat before the rice and dal becomes dry.'

They sat in the shop, talking till late in the night, Ishvar and Om taking care to soften the details of their trials. They did this instinctively, wishing to spare Ashraf Chacha the pain, seeing how he winced in empathy with everything they described.

Around midnight Om began nodding off, and Ashraf suggested they go to bed. 'My old head could stay up listening all night, it has not much need of sleep. But you two must rest.'

Ishvar moved aside the chairs to make space for bedding on the floor. Ashraf stopped him. 'Why here? There is just me upstairs. Come on.' They climbed the steps from the shop to the room above. 'What life there was in this place once. Mumtaz, my four daughters, my two apprentices. What fun we had together, nah?'

He got extra sheets and blankets from a trunk smelling of naphthalene. 'My Mumtaz packed it all away after our daughters married and left. She was so careful – every year she would air it out, and put in new moth-balls.'

Om was asleep as soon as his head touched the pillow. 'Reminds me of you and Narayan,' whispered Ashraf. 'When you first came here as little boys, remember? You would go down to the shop after dinner and spread your mats. You would fall asleep so peacefully, as though it was your own house. You could have paid me no greater compliment.'

'The way you and Mumtaz Chachi looked after us, it felt like our own house.' They reminisced a few minutes longer before switching off the light.

Ashraf wanted to present new shirts to Ishvar and Om. 'We'll go for them this afternoon,' he said.

'Hoi-hoi, Chachaji. That's too much to take from you.'

'You want to cause me unhappiness, refusing my gift?' he protested. 'For me, too, Om's marriage is very important. Let me do what I want to do.' The shirts were to wear at the four bride-viewing visits. The wedding garments would be negotiated later, with the family of the girl they selected.

Ishvar relented, but on one condition – that he and Om would help him make the shirts. Chachaji toiling alone at the sewing-machine was out of the question.

'But nobody needs to sew,' said Ashraf. 'There is the new ready-made shop in the bazaar. The one that stole our customers. How can you forget? That shop was the reason you had to leave.'

He told them about the faithful clients who, one by one, had abandoned Muzaffar Tailoring, including those whose families had been customers since his father's time. 'The loyalty of two generations has vanished like smoke on a windy day, by the promise of cheaper prices. Such a powerful devil is money. Good thing you left when you did, there is no future here.'

It was not long before Om brought up the other, always unspoken, reason for their flight to the city. 'What about Thakur Dharamsi? You haven't mentioned him. Is that daakoo still alive?'

'The district has put him in charge of Family Planning.'

'So what is his method? Does he murder babies, to control the population?'

His uncle and Ashraf Chacha exchanged uneasy glances.

'I think our people should get together and kill that dog.'

'Don't start talking nonsense, Omprakash,' warned Ishvar. His nephew's old unhappy rage seemed to be on the verge of returning, and it worried him.

Ashraf took Om's hand. 'My child, that demon is too powerful. Since the Emergency began, his reach has extended from his own village to all the way here. He is a big man now in the Congress Party, they say he will become a minister in the next elections – if the government ever decides to have elections. Nowadays, he wants to look respectable, avoids any goonda-giri. When he wants to threaten someone, he doesn't send his own men, he just tells the police. They pick up the poor fellow, give him a beating, then release him.'

'Why are we wasting our time talking about that man?' said Ishvar angrily. 'We are here for a joyous occasion, we have nothing to do with him, God will deal with Thakur Dharamsi.'

'Exactly,' said Ashraf. 'Come on, let's go buy the shirts.' He hung out a sign that the shop would reopen at six. 'Not that it matters. Nobody comes.' He struggled with the steel collapsibles, and Om went to help. The grating stuck in its track, demanding to be reversed, shaken loose, coaxed forward.

'Needs oiling,' he panted. 'Like my old bones.'

They took the dirt road to the bazaar, treading the hard, dry earth past grain sheds and labourers' hovels. Their sandals crunched lightly and kicked up tiny tongues of dust.

'How was the rain in the city?'

'Too much,' said Ishvar. 'Streets were flooded many times. And here?'

'Too little. The devil held his umbrella over us. Let's hope he shuts it this year.'

The way to the clothes shop led past the new Family Planning Centre, and Om slowed down, peering inside. 'You said Thakur Dharamsi is in charge here?'

'Yes, and he makes a lot of money out of it.'

'How? I thought government pays the patients to have the operation.'

'The rogue puts all that cash in his own pocket. The villagers are helpless. Complaining only brings more suffering upon their heads. When the Thakur's gang goes looking for volunteers, the poor fellows quietly send their wives, or offer themselves for the operation.'

'Hai Ram. When a demon like this is allowed to prosper, the world must really be passing through the darkness of Kaliyug.'

'And you tell me I am talking nonsense,' said Om scornfully. 'Killing that swine would be the most sensible way to end Kaliyug.'

'Calm down, my child,' said Ashraf. 'He who spits paan at the ceiling only blinds himself. For the crimes in this world, the punishment occurs in the Next World.'

Om rolled his eyes. 'Yes, definitely. But tell me, how much money can he make from that place? The operation bonus is not very big.'

'Ah, but it's not his only source. When the patients are brought to the clinic, he auctions them.'

'What does that mean?'

'You see, government employees have to produce two or three cases for sterilization. If they don't fill their quota, their salary is held back for that month by the government. So the Thakur invites all the school-teachers, block development officers, tax collectors, food inspectors to the clinic. Anyone who wants to can bid on the villagers. Whoever offers the most gets the cases registered in his quota.'

Ishvar shook his head in despair. 'Come on, let's go,' he said, putting his hands over his ears. 'Bas, I don't want to hear any more of this.'

'I don't blame you,' said Ashraf. 'To listen to the things happening in our lifetime is like drinking venom – it poisons my peace. Every day I pray that this evil cloud over our country will lift, that justice will take care of these misguided people.'

As they were moving away from the building, someone from the Family Planning Centre came to the door. 'Please step inside,' he said. 'No waiting, doctor is on duty, we can do the operation right away.'

'Keep your hands off my manhood,' said Om.

The fellow started explaining wearily that it was a misconception people had about vasectomy, the manhood was not involved, the doctor did not even touch that part.

'It's all right,' smiled Ashraf. 'We know. The boy is only teasing you.' He waved genially, and they continued on their way.

Outside the ready-made shop, shirt-and-pant combinations flapped on wire hangers, suspended from the awning like headless scarecrows. The main stock was in cardboard boxes on shelves. Having assessed their sizes, the salesman proceeded to display some shirts. Om made a face.

'You don't like?'

Om shook his head. The man pushed the boxes aside and showed a battery of alternate selections. He watched his customers anxiously.

'That's a nice one,' said Ishvar, out of consideration for the man. He examined a short-sleeved shirt with checks. 'Just like the one Maneck has.'

'Yes, but look how badly the buttons are sewn,' objected Om. 'One wash and they will come off.'

'If you like the shirt, take it,' said Ashraf. 'I will strengthen the buttons for you.'

'Let me show you more,' said the salesman. 'This box has our special patterns, top quality, from Liberty Garment Company.' He fanned out half a dozen specimens along the counter. 'Stripes are very popular nowadays.'

Om picked up a light-blue shirt with dark-blue lines and slid off the transparent plastic bag. 'Look at that,' he said disgustedly, shaking it open. 'The pocket is crooked, the stripes don't even meet.'

'You are right,' the salesman admitted, uncovering more boxes. 'I just sell the clothes, I don't make them. What to do, no one takes pride in good workmanship anymore.'

'Very true,' said Ishvar. 'It's like that everywhere.'

Lamenting the changing times, it became easier to find acceptable shirts. The man folded their choices along the original creases and slipped them back in the transparent bags. The cellophane crackled opulently. The illusion of value and quality was restored, while string and brown paper secured it in place. He gnawed through the string to sever the required length from the large reel. 'Please come back, I will be happy to serve you.'

'Thank you,' said Ashraf.

They stood in the street and debated what to do next. 'We could roam in the bazaar,' said Om, 'see if there is anyone we know.'

'I have a better plan,' said Ashraf. 'Tomorrow is market day. Let's come in the morning. Everyone from the villages will be here, you will get to meet lots of friends.'

'That's a good idea,' agreed Ishvar. 'And now let me treat you to paan, before we go home.'

'Don't tell me you've picked up the paan habit,' said Ashraf disapprovingly.

'No no, it's only because this is a special day, we are seeing you after so long.'

Their mouths bulging with the mixture of betel nut, chunam, and tobacco, they walked back towards Muzaffar Tailoring, passing the Family Planning Centre again, where Ashraf relieved his juice-laden mouth in the ditch and pointed to a parked car. 'That's Thakur Dharamsi's new motor. He must be inside, counting his victims.'

Ishvar immediately began steering them across the road.

'What are you running for?' said Om. 'We don't have to be scared of that dog.'

'Better to avoid any trouble.'

'I agree,' said Ashraf. 'Why see the demon's face if you can help it?'

Just then, Thakur Dharamsi emerged from the building, and Om strode boldly towards him on a collision course. Ishvar tried to pull him back beside Ashraf Chacha. The smooth leather soles of Om's sandals slipped on the pavement. He felt foolish. His uncle was winning the tug of war, and his defiance was turning into humiliation before the Thakur.

Om spat.

The arc of red ended several feet short; the sticky juice soaked the earth between them. The Thakur stopped. The two men with him awaited instructions. In their vicinity, people faded like the light, fearful of witnessing what might follow.

The Thakur said very softly, 'I know who you are.' He got in the car, slammed the door, and drove off.

The rest of the way home, Ishvar was frantic with rage and anxiety. 'You are mad! Bilkool paagal! If you want to die why don't you swallow rat poison? Have you come for a wedding or a funeral?'

'My wedding, and the Thakur's funeral.'

'Leave your clever talk! I should give your face one backhand slap!'

'If you hadn't stopped me, I could have spat over him. Exactly in his face.'

Ishvar raised his hand to strike, but Ashraf made him desist. 'What's happened has happened. We have to stay out of that demon's way from now on.'

'I'm not scared of him,' said Om.

'Of course you're not. We just don't want any trouble to spoil the wedding preparations, that's all. Our joy doesn't need to be darkened by that demon's shadow.'

He had to keep applying his words like balm upon Ishvar's anguish. But now and again the terror broke through, erupting in a bitter condemnation of his nephew's stupidity. 'Acting like a hero and thinking like a zero. My fault only, for buying paan for you. A bad-tempered owl, as Dinabai used to call you. What has become of your humour and your joking? Without Maneck you have forgotten how to laugh, how to enjoy life.'

'You should have brought him with you, if you think he's so wonderful. I would have stayed back.'

'You are talking bilkool nonsense. We are here for just a few days. Soon we return to our jobs. You can't behave sensibly even for this short time?'

'That's what you said in the city – that we would be there for a short while only, and soon go back to our native place.'

'So? Is it my fault that it's tougher than we expected, making money in the city?'

Then they abandoned the topic altogether. Quarrelling on would have meant Ashraf Chacha learning about the misery concealed in the details they had spared him.

Market day was noisier than usual because the Family Planning Centre was promoting its sterilization camp from a booth in the square, its loudspeakers at full blast. Banners were strung across the road, exhorting participation in the Nussbandhi Mela. The usual paraphernalia of the fairground – balloons, flowers, soap bubbles, coloured lights, snacks – were employed to lure the townsfolk and visiting villagers. The film songs were interrupted often with announcements about the nation's need for birth control, the prosperity and happiness in store for those willing to be sterilized, the generous bonuses for vasectomies and tubectomies.

'Where will they perform the operations?' wondered Om. 'Right here?'

'Why? You want to watch or what?' said Ishvar.

Ashraf said the Centre usually erected tents outside town. 'They set it up like a factory. Cut here, snip there, a few stitches – and the goods are ready to be shipped.'

'Sounds just like the tailoring business, yaar.'

'Actually, we tailors take more pride in our work. We show more consideration for fabric than these monsters show for humans. It is our nation's shame.'

Not far from the birth-control booth was a man selling potions for the treatment of impotency and infertility. 'The quack is getting a bigger crowd than the government people,' said Ishvar.

The man, his hair combed out in a black shiny halo, wore an animal pelt over his shoulders. His chest was bare, and a tight thong cutting into his upper right arm made his veins stand out in a show of power all the way along his limb. He brandished his muscular forearm, engorged and hard, whenever some reproductive matter needed graphic illustrating.

Spread out on a mat before him were several jars containing herbs and chunks of bark. And lest these be mistaken for the trappings of an insipid apothecary, he had interspersed among them an assortment of dead lizards and snakes, to imbue the display with a feral virility, a reptilian electricity. In one corner sat a human skull. The centre of the mat was occupied by a bear's head, the eyes large and gleaming, jaws open wide. This trophy had suffered in its travels, losing two teeth; tiny wooden cones painted white had taken their place. The risible dentures undercut the bear's ferocious glare, and the overall effect was clownish.

The Potency Pedlar pointed with a stick at charts listing symptoms and cures, and at diagrams that might have depicted electrical circuits. Midway through the exegesis, he raised the hem of his dhoti and pulled it up – up until it revealed his calves, his knees, and finally his muscular thighs. His dark-brown skin shone under the sun. For a hairy-chested man, his legs were questionably smooth. Then, to emphasize what he was saying, he slapped the firm flesh of his thighs several times. The report was sharp, like the clapping of perfect hands.

His sales pitch followed a question-and-answer routine. 'Are you having difficulty in producing children? Is your hathiyar reluctant to rise up? Or does it sleep and forget to wake?' His pointer drooped disconsolately. 'Fear not, there is a cure! Like a soldier at attention it will stand! One, two, three – bhoom!' He whipped up his pointer.

Some in the audience sniggered, others were bold in their loud laughter, while a few produced dark, censorious frowns.

'Does it stand, but not straight enough? Is there a bend in the tool? Leaning left like the Marxist–Leninist Party? To the right, like the Jan Sangh fascists? Or wobbling mindlessly in the middle, like the Congress Party? Fear not, for it can be straightened! Does it refuse to harden even with rubbing and massage? Then try my ointment, and it will become hard as the government's heart! All your troubles will vanish with this amazing ointment made from the organs of these wild animals! Capable of turning all men into engine-drivers! Punctual as the trains in the Emergency! Back and forth you will shunt with piston power every night! The railways will want to harness your energy! Apply this ointment once a day, and your wife will be proud of you! Apply it twice a day, and she will have to share you with the whole block!'

The last bit provoked a great quantity of laughter from some young men. Women hid their smiles behind their hands; a few giggles escaped before they could be strangled. The frowning censors walked away in disgust.

The Potency Pedlar picked up the grinning human skull and held it aloft. 'If I were to rub my ointment on this fellow's head, even he would start jumping! But I dare not, I have to think of the ladies present, and the safety of their virtue!' The audience applauded heartily.

He continued in this vein for a bit longer before addressing women's problems. Now he spoke in his alternate role – the fakir of fertility. 'Is there sadness in your life because your neighbour has more children than you? Do you need more hands to help you with the endless work in the fields, to carry water, to search for firewood? Are you worried about who will look after you in your helpless old age, because you have no sons? Fear not! This tonic will make strong children flow forth from your belly! One spoon a day, and you will give your husband six sons! Two spoons, and your womb will produce an army!'

Despite the large crowd around the vendor, actual customers were few. Mainly, they were there for the entertainment. Besides, to purchase the products in broad daylight meant a public admission of inadequate loins. The sales would take place later, after the performance wound down and the fun-seekers drifted away.

'Are you planning to buy?' Ishvar tickled Om in the ribs, who was listening with grave intent.

'I don't need all this rubbish.'

'Of course not,' said Ashraf, putting his arm over Om's shoulder. 'Inshallah, sons and daughters will appear at the proper time.'

They resumed their stroll through the bazaar till they came to the Chamaar stalls. 'Don't say anything, just stand quietly,' said Om. 'Let's see how long before they spot us.'

They pretended to inspect the sandals, waterskins, purses, belts, barber's strops, harnesses. The rich smell of fresh leather travelled deep, waking forgotten memories. Then someone from their village recognized them.

A shout of delight went up, echoed by others. The welcome was euphoric. People gathered around, and the conversation began to overflow. Everyone was eager to fill the void the tailors' lengthy absence had created.

Ishvar and Om learned from the villagers that Dukhi's lifelong friend, Gambhir, who had had molten lead poured in his ears many years ago, had died recently. Though the burn injury had always festered, it was blood poisoning from cutting his leg on a rusty scythe that had finally taken him. The old women, Amba, Pyari, Padma, and Savitri, were well. They were the ones who most remembered the tailors' family; their favourite story was still the one about going by bus with Roopa and Dukhi and several dozen others to inspect Narayan's wife-to-be.

After homage was paid to the dead and the elderly, they turned to the present. News of the impending bride-viewing had spread in the Chamaar community. Two men lifted Om to their shoulders and paraded him like a conquering hero, as though the wedding was already accomplished. Felicitations poured from every mouth, embarrassing

Om. For once, he was left incapable of making a smart retort, while his uncle beamed and nodded.

For those who had known his father, the occasion had a special significance. They were happy that the line of one as remarkable as Narayan, the Chamaar-turned-tailor who had defied the upper castes, was not going to die out. 'We prayed that the son will return one day,' they said, 'and our prayers are answered. Om must carry on the work of his father. And the grandsons will do likewise.'

To Ishvar's ears the yearnings of his community were ill-considered, and recklessly tempted fate. The fear born out of Om's foolhardiness with Thakur Dharamsi yesterday was still trembling in his veins. He cut short the well-wishers. 'There is no chance of coming back. We have very good jobs in the city. The future there is bright for Omprakash.'

The Chamaars talked about the years when Ishvar and his brother had first left the village as apprentices to Muzaffar Tailoring. They told Om what a brilliant tailor his father had been, while Ashraf, the proud teacher, smiled, nodding to indicate that yes, it was all true. 'It was like magic,' they said. 'Narayan could take the discards of a fat landlord and alter them with his machine to fit us like brand-new. He could take our rags and turn them into clothes suitable for a king. We will never again see the like of him. So generous, so brave.'

Ishvar changed the subject once more, worried about the effect their reminiscing would have on his nephew. 'Ashraf Chacha has been talking to us of the old days ever since we arrived,' he said. 'Tell us what is happening in these new days.'

So Ishvar and Om learned that recently a stream had run dry, and in its bed was discovered a perfectly spherical rock with sickness-curing properties. In another village, a sadhu had meditated under a tree, and when he departed, furrows developed on the trunk in the image of Lord Ganesh. Elsewhere, during the religious procession of Mata Ki Sawari, someone had entered a trance and identified a Bhil woman as the witch causing the community's woes. She was beaten to death, and the village was expecting better times; unfortunately, a year later they were still waiting.

Before the conversation could stray again into the past, Ishvar said, 'We'll see you at the wedding, if everything goes well,' and they took their leave to cheers and laughter.

They wandered into the vegetable section of the market where he selected peas, coriander, spinach, and onions. 'Tonight I'll cook my specialty for us.'

'And the chapati expert will favour us with his skills,' said Ashraf, putting his arm around Om again. It was hard for him to restrain himself from constantly touching and embracing the two who were like son and grandson to him. Besides, he was trying to ward off the dreaded day of departure that would dawn when the celebrations were over.

'One more stop before we go home,' said Ishvar. He led them towards the religious merchandise, and purchased an expensive string of prayer beads. 'A small gift from us,' he said to Ashraf. 'We hope you will use it for many years to come.'

'Inshallah,' he said, and kissed the beads of amber. 'You have chosen the right item for me.'

'My idea,' claimed Om. 'We noticed you are spending more time in prayer.'

'Yes, awareness of death and old age tend to have that effect on us mortals.' He stopped the vendor, who was making a newspaper pouch to package the beads. 'No need for that,' he said, and wound the precious string round his fingers.

Nearby, the candy-floss man issued his inviting call: 'Aga-ni-dadhi! Aga-ni-dadhi!'

'I want one,' said Om.

'Aray eat more, have two!' he tinkled his little brass bell.

Ishvar held up one finger, and the candy-floss man switched on the machine.

They watched the whirring, humming centre spin out wisps of pink. The man whisked a stick around inside the tub, stroking the air to harvest the sweet strands. When the ball reached the size of a human head, he switched off the machine.

'You know how that works, nah?' said Ashraf. 'There is a large spider sitting inside the machine, feeding on sugar and pink dye. At the man's command, it starts spinning its web.'

'For sure,' said Om and chucked him under the chin, fingering his fine white beard. 'Is that how your dadhi was also made?'

It was a little before noon. Empty trucks rumbled up the main road and parked outside the market square. No one paid attention. Traffic was always heavy on this day of the week.

'Want to taste?' Om held out the stick.

Ishvar declined. Ashraf decided to try some, gamely negotiating the fluff through his whiskers. Bits of it stuck, pink on white, and Om roared. He led him to the window of a sari shop and showed him his candy-floss beard. 'Looks very handsome, Chachaji. You could start a new style.'

'Now you know why it's called aga-ni-dadhi,' said Ashraf, plucking the wisps out of his hair.

Ishvar watched contentedly, smiling with happiness. In spite of everything, life was good, he thought. How could he complain when Om and he were blessed with the friendship of people like Ashraf Chacha, and Dinabai, and Maneck.

More trucks appeared around the square, occupying the lanes leading into the bazaar. These were garbage trucks, round-roofed with openings at the rear.

'Why so early?' wondered Ashraf. 'Market still has many hours to go, cleanup does not begin till evening.'

'Maybe the drivers also want to do some shopping.'

Suddenly, horns blaring, police vans swept into the marketplace. The sea of humans parted. The vehicles stopped in the centre and disgorged a battalion of constables who took up positions inside the square.

'A police guard for the bazaar?' said Ishvar.

'Something is wrong,' said Ashraf.

The shoppers watched, perplexed. Then the police began to advance and grab people. The bewildered captives resisted, shouting and questioning, 'First tell us! Tell us what we've done! How can you catch people just like that? We have a right to be here, it's market day!'

The constables answered by moving relentlessly through the crowd. Resistance was met with swinging lathis. Panic filled the marketplace as people pushed, pleaded, struggled with the police, tried to break through the cordon. But the square had been efficiently surrounded. Those who made it to the periphery were beaten back into the waiting hands of more police.

Stalls and stands came crashing down, baskets were overturned, boxes smashed. In seconds the square was littered with tomatoes, onions, earthen pots, flour, spinach, coriander, chillies – patches of orange and white and green, dissolving in chaos out of their neat rows. The Potency Pedlar's bear was trampled underfoot, losing more of its teeth, while his dead lizards and snakes died a second death. The music from the Family Planning booth continued to blare over the screams of people.

'Come to this side, quick,' said Ashraf. 'We will get shelter here.' He led them into the doorway of a textile-merchant who used to refer customers to Muzaffar Tailoring. The shop was closed, and he rang the bell. There was no answer. 'Never mind, we'll just stay here till things are quiet. Police must be looking for criminals in the crowd.'

But the police were snatching people at random. Old men, young boys, housewives with children were being dragged into the trucks. A few managed to escape; most were trapped like chickens in a coop, unable to do anything except wait to be collected by the law enforcers.

'Look,' urged Ashraf, 'that corner has only one havaldar. If you run fast you will get through.'

'What about you?'

'I'll be safe here, I'll meet you later at the shop.'

'We have done nothing wrong,' said Ishvar, refusing to leave him. 'We don't need to run like thieves.'

They watched from the doorway while the police continued to chase the ones tearing frenziedly amid the spilled fruit and grain and broken glassware. Someone tripped, fell upon the shards and cut his face. His pursuer lost interest, picking a new quarry.

'Hai Ram!' said Ishvar. 'Look at that blood! And now they are ignoring him! What is going on?'

'I wouldn't be surprised if that demon Dharamsi is behind it,' said Ashraf. 'He owns those garbage trucks.'

As the vehicles filled up, the numbers in the square began to dwindle. The police had to work harder to catch the remainder. Before long, six constables targeted the tailors. 'You three! Into the truck!'

'But why, police-sahab?'

'Just come on, don't argue,' said one, raising his lathi.

Ashraf flung up his hands before his face. The constable grabbed the prayer beads round his fingers and pulled, breaking the string. The beads rolled lazily about the pavement.

'Oiee!' yelled two others as they slipped on the tiny amber spheres. Seeing his comrades fall, the first one reacted by lashing out angrily with his lathi.

Ashraf groaned and crumpled slowly to the ground.

'Don't hurt him, please, it was a mistake!' pleaded Ishvar. He and Om knelt to cradle his head.

'Stand up,' said the constable. 'He's okay, just pretending. I gave him just a light blow.'

'But his head is bleeding.'

'Just a little. Come on, get in the truck.'

The tailors ignored the command in favour of Ashraf Chacha. The constable kicked them, once each. They yelped and clutched their ribs. As he drew his foot back to kick again, they stood up. He shoved them towards the trucks.

'What about Ashraf Chacha?' screamed Ishvar. 'You're going to leave him on the pavement?'

'Don't yell at me, I'm not your servant or something! Saala, one tight shot on your face I'll give!'

'Sorry, police-sahab, please forgive! But Chachaji is hurt, I want to help him!'

The constable turned to look again at the injured old man. Blood was oozing through the skimpy white hair, dripping in a slow trickle onto the kerb. But the police had been instructed not to load anyone unconscious onto the vehicles. 'Others will take care of him, it's not your worry,' he said, pushing the two aboard a truck.

On the pavement a dog sniffed at the candy-floss Om had dropped. The fluff stuck to its muzzle. The animal worried the pink beard with a paw, and a child in the truck, sitting on its mother's lap, laughed at the creature's antics. The police discontinued the roundup when the garbage trucks were full. The people remaining in the square suddenly found themselves at liberty to leave.

—

The sterilization camp was a short ride from town. A dozen tents had been pitched in a field on the outskirts, where the stubble of the recent harvest still lingered. Banners, balloons, and songs identical to those at the marketplace booth welcomed the garbage trucks. The passengers' terrified wailing grew louder as the vehicles were parked in an open area behind the tents, alongside an ambulance and a diesel generator.

Two of the tents were larger and sturdier than the rest, with electric cables running to them from the generator that throbbed powerfully beneath the music. Red cylinders for gas stoves squatted outside the canvas. Inside, office desks covered with plastic sheets had been set up as operating tables.

The medical officer in charge of the camp wrinkled his nose in the vicinity of the garbage trucks. The putrid smell of their usual cargo clung to them. He had a word with the police. 'Wait for ten minutes, we'll finish our tea by then. And bring only four patients at a time – two men and two women.' He didn't want more in the tents than could be handled by the attending doctors, or it would lead to greater panic.

'No one is offering us any tea,' the constables grumbled among themselves. 'And this stupid music. Same songs over and over.'

Half an hour later they got the go-ahead. Four persons were selected from the nearest truck, dragged screaming to the two main tents and forced onto the office desks. 'Stop resisting,' said the doctor. 'If the knife slips it will harm you only.' The warning frightened them into silent submission.

The constables watched the tents carefully, trying to maintain a steady supply according to instructions. But several who couldn't read kept getting confused. They escorted women to the vasectomy tent. The mix-up was understandable: except for the handwritten signs, both tents were identical, and the medical personnel in white coats all looked alike.

'Men to the left tent, women to the right,' the doctors reminded them repeatedly. Their annoyance grew with the suspicion that it was being done on purpose – perhaps some kind of inane police humour. Finally, a medical assistant improved the signs. With a black marker he drew figures on the signboards, of the sort found on public latrines. The turban on the male, and the sari and long plait on the female were unmistakable, and now the constables were able to work with greater accuracy.

As the sterilizations proceeded, an elderly woman tried to reason with her doctor. 'I am old,' she said. 'My womb is barren, there are no more eggs in it. Why are you wasting the operation on me?'

The doctor approached the district official keeping a tally of the day's procedures. 'This woman is past child-bearing age,' he said. 'You should take her off your list.'

'Is that a medical conclusion?'

'Of course not,' said the doctor. 'There is no equipment here for clinical verification.'

'In that case, just go ahead. These people often lie about their age. And appearances are deceptive. With their lifestyle, thirty can look like sixty, all shrivelled by the sun.'

Two hours into the campaign, a nurse hurried to the policemen with new instructions. 'Please slow down the supply of lady patients,' she said. 'There is a technical problem in the tubectomy tent.'

A middle-aged man took the opportunity to appeal to the nurse. 'I beg you,' he wept. 'Do it to me, I don't mind – I have fathered three children. But my son here is only sixteen! Never married! Spare him!'

'I have no authority, you must speak to the doctor,' she answered, and hurried back to attend to the technical problem. The autoclave was not working, she had to boil water to disinfect the instruments.

'See, I was right,' Ishvar whispered to Om, holding him close in his trembling arms. 'The doctor will let you go, that's what the nurse just said. We must talk to the doctor and tell him you don't have children yet.'

In the truck with the tailors a woman was feeding her baby, unaffected by the anguish around her. She softly hummed a song, swaying her body to help the infant fall asleep. 'Will you hold my child for me when my turn comes?' she asked Ishvar.

'Hahnji, don't worry, sister.'

'I'm not worried. I'm looking forward to it. Five children I already have, and my husband won't let me stop. This way he has no choice – government stops it.' She began singing again, 'Na-na-na-na Narayan, my sleepy little Narayan . . .'

By and by, the constable beckoned to her, and she removed the child from her breast. The swollen nipple separated with a tiny pop. Om watched her tuck her breast back into her choli. Ishvar eagerly held out his arms and took the child. It started to cry as the mother was climbing down from the truck.

He nodded to reassure her, and rocked the child gently in his lap. Om tried to distract the infant by making funny faces. Then Ishvar began singing like the mother, imitating her little tune, 'Na-na-na-na Narayan, my sleepy little Narayan.'

The baby stopped crying. They exchanged triumphant looks. Minutes later, tears were rolling down Ishvar's cheeks. Om turned away. He did not need to ask the reason.

Frustrated by the malfunctioning equipment, the doctors operated slowly through the afternoon, and the Nussbandhi Mela was extended beyond its closing time of six p.m. The second autoclave had broken down as well. Around seven o'clock, a senior administrator from the Family Planning Centre arrived with his personal assistant.

The constables shuffled their feet and stood a little more erect while the camp was inspected. The administrator conveyed his displeasure regarding the number of patients still in the trucks. Then he came upon the doctors by the gas stoves, waiting for a fresh pot of water to boil, and decided to give them a piece of his mind.

'Stop wasting time,' he snapped as they wished him good evening. 'Have you no sense of duty? There are dozens of operations left to do. A chupraasi can make tea for you.'

'We are not making tea. The water is for cleaning instruments. The machine is not working.'

'Instruments are clean enough. How long do you want to heat the water? Efficiency is paramount at a Nussbandhi Mela, targets have to be achieved within the budget. Who's going to pay for so many gas cylinders?' He threatened that they would be reported to higher authorities for lack of cooperation, promotions would be denied, salaries frozen.

The doctors resumed work with partially sterile equipment. They knew of colleagues whose careers had suffered similarly.

The administrator watched for a while, clocking the operations and working out the average time per patient. 'Too slow,' he said to his personal assistant. 'A simple job of snip-snip-snip they turn into a big fuss.'

Before leaving, he delivered the final threat in his arsenal. 'Remember, Thakur Dharamsi will be coming later to check the totals. If he is not pleased with you, you may as well send in your resignations.'

'Yes, sir,' said the doctors.

Satisfied, he went to inspect the other tents. His personal assistant stayed by his side like an interpreter, letting his facial expressions illuminate his superior's speech.

'We have to be firm with the doctors,' confided the administrator. 'If it is left to them to fight the menace of the population explosion, the nation will drown, choked to death, finished – end of our civilization. So it's up to us to make sure the war is won.'

'Yes, sir – absolutely, sir,' said the aide, thrilled to receive this private pearl of wisdom.

The sun was disappearing at the horizon when it was the tailors' turn. Ishvar said beseechingly to the constable who gripped his arm, 'Police-sahab, there has been a mistake. We don't live here, we came from the city because my nephew is getting married.'

'I cannot do anything about that.' He lengthened his stride.

Ishvar's feet skipped in an effort to keep from being dragged. 'Can I see the man in charge?' he panted, his voice uneven.

'Doctor is in charge.'

Inside the tent, Ishvar spoke timidly to the doctor. 'There is a mistake, Doctorji. We don't live here.'

The exhausted man made no response.

'Doctorji, you are like mother-father to us poor people, your good work keeps us healthy. And I also think nussbandhi is very important for the country. I am never going to marry, Doctorji, please do the operation on me, I will be grateful, but please leave out my nephew, Doctorji, his name is Omprakash and his wedding is happening soon, please listen to me, Doctorji, I beg of you!'

They were pushed onto the desks and their pants were removed. Ishvar started to weep. 'Please, Doctorji! Not my nephew! Cut me as much as you like! But forgive my nephew! His marriage is being arranged!'

Om said nothing. He blocked out the humiliating appeals, wishing his uncle would behave with more dignity. The canvas ceiling undulated slightly in a breeze. He stared numbly as the guy ropes creaked and the electric lights swayed.

Dusk had turned to night when the tailors were helped off the table by the nurses. 'Aiee!' said Om. 'It hurts!'

'Soreness is normal for a few hours,' said the doctor. 'Nothing to worry about.'

They were led limping through the dark field towards the recovery tent. 'Now why are you keeping us here?' sobbed Ishvar. 'Can't we go home?'

'You could,' said the nurse. 'But better to rest for a while.'

Half a dozen steps later, the pain was sharper. They decided to heed her advice and lie down on the straw mattresses. No one took notice of Ishvar's crying; grief and tears were general throughout the tents. They were given water and two biscuits each.

'Everything is ruined,' he wept, passing his biscuits to Om. 'The four families will never accept us now for their daughters.'

'I don't care.'

'You are a stupid boy, you don't understand what it means! I have let down your dead father! Our family name will die without children, it is the end of everything – everything is lost!'

'Maybe for you. But I still have my dignity. I'm not crying like a baby.'

A man on the next pallet was listening intently to their conversation. He raised himself on one elbow. 'O bhai,' he said, 'don't cry. Look here, I've heard the operation is reversible.'

'But how can that be? After the nuss has been cut?'

'No, bhai, it's possible. Specialists in big cities can reconnect the nuss.'

'Are you sure?'

'Absolutely sure. Only thing is, it's very expensive.'

'You hear that, Om? There is still hope!' Ishvar wiped his face. 'Never mind how expensive – we will get it done! We will sew like crazy for Dinabai, night and day! I will get it reversed for you!'

He turned to his benefactor, the creator of hope. 'God bless you for this information. May you also be able to reverse it.'

'I don't want to,' said the man. 'I have four children. A year ago I went to my doctor and had the operation of my own free will. These animals did it on me today for the second time.'

'That's like executing a dead man. Don't they listen to anything?'

'What to do, bhai, when educated people are behaving like savages. How do you talk to them? When the ones in power have lost their reason, there is no hope.' Feeling a sharp pain in his crotch, he lowered his elbow to lie down.

Ishvar wiped his eyes and lay down too. He reached over to the next mattress and stroked his nephew's arm. 'Bas, my child, we have found our solution, no need to worry now. We will go back, reverse the nussbandhi, and come next year for the wedding. There will be other families interested by then. And maybe by then this accursed Emergency will also be over, and sanity will return to government.'

A sound like a tap was heard, and a hissing; someone was urinating outside. His loud stream hitting the ground angered the twice-vasectomized man in the tent. He rose again on his elbow. 'See? Like animals, I told you. These policemen don't even have the decency to go to the end of the field to pass water.'

Darkness was falling, and the doctors were down to their last few operations when Thakur Dharamsi arrived. The policemen and Family Planning workers flocked to bow before him, jostling to touch his feet. He spoke briefly to the doctors and nurses, then strolled through the recovery tents, waving to the patients, thanking them for their cooperation in making the sterilization camp a success.

'Quick, turn your face, Om,' whispered Ishvar urgently, as the Thakur approached their row. 'Cover it with your arms, pretend you are asleep.'

Thakur Dharamsi stopped at the foot of Om's mattress and stared. He murmured a few words to someone at his side. The man left, returning a moment later with one of the doctors.

The Thakur spoke to him softly, and the doctor recoiled, shaking his head vehemently. The Thakur whispered again. The doctor went pale.

Shortly, two nurses arrived and helped Om to his feet. 'But I want to rest,' he protested. 'It still hurts.'

'Doctor wants to see you.'

'Why?' shouted Ishvar. 'You already finished his operation! Now what do you want?'

In the operating tent, the doctor was standing with his back to the entrance, watching the water come to a vigorous boil. The scalpel lay at the bottom, shining below the bubbles. He motioned to the nurses to get the patient on the table.

'Testicular tumour,' he felt obliged to explain to them. 'Thakurji has authorized removal, as a special favour to the boy.' The quaver in his voice betrayed the lie.

Om's pants were taken off for the second time. A rag soaked in chloroform was gripped at his nose. He tore at it briefly, then went limp. With a swift incision the doctor removed the testicles, sewed up the gash, and put a heavy dressing on it.

'Don't send this patient home with the others,' he said. 'He will need to sleep here tonight.' They covered him with a blanket and carried him to the recovery tent on a stretcher.

'What have you done to him?' screamed Ishvar. 'He went out on his feet! You bring him back senseless! What have you done to my nephew?'

'Quiet,' they admonished, sliding Om from the stretcher onto the pallet. 'He was very sick, and Doctor did a free operation to save his life. You should be grateful instead of simply shouting. Don't worry, he'll be all right when he wakes up. Doctor said for him to rest here till morning. You can also stay.'

Ishvar went to his nephew's side to see for himself. He sought verbal assurances. Sound asleep, Om did not answer. Ishvar pulled down the blanket and began examining him: his hands, fingers, toes were intact. He checked the back – there were no bloody welts of whiplashes. And the mouth was fine, the tongue and teeth were undamaged. His fear began to abate, perhaps the Thakur had left him alone.

Then he found bloodstains on the underside of the trouser crotch. Could it be from the nussbandhi operation? He looked down at himself – there was no blood. Fingers shaking, he undid Om's trousers and saw the large dressing. He unbuttoned his own trousers to compare: there was only a small piece of gauze and surgical tape. He put his fingers on Om's bandage and felt the absence. Swallowing hard, he moved his fingers around frantically, hoping to locate the testicles somewhere, refusing to believe they were missing.

Then he howled.

'Hai Ram! Look! Look what they have done! To my nephew! Look! They have made a eunuch out of him!'

Someone came from the main tent and told him to be quiet. 'What are you shouting for again? Didn't you understand? The boy was very sick, that part had a dangerous growth in it, a gaanth full of poison, it needed to be removed.'

The twice-vasectomized man had already departed. The remaining occupants of the tent were busy nursing their own sorrow and trying to cope with nausea and dizziness. One by one, when they felt strong enough, they rose and returned shamefaced to their homes. There was no one left to comfort Ishvar.

Alone through the night, he howled and wept, slept for a few minutes when exhausted, then wept once more. Om came out of the chloroform past midnight, retched, and fell asleep again.

———

After the roundup in the market square, Ashraf Chacha had been carried to the municipal hospital, and his relatives at the lumberyard were notified. He died a few hours later. The hospital, following standing orders, put down the cause of death as accidental: 'Due to stumbling, falling, and striking of head against kerb.' His relatives buried him beside Mumtaz Chachi the next day, while Ishvar and Om were still making their way back from the sterilization camp.

Apart from a soreness in the groin, Ishvar felt no discomfort. But Om was in grave pain. The bleeding resumed when he took a few steps. His uncle tried to carry him on his back, which was more agonizing. Flat in his arms like a baby was the only comfortable position for Om, but too exhausting for Ishvar. He had to put him down every few yards along the road.

Towards afternoon, a man passing with an empty handcart stopped. 'What is wrong with the boy?'

Ishvar told him, and he offered to help. They placed Om on the cartbed. The man removed his turban to make a pillow. Ishvar and he pushed the handcart. It was not heavy to roll, but they had to move very slowly over the rutted road. The jolts knifed their way through Om, and the distance was measured by his harrowing screams.

It was dark when they reached Muzaffar Tailoring. The handcart-man refused payment. 'I was travelling in this direction anyway,' he said.

Ashraf's nephew from the lumberyard was inside, come to secure the shop. 'I have sad news,' he said. 'Chachaji had an accident and passed away.'

The tailors were too distraught, however, to be able to mourn the loss or fully comprehend it. Yesterday's events in the market square had merged with all the other tragedies in their lives. 'Thank you for coming to inform us,' Ishvar kept saying mechanically. 'I must attend the funeral, and Om will also come, yes, he'll be better tomorrow.'

The man repeated it four times before they realized that Ashraf Chacha had already been buried. 'Don't worry, you can stay here till you are well,' he said. 'I haven't yet decided what to do with this property. And please let me know if you need anything.'

They went to sleep without eating, having no desire for food. To avoid climbing the flight of steps, Ishvar prepared a mattress downstairs beside the shop counter. During the night Om thrashed around in delirium. 'No! Not Ashraf Chacha's shears! Where's the umbrella? Give me, I'll show the goondas!'

Ishvar awoke in fright and groped for the light switch. He saw a dark blotch on the sheet. He cleaned Om's wound and sat up the rest of the night to restrain him, lest the dressing tear open.

In the morning he half-dragged, half-carried him to a private dispensary in town. The doctor was disgusted by the castration but not surprised. He treated victims of caste violence from time to time, from the surrounding villages, and had given up trying to get the law to pursue the cause of justice. 'Insufficient evidence to register a case' was the routine response, whether it was a finger or hand or nose or ear that was missing.

'You are lucky,' said the doctor. 'This was done very cleanly, and stitched properly. If the boy rests for a week, it will heal.' He disinfected the wound and put a new dressing on it. 'Don't let him walk, walking will make it bleed again.'

Ishvar paid the fee out of the wedding money, then asked, despite knowing the answer, 'Will he be able to father children?'

The doctor shook his head.

'Even though the pipe is intact?'

'The vessels which produce the seed have been cut off.'

Remembering the doctor's advice, Ishvar staggered home with his nephew in his arms and put him to bed. He found a bottle and a pan so Om could relieve himself without having to walk to the lavatory. Ashraf Chacha's neighbours avoided them. In the tiny kitchen where Mumtaz Chachi had cooked for her family of six, plus two apprentices, Ishvar prepared the joyless meals. The friendly ghosts of his childhood were unable to comfort him, and they ate in silence at Om's bedside.

At the end of seven days, Ishvar carried him again to the private dispensary. In the street it was easy to spot the victims of forced vasectomies, especially among those who possessed only one set of garments. Pus stains at the crotch told the story.

'The healing is almost complete,' said the doctor. 'It is all right to walk now – but no hurrying.' He did not charge for the second visit.

From the dispensary they took small, careful steps to the police chowki and said they wanted to register a complaint. 'My nephew was turned into a eunuch,' said Ishvar, unable to control a sob as he spoke the word.

The constable on duty was perturbed. He wondered if this meant a fresh outbreak of inter-caste disturbances, and headaches for his colleagues and himself. 'Who did it?'

'It was at the Nussbandhi Mela. In the doctor's tent.'

The answer relieved the policeman. 'Not police jurisdiction. This is a case for the Family Planning Centre. Complaints about their people are handled by their office.' And in all probability, he thought, it was just another instance of confusing sterilization with castration. A visit to the Centre would sort things out.

The tailors left the police chowki and walked very slowly to the Family Planning Centre. Ishvar was grateful for the unhurried pace. A terrible ache had grown around his own groin in the last three days, which he had ignored in his concern for his nephew.

Om noticed the peculiar walk, and asked his uncle what the matter was. 'Nothing.' He winced as waves of pain rolled leisurely down his legs. 'Just stiffness from the operation. It will go.' But he knew that it was getting worse; this morning, a swelling had begun in the legs.

At the Family Planning Centre the moment Ishvar said eunuch, they refused to listen further. 'Get out,' ordered the officer. 'We are fed up with you ignorant people. How many times to explain? Nussbandhi has nothing to do with castration. Why don't you listen to our lectures? Why don't you read the pamphlets we give you?'

'I understand the difference,' said Ishvar. 'If you take just one look, you will see what your doctor has done.' He motioned to Om to drop his pants.

But as Om began undoing the buttons, the officer ran and grabbed the waistband. 'I forbid you to take off your clothes in my office. I am not a doctor, and whatever is in your pants is of no interest to me. If we start believing you, then all the eunuchs in the country will come dancing to us, blaming us for their condition, trying to get money out of us. We know your tricks. The whole Family Planning Programme will grind to a halt. The country will be ruined. Suffocated by uncontrolled population growth. Now get out before I call the police.'

Ishvar begged him to reconsider, to at least take one quick look. Om spoke in his uncle's ear, warning him not to start crying again. The man kept advancing threateningly. They were forced to back up. When they were out in the street, the door was shut and a Closed For Lunch sign hung on it.

'You really thought they would help?' said Om. 'Don't you understand? We are less than animals to them.'

'Keep your mouth shut,' said Ishvar. 'Your foolishness has brought this on us.'

'How? For my foolishness I lost my balls. But how is your nussbandhi my fault? That would have happened anyway. It happened to everyone in the market.' He paused, then continued bitterly, 'In fact, it's all *your* fault. *Your* madness about coming here and finding a wife for me. We could have been safe in the city, on Dinabai's verandah.'

Ishvar's eyes filled with tears. 'So you are saying we should have stayed hidden on the verandah for the rest of our days? What kind of life, what kind of country is this, where we cannot come and go as we

please? Is it a sin to visit my native place? To get my nephew married?'
He could walk no further, and sank to the pavement, shaking.

'Come on,' hissed Om, 'don't do a drama on the street, it's looking bad.'

But his uncle continued to weep, and Om sat down beside him. 'I did
not mean it, yaar, it's not your fault, don't cry.'

'The pain,' shivered Ishvar. 'It's everywhere . . . too much . . . I don't
know what to do.'

'Let's go home,' said Om gently. 'I'll help you. You must rest with
your feet up.'

They rose and, with Ishvar limping, dragging, trembling with agony,
they reached Ashraf Chacha's shop. They agreed that a good night's
sleep would cure him. Om arranged the mattress and pillows comfortably for his uncle, then massaged his uncle's legs. They both fell asleep,
Ishvar's feet clasped in his nephew's hands.

A week later Ishvar's legs were swollen like columns. His body burned
with fever. From the groin to the knee the flesh had become black. They
returned to the Family Planning Centre and peered timidly from the
entrance. Fortunately, a doctor was present this time, and the man they
had spoken to on the last visit was not around.

'The nussbandhi is fine,' said the doctor after a cursory glance. 'It's not
connected to the sickness in your legs. There is a poison in your body
which is causing the swelling. You should go to the hospital.'

Seeing that this was a reasonable man, Ishvar mentioned his nephew's
castration, and the doctor was instantly transformed. 'Get out!' he said.
'If you are going to talk nonsense, get out of my sight this moment!'

They went to the hospital, where Ishvar was given a course of pills:
four times a day for fourteen days. The pills reduced the fever, but there
was no improvement in his legs. At the end of the fortnight's treatment
he could not walk at all. The blackness had spread downwards like a
stain, towards the toes, reminding him of the leather dye that used to
impregnate his skin as a boy, when he worked with his father and the
Chamaars.

Om found the handcart-man in the market that afternoon, and
requested his help. 'It's my uncle this time. He cannot walk, he has to be
taken to hospital.'

The man was unloading a consignment of onions from the cart. A few
bulbs had been crushed during transit, and the air was charged with the
pungent reek. He wiped his eyes, hoisted a sack over his shoulders, and
took it to the godown. The vapours travelled into Om's eyes too, though
he stood at some distance.

'Okay, I'm ready,' said the handcart-man twenty minutes later. He dusted off the cartbed and they went to Muzaffar Tailoring to collect Ishvar. They positioned the cart close to the steps and hoisted him upon it. The neighbours watched, hidden behind curtains, as the rickety wheels trundled off towards the hospital.

The handcart-man waited outside the building while Ishvar huddled in the entrance and Om went in search of the emergency ward. 'The pills have not worked,' the doctor on duty announced after the examination. 'The poison in the blood is too strong. The legs will have to be removed in order to keep the poison from spreading upwards. It's the only way to save his life.'

Next morning the blackened legs were amputated. The surgeon said the stumps would be observed for several days, to make sure all the poison had drained out. Ishvar spent two months in hospital. Om went every morning with food, and stayed till night.

'You must send a letter to Dinabai,' Ishvar reminded Om repeatedly. 'Tell her what happened, she will be worrying about us.'

'Yes,' said Om, but he did not dare attempt the task. What would he write? How could he even begin to explain on a piece of paper?

At the end of the two months, the handcart-man returned to the hospital and helped to take Ishvar home to Muzaffar Tailoring. 'My life is over,' wept Ishvar. 'Just throw me in the river that runs by our village. I don't want to be a burden to you.'

'Leave it, yaar,' said Om. 'Don't talk rubbish. What do you mean, life is over? Have you forgotten Shankar? He doesn't even have fingers or thumbs. You still have both hands, you can sew. Dinabai has an old hand-machine, she will let you use it when we go back.'

'You are a crazy boy. I can't sit, I can't move, and you are talking of sewing.'

'Let me know if you need more transport,' said the handcart-man, adding quickly, 'I will take you for the price of a bus ticket from now on.'

'Yes, we'll pay you, don't worry,' said Om. 'My uncle will need to go to the hospital. And maybe in a few weeks, once he feels stronger, you can take us to the train station. We'll soon be returning to our city.'

The recovery was slow. Their money was running out. Ishvar ate poorly, and his nights continued to pass in the embrace of fever and nightmares. He often woke up crying. Om comforted him, asked him what he would like.

'Massage my feet, they are aching too much,' he always said.

One evening, Ashraf Chacha's nephew from the lumberyard came to see them. He had found a buyer for the shop. 'Very sorry to make you leave. But who knows when I will get another offer?' He proposed alternate accommodation in a shed or shack, certain that some corner of the lumberyard could be found for them.

'No, it's okay,' said Om. 'We'll just return to the city and start sewing again.'

This time Ishvar agreed with him. It was better to go, he felt, than to stay in this place that had brought them nothing but misery. Each day now was mortifying, with the people who knew them, especially the neighbours, staring at them on their trips to and from the hospital, whispering among themselves, shying away when they saw the handcart coming.

'Can you do us one last favour?' Om asked Ashraf Chacha's nephew. 'Can you get your carpenter in the lumberyard to make a little trolley with small wheels, for my uncle?'

He said it would be an easy matter. The next day he delivered the rolling platform to the shop. There was a hook at the front end, with a rope for Om to pull the platform.

'This rope is unnecessary,' insisted Ishvar. 'I will roll the gaadi with my own hands, like Shankar. I want to be independent.'

'Okay, yaar, we'll see.'

They removed the rope, and Ishvar began practising indoors. He needed to learn how to slump his body so it would be stable without the counterweight of legs. His frustration mounted. In his weakened state he could not propel the platform. There was no question of venturing into the street.

'Patience,' said Om. 'You will be able to do it as you get stronger.'

'What patience,' sobbed Ishvar. 'Patience is not going to make my legs grow back.' Hopelessly defeated, he allowed the towing rope to be reconnected.

Almost four months after coming to make wedding arrangements, the tailors set off for the railway station, for the return journey to the city. Along the way they stopped at the graves of Ashraf Chacha and Mumtaz Chachi. 'I envy them,' said Ishvar. 'Such peace now.'

'Don't be talking nonsense again,' said Om, shifting the platform around to leave.

'Can't we stay here a little longer?'

'No, we have to go.' Om tugged at the rope, and the castors jolted over the earth of the graveyard. How light is my uncle, he thought, light as a baby, pulling him is no strain at all.

XVI The Circle Is Completed

THE FIRST THING Zenobia saw when Dina opened the door was the patchwork curtain rigged down the middle of the verandah. 'What's this, your washing?' she giggled. 'Or are you starting a dhobi service?'

'No, that's the bridal suite,' said Dina, breaking into laughter. She had endured four weeks of enforced solitude with resentment. Her friend dropping in was a great relief.

Zenobia found the joke hilarious without understanding what it meant. They went into the front room. Between renewed bursts of laughter, she learned why the verandah was partitioned.

'They should be back any day now,' said Dina. 'The curtain isn't thick enough to muffle the newlyweds' noises, but it's the best I can do.'

Zenobia no longer thought it funny. She stared at Dina as though she had gone mad. 'How you've changed. Are you listening to what you are saying? Only a year ago you were against keeping a harmless paying guest. It took me days to convince you that Aban Kohlah's son was no threat, that he was not going to eat up your flat.'

'And you were absolutely right – Maneck is a lovely boy. Two more weeks, and he'll be back too. Look at this quilt I made. It's going to be Om's wedding present.'

Zenobia ignored it and continued. 'Suddenly you became very brave, letting the tailors live here. That was bad enough. Now you are allowing them to bring a wife? You'll regret it, believe me. The whole jing-bang clan will end up on the verandah. Half their village. And you'll never be able to get rid of them. The place will turn into a pigsty, with all their primitive unhygienic habits.'

The grim prognostication amused Dina, but this time she was laughing alone. To placate her friend she employed a more serious tone. 'They would never take advantage of me. Ishvar is a perfect gentleman. And Om is a good, intelligent boy, just like Maneck. Only less fortunate.'

Zenobia stayed for another half-hour, pleading, threatening, cajoling, doing her best to change her friend's decision. 'Don't be foolish, just let them go. We can always find new tailors for you. Mrs. Gupta will help us, I'm sure.'

'But that's not the point. I would let them stay even if they weren't working for me.'

By the time Zenobia realized she was getting nowhere, she had already invested her emotions in the argument. To rescue her pride, she departed in a huff.

━━

The letter from Maneck made Dina's hands shake as she opened it. 'Dear Aunty,' she read, 'I hope you are well and in the pink of perfection, as are all of us at our end. Mummy and Daddy send you their best wishes. They said they were very happy to see me, and that they missed me.

'I finally heard from my college. Sorry to write that my marks were not very good. They have refused me admission to the degree programme, so I will have to be satisfied with my one-year certificate.'

She knew what was coming, but read on, trying to ignore the sick feeling in the pit of her stomach. 'You should have seen the acting that went on when the news arrived. If you remember, when I first suggested doing three more years, my parents had been against it. But now they got upset with me for the opposite reason. What are you going to do with your life, Daddy kept repeating, finished, it's all finished, this boy has no idea what a disaster this is, all my life has been one disaster after another, I thought my son would change the pattern, but I should have known better, the lines on my palm are permanent, no alterations permitted, it is my fate, I cannot fight it.

'Do you remember Ishvar's theatrics about finding a wife for Om? That was nothing, Aunty, compared to Daddy's performance. I should never have told them I was planning to take that silly degree programme.

'Fortunately, after all the acting was over, a friend of my parents brought some good news. Brigadier Grewal has contacts in those rich Arab countries in the Gulf, where money grows on trees. He has promised me a good job in a refrigeration and air-conditioning company in Dubai. The Brigadier thinks he is a great comedian. He said everyone owns a unit to cool their tent in the desert, and with sandstorms and simoons choking the motor and fan, there is constant demand for new air-conditioners and maintenance work.

'Due to Brigadier Grewal's pathetic sense of humour, I have decided to accept the job. If I go to Dubai, I won't have to listen to his jokes. And the salary, benefits, living allowance is fantastic. They say over there a person can save a small fortune in just four or five years. Maybe I will be able to come back and start my own air-conditioning business in the city. Or even better, we could start a tailoring business. With all my experience last year, I would be the boss, of course. (Ha ha, just joking.)'

It was getting difficult to read with the tears stinging her eyes. She blinked rapidly a few times and took a deep breath. 'I have to be in Dubai in three weeks, so Mummy is driving everyone crazy trying to get things ready for me. It's a repeat performance of what she went through last year when I was leaving for college. And Daddy is the same as before. He hasn't talked properly to me even once since I returned, although I've done exactly what he wanted. He now makes it sound like I am abandoning him and the General Store. He wants to have his cake and eat it too. What does he expect if he runs things in his same old-fashioned way. When I try to make suggestions, he just gives me that tragic look of his. He'll feel better once I've gone, he just does not enjoy having me around. I knew it the day he sent me to boarding school in the fifth standard.

'Please tell Om I am sorry not to be there to meet his wife. I am sure she will be very happy with a wonderful mother-in-law like you. (Ha ha, joking again, Aunty.) But next year, when I come home from the Gulf on vacation, I am planning to stop over and see all of you.

'Lastly, I want to thank you for letting me stay in your flat, and for looking after me so well.' The next sentence had been cancelled out, but she could decipher two fragments under the heavy scratches: 'the happiest' and 'life.'

There was not much more after this. 'Good luck with the tailoring. Lots of love to Ishvar and Om, and to you.'

Below his name he had added a postscript. 'I have asked Mummy to write the enclosed cheque for three months' rent, since I did not give proper notice. I hope this is all right. Thanks again.'

The writing went quite blurry now. She removed her spectacles and wiped her eyes. Such a wonderful boy. Would she ever get used to being without his company? His teasing, his constant chatter, his helpful nature, the good-morning smile, his antics with the cats, even if his ideas about life and death were a bit grim. And how generous the cheque was; she was certain he had pressured his mother into writing it.

But it was selfish to feel sad, she thought, when she should be happy about Maneck's opportunity. He was right, lots of people had made fortunes by working in these oil-rich countries.

Two days after receiving the letter, Dina went to the Venus Beauty Salon. The receptionist returned from the rear and announced that Zenobia was with a customer. 'Please wait in the waiting area, madam.'

Dina sat near a withered plant and picked up a stale issue of *Woman's*

Weekly, smiling to herself. Clearly, Zenobia was still miffed about the business of Om's wife, and this was her way of letting her know, or she would have come running, clutching scissors and comb, breathless, said hello, and run back.

Forty-five minutes passed before Zenobia emerged to escort her customer to the door. The extravagantly coiffed woman was none other than Mrs. Gupta. 'What a surprise to see you here, Mrs. Dalal,' she said. 'Is Zenobia doing your hair?' Despite the smile, something about the left corner of her upper lip suggested she did not approve of the idea.

'Oh no, I could never afford her services! I just dropped in to chat.'

'I hope her charges for chatting are more reasonable than for hair-styling,' tittered Mrs. Gupta. 'But I'm not complaining, she is a genius. Just look – what a miracle she has performed today.' She moved her head in a slow rotation from left to right and back again, letting it come to rest statuesquely in a gaze frozen at the ceiling fan.

'So lovely,' said Dina without wasting time. Mrs. Gupta was capable of holding her pose indefinitely if a compliment was not forthcoming.

'Thank you,' she said coyly, and allowed her cranium to move again. 'But when are we going to see you at Au Revoir? Have your tailors returned or not?'

'I think we'll start next week.'

'Let's hope they don't ask for honeymoon leave when their wedding leave finishes. Or there will be another population increase.' Mrs. Gupta tittered again, glancing in the mirror behind the reception counter. She patted her hair and departed reluctantly; the angle of that particular glass had given her immense satisfaction.

Alone with her friend, Dina smiled confidentially, sharing a wordless opinion of Mrs. Gupta. But Zenobia's response was cold. 'You wanted to ask me something?'

'Yes, I got a letter from Maneck Kohlah. He doesn't need my room anymore.'

'I'm not surprised,' she sniffed. 'Must be fed up of living with tailors.'

'Actually, they all got along very well.' She was aware, as she mouthed the words, that the statement did not do justice to her household. But what else to say? Could she describe for Zenobia the extent to which Maneck and Om had become inseparable, and how Ishvar regarded both boys like his own sons? That the four of them cooked together and ate together, shared the cleaning and washing and shopping and laughing and worrying? That they cared about her, and gave her more respect than she had received from some of her own relatives? That she had, during these last few months, known what was a family?

It was impossible to explain. Zenobia would say she was being silly and imagining fancy things, turning a financial necessity into something sentimental. Or she would accuse the tailors of manipulating her through fawning and flattery.

So Dina merely added, 'Maneck isn't coming back because he has got a very good job in the Gulf.'

'Well,' said Zenobia. 'Whatever the real reason, you need a replacement paying guest.'

'Yes, that's why I'm here. Do you have someone?'

'Not right now. I'll keep it in mind.' She rose to return to work. 'It's going to be difficult. Anyone who sees your Technicolour curtain and a tribe of tailors on the verandah will run from that room.'

'Don't worry, I'll remove the curtain.' Dina expected her friend would come through; when Zenobia was upset, she took a few days to recover, that was all.

She went home and made sure Maneck's room was spotless. But she must stop thinking of it now as Maneck's room, she resolved. Dusting and cleaning, she found the chess set in the cupboard. Should she send it to Maneck? By the time it reached the hill-station, he would have left for the Gulf. Better to save it till he visited next year, as he had written.

Dina liked this idea, and tucked away the set among her own clothes in the sewing room. It seemed to fix Maneck's visit more definitely in time. It was a comforting thought, drowning the other, painful one – that he would never live here again.

At night, she went to the kitchen window and fed the cats, calling them by the names he had given them.

━━

The full six weeks had elapsed, and yet she kept waiting patiently, certain at every ring of the doorbell that Ishvar and Om had returned. Then the hire-purchase man arrived to demand the overdue amount on the two Singers.

'The tailors are coming next week,' she stalled. 'You know how busy it gets when there is a wedding.'

'They have been late too often,' grumbled the man. 'The company shouts at me that I am not collecting on time.' He agreed to wait for seven more days.

Later that morning, the doorbell rang again. She ran to the verandah.

It was Beggarmaster. He was carrying a small wedding gift. 'An aluminium tea kettle,' he said, disappointed that the tailors were not yet back.

'I'm hoping for next week, latest,' said Dina. 'The export company is also getting impatient.'

'I'll bring the gift next Thursday.'

She knew what he was getting at: his instalment, like the hire-purchase man's, was overdue. 'There won't be any problem with the landlord, will there? Because the tailors haven't paid? I can give you a little right now, if you insist.'

'Not at all. I am looking after the flat, don't worry. With such good people I am not concerned about temporary arrears. You came to Shankar's funeral, I won't forget that.'

He made a collection note in his diary and shut the briefcase. 'Yesterday I finally made the donation to the temple in Shankar's memory. There was a small puja, and as the priest was ringing the bell, I felt such peace. Maybe it's time for me to give up this business, devote myself to prayer and meditation.'

'Are you serious? What will happen to all your beggars? And to the tailors and me?'

Beggarmaster nodded wearily. 'That's the thing. For the sake of my worldly duties, I must keep in check my spiritual urges. Don't worry, I will not abandon any of my dependants.' The briefcase chain on his wrist rattled softly as he left. She noticed it had started to rust.

The reassurance bestowed by his solemn pledge evaporated within minutes. After the morning's two visitors, the anxiety she had kept at bay began closing in, prowling and circling like a predator. Now she was certain that the tailors' failure to return meant more than a brief delay. And not even the courtesy of a postcard. What could have happened that they could not let her know in a few words: please excuse us Dinabai, we have decided to settle again in our village, Om and his wife prefer it. Just a few lines. Was that too much to expect? Zenobia was right, it was foolish to trust their type of people. They had used her, and discarded her.

To complete the day, the bell taunted her a third time, late in the afternoon. She turned the knob without putting on the chain. The bright sun made the precaution seem unnecessary. Then the opening door presented a fearful apparition.

'Ohhh!' she screamed, badly scared. The man, wasted and with freshly healed scars on his forehead, a wild gaze about his eyes, looked as though he had risen from his deathbed.

She tried to push the door shut. But he spoke, and her fears diminished. 'Don't be frightened, ma-ji,' he gasped. 'I mean no harm.' It was the pitiful whine of a wounded creature, the wheezing of damaged lungs. 'Two tailors work here? Ishvar and Omprakash?'

'Yes.'

The man almost collapsed with relief. 'Please, can I see them?'

'They are away for a few days,' said Dina, stepping back; his smell was strong.

'They will come back soon?' his words groped desperately.

'Maybe. Who are you?'

'A friend. We lived in the same jhopadpatti, till government flattened it.'

For a moment Dina wondered if this could be Rajaram, the one who wanted to renounce the world and become a sanyasi. She had seen him only once or twice – could the hardship of sanyas have already altered him so greatly? 'You are not the hair-collector, are you?' she asked.

He shook his head. 'I am Monkey-man. But my monkeys are dead.' He fingered his forehead, touching the itchy scars delicately. 'The tailors had told me they worked in this neighbourhood. Since yesterday, I've been going to every building on this road, knocking at every flat. And now – they are not here.' He looked ready to cry. 'Ishvar and Om are still with Beggarmaster, yes?'

'I think so.'

'You know where he lives?'

'No. Beggarmaster always comes here to collect. In fact, he was here today.'

Monkey-man's eyes lit up. 'How long ago? Where did he go?'

'I don't know – hours ago, in the morning.' The hope vanished from his face. Like light from a bulb, she thought, on and off.

'I have very important business with him. And I don't know how to find him.'

His helplessness, the sight of his battered body, the despair in his voice made Dina wince. 'Beggarmaster is coming again next Thursday,' she volunteered.

Monkey-man touched his forehead and bowed. 'May God bless you and grant all your wishes for helping a wretch like me.'

The hire-purchase man returned the following week and said he could not wait any longer for payment. Expecting more excuses from Dina, he was determined to be firm this time.

'I don't want you to wait,' she snapped. 'Take the machines right now, I refuse to keep them another minute.'

'Thank you,' he said, astonished. 'Our van will pick them up tomorrow morning.'

'Did you hear me? I said right now. If they are not gone in one hour, I will push them out of my flat. I'll leave them in the middle of the road.' The man hurried off to telephone the office for an urgent pickup.

Expelling the sewing-machines made her feel better. Let the rascals come back and find their Singers vanished, she thought. That would teach them a lesson for life.

Next, she waited for Beggarmaster and his wedding gift. With him, too, she decided to change tactics and let him know the tailors had disappeared. His missing instalments would make him act quickly, track them down wherever they were.

But Beggarmaster did not keep his appointment. How unlike his punctual habit, she thought, as the day passed. Could he and the tailors have formed a wicked alliance against her, planning to get rid of her and take over the flat? Anxiety stimulated her imagination, causing nefarious plots to flower, to plague her with their scent till next morning, when a knock on the door finally revealed the truth.

Disappointment, betrayal, joy, heartache, hope – they all entered her life through the same door, she thought. She listened for the clink of Beggarmaster's briefcase chain. Nothing. And then another soft knock. Whoever it was, was staying clear of the jangling bell. She opened the door, leaving on the security chain.

A wisp of white beard came through the crack, and then the voice: 'Please sister, let me in! I'll be punished if someone from the office sees me, I'm not supposed to be here!'

Reluctantly, she unhooked the chain and allowed Ibrahim inside. 'What do you mean, not supposed to be here? You're the rent-collector.'

'Not anymore, sister. Landlord dismissed me last week. He said I was destructive with office property, that I was breaking too many folders. He showed me the stationery records since I started there forty-eight years ago. Seven folders I had been through – one leather-bound, three buckram, and three plastic. Seven is the limit, the landlord told me, seven folders and you're out.'

'What nonsense,' said Dina. 'You were always so careful with it, keeping it clean, opening and shutting it gently. It's not your fault if they give you cheap-quality folders that fall apart in a few years.'

'He just wanted an excuse to get rid of me, sister. I know the real reason.'

'What is the real reason?'

He waited, as though debating whether to share it with her, and sighed. 'The real reason is: I no longer have a passion for my duties. I am no longer mean enough with the tenants, I do not menace them in a way that scares them, I have lost my fire. And so I am useless to the land-lord.'

'Can't you try harder? Use more threatening language or something?'

He shook his head. 'Once the flame goes out, it cannot be rekindled. It came to pass right here, in this flat, sister. Don't you remember? The night I brought those goondas, months ago? After what happened here, I couldn't frighten a little baby. And I thank God for that.'

She reminded herself of the terror he had inflicted upon her that night, but instead of anger she felt somehow responsible for the loss of his job. 'Have you found other work?'

'At my age? Who will hire me?'

'Then how are you managing?'

He looked shamefully at the floor. 'Some of the tenants help me a lit-tle. Recently, I have made a few friends among them. I stand outside the building and they, you know, give me – help. But never mind all that, sister, let me tell you the reason for my visit. I have come to warn you, you are in great danger from the landlord.'

'I'm not scared of that rascal. Beggarmaster is looking after me.'

'But sister, Beggarmaster is dead.'

'What are you saying? Have you gone crazy?'

'No, he was murdered yesterday. I saw it all, I was standing outside, it was horrible! Horrible!' Ibrahim started to tremble, staggering side-ways. She led him to a chair and made him sit.

'Now take a deep breath and tell me properly,' she said.

He took a deep breath. 'Yesterday morning I was standing near the gate with my tin can, waiting for help from my tenants – I mean, my friends. I was able to see everything. The police said I was their star wit-ness, and took me along to give a full statement. They kept me till night, asking questions.'

'Who killed Beggarmaster?'

He took another deep breath. 'A very sick-looking man. He was hid-ing behind the stone pillar at the gate. When Beggarmaster entered, he jumped upon his back and tried to stab him. But he was such a weak fel-low, his blows were too soft, the knife would not go in. Anyone could have escaped such a feeble attacker.'

'Then why didn't Beggarmaster?'

'Because Beggarmaster's luck was not with him that day.'

What was with him, explained Ibrahim, was the large bag full of coins, chained to his wrist, which he had been out gathering from his beggars. Anchored to the ground by this deadweight, one hand immo-bilized, he was trapped. He thrashed and flailed with the free arm, kicking his legs about, while the frail murderer laboured on, sitting astride his victim's back, trying to make the blade pass through the clothes, break the skin, enter the flesh and pierce the heart.

'At first it looked so comic. As if he was playing with a plastic folding knife from the balloonman. But he took his time, and finally Beggarmaster stopped moving. He who had lived by the beggings of helpless cripples died by those beggings, rooted by their heaviness. You see, sister, once in a while there is a tiny piece of justice in the universe.'

But Dina was remembering all the beggars at Shankar's funeral. True, they were free now. But of what use was freedom to them? Scattered about the miserable pavements of the city, orphaned, uncared for – weren't they better off in Beggarmaster's custody?

'He wasn't a completely bad man,' she said.

'Who are we to decide the question of good or bad? It's just that for once, the scales look level. To be honest, sister, yesterday morning as I saw Beggarmaster approach, even I was thinking of asking him for help – to set me up somewhere in a good location. But the killer got to him first.'

'Did he try to steal the money?'

'No, he wasn't interested in the bag. And if he was, he would have had to chop the wrist. No, he just threw down his knife and shouted that he was Monkey-man, he had killed Beggarmaster for revenge.'

Dina turned pale and slipped into a chair. Ibrahim struggled out of his own to touch her arm. 'Are you all right, sister?'

'The one who said he was Monkey-man – did he have a big scar on his forehead?'

'I think so.'

'He came here last week, wanting to meet Beggarmaster for some business. I told him he was visiting on Thursday – yesterday.' She bunched her fingers in a fist and covered her mouth with it. 'I helped the murderer.'

'Don't say that, sister. You didn't know he was going to kill.' He patted her hand, and she saw his nails were dirty. A few months ago she would have been repulsed by the touch. Now she was grateful for it. His skin, wrinkled and scaly, like a harmless reptile's, filled her with wonder and sorrow. Why did I dislike him so much, she asked herself? Where humans were concerned, the only emotion that made sense was wonder, at their ability to endure; and sorrow, for the hopelessness of it all. And maybe Maneck was right, everything did end badly.

'Don't blame yourself, sister,' he said, patting her hand again.

'Why do you keep calling me sister? You are more my father's age.'

'Okay, I'll say daughter, then.' He smiled, and it was not his automatic smile. 'You see, this Monkey-man fellow would have found Beggarmaster sooner or later, whether you helped him or not. The police said he is a mental case, he didn't even try to run, just stood there and shouted all kinds of nonsense, that Beggarmaster had stolen two children from him while he was unconscious, and cut off their hands, blinded them, twisted their backs, and turned them into beggars, but now he had fulfilled the prophecy, now his vengeance was complete. Who knows what devils are tormenting the poor man's mind.'

He touched her hand again. 'Now that Beggarmaster is dead, the landlord will soon send someone to throw you out. That's why I came to warn you.'

'There is not much I can do against his goondas.'

'You must act before he does. You may have a little time. Your paying guest and tailors are gone, so he will need a new excuse. Get a lawyer and –'

'I can't afford expensive lawyers.'

'A cheap lawyer will do. He must –'

'I don't know how to find one.'

'Go to the courthouse. They will find you. Soon as you walk through the gate, they will come running to you.'

'And then?'

'Interview them, select one you can afford. Tell him you want to seek an injunction against the landlord, to cease and desist from threatening actions and other forms of harassment, that the status quo must be maintained until such time as –'

'Let me write this down, I won't remember.' She fetched paper and pencil. 'You think it will work?'

'If you are quick. Don't waste time, my daughter. Go – go now.'

She dug into her purse and found a five-rupee note. 'Just till you find a job,' she said, pressing it into his scaly hand.

'No, I cannot take from you, you have enough troubles.'

'Can a daughter not help her old father?'

His eyes were wet as he accepted the money.

The courthouse gates swarmed with the bustle of an impromptu bazaar set up right outside the precinct, where people who had spent hours in the pursuit of justice, and had days, weeks, months more to go, were trying to purchase sustenance from vendors. Spotting the experienced litigants was easy – they were the ones come prepared with food packets, standing to the side and munching calmly. The man frying bhajia had drawn a large hungry crowd. No wonder, thought Dina, the aroma was delicious. Next to him, there was pineapple chilling on a large slab of ice. She admired the neatly serrated round slices, watching the woman notch the fruit with her long, sharp knife to remove the eyes.

Central to the activity outside the courthouse were the typists. They sat cross-legged in their stalls before majestic Underwoods as though at a shrine, banging out documents for the waiting plaintiffs and petitioners. On sale was legal-sized paper, paperclips, file folders, crimson cloth ribbon to secure the typed briefs, blue and red pencils, pens, and ink.

Black-jacketed members of the legal profession prowled among the crowds, hunting for cases. Dina avoided them carefully, deciding to first look around the courthouse compound. 'No, thank you,' she repeated to those who offered their help.

Nearer the main building, the crowds grew dense, and an overwhelming sense of chaos hung over the area. People were surging in and out through the entranceway, those inside gesticulating frantically to their contacts in the compound, others on the outside yelling to the insiders to come out. Every now and then someone dropped their precious documents, and in trying to retrieve them, set off a scrimmage during which other things like hankies, chappals, caps, dupattas were lost.

While one great surge was flowing inwards, Dina allowed herself to be carried along. She found herself in a corridor overlooking the compound. Here, too, people were in perpetual motion, pouring into or out of overbrimming courtrooms, up and down the stairs, as though an epidemic of disorientation had overcome everyone. The rooms and hallways resounded in a constant din of voices. Sometimes it was a steady buzz with intermittent flashes of clamour. Dina wondered how anyone could follow the legal arguments.

She stood awhile in a doorway where a case appeared to be in progress. The judge sucked the stem of his spectacles meditatively. The defence lawyer had the floor. Not a word could be heard. His precise hand movements and bulging throat tendons were the only signs that he was engaged in presenting the facts.

Occasionally, people stopped dead in their tracks in the corridor and urgently yelled out a name or a number. Sometimes the search party split up and dashed off in various directions with that name or number on their lips. Could something have gone wrong in the judicial system, wondered Dina, a strike, perhaps? Maybe the peons and clerks and secretaries had phoned in sick, thus plunging the courthouse into this mad muddle.

She decided to closely follow one family who seemed to know what they were doing. She ran where they ran, she listened to what they said, she followed the gaze of their eyes. And after careful observation, she began to see a pattern emerge from the turmoil and disorder. Just like working with a new dress, she thought. Paper patterns also seemed haphazard, till they were systematically pieced together.

Now she was able to realize that all of the frantic commotion was part of a normal day at the courthouse. The stampeding crowds in the corridors, for example, were merely trying to find the notice board displaying their case number with the room location where the case would be heard. The groups huddling suspiciously in dark corners were middlemen negotiating bribes. The ones yelling out names were lawyers looking for their clients, or vice versa, because their cases were about to come up. After waiting for months, and sometimes years, the litigants' frenzy was understandable. Nothing would have been more devastating than to have the bench reschedule the hearing because the solicitor had chosen that crucial moment to go to the toilet, or for a cup of tea, without informing the clerk.

Once Dina had traced the filament of order within the confusion, she felt more confident. She returned outside to the compound and inspected the lawyers for hire. Some were displaying handwritten signs listing their services and specialities: DIVORCE CASES HANDLED HERE; WILLS AND PROBATES; KIDNEY SALES ARRANGED; DEPOSITIONS DRAFTED WITH QUICKNESS & CLARITY IN GOOD ENGLISH.

Others preferred to call out their offerings like vendors in the marketplace: 'True copies, five rupees only! Affidavits, fifteen rupees! All cases, all offences, low rates!'

She stopped by one whose billboard stated, at the top of the menu: RENT ACT DISPUTES – RS. 500 ONLY. As she was preparing to speak to him, a horde of them, sensing an opportunity, descended on her, their black jackets flapping. Many of these barely passed for black, the dye having faded to grey in the wash.

The lawyers jostled for her attention but maintained their dignity by keeping the contest impersonal. The professional rivalry did not show on their faces; there was not a frown or a cross word among them. Each seemed oblivious to the others' presence while pleading to be considered.

One got in front of the rest and thrust his law credentials under her face. 'Please, O madam! Look at this – genuine degree from good university! Lots of crooked fellows are pretending to be lawyers! Whoever you pick, be careful, always remember to check the qualifications!'

'Special offer!' yelled a man from the rear of the pack. 'No extra charges for typing of documents – all inclusive in one low fee!'

They had her completely surrounded. Harried by the unwanted attention, she tried to extricate herself from the melee. 'Excuse me please, I am –'

'What are the charges, madam?' shouted someone standing on his toes to be seen. 'I can handle criminal and civil!'

Specks of his spit landed on her glasses and cheeks. She flinched, and tried again to free herself. Then, in the crush, a hand squeezed her bottom, while another passed neatly over her breast.

'You rogues! You shameless rascals!' She struck out with her elbows, and managed to kick a shin or two before they scattered. She wished she had her pagoda parasol with her – what a lesson she would teach them.

Her hands were shaking, and she had to concentrate hard to place one foot in front of the other without losing her step. She retreated to a less crowded part of the compound, at the side of the building. Devoid of lawyers, the area was quiet. Wooden benches lined the compound railing. People were resting on the grass, taking naps with their sandals under their heads for safekeeping and for pillows. Others were eating from shiny stainless steel tiffin boxes. A mother peeled a chickoo with a penknife and fed the sweet brown fruit to her child. Music from a soft transistor radio buzzed like a dragonfly through the hot afternoon.

In this tranquil setting, on a broken bench, sat a man gazing up into a mango tree. Three little boys were throwing stones at the hard green fruit while their parents dozed on the lawn. Their efforts managed to dislodge one mango. They took bites and passed it around, the tart raw flesh making their mouths shrink. Shuddering with delight, eyes tightly shut, they clenched their teeth to savour its astringent pleasures.

The man on the broken bench smiled and nodded, relishing memories evoked by the children. His shirt pocket bulged with pens clipped inside a special plastic case. At his feet was a cardboard rectangle, about fifteen inches by ten, propped up with a brick.

Curious, Dina went closer and read the inscription on the board: Vasantrao Valmik – B.A., LL.B. Strange, she thought, that he should be content to sit here passively if he was a lawyer. And without so much as a black jacket, making no effort to obtain business.

'Madam, on behalf of my profession, I would like to apologize for that disgraceful display near the entrance,' said Mr. Valmik.

'Thank you,' said Dina.

'No, please, I must thank you for accepting the apology. It was shameful, the way they mobbed you. I saw it all from here.' He uncrossed his legs, and his toe nudged the cardboard sign, making it collapse. He straightened it and adjusted the supporting brick.

'From my seat here on the bench, there is much that I observe every day. And most of it makes me despair. But what else to expect, when judgement has fled to brutish beasts, and the country's leaders have exchanged wisdom and good governance for cowardice and self-aggrandizement? Our society is decaying from the top downwards.'

He shifted to the edge of the ramshackle bench, making room for her on the less broken part of it. 'Please, do sit down.'

Dina accepted, impressed by his speech and manners. She felt he was out of place in these surroundings. A tastefully appointed office with a mahogany desk leather-upholstered chair, and well-stocked bookcases would have better suited him. 'On this side of the courthouse everything is so calm,' she said.

'Yes, isn't it nice? Families relaxing peacefully, passing the time till the Wheels of Justice grind out their cases. Who would believe that this beautiful locale is really the shabby theatre for rancour and revenge, the splintered stage where tragedies and farces are played out? Out here it looks more like a picnic ground than a battlefield. A few months ago I even witnessed a woman going into labour and giving birth right here, most happily. She didn't want to go to hospital, didn't want any more postponements of her case. She was my client. We won.'

'So you are also a practising lawyer?'

'Yes, indeed,' he pointed to the sign. 'Fully qualified. But once upon a time, many years ago, when I was in college, in First Year Arts, my friends used to say I didn't need to study, that I was already an LL.B.'

'How was that?'

'Lord of the Last Bench,' said Mr. Valmik, smiling. 'They gave me this honorary degree because I always took the rearmost seat in the classroom – it gave me a good view of things. And I must confess, the location taught me more about human nature and justice than could be learned from the professors' lectures.'

He touched the sheaf of pens in his shirt pocket as though to make sure they were all present and accounted for. They bristled formidably in their plastic protector, like a quiverful of arrows. 'Now here I am, with a new degree: L.BB. – Lord of the Broken Bench. And my education continues.' He laughed, and Dina joined him politely. Their rickety seat shook.

'But why is it, Mr. Valmik, that you are not out in front like the other lawyers, trying to get clients?'

He directed his gaze into the mango tree and said, 'I find that kind of behaviour utterly uncouth, quite *infra dig*.' Quickly he added, 'It's below my dignity,' worried that she might construe the Latinism as a form of snobbery.

'But if you just sit here, how can you make a living?'

'My living makes itself. A little at a time. Eventually people discover me. People like you, who are disgusted with those legal louts and tawdry touts. Of course, they are not all bad characters – just desperate for work.' He waved genially at a passing court clerk and touched his pens again. 'Even if I had the temperament for vulgar conduct, my vocal disability would not let me compete in that loud contest. You see, I have a serious throat impediment. If I raise my voice, I lose it altogether.'

'Oh, how unfortunate.'

'No, not really,' Mr. Valmik reassured her. He considered genuine sympathy a precious commodity, and hated to see it squandered. 'No, it matters not a jot to me. There is not much call these days for lawyers who can make their voices ring out sonorously through the courtroom, holding judge and jury spellbound in webs of brilliant oratory.' He chuckled. 'No demand here for a Clarence Darrow – there are no more Scopes Monkey Trials taking place. Although monkeys there are in plenty, in every courtroom, willing to perform for bananas and peanuts.'

He sighed heavily, and his sarcasm was displaced by grief. 'What are we to say, madam, what are we to think about the state of this nation? When the highest court in the land turns the Prime Minister's guilt into innocence, then all this' – he indicated the imposing stone edifice – 'this becomes a museum of cheap tricks, rather than the living, breathing law that strengthens the sinews of society.'

Touched by the weight of his anguish, Dina asked, 'Why did the Supreme Court do that?'

'Who knows why, madam. Why is there disease and starvation and suffering? We can only answer the how and the where and the when of it. The Prime Minister cheats in the election, and the relevant law is promptly modified. *Ergo*, she is not guilty. We poor mortals have to accept that bygone events are beyond our clutch, while the Prime Minister performs juggling acts with time past.'

Mr. Valmik stopped suddenly, realizing that he was rambling while a potential client sat beside him. 'But what about your case, madam? You seem like a veteran of this institution.'

'No, I've never been to court before.'

'Ah, then you have led a blessed life,' he murmured. 'I don't want to be inquisitive, but is there need for a lawyer?'

'Yes, it's concerning my flat. The trouble started nineteen years ago, after my husband passed away.' She told him everything, starting with the landlord's first notice a few months after Rustom's death on their third wedding anniversary, and about the tailors, the paying guest, the rent-collector's continuing harassment, the goondas' threats, Beggarmaster's protection, and Beggarmaster's death.

Mr. Valmik steepled his fingertips and listened. He did not move once, not even to caress his beloved pens. She marvelled at how carefully he attended – almost as carefully as he spoke.

She finished, and he put his hands down. Then he said in his soft voice, which was beginning to turn hoarse, 'It's a very difficult situation. You know, madam, sometimes it may appear expeditious to act *ex curia*.' Seeing her quizzical, he added, 'That is, out of court. But in the end it leads to more problems. True, there are goondas galore in the wilderness of our time. After all, this is a Goonda Raj. So who can blame you for taking that route? Who would want to enter the soiled Temple of Justice, wherein lies the corpse of Justice, slain by her very guardians? And now her killers make mock of the sacred process, selling replicas of her blind virtue to the highest bidder.'

Dina began to wish Mr. Valmik would stop talking in this high-flown manner. It had been entertaining for a while but was rapidly becoming wearisome. How people loved to make speeches, she thought. Bombast and rhetoric infected the nation, from ministers to lawyers, rent-collectors to hair-collectors.

'So are you saying there is no hope?' she interrupted him.

'There is always hope – hope enough to balance our despair. Or we would be lost.'

Now he took out a writing pad from his briefcase, lovingly selected a pen from the well-stocked pocket, and began making notes. 'Perhaps the ghost of Justice is still wandering around, willing to help us. If a decent judge hears our petition and grants the injunction, you will be safe till the case is tried. Your name, madam?'

'Mrs. Dalal. Dina Dalal. But how much do you charge?'

'Whatever you can afford to pay. We'll worry later about that.' He jotted the landlord's name and office address, and relevant details about the case history. 'My advice to you is, don't leave the flat unoccupied. Possession is nine-tenths of the law. And goondas are basically cowards. Is it possible to have someone, relatives or friends, stay with you?'

'There is no one.'

'Yes, never is, is there? Forgive my question.' He paused, then broke into a fearful coughing fit. 'Excuse me,' he croaked, 'I think I have exceeded my throat's quota of conversation.'

'My goodness,' said Dina, 'it sounds really bad.'

'And this is after treatment,' he said, in a tone that sounded like bragging. 'You should have heard me a year ago. All I could do was squeak like a mouse.'

'But what was it that damaged your throat so badly? Were you in an accident or something?'

'In a manner of speaking,' he sighed. 'After all, our lives are but a sequence of accidents – a clanking chain of chance events. A string of choices, casual or deliberate, which add up to that one big calamity we call life.'

Here he goes again, she thought. But his words did ring true. She tested them against her own experience. Random events controlled everything: her father's death, when she was twelve. And the tailors' entire lives. And Maneck – one minute coming back, next minute off to Dubai. She would probably never see him again, or Ishvar and Om. They came from nowhere into her life, and had vanished into nowhere.

Mr. Valmik, meanwhile, to answer her question, stroked his precious pens and began his story. Dina felt there was something slightly obscene about this habit of his. Still, touching pens was preferable to touching crotches, the way some men did, to push their things to left or right, or for no reason at all.

His voice was guttural as he told of the enthusiastic young student at law college whose promise was recognized early by his teachers, but who, after being called to the bar, craved peace and solitude, and found it in proofreading. 'For twenty-five years I enjoyed the civilized companionship of words. Till one day, when my eyes turned allergic, and my world turned upside down.'

The rasping noises from his throat were so distorted that Dina was having trouble understanding him. But her ears became attuned to the rare timbres and bizarre frequencies. She realized that although Mr. Valmik depicted life as a sequence of accidents, there was nothing accidental about his expert narration. His sentences poured out like perfect seams, holding the garment of his story together without calling attention to the stitches. Was he aware of ordering the events for her? Perhaps not – perhaps the very act of telling created a natural design. Perhaps it was a knack that humans had, for cleaning up their untidy existences – a hidden survival weapon, like antibodies in the bloodstream.

As he spoke, he absently pulled out a fountain pen, unscrewed the cap, and put the nib to his nose. She watched, perplexed, as each nostril in turn was pressed shut and the ink fragrance inhaled deeply.

Fortified by his fix of Royal Blue, he continued, 'Now I had to contend with the noisy world of morcha productions and protest marches, in order to put food in the tummy-tum-tum. Slogan-making and slogan-shouting became my new profession. And thus began the devastation of my vocal cords.'

The lawyer's tale reminded her of her languishing patchwork quilt. Om's wedding gift. And Mr. Valmik had his own fragments to fashion his oral quilt, which he was now reciting for her benefit. Like a conjuror pulling an endless chain of silk scarves from his mouth.

'Ultimately, it was just another chance event – my finding the sergeant-major when I did. Shouting was second nature to him. He shouted even when there was no need. His rawhide throat thrived on it, and I was finally able to give mine a rest.'

He stopped to offer her a cough lozenge; she declined. He popped one in his own mouth. 'Such plans I had, to expand, to open branch offices in every big city. I envisioned buying a helicopter and training a unit of Flying Sloganeers. Wherever there was a strike or unrest, whenever a protest march was required, one phone call and my men would descend from the sky, banners at the ready.'

The entrepreneurial gleam in his eye faded with reluctance. 'Unfortunately, during this Emergency, morchas and demonstrations are banned by the government. So for the past year I have sat on this broken bench, armed with my law degree. The circle is completed.'

He crunched up the half-sucked lozenge, having run out of patience with shifting it from cheek to cheek. 'How much I have lost, in describing the circle. Ambition, solitude, words, eyesight, vocal cords. In fact, that is the central theme of my life story – loss. But isn't it the same with all life stories? Loss is essential. Loss is part and parcel of that necessary calamity called life.'

She nodded, not quite convinced.

'Mind you, I'm not complaining. Thanks to some inexplicable universal guiding force, it is always the worthless things we lose – slough off, like a moulting snake. Losing, and losing again, is the very basis of the life process, till all we are left with is the bare essence of human existence.'

Now Dina grew extremely impatient with Mr. Valmik. This last bit sounded like a lot of tiresome nonsense. 'The snake has a brand-new skin underneath,' she cut him off. 'I would prefer not to lose my flat, unless a new one will rise in its place.'

Mr. Valmik looked as though he had been struck in his diaphragm. But he recovered quickly and smiled, appreciating her argument. 'Very good. Very good indeed, Mrs. Dalal. That was a poor example I gave. And you caught me. Very good. And a good sense of humour too. One of the drawbacks of my profession is the total lack of humour. The Law is a grim, unsmiling thing. Not Justice, though. Justice is witty and whimsical and kind and caring.'

He picked up his signboard and packed it away, stowing the brick under the bench till he should need it again. He dusted its red powder off his hands and declaimed, 'I will arise and go now, and go to write this plea, and a convincing petition build, of words and passion made.'

The strange diction made her regard Mr. Valmik curiously. She wondered if she had chosen the right lawyer after all.

'Don't mind me,' he said. 'I'm inspired by the poet Yeats. I find his words especially relevant during this shameful Emergency. You know – things falling apart, centre not holding, anarchy loosed upon the world, and all that sort of thing.'

'Yes,' said Dina. 'And everything ends badly.'

'Ah,' said Mr. Valmik. 'Now that is too pessimistic for Mr. Yeats. He could never have written that line. But please come to my office, day after tomorrow, and I will bring you up to date.'

'Office? Where?'

'Right here,' he laughed. 'This broken bench is my office.' He tenderly patted the pen he had reinserted into the plastic sheath. 'Mrs. Dalal, I must thank you for listening to my story. Not many people have the time these days to indulge me. The last opportunity I had was a year ago, with a college student. We were both on a very long train journey. Thank you again.'

'You're welcome, Mr. Valmik.'

After he left, a fresh group of youngsters became engrossed in plundering the mango tree's sparse green treasures. Their effort and excite-

THE CIRCLE IS COMPLETED

ment were amusing to observe. Dina sat for a few minutes longer before starting back to her flat.

====

A police sergeant and constable were joined in argument with two men over the question of the padlock on the front door. The scene had been rehearsed frequently in Dina's mind; she felt no sense of crisis. One phase of life was concluding, another beginning. Time for the latest instalment, she thought. A new patch in the quilt.

She recognized the two men, the landlord's goondas. Their hands looked so different, she realized, thanks to Beggarmaster. The fingers were bent in grotesque ways, misshapen, of incongruous lengths, as in a child's drawing. The man was dead but his work lived on.

'What is it, what do you want here?' she bluffed.

'Sergeant Kesar, madam,' he said, plucking his thumbs out of his belt where he had stuck them aggressively while addressing the goondas. 'Very sorry for the trouble. There is an eviction order for this flat.'

'You can't do that. I've just come from my lawyer, he is applying for a court injunction.'

The bald goonda grinned. 'Sorry, sister, we were first.'

'What do you mean, first?' She appealed to Sergeant Kesar: 'It's not a race or something, I have a right to go to court.'

He shook his head sadly; he had a long professional acquaintance with the goondas, and was waiting for the day when they could be put away in the lockup. 'Actually speaking, madam, there is nothing I can do. Sometimes the law works just like a lemon-and-spoon race. The eviction has to take place. You can appeal later.'

'I might as well bang my head against a brick wall.'

The goondas agreed with her, nodding sympathetically. 'Courts are useless. Arguments and adjournments, testimony and evidence. Takes forever. All those stupid things are unnecessary under the Emergency.' His partner rattled the padlock, reminding the law to get a move on.

'Please, madam,' said Sergeant Kesar, 'will you open it now?'

'If I refuse?'

'Then I would have to break the lock,' he said sorrowfully.

'And what will happen after I open it?'

'The flat will be emptied out,' he murmured, shame making his words indistinct.

'What?'

'Emptied out,' he repeated a little louder. 'Your flat will be emptied out.'

'Thrown out on the pavement? Why? Why do they behave like animals? At least give me a day or two so I can make arrangements.'

'Actually speaking, madam, that's up to the landlord.'

'Time has run out,' said the bald goonda. 'As the landlord's agents, we cannot allow any delaying tactics.'

Sergeant Kesar turned to Dina. 'Don't worry, madam, your furniture will be safe. I will make sure they treat everything carefully. My constable will guard it. If you like, I can send him to hire a truck for you.'

She found the key in her purse and unlocked the door. The goondas tried to rush in, as though it might spring shut again, but were foiled by Sergeant Kesar's arm. Like a traffic policeman, he held it up to block them.

'After you, madam,' he bowed, following behind.

The first things they saw were the tailors' cardboard cartons stacked in a corner of the verandah. The goondas started to take them out.

'Those are not my boxes, I don't want them,' Dina burst out, directing her anger at the absent ones – *they* had abandoned her, *they* had left her to face this alone.

'Not yours? Good, then we'll take the boxes.'

She put away clothes and knickknacks into drawers and cupboards, trying to stay a few steps ahead of the goondas as they began to carry the furniture outside. Sergeant Kesar waddled about after her, anxious to help. 'Have you decided where to transport everything, madam?'

'I'll go to Vishram and phone my brother. He will be able to send his office truck.'

'Okay, I'll keep an eye on those two. Anything else I can do while you are gone, madam?'

'Are you allowed to help a criminal?'

He shook his head sadly. 'Actually speaking, madam, the criminals are those two, and the landlord.'

'And yet I am being thrown out.'

'That's the crazy world we live in. If I did not have a family to feed, you think I would do this job? Especially after the ulcers it has given me? Since the Emergency began, my ulcers began. At first I thought it was just stomach acidity. But doctor has confirmed the diagnosis, I have to be operated soon.'

'I am very sorry to hear that.' She found the screwdriver on the kitchen shelf and handed it to him. 'If you like, you can remove the nameplate for me from the front door.'

He seized the tool with joy. 'Oh, most certainly. I will be happy to, madam.' He went off, his guilt a tiny bit assuaged, and was soon huffing and puffing over the tarnished brass plate, sweating as he wrestled with the screws.

'What?' screamed Nusswan through the telephone. 'Evicted? You call me after the furniture is on the pavement? Digging a well when the house is on fire?'

'It happened suddenly. Can you send your truck or not?'

'What choice do I have? It's my duty. Who else will help you if I don't?'

The men had almost finished when she returned to the flat. Pots and pans and the stove from the kitchen were the last to be carried out. The constable stood guard over all of it on the footpath. Her household, stacked in this manner, did not seem like very much, she thought, did not seem capable of filling the three rooms, or the twenty-one years of her life spent in them.

Sergeant Kesar was relieved that rescue was on the way. 'You are so fortunate, madam, at least you have somewhere to go. Daily I see cases where people end up making the pavement their home. Lying there exhausted, lost, defeated. The amazing thing is how quickly they learn to use cardboard and plastic and newspaper.'

He requested Dina to inspect the rooms before handing over custody of the flat. 'Are you sure you don't want the stuff on the verandah?' he whispered.

'It's not mine – garbage, as far as I care.'

'You see, madam, whatever is left here automatically becomes the property of the landlord.'

'That's us,' said the goondas, grabbing the boxes. They shut the front door and slipped a fresh padlock on the hasp. Sergeant Kesar completed the formalities; cyclostyled documents were signed in triplicate.

Then the two goondas turned their attention to the boxes, eager to examine their unexpected bonus. 'Wait a second,' said the bald one, lifting out a handful of black tresses. 'What rubbish is this?'

'Why rubbish?' laughed his partner. 'Hair is just what you need.'

The bald one was not amused. 'See what's in the other box.'

Sergeant Kesar watched them for a minute, then hitched his thumbs in his belt. He was ready for action. He remembered the murders of the two beggars – the infamous Case of the Hair-Hungry Homicide. Here was the chance he was waiting for. He unbuttoned the flap of his holster, just in case, and whispered instructions to the constable.

'Excuse me,' he said politely to the goondas. 'You are both under arrest for murder.'

They laughed. 'Heh-heh, Sergeant Kesar is becoming a joker.' When their wrists were smartly handcuffed by the constable, they protested that the joke had gone too far. 'What are you talking about? We haven't murdered anybody!'

'Actually speaking, you have: two old beggars. This is a perfect prima facie case. The murdered beggars' hair was chopped off and stolen. Now the hair is in your possession. It tells the whole story.'

'But we just found it here! You saw us open the box!'

'Actually speaking, I didn't see anything.'

'You have no evidence of murder! How do you know it's the same hair?'

'Don't worry about that. As you were saying earlier, silly things like evidence are not necessary anymore. Nowadays, we have nice things like the Emergency and MISA.'

'What's MISA?' asked Dina.

'Maintenance of Internal Security Act, madam. Very convenient. Allows detention without trial, up to two years. Extensions also available on request.' He smiled sweetly and turned to the goondas again. 'I almost forgot to tell you – you have the right to remain silent, but if you do, my boys at the station will process your bones to help you confess.'

The two were made to squat with their handcuffed hands draped over their heads. Sergeant Kesar was not yet ready to take them in. He stuffed the hair back in the box. 'Exhibit A,' he said to Dina. 'Don't worry, madam, I'm waiting here till your truck comes. Who knows how many of your possessions will vanish if I leave. Once you are safely on your way, I'll take these dogs to the station.'

'Thank you very much,' said Dina.

'No, thank you. You have made my day.' He checked if his holster flap was secure. 'You like Clint Eastwood films, madam? *Dirty Harry*?'

'I've never seen them. Are they good?'

'Very thrilling. Highly action-packed dramas.' He added with a wistful smile, 'Dirty Harry is a top-notch detective. He delivers justice even when the law makes it impossible.' Lowering to a whisper, he asked, 'By the way, madam, how did the hair come to your verandah?'

'I'm not sure exactly. There were two tailors working for me, and they had a friend, a hair-collector, and – I'm not sure, they've all disappeared.'

'Lots of people have disappeared in the Emergency,' he said, shaking his head. 'But you know, you may have been unknowingly mixed up with homicidal maniacs. Thank your stars, madam, that you escaped unharmed.'

'But then, these two goondas are not really guilty, are they?'

'Actually speaking, they are – of other crimes. They definitely deserve jail, madam. It's like debit and credit, double-entry bookkeeping. In a way, Dirty Harry is also an accountant. The final balance is what's important to him.'

She nodded, watching a flock of crows rooting in the congealed gutter across the street. They jostled and squabbled over tidbits. Then the truck arrived.

'You have children?' she asked Sergeant Kesar, while Nusswan's men loaded the furniture.

'Oh yes,' he said proudly, pleased by her question. 'Two daughters. One is five years, other is nine.'

'They go to school?'

'Oh yes. The older one is taking sitar lessons also, once a week after school. Very expensive, but I do overtime for her sake. Children are our only treasure, no?'

When the truck was ready, she climbed in beside the driver and thanked Sergeant Kesar again for his help. 'My pleasure,' he said. 'All the best, madam.'

'The same to you. I hope your ulcer operation goes well.'

The driver took a while to reverse the truck, for the way was narrow. Emerging through the gate, she saw Ibrahim behind the pillar, holding out his tin can to passersby.

As the truck passed, he tried to lift his hand to his fez in farewell. But the pain in his shoulder stopped him. He tugged at the collar of his sherwani instead, and waved.

'Sorry I'm late,' said Nusswan, kissing Ruby's cheek and then hugging his sister. 'These never-ending meetings.' He rubbed his brow. 'The truck brought everything safely?'

'Yes, thank you,' said Dina.

'I suppose your beggars and tailors and paying guest have all wished you Au Revoir.' He laughed at his joke.

'Stop it, Nusswan,' said Ruby. 'Be nice to her, she has been through a lot.'

'I'm only teasing. I can't tell you how happy I am that Dina is back.' His voice grew softer, and filled with emotion. 'For years and years I have prayed to God to bring you home. It hurt me so much, you choosing to live alone. In the end, only family will be of help – when the rest of the world turns its back on you.'

He swallowed a lump in his throat, and Dina was touched. She helped Ruby set the table, fetching the water jug and glasses. They were in their usual place in the sideboard. Nothing had changed here in these many years, thought Dina.

'No more humiliation with tailors or beggars,' said Nusswan. 'No need for them, you don't have to worry about money anymore. Just make yourself useful in the house – that's all I ask.'

'Nusswan!' scolded Ruby. 'Poor Dina always used to help me. One thing she is not is lazy.'

'I know, I know,' he chuckled. 'Stubborn is what she is, not lazy.'

After dinner, they examined the household effects from the flat. Nusswan was appalled by it. 'Where did you find this junk?'

She shrugged. A verbal answer was not always necessary. That was one useful thing she had learned from Maneck.

'Well, there is no room for it here. Look at that ugly little dining table. And that sofa must be from Bawa Adam's time.' He promised to call a jaripuranawalla and dispose it of within a few days.

She did not argue with him. She did not plead for the memories which fleshed the ribs of her meagre belongings.

Nusswan wondered about the change in his sister. Dina was too docile, far too meek and quiet, not like her old self at all. It made him a little uneasy. Could she be pretending? Was it part of some plan which she would spring when he least expected it?

They transferred the contents of her chest of drawers into the wardrobe standing in her old room. 'It's been waiting for you,' confided Ruby. 'Your father's cupboard. I'm really happy you've come back.'

Dina smiled. She removed the cover from the mattress and stored it in the bottom of the wardrobe. In its place she draped her own quilt, folded, at the foot of the bed.

'That is beautiful!' said Ruby, spreading it out to admire. 'Absolutely gorgeous! But what happened in that one corner, why the gap?'

'I ran out of cloth.'

'What a pity.' She thought for a moment. 'You know, I have some lovely material, it will provide the perfect finishing touch. You can complete it with that.'

'Thank you.' But Dina had already decided there was nothing further to add.

At night in bed, she covered herself with the quilt and took to recounting the abundance of events in the tightly knit family of patches, the fragments that she had fashioned with needle, thread, and affection. If she stumbled along the way, the quilt nudged her forward. The streetlight through the open window was just bright enough to identify the motley of its making. Her bedtime story.

Once, after midnight, Nusswan and Ruby knocked on the door and barged in while she was halfway through the narrative. 'Dina? Do you need something?'

'No.'

'Are you okay?'

'Of course I am.'

'We heard voices,' said Ruby. 'We thought you were talking in your sleep, having a bad dream or something.'

Then Dina knew she had slipped from a silent recitation into reading aloud. 'I was only saying my prayers. Sorry I disturbed you.'

'It's all right,' said Nusswan. 'But I couldn't recognize the passage at all. You better take some lessons from Dustoor Daab-Chaab's successor at the fire-temple.' They laughed at his joke and returned to bed.

He whispered to Ruby, 'Remember how she was, after Rustom's death? How she would call out his name almost every night?'

'Yes, but that was a long time ago. Why should she still be upset about that?'

'Maybe she never got over it.'

'Yes. Maybe you never recover from certain things.'

In her room, Dina folded up the quilt. The patchwork had transformed her silence into unbidden words; it had to be locked away now in the wardrobe. She was frightened of the strange magic it worked on her mind, frightened of where its terrain was leading her. She did not want to cross that border permanently.

Nusswan gave up teasing Dina because it was no fun if she did not retaliate. There were times when he sat alone in his room, recalling the headstrong, indomitable sister, and regretted her fading. Well, he sighed to himself, that was what life did to those who refused to learn its lessons: it beat them down and broke their spirit. But at least her days of endless toil were behind her. Now she would be cared for, provided for by her own family.

Not long afterwards, the servant who came in the mornings to sweep and swab, and dust the furniture was dismissed. 'Bloody woman wanted more money,' Nusswan offered by way of explanation. 'Saying there was an extra person in the house, creating more work for her broom and mop. The excuses these rascals come up with.'

Dina took the hint and assumed the chores. She absorbed everything like a capacious sponge. During her private moments she wrung herself out and then was ready to blot up more.

Ruby was gone most of the day now. But before leaving, she always inquired if she could help. Dina encouraged her to run along, preferring to be alone.

'It's thanks to Dina that I am at last able to use my Willingdon Club membership,' she told Nusswan in the evening. 'Previously the fees were all going to waste.'

'Dina is one in a million,' he agreed. 'I have always said that. We had many fights and arguments, right, Dina? Especially about marriage. But I've always admired your strength and determination. I'll never forget how bravely you behaved when poor Rustom passed away on your third anniversary.'

'Nusswan! Do you have to remind us at dinner and upset poor Dina?'

'Sorry, very sorry.' He obediently changed the topic, to the Emergency. 'Problem is, the excitement has gone out of it. The initial fear which disciplined people, made them punctual and hardworking – that fear is gone. Government should do something to give a boost to the programme.'

The subject of marriage was no longer brought up in their dinner conversations. At forty-three the matter was exhausted and the goods quite shopworn, he confided to Ruby.

On Sunday evenings they played cards. 'Come on, everybody,' Nusswan summoned them promptly at five o'clock. 'Time for cards.'

He observed the session religiously. It breathed a feeble reality into his dream of a close family. Sometimes, if a visiting friend made a fourth, they played bridge. More often, though, it was just the three of them, and Nusswan steered the hours through round after round of rummy, doggedly enthusiastic in his pursuit of familial happiness.

'Did you know that playing cards originated in India?' he asked.

'Really?' said Ruby. Such items from Nusswan always impressed her very much.

'Oh yes, and so did chess. In fact, the theory is that playing cards were derived from chess. And they did not make their way to Europe till the thirteenth century, via the Middle East.'

'Imagine that,' said Ruby.

He rearranged his hand, discarded a card face-down and announced, 'Rummy!'

After presenting his completed sequences, he analysed the errors the others had made. 'You should never have thrown away the knave of hearts,' he told Dina. 'That's why you lost.'

'I took a chance.'

He gathered up the cards and started shuffling. 'Okay, whose deal is it?'

'Mine,' said Dina, and accepted the deck.

Epilogue: 1984

IT WAS MORNING when the gulf flight bringing Maneck home landed in the capital after a delayed departure. He had tried to sleep on the plane but the annoying flicker of a movie being shown in the economy cabin kept buzzing before his eyelids like malfunctioning fluorescent lights. Bleary-eyed, he stood in line for customs inspection.

An airport expansion scheme was in progress, and the passengers were packed into a temporary corrugated-iron structure. Construction was just beginning when he had left for Dubai eight years ago, he remembered. Waves of heat ricocheted off the shimmering sun-soaked metal, buffeting the crowds. The smell of sweat, cigarette smoke, stale perfume, and disinfectant roamed the air. People fanned themselves with passports and customs declaration forms. Someone fainted. Two peons tried to revive the man by arranging him in the stream of a customs officer's table fan. Water was sent for.

The baggage searches resumed after the interruption. A passenger behind Maneck grumbled about the slowness, and Maneck shrugged his shoulders: 'Maybe they received a tip that a big smuggler is coming today from Dubai.'

'No, it's like this all the time,' said the man. 'With all flights from the Middle East. What they are looking for is jewellery, gold biscuits, electronic goods.' He explained that customs had become more zealous because of a recent government directive, which offered special bonuses – a percentage of each officer's seizures. 'So they are harassing us more than ever now.'

'All my carefully folded saris will get crumpled,' complained the man's wife.

The officer looking through Maneck's suitcase pushed his fingers under the clothes and felt about. Maneck wondered if there would be a penalty for setting a mousetrap inside one's luggage. After much groping, the officer withdrew his hands and let him through grudgingly.

Maneck squeezed the bag shut, rushed outside to a taxi and asked to be driven to the railway station. The driver was unwilling to make the journey. 'It's right in the middle of the rioting. Too dangerous.'

'What rioting?'

'Don't you know? People are being beaten and butchered and burnt alive.'

Rather than argue with him, Maneck tried elsewhere. But every taxi driver he approached refused the fare with the same warning. Some advised him to check into a hotel near the airport till things quietened.

In frustration, he decided to offer an incentive to the next one. 'You'll get double of what is on the meter, okay? I have to get home, my father has passed away. If I miss the train I will miss my father's funeral.'

'It's not the meter I am worried about, sahab. Your life and mine are worth much more. But get in, I'll try my best.' He reached for the meter, flipping the FOR HIRE indicator upside-down with a clang.

The taxi extricated itself from the swarm of vehicles that throttled the airport lanes, and soon they were on the highway. In between checking for traffic, the driver observed his passenger through the rearview mirror. Maneck could feel the man's eyes on him.

'You should think about shaving off your beard, sahab,' the driver spoke. 'You might be mistaken for a Sikh.'

Maneck was very proud of his beard; and so what if people thought he was a Sikh? He had started growing it two years ago, grooming it carefully to its present state. 'How can I be mistaken for a Sikh? I don't have a turban.'

'Lots of Sikhs don't wear turban, sahab. But I think clean-shaven would be much safer for you.'

'Safer? Meaning what?'

'You are saying you don't know? Sikhs are the ones being massacred in the riots. For three days they have been burning Sikh shops and homes, chopping up Sikh boys and men. And the police are just running about here and there, pretending to protect the neighbourhoods.'

He pulled over to the extreme left of the road as a convoy of army lorries approached the taxi from behind. He shouted to Maneck over his shoulder, over the thunder of the vehicles. 'That's the Border Security Force! The newspaper said it was being sent in today!'

The convoy passed, and his voice returned to normal. 'Our best soldiers, the BSF. First line of defence against enemy invasion. Now they must guard borderlines within our cities. How shameful for the whole country.'

'But why Sikhs only?'

'Sahab?'

'You said only Sikhs are being attacked.'

The driver gazed into the rearview mirror with disbelief. Was the passenger feigning ignorance? He decided the question was indeed asked in earnest. 'It started when the Prime Minister was killed three days ago. She was shot by her Sikh bodyguards. So this is supposed to be revenge.'

Now he turned and looked directly at Maneck. 'Where have you been, sahab, you didn't hear anything of what has happened?'

'I knew about the assassination but not the riots.' He studied the cracks in the vinyl seat in front of him and the driver's frayed collar visible above the seatback. Small boils, not yet ready to burst, shone upon the man's neck. 'I've been very busy, trying to come back in time for my father's funeral.'

'Yes,' said the driver sympathetically. 'Must be very difficult for you.' He swerved to avoid a dog in the road, a yellow mongrel, mangy and skeletal.

Maneck glanced through the rear window to see if the animal made it to safety. A lorry behind them squashed it. 'The problem is, I've been out of the country for eight years,' he offered as a further excuse.

'That's a very long time, sahab. That means you left before the Emergency ended – before the elections. Of course, for ordinary people, nothing has changed. Government still keeps breaking poor people's homes and jhopadpattis. In villages, they say they will dig wells only if so many sterilizations are done. They tell farmers they will get fertilizer only after nussbandhi is performed. Living each day is to face one emergency or another.' He beeped a warning to someone trudging along the shoulder. 'You heard about the attack on the Golden Temple, no?'

'Yes. Things like that are hard to miss,' said Maneck. Where did the fellow think he was returning from, the moon? In the silence that followed, he realized that in fact he knew very little about the years he had been away. He wondered what other tragedies and farces had unfolded in the country while he was supervising the refrigeration of the hot desert air.

He encouraged the driver to keep talking: 'What's your opinion about the Golden Temple?'

The man was pleased at being asked. He turned off the highway near the outskirts of the capital. They passed the burned-out carcass of a vehicle, its wheels in the air. 'I will have to take a longer way to the station, sahab. Some roads are better avoided.' Then he came back to Maneck's question. 'The Prime Minister said Sikh terrorists were hiding inside the Golden Temple. The army's attack was only a few months ago. But the important thing to ask is how the problem started many years ago, no?'

'Yes. How?'

'Same way all her problems started. With her own mischief-making.

Just like in Sri Lanka, Kashmir, Assam, Tamil Nadu. In Punjab, she was helping one group to make trouble for state government. Afterwards the group became so powerful, fighting for separation and Khalistan, they made trouble for her only. She gave her blessing to the guns and bombs, and then these wicked, violent instruments began hitting her own government. How do they say in English – all her chickens came home for roasting, isn't it?'

'Came home to roost,' murmured Maneck.

'Yes, exactly,' said the driver. 'And then she made the problem worse and worse, telling the army to attack the Golden Temple and capture the terrorists. With tanks and what-all big guns they charged inside, like hooligans. How much damage to the shrine. It is the most sacred place for Sikhs, and everybody's feelings were hurt.'

Maneck was touched by the poignant understatement. 'She created a monster,' the driver went on, 'and the monster swallowed her. Now it swallows innocents. Such terrible butchery for three days.' His fingers clenched the steering wheel, and his voice was shaking. 'They are pouring kerosene on Sikhs and setting them on fire. They catch men, tear the hair from their faces or hack it with swords, then kill them. Whole families burnt to death in their homes.'

He drew a hand across his mouth, took a deep breath, and continued to describe the slaughter he had witnessed. 'And all this, sahab, in our nation's capital. All this while police do their shameless acting, and the politicians say the people are upset, they are just avenging their leader's murder, what can we do. This is what I say to the stinking dogs – *phthoo!*' He spat through the window.

'But I thought the Prime Minister was not much liked by the people. Why are they so upset?'

'It's true, sahab, she was not liked by ordinary people, even though she went about like a devi in a white sari. But let's suppose she was beloved – do you think ordinary people will behave in this way? Aray, it's the work of criminal gangs paid by her party. Some ministers are even helping the gangs, providing official lists of Sikh homes and businesses. Otherwise, it's not possible for the killers to work so efficiently, so accurately, in such a big city.'

They were passing through streets now where smouldering ruins and piles of rubble lined the road. Women and children sat amid the debris, dazed or weeping. The driver's face contorted, and Maneck thought it was fear. 'Don't worry,' he said. 'There will be no trouble because of my beard. If we are stopped, they'll at once know I'm a Parsi – I'll show them the sudra and kusti I am wearing.'

'Yes, but they might want to check my licence.'

'So?'

'You haven't guessed? I am a Sikh – I shaved off my beard and cut my hair two days ago. But I'm still wearing my kara.' He held up his hand, displaying the iron bangle round his wrist.

Maneck studied the driver's face, and suddenly the evidence became plain: his skin, unused to the razor's scrape, had been cut in several places. Suddenly, all the incidents narrated by the man – of mutilation and bludgeoning and decapitation, the numerous ways that mobs had of breaking bones, piercing flesh, and spilling blood – everything that Maneck had been listening to with detachment now achieved a stark reality in the razor's nicks. The coagulated specks of red on the chin and jowls might have been rivers of blood, so intense was their effect against the pale, newly shaven skin.

Maneck was nauseated, his face felt cold and sweaty. 'The bastards!' he choked. 'I hope they are all caught and hanged!'

'The real murderers will never be punished. For votes and power they play with human lives. Today it is Sikhs. Last year it was Muslims; before that, Harijans. One day, your sudra and kusti might not be enough to protect you.'

The taxi drew up to the railway station. Maneck checked the meter and counted out twice the amount from his wallet, but the driver refused to take more than the actual fare. 'Please,' said Maneck, 'please take it.' He pressed the money on him, as though that would help him survive the terror, and the driver finally accepted.

'Listen,' said Maneck, 'why don't you remove your kara and hide it for the time being?'

'It won't come off.' He held up his wrist and pulled hard at the iron bangle. 'I was planning to have it cut. But I have to find a reliable Lohar, one who won't tell the wrong people.'

'Let me try.' Maneck grasped the driver's hand, tugging and twisting the kara. It would not budge past the base of the thumb.

The driver smiled. 'Solid as a handcuff. I am manacled to my religion – a happy prisoner.'

'At least wear long sleeves, then. Cover it up, keep your wrist hidden.'

'But sometimes I have to stick my hand out, to signal my turns. Or the traffic police will catch me for bad driving.'

Maneck gave up, releasing the kara. The driver took Maneck's hand in both of his and clasped it tight. 'Go safely,' he said.

Aban Kohlah began to weep when her son arrived. How wonderful it was to see him again, she said, but why had he stayed away for eight years, was he angry about something, did he feel he was not wanted? She hugged him and patted his cheeks and stroked his hair while speaking.

'But I like your beard,' she said dutifully. 'Makes you look very handsome. You should have sent us a photo, Daddy could also have seen it. But never mind, I am sure he is watching from above.'

Maneck listened silently. Not one day had passed during his long exile that he did not think about his home and his parents. In Dubai, he had felt trapped. Trapped, he thought, as surely as that young woman he had met during one of his domestic maintenance calls to service a refrigerator. She had come to the Gulf as a maidservant because the money promised had seemed so good.

'What is it, Maneck?' pleaded Mrs. Kohlah. 'Don't you want to live here in the hills anymore – is that it? Do you find this place too dull?'

'No, it's beautiful,' he said, patting her hand absently. He could not stop wondering what had become of that maidservant. Overworked, molested repeatedly by the men of the house, locked up in her room at night, her passport confiscated, she had begged him for help, speaking in Hindi so her employer would not understand. But she had been called away from the kitchen before Maneck could say anything. Uneasy about intervening, all he had done was anonymously telephone the Indian Consulate.

How fortunate he was compared to that poor woman, he thought. Why, then, did he feel as helpless as she was, even here, at home?

And now, as his mother wept, he wished he had answers to her questions. But he was unable to explain, either to her or to himself. All he could offer were the trite, customary excuses: a demanding job, pressures at work, lack of time – a repeat of the empty words he would scribble in his annual letter to her.

'No, tell me the real reason,' she said. 'Never mind, we will talk later, after you have rested. Poor Daddy, how much he missed you, and yet he never, ever complained. But I knew that inside it was eating him up.'

'So now you are blaming the cancer on me.'

'No! I didn't mean it like that! I didn't!' His mother held his face in her hands, repeating the denial till she was certain he believed her. 'You know, Daddy once told me it was the worst day of his life when he let Brigadier Grewal persuade him that a job in the Gulf would be a good thing for you.'

They sat on the porch while she told him about the funeral arrangements for the next morning: dustoors were coming from the nearest fire-temple, which was still a considerable distance. It had been an effort to find two who were willing to perform the ceremony. Most had refused the assignment when they discovered the deceased was to be cremated, saying their services were available only to Zoroastrians bound for the Towers of Silence – never mind if it was a long trip by railway.

'How narrow-minded these people are,' she said, shaking her head. 'Of course, we are cremating because it was Daddy's wish, but what about people who cannot afford to transport the body? Would these priests deny them the prayers?'

It wasn't going to be an open-air pyre, she explained. The electric crematorium had been booked in the valley – it would be more decorous. And Daddy wasn't really specific on this point, so it didn't matter.

The General Store had remained closed since his death. She meant to reopen it next week and continue as usual. 'Are you planning to settle back here?' she ventured timidly, afraid of appearing to pry into his affairs.

'I haven't thought about it yet.'

Daylight was starting to fade about them. He watched a lizard, motionless upon the stone wall. Every now and then, its thin body shot forward like an arrow to catch a fly.

'Are you happy in Dubai? Is your job interesting?'

'It's okay.'

'Tell me more about it. You wrote that you are a manager now?'

'Supervisor. Looking after a maintenance team – central air-conditioning.'

She nodded. 'And what is Dubai like?'

'It's okay.' He searched his mind for things to add, and realized he did not know the place, didn't want to. The people, their customs, the language – it was all as alien to him now as it had been when he had landed there eight years ago. His uprooting never seemed to end. 'Lots of big hotels. And hundreds of shops selling gold jewellery and stereos and TVs.'

She nodded again. 'Must be a very beautiful place.' His unhappiness afflicted her like something palpable. She felt the moment was right to talk again about his returning home. 'The shop is yours, you know that. If you want to come back and run it, modernize it. Whatever you like. If you prefer to sell it and use the money to start your own refrigeration and air-conditioning business, that's also possible.'

He heard the diffident note in her voice and felt miserable. A mother scared to talk to her own son – was he really so intimidating? 'I haven't thought about all that,' he repeated.

'Take your time, there is no rush. Whatever you wish.'

He winced at her efforts to mollify him. Why didn't she say she was disgusted with his behaviour, with his long absence, his infrequent, superficial letters? And if she did say it – would he defend himself? Would he give reasons, try to explain how meaningless every endeavour seemed to him? No. For then she would start crying again, he would tell her to stop being silly, she would ask for details, and he would tell her to mind her own business.

'I was thinking,' said Mrs. Kohlah, shifting to a less risky subject. 'Since you have come after so many years, maybe you should take the chance and visit our relatives. Everyone in the Sodawalla family is dying to see you again.'

'It's too far to go, I don't have time.'

'Not even two-three days? You could also say hello to the lady you lived with when you were in college. She would be so happy to see you.'

'She's forgotten me after all this time, for sure.'

'I don't think so. If it wasn't for her, you wouldn't have finished your certificate. You didn't like the college hostel, you wanted to come straight back home, remember? You owe your success to Dina Dalal and her accommodation.'

'Yes, I remember.' Hearing his mother say 'success' made him cringe.

Dusk fell, and the lizard he had been watching began melting into the stone wall. When it moved, it became sharply visible again. But the creature's appetite must have been sated, he thought, for it no longer darted at flies – its belly seemed distinctly bloated.

'Maneck.' She waited till he turned his head towards her. 'Maneck, why are you so far away?'

He narrowed his eyes to examine her face – his mother was not usually given to such inanities. 'It's because my job is in Dubai.'

'I wasn't referring to that distance, Maneck.'

Her answer made him feel foolish. Gently touching his shoulder, she said, 'Time to start dinner,' and went inside.

He listened to the kitchen noises travelling to the porch, timid as his mother's words. Pots and pans, and then the knife – a flurry of taps against the board while she chopped something. Water running in the sink. A thud, and a bolt rattling into place, as she shut the window to keep out the evening cold.

Maneck shifted uneasily in his chair. The cooking sounds, the twilight chill, the fog rising from the valley began escorting a host of memories through his troubled mind. Childhood mornings, waking, standing at the enormous picture window of his room, watching the snow-covered peaks as the sun rose and the mountain mists commenced their dance, while Mummy started breakfast and Daddy got ready to open the shop. Then the smell of toast and fried eggs made him hungry, so he pushed his warm feet into the cold slippers, enjoying the shiver that shot through him, brushed his teeth, and hurried downstairs, gave Mummy a good-morning hug and snuggled into his chair. Soon, Daddy came in rubbing his hands, and took great gulps of tea from his special cup while standing, gazing out upon the valley before sitting to eat his breakfast and drink more tea, and Mummy said . . .

'Maneck, it's getting chilly outside. Do you want a pullover?'

The intrusion jolted the elbow of memory; his thoughts collapsed like a house of cards. 'No, I'll be in soon,' he called back, irritated by the interruption, as though he could have recaptured, reconstructed, redeemed those happy times if only he had been given long enough.

The lizard still clung to the stone wall, camouflaged within the stone colouring. Maneck decided he would go inside when the fading light made the creature disappear completely. He hated its shape, its colour, its ugly snout. The manner in which it flicked its evil tongue. Its ruthless way of swallowing flies. The way time swallowed human efforts and joy. Time, the ultimate grandmaster that could never be checkmated. There was no way out of its distended belly. He wanted to destroy the loathsome creature.

He took a walking-stick leaning in the corner of the porch, crept forward, and swung at the lizard. The stick made a flat *thwack* upon the stone. He stepped back quickly, examining the ground at his feet, ready to deliver a second blow if required. But there was nothing there. He looked at the wall. Nothing. He had swung at thin air.

Now he felt relief that he had not killed the lizard. He wondered at what point it had departed, leaving him to conjure up its saurian presence. He looked closely at the wall's texture. He ran his fingers over the surface to find the spot. There must be some curious marking in the stone, a bump or crack or hollow that had tricked his eyes.

But the outline had vanished. Try as he might, he could not bring back the picture. The imagined lizard had escaped as cleanly as the real one.

——

The morning after the cremation, Maneck and his mother set off with the wooden box to scatter his father's ashes on the mountainside where he had loved to walk. He had wanted to be strewn throughout these vistas, as far and wide within the panorama as human effort could accomplish. *Hire a Sherpa if you have to*, he had joked. *Don't dump me in one spot*.

'I think Daddy is forcing me to take at least one long walk with him,' said Mrs. Kohlah, brushing away her tears with the back of her hand, keeping her fingers dry for the ashes.

Maneck wished he had accompanied his father more often on his outings. He wished the delight, the eagerness he had shown as a child could have endured in later years, when his father needed him most. Instead, he had succumbed to embarrassment in the face of his father's growing effusiveness about streams and birds and flowers, especially after the townspeople started talking about Mr. Kohlah's strange behaviour, his patting of rocks and stroking of trees.

The air was calm this morning. There was no breeze to help disperse the ashes. Maneck and his mother took turns dipping into the box and sprinkling the grey powder.

When half the ashes were gone, Aban Kohlah felt a pang of guilt, felt they were not doing it as thoroughly as her husband would have liked. She ventured into more difficult places, trying to throw a fistful in a hesitant waterfall, mingle some in an inaccessible clump of wildflowers, spread a little around a tree that grew out of an overhang.

'This was Daddy's favourite spot,' she said. 'He often described this tree, how strangely it grew.'

'Be careful, Mummy,' warned Maneck. 'Tell me where you want to scatter it, don't lean so much over the edge.'

But that would not be the same thing, she thought, and persevered in her precarious clamberings down steep paths. Finally, what Maneck had feared came to pass. She lost her footing and slipped down a slope.

He ran to where she crouched, rubbing her knee. 'Ohhh!' she said, rising and trying to walk.

'Don't,' he said. 'Just wait here, I'll get help.'

'No, it's okay, I can climb up.' She took two steps and sank to the ground again.

He tucked the box of ashes safely behind a boulder, then hurried to regain the road, shouting to someone going by that his mother was injured. Within thirty minutes, a group of friends and neighbours came to the rescue, headed by the formidable Mrs. Grewal.

The wife of Brigadier Grewal had become more and more leaderly in her demeanour since her husband's death. Wherever she found herself, she automatically took control of things. Most of her friends welcomed this, for it meant less work for them, whether it was planning a dinner party or arranging an outing.

Sizing up Mrs. Kohlah's predicament, Mrs. Grewal sent for two porters who now worked as waiters in a five-star hotel. In the old days, the duo would carry elderly or infirm tourists in a long-armed viewing chair along the mountain paths and trails to enjoy the scenery. When the new road was built, wide enough to accommodate sightseeing buses, it put the porters out of business.

But the two were happy to get the palkhi out of storage for Mrs. Kohlah. Maneck asked if they would be able to carry her safely, since they might have lost their surefootedness after years in their soft hotel jobs, padding between kitchen and dining room.

'Have no fear, sahab,' they said. 'This work was our family tradition, it is in the blood.' They were visibly excited about the chance, however brief, to exercise their old skills.

'Maneck, will you stay and finish the box?' asked Mrs. Kohlah, as she was helped into the palkhi.

'Yes, he will stay,' said Mrs. Grewal, deciding for them. 'Maneck, you finish the ashes and catch up with us later. Your mummy will be safe with me.'

She motioned to the porters; they hoisted the palkhi to their shoulders and trotted off in perfect unison, their legs and arms moving like well-oiled machinery, finding a smooth rhythm over the rugged paths to spare the passenger unnecessary jolts. Maneck was reminded of the steam engine his father had once shown him at close quarters . . . Daddy lifting him in his arms at the railway station, the engine-driver blowing the whistle . . . shafts and cranks and pistons, darting and thrusting in a powerful, clanking symmetry . . .

'Oh, if only Farokh could see this,' said Mrs. Kohlah, smiling and crying. 'His wife going home in a palkhi after scattering his ashes. How he would laugh at my stylish clumsiness.'

Maneck watched the porters disappear around the next bend, then retrieved the box hidden by the boulder. He resumed scattering the ashes. By and by, a wind came up. The slow clouds, drifting lazily, now began a rowdy race across the sky, their shadows threatening the valley below. He let the ashes trickle from his fingers into the clutches of the wind. He scraped the inside of the box, turned it over, and tapped on the outside. The last traces flew away to explore the vastness.

From time to time, Mrs. Grewal, striding right behind the porters, called out instructions for them. 'Careful, that branch is very low. You don't want Mrs. Kohlah to bang her head.'

'Have no fear, memsahab,' they panted. 'We haven't forgotten our work.'

'Hmm,' said Mrs. Grewal, doubtful. 'Watch out now, that's a very big stone, don't stumble.'

This time, Mrs. Kohlah did the reassuring on the porters' behalf. 'Don't worry, they are experts. I am very comfortable.'

The friends and neighbours following after them gave the two palkhi-wallas a round of applause as they emerged from the mountain path and continued along the road into town. It had been years since anyone had seen a palkhi float through the streets. The ghost from the past was greeted with delight by all who met it on its journey. Many decided to tag along, swelling the ranks of the spontaneous celebration.

Now and again, the chair party had to stop at the side to allow lorries and buses to pass. After the fifth such halt, Mrs. Grewal became indignant. 'Enough of this nonsense,' she said. 'Come on, everybody. Step out, all the way out – into the middle of the road. We shall not move for anybody. Not today. Mrs. Kohlah has the right of way, this is a special day for her. The traffic can wait.'

Everyone agreed with Mrs. Grewal, and for thirty-five glorious minutes they marched into town in a determined procession, trailed by lines of impatient vehicles, the drivers honking and shouting. For the most part Mrs. Grewal ignored them, determined not to dignify their cheap cacophony with a retort. Occasionally, though, her outrage made her pause and shout back, 'Show some respect! The woman is a widow!'

About an hour after they had started, the rescue party reached home safely, and Mrs. Kohlah was made comfortable in an easy chair, with an ice pack round her knee. Mrs. Grewal sat opposite her in a straight-backed chair, erect as a sentry. She refused to leave with the others, declaring firmly, 'You cannot remain all by yourself on the day after the funeral.'

Mrs. Kohlah was a little amused at her manner, and grateful for the company. They reminisced about the General Store, the prosperous old times, the tea parties and dinners, the cantonment days. How wonderful life used to be, how sweet and healthy the air – any time you felt sick or tired, all you had to do was step outdoors, breathe deeply, and you felt better immediately, no need to swallow any medicine or vitamin tablets. 'Nowadays the whole atmosphere only has changed,' said Mrs. Grewal.

Just then Maneck walked in, and there was an awkward silence. He wondered what they had been discussing.

'You are back very fast,' observed Mrs. Grewal. 'Young people, strong legs. And you managed all right with the ashes?'

'Yes, thank you.'

'You are sure you did it properly, Maneck?' inquired his mother.

'Yes.'

There was another little silence.

'And what have you been doing in Dubai?' asked Mrs. Grewal. 'Besides growing a beard?'

He smiled in reply.

'Very secretive. Making lots of money, I hope.'

He smiled again. She left a few minutes later, saying there was no need for her to stay any longer. 'You can look after your mother now,' she added meaningfully.

Maneck checked the ice pack, then offered to make cheese sandwiches for lunch.

'My son visits after eight years and I can't even prepare his food,' lamented his mother.

'What difference is it who makes the sandwiches?'

She took the warning in his voice and retreated, then tried again. 'Maneck, please don't get angry. Won't you tell me the reason you are so unhappy?'

'There is nothing to tell.'

'We are both sad because of Daddy's death. But that cannot be the only reason. We were expecting it ever since his colon cancer was diagnosed. There is something different about your sadness, I can sense it.'

She waited, watching him as he cut the bread, but his face remained impassive. 'Is it because you did not visit while he was still alive? You shouldn't feel bad. Daddy understood that it was difficult for you to come.'

He put down the bread knife and turned. 'You really want to know why?'

'Yes.'

He picked up the knife again, slicing the loaf carefully while keeping his voice level. 'You sent me away, you and Daddy. And then I couldn't come back. You lost me, and I lost – everything.'

She limped to his side and took his arm. 'Look at me, Maneck!' she said tearfully. 'What you think is not true, you are everything to me and

Daddy! Whatever we did, we did for you! Please, believe me!'

He withdrew his arm gently, and continued with the sandwiches.

'How can you say something so hurtful and then become silent? You always used to complain that Daddy was fond of dramatics. But now you are doing just that.'

He refused to discuss it further. She followed him around the kitchen, hobbling, pleading with him.

'What's the point of me making the sandwiches if you are going to keep marching with that knee?' he said, exasperated.

She sat down compliantly till he finished and lunch was on the table. While they ate, she studied his face in snatches, when she was sure he wasn't looking. The sky started to darken in earnest. He washed their plates and put them on the rack to dry. The rumble of thunder rolled over the valley.

'We were so lucky this morning,' she said as the drizzle commenced. 'I'm going up to rest now. Will you shut the windows if the rain comes in?'

He nodded, and helped her climb the stairs. She smiled through the pain, leaning with pleasure on her son's shoulder, taking pride in its strength and firmness.

After his mother was in bed, Maneck returned downstairs and stood at the window to watch the display of lightning, to revel in the thunder-claps. He had missed the rains in Dubai. The valley was disappearing under a blanket of fog. He strode restlessly about the house, then went into the shop.

He examined the shelves, savouring the brand names on the jars and boxes that he had not seen for years. But how small, how shabby the shop was, he thought. The shop that was once the centre of his universe. And now he had moved so far away from it. So far that it felt impossible to return. He wondered what was keeping him away. Not clean and gleaming Dubai, for sure.

He descended the steps into the cellar where the bottling machinery slept. Cobwebs had taken over, shrouding the defeated apparatus. Demand for Kohlah's Cola had almost vanished in recent times, his parents had written – just half a dozen bottles a day, to loyal friends and neighbours.

He pottered around amid the empty bottles and wooden crates. In a corner of the cellar stood a stack of mouldering newspapers, partially hidden by a bundle of gunnys. He stroked the coarse jute sacking, feeling the bite of the fibre, breathing in its extravagant green smell of wood and vegetation. The newspaper dates went back ten years, and jumped haphazardly over the decade. Strange, he thought, because Daddy used them up regularly in the store, for wrapping parcels or padding packages. These must have been overlooked.

He decided to take them upstairs and browse through them. Reading old newspapers seemed a fitting way to spend the gloomy, rain-filled afternoon.

He settled in a chair by the window and opened the yellow, dusty sheets of the first issue in the pile. It was from the period after the post-Emergency elections that the Prime Minister lost to the opposition coalition. There were articles about abuses during the Emergency, testimony of torture victims, outrage over the countless deaths in police custody. Editorials that had been silenced during her regime called for a special commission to investigate the wrongdoings and punish the guilty.

He skipped to another paper, impatient with the repetitious reportage. The new government's dithering over how to deal with the ex-Prime Minister did not make stimulating reading either, except for one article which quoted a cabinet minister as saying: 'She must be punished, she is a terrible woman, wicked as Cleopatra.' And the only unanimous decision of the paralysed government was to expel Coca-Cola from the country, for refusing to relinquish its secret formula and its managing interest; with a little twisting and turning, the action suited all ideologies in the coalition brew.

Not many newspapers later, the coalition had vaporized in endless squabbles, and fresh elections were to be held. The ex-Prime Minister was poised to shed her prefix and return to power. The editorials now reined in their rhetoric against her, adopting the obsequious tone reminiscent of the Emergency. One grovelling scribe had written: 'Can the Prime Minister have incarnated at least some of the gods in herself? Beyond doubt, she possesses a dormant power, lying coiled at the base of her spine, the Kundalini Shakti which is now awakening and carrying her into transcendence.' There was no sarcasm intended, it being part of a longer panegyric.

Fed up, Maneck looked for the sports pages. There were pictures from cricket matches, and the statement by the Australian captain about a 'bunch of Third World beggars who think they can play cricket.' And then the jubilation and fireworks and celebration when the bunch of beggars defeated Australia in the Test Series.

He began going more rapidly through the newspapers. After a while even the pictures looked the same. Train derailment, monsoon floods, bridge collapse; ministers being garlanded, ministers making speeches, ministers visiting areas of natural and man-made disasters. He flipped the pages between glances out the window, at the theatre of weather – the lashing rain, windswept deodars, bolts of lightning.

Then something in the paper caught his eye. He turned back for a second look. It was a photograph of three young women. Dressed in cholis and petticoats, they were hanging from a ceiling fan. One end of each of their saris was tied to the fan hook, the other round their necks. Their heads were tilted. The arms hung limp, like the limbs of rag dolls.

He read the accompanying story, his eyes straying repeatedly to the scene that floated like a ghastly tableau. The three were sisters, aged fifteen, seventeen, and nineteen, and had hanged themselves while their parents were out of the house. They had written a note to explain their conduct. They knew that their father was unhappy at not being able to afford dowries for them. After much debate and anxiety, they had decided to take this step, to spare their mother and father the shame of three unmarried daughters. They begged their parents' forgiveness for this action which would cause them grief; they could see no alternative.

The photograph dragged Maneck's eyes back to it, to the event that was at once unsettling, pitiful, and maddening in its crystalline stillness. The three sisters looked disappointed, he thought, as though they had expected something more out of hanging, something more than death, and then discovered that death was all there was. He found himself admiring their courage. What strength it must have taken, he thought, to unwind those saris from their bodies, to tie the knots around their necks. Or perhaps it had been easy, once the act acquired the beauty of logic and the weight of sensibleness.

He tore his eyes away from the photograph to read the rest of the article. The reporter had met the parents; he wrote that they had suffered more than their fair portion of grief – they had, during the Emergency, lost their eldest under circumstances that were never satisfactorily explained. The police claimed it was a railway accident, but the parents spoke of wounds they had seen on their son's body at the morgue. According to the reporter, the injuries were consistent with other confirmed incidents of torture: 'Moreover, in view of the political climate during the Emergency, and the fact that their son, Avinash, was active in the Student Union, it would appear to be one more case of wrongful death in police custody.'

The article proceeded to comment on the parliamentary committee's inquiry into the Emergency excesses, but Maneck had stopped reading.

Avinash.

The rain was pounding on the roof and coming in through the windows. He tried to fold the discoloured newspaper neatly along its crease, but his hands were shaking, and it flapped and crumpled untidily in his lap. The room was airless. He struggled to push himself out of the chair. The paper, with its cellar smell of mould and decay, rustled to the floor. He went to the porch, stealing deep gulps of the rich rainladen air. The wind rushed through the open door. The fallen pages were blown around the room while the curtains whipped against the window. He closed the door, paced the damp porch a few times, then walked out into the rain, tears streaming down his face.

His clothes were soaked within seconds; wet hair plastered his forehead. He circled the house: down the slope, into the back yard, around the lower level, and up from the other side. Through the wall of falling rain he saw the steel cables tethering the foundation to the cliff. The trusty cables, that had held strong for four generations. But he could swear the house had shifted in the years he had been away. *A house with suicidal tendencies,* Avinash had called it. A little bit, and then a little more – and eventually it would rip out the anchors, tumble headlong down the hill. It seemed fitting. Everything was losing its moorings, slipping away, becoming irrecoverable.

He took the road out of the town square, almost running now. He did not notice the people who stared. He saw only that photograph. Three saris gripping those fragile necks . . . Avinash's three sisters . . . he used to enjoy feeding them when they were little, they used to bite his fingers in fun. And the poor parents . . . What sense did the world make? Where was God, the Bloody Fool? Did He have no notion of fair and unfair? Couldn't He read a simple balance sheet? He would have been sacked long ago if He was managing a corporation, the things He allowed to happen . . . to the maidservant, and the thousands of Sikhs killed in the capital, and my poor taxi driver with a kara that wouldn't come off.

Maneck looked up at the sky. Daddy's ashes, scattered that morning. Getting wet, getting washed away. The thought was unbearable, because then there would be nothing . . . and Mummy, left all alone . . .

He raced along the path, which was fast becoming soft and slippery. Running, sliding, stumbling, hoping to find a place that was still green and pleasant, a place of happiness, serenity, where his father would be walking, sturdy and confident, his arm over his son's shoulder.

Squelching through the mud, he skidded; his arms shot out sideways to keep him from falling. Now he felt the despair his father had felt as the familiar world slipped from around him, the valleys gashed and ugly, the woods disappearing. Daddy was right, he thought, the hills were dying, and I was so stupid to believe the hills were eternal, that a father could stay forever young. If only I had talked to him. If only he had let me get close to him.

But the ashes – they lay in the cold, driving rain. He ran to where he had emptied the wooden box in the morning. Panting, he stopped at each familiar spot where his mother had lingered, but could find no trace of the grey ash. His breath coming in great sobs, he brushed aside leaves, kicked over a rock, shifted a broken bough.

Nothing. He was too late. He stumbled and fell on his knees, his fingers in the ooze. The rain descended pitilessly. He felt unable to rise. He covered his face with his muddy hands and wept, and wept, and wept.

A dog pattered lightly in the muck towards Maneck. He couldn't hear it through the noise of rain. It came closer, sniffing. He started and uncovered his face when he felt its muzzle upon his hand. The dog licked his cheek. He patted it; was this one of the pack that Daddy used to feed on the porch? He noticed a suppurating ulcer on its haunch, and wondered if the homemade ointment with which his father treated the strays was still on the shelf below the counter.

The downpour was less heavy now. He stood up, wiping his face on his wet sleeve, and looked out across the hillside. Breaks were beginning to appear in the clouds, and fragments of the valley were emerging from the fog.

He stayed where he was till the rain had almost stopped. Now it was a very fine drizzle, so fine it felt lighter than human breath upon the skin. He returned to the place where the tree grew out of the overhang. The dog followed him for a while. The abscess was making it limp, the infection had probably penetrated the bone. Only a few weeks of life left for the poor creature, thought Maneck, no one to nurse it and heal it. Without Daddy around, who will care?

Tears returned to his eyes, and he began walking homewards. The rain had created numerous little rivulets that were coursing down the hill. They would go to swell the mountain streams and strengthen the impromptu waterfalls. Tomorrow everything would burst with green and freshness. He pictured the ashes, carried by all this shining water, travelling everywhere over the mountainside. His father had got his wish – he was being strewn abundantly, with more thoroughness than any human could have exercised: nature's mighty and scrupulous hand had taken charge, and he was everywhere, inseparable from the place he had loved so deeply.

Wrapped in a Kashmiri shawl, Mrs. Kohlah waited anxiously on the porch, gazing down the road. She waved frantically when Maneck came into view. He picked up his pace.

'Maneck! Where were you? I woke from my nap and you were gone! And it was raining so heavily, I got worried.' She grasped his arm. 'Look at you, you're soaking! And there is mud on your face and clothes! What happened?'

'It's all right,' he said gently. 'I'm fine, I felt like taking a walk. I slipped,' he added to explain the mud.

'You're just like Daddy, doing crazy things. He also loved rain walks. But go, change your clothes, I'll make tea and toast for you.' The rain had made the years fall away. He was her little boy again, drenched and helpless.

'How's your knee?'

'Much better. The ice pack helped.'

He went up to his room, washed, and changed into dry clothes. The tea was ready when he returned downstairs. His mother added two spoons of sugar for him and one for herself. His had been poured in his father's cup. She stirred it before moving it towards him. 'You remember how Daddy always used to drink the first cup, strolling about the kitchen?'

He nodded.

She smiled. 'Getting in my way when I was busiest. But he stopped doing that in the last few years. He would just come in and sit down quietly.' Leaning sideways in her chair, she touched Maneck's head lightly with her fingers. 'Look at that, your hair is still dripping.'

She got a napkin from the linen cupboard and began to dry it. Her vigorous towelling with short, rapid strokes made his head roll back and forth. He was on the verge of protesting, but found it relaxing and let her continue. His eyes closed. He could see the masseurs in the city, eight years ago with Om at the beach, where customers sat in the sand to have their heads kneaded and rubbed and pummelled. Waves breaking in the background, and a soft twilight breeze. And the fragrance of jasmine, wafting from vendors selling chains of the milk-white flowers for women to twine in their hair.

'I think I *will* visit our relatives. And also Dina Aunty.' Her brisk efforts with his wet hair added a curious vibrato to his voice.

'How funny you sound. As if you were trying to talk and gargle at the same time.' She laughed and put away the napkin. 'They'll be so happy to see you. When will you leave?'

'Tomorrow morning.'

'Tomorrow?' She wondered if it was a ruse to get away from her.

'And when will you return here?'

'I think I'll go back to Dubai straight from there. More convenient.'

She knew the hurt was showing in her face, and he did not seem aware of it. His words grew indistinct to her ears, already travelling the distance he was to put between them.

'What I want to do,' he continued, 'is get back to my job quickly – give them notice, find out how soon they will release me.'

'You mean, resign? And then?'

'I've decided to come back and settle here.'

Her breath quickened. 'That's a wonderful plan,' she said, restraining, as best she could, the tide of emotion that swept through her. 'You can start your own business by selling the shop and –'

'No. The shop is why I'm coming back.'

'Daddy would like that.'

He left the table and went to the window. It did not always have to end badly – he was going to prove it to himself. First he would meet all his friends: Om, happily married, and his wife, and at least two or three children by now; what would their names be? If there was a boy, surely Narayan. And Ishvar, the proud grand-uncle, beaming away at his sewing-machine, disciplining the little ones, cautioning them if they ventured too close to the whirring wheels and galloping needles. And Dina Aunty, supervising the export tailoring in her little flat, orchestrating the household, holding sway in that busy kitchen.

Yes, he would see all this with his own eyes. If there was an abundance of misery in the world, there was also sufficient joy, yes – as long as one knew where to look for it. Soon, he would return to take charge of Kohlah's Cola and the General Store. The foundation cables needed attention. The house would be refurbished. He would install new bottling machinery. He had more than enough money saved up.

Mrs. Kohlah went to stand beside him at the window. His hands were on the sill, clutching it tight, the knuckles white. They were strong hands, like his father's, she thought.

'It's getting cloudy again,' he said. 'There'll be lots more rain tonight.'

'Yes,' she agreed, 'which means everything will be green and fresh tomorrow. It will be a beautiful day.'

He put his arm around his mother and gave her the good-morning hug of his childhood although it was evening. Her contented sigh was almost inaudible. Her grip on his hand, where it rested on her shoulder, was tight and warm.

The rain followed Maneck down the country, down the hills and across the plains, for thirty-two hours on the southbound train. He had almost missed the train; the bus from the town square to the railway station had been delayed by mud slides. Yesterday's promise of sun and green and freshness remained unfulfilled, the storm still going strong. And at journey's end, when he emerged from the crowd and clamour of the station concourse, the city streets were shining wet from a heavy downpour.

The taxi stand was empty. He waited at the kerb, surrounded by puddles. There was nowhere to put his suitcase, and he shifted the bag to the other hand.

Then he noticed the crack in the flagstones behind him. Worms were pouring out of it, slithering dark red across the rain-slick pavement. *Phylum Annelida.* Several had been pulped under the feet of pedestrians. Dozens more continued to emerge, gliding along on a film of water, undulating over the dead ones.

While he watched, the gears of time slid effortlessly into reverse, and the busy pavement became Dina Aunty's bathroom. It was his first morning in her flat, he could hear her calling through the door, and he froze, keeping an eye on the wiggling battalion's advance. How she had teased him afterwards. He smiled at the memory. The crack in the flagstones was now almost depleted of worms, as the last stragglers dragged themselves to the safety of the gutter.

He decided to spend the evening with his mother's relatives, get that task out of the way. Then tomorrow could be devoted entirely to Dina Aunty and Ishvar and Om.

A taxi rattled up beside him. The driver, his arm hanging out the window, looked expectant, smelling a fare.

'Grand Hotel,' said Maneck, opening the door.

He washed, changed his shirt, and set off to suffer the fond attentions of the Sodawalla family. During the course of the evening he patiently allowed himself to be called Mac, flinching while they hugged and patted and fawned over him. It was a bit like being the prize dog at a kennel show.

'What a terrible shock it was when we heard that your daddy passed away,' they said. 'And you people live so far away, we couldn't even go to the funeral. So sorry.'

'It's all right, I understand.' He remembered what Daddy used to say about the Sodawalla relatives – no fizz, dull as a flat soda, in danger of boring themselves to death. And in the end, Daddy had lost his own effervescence.

Maneck felt suddenly oppressed in the house, exhausted by the visit. He thought he would collapse if he spent any more time with his relatives. He rose and held out his hand. 'It was very good seeing you again.'

'Stay a little longer, spend the night with us,' they insisted. 'It will be so nice. In the morning we will eat omelette, and make some fresh prawn patia.'

He refused firmly. 'I have a business appointment for dinner. Also some early breakfast meetings. I must get back to the hotel.'

They were understanding about this, suitably awed by the idea of breakfast meetings. They saw him off with blessings and good wishes, and instructions to come soon for another visit. 'Don't make us starve again so many years,' they said.

On his way back to the hotel, he stopped at the airline office and checked his reservation. The agent confirmed the booking: 'It's for day after tomorrow, sir. And your flight departure time is eleven-thirty-five p.m. Please be at the airport before nine p.m.'

'Thank you,' said Maneck.

At the Grand Hotel, he ate a plate of mutton biryani in the dining room. Afterwards, he read the newspaper in the lobby for a few minutes, then collected his key and went to bed. He fell asleep thinking about Dina Aunty, and the time they had sat up late into the night, completing the dresses for Au Revoir when Ishvar and Om had gone missing. The time of trouble with a capital t.

———

Renovations had transformed the place beyond recognition, and for a moment Maneck thought he was at the wrong address. Marble stairways, a security guard, the foyer walls faced with gleaming granite, air-conditioning in every flat, a roof garden – the low-rent tenement had been converted into luxury apartments.

He checked the nameplates listed in the entrance. The bastard landlord had finally done it, got rid of Dina Aunty – it *had* ended badly for her. And what about the tailors, where were they working now?

Outside, he felt the returning grip of despair, the sun pounding his head. Perhaps Dina Aunty would know where Ishvar and Om were. There was only one place she could have gone: to her brother, Nusswan. But he didn't have the address. And why bother – would she really be pleased to see him? He could look it up in the telephone directory. Under what surname?

He rattled his memory for Dina Aunty's maiden name. She had mentioned it once. One night, all those years ago, when Ishvar and Om and he had sat listening to her tell them about her life. It was after dinner, and she had the quilt in her lap, connecting a new patch. *Never look back at the past with regret*, Dina Aunty had said. And something about her bright future lost ... no, clouded ... back when she was still a schoolgirl, and her name was – Dina Shroff.

He stopped at the chemist's to consult the telephone directory. There were several Shroffs but only one Nusswan Shroff, and he noted the address. The clerk said it wasn't far. He decided to walk.

After leaving behind the old neighbourhood, the road became unfamiliar. He asked directions of a carpenter sitting by the kerb with his tools in a sack. The carpenter's thumb was heavily bandaged. He told Maneck to turn right at the next intersection, past the cricket maidaan.

There was a marquee set up at the edge of the field, although no cricket match was in progress. Inquiring crowds were milling around it, peering inside. Over the entrance a sign proclaimed: WELCOME TO ONE & ALL FROM HIS HOLINESS, BAL BABA – DARSHAN AVAILABLE FROM 10.00 A.M. TO 4.00 P.M. EVERY DAY INCLUDING SUNDAY & BANK HOLIDAY.

A hardworking godman for sure, thought Maneck, wondering what his specialty was – producing gold watches out of thin air, tears from the eyes of statues, rose petals from women's cleavages?

But his name suggested a trick to do with hair. He asked someone at the entrance, 'Who is Bal Baba?'

'Bal Baba is a very very holy man,' said the attendant. 'He has returned to us after many many years of meditationing in a Himalayan cave.'

'What does he do?'

'He has a very especial, very saintly power. He tells you any sort of thing you will want to know. All he needs is to hold some of your hairs between his holy fingers for ten seconds only.'

'And what's the charge for it?'

'Bal Baba has no charges,' said the man indignantly. Then he added, with an oily smile, 'But all donations are mostly welcome by the Bal Baba Foundation, anymuch amount.'

Maneck grew curious, and went in. Just for a quick look, he decided – at the latest fakeologist in the city, as Om would say. It would be amusing to tell the tailors what he saw. Something to laugh about together, after eight years.

The crowds were bigger outside the marquee than inside. Only a few people were waiting near a screen behind which sat the very very saintly Bal Baba. Shouldn't take long, thought Maneck, at the rate of ten seconds per meditation per customer. This was assembly-line darshan and consultation.

He joined the queue, and soon it was his turn. The man behind the screen, in a saffron robe, was bald and clean-shaven. Even his eyebrows and eyelashes had been plucked clean. Not a hair was visible on his face or on the skin left uncovered by the robe.

Despite the bizarrely smooth and shining countenance, however, Maneck recognized him. 'You're Rajaram the hair-collector!'

'Eh?' jumped Bal Baba, startled enough to let the unsaintly ejaculation escape him. Then he regained his composure, raised his head, and enunciated beatifically, embroidering his words with graceful hand and finger movements: 'Rajaram the hair-collector renounced his life, his joys and sorrows, his vices and virtues. Why? So that Bal Baba could be incarnated, and could use his humble gift to assist humanity along the pathway to moksha.'

The fancy mannerisms were discontinued after this declaration. He inclined his head and asked in a normal voice, 'But who are you?'

'Remember Ishvar and Om? The tailors who used to lend you money in your previous incarnation – your hairy days? I lived in that same flat with them.' While the hair-collector took this in, Maneck added, 'I've grown a beard. Maybe that's why you don't recognize me.'

'Not at all. No hairstyle or beard on earth can deceive Bal Baba,' he said grandly. 'So what is your question for me?'

'You're joking.'

'No, just try me. Go ahead, ask. Ask about job, health, marriage prospects, wife, children, education, anything. I'll give you the answer.'

'I already have the answer. I'm searching for the question.'

Bal Baba looked askance at him, annoyance shadowing the glabrous face – enigmatic utterances of this sort were his preserve. But he controlled his displeasure and reattached the requisite smile of enlightenment.

'On second thoughts, I do have a question,' said Maneck. 'How would you help someone who has a bald head like yours?'

'That is only a small obstacle. The Bal Baba Foundation sells a special hair tonic at cost price – postage and handling charges extra. Made from rare Himalayan herbs, works like magic. In a few weeks, the bald head is covered with thick hair. Then the person comes here, I hold the newly grown hair for meditation, and answer the question.'

'Do you ever feel like chopping it off? For your collection?'

Bal Baba grew enraged. 'That was another life, another person. That's all finished, don't you understand?'

'I see. And have you visited Ishvar and Om since you returned from your cave? They might have questions for you.'

'Bal Baba cannot afford the luxury of visiting anybody. He is bound to this place, to allow people the opportunity for darshan.'

'Right,' said Maneck. 'In that case I better not waste your time. There are thousands waiting outside.'

'May you soon find the bliss of contentment,' said Bal Baba, raising one hand in a transcendent farewell. His eyes were still furious.

Maneck decided to come again next morning, bring Om and Ishvar with him – he didn't have to leave for the airport till tomorrow night. It would be a great joke, and lots of fun to deflate Bal Baba's pomposity. Take him down a notch or two, make him look back at his yesterdays.

The way out was through the rear of the marquee, past a man writing at a wobbly table stacked with letters and envelopes. Maneck stared, trying to remember where they had met. Then he spotted the plastic case in the man's shirt pocket, with its battery of pens and ballpoints. It came back to him – the train, the passenger with the hoarse voice.

'Excuse me, you're the proofreader, aren't you?'

'Erstwhile,' he said. 'Vasantrao Valmik, at your service.'

'You don't recognize me because I've grown a beard, but I was the student on the train with you, many years ago, when you were travelling for specialist treatment for your throat problem.'

'Say no more,' said Mr. Valmik, smiling with delight. 'I remember perfectly, I've never forgotten you. We talked a lot on that journey, didn't we.' He chuckled, and screwed the cap on his pen. 'You know, it's so very rare to find a good audience for one's story. Most people get restless when a stranger tells them about his life. But you were a perfect listener.'

'Oh, I enjoyed listening. It shortened the journey. Besides, your life is so interesting.'

'You are very kind. Let me tell you a secret: there is no such thing as an uninteresting life.'

'Try mine.'

'I would love to. One day you must tell me your full and complete story, unabridged and unexpurgated. You must. We will set aside some time for it, and meet. It's very important.'

Maneck smiled. 'Why is it important?'

Mr. Valmik's eyes grew wide. 'You don't know? It's extremely important because it helps to remind yourself of who you are. Then you can go forward, without fear of losing yourself in this ever-changing world.'

He paused, touching his pen pocket. 'I must be truly blessed, for I have been able to tell my whole story twice. First to you on the train, then to a nice lady in the courthouse compound. But that was also many years ago. I'm thirsting to find a new audience. Ah, yes, to share the story redeems everything.'

'How?'

'How, I don't know exactly. But I feel it here.' He put his hand over his shirt pocket again.

He felt it in his pens? Then Maneck realized that the proofreader meant his heart. 'And what are you doing nowadays, Mr. Valmik?'

'I am in charge of Bal Baba's mail-order business. He does prophecies by correspondence too. People send in clippings of hair. I open the envelopes, throw away the hair, cash the cheques, and write answers to their questions.'

'Are you enjoying it?'

'Very much indeed. The scope is unlimited. I can use all kinds of devices in my replies – essay form, prose poem, poetic prose, aphorism.' He patted the pen pocket and added, 'My little darlings are at full flow, creating fiction after fiction, which will become more real in the recipients' lives than all their sad realities.'

'It's been good to see you,' said Maneck.

'And when shall we meet again? You really must tell me all about yourself.'

'Maybe tomorrow. I'm planning to bring two friends of Bal Baba.'

'Good, good. See you soon.'

At the exit, the attendant held out a brass bowl containing a little loose change. 'Anymuch donation is welcome.'

Maneck threw in some coins, feeling he had certainly got his money's worth.

The door took a while to open in answer to Maneck's ring. The stick-wristed figure looked nothing like the Dina Aunty he had left eight years ago. Eight years in passing were entitled to take their toll; but this – this was more than a toll, it was outright banditry.

'Yes?' she asked, leaning forward. Her eyes were pinpoints through lenses twice as thick as he remembered them. The grey in her hair had thoroughly subjugated the black.

'Aunty,' his voice snagged on the obstacle course his throat had become. 'It's Maneck.'

'What?'

'Maneck Kohlah – your paying guest.'

'Maneck?'

'I've grown a beard. That's why you don't recognize me.'

She came closer. 'Yes. You've grown a beard.'

He felt the coldness in her voice. Stupid of me to expect anything else, he thought. 'I went to your flat . . . and . . . you were not there.'

'How could I? It's not my flat.'

'I wanted to see you again, and the tailors, and –'

'There are no more tailors. Come inside.' She shut the door, leading the way with small, careful steps, using the walls and furniture to guide herself in the dark hallway.

'Sit,' she said, when they reached the drawing room. 'You have appeared suddenly. Out of nowhere.'

He heard the accusation, and nodded. He had no defence.

'That beard. You should shave it off. Makes you look like a toilet brush.'

He laughed, and so did she, a little. He was relieved to hear the silver flash in hers, but it was not entirely enough to cancel the chill. The room they sat in was opulent. Rich old furniture, antique porcelain in showcases, an exquisite silk Persian carpet on one wall.

'Next time you see me, the beard will be gone for sure, Aunty, I promise.'

'Maybe then I will recognize you sooner.' She struggled with a hairpin and patted it down. 'My eyes are terrible now. Those carrots you forced me to eat were wasted. Nothing can save these eyes.'

He laughed tentatively, but this time she did not join in.

'You came after very long. A few more years, and I won't see you at all. Even now, you're a shadow in this room.'

'I was away, working in the Gulf.'

'And what was it like?'

'It was . . . it was – empty.'

'Empty?'

'Empty . . . like a desert.'

'But it is a desert country.' She paused. 'You didn't write to me from there.'

'I'm sorry. But I didn't write to anyone. It seemed so . . . so pointless.'

'Yes,' she said. 'Pointless. And my address changed, in any case.'

'But what happened to the flat, Aunty?'

She told him.

He leaned forward to whisper, 'And you are okay here? Nusswan treats you all right?' He lowered his voice still further. 'Does he give you enough to eat?'

'You don't have to whisper, no one is home to hear you.' She removed her spectacles, wiped them with the hem of her skirt, and put them on again. 'There is more food than I have an appetite for.'

He shifted uncomfortably. 'And what about Ishvar and Om? Where are they working now?'

'They are not working.'

'Then how are they managing? Especially with Om's wife, and children?'

'There is no wife, no children. They have become beggars.'

'Sorry – what, Aunty?'

'They are both beggars now.'

'That's impossible! Sounds crazy! I mean – aren't they ashamed to beg? Couldn't they do some other work, if there's no tailoring? I mean –'

'Without knowing everything you want to judge them?' she cut him off.

Her scathing tone made him curb his outburst. 'Please tell me what happened.'

While she spoke, cold like a knife sliced through his insides. He sat frozen, like one of the figurines in the glass-fronted cabinets around him.

When she reached the end, he had still not stirred. She leaned forward to shake his knee. 'Are you listening?'

He gave a slight nod. Her eyes missed the small movement, and she asked again, irritated, 'Are you listening or am I wasting my breath?'

This time he used words for his answer. 'Yes, Aunty. I am listening.' His voice was lifeless.

Empty as his face, she thought. 'You wouldn't recognize them if you saw them. Ishvar has shrunk, not just because his legs are gone – all of him. And Om has become very chubby. One of the effects of castration.'

'Yes, Aunty.'

'You remember how we used to cook together?'

He nodded.

'You remember the kittens?'

He nodded again.

She tried once more to breathe life into him. 'What time is it?'

'Twelve-thirty.'

'If you are not in a rush, you could meet Ishvar and Om. They will come here at one o'clock.'

Emotion re-entered his voice, but not the sort she was hoping for. 'I'm sorry – I cannot stay.' The refusal was tinged with terror, his words spilling out in a rush. 'I have so many things to do . . . before my plane leaves tomorrow. My mother's relatives, and some shopping, and then to the airport. Maybe when I come next time.'

'Next time. Yes, okay. We'll all be waiting for you next time.'

They rose and walked down the hallway. 'Wait,' she said when they reached the door. 'I have something for you.'

She returned with her small, careful steps. 'You left this behind in my flat.'

It was Avinash's chess set.

'Thank you.' He swayed, but his voice remained calm. He put out a hand to accept the board and the maroon plywood box. Then he said, 'I don't really need it, Aunty. You keep it.'

'And what would I do with it?'

'Give it to someone . . . to your nephews?'

'Xerxes and Zarir don't play. They are very busy men.'

Maneck nodded. 'Thank you,' he said again.

'You're welcome.'

He hesitated, turning the box around and around in his hands, gently running his fingers along the edge. 'Bye-bye, Aunty.'

She nodded silently. He leaned forward and kissed her cheek lightly, quickly. She raised her hand as though to wave, stepped back, and began to close the door. He turned and hurried down the cobbled walkway.

He stopped when he heard the door shut. He was under a tree at the end of the path. A bird sang in the branches. He listened, staring at the board and box in his hands. Something fell on his head, and he jumped aside to avoid a second dropping. His fingers felt the sticky splotch. Using leaves from the tree, he wiped his hair and looked up. There was only a crow, the singing bird had flown. He wondered which one was in his hair. Daddy used to say a common crow's droppings brought uncommon good luck.

He glanced at his watch: twenty to one. Ishvar and Om would be arriving soon. If he spent a few minutes here, he could see them. And they would see him. But – what would he say?

In the quiet street outside the house, he began strolling along the foot-path. Up, towards the end of the street, then down again, to Dina Aunty's house. After several turns, he saw two beggars rounding the corner from the main road.

One sat slumped on a low platform that moved on castors. He had no legs. The other pulled the platform with a rope slung over his shoulder. His plumpness sat upon him strangely, like oversized, padded clothes. Under his arm he carried a torn umbrella.

What shall I say? he asked himself desperately.

They drew nearer, and the one on the platform jiggled the coins in his tin can. 'O babu, ek paisa?' he pleaded, looking up shyly.

Ishvar, it's me, Maneck! Don't you recognize me! The words raced uselessly inside his head, unable to find an exit. Say something, he commanded himself, say anything!

The other beggar demanded, 'Babu! Aray, paisa day!' His voice was high-pitched, challenging, his look direct and mocking. They stopped expectantly, hand held out, tin rattling.

Om! Sour-lime face, my friend! Have you forgotten me!

But his words of love and sorrow and hope remained muted like stones.

The legless beggar coughed and spat. Maneck glanced at the gob; it was tinged with blood. The platform started to roll past him, and he saw that Ishvar was sitting on a cushion. No, not a cushion. It was dirty and fraying, folded to the size of a cushion. The patchwork quilt.

Wait, he wanted to call out – wait for me. He wanted to hurry after them, go back to Dina Aunty with them, tell her he had changed his mind.

He did nothing. The two turned into the cobbled walkway and disappeared from sight. He could hear the castors clattering briefly over the uneven stones. The sound died; he continued on his way.

Past the cricket maidaan, past Bal Baba's marquee, past the injured carpenter by the kerb, Maneck hurried till he was in familiar surroundings again. He saw the new neon sign of the Vishram Vegetarian Hotel. The place seemed like a prosperous restaurant now, enlarged by having swallowed the shops on either side, its lights humming and flickering fatuously in the afternoon sun. EAT DRINK, ENJOY IN OUR AIR-CONDITIONED COMFORT, said the smaller board under the neon.

He entered, and was shown to a shiny glass-topped table. A neat, uniformed waiter appeared, bearing a large, glossy menu. Maneck placed the chess set on an empty chair beside him and ordered a coffee.

The eating house was busy; it was lunchtime. The waiter hurried back with a glass of water. 'Making fresh coffee, sahab. Two more minutes.'

Maneck nodded. On a high shelf behind the cash desk, a loudspeaker emitted vapid instrumental music, purposeless above the restaurant bustle. He gazed at the tables around him, at office workers in bush shirts, ties, jackets, eating energetically, their animated conversations supplementing the clatter of cutlery – office talk, about management treachery and dearness allowances, budgets and promotions. This was a new class of clientele, far removed from the peons and sweaty labourers who used to eat here in the old days.

The coffee arrived. Maneck added sugar, stirred at length, sipped a little. Immediately the waiter, lingering nearby, stepped forward. 'Is it good, sahab?'

'Yes, thank you.'

The man adjusted the salt and pepper containers and wiped the ashtray with vigour. 'So, sahab, the Prime Minister's son has taken over. You think he will be a good ruler?'

'Who knows. We'll have to wait and see.'

'That's true. They all say one thing, do something else.' He left to attend another table, where the customers had finished eating. Maneck watched him stack the plates, then add to this stack at the next table, and the next, before staggering off to the kitchen with the lot.

He soon returned and inspected Maneck's half-empty cup. 'Anything to eat, sahab?'

Maneck shook his head.

'We have nice tasty ice cream also.'

'No, thank you.' The over-attentiveness was getting on his nerves – the polite smile like part of the new decor, he felt, in the new Vishram. Where he was alone. In the old Vishram, he had always come with Om and Ishvar. Afternoons, at that single, smelly table. And Shankar rolling outside, waving his incomplete hands, wiggling his truncated legs, smiling, rattling his tin. And then his funeral pyre. The priest's chanting, the burning sandalwood, the fragrant smoke. Completeness. In the crematorium with Daddy this was missing, an open pyre was definitely better. Better for the living . . .

A group of customers noisily pushed back their chairs to leave; a new batch took their place. They greeted the staff by name. Regulars, apparently. Maneck picked up the maroon plywood box and pushed open the sliding lid, fishing out a piece at random. A pawn. He rolled it between his thumb and fingers, observed that the green felt on its base was peeling.

The waiter saw it too. 'You should use Camel Paste, sahab, it will stick it strong.'

Maneck nodded. He drank what remained of the coffee and dropped the pawn back in the box.

'My son also plays this game,' said the waiter proudly.

Maneck looked up. 'Oh? Does he have his own set?'

'No, sahab, it is too expensive. He plays in school only.' Noticing the empty cup, he offered the menu again. 'Two o'clock, sahab, kitchen is closing soon. We have very nice karai chicken, also biryani. Or some small thing? Mutton roll, pakora with chutney, puri-bhaji?'

'No, just one more coffee.' Maneck rose and went to the back, looking for the WC.

It was occupied. He waited in the passage, where he could observe the brisk kitchen activity. The cook's perspiring helper was chopping, frying, stirring; a skinny little boy was scraping off dirty plates and soaking them in the sink.

Despite the chrome and glass and fluorescent lights, something of the old Vishram remained, thought Maneck – kerosene and coal fuelled the stoves. Then the WC door creaked open, and he went in.

When he came out, the table nearest the kitchen had been vacated. He decided to take it. The waiter darted across to remind him his second coffee was waiting at the other table.

'I'll have it here,' said Maneck.

'But it's not good, sahab. Kitchen noise, and smell and all, over here.'

'That's okay.'

The waiter complied, fetching the coffee and the chess set before retreating to discuss with a colleague the whims and idiosyncrasies of customers.

Someone called out an order of shish kebab to the kitchen. The cook's helper stoked the coals and, when they had caught, arranged a few on a brazier. Skewers loaded with chunks of lamb and liver were placed over it. The coals perked up as they were fanned.

How they glowed, thought Maneck – live creatures breathing and pulsating. Starting small, with modest heat, then growing to powerful red incandescence, spitting and snapping, their tongues of flame crackling, all heat and passion, transforming, threatening, devouring. And then – the subsidence. Into mellow warmth, compliance, and, finally, a perfect stillness . . .

The Vishram's lunch hours had ended. Past three o'clock, the waiter began hinting apologetically, with a weak attempt at humour. 'Everybody ran back to office long time ago, sahab,' he smiled. 'Scared of their bosses. But you must be a very big boss, only you are left behind here.'

Yes, only I, thought Maneck. *Only slow coaches get left behind*.

'You are on holiday?'

'Yes. Bill, please.' He glanced inside the kitchen again. The stoves were off; the cook's helpers were cleaning the place to get ready for the dinner patrons. On the brazier, the coals had crumbled to ashes.

The total for two coffees was six rupees. Maneck placed ten in the saucer and walked to the door.

'Wait, sahab, wait!' called the waiter, running after him. 'Sahab, you forgot your paakit on the chair! And also your game!'

'Thank you.' Maneck slipped the wallet into his hip pocket, and took the chess set.

'All your things you are forgetting today,' the waiter laughed a little. 'Be careful, sahab.'

Maneck smiled and nodded, then opened the door, stepping from the air-conditioned chill of the Vishram into the afternoon sun's harsh embrace.

Gradually, it became difficult for Maneck to make his way along the pavement. He realized he was walking against the flow. Evening had fallen while he had wandered the city streets; people were spilling urgently out of office buildings, heading for home. His watch showed a quarter after six. He turned towards the railway station, to let the human tide carry him forward.

The brunt of the rush hour had passed, but the high-ceilinged concourse continued to reverberate with the thunder of trains. There was a line at the ticket-window. He remembered a story he had heard about ticketless travel, once upon a time.

Abandoning the queue, he jostled through the crowds to get to the platform. The display indicated that the next train was an express, not scheduled to stop here.

He looked around at the waiting passengers – lost inside newspapers, fidgeting with luggage, drinking tea. A mother was twisting her child's ear to drive home some lesson. A distant rumbling was heard, and Maneck moved to the front of the platform. He stared at the rails. How they glinted, like the promise of life itself, stretching endlessly in both directions, silver ribbons skimming over the gravel bed, knitting together the blackened, worn-out wood of the railway ties.

He noticed an elderly woman in dark glasses standing next to him. He wondered if she was blind. It could be dangerous for her so close to the edge – perhaps he should help her move to safety.

She smiled and said, 'Fast train, not stopping here. I checked the board.' She took one step backwards, motioning with her hand to draw him back too.

Not blind then, just stylish. He returned her smile and remained where he was, hugging the chess set to himself. Now the express could be seen in the distance, having cleared the bend in the tracks. The rumble was louder, growing to a roar as it approached. When the first compartment had entered the station, he stepped off the platform and onto the gleaming silver tracks.

The elderly woman in dark glasses was the first to scream. Then the shriek of the pneumatic brakes drowned all other sounds. The fast train took several hundred yards to stop.

Maneck's last thought was that he still had Avinash's chessmen.

Under the tree where the cobbled walkway met the pavement, Om dropped Ishvar's towrope, and they settled down to wait. A bird startled in the dense foliage above them. They kept glancing at the wristwatches of passersby whom they pestered for alms.

At one o'clock they left the pavement and trundled over the cobbles. The shrubbery and the garden wall of the Shroff residence shielded them from the neighbours' view. They made straight for the back door, keeping close to the side of the house, and knocked softly.

Dina ushered them in. She filled water glasses for them and, while they drank, dished out masoor in plates from Ruby's everyday set on the sideboard. How many more years could she do this before Ruby or Nusswan found out, she wondered. 'Anyone saw you come in?'

They shook their heads.

'Eat fast,' she said. 'My sister-in-law is coming back earlier than usual.'

'It's very tasty,' said Ishvar, carefully balancing the plate on his lap.

Om grunted his affirmation, adding, 'Chapatis are a little dry, not as nice as yesterday. You didn't follow my method or what?'

'This fellow thinks he's too smart,' she complained to Ishvar.

'What to do,' said Ishvar, laughing. 'He's the chapati champion of the world.'

'They are from last night,' said Dina. 'I didn't make fresh ones. I had a visitor. You'll never guess who.'

'Maneck,' they said.

'We saw him passing half an hour ago. We knew him in spite of his beard,' said Ishvar.

'Didn't you talk to him?'

They shook their heads.

'He didn't recognize us,' said Om. 'Or he ignored us. We even said 'Babu, ek paisa' to get his attention.'

'You have altered very much from when he knew you.' She held out the platter of chapatis. 'Have another.' Ishvar took one and shared with Om, tearing it in half.

'I told him you would come at one o'clock,' she continued. 'I asked him to wait but he was getting late. Next time, he said.'

'That will be nice,' said Ishvar.

Om shrugged angrily. 'The Maneck we knew would have waited today.'

'Yes,' said Ishvar, scooping up the last bit of masoor from his plate. 'But he went so far away. When you go so far away, you change. Distance is a difficult thing. We shouldn't blame him.'

Dina agreed. 'Now remember, tomorrow is Saturday, everyone will be home – you mustn't come for the next two days.' She put their plates in the sink and opened the door to let them out.

'Hoi-hoi,' said Ishvar. 'What's this?' A thread had unravelled from the quilt he was sitting on, and was tangled in one of the castors.

'Let me see.' Om reached down to slide the quilt out as his uncle levered himself up slightly on his arms. They found the patch from which the thread had strayed.

'Good thing you saw it,' said Dina. 'Or that piece might have fallen off completely.'

'It's easy to fix,' said Ishvar. 'Can I borrow your needle, Dinabai? For a few minutes?'

'Not now. I told you my sister-in-law is returning early.' But she went to her room and fetched a spool of thread with a needle stuck into it. 'Take this with you.' She opened the door again for them. 'Don't forget the umbrella.' She tucked it under Om's arm.

'It was very useful last night,' he said. 'I hit a thief who tried to grab our coins.' He raised the rope and hauled. Ishvar made a clacking-clucking sound with his tongue against the teeth, imitating a bullock-cart driver. His nephew pawed the ground and tossed his head.

'Stop it,' she scolded. 'If you behave that way on the pavement, no one will give you a single paisa.'

'Come on, my faithful,' said Ishvar. 'Lift your hoofs or I'll feed you a dose of opium.' Chuckling, Om trotted away plumply. They quit clowning when they emerged into the street.

Dina shut the door, shaking her head. Those two made her laugh every day. Like Maneck used to, once. She washed the two plates, returning them to the sideboard for Nusswan and Ruby to dine off at night. Then she dried her hands and decided to take a nap before starting the evening meal.